Praise for *Lucky*

"The jeopardy in which the characters are placed is so urgent, a night without sleep seems a small price to pay for finding out whether they live happily ever after. . . . If you take *Lucky* to the beach for sunbathing company, you may still be lying there reading when the moon comes up."

—*Cosmopolitan*

"A chaotic fairy tale of the unrepentantly rich . . . [told with] breathless, perfumed abandon."

—*The Washington Times*

"*Lucky* reads like the publishing equivalent of a firecracker."

—*The Hollywood Reporter*

"Steamy."

—*The Philadelphia Inquirer*

"Like *Gone With the Wind*, considered raunchy in its time, *Lucky* is a strong, true-to-life story that defies putting down."

—*The Charlotte Observer*

"So hot, it will have to be printed on asbestos."

—*New York Daily News*

"Marvelous . . . Fast-moving . . . Suspense-filled."

—*Houston Chronicle*

"Impossible to put down."

—*The Wall Street Journal*

Praise for Jackie Collins

Also by Jackie Collins

Jackie Collins

Lucky

POCKET BOOKS

New York   London   Toronto   Sydney   New Delhi

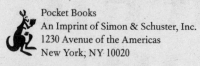

Pocket Books
An Imprint of Simon & Schuster, Inc.
1230 Avenue of the Americas
New York, NY 10020

This book is a work of fiction. Any references to historical events, real people, or real places are used fictitiously. Other names, characters, places, and events are products of the author's imagination, and any resemblance to actual events or places or persons, living or dead, is entirely coincidental.

Copyright © 1985 by Jackie Collins
Foreword copyright © 2019 by Peebo & Pilgrim Ltd.

This Pocket Books paperback edition December 2022

POCKET and colophon are registered trademarks of Simon & Schuster, Inc.

For information about special discounts for bulk purchases, please contact Simon & Schuster Special Sales at 1-866-506-1949 or business@simonandschuster.com.

The Simon & Schuster Speakers Bureau can bring authors to your live event. For more information or to book an event, contact the Simon & Schuster Speakers Bureau at 1-866-248-3049 or visit our website at www.simonspeakers.com.

Interior design by Erika R. Genova

Manufactured in the United States of America

10   9   8   7   6   5   4   3   2   1

ISBN 978-1-6680-0519-4

In memory of Kimberly.
You are not forgotten.

INTRODUCTION

Looking back on the success of her first novel, *The World Is Full of Married Men*, published in 1968, Jackie Collins observed: "Women didn't write about sex then. They wrote about going off to the Cotswolds to have a nervous breakdown over a man." After I'd stopped laughing, I realized the power behind her statement. Collins was saying that women didn't have to center around men, either in books or in life. Women could have their own adventures. Women could live in the sunshine, not cottages in Chipping Campden where the only thing rising was the damp.

I recognize the sort of book Collins was talking about: the worthy mix of psychological and lyrical, the oblique male influence on repressed female lives which end with a whimper not a bang (usually under a full moon), invoking our feminist rage and pity. Given the patriarchal bibliography that women writers were—and continue to be—subject to, the existence of these books is important. But Jackie's books are also important, because writing a woman's life in leopard print doesn't make it any less valid. We should be grateful that Jackie served us up the other side of the moon.

She simply did what she wanted to do, and I don't think we realize quite how revolutionary an act that was. When discussing Lucky Santangelo—probably her most popular heroine with readers and definitely with Collins ("She is my favorite, favorite, *favorite* character.")—Collins declared that she was the woman who did everything we wanted to do. And definitely, Lucky Santangelo is a boon companion—witty, warm, assertive, sexually confident and self-aware. Collins said she never wrote about her own sex life or her experience of wealth, she wrote about other people's—but I do think Lucky is a recalibrated, amplified version of the writer, the kind of woman who rode the Pacific Coast Highway in an Aston Martin after she'd done her pages.

Knowing her own worth was yet another revolutionary act. Collins knew the label "bonkbuster" was pejorative, but her response was robust: "A lot of people think they can write like me," she said. "But they can't." She had a point: half a billion copies sold in forty languages, and every one of her thirty-one novels making it to the *New York Times* bestseller list. She said she liked to write by the pool "listening to Lionel Richie, surrounded by all those phallic cacti." Again, I laughed. You can hear the self-awareness of the sybarite-millionaire, but the work ethic is clearly evident. The cacti might be phallic (of course they are, it's Jackie Collins), but even by the pool, it's the woman who is writing. Seven days a week, in fact. Without fail.

And what is she writing? Not interiority, not subordination, not helplessness—these themes never interested Collins much, and if ever they appeared in her work they were determinedly overcome. "I can write about anything I want," she once said. "I can create anyone I want, kill off anyone." Confidence and control appealed to her. (When asked what she disliked most about her appearance, Collins replied, "Nothing—I try to make the most of what I have." And when pressed for her most embarrassing moments, she said there were none, because "I think I've blocked them all out.") As in life, so in her books: there is irrepressibility, humor, glamour, uncomplicated sex. Beautiful locations, lavish homes. Fallible people with infallible genes. It's a phenomenal shopping list, and all of it is here in *Lucky*.

Collins wasn't really just writing by the pool, of course. That was only part of her persona. She wrote on the school run and cooking her children's dinner, and my guess is she offered her heroines' escapades for all those women locked in the repetition of domesticity. Because what Collins really writes about is power, and this is why readers have endured with her for over forty years. "I certainly don't think of my books as literature, more a mild send-up," she demurred, before coming up with the rejoinder: "It's the success I love, and, of course, the power." Her books gift the reader the power of escape, of entertainment—and perhaps above all, the power of pleasure.

But on the other side of the moon there's also darkness. Adversity, failure and poverty all crop up in Jackie's novels, and her morality has a taste of the Old Testament; the baddies always get it in the end. Her attention does not shy from casual domestic violence, racism and misogyny, depicted in ways which these days might raise an editor's eyebrow. Collins always said her plots were tame compared to the real-life stories she knew, but whilst some of the sentences in *Lucky* might have passed the censor in the 1980s, I wonder if she'd get away with them now.

This doesn't make her writing a museum piece—it's more a case of witnessing a creative mind unshackled by identity politics or concern for what her critics might think. "I've always tried to write for everybody, gay, straight, Black, white, Hispanic, whatever," she observed—and that "whatever" is important. It's the individual who mattered to Collins, not the color of a person's skin, or their gender. Idealistic, perhaps, but she never wanted the world to restrict her because she was a woman, and she wanted the same for her reader.

• • • • •

During my own (far shorter and less glamorous) experience of being a woman who loves to write books—but who also loves clothes, jewels, and cocktails by the pool—Jackie Collins has often felt like the only literary angel I can find. We like to think the times have moved on, but cultural discourse still seems to struggle with a woman who is many things. The world may still be full of married men but it's also still brimming with binary opinions—and Jackie, just like her heroines, always defied both the conscious and unconscious messages that said a woman could only be one thing.

She never saw the need to compromise her various self-hoods. Her own daughter, Rory, described her as weaving "seamlessly" between the domestic and the glamorous, and it wasn't just that one dichotomy: "I realized from a young age that if Mum was two people in our day-to-day lives, in her writing life she morphed into many." To be a shape-shifter like that, you have to act generously, you have to be in love with living, you have to concentrate. Jackie Collins embodied all these qualities. She is my patron saint of women who write in the public eye. I have often flirted with the idea of getting one of those religious bracelets that spell WWJD—except my acronym would stand not for Jesus, but *What Would Jackie Do?*

When I was in Hollywood, I took a pilgrimage to Jackie's grave. In gold and onyx, engraved with a panther of course, her epitaph reads: SHE GAVE A GREAT DEAL OF PEOPLE A GREAT DEAL OF PLEASURE. I beamed when I saw those words glinting in the California sun. It was how she'd said she wanted to be remembered, and she certainly succeeded. Whenever I told people I was writing this preface, their eyes lit up—a unanimous, unprecedented reaction from all ages and reading tastes. It's the Jackie Collins effect. Ever in control, she chose the words on her gravestone well. There was no one like Jackie—and even in passing, she knew that no other sentence, or writer, would have put it better.

Jessie Burton
2019

PROLOGUE

The jury filed silently into the courtroom. The judge made his entrance a moment later, and a hiss of expectation raged through the packed room.

Lucky Santangelo stood tensely in the dock. She stared straight ahead. Impassive. Wildly, darkly beautiful. In spite of everything.

The judge took his place, adjusted his heavy horn-rim glasses and cleared his throat. "Ladies and gentlemen of the jury, have you reached your verdict?" he asked tersely.

The foreman of the jury stepped forward. He was a sallow-faced man with a most unfortunate facial tic. "Yes, Your Honor," he said indistinctly, causing the judge to bark an irritable "Speak up!"

"Yes, we have, Your Honor," the foreman repeated, his nervous tic becoming distractingly obvious.

"Then pass your verdict to the court clerk, if you please," snapped the old judge waspishly.

The foreman did as he was bade. The clerk accepted the folded verdict form and took it directly to the judge, who peered at it intently.

An expectant hush hung over the crowded courtroom—a silence so heavy that to Lucky it seemed more like an accusing roar.

She did not look at the judge, but she saw him read the paper, saw him pass it back to the court clerk, and she closed her black opal eyes for one brief moment of secret prayer. She, Lucky Santangelo, was accused of murder, and the next few minutes would decide her fate.

She tried to breathe evenly and deeply. Tried to remain calm, to concentrate, to think only positive thoughts.

The court clerk began to speak.

Oh, God! This couldn't be happening to her. Not to Lucky Santangelo. *Not to her.*

She held her head high. She was a true Santangelo. Nothing could get her down. Nothing.

After all, she was innocent.

Wasn't she?

Wasn't she . . . ?

Book One

THE SUMMER OF 1978

1

Lennie Golden had not set foot in Vegas for thirteen years, even though it was the city of his conception, birth and first seventeen years of life.

He looked around as he stepped off the plane, sniffed the air and took a deep breath. The place still smelled the same.

The airport was doing a roaring trade in visiting gamblers, tourists and middle America out to have fun. Fat male butts waddled alongside plump, peroxide ladies in polyester pant suits and fake jewelry. Small children whined and complained. Traveling hookers in halter tops, hot pants tightly outlining their crotches, arrived to do business. Swarthy foreigners clutched black leather attaché cases and breathed garlic over their accompanying yellow-haired mistresses.

Jess was there to meet him. Five feet tall, startlingly pretty, she still had the air of a tomboy about her—which is what she had been at school. She had always preferred to hang out with the boys. Especially Lennie. They had been best friends since first grade, their somewhat unexpected and platonic relationship surviving and getting stronger each year—even though they didn't see much of each other since he had moved from Vegas to New York.

They made an ill-assorted couple. Lennie, so tall and lanky, with dirty-blond hair and ocean-green eyes. An overgrown Robert Redford with more than a touch of Chevy Chase. And Jess, petite and wide-eyed, with a mop of orange hair, freckles and a *Playboy* centerfold body in miniature.

She hurled herself into his arms. "It's *so* good to see you! You look fantastic. For a guy who spends his life screwin' around I don't know how you do it."

"Hey—" He swung her in the air like a rag doll. "Look who's talking."

She giggled and hugged him tightly. "I love you madly, Lennie Golden. Welcome back."

"I love you too, monkey face."

"Don't call me that!" she screeched. "I'm married now. I'm respectable. I got a kid, the whole bit. So c'mon, Lennie— treat me like a lady."

He burst out laughing. "If *you're* a lady, *I'm* Raquel Welch."

She grabbed his arm. "You got great tits!"

Laughingly they strolled toward the exit.

"So how was the flight?" she asked, trying to grab his battered suitcase.

He wrestled it away from her. "Long and boring. If God had meant us to fly he'd have given us more stewardesses.

"Didja score?" She winked knowingly.

"Affirmative."

"Really?"

"Would *I* lie to *you?*" he deadpanned.

She laughed. She had a maniacal guffaw that caused people to turn and stare. "You'd lie to the Pope if you thought it would get you through the day."

"And there she goes . . ." he singsonged.

"Who? Where?" Automatically she turned to check out his conquest. A nun walked serenely by.

"I told you my tastes are changing," he said gravely.

"Very funny!" She aimed a punch at his stomach.

He held up a protesting hand. "Lay off. I just had surgery of the tongue."

"Huh?"

"Remember the taping of the *Lee Bryant Show?* The one I told you I was doing?"

"Yeah."

"They cut my four-minute spot to thirty seconds. If you fart you miss me."

She frowned. "Schmucks. They know from nothin'. Anyway, you're back in Vegas now. Your kind of comedy schtick's gonna kill 'em here."

"Oh sure, in the lounge of the Magiriano Hotel I'm really going to cause a riot."

"It's a change of scene. Could be just what you need. Who knows *what* it'll lead to?"

"C'mon, Jess. You sound like my agent. Do this shit, that piece of crap, and before you know it you'll have a regular spot on Carson."

"Your so-called agent is a New York jerk-off artist." She wrinkled her nose. "You're a *great* comedian. *I* should be handling you. I mean, I got you this gig, didn't I?"

"What do you want—ten percent?"

She laughed wildly. "You think I wanna give up the title of best blackjack dealer in Vegas? You think I'm crazy or somethin'? Stick your commission where the sun don't give you a tan!"

They were passing a ladies' room. "Wait a sec," she said. "I'm so excited to see you I gotta take a pee."

He laughed and leaned against the wall while she dashed inside. Jess was a friend indeed. He had called her two weeks ago and said he had to get out of New York.

"No problem," she replied without hesitation. "Matt Traynor, the entertainment director of the hotel I work at, has the hots for me. Send me a tape and I'll get him to hire you."

He had sent the tape. She had come through with the gig. Some good friend.

Idly he watched a dark-haired girl in black leather pants and a red shirt stride by. She cut through the crowd as if she owned the place. He liked her style, not to mention her body.

Jesus! Was he free yet? He and Eden had split six months ago, yet every time he saw an attractive woman he couldn't help comparing the two. He was still doing it. Eden Antonio and he were unfinished business—why didn't he just face it?

Jess emerged from the ladies' room and squeezed his hand.

"It is *sooo* great to have you here," she said. "I want to hear all about everything."

"Hey—everything is a career going nowhere and a fucked-up sex life."

"Sounds exciting. So what else is new?"

They were outside now and the desert heat enveloped them.

"Jeez!" he exclaimed. "I forgot how hot it is here."

"Aw, stop bitching. You could do with a tan. You look like Nightclub Charlie."

They approached a dented red Camaro waiting in the parking lot.

"I see you're still an ace driver," he remarked dryly, throwing his suitcase in the trunk.

"*I* didn't do that," she replied indignantly. "My old man can't drive around the block without gettin' into trouble."

He wondered what kind of man took on crazy Jess for a wife. Someone special, he hoped.

"C'mon," she said, sliding behind the steering wheel. "Wayland is makin' lunch. The baby's makin' noise, and Lennie, *you* are gonna *love* it here. It always was your kinda town."

He nodded grimly. "Yeah. That's what I'm afraid of."

· · · · ·

Lucky Santangelo stood out as she strode briskly through the crowd at the airport. She was a strikingly beautiful woman of twenty-eight, with an unruly mass of jet curls, black gypsy eyes, a wide sensual mouth, a deep suntan and a lean, loose-limbed body. She wore soft black leather pants, a red silk shirt casually unbuttoned to the limit, and a wide belt studded with silver. From her ears hung plain silver hoops, and on her right hand was a square-cut diamond of such size and brilliance that one would be forgiven for thinking it was not real. It was.

No conventional beauty, she had a style and bearing all her own. Confidence wafted from her like the exotic scent she drenched herself with.

"Hey, Boogie." With affection she greeted the skinny, long-haired man in army fatigues who stepped forward to greet her. "How's everything?"

"The same," he said, low-voiced, his slit eyes darting this way and that, observing everyone and everything as he took her black leather tote bag and the claim check for the rest of her luggage.

"No exciting news? No gossip?" she questioned, grinning, delighted to be back.

He had gossip, but *he* didn't want to be the one to give it to her.

She talked excitedly as they walked toward the stretch Mercedes limousine parked on a red line.

"I think I put it all together, Boog. The Atlantic City deal is ready to fly. And I did it. Me! All I need is an okay from Gino and the record'll spin. I feel *great!*"

He was pleased to see her in such a good mood. He nodded and said, "If you want it you'll get it. I never doubted you."

Her eyes gleamed with excitement. "Atlantic City," she said. "We'll build a hotel to beat everything!"

"You'll do it," he agreed, opening up the rear door.

"Hey," she complained, "you know I always sit up front with you."

He switched doors, settled her in the passenger seat and loped off to get the rest of the baggage.

* * * * *

Gino Santangelo awoke with a start. For a moment he was disoriented, but only for a moment. He might be old, but he certainly wasn't senile, thank God. Besides, seventy-two nowadays was not exactly fertilizing-oranges time. In fact, last night in bed, he had felt like a kid again. And why not, with Susan Martino for company?

Susan Martino. Widow of the late, great Tiny Martino, a multitalented veteran of television and the movies. A comedian whose name ranked alongside Keaton, Chaplin and

Benny. Tiny had died of a stroke two years previously. Gino had attended the funeral in Los Angeles, conveyed his respects to the widow—and had not seen her again until she turned up in Vegas three weeks ago at a charity benefit. Now he was waking up in her bed for the fifth morning in a row, and feeling no pain.

As if she knew he was thinking sweet thoughts about her, Susan entered the room. She was an attractive, well-groomed woman of forty-nine, who looked at least ten years younger. Her eyes were pale china blue, cheekbones high, skin white and smooth. Her silver-blond hair was neatly drawn back in a chignon, even though it was only nine in the morning. She wore a white silk peignoir over her understated but perfect body, and she carried a tray with a glass of freshly squeezed orange juice, a soft-boiled egg, and two pieces of lightly buttered toast cut into thin slices.

"Good morning, Gino," she said.

He struggled to sit up, pushing his hands through his unruly black hair, which, although graying at the temples, was just as thick and curly as it had been in his youth. He was still a man to be reckoned with. Age had by no means dulled his vitality and ceaseless energy, although a nearly fatal heart attack a year ago had slowed him down a mite. Like Susan, he did not look his age.

"What's all this?" He indicated the laden tray.

"Breakfast in bed."

"And what did I do to deserve it?"

She smiled. "What *didn't* you do."

He grinned, remembering. "Yeh. Not bad for an old man, huh?"

She placed the tray in front of him and sat on the edge of the bed. "You're the best lover I ever had," she said gravely.

He liked that. He liked it a lot. Susan Martino was no tramp, but she'd had a reputation of sorts before marrying Tiny Martino twenty-five years earlier. Aly Khan, Rubirosa, even Sinatra were rumored to be in her past. Enough for Gino to feel more than flattered by her compliment.

Not, of course, that he had ever questioned her about her past, just as she had never asked him about his.

"I wanna know somethin'," he said, interested enough now to start finding out.

"What?" she replied, carefully peeling the shell from his egg.

"When you were married to Tiny—you ever cheat around?"

She did not hesitate. "Never," she replied firmly. "Although why I should tell you . . ."

He suddenly felt possessive of this woman. This classy blond *lady*. And how many of *them* were there around today?

Women. Love 'em and leave 'em had been his life's motto. With very few exceptions. In the last year, taking them to bed had become boring. Another body. Another pretty face. Another thousand-dollar bill for a trinket because he didn't like to dismiss them empty-handed. When they left Gino Santangelo's bed he wanted them to *know* they had been somewhere. Not that he had to pay. Ever. The very thought was crazy.

"Can we spend the day together?" Susan asked, dipping a sliver of toast into the egg and feeding it to him.

He was just about to say yes when he remembered. Lucky was coming back today. His daughter. Beautiful, wild Lucky—with *his* eyes and *his* deep olive skin and *his* jet hair and *his* zest for living. How could he have forgotten? She had been away for three weeks on a business trip to the East. He would be missing her badly if it weren't for Susan.

"Why don't we make it tomorrow? I got things to do today," he said, pushing the fork away.

"Oh." She looked disappointed.

He wondered how Lucky would feel about Susan's joining them for dinner and knew instinctively that she would hate it. He could understand. After all, it was her first night back, and they would have a lot to talk about.

There was time enough to introduce Susan into their lives, and he fully intended to. Susan Martino was too much a lady to be just a one-week stand.

• • • • •

During the drive from the airport Lucky continued to fill Boogie in on her trip. He was more than her driver and sometime bodyguard when the climate indicated she was in need of protection. He was her friend, and she trusted him implicitly. In times of trouble Boogie came through. As he had proved in the past, he was loyal, smart and usually silent, unless he had something worth saying—which suited Lucky just fine.

He drove her to the front of the Magiriano Hotel on the Strip. She got out of the car and stood for a minute feeling the usual thrill of coming home to *her* hotel.

The Magiriano—a combination of her parents' names— Maria and Gino. Gino's dream, put into being by her while Gino sweated out a seven-year tax exile in Israel. She would always be proud of her achievement. The Magiriano was very special.

In the lobby there was the usual melee of tourists and noise. The casino was crowded with morning gamblers. No windows. No clocks. Twenty-four hours nonstop fun.

Lucky did not gamble. Who needed to play the tables when it all belonged to her and Gino anyway? She strode across the lobby to her private elevator concealed behind an arrangement of potted palms and inserted a code card to gain entry.

It was good to be back.

She couldn't wait to see Gino. She had so much to tell him.

• • • • •

Jess did not live in luxury, but the small tract house in front of which she stopped the car at least had its own tiny swimming pool. "This place is okay, but we're movin' on soon," she explained airily, opening up the front door. "We've seen a development in Lake Tahoe we're lookin' to buy into."

"Yeah?" said Lennie, and wondered who was looking to buy into it. From the small amount of information Jess had divulged about her husband, it seemed he didn't do much at all except look after their ten-month-old baby while she brought in the money.

"Anyone around?" she called out, as a scruffy mongrel dog appeared and wagged its sorry-looking tail. She bent to pet the animal. "This is Grass," she explained. "Found him dumped in the garbage when he was a pup. Cute, huh?"

Wayland appeared, or at least Lennie presumed it was he. From the look of him, Jess had found herself another stray. He was dressed in grubby white chinos and a loose, embroidered shirt, and his dirty feet were bare. He had shoulder-length yellow hair with a center part, and a long, pallid face. Jess—who wrote wonderful letters—had mentioned that he painted. Exactly what he painted she hadn't gone into.

"Greetings, man," said Wayland, stoned to the eyeballs. "Welcome to our home." And he extended a thin, shaking hand.

"Where's the baby?" Jess demanded.

"Asleep."

"You sure?"

"Go see."

For a moment her pretty features clouded over, and Lennie sensed all was not well in this year-old marriage. That's just what he needed, to be stuck right in the middle of some miserable scene. He had enough problems of his own.

Lunch turned out to be a large bowl of brown rice and some wilted lettuce coated with stale yogurt. Jess tried to conceal her aggravation—she had been at work all night and had left instructions for Wayland to fix something special—but she did it with difficulty. Lennie knew her well enough to realize she was pissed off.

The baby—a boy named Simon—woke briefly and accepted a bottle.

"I wanna take Lennie over to the hotel," Jess said restlessly, when the baby was asleep again.

Wayland nodded. He didn't have much to say about anything.

Out in the car she lit up a joint, blew smoke in Lennie's face and said aggressively, "I don't want to talk about it, okay?"

"Who's asking?" he replied calmly.

She gunned the car into action and sped all the way to the Magiriano, where she drew up to the entrance without cutting the engine. "I'll meet you here in a couple of hours," she said. "Ask for Matt Traynor. He's the guy who booked you. He'll get someone to show you around."

"Where are *you* going?"

"I got an . . . er . . . appointment."

"Screwin' around already?"

"Give me a reason not to."

Having met Wayland, he couldn't think of one.

Matt Traynor was a fifty-five-year-old silver-haired fox in a three-piece beige suit. Apart from being the best entertainment director in Vegas, he had points in the hotel. Lucky Santangelo had personally pursued him to take the job, and only the lure of a piece of the action had persuaded him.

He told Lennie he loved the videotape Jess had shown him of his work and then proceeded to fire off questions about her as if hoping to find out every detail of her life.

Lennie made a stab at a few answers, but when Matt started asking about her marriage, Lennie felt the time had come to move on. Quickly he said he wanted to check out the lounge he would be appearing in and generally get the feel of the place. Matt Traynor agreed, gave a few vague directions and waved him on his way.

Las Vegas. The heat. The special smell. The hustle.

Las Vegas. Home. From birth to seventeen.

Las Vegas. Youthful memories crowding his head. The first time he got laid, drunk, stoned, busted. The first time he fell in love, ran away from home, stole his parents' car.

Mom and Pop. The odd couple.

Pop, an old-fashioned stand-up comic. Jack Golden. Dependable, a real hack. But a name everyone in show business knew—everyone except the general public. Dead thirteen years now. Cancer of the gallbladder.

And Mom, Alice Golden, formerly known as "the Swizzle"—one of the hottest strippers in town. Good old Mom, fifty-nine years old and living in a condo in California. From Las Vegas to Marina del Rey in one fell swoop with a used-car salesman from Sausalito. Alice was not your average Jewish mother. She wore short shorts, strapless tops, dyed her hair, shaved her legs and got laid a lot after the Sausalito salesman skipped town with ten thousand dollars' worth of her jewelry.

Alice . . . she was something else. He had never felt close to her. When he was a kid she bossed him around, sent him on endless errands and used him as a lackey. She never cooked a meal in her life. While other kids took neat brown bags to school with homemade meatloaf sandwiches, cookies and cheese, he was lucky to scrounge an apple from a tree in the garden.

"You gotta learn to be independent," Alice told him when he was about seven.

He had learned the lesson well.

Living with Alice and Jack *was* exciting. Their untidy apartment was always filled with dancers and singers, casino people and general show biz. Life was fun, if you forgot about childhood.

Alice. A real character. He had learned to accept the way she was.

Las Vegas. Why had he come back?

Because a job was a job was a job. And as he'd told Jess, he had to get out of New York. The police were on his case after he'd punched out a fat drunk who was heckling him during his act at a Soho club. The fat drunk turned out to be a shyster lawyer, who, when he woke up the next morning with a black eye and a split lip, decided Lennie Golden needed to be put away and set about doing so. The aggravation of a lawsuit was not something Lennie needed in his life. Leaving town seemed the best way to deal with it. Beside, Eden was on the West Coast, and for months he had been thinking about following her. Not that they had parted friends.

After Vegas he planned to move on to Los Angeles.

Not just to see Eden.

Yeah. To see Eden.

Admit it, schmuck, you're still hooked.

•　•　•　•　•

Lucky entered the pool area and paused for a moment until she caught the eye of Bertil, the Swedish head honcho of all pool activity.

He spotted her immediately. She was impossible to miss in a one-piece black swimsuit covering a supple tanned body with the longest legs in town. He jumped to attention, remembering she was the boss, and hurried toward her, greeting her with just the right amount of deference and enthusiasm. "Welcome back, Miz Santangelo."

She nodded briefly, scanning the mass of bronzed bodies. "Thank you, Bertil. Any problems while I was away?"

"Nothing to bother *you* with."

"Bother me," she said softly. "I like to know everything."

He hesitated, then launched into a short story about two lifeguards who had been hitting on female guests.

"Did you fire them?" she asked.

"Yes, but they're planning to sue."

"Have you talked to our lawyers?"

"Yes."

"Then it's all taken care of," she said, satisfied.

He escorted her to a poolside lounger, and she settled back to observe the action.

"Bring me a phone," she requested.

He did as she asked, then left her alone.

She tried Gino for the third time. He was still out. Where the hell was he? Why wasn't he awaiting her arrival?

2

Olympia. You are a princess. A goddess. A queen."

Olympia Stanislopoulos's golden rounded body quivered with delight. "More, Jeremy, tell me more."

The English lord shifted position on top of the Greek shipping heiress's nubile naked body and continued his litany of praise. "Your eyes are the Mediterranean. Your lips ruby jewels. Your skin the smoothest velvet. Your . . ."

"Ahhhhhh . . ." Her loud cry of ecstasy silenced him. She spread her legs wide, then brought them tightly together, scissoring him in a painful embrace. While doing this, her long talonlike nails scratched a lethal trail across his back, drawing blood.

His yell of pain joined her shout of ecstasy. "For God's sake, Olympia!"

She was uninterested in his complaints. Casually she pushed him from her.

"I haven't come," he complained.

"Too bad," she retorted sharply, and rolled off the bed.

Olympia Stanislopoulos had never been known for her warm and compassionate nature. She bounced quickly into the bathroom, slammed the door and confronted her reflection in a full-length mirror.

Fat! Rolls of unwanted cellulite-dimpled fat! Angrily she grabbed a fold of flesh around her waist and squealed with fury. God*damn* that phony French doctor who had given her three months of treatment, a few lousy fucks, and charged her thirty thousand dollars. He'd certainly seen *her* coming—in more ways than one. She stuck her tongue out at her reflection, hating what she saw.

What she saw was a twenty-eight-year-old, five-foot-three, very curvacious woman, with great bouncy breasts, an abundance of thick blond curls and a pretty face. Her eyes were small and blue. Her nose nondescript. Her lips pouting rosebuds. Men loved her. She looked very sexy. A regular sex bomb. But a sex bomb with a difference.

On her twenty-first birthday Olympia Stanislopoulos had inherited seventy million dollars. Wisely invested, the millions had made her now worth more than twice that.

She had been married three times. First, at seventeen, to a fledgling Greek playboy of twenty whose family had lineage but little money. They were married aboard her father's— Dimitri's—yacht, conveniently moored beside his private island. The occasion had been more than festive: two princes, a scattering of princesses, a deposed king and most of Europe's idle jet set. The happy couple honeymooned in India, lived for three months in Athens, and divorced in Paris when Olympia discovered her new husband on all fours being roughly serviced by the butler. She was no prude, but there *was* such a thing as decorum. Dimitri consoled his petulant daughter with a magnificent apartment on the Avenue Foch—two blocks away from the family mansion.

Soon she met an Italian business tycoon. Or at least, that's what he *said* he was. A man of forty-five with charm, smooth lines, a reputation as a womanizer, and a great wardrobe. He courted her through the discotheques of Europe and married her on her nineteenth birthday. They stayed together a year. She bore him a baby daughter, Brigette, while he spent as much of her money as he could. His indiscretions hit the newspapers and magazines once too often. Olympia was furious to discover he had been dancing the night away while she was screaming the night away delivering their child.

Dimitri arranged the divorce for her. She settled two Ferraris and three million dollars on her second mistake. He never had time to enjoy them. Three months after the divorce, he stepped out of a car in Paris and was blown to pieces by a terrorist bomb. Olympia had no time to mourn—she was too busy making mistake number three, an impoverished Polish count. Take out the *o* and you had his number. He lasted sixteen weeks and left her with a title and all his debts.

Olympia decided marriage was out, and she indulged in a great many affairs, none of which satisfied her. She began to travel frequently, dividing her time between her Paris apartment, a *pied-à-terre* in Rome and the Connaught in London. Summers she spent in the south of France. Gstaad at Christmas. Acapulco when she felt like it. She went through men fast. Most of them bored her after she had sampled their bodies. She needed more than sex—she needed an added thrill.

Married men were fun. And famous men. And powerful men. The more unobtainable they were, the better.

Laying them was the kick. After the initial encounter, what was left? She needed a challenge. For she discovered something she had known all along—most men were easy lays. And who needed easy?

Olympia's first lover had taken possession of her body when she was a mere sixteen. The setting was southern France, in a villa she and her girlfriend, Lucky Santangelo, had "borrowed" from Olympia's aunt. They were on the run from boarding school, two adventurous little girls with time on their hands, money to burn, a white Mercedes and inquisitive natures. Often Olympia looked back on those illicit carefree days as the happiest time of her life. No pressures or sneaking photographers behind every bush. No great expectations.

Warris Charters. She remembered him well. Handsome, with corn-colored hair and slitted green eyes. An older man. A film producer. A broke hustler with an exceedingly active cock.

Sometimes she wondered what had happened to him. Warris Charters, caught with her sixteen-year-old golden curls between his legs, giving him a blow job. Caught by her father and Lucky's father when the two men traveled to the south of France in search of their errant daughters.

The last she had seen of Warris was a nervous figure scurrying into the storm-ridden night clutching two Gucci suitcases and an earful of threats from Dimitri.

She had never heard from him again. Understandably so.

She had never heard from her best friend Lucky Santangelo again either. Not so understandable. After all the experiences they had shared, she would have expected at least a phone call. It never occurred to her that Lucky, like her, had been forbidden further contact. What *did* occur to her was that Lucky might have betrayed them. Summoned the two fathers to come and collect them, because she, Olympia, was having all the fun.

Who needed Lucky anyway?

"*Olympiaaa.*" The plaintive cry was accompanied by a sharp pounding on the bathroom door. "My beauty. What are you doing in there?"

What did the fool *think* she was doing? Playing with herself?

She flung open the door impatiently.

Lord Jeremy's naked erectness faced her.

She sighed.

It was a rainy afternoon in Paris.

What else was there to do on a rainy afternoon?

3

Bikini'd bodies, oiled and gleaming, lay in various stages of undress beside the Magiriano pool. Lennie sauntered aimlessly among them, and remembered the countless times he and Jess had crashed out beside many of the better hotel pools while playing hooky from school. It had become one of their most interesting games, along with cruising the casinos, feeding the slot machines without getting caught and trying to sneak into the lavish shows. In the end, every security guard in town knew their faces, which kind of cramped their style— but certainly not their energy.

Leaving Vegas for New York, at seventeen, was easy. Leaving Jess behind was not. But New York beckoned, and who was he to argue? He looked at least twenty, and was six feet two, with a great body and a tousled handsomeness. A variety of jobs kept him going while he made up his mind what he wanted to do. He had no trouble getting by. A room in Greenwich Village became his home, and there was never a shortage of girlfriends as he coasted along for a couple of years just enjoying the freedom of being in the big city. To survive he did everything from slicing lox in a Sixth Avenue deli to selling watches in Bloomingdale's. The summers he spent in the Catskills, doing busboy duties at one of the busier hotels. It was there he learned that there was more to comedy than pie in the face, drop your pants, Jack Golden style. He discovered the records of the late great Lenny Bruce (he fantasized for a while that his mother had named him after Lenny Bruce. Just a fantasy. She had named him after a dumb cousin of hers in Miami). He discovered political humor, irreverent humor and the straight monologue. At last he realized what he wanted to do with his life, and he set about it with a vengeance.

Writing came first. Routines. Schtick. Brief sketches. Then

he found himself an agent who began to sell some of his stuff. Not enough to give up his other jobs—but it was a start.

He had a flair for pithy, original material. Sometimes it was a little too wild, but gradually his agent developed a steady market of buyers for anything he came up with. By the time he was twenty-four he was able to concentrate full time on creating. He wasn't making a fortune, but things were moving along nicely, lots of girlfriends and plenty of good times.

Being back in Vegas was strange.

He passed a Slavic blonde with cheekbones that could cut butter. She threw him a long, slow look as she suggestively rubbed suntan oil on her thighs. He was not in the mood for a pickup. Now that he was thirty, there had to be more than just getting laid. She did look a little like Eden though. The same high cheekbones, icy blondness and cool, narrow eyes. Cat eyes.

Eden Antonio. He would never forget the first time he saw her. He was living with a girl named Victoria, a photographic model who looked like Miss Prom Queen—all long, lean limbs and whiter-than-white teeth. He had thought they had a pretty good thing going for the two years they were together. She adored him and gave him all the home comforts he had never received at home. Then one day she introduced him to another model, Eden Antonio.

When he first set eyes on Eden he knew Victoria had merely been the hors d'oeuvre. Eden was the main course. She had just returned from a successful working trip to Europe, and was as feline and sleek as a cat. Unlike Victoria, she did not look like Miss anything. She was pale and exotic-looking, with finely etched porcelain features and a startling bone structure. She was also making more money than he was, but things were getting better all the time. He had gotten himself involved in the pilot for a new kind of television show, aptly titled *Off the Wall*; for the first time he was actually performing, and he loved it. Audience reaction was a charge he had never thought would turn him on to the extent it did. The show was given a weekly spot on a local station. He was twenty-seven and running on all cylinders. Not bad for a boy who had arrived in New York without a pot to piss in.

Eden was neurotic, ambitious, and just about the most exciting woman he had ever met. Although she was four years younger than he, she seemed to know so much about life. She had traveled around the world, had dallied with numerous lovers and struck Lennie as being incredibly sophisticated. Of course, that was in the beginning. After three and a half years of a love-hate relationship, he knew her supposed sophistication for the sham it was. Eden Antonio was the most insecure person he had ever met. At times he felt sorry for her; other times she made him so jealous he could kill.

Eden! What she had put him through. He had physical as well as mental scars from their intense, volatile relationship. And yet . . . still he wanted more. They might have fought constantly, but the making up was always worth it.

"You are what is commonly known as pussy-whipped," his friend Joey Firello had told him on many occasions. "She fucks up your head, and you come back for more. Dump her, Lennie. She's just a user. A classy tramp."

Sure she was. He knew that. But he couldn't help himself.

"She's got you by the balls," Joey said.

"No way," Lennie replied. But it was true.

Eden adored being seen. Every night she liked to go out on the town. Weekends she attended some half-assed acting class. She wanted to be discovered and become a movie star. She already thought she was a star of sorts. When Lennie's television show was canceled after one season, her only comment was, "Jesus! And I was just about ready to do a guest shot for you."

She thought his career was a dead end and often told him so. Not that she gave a damn. Eden never cared about anyone except herself.

She was a terrible actress. Lennie saw her in several class productions and found her embarrassingly inept. As a model, nobody could beat her. "Why don't you stick to modeling?" he asked one Sunday afternoon, having watched her murder a scene from *Cat on a Hot Tin Roof*.

"Fuck you, you sonofabitch!" she screamed. "Are you telling me I'm no good?"

"I'm telling you you'd be better off doing what you do better than anyone around."

"You bastard!" A bottle of scent came flying through the air. "You cocksucker!" Followed by a hefty glass ashtray. "You jealous *asshole!*"

Two months and many fights later she had taken off for California with an actor from her class, a long-haired jerk named Tim Wealth.

Lennie missed her. Even though he was into performing at small off-beat clubs. Even though he loved every minute of it. Even though audience reaction was very positive and gradually he was beginning to build a small but hard-core following.

Reviews—when he got them—were excellent. The money was nothing to get excited about, but he supplemented his salary with writing assignments. His material was always in demand.

In the back of his mind he knew he would follow her to California. Las Vegas was the starting point. If he could make an impression there, then he could head for L.A. with a real shot. Eden was impressed by success. If he ever made it, she'd come running. . . .

The Slavic blonde beckoned, and he realized he must have been staring. Quickly he moved on, skirting the pool, looking around. A girl lay on a lounge chair in a black one-piece swimsuit. He remembered seeing her stride through the airport earlier. There had been a lot of women since Eden, but none of them had helped. Each time he thought the next one would be different. They never were.

Without pausing, he was beside the girl in the black swimsuit, mentally zeroing in on which of his many successful lines he should go with. He decided safe was best, and besides, it always worked. Turndowns were something Lennie Golden knew little about.

"You," he said, "are too beautiful to be alone. So what's it to be? A drink? Breakfast? Or how about diamonds? I give great heist."

Usually they responded in one of two ways. They either laughed or made a quick request for diamonds. Whatever they did, a dialogue was created, and from there it was all the way home. Make 'em laugh first, *then* move in for the kill.

Lucky raised her shades slowly and stared at him coldly.

He fell into her black opal eyes and almost gave up blondes forever.

"You've got to promise to respect me in the morning," he said quickly. "I'm *very* sensitive." He grinned in what he had been told countless times was an irresistible way and waited for her comment.

"Back off, schmuck," she said disinterestedly. "Try the cupcake posing under the palm tree, she looks like she could use a little of your corn syrup. More your style, y'know what I mean?" She lowered her shades dismissively.

"Wait a minute, who's writing your script—me?" She was a touch icy, but nothing he couldn't thaw.

Before he could continue further a hand descended on his shoulder and a burly Swede in blue swim shorts said, "This is not a pickup joint, mister. Please leave."

He tried to shake the hand off, but Bertil's grip was firm. "Hey, c'mon, man, I'm a guest here," he objected.

"Show me your room key," said Bertil, propelling him away from Lucky.

He didn't like being strong-armed. Nor did he like being made to look a fool. "Do yourself a favor," he exclaimed in disgust. "Take your hands off me. I'm appearing here in the Bahia Lounge. My name's Lennie Golden. I'm *talent*, for crissakes."

The scream of a distraught mother distracted everyone. "My little girl, she can't swim!" yelled the hysterical woman.

Bertil loosened his grip. Two lifeguards and Lennie leaped into the pool. He reached the child first, pulled her up by a mop of hair and hauled her to the side, where Bertil lifted her from his arms and handed her, unhappy but unharmed, to the grateful mother. Lennie pulled himself out and stood dripping in ruined white pants and a shrinking sweater, not to mention waterlogged tennis shoes. The two lifeguards shot him filthy looks. Bertil ignored him. The mother was too interested in her rescued offspring to even glance in his direction.

He looked for the girl with the black eyes. How could she resist him now?

She was long gone.

So much for heroics.

• • • • •

"I thought," said Lucky, "that I would come over and bring you up-to-date on everything. I have so much to tell you."

It was past noon and she had finally located Gino. They spoke on the phone.

"I'm tired, kid," he said. "Gonna take a nap and get myself in shape."

She had been away three weeks and he was too tired to see her. What was going on?

"Where were you? I called four times," she said lightly, knowing that with Gino it was best not to push.

"Around," he replied.

Shacked up with some sleazy showgirl, she thought. *Seventy-two and still out getting laid.*

She gave him a little silent disapproval.

"I'll pick you up tonight," he offered. "We'll have a quiet dinner, just the two of us. Does eight o'clock suit you?"

An edge of sarcasm. "You're sure you won't be too tired?"

"Come *on*, kid. When am I ever too tired for you?"

Now, she wanted to say. But she didn't. She agreed that

eight o'clock was fine, and spent an impatient afternoon waiting to tell him all about her trip, and the deals she had in the works. He would be so proud of her. She couldn't wait!

• • • • •

"What happened to you?" demanded Jess.

"I wanted to see if this sweater was shrinkproof," replied Lennie sarcastically.

"It's not."

"Oh, really? Then remind me never to go swimming in it again."

He climbed into the car and she sped off. Her eyes glittered dangerously as she gunned the red Camaro down the Strip at full speed, narrowly missing a lumbering tourist in an "I Love Chicago" T-shirt.

"Shit!" she muttered.

"What's the matter?"

"Haven't had a hit in years."

"You could have fooled me."

She whirled the car into the parking lot of a supermarket and killed the engine.

"Gotta get dog chow," she announced. "And baby stuff, food, things like that."

"Doesn't your old man take care of the shopping?"

"You experienced lunch. What can I tell you?" She grimaced.

"I think we've got to talk," he said.

She nodded. "We will."

He followed her into the market. A six-foot redhead in pink Spandex pants and a crocheted boob tube smiled at him. He smiled back.

A short bad-tempered man in a wrinkled white suit whacked the redhead on the ass. "Quit it," the man said tersely.

The redheaded woman tossed long swirls of hair and pouted.

"Vegas is full of hookers," Jess remarked.

"Tell me about it," replied Lennie.

The groceries came to sixty-three dollars. Lennie insisted on paying, but Jess fought him all the way.

"You're broke," she said.

"Not at all."

"It's unnecessary."

"Says who?"

"Me."

"Take a walk, monkey face."

"Don't call me that!"

The line behind them applauded when she finally allowed him to pay.

They fell into the parking lot, laughing.

A fat boy with long greasy hair was trying to gain entry to the Camaro.

"Hey!" yelled Jess indignantly.

The boy continued his assault on the passenger window with a wire coat hanger.

Jess dropped two paper sacks of groceries and charged.

Lennie followed suit. Together they dragged the fat boy from his task. Stoned eyes signaled venom. He lumbered across the parking lot and set to work on a Ford.

"I don't *believe* it," Lennie said.

"You're a New Yorker now, you should believe anything," Jess responded sagely.

They retrieved scattered groceries and made it to the house in record time.

Wayland floated on a blue striped mattress in the pool, smoking a joint.

Simon cried wildly on a dirty Navajo blanket.

"Shit!" muttered Jess.

It appeared to be her favorite expression.

Lennie wondered if he should have booked into a hotel. It looked like Jess had enough problems without a houseguest to complicate matters.

4

"Hey, you're lookin' good, kid. Atlantic City agreed with you, huh?" He winked at his daughter.

"You know something, Gino, for an old man you're looking pretty good yourself."

She never called him Daddy. Only sometimes, in her mind, when it was late and she was tired and the memories came creeping back to haunt her . . .

"Cut out the 'old,' " he snapped.

They grinned at each other, linked arms and proceeded to her private elevator.

How alike the two of them were. The same smoldering eyes, dark olive skin, jet hair and wide sensual mouths.

They enjoyed the perfect relationship. So similar in every way. From food to movies to books to people, they almost always formed the same opinions. Gino would say, "I don't trust that guy—not with my left ball I don't trust him." And Lucky would add, "Lock up your right one—that dude is bad news." Then they would break up laughing, black eyes locking fondly with black eyes.

They maintained separate penthouse apartments atop the two hotels they owned. Gino lived at the Mirage. And Lucky resided in the Magiriano. Together they shared a house outside New York in East Hampton. An old-fashioned white mansion filled with so many memories—so much of their past. . . .

Once they had lived in the house as a family. Gino and his wife, Maria, with their children, beautiful, dark Lucky and her blond brother, Dario.

Now there were only Gino and Lucky—the two of them against the world. There existed a special bond between them no one could break.

It hadn't always been that way. . . .

• • • • •

Gino Santangelo was born in Italy, and in 1909, at the age of three, he traveled to America with his parents, a young, strong couple, filled with ambition and a desire to capture the great American dream. But jobs were not easy to come by. Too many immigrants, all with the same idea, all brimming with energy and enthusiasm.

By the time Gino was six, the great American dream had soured. His mother ran off with another man, and Paulo, embittered and disillusioned, embarked on a life of petty crime, drink and loose women.

When Paulo was in jail, which was often, it didn't bother Gino. He found himself shuttled between foster homes, and it taught him to be fast and smart, a true street kid with big ambitions. At fifteen he was caught stealing a car, and sent to the New York Protectory for Boys—a tough home in the Bronx for orphans and first-time offenders. The brothers in charge were a hard bunch. Discipline was the order of the day, and messing with the boys the order of the night. Gino was able to protect himself, but some of the younger boys were not so fortunate. A scrawny kid named Costa Zennocotti was hit on constantly. His cries for help went unanswered, until one day Gino could stand the agonized screams coming from a back room no longer. Unthinkingly he picked up a scissors and slipped into the room. Costa was bent across a table, his trousers and shorts around his ankles, while one of the brothers plunged his erectness into the skinny child's ass. Gino lunged with the scissors.

The result was a stay in the Bronx County jail, six months' probation, and a friend for life in Costa, who, as a result of the publicity, was adopted by a well-to-do family in San Francisco.

By the time Gino hit the streets again he was older and sharper, with a strong urge to make money and beat the system. He had no desire to live with his father—still in and out of jail and now married to a prostitute named Vera. So he looked around and observed the heroes of the day—men like Salvatore Charlie Luciana (later to be known as the notorious Lucky Luciano), Meyer Lansky and Bugsy Siegel. They were the guys with the money, the sleek cars and beautiful women, the power and the respect.

Gino saw. Gino wanted. Gino got.

His rise to the top was long and hard but eventually worthwhile. After starting off small, he went into business for himself, operating a thriving bootleg racket. By the time he was twenty-two he had a pretty girlfriend named Cindy and a rich society mistress by the name of Clementine Duke, whose Senator husband introduced him to the world of investments and real money. Senator Duke made Gino's money legitimate. When the great stock-market crash came in 1929 he was prepared, and thanks to the Senator walked away unscathed.

Along the way he had acquired a business partner, Enzio Bonnatti, and by 1933 their interests included gambling, loan-sharking and the numbers racket. Gino refused to touch prostitution and drugs, in spite of pressure from Enzio. Because of this conflict they split their interests in 1934 and went their separate ways.

For recreation Gino opened a nightclub, called it "Clemmie's," and became a minor celebrity. Clementine Duke was delighted. However, she was not so delighted by his amazing success with women. She persuaded him to marry Cindy—in the hope that this would take him off the market. But women to Gino were a fatal attraction. He truly loved to make love, having been initiated by one of his foster mothers at the age of twelve, then led to new levels of accomplishment by the very versatile Mrs. Duke. Now his conquests were many and often.

Cindy soon became as angry and jealous as Mrs. Duke. She plotted revenge, slept around and threatened him with exposure to the Internal Revenue Service for tax evasion.

In 1938 she fell to her death from a window in their penthouse apartment—an unfortunate accident. Gino gave her a magnificent funeral.

By 1939 rumblings of a war in Europe were shaking America. Senator Duke sat down with Gino one day and worked out ways to benefit from the situation. Gino went along with everything the older man suggested. The Senator had never advised him badly.

Gino often wondered how he would be involved if the war spread to America. He needn't have worried. On New Year's Eve

1939 he found his father in a tawdry hotel beating up Vera. She was just a cheap whore, but she had been kind to him over the years. And in return he had helped her when he had the means.

As Gino came upon the sordid scene, Vera raised the .38 she was holding and blew Paulo's brains out. Gino wrestled the gun from her—and later that night was accused and arrested for his own father's murder. He spent the war years behind bars, punished for a crime he never committed.

His old-time friend and now lawyer, Costa Zennocotti, managed to extract a written and witnessed confession from Vera just before her death from alcoholism seven years later. Gino got a pardon and a paltry offer of compensation. What amount of money could possibly compensate for seven years of his life?

In 1949 he decided he needed a change of scene, new interests. Las Vegas was an appealing prospect—and an old friend of his, Jake the Boy, was bugging him to invest. He put together a syndicate, and they financed the building of the Mirage Hotel. Las Vegas was just beginning. Bugsy Siegel had already opened up the Flamingo Hotel and casino (later he was murdered for skimming money), and Meyer Lansky had financed the Thunderbird. Gino wanted in. It was an exciting time. He wanted to enjoy it, have fun and forget the dark years of being locked away.

And then he met his wife-to-be, Maria. She was young, innocent, only twenty—with pale-gold hair and the face of a fragile madonna. They were married almost immediately. And in 1950 Lucky was born. Even as a baby she looked just like him.

They lived in a large white mansion in East Hampton, with eucalyptus trees in the garden and the smell of peace and tranquility all around.

To make their world complete Maria gave birth to a son eighteen months later. They named him Dario. He looked just like his mother.

• • • • •

The elevator ground to a halt, and Lucky stepped out into the milling crowds filling the casino. She had planned the location of the elevator so that it delivered her right into the center of action—unlike Gino, whose own private elevator in the Mirage took him straight to a basement garage where his limousine and driver were on call twenty-four hours a day.

Gino hung back for a moment, his eyes ever watchful. Once a street kid, always a street kid. You could have all the power and money in the world, but it was never enough to protect you 100 percent.

He felt the slight pressure of his gun carefully concealed in a hidden shoulder holster and, reassured, stepped forward.

Lucky turned to him with a wide grin. "Business is booming, huh, Gino?"

"Yeah, kid. Things are hot."

Things were always hot in Vegas. The suckers were always on parade with their quarters and dollars, ready and willing to take a gamble, run a risk, win or lose, it didn't really matter as long as they got their shot.

They ate in the hotel at the secluded Rio restaurant, just the two of them. Lucky spoke of her trip nonstop, her eyes shining with enthusiasm, her cheeks flushed.

"I've set up exactly the deal we've been looking for," she said. "The right property on the boardwalk. The right investors. I've even got architects and builders coming up with bids. If we move fast we can start work within the next couple of months. It's all set. All you have to do is give the go-ahead." She paused for breath. "Of course we'll need building permits, licenses. But everything's in hand. I have it covered." She grinned triumphantly.

Gino listened carefully. She was smart, his daughter. Smart and fast. Beautiful and bright. Tough and wild. Daddy's little girl. She made him proud. Her business acumen was as sharp as his.

He had never thought a woman could equal him—but his daughter could. His Lucky.

· · · · ·

Right from the beginning Lucky Santangelo was a bright-eyed, excitable child. Her younger brother, Dario, was smaller, more delicate. There were only eighteen months between them, but even when they were young, Lucky took charge.

Maria was a wonderful mother. Gino spoiled them rotten. All the time it was presents and kisses and hugs. And special hugs for Lucky, who responded to him far more than Dario.

On her fifth birthday they threw her a fantastic party for fifty children. Clowns. Donkey rides. A huge chocolate cake. And Gino on hand to sweep her up in his arms and smother her with love. Lucky remembered it as the happiest day of her life.

A week later Gino left on a business trip. Lucky hated it when he went away, but there were compensations, such as taking his place in the big double bed he shared with Mommy, and all the wondrous presents when he came home.

Only this time there were no presents, or kisses, or laughter. This time there was only the pain of her mother's sudden and brutal murder, her naked body left floating on a raft in the center of the swimming pool for Lucky to discover when she got up in the morning.

Memories, for a while, were a blur. Policemen. Photographers. Guards. Then a plane trip to California. A new house with bars on the windows, alarms and guards with dogs patrolling the grounds. Life changed completely for Lucky and Dario. Maria gone forever. And Gino so different, angry and sad. No more laughter and playing, or hugs and kisses. In fact, he was hardly ever there. He was either in his New York apartment or his Vegas hotel. It was almost as if he didn't want to spend any time with them. They were cared for by nannies and tutors and maids.

The pain hardened inside Lucky, while Dario withdrew into a world of make-believe. They had everything money could buy. But all they really had was each other.

When Lucky was almost fifteen a decision was made to send her to a boarding school in Switzerland. She was both excited and fearful at the prospect, but the thought of getting away from the Bel Air mansion was certainly tempting.

L'Evier turned out to be a strict private school run by a thin-

nosed woman who demanded "respect and obedience" from her girls. If it hadn't been for her roommate, Olympia Stanislopoulos, Lucky would have hated it. Olympia's attitude was "Screw school. Let's get out and have fun." And Lucky did not argue. Together they obeyed the rule of lights out at 9:30 P.M. And at 9:35 it was Lucky and Olympia climbing out a convenient window. It was only a ten-minute ride to the nearest village, where waited boys, booze and fun. It took them exactly two semesters to get expelled.

Gino arrived to collect his rebellious daughter, his face a mask of thunder. He flew her back to New York and promptly enrolled her in an even stricter school in Connecticut. It did not take her long to contact Olympia in Paris, and together they planned an escape. With a little help from a couple of credit cards she was able to get a flight to France, where Olympia met her. Then it was a fast drive in a white Mercedes convertible all the way to the south of France where they broke into Olympia's aunt's villa and took up residence. The memories were sweet. Even when Olympia moved in her boyfriend, "Warris the hustler," as Lucky christened him.

The memories were not so sweet the night their fathers arrived. Gino Santangelo and Dimitri Stanislopoulos. Then it was back to the Bel Air mansion. Dario was now away at school.

There were times when she hated her father—a furious, blazing hate that burned deep. Other times she loved him more than anything else in the world. And she wished it could be like it once was. Desperately she craved his attention, but that seemed the last thing he was prepared to give her.

On her sixteenth birthday he surprised her by flying her to Las Vegas. Once there he arranged for her to have her hair styled, bought her a designer dress and gifted her with exquisite diamond ear studs. Then he said she was to accompany him to an important charity benefit he was giving for Mrs. Peter Richmond—Senator Richmond's wife. Lucky was thrilled. Things were looking up. But at the dinner he sloughed her off at another table next *to Mrs. Richmond's creepy son, Craven, and ignored her all night.*

Later she sneaked away, changed into jeans, cruised the Strip and ended up fighting off a drunk in the parking lot.

Gino was waiting when she arrived back at 3 A.M., her clothes torn and dirty.

He came straight to the point. She was a little tramp whose only thought in life was to screw around, so he was marrying her off and that was that.

If she didn't like it . . .

Tough.

· · · · ·

Gino had not thought of Susan Martino all night. Nor had the moment been right to mention his involvement to Lucky. So it gave him a jolt when Susan entered the restaurant with a man, smiled, waved and sat down at a nearby table.

Lucky said, "Who's that?"

"Hey—" He stalled for a moment. Had somebody told her already? "Don't you know Tiny Martino's widow?"

"Not the woman," Lucky replied dismissively. "The old guy with her, he looks familiar."

Gino squinted—his eyes were going, but pride prevented him from wearing glasses. "Yeh," he agreed. "I think I know the face."

He began a slow burn. The man was over six feet tall, impeccably groomed, with bushy white hair and hard but handsome features, marred only by a too-prominent nose. And the sonofabitch was sitting down next to Susan.

Gino scowled.

She couldn't possibly be his date.

Could she?

He burned even more, and signaled for the captain. "Who are the people at that table?" he demanded.

"Guests of Mr. Traynor's," the captain replied.

"Where the fuck *is* Mr. Traynor?"

"Coming in now, Mr. Santangelo." The captain backed away nervously.

"What's the matter?" said Lucky calmly, used to her father's outbursts. "Is he someone we shouldn't have in here?"

"I'll find out soon enough," replied Gino grimly. "Hey—Matt. Over here," he yelled, ignoring the other diners, who turned to stare.

Matt Traynor bore down on them, all smiles, his silver hair gleaming in the candlelit room. "Lucky. Welcome back. You look beautiful. And Gino. It's a pleasure."

"Who the fuck is that asshole with Susan Martino?"

Matt Traynor blinked rapidly while he tried to figure out what he'd done wrong. He had heard rumors of Gino Santangelo's interest in Tiny's widow, but he hadn't figured it to be anything serious, so why was Gino bellowing like a jilted lover?

"Susan's not *with* anyone," he explained quickly. "I thought she might enjoy a little company, so I asked her to join me and some of my friends." He paused, threw in the punch line with sad sincerity. "Tiny was like a brother to me, you know."

Gino was untouched. "Who's the prick?" he growled.

"Am I missing something here?" interrupted Lucky.

"If I thought it would upset you, Gino—" Matt said solicitously.

"Who the fuck's upset?" screamed Gino. And he stood up.

"Dimitri Stanislopoulos," Matt said hurriedly. "He arrived this evening. He's here for the Francesca Fern tribute dinner. We're comping him in the Presidential Suite—everything complimentary. Usually he stays at the Sands, and *loses* at the Sands—if you get my drift. But I met him in Monte Carlo last month and persuaded him the Magiriano would be more to his taste. The guy has more money than Onassis. And loves to play baccarat."

"Of course!" exclaimed Lucky. "Olympia's father. No wonder he looks familiar."

"Olympia?" said Gino blankly.

"You remember," Lucky continued excitedly. "Olympia was my best friend at school—we ran away to the south of France and you and Dimitri tracked us down. It's him all right. I could never forget *that* face."

Gino gestured impatiently. He was in no mood for the past. "Matt," he said brusquely, "you'll join us."

It was more command than invitation.

"I'm sure we'd love to," Matt replied easily, although he was aggravated at being treated like hired help. Still, when Gino Santangelo spoke—everyone jumped. "My date will be here in a minute with a girl for Dimitri. You want us *all* to join you?"

"Sure. Bring Susan and whatshisname over now, and the others when they get here."

"Good idea," said Matt, thinking it was a lousy idea.

As soon as he left their table Lucky said, "Why do you want *them* to come over? We have so much left to talk about."

"Why not?" replied Gino, sitting down again. "You'll like Susan Martino, she's a lovely woman."

Like hell I will, thought Lucky. It was becoming increasingly clear that while she was away Gino had been at play. And this time not with some two-bit showgirl. She could tell she had lost his attention and it infuriated her.

"Have you been seeing her?" she asked lightly.

"Once or twice," he replied, equally casual.

Once or twice, my ass. You've got a hot nut the whole room can see.

Inexplicably she felt jealous.

Why?

Why not?

He was her father.

Daddy.

Gino.

• • • • •

The invitations, hurriedly printed, invited guests to attend the wedding of Lucky Santangelo to Craven Richmond.

Craven Richmond. Tall, skinny son of Senator Peter Rich-mond and his athletic wife, Betty.

Craven Richmond. Attentive, polite, boring.

Craven Richmond. A husband chosen by Gino for Lucky with-out her approval or consent.

She dared not disobey her father. So she and Craven were married one week after her sixteenth birthday. It was a marriage doomed to failure. They honeymooned in the Bahamas. A big joke. Although Gino thought she was some hot little nympho and had married her off to protect the great Santangelo name, she was actu-ally still a virgin in the technical sense, never having done more than a lot of heavy petting. Craven, at twenty-one, was totally inexperienced, and unwilling to indulge in more than three fast minutes of sex a night.

Before their honeymoon was over Lucky took her first lover. And from then on she never looked back. How else would she have gotten through four years of being married to a man who had been paid to marry her? Yes, paid—a sad fact she had found out from Betty Richmond one day during the course of a family fight. Gino had paid Craven and blackmailed Betty and Peter to allow it to happen.

So—she was stuck in a loveless marriage to a man she couldn't stand. And her future seemed bleak. They lived in a Washington apartment not five minutes from the Richmond palatial spread. Craven had no job. He spent his days playing tennis with his mother and hung around his father's campaign headquarters get-ting in everyone's way. Lucky filled her days with shopping, read-ing and drifting up and down the freeways in her red Ferrari—a wedding present from Big Daddy. It was not the way she wished to spend her life.

Once she had indicated to Gino that she wanted to follow him into the family business, but he had looked at her as if she were mad and said that only boys went into business—girls got mar-ried, stayed home, and had babies.

She felt trapped in a life Gino had forced upon her. She

hated him with a passion. Yet she desperately wanted to please him.

Staying married pleased him.

Fucking around pleased her.

So she did.

A lot.

Until one day, four years into her marriage, came the phone call summoning her to New York. Gino wanted to see her, and for once without Craven. She was delighted. Anything to get away, and it had been months since she'd seen her father—maybe he was missing her.

In New York she discovered that Dario had also been sent for. The brother she had once been so close to was now a secretive stranger. He attended an art institute in San Francisco and never communicated with her in any way.

Gino presided over the family dinner, which dragged until he made the announcement they had both been waiting for. It seemed he was in trouble with the tax authorities and faced an upcoming subpoena and chance of jail. He had to get out of the country for a while.

"As a precaution," he said, "I'm signin' over a lot of things to you two. Nothin' to bother yourselves with—you'll just have to put your signature on some papers occasionally. Costa will have my power of attorney, he'll take care of everything. And Dario, I want you to move to New York. There's a lot of things you should know about. Costa'll start teachin' you."

"Move to New York!" Dario cried. "Why?"

"You're a Santangelo, that's why. And you've bin pissin' around at that dumb art school for long enough. It's time you came into the business."

"What about me?" Lucky demanded.

"What about you?"

"If Dario's going to learn the business, I want to as well."

"Don't be a silly girl," Gino said mildly.

She felt four years of frustrated rage boiling up inside her. "Why not?" she demanded. "Why not?"

"Because you're a married woman who will stay by her hus-

band's side and behave like a proper wife. And *it's about time you had a baby. What are you waiting for anyway?*"

"What am I waiting for?" she exploded. "I'm waiting to have a life first—that's what I'm waiting for."

Gino threw up his hands in mock despair. "She wants a life. It isn't enough she's had the best money can buy——"

"Including a husband," Lucky yelled angrily. "You bought me a husband with your lousy money. You——"

"That's enough."

"It's not enough. I want more," she screamed. "Why should Dario get a chance and not me?"

"Cut it out, Lucky." His voice was ice.

"Why the fuck should I?"

His black eyes were as deadly as hers. "Because I'm *tellin'* you. And watch your language. Ladies don't talk like you."

She put her hands on her hips and arrogantly faced him. "I ain't no lady," she mocked. "I'm a Santangelo. I'm just like you—and you ain't no gentleman."

He stared at his wild daughter and thought, *Christ! What have I raised here? I've given her everything.* What more does she want?

"Why don't you just shut up and sit down?" he said wearily.

This made her even angrier. "Oh, sure! Shut her up, marry her off, and who cares whether she's happy or not? You're a fucking male chauvinist who thinks women are only good for screwing and cooking. Keep 'em in the kitchen or the bedroom where they belong. Is that what you did with Mommy before she was murdered? Did you lock——?"

He cut her words off abruptly by slapping her across the face.

Desperately she tried to control the burning tears. "I hate you," she hissed. "I never want to see you again."

She stormed from the room. Behind her she heard him say, "Kids! What can you do? You try your best. . . . A woman in business . . . you gotta be nuts . . . emotional . . . Jeeze, they're all so goddamn emotional. . . ."

Lucky was full of a hard, cold anger.

Gino left the country shortly after. He settled in Israel for an undetermined period of time. A few weeks later Lucky heard from Costa. There were papers to be signed and he would be sending them to her.

When she received the documents, she studied them carefully in spite of a note from Costa that read, "Don't bother reading— just sign by the pencil mark, purely a formality."

If she was signing, she was reading.

She then decided, why bother sending them back if she could deliver them personally?

Within hours she was on a plane to New York.

• • • • •

Susan Martino was groomed from the top of her perfectly coiffed head to the tip of her Charles Jourdan gold pumps. She wore a simple little Adolfo and a few hundred thousand dollars' worth of blazing sapphires. They matched her eyes, so delicately made up—nothing obvious.

She was the sort of woman, Lucky decided, who looked like she never went to the bathroom. The thought of Susan and Gino in bed together was laughable.

"I'm so pleased to meet you, dear," she said to Lucky. "Your father mentions you all the time."

Lucky manufactured a smile, and wondered what had happened to the cozy evening for two she and Gino had been enjoying. Susan Martino, Dimitri Stanislopoulos and Matt Traynor joined them at their table. With difficulty, Lucky controlled her impatience.

Dimitri and Gino recalled their previous meeting. They laughed about it. So long ago and far away. And now the two delinquent daughters grown women.

"Say hello to Lucky," said Gino to Dimitri with a grin. "She sure remembers you." Once he had established that Susan was not Dimitri's date, he had calmed down. And why not? With Susan beside him, so womanly and such a lady in the true sense of the word.

"My pleasure, Lucky," said Dimitri, taking her hand and bringing it to his lips, where he brushed it with a kiss.

Old-fashioned bullshit artist. She remembered him on his Greek island the summer she had vacationed there with Olympia. He had been sleeping with one woman, a soignée brunette, and making it on siesta afternoons with another houseguest—a long-haired actress with horny eyes and an easygoing husband. According to Olympia, if it moved, her father felt obliged to fuck it! Not so different from Gino, Lucky had thought at the time.

Two showgirls approached the table. All teeth, tits and hair. One was Matt Traynor's date—he had the taste of a tomcat—and the other a fix-up for Dimitri. Both girls were visibly impressed by the group they were joining.

Lucky thought about leaving. But why should she? She decided to sit it out and observe Susan Martino in action.

The blond woman did not disappoint. She handled Gino expertly. Every move was the right one. She was a practiced courtesan who had found someone she wanted and had every intention of getting him.

Lucky was not fooled by the act.

Gino was.

Why am *I* concerned? Lucky thought. It's his life.

Like hell it is.

It's *our* life. And has been for the last year.

• • • • •

New York was exciting. So was being away from the Richmond family. Learning about Gino's business interests was the most exciting of all.

Lucky found a ready teacher in Costa, who fell for her wide-eyed interest, and cooperated fully, although he knew Gino would not approve. Day after day she appeared at the office, and he began to explain the workings of the various companies. "Of course, you're only a figurehead," he said. "You'll never be called upon to get involved."

Oh, no? That's what he thought. Like a sponge she absorbed every bit of information. When Craven called angrily from Washington demanding her return, she told him their marriage was over. It was easy to make the move without Gino looking over her shoulder.

And when Dario arrived reluctantly from San Francisco and found his sister doing what he should be doing, he was relieved. Business had never interested him; now he could concentrate on his social life and do all the things Gino would never have allowed. Dario's main interest was boys, not girls.

Within a year Lucky knew everything there was to know about the various Santangelo operations. Like Gino before her, she was a quick study.

Gino had set up a syndicate of investors to finance the building of the Magiriano. Construction on the hotel had just begun, and the weekly payroll was vast. Since Gino's exile from America, some of the investors were stalling on paying out.

"Don't we have agreements with these people?" Lucky demanded.

Costa shook his head. "No. It was all done on a handshake basis."

"They gave Gino their word, didn't they? What would he *do if they didn't come up with the money?"*

Costa cleared his throat nervously. "He had his own ... methods."

"You're supposed to be running things for him. Why don't you *use his methods?"*

"Certain things are best left alone until the moment is right. We must wait for Gino."

She stared at him hard. "We can't wait. We don't know how long he'll be away. Even you say it could be years. If they gave their word, they have to be made to keep it. I want a list. I think I can work something out."

He laughed in disbelief. "Don't be a silly girl, these are hard men——"

Her eyes were ice-cold. "Don't ever call me a silly girl again, Costa. You understand?"

He remembered Gino at the same age. And he knew there was

*no way he was going to stop her from taking over while her father
was away.*

· · · · ·

"There's a new comedian opening in the Bahia Room tonight," Matt said to Lucky. "Why don't we have our coffee in
there and catch the second show?"

"Is he funny? I need a laugh."

"Would I hire a comedian who isn't funny?"

She glanced at his date, an over-made-up nineteen-year-
old Barbie doll. "There's a lot of things you do that make me
wonder, Matt."

She was fed up with the entire evening. It pained her to
see Gino making such a fuss of the groomed-to-the-eyeballs
Susan Martino. Dimitri Stanislopoulos was loud and overbearing, and the two showgirls an embarrassment.

"Shall I suggest it?" Matt indicated Gino, lost in the azure
blue of Susan's eyes.

"Do what you like," snapped Lucky. For a year nobody
had come between her and Gino. Nobody got closer to him
than an hour or two in his bed. And what did that mean? A
quick physical act with some undemanding bimbo. For a man
of his age he sure liked to indulge. But indulging was one
thing—becoming involved another.

What did he need it for? She frowned. It would be different
if Susan was a warm and wonderful person, but she wasn't. She
came across as an icy, controlled bitch, with a thin veneer of
saccharine charm. And Lucky wanted the best for her father,
not some ball-breaking Beverly Hills widow who probably saw
him as an ongoing meal ticket. It was obvious she liked money.
Judging from her jewelry, the more the merrier. Why didn't she
turn on to Dimitri, who probably crapped gold bars?

Contemplatively Lucky lit a cigarette and blew perfect
smoke rings while Matt got the party together for the move
into the Bahia Room. She hadn't slept with a man for months.
The urge just wasn't there.

Lucky Santangelo, celibate. The thought amused her.

There had been a time when she might have bedded one or two different men a week. If they were attractive, appealed to her, didn't want any entanglements and were prepared for her brisk "Don't call me, I'll call you." Sexually she had always lived her life like a man, and why not? As long as she wasn't hurting anyone. Sexual hypocrisy outraged her. Who thought up the double standard anyway? Why did society call a man who slept around a stud, and a woman a nymphomaniac? To hell with that rhetoric. She just liked getting laid when she felt like it without the hassle of a relationship.

Of course, there was always the exception. In Lucky's life there had only been one exception. Marco.

• • • • •

Marco entered Lucky's life when she was a mere fourteen and he was around thirty. Dark and brooding, he was, she thought, the most attractive man she had ever seen. Unfortunately the feeling was not mutual. He regarded her as nothing more than a dumb kid and treated her as such. He worked for Gino and sometimes did duty as a bodyguard-chauffeur when either Dario or Lucky went shopping or to the movies—which wasn't often. Gino did not encourage outings. After Maria's death, he liked his children safely behind the gated security of the Bel Air mansion.

When she went away to school it was Marco who accompanied her to the airport. When she returned on vacations he was always there. When Gino took her to Las Vegas for her sixteenth birthday and announced he was marrying her off, she had thought for one wild and wonderful moment he meant to Marco. But that was not to be, and it was Craven Richmond, Washington, and Marco out of her life—perhaps forever.

Occasionally, along the path of an annihilatingly boring marriage, she met a man or two who reminded her of Marco. Maybe it was the dark eyes, or the way his hair curled over the back of his collar, or perhaps just a gesture. Whatever. It was enough to send her into their beds. But Marco clones were never the real thing.

With Gino out of the country and her marriage behind her, she tried to forget him and threw herself into solving the problem of the reluctant investors. Costa was a nice man, and a brilliant lawyer, but obviously not a man of action. It was imperative that work on the Magiriano continue, and she had to make sure it did, so she went to see Gino's old business partner, Enzio Bonnatti. Costa had taken her to meet him months before, and they hit it off immediately. At their first meeting he had declared himself her godfather, and as such, she felt she could go to him for his advice and help.

"Costa will not act," she said, after explaining the situation, "but I am prepared to do whatever my father would do."

Enzio chuckled. "Gino never took no shit from no one—excuse my language. You want to be like him, why not? I lend you a couple of soldiers. You frighten the crap outa number one on the list, you ain't got no problems with the rest. You want I should take care of it for you, my pleasure."

She shook her head. "Just let me have the assistance."

She started off with the biggest investor, paying a visit to Rudolpho Crown, a slick-haired "investment banker." He sat behind a massive desk in his office and leered insolently while she discussed the money he had promised but failed to put up.

"You gave your promise, Mr. Crown," she said coolly. "You are part of a syndicate. If you try to drop out, others will follow, and then work on the hotel will have to be stopped."

"I gave my word to Gino. And when he comes back I'll honor it."

Her voice was very soft. "It makes no difference where Gino is. You gave your promise. He wants it honored—now."

Rudolpho grinned. "He's hardly in a position to want anything. Word is out he won't be back for a long, long time—if ever."

She smiled sweetly. "Risk it, Mr. Crown."

A week later he was wakened at midnight by the touch of cold steel on his balls. He opened his eyes, panic-stricken. Two men *were holding knives to his shriveled penis. He started to scream, to cry, to beg.*

He saw a shadow by the door and a woman's voice said, "This is only a dress rehearsal, Mr. Crown. If your money isn't forthcoming immediately, the first performance will be next week."

Rudolpho Crown put his money up—fast. Other investors followed equally fast. The Magiriano was back in business.

Shortly after settling the business of the reluctant investors, Lucky flew to Las Vegas to see for herself the building progress being made on the Magiriano. Naturally enough she stayed at the Mirage. And there was Marco to greet her. She hadn't seen him since her wedding day.

"You look sensational," he said.

"You look a little ragged yourself." Quickly she worked out how old he must be now: forty-one. His exceptional good looks had not faded at all. He was still the most attractive man she had ever seen, and she burned to go to bed with him.

"How long are you staying?" he asked politely.

Just as long as it takes me to get you into bed. She gestured vaguely. "A few days, maybe a week."

"Good. I want you to meet my wife."

His wife! "How long have you been married?" she asked, hardly able to catch her breath.

"Exactly forty-six hours. You just missed the wedding."

It took time for Marco to sense the heat of her desire. She stepped back and treated him just like any other employee.

"I want the Mirage renovated," she told Costa. "It looks tacky."

Marco was furious. "What's going on here?" he screamed at Costa over the phone when the decorators descended. "Get Lucky off my back. She's disrupting everything."

"I can't," Costa replied simply. "She's the major shareholder. She can do what she wants."

Wild with fury, Marco noticed her all right. By the time he noticed her enough to want her, she was businesslike and remote. She had no intention of sharing him with his wife.

Their relationship simmered. Lucky was in and out of Las Vegas watching the work on the Magiriano. There were problems—then more problems. Nothing she couldn't deal with.

Marco was always around to greet her.

"Still married?" she would ask lightly, although her stomach churned with the anticipation that he might have gotten a divorce.

"Sure am. And you? Still screwing around?"

"Give me a better hobby and I'll try it," she drawled jokingly. She knew her casual sex life pissed him off.

One night, when his wife was out of town, he finally made a move. They had dined together, discussed old times, and when she was at the door of her suite, he said, "I'll come in."

He was so close she could feel his breath on her cheek. She desired him more than she had desired anyone in her life. Sweetly she said, "Goodnight, Marco. Sleep warm," and closed the door before she could weaken.

When she had him she wanted it to be for keeps. That's the way it had to be.

As time passed, Lucky worked hard and played hard. She was a resolute businesswoman, demanding and getting the best from the people she employed. She flew back and forth to Las Vegas constantly, noting that Marco remained firmly married. She still wanted him, but it had to be on her terms.

Very rarely she thought of Gino, whose empire she was taking over. She was building his hotel, realizing his dream—yet they had not spoken or been in touch at all. And that was the way she liked it. It would suit her if he never returned to America.

In 1975 the Magiriano was finally completed. Opening night, and Lucky glowing in a black Halston dress, Marco resplendent in black tie—the electricity charging between them like firecrackers. The time was right. Somehow the fact that he still had a wife didn't seem to matter anymore.

Lucky got through the evening in a heightened state of sexual anticipation. Marco felt the same way.

Later they came together in exultant ecstasy. A wild ritual of incredible sex, followed by the release of being with each other at last. It was a joining of soul mates. A fusion of energies.

Plans were made. He would tell his wife immediately and arrange a quick divorce. There would be no more separations. Now that it had happened, it would be forever.

When he left her bed in the morning, Lucky knew she had finally found what she had been searching for—a man she could look up to, live with and love. Marco was everything and more. Marco was her world.

At 2:30 P.M. that day, as Lucky sat with Costa in the Patio restaurant waiting for Marco to join her for lunch, she noticed Boogie— her bodyguard—heading swiftly across the room toward her.

As he approached, she felt a chill of apprehension.

"There's been a shooting," he said.

She knew it was Marco.

She knew it was her future.

She closed her eyes to pray, but with a feeling of foreboding she knew it was too late.

• • • • •

The Bahia Lounge was crowded, but a table was made immediately available for the Santangelo party.

Lucky found herself seated beside Dimitri Stanislopoulos. "How's Olympia?" she asked. Not that she cared. Over the years Olympia had never once tried to get in touch with her. They had not spoken since that fateful night in France thirteen years before. Sometimes Lucky read about her in the newspapers and was bored by the antics of the puffy-looking blonde with too much money and too many husbands. They might have been best friends once, but they were total strangers now.

"She's divorced again," Dimitri said shortly. "For the third time."

He had extremely penetrating eyes, steel gray, and a deep Mediterranean suntan. His eyes lingered on the wildly beautiful Lucky for a moment, then his showgirl friend-for-the-night tugged on his sleeve and asked him some inane question.

Lucky turned to Gino, but his attention was on Susan. She thought she might leave, but decided to stay for the comedian, who was adjusting the mike and opening with a few deadpan comments on the day's news.

A ripple of laughter drifted through the room. He was quick to grab the audience's attention, an audience more attuned to discussing their losses and/or wins rather than to listening to a stream of jokes.

He didn't tell jokes. He commented on life.

He was cutting, satirical and painfully truthful.

"What's his name?" Lucky asked Matt.

"Lennie Golden. You like him?"

"Not bad."

Matt smiled. Jess had come up with a winner, thank Christ. He had taken a risk in booking the guy just because she wanted him to. But he had the hots for little Jess, and now he'd done her a favor, wasn't it about time she returned the compliment? It was funny, really—he had never liked short girls, had always gone for the statuesque type. However, five-foot-nothing Jess had him under her spell. He wanted to get her into bed in the worst way.

Halfway through Lennie Golden's performance Gino leaned over to Lucky and said, "Susan's tired. I'm taking her home. I'll see you tomorrow, kid."

He helped Susan from her seat.

For a moment Lucky was speechless. *Her* evening with *her* father, and he was taking Grace Kelly home. Shit!

"Goodnight, dear. So nice meeting you," said Grace.

Was it her imagination or was there the glint of triumph in Susan's icy blues? Lucky manufactured yet another smile. Better to charm the enemy than to kick them in the teeth. "Nice meeting *you*."

After they left, Lucky was too restless to sit still. She was annoyed *she* hadn't made the first exit. Let Gino see how much it mattered if he wanted to ruin their evening together.

She glanced at the comedian, still getting laughs; noted

Dimitri's strong hand on the thigh of his date; hated the way Matt Traynor waved the front of his silver hair.

Fuck 'em. What a dull group.

"I'll be back," she whispered, although she had no intention of returning.

Outside the lounge the huge casino rocked with action. She cruised around for a while, greeting staff, watching the pit bosses keeping a sharp eye on the croupiers, noting the paying customers in their weird and wonderful outfits. Where else would you see Bermuda shorts beside Balmain gowns? Halter tops next to Halston tuxedos? Hookers and housewives, playboys and punters.

I want to get laid, she thought. *Oh, God, do I want to get laid.*

She went to the front desk and selected the keys to an empty suite. Then she started to cruise. It couldn't be just anybody. There had to be a certain sexual chemistry. After all, it had been a long time.

There was a man playing alone at a roulette table. He was dark, moody-looking. He reminded her of Marco.

No!

Abruptly she turned away.

She felt lonely. What she needed was anonymous sex with an anonymous lover who would give her what she wanted, then just quietly disappear.

A hand gripped her by the arm. A voice said accusingly, "You walked out on me. What's the matter with you? Don't you appreciate exceptional talent when you see it?"

She turned, hesitated for only a second, then smiled dazzlingly. "Lennie Golden," she said. "You're just the man I'm looking for."

5

New York in the summer was not Olympia's favorite place. Too hot, crowded and dirty. She tried to visit as little as possible, but there were times when she had to make the trip. And her mother's third wedding was one of them.

She traveled by Concorde from Paris with her nine-year-old daughter, Brigette, and the girl's English nanny, Mabel. Brigette was a pretty child. She had inherited her mother's thick blond hair and blue eyes, and her father's patrician features and lithe body. She had also inherited Olympia's willful streak.

Nanny Mabel was a frustrated fifty-year-old woman, who, after thirty-five years of "service," considered she had wasted her life looking after other people's children. Olympia was the latest in a long line of wealthy employers, and although she had worked for her for only six months, she had grown to loathe the capricious blond heiress. The child was not much better. Spoiled, selfish and destructive. A miniature version of her mother. Fortunately, the money more than compensated, and Nanny Mabel also enjoyed the limousines, private planes, and first-class service. When in Paris, Olympia rarely visited what she referred to as the "nursery floor" in her duplex apartment on the Avenue Foch, so Nanny Mabel hardly had to put up with her at all.

Olympia was more than a little annoyed that she had been forced to bring Brigette and Nanny with her. But her mother had insisted the child be flower girl at the wedding, and Olympia was unable to summon up a suitable excuse.

Her mother, Charlotte, was a chic American society matron. She had married Dimitri Stanislopoulos at the age of twenty against violent parental objections, given birth to Olympia nine months later and divorced her husband after a year. Then she had returned to America, and within a year remarried, this time to a Wall Street banker, with her parents' full approval. For the first twelve years of her life Olympia had lived with them in America, but when puberty struck, she became unmanageable and screamed to be allowed to live with her father, who flitted between his Greek island, his yacht and his mansion in Paris. They compromised, and sent her to a series of boarding schools—all of which she managed to get thrown out of. Eventually she got her wish and moved in with Dimitri, who treated her as just another houseguest.

Charlotte's banker husband, a stepfather who Olympia never warmed to, had passed away a year ago. Now Charlotte had a new prospect ready for the altar—a film producer who Olympia had no desire to meet.

"Mama," said Brigette, as they were escorted out of customs. "I see the men with the cameras." At nine she spoke three languages fluently.

"Head down, eyes straight ahead," warned Nanny Mabel sternly. "Never acknowledge their presence."

Olympia touched her golden curls, fluffed them out a little. She hated the paparazzi, but if they were going to catch you— well, one may as well appear at one's best. It wouldn't do to be seen looking like Christina Onassis. She adjusted her dark glasses and smoothed down the skirt of her St. Laurent suit.

The cameramen leaped into action.

It wasn't easy being one of the richest women in the world.

• • • • •

Dimitri Stanislopoulos was not interested in the showgirl Matt Traynor had arranged for his pleasure. She was young and not even all that pretty. He was sixty-two years old. He did not need the boring conversation of a woman forty years younger. He preferred to play baccarat, so Matt set him up at a private table with several other high-rolling guests. There was a male singing star wearing a bad toupee; a French princess with skin the color and texture of baked mud; two Japanese electronics kings; and the English girlfriend of an Arab munitions dealer.

Dimitri knew the woman. He nodded at her. She nodded back. He found her a far more interesting proposition than the vacuous showgirl.

"Where is Saud?" he asked, swooping to kiss her hand.

"L.A.," she replied. "He'll be back tomorrow. I'm keeping his seat warm."

And more than that, Dimitri thought. He liked English-women. In bed, they had a certain whorelike quality. Very appealing. And he should know—his mistress for the last eight years had been a world-renowned English stage actress, Francesca Fern—an immense talent and a flamboyant personality. She was fifty years old, with flame-red hair, piercing eyes, succulent lips and a beaky nose to rival his own. Francesca. What a woman! He loved her power, her dramatic presence and her passion.

Ah . . . her passion. She was the most exciting woman he had ever bedded. And that was saying something, since he had slept with many of the most beautiful and cultured women in Europe.

Dimitri liked expensive women who knew all about the finer things in life. He liked them clad in sable, with jewelry from Cartier and Asprey and Bulgari. He liked them in Dior clothes with designer underwear and five-hundred-dollar shoes. He liked them to know all about good food, fine wine, classical music, opera and the ballet.

He liked breeding. And he did not mind paying for it.

During their affair, he had gifted Francesca with a king's ransom in jewelry. She accepted everything he gave her with a knowing glint in her eye and a husky "Thank you, darling" as if the prizes he found for her were no more than trinkets.

He admired her tremendous style. He did not admire her husband, a puny little man called Horace whom she resolutely refused to divorce. They had enjoyed some of their hotter fights concerning Horace.

"Leave him!" Dimitri would bellow.

"I can't," Francesca would reply dramatically. "It will kill him. I am his life." And tears would fill her heavily outlined eyes.

"But I want to marry you," Dimitri would shout.

"One day," Francesca would husk vaguely, "we will be together forever."

In the meantime, Horace did not interfere with their tempestuous *affaire*. He put up with it, as he put up with most things in life, and stayed quietly in the background of his wife's volatile life. Once a year they rendezvoused on Dimitri's palatial ocean-going yacht—Francesca and Horace, accompanied by her personal maid, her own hairdresser, and sometimes her two ancient Pekinese dogs.

Dimitri always invited other guests for the August cruise. It was a time he looked forward to because he had Francesca to himself—well, almost. She spent every night in his stateroom. He never *had* found out how she explained this to Horace. He never really cared. Horace must know. Horace was complaisant.

Occasionally they met in other parts of the world. New York, Paris, Rome. Even when he married for the second time they continued to meet. His second marriage lasted no longer than his first. Dimitri Stanislopoulos was not an easy man to live with.

The baccarat game was starting. "What's the limit at this table?" Dimitri asked one of the steely-eyed croupiers.

"Six thousand dollars, Mr. Stanislopoulos," replied the man, expressionless.

"Give me two hundred thousand dollars' worth of chips."

Deftly the man piled gold five-hundred-dollar chips in neat stacks and pushed them in front of him. Unobtrusively a marker was produced for his signature.

Dimitri liked to gamble. It relaxed him. And he needed to relax, for Francesca was arriving in two days' time to attend a televised gala evening in her honor, and he had finally decided. Eight years was long enough. One way or another, Horace had to go.

6

"Hey," said Lucky. "What's the matter with you?"

"What's the matter with *me?*" replied Lennie, outraged.

They faced each other warily in the opulent luxury of the darkened hotel suite. She had said, "You're just the man I'm looking for." Then she had taken him by the hand, adding mysteriously, "Come with me." And had led him to the nearest elevator. Once inside the suite she had pressed against him, kissed him long and hard, then groped him intimately.

He was not yet in a gropable state. In fact, he was trying to figure out what the hell was going on.

"Are you selling it?" he had asked.

"Are you kidding?" she had replied, and proceeded to remove her dress.

He had said, "Hold it, I don't want you to do that."

Now they were ready for battle.

"You got a problem?" she sighed.

"Yeah. I think I got a problem."

A shrug of impatience. Obviously she had picked the wrong guy.

"What is it?" she asked disinterestedly, zipping up the soft leather dress she had been about to step out of. May as well end *this* scene. And fast.

Lennie stared at her in amazement. He did not believe what was happening. Here was this woman—this strikingly *beautiful* woman whom he had first spotted at the airport, spoken to by the pool—and been insulted for his trouble. Then she had appeared in the Bahia Lounge and *walked out on his act.* Now she was coming on to him like a steam roller, and expected instant action. What did she think he was—a traveling stud with no feelings? She could be the most gorgeous woman in the world, but sex with no communication was just not for him. He wasn't sixteen and desperate to get laid.

"My problem is I don't even know your name, let alone what's going on," he said tightly.

"Oh, and if I tell you my name, will that make everything all right?" she mocked, all zipped up and ready to leave.

"You know what I mean," he said angrily.

"No. I don't know what you mean." Coolly she strolled toward the door. "It's simple really. I saw you. Liked you. Thought that maybe the two of us might equal great sex. Obviously I was wrong."

"How come you didn't think we equaled great sex this afternoon?" he said quickly.

"What are you talking about?"

"This afternoon. Out by the pool. When I spoke to you and you gave me the icy treatment."

"Was that you?"

Jesus! She didn't even remember him. And he was supposed to get a hard-on?

"Look," she said impatiently, hand on the doorknob, "I'm sure we've all made mistakes before. Why don't we just forget the whole thing?"

Lennie had been through a lot of women in his time, but this one took the prize. Even Eden would never behave like this.

He wished she wasn't so goddamn horny-looking. How could he let her walk out when she was offering a trip he'd probably never forget?

He decided to put a little charm back into his act. "You know what I think?" he said. "I think that maybe we should start from page one, go downstairs, find a bar, have a drink and get to know each other. Hey—at least exchange names. And then, beautiful lady, we can have *really* great sex. What do you say?"

She was bored with Lennie Golden. The entire incident was a mistake. She opened the door and headed for the elevator. "Let's just forget it," she said offhandedly.

He followed, grabbed her by the arm. "Let's not."

Now that he couldn't get it up, he was not going to be easy to shake. Masculine pride or some such crap. "Hmmm . . ." she said. "That's not a bad idea."

He had her. They were all easy. One drink, maybe two, *then* they would go to bed, with *him* calling the shots.

"You go on down to the Bahia, order me a Bloody Mary. I just want to freshen up." She smiled. "Five minutes, okay?"

• • • • •

Lennie leaned across the green baize of Jess's blackjack table. She dealt like greased lightning, her eyes never leaving the shiny box known as the shoe, which held the cards.

"Don't bother to wait, I won't be coming home tonight," he said.

"Why not?" she muttered out of the corner of her mouth.

"Why do you think not? The Golden charm works again."

"Really? Who'd you score with this time?"

"Are we playin' or talkin'?" demanded a belligerent blonde in a sequinned tank top. "Gimme a card."

Jess grimaced, pulled a three from the shoe, with sleight of hand magically turned it into a nine—thereby putting sequinned tank top over twenty-one and out.

"Aw, crap!" the woman exclaimed loudly.

Jess allowed herself a secret wink in Lennie's direction. "Call me," she mouthed. She didn't usually play God with the cards, but sometimes she just couldn't help it.

Lennie grinned and strolled away. Now that his evening was set he felt pretty good. They had loved him in the Bahia Lounge—given him a great reception. His two-week gig was going to be a big success—he could feel it. Now he had this wild-looking female to deal with, and she looked like more than enough to occupy him for two weeks. Maybe even make him forget Eden, although he doubted if she could do that. He wondered what her name was, what she was doing in Vegas, what she would be like in bed. . . .

Yeah—a two-week relationship would suit him fine. He

had had it with heavy involvements. First they stayed the night, next the weekend, finally they took over everything, until taking a shower was one long obstacle course strewn with panty hose and bras.

He hurried into the Bahia Lounge, ordered himself a beer and a Bloody Mary for her—whatever her name was. He would know soon enough. He would know more than her name.

• • • • •

Matt Traynor's apartment was decorated in early nouveau riche. A lot of ornamental gilt, black fur, fake marble and damask-covered couches. A sign behind the bar read "Matt's Place," and his lead crystal glasses were embossed with his initials, as were his shirts, socks, undershorts, sheets, towels and pajamas.

"Wow!" exclaimed his date, six months out of Ohio and impressed. "What a *fabulous* place."

He poured her undiluted Scotch, switched Sinatra on the stereo and adjusted the pink lighting to low.

"Wow!" said Miss Ohio. "What a *fabulous* singer. Who is it?"

"Are you jesting with me, young lady?"

"What?"

He wondered if she gave blow jobs.

"Sinatra," he said.

"Oh. *Fabulous!*"

"*You're* fabulous."

She giggled inanely and sucked suggestively on an ice cube.

"In fact," he continued, "you're the most fabulous girl I've seen all year."

"Really?"

"Really."

He reached for her left boob and circled the nipple with his thumb.

She took a swig of Scotch, put the glass down and leaned back on the couch.

He kept his thumb twirling and bent to kiss her.

She responded nicely while Sinatra crooned "Strangers in the Night."

He maneuvered her boob from the confines of her scoop-neckline sweater and bent his head to the erect nipple.

"Fabulous!" she murmured.

He unzipped his fly, allowing what he considered to be a healthy hard-on to escape. Then he took her right hand and placed it where it would find gainful employment.

The phone rang. He had forgotten to put on the answering machine.

"Goddamn it!" he said.

"Don't answer," she said.

His hard-on deflated. He picked up the offending instrument. "Yes?" he snapped.

"Matt. This is Lucky. I want you here. Now. There's something I need taken care of."

"Can't it hold until tomorrow?"

"No."

For the second time that night he was more than pissed off with the Santangelos. First Gino, now Lucky. The pair of them were a pain in the ass.

"If it's important—"

"It is. Come to my apartment."

"I'll be there."

"Fast."

He banged the receiver down and stood up. His penis hung out of his trousers, a sorry reminder of what might have been. Quickly he zipped it from sight.

"I've got to go out," he said.

"Oh, what a shame!"

"Can you wait for me?"

"Well . . ."

"There's television, and you can have fun in the Jacuzzi. I won't be long."

She wasn't hard to persuade. "Fabulous!" she said, and
Sinatra crooned on.

• • • • •

Lennie glanced at his watch. Half an hour had passed and she
obviously had no intention of showing up. Bitch! They were
all the same. And this one was a wacko anyway, it was better
she *didn't* show.

But still . . . He was mad—at himself more than anything.
If he thought she was so horny-looking, why hadn't he taken
her up on her offer? *Wham bam, thank you ma'am.* And goodbye, Charlie.

For Christ's sake, what was so threatening about a woman
instigating the proceedings? He could deal with that.

She had probably not shown because she figured him for a
jerk. And rightfully so. No doubt he had turned down a great
experience. Jesus! He couldn't wait to tell Jess about it. They
would at least get a few laughs out of Lennie Golden—the
reluctant fuck! Hey—he might be able to work it into some
great comedy schtick.

He thought he might call her. What did he have to lose?
And maybe it wasn't too late.

Suite eleven twenty-two—the memory never let him down.
He hurried to a house phone. No answer. Maybe she was out
cruising, busy finding a replacement for Mr. Reluctant.

Why was he feeling jealous of someone he didn't even
know?

Why could he see her face, that beautiful face?

And why could he feel her lips, full and sensual and . . .

Knock it off, schmuck. You blew it. Don't sweat it. Forget it. At
least his routine had been a smash.

Tonight the Magiriano.

Tomorrow the Carson show.

Why not?

He had worked his balls off for it.

7

"Fire the comedian," said Lucky.

Matt frowned. "What?"

"Lennie Golden. That's his name, isn't it?"

"You mean Lennie Golden who went on tonight in the lounge?"

"Do we have two Lennie Goldens working for us?"

"I don't understand. He opened great. The audience loved him. Even *you* said he was good."

Coolly she lit a cigarette and stared out at the spectacular view over the Strip. "I never said he wasn't good. I just said I want you to fire him."

"Is that what you summoned me for?"

"Yes."

"Jesus Christ, Lucky." A vein throbbed angrily near his temple. "Jesus Christ! I'm not some lackey you can jerk around on a string. It's two o'clock in the morning. Why didn't you tell me on the phone?"

She wondered if he would dare speak to Gino like that. Decided he wouldn't.

"Do you like your job here?" she asked mildly.

"It's not a job. I got points in the place. I'm a director of the company."

"Sure. *I* made you a director, and I can move you out any time I want."

"So do it," he snorted.

"Maybe I will."

They glared at each other. He broke the stare first. Working for the Santangelos gave him more power than he'd ever had in his life. He didn't want to blow it. "So what is it you want me to do?" he said sourly.

"Pay him. Fire him. Get him off the premises."

"May I at least ask why?"

"Because he's *too* good for the lounge. He makes people think. He makes them laugh. He stops them drinking and playing the tables. I want you to fire him tonight and get him out of here."

"If that's what you want."

"It's *exactly* what I want."

After he left, she finished her cigarette, then went to the bureau and fished out a joint. She would get high instead of laid. Probably more satisfying in the long run.

How nice to phone Gino now, have a father-daughter chat.

Ha! She laughed aloud. They had never had that sort of a relationship. Not since she was five years old. Not since her mother was murdered. . . .

Flashes of white-hot pain. She could still picture the scene as vividly as if it were yesterday. The pink pool . . . Maria's naked body floating on a raft . . . her long blond hair fanning out in the water . . .

Abruptly she closed her eyes, but the image became even more vivid. For a year she and Gino had been wonderfully close, but never close enough to discuss what had happened to Maria, never close enough . . .

She began to cry. But she didn't know she was crying until the tears rolled down her cheeks.

Lucky Santangelo crying. Never.

Angrily she wiped her face. Goddamn it! Gino found himself a girlfriend and she went to pieces. She hadn't even missed him when he was seven years in exile. Hadn't given him so much as a second thought when she took over his empire. Now he was shacking up and she was breaking down. What *was* this crap?

• • • • •

In 1977 Gino returned to America. A six-million-dollar settlement with the IRS plus pulling a few strings made it possible.

Lucky awaited his return with trepidation. He needn't think he was taking over. She had worked hard, made her mark, and now she planned to stand firm. Of course, it would mean returning to Vegas, a city she had stayed away from since Marco's murder.

Enzio Bonnatti had been wonderful. He had tracked the assassin, dealt with the slime and taken over the running of the Magiriano until she wished to go back.

With Gino's imminent reentry into America, the time had come.

Costa arranged a meeting two days after Gino's return. They met at the Pierre Hotel in New York. Father and daughter. Seven years apart. Seven years of silence. Lucky was hostile and uneasy, although Gino seemed friendly enough. He could see at once that this was not the spoiled girl he had left behind. This was a woman, self-assured, confident.

He smiled and held open his arms. "Lucky."

She was taken aback. Did he honestly expect it to be that easy?

He stared at her quizzically and tried to turn his arms into a gesture, a shrug. "Well, well," he said, "look at you. All grown up."

She regarded him coldly. "I thought I was all grown up when you married me off at sixteen."

"So it didn't work out. But it kept you out of trouble, right? You goin' to hold a grudge forever, kid?"

She spotted a bottle of Scotch and poured herself a hefty glass.

Gino did not take his eyes off her. "I guess we better talk," he said at last.

She was unnerved by his steady stare. "Yes," she said defiantly. "A lot of things have changed while you've been away. I'm involved now, I'm part of it."

"So I heard."

She turned to face him, her eyes blazing. "I can tell you this— no way are you shoving me out. No way. Vegas is mine, and I'm going back."

"A little late in the day."

"What do you mean?"

"Come on, Lucky—you seem like a smart girl. You gave Vegas to Bonnatti—handed it to him. You think he'll just step down with a smile?"

"I know how to handle him."

He laughed aloud. "Don't you realize Bonnatti is no longer our friend?"

Yes, she knew. Although she wasn't about to admit it to Gino. Earlier that day, Boogie had flown in from Vegas with stories of betrayal that made her cold with fury and hot for revenge. It seemed she'd been taken for dumb pussy. Bonnatti had arranged Marco's murder. He had wanted her out of Vegas—and getting rid of Marco did the job. She had fled, just like the bastard knew she would. And now he had control. But not for long—she had her plans. And Gino was not going to screw them up.

Before they could discuss the matter further, Dario arrived.

Lucky wasn't pleased. This was supposed to be a business meeting and it was turning into a family reunion.

Dario did not stay long. He was a jumpy, nervous wreck, and after ten minutes of stilted conversation he ran from the room like a thief.

"What the fuck is the matter with that kid?" Gino stormed. "Get him back, Costa. I think it's about time I straightened the little pansy out." Much to his chagrin Costa had relayed his son's sexual preferences to him.

"Oh," said Lucky. "I think you've left that a bit late. If you had paid more attention to him when he was a teenager—"

Gino whirled on her. "And who do you think you're talkin' to?"

She didn't back down. "When Dario and I were little we had no family life. Shut up in that Bel Air mausoleum like a couple of lepers. No wonder Dario is screwed up today."

He glared at her. "Terrible life you had. A beautiful home. The best money could buy."

She raised her voice excitedly. "Money. Who cares about money? I wanted you when I was growing up. I wanted you to care—to be with me. I wanted you to be a proper father."

Her words cut into him. "I always did the best for both of you," he growled. "The best I knew how—"

"Well, it wasn't enough," she said triumphantly.

Police sirens wailed in the street outside. Costa went to the window and tried to see what was going on.

"Get the fuck out of here and bring Dario back," *Gino screamed. Costa left hurriedly.*

"I'm going," *Lucky said.* "You and I—we can't communicate. We never could."

"You talk about me bein' a proper father," *he steamed.* "How about you bein' a proper daughter? Runnin' away from school. Screwin' anything in pants. Goin' from—"

"I didn't," *she interrupted, furiously.* "And even if I did, so what?"

"So what? she says. So what?" *He shook his head sadly.* "You're right, Lucky. You an' I—we just aren't on the same wavelength. Why don't you go? Seven years an' not even a lousy postcard. That's a* daughter?" *He felt suddenly tired. Someone was pounding on the door. He opened it and Costa burst in, white and trembling.* "Dario's been shot," *he gasped,* "outside the hotel. He's dead."

"Holy Christ!" *Gino cried out.* "Holy Mother of Christ!"

Lucky stood transfixed.

Suddenly Gino clutched his chest and staggered toward the couch. A low moan escaped his lips.

"What is it?" *Lucky asked urgently.* "What is it?"

He moaned again, his face gray. All at once he looked every one of his seventy-one years.

"I...think...it's...my...heart..." *he mumbled.* "You'd... better...get...me...a...doctor...fast."

It took her father's near death for Lucky to realize how much she really loved him. He had his faults, but he was still Daddy ... Gino. And when he whispered from his hospital bed, where he hovered between life and death, for her to take revenge, honor the family name, she knew at once that she would do as he had asked, with no question.

Enzio Bonnatti.

Friend.

Godfather.

Assassin.

Betrayer.

She drove to his mansion out on Long Island, filled with an icy calm.

Revenge. Why not?

Revenge for the Santangelos and for Marco. There was no son to do the job—it fell upon her shoulders, and she did not flinch from family responsibilities.

The shooting of Enzio Bonnatti was a clearcut case of self-defense. Apparently the man had tried to rape Lucky Santangelo, and she had shot him with his own gun. The case never even came to court.

With Lucky by his side, Gino recovered quickly, and gradually they rediscovered the closeness they had once shared before Maria's death. They moved back to Vegas. "You take the Magiriano, kid," Gino said. "I'll have the Mirage. One of these days we'll build a place together."

It was a dream. But Lucky always knew it could become a reality.

For one year they had been inseparable. Now there was the widow Martino to contend with.

• • • • •

An old Clint Eastwood movie played on television. Lucky finished the joint and watched it for a while. She liked Eastwood. He had a sort of silent eroticism that appealed to her. He was probably a great lay.

Gradually she drifted off to sleep, only to be jolted awake at dawn by a forgotten nightmare.

She got up, pulled a silk kimono over her nakedness, and watched the sun rise over the desert. It was a beautiful sight. Once she might have phoned Gino, woken him and allowed him to share it with her. But in the morning light she realized it was okay if he'd found someone to spend the night with. She could be a lot of things to him, but she could never be his lover. And perhaps he needed the closeness of a woman to hold.

Maybe Susan Martino would be good for him.

Maybe.

8

Once in a while Olympia decided she should play the perfect mother role. Not often. It was hardly a part she relished. However, a meeting with her own mother required that she make the effort.

Charlotte intimidated her. She was so annoyingly correct. She did not smoke or drink. She certainly did not do drugs. She was slim, active, and an utter bore. She was also very rich—although that was one area where Olympia beat her out. It would be hard to top Olympia's massive fortune.

Unfortunately, being in Charlotte's presence always made her feel like a child again, so before leaving, Olympia sat in the luxurious bathroom of her father's Fifth Avenue penthouse and snorted three lines of coke. The insidious white powder made her feel marvelous. A deep breath, a glance in the mirror, and she was ready for anyone and anything.

Nanny Mabel and Brigette waited by the front door. The child gazed up at her mother, huge saucer eyes in a picture-pretty face. "Mama," she said, "please can I have a hot dog?"

"What?" snapped Olympia, adjusting the collar of her sable jacket in the hall mirror.

"An American hot dog," the small girl repeated patiently.

"Certainly not," scolded Nanny Mabel. "Wherever do you get such ideas?"

"Mama?" questioned Brigette, ignoring her nanny. "Can I?"

"Hmmm . . ." Olympia replied vaguely, licking her lips and sucking in her cheeks. "Whatever Nanny says . . ."

"Nanny says no," whined Brigette.

Olympia's voice rose slightly. "Then *listen* to Nanny. Do come on."

She marched out of the apartment, followed by the two of them. Into the elevator, onto the sidewalk.

The chauffeur leaped out of the waiting limousine and held open the door. Two idling paparazzi raised their cameras.

Olympia manufactured a condescending smile and reached for Brigette's hand. The child suddenly stood stock still and screamed, "I *haaate* everyone!"

"Brigette," exclaimed a furious Nanny Mabel, "stop this behavior *at once!*"

The two photographers, sensing something more than the usual polite picture, began to snap in earnest.

Brigette, now the center of attention and enjoying it, yelled even louder.

Olympia wanted to jump in the car and distance herself from the whole embarrassing scene. But how could she? The screaming brat was *her* child—unfortunately—and she was playing perfect mother for the day.

"Do something," she hissed at Nanny.

"I can't, madam." Her attempts to pull Brigette toward the car were unsuccessful.

"Oh, God!" exclaimed Olympia. A flash exploded in front of her face. "Go away, you stupid little man," she shouted at the photographer.

An amused crowd was gathering. Olympia could stand it no longer. She turned on Brigette in a fury, smacked her across the face, picked the surprised child up and flung her into the car.

The cameras captured every moment.

· · · · ·

A day later Dimitri viewed the photograph of his grandchild being set upon by his daughter with a mixture of annoyance and anger. The annoyance was because he had constantly implored Olympia to avoid publicity. And the anger was because she had struck his precious little Brigette, a child he doted upon.

He flung the newspaper to the ground and picked up the phone. Within seconds he had Nanny Mabel on the line.

"Madame is resting," she said.

"Wake her," thundered Dimitri.

"I'm not allowed to."

"Do it!"

Grumbling to herself, the woman did as she was told.

Olympia hurled abuse and picked up the phone. "What is it?" she demanded. She had long ago stopped being in awe of her father, ever since she had inherited her fortune at twenty-one.

He complained for a while.

She listened fitfully.

He gave orders on how she should conduct herself publicly.

She ignored him.

"Why are you in Las Vegas?" she asked, when he paused for breath.

A moment's silence, then, "Francesca Fern is being honored. As I am such a close friend, she and Horace begged me to attend."

Olympia stifled a rude laugh. God! He made her so mad. He honestly believed no one knew about his affair with prima donna Fern. The whole world knew. They had fucked their way from one end of the globe to the other.

And he had a nerve complaining to *her* about the paparazzi. They had captured *him* doing everything short of actually making it with one of his society whores.

"Who on earth gets honored in a dump like Las Vegas?" she sneered.

He changed the subject. "I want to see Brigette."

"We're staying in New York until Monday."

"I'll try and fly in on Saturday, then we can return to Paris together."

"Good." She was pleased. Better than traveling on a commercial airline. She liked Dimitri's Lear Jet with all its luxuries. When she found the time, maybe she'd buy one for herself.

Once off the phone, she stretched out on the bed and decided New York was turning out to be a fun place after all, if one ignored the paparazzi—and they were everywhere since the now famous photo had appeared on the front of *The New York Post* that very morning.

Tea with Charlotte the day before had gone well. Brigette, after her outburst, behaved perfectly. And Charlotte was so preoccupied with her impending wedding she hardly found time to criticize, although she did mention that Olympia was ten pounds overweight and needed a good facial. Later, Olympia met with friends and had a perfectly wonderful time, ending up at 2 A.M. at Studio 54, which she loved.

Today she had lunched at "21," shopped along Madison, and now she was resting before another evening on the town. She wondered if she would meet Mr. Wrong, and hoped so. Two days without sex was two days too many.

9

Jess presented herself in Matt Traynor's office at noon the day after Lennie's dismissal. She was full of righteous indignation.

"Why did you fire Lennie?"

Matt stared at the angry girl confronting him across his desk. She was so pretty, so stacked, so *short*.

"Jessie baby—" he began.

"Don't call me Jessie, and don't call me baby. Just give me an answer."

He knew what he would like to give her—she made him uncomfortably hot. Instead he shrugged noncommittally and said, "House policy."

"House bullshit. I hear he was great."

"Yes he was, and I told him so, but he stopped people from playing the tables."

She snorted disbelievingly. "Well, if *that's* the reason, why don't you fire Ann-Margret, Diana Ross, Tom Jo—?"

He held up an authoritative hand and wondered if she gave great head. He was sure she did. "Okay, okay. I don't need a list. Why don't you have dinner with me tonight, and I'll try to explain it to you properly."

"I'm working."

"Tomorrow night?"

"Ditto."

"When's your night off?"

"I'm also married. Remember?"

"How about a late supper after your shift tonight?"

"Where?"

He had been asking her out for two months. This was the first breakthrough. "My place," he said quickly.

She laughed loudly. She had a laugh like a hyena and eight

thousand freckles and crazy orange hair. He thought she was the most attractive girl he'd seen in months.

"What's wrong with my place?" he asked belligerently.

"Nothing. Except that every showgirl in town knows its location, size, even the color of your sheets."

"I give a lot of parties," he said defensively.

"That's not all you give. I'm surprised you're not riddled with the clap."

He managed a laugh, quite flattered she knew so much about him. As a matter of fact he had never had the clap, but the rest was accurate. And why not? He was making up for lost time. Married for twenty-four years, he had been divorced by his wife five years ago. *She* divorced *him*. The woman was mad. Nobody could have been a better husband. For the first six months he missed her, and then, like a revelation, the joys of being an affluent, powerful *single* man hit him. And then he found out that while he was married things had changed. The sexual revolution had taken place, and you no longer had to fight and scheme, promise and declare undying love to get a girl into bed. From that moment on Matt lived every second to its fullest. And when his ex-wife—a retarded feminist—decided they should get back together, he told her exactly where to stick the idea.

"Will you have dinner with me or not?" he asked.

Jess chewed on her thumb for a moment—a childhood habit she was unable to break. She really wanted to find out why Lennie had been so unceremoniously dumped. But dinner with Matt Traynor—ugh! With his silver waved hair and his gold chains and his perpetual leer . . .

At least if she went to his place nobody would see them together. It would be too humiliating for people to think she had been added to his list of conquests. She couldn't understand why he wanted her anyway. She was hardly his style. But he had a very obvious yen for her—one she had taken advantage of by getting Lennie the job in the first place. All she'd had to do was show Matt a videotape of his work and a few key reviews—one a rave from *The Village Voice*—and Matt had said, "Sure. We'll book him. If *you* say he's good, that's enough for me."

Lennie's being fired like that had made *her* look a fool. He had hired a car and stormed off to L.A. in the middle of the night with "I don't *need* this shit. Thanks a lot, Jess."

She knew that as soon as he calmed down he would realize it was not her fault, and she hoped by the time he called to apologize she would know exactly what *had* happened.

So dinner with Matt it was.

"Okay," she said.

He looked pleased. "Later?"

She sighed, "I guess."

"Don't look so thrilled about it. Who knows? You might enjoy it."

"I'm a vegetarian."

He wondered if that meant she didn't give head. Decided not to pursue it. "Tonight," he said, "I'm delighted."

"I'm glad someone is," she muttered.

"What?"

"Nothing."

· · · · ·

The rented Chevrolet got Lennie into Los Angeles at eight o'clock in the morning. Not bad considering he hadn't left Vegas until 3:30 A.M.

The city was already hot, a steamy smoggy heat that promised a long and sultry day.

He came off the freeway at the Sunset Boulevard exit, turned left and realized he had no idea of where to go or what to do. He had only been to L.A. once before, and that was on his thirteenth birthday with Mom and Dad. They had stayed with an aunt in the valley for five uneventful days. The highlight of the trip was a visit to Disneyland—memorable because Mom got stoned on excitement and sang "The Star-Spangled Banner" to a wooden Indian.

So—he did not exactly know his way around. However, he did know that getting out of Vegas immediately was an absolute necessity after the silver-haired smarm had told him he was out.

He, Lennie Golden, was out.

OUT.

Dropped.

Bounced.

Fired.

Shit!!

He pulled over to the side of the street and groped in the pocket of his faded work shirt for the infamous Golden black book. It was his lifeline and he carried it everywhere. There were two pages crammed with L.A. numbers. Friends. Contacts. Friends of friends. Agents. Clubs. Connections. And dear old Mom. Feisty Alice Golden—the Jewish mother who would *not* cook him chicken soup or ask about his love life. More likely she would offer him a joint and tell him about hers.

Alice. Maybe he would crash at her place for a couple of days while he thought out his next move. But then he thought about her new boyfriend—the one she had brought to New York last year. A total jerk with false teeth and an uneasy laugh. Lennie was not in the mood for *his* company. He moved down the list.

There was Jennifer. A perfectly delectable sugar-lipped blonde who had abandoned acting class in New York to try her luck in L.A.

There were Suna and Shirlee. The twins. Would-be singers and actresses now doing commercial voice-overs.

There was his friend Joey Firello, a fellow comedian who had arrived in L.A. several months earlier and was already a regular on a weekly TV show.

And then of course there was Eden. They had not parted friends. She had stormed out of his life bad-mouthing him at full volume.

Ah . . . Eden, the queen of all bitches. A beautiful, mean, fucked-up, difficult *cunt*.

He wanted to see her.

He needed to see her.

Maybe she'd dumped her actor friend and was ready for a reunion.

Without hesitation he searched for a dime and a phone booth.

A male voice answered on the third ring. An unfriendly "Yeah?" Was this the actor? Or a new guy? Or maybe just an answering service?

"Eden Antonio," he said briskly.

"Who wants her?" growled the voice.

"Uh, tell her Lennie."

Why did he feel like a twelve-year-old trying to make out? And why was he calling her anyway? What was he going to say? I'm here. Just like that. No job. No place to stay. I'm here. Eden would tell him to shove it.

"She ain't around," said the voice, and cut the connection.

• • • • •

Eden Antonio was not a star, nor even close, but she worked occasionally on a daytime soap, and she knew that eventually it would lead to more important roles.

She sat in the middle of her queen-size bed painting her toenails and said to her current boyfriend—a short bald man wearing an expensive custom-made dark suit—most un-Californian—"Who was that, sweetie?"

Santino Bonnatti shrugged dismissively as he dumped the phone down. "Some jerk." His beady nugget eyes darted around the room. This Eden broad was something, but her apartment was not. "I been thinkin'," he said. "How about if I move ya out of this place an' set y'up in a decent joint. Would y'like that?"

Eden concentrated on her toenails. She had known Santino Bonnatti for six weeks, and she had been sleeping with him for five. He was hardly Paul Newman, but according to her girlfriend Ulla, who had introduced them, he was loaded, and might not be averse to investing in a movie if the right deal came along. "What business is he in?" she had asked Ulla.

Her friend looked vague. "I'm not really sure. Commodities, I think. Import. Export. Important stuff."

That had been enough to pique Eden's interest. For once in her life she wanted a rich boyfriend, not just a good-looking bum with nothing but big dreams and a hard-on.

The fact that Santino had a wife and four kids stashed in a Beverly Hills mansion did not bother her at all. She didn't want to marry him, just use him until he got her where she wanted to be.

"Exactly what did you have in mind?" she asked coolly.

He straightened his tie and peered at his reflection in a mirrored closet. "I dunno," he said vaguely. "I could set ya up in a house. It'd make it easier for me."

"Do you mean buy me a house?" inquired Eden, never one to let the grass grow.

"Yeah," he replied expansively. "Why not?"

Why not indeed? she thought excitedly. I'm screwing your hairy little body, it's about time compensation was forthcoming. A house would be very nice indeed.

She stretched out a long pale leg and admired her blood-red toenails. The black peignoir she wore fell back and exposed a glorious mound of pale-blond pubic hair. She had it dyed regularly.

"I think I would like that a lot," she said slowly.

His beady eyes fixed on her pubis. What a horny broad this one was. A few weeks into the relationship and he was already springing for a house. He felt like slamming another fuck into her, but business called, and she would be available later. "I'll contact a real estate friend who owes me a favor," he said. "We'll find ya somethin' nice."

She smiled. She had thin lips and small perfect teeth. "I'm sure you will, sweetie."

"Gotta go," he said.

"A hard day at the office?" she asked sympathetically.

"Naw. I don't like sittin' behind a desk. I got some foreign shipments comin' in."

She had no idea *what* he did. Every time she asked, he told her something different. One day he was importing olive oil from Italy, the next Colombian coffee. Whatever it was, he was rolling in money.

She held out her arms invitingly. "Do I get a goodbye kiss?"

He obliged.

She waited until the front door slammed behind him, then she rolled onto her stomach, reached under the bed, and pressed the playback on a hidden tape machine connected to the phone. If Santino thought he could censor her calls, he had another think coming. Besides, taping *his* conversations was fascinating—especially when he spoke to his crabby wife with the whining Italian accent.

He had made two calls the previous evening. One a complicated business conversation dealing with shipments and vast sums of money. And the other to tell wifey he was in San Francisco and would not be home.

Lying little shit. Well, they were all liars. And all shits. Eden knew about such things.

"Some jerk" turned out to be Lennie Golden. For a moment Eden felt a rush of excitement—what was *he* doing in town? If indeed he was. Maybe he was calling from New York. She played back the tape.

Lennie Golden. A luxury she had allowed herself. A loser. But sexy and smart and funny, with a great body. Oh, yes—she missed their lovemaking. In a way she missed their fights. And they had had some humdingers!

Then she remembered. Lennie Golden. A one-way street to nowhere. He would always be a nothing. And she, Eden Antonio, was going all the way to the top—with a little help from a friend.

• • • • •

In the underground garage waited Santino's car and driver. His bodyguard, Blackie, had already joined him at the elevator. Santino never traveled anywhere without protection. In his business he needed it. There was no reason to take unnecessary risks, and that's what Eden's crummy apartment was.

"Remind me," he said to Blackie, "I gotta get this broad set up in a house."

"Yes, boss." Blackie nodded.

Santino took a breath spray from his pocket and squirted it into his mouth. Eden intrigued him. She was beautiful and cold and a user. It would be interesting breaking her in. She thought he was a mark, ready to be fleeced. But she didn't know him, did she?

She would. When he was ready. And only then.

• • • • •

Wayland did not bother asking where Lennie was, so Jess felt no need to explain his abrupt exit.

She returned home after meeting with Matt, stripped off her clothes and flopped out on the overgrown grass beside the dirty pool.

Wayland was in a daze—as usual, so stoned he didn't care what happened to anyone. The baby was asleep in a wicker carry-basket under a tree. Jess bit on a hangnail and thought about her life. It wasn't perfect. Whose was? But it could certainly be a lot better.

Why had she married Wayland?

Was being seven months pregnant a good enough reason?

Maybe. Maybe not. Plenty of people had kids without getting married. Yeah, but maybe they didn't have a mother dying of cancer in the hospital. A mother whose fervent wish was to see her only daughter married.

Funny, really, for all of her thirty years she and her mother had fought over everything. Came the crunch, and she found she would do anything for the woman who had brought her into the world. So she married Wayland, who at least before they did the deed seemed like a fairly normal human being— not the stoned zombie she had ended up with.

He had *really* fallen into a soft patch. A wife who worked her ass off, cleaned the house, looked after the baby *and* kept him in drugs. What more could a man ask for? Man. That was a laugh. He hadn't been near her in months. He preferred to get high rather than laid. The two did not always go together. Not that she cared. She would rather he *didn't* touch her. He never showered, his hair was always dirty, and his teeth were beginning to rot because of the nasty little habit he had of ingesting pure sugar—just spooning it straight from the package. Disgusting!

She gave a long-drawn-out sigh. She was depressed by Lennie's leaving. They had spent hardly any time together, and she had harbored the hope that once they talked—*really* talked—he would help and advise her. In fact she had been counting on him to get her out of the mess she was in. She hadn't told him about her mother, had not wanted to upset him on his first day in town. Now it was too late. He had thought she was out screwing around. Ha! Who had the time, energy or inclination? Her hours were spent between home, hospital and the casino.

She stared at Wayland and hated him. When they first met he had seemed like a gentle, easygoing, kind person. A touch eccentric, but he was an artist. He had shown her a portfolio of brilliant drawings. Since they were married he had not put pen to paper, let alone brush to canvas.

For gentle, read weak; for easygoing, lazy; for kind, dumb. She snorted in disgust, and the baby started to cry. Wayland did not budge—naturally. Jess jumped up and scooped Simon from his basket. At least she had a gorgeous baby—the relationship had produced *something* of value.

She walked slowly into the house and thought about dinner with Matt Traynor. Not an event she relished, but maybe if she found out the truth she could persuade him to rehire Lennie.

Oh, if only she could! She needed a friend, and she needed him now.

• • • • •

So much for Eden. In a way Lennie was relieved, because he really wasn't prepared to talk to her. Best to get settled first and *then* give her a call.

While he was near a phone he decided he would check out his mother. Maybe the boyfriend had moved on—one never knew with Alice. She had gotten herself an answering machine, and there she was in high spirits and gravelly voice saying, *"Hi-de-ho! This is Alice. I am out. Disappointed? Don't be. Leave your name, your number, and (giggle, giggle) vital statistics. If your luck is in, I will call you back."*

Why did she make him cringe with embarrassment? Shouldn't he have learned to accept her by now? He tried Joey Firello. Also out. Then he called the twins.

Shirlee answered, screamed a greeting, and insisted he come by for breakfast immediately. It seemed like a good idea. Besides, he had nowhere else to go.

10

In the morning Lucky felt great. She was back, the sun was shining, and she couldn't imagine why she had been so uptight about Gino and the widow Martino the night before. It was nothing. It was a lay. Someone different. A constant parade of showgirls was enough to get anyone down.

She grinned. Good old Gino. He still had it. She should be proud of him, not mad. And today they would get everything settled—it would be business as usual.

In high spirits she leaped out of bed, did a few isometrics, then threw herself under an icy shower. For a split second she saw Marco's smiling face, so handsome and dark. . . .

She forced the image away and thought instead about the casual pickup the night before. Fortunately he had not been hot to trot, because she would have regretted it in the morning. How dumb of her to have picked an employee—she hoped Matt had done as she asked and fired him.

She stepped from the shower, shook drops of water from her glistening black hair and slipped into a white toweling track suit. In Atlantic City she had run for the first time and had liked it. There was a jogging track on the grounds of the Magiriano and she planned to use it.

Downstairs early-morning gamblers filled the casino. The ping of the slot machines was a twenty-four-hour sound. It reassured Lucky that all was in order. She stopped for an orange juice in the coffee shop, chatted with a couple of security guards, then made her way down to the gym, where she found Boogie working out with weights.

"Hey–hey–hey!" she exclaimed. "What's with you?"

Boogie looked sheepish at having been caught. He was tall and quick and skinny—never thought about developing a muscle in his life.

"It must be love," Lucky crooned, and with a wave made her way outside to the running track.

• • • • •

Gino's morning progressed at a more leisurely pace.

Susan awoke him, again with a tray of goodies, kissed him lightly on the lips and said, "I never realized anyone could make me as happy as you do."

He struggled awake with a grin. This sure was some classy broad. "You don't do a bad job yourself," he said, and decided he would buy her a present, maybe an important piece of jewelry.

She smiled, all pearly teeth and swept-back hair. She looked like a million bucks in the morning.

He fingered the décolleté of her beige lace peignoir. "Anyone ever tell you you got great tits?"

"Gino!"

"Wassamatter? No one ever told you that?"

"Not in quite such a way."

He gave a dirty laugh. "You're such a goddamn lady. That's what I like about you."

"Ah . . . so that's what you like," she murmured teasingly.

"That and your great tits!"

He dug his hands in and she imperceptibly flinched, but did not draw back.

He played with her nipple and guided her hand to his penis. Deftly she moved away. "Breakfast time," she said sweetly.

Obligingly his hard-on slid into oblivion.

"Hey," he objected, "last person who told me to eat my breakfast was a six-foot nurse with hair on her chin."

"Eat up."

He grinned. "I'd sooner eat your pussy."

"Gino! Sometimes I wonder if you're seventy or seventeen."

"Just keep wondering, sweetheart. I like to keep 'em guessing."

• • • • •

After running around the track for twenty minutes, Lucky took a brisk swim in the super-Olympic-size pool. She managed twenty-five laps, which pleased her, considering she was out of practice. On her way back upstairs, she stopped by Matt's office, but he was not in.

She sat on his desk and called Gino. He was not there either. For a moment her face clouded over. Two nights in a row with the widow Martino? Two all-nighters, when he loved his own bed? Two nights of solid fucking—which was not good for a seventy-two-year-old man with a heart condition.

She frowned. Her day did not seem quite so bright. She needed answers, and he was out getting laid.

"Have him call me the minute he gets back," she said to the operator. "Oh, and you can tell him it's urgent."

• • • • •

By the time Gino was dressed and ready to leave the comfort of Susan's rented house, it was past noon. Susan, dressed in a crisp white tennis dress, sat under an umbrella on the patio sipping iced mint tea.

"Would you care for some?" she said.

He was still in a joking mood. "What did you have in mind?"

"Tea, dear. Not even Superman could manage anything else today."

"Hey—" he said. "How about tonight? You wanna have dinner with me and Lucky?"

A tiny note of surprise crept into her carefully modulated tone. "Do you always dine with your daughter?"

"Huh? Yeh . . . well, most times. We kinda got into the habit."

"Doesn't she have a boyfriend?"

He shrugged. "She was married to this guy—a real nothing. My fault."

"Why was it your fault?"

"I married her off when she was very young. Thought I was keepin' her out of trouble 'stead of gettin' her into it. She divorced him when I was out of the country. Now she's wrapped up in the business—knows as much about things as I do."

"And you spend all your time together?" Susan stated dryly.

"Suits both of us."

It doesn't suit me, she thought, but did not say. Instead she beamed and murmured, "Lovely. We'll all have dinner. Lucky sounds like such an interesting girl. I shall enjoy getting to know her."

• • • • •

Matt reached Lucky before Gino. His tone was cool.

"Are you pissed at me?" she questioned.

"Why should I be? I dig getting out of bed at two o'clock in the morning and firing a first-class comedian who didn't do a thing to deserve it."

"Don't say 'dig.' It makes you sound like some creep from the stone age."

"Thank you."

"You're welcome." A long silence, which *she* finally broke. "Who will you replace him with?"

"A singing nun. Should send people to the tables in droves."

"Ha, ha. Was he upset?"

"Of course the poor bastard was upset. His ego took a nosedive."

"Tough." She paused, then added, "You paid him for the whole two weeks?"

"I even gave him a bonus."

"Then that's okay."

"If you say so."

She put the phone down and hoped she would never set eyes on Lennie Golden again. He was the first man ever to reject her advances. Still . . . even if he *had* performed she would have fired him. He had gotten himself caught in a no-win situation. It was his own fault anyway. He had started the whole thing by the pool in the afternoon, coming on to her like stud of the year. Of course, physically, he *was* undeniably attractive. Not *her* type, she didn't go for the Robert Redford look. She liked her men dark and hard with a certain menace about them. Who did the creep think he was anyway? She hated guys like that.

Suddenly she saw the funny side of it. Mr. Come-on couldn't get it up. The only way *he* made it was *his* way.

She hoped he had learned his lesson.

* * * * *

The pure yellow diamond ring on the widow Martino's pinky sparkled brightly.

Gino could not wipe the grin from his face.

Lucky scowled.

Another sensational evening. Just the three of them this time. And the bitch giving Lucky digs that she recognized as major danger signals.

Naturally it was all very civilized. Susan, calm and charming. Only Lucky caught every one of the zingers that came her way.

She did not rise to the bait. She knew she was being set up, and there was no way she was blowing it in front of Gino. Susan *wanted* her to blow. Susan *wanted* a confrontation.

So Lucky stayed cool. She smiled and fended impertinent questions and laughed and joked, while all the time her black eyes shone with fury that this grasping woman had somehow invaded their lives.

"What do you think?" Gino asked proudly, when Susan finally went to the ladies' room.

I think you're getting senile.

I think she's a cunt.

"I think she's very . . . uh . . ." she groped for a suitable adjective ". . . attractive." Jokingly she added, "But isn't she a touch ancient for Gino the Ram?"

She used the nickname he had carried in his youth. Costa had told her all about *that* part of his life.

Gino fingered the almost faded scar on his cheek, another reminder of far-off days, and smiled ruefully. "I don't want the twenty-year-olds, they got no conversation. I don't want the thirty-year-olds, they're all lookin' to get hitched. Susan's just right for me."

"How old *is* she?"

"I don't know, and I ain't bothered. Forty something. Who gives a shit?"

Forty something, my ass. She has to be over fifty at the very least.

"She must have been awfully young when she married Tiny. Weren't they together thirty years?" Lucky asked artlessly.

"Nah. More like twenty."

"Oh. I read somewhere it was thirty."

"Yeh?"

At least she had implanted the suspicion that the widow Martino was older than he thought.

"Excuse me, dear." Susan returned to the table freshly powdered and lipsticked, and smelling of Estée Lauder's Youth Dew.

Lucky stifled her fury. She was not about to sit there any longer. "I think I'll stroll around the casino. You don't mind, do you?"

Mind? They couldn't care less if she took a running dive off the roof of the hotel.

11

The twins greeted Lennie exuberantly. He hadn't seen them in eighteen months and was amazed at the transformation. In New York they had been two fairly ordinary-looking girls. Not unattractive, but no raving beauties. Now they were traffic stoppers. Platinum blondes (previously the hair was mouse) with matching nose jobs, gleaming suntans, gorgeous bodies and pneumatic breasts (California silicone at its best).

"I don't believe it!" he exclaimed.

"It cost a *fortune*—but it's worth every red cent," drawled Suna.

"Sure is," agreed Shirlee.

"You look awful," they chorused.

"Thanks a lot," he replied. He really needed this.

They lived in a tiny wooden one-story house on Keith Avenue, with dead plants hanging on the porch in their macramé baskets, and a withered grapevine clinging hopelessly to its side. The house was filled with a hodgepodge of Salvation Army furniture and junk. There was a minute backyard, and a clapped-out Volkswagen parked in front.

The two girls wore brief striped leotards and high-heeled white sandals. They were identical.

"What are you doin' here, Lennie?" they chorused, settling him on a couch with busted stuffing and sitting down on either side of him.

He laughed. "I honestly don't know. Drove in last night with nothing in mind."

"From New York?" asked Shirlee.

"Some drive," added Suna.

"From Vegas," he said.

"Vegas," they exclaimed. "What were you doing there?"

"It's a short story. Boring. I thought I'd give L.A. a shot."

Shirlee stood up and stretched. He couldn't get over the

bodies they had acquired. She stared at him significantly. "Have you seen Eden?" she asked.

"Eden who?" he deadpanned.

"Come off it, Lennie," sighed Suna.

He tried to look nonchalant. "Is Eden still here?" he asked casually.

"Yes," said Shirlee.

"And *how*," added Suna.

Where is she? he wanted to ask. *Who is she with? Does she still look great? Does she miss me?*

He managed a calm "Is she still going with that half-assed actor? What was his name? Tim Wealth or something."

The two girls exchanged looks. Neither wished to tell him Eden Antonio had hooked up with a short, bald, married mystery man and was nothing more than a kept woman.

"Don't think so," Shirlee said and abruptly changed the subject. "Do you have an agent here?" she asked.

"No. But plenty of numbers to call."

Suna shook her head knowingly. "You need an agent. Nobody gets anywhere without one. This isn't New York, where you use who you know."

"So I'll get an agent. No hassle. What are you two doing? Apart from looking like the reincarnation of Marilyn Monroe."

"We're *hot!*" exclaimed Shirlee.

"Well, almost," added Suna.

"We're up for a series," said Shirlee.

"No more voice-overs. From now on it's all or nothing," enthused Suna.

"This house might look like a dump to you," Shirlee said seriously. "But it's central. One block from Santa Monica and *three blocks* from Beverly Hills. Do you realize how important location is?"

No, but he realized these two Barbie dolls were not the girls he had known and liked in New York. It was not merely their bodies that had undergone a transformation.

"Do you ever run into Eden?" he asked casually, unable to keep off the subject.

"When we first came out here," said Suna.

"Yeah, before she got big time and stopped returning our calls," snorted Shirlee.

"Big time?"

"She does a bit on some soap opera. Thinks that makes her better than everybody else. Anyway, I thought it was over with you two," Suna said.

"Yeah, it's over. I just wondered how she is doing, that's all. Can I use your phone?"

"Sure," they chorused. "Just put the money in the appropriate box."

Next to the phone, located in a dish-strewn kitchen, were two boxes. One was marked "local" and the other "long distance." He had no idea which Marina del Rey was, so he stuffed a dollar in each opening. Mother's answering machine was still keeping vigil.

On impulse he dialed the operator and requested the Magiriano Hotel in Vegas. For some reason he felt like speaking to the girl with the black opal eyes.

When the switchboard operator answered, he asked for suite eleven twenty-two.

"Sorry," said the operator. "That suite is unoccupied."

Had she checked out? So soon?

"Well, give me the name of the person who was registered there yesterday."

"Suite eleven twenty-two has been unoccupied for five days."

"That's impossible."

"I'm sorry, sir. Suite eleven twenty-two has had no guests for five days."

The operator disconnected him.

Shit! He must have remembered the wrong number. Now he had no way of finding out her name, and even though he had acted like schmuck of the decade, he still wanted to see her again. Why should *she* get to make the last move?

"What's the matter, Lennie?" murmured Suna, strolling casually into the kitchen.

She was probably checking to see if he'd deposited his money in the box.

"Nothing. I just can't get through to anyone."

"Story of my life," she said, sticking her finger into an open jam pot, then sucking it.

He wondered if they were going to offer him the promised breakfast—even a cup of coffee would be welcome.

Shirlee drifted into the kitchen. "Where are you staying?"

"I don't know. I'll give you a call when I'm settled."

"Please," said Suna.

"Yes, please," echoed Shirlee.

"Goodness me!" exclaimed Suna, catching sight of the kitchen clock. "I must rush, I'll be late for my dancing lesson."

"Me too!" added Shirlee.

So much for breakfast.

Lennie made a fast exit.

· · · · ·

"Why did we have to meet in the parking lot?" Matt grumbled.

"Why not?" replied Jess, and jumped quickly into the passenger seat of his fifty-thousand-dollar white Excalibur, in the hope she would not be seen.

"Anybody would think," he said gruffly, "that you don't want to be *seen* with me."

"Nonsense," she answered briskly. "This just seemed like the most convenient place."

"Sure it is," he said, playing with his gold chains.

"Let's go," she said impatiently.

"What's your hurry?"

"No hurry. We'll sit here all night if that's what turns you on."

"*You* turn me on."

"Are we going or what?"

He started the car and drove at show-off speed all the way

to his apartment. Jess was unimpressed. Even more so when they entered his shrine to bad taste.

"This place looks like something out of *Playboy*," she exclaimed.

He took it as a compliment and thanked her.

She stifled several more comments, deciding if she was to get any information out of him she'd better try to be civil. Frankly, she found him pathetic—an aging swinger who wouldn't give up. If he just acted his age, got rid of the gold chains, the wave in his hair, the too-young clothes, he would be quite an attractive older man. Tom Jones pants at age fifty were not a pretty sight. He had to be at *least* fifty—the lines on his face told her that. What was next? A face-lift?

He touched a few switches, and the lights dimmed to a soft pink glow, Sinatra came on the stereo, and the sign behind the bar that read "Matt's Place" blinked on and off.

"Jesus!" Jess muttered under her breath, sinking into a damask-covered couch.

"Scotch?" Matt questioned solicitously, already behind the bar and pouring.

"Coke," she said quickly.

"I don't have any," he replied. "But I do have some grass if you're interested."

"I *meant* Coca-Cola."

"With Scotch?"

"Plain."

"You don't drink?"

"Sometimes."

"Not tonight?"

"Maybe later."

The "Maybe later" made him feel good. That meant she was planning to stay awhile. Perhaps all night if he was fortunate. Or if *she* was, depending on which way you looked at it.

She obviously loved the apartment. She hadn't stopped looking around from the moment she'd walked in.

"Would you like the grand tour?" he asked, handing her

a Coca-Cola in an initialed glass. Wait until she saw the bedroom!

"Not right now."

"Why not?"

"Because I'm hungry, and you invited me for dinner. Remember?"

How could he forget? He had arranged a magnificent dinner. Only it was not due to arrive for another hour. He had hoped that maybe he could get her into bed *before* the food arrived. He hated making love on a full stomach—it gave him heartburn.

"Jess," he said smoothly, "I want you to know that you are the most fantastic girl I've seen all year."

He sat next to her, put his arm around her shoulders, then let his hand casually slip down to her right breast.

She jerked away. "Cut it out, Matt. I came here for food and information—so please don't grope me while coming on with dumb bullshit lines. Okay?"

• • • • •

The twins depressed Lennie. He hated the transformation. They didn't look real anymore, more like a couple of blow-up dolls—the kind you purchased in the porno shops around Times Square. A lot of people in New York put L.A. down. They said it was fantasy land—all sucking and fucking, sunshine and sex.

So what was so bad about that?

Plenty. If there was nothing else. Suna and Shirlee looked like there was nothing else.

He stopped for coffee and eggs, and tried Marina del Rey Alice for the third time. She answered on the second ring.

A breathy, "Hi, this is Alice Golden. What can I do for you?"

"You're asking for an obscene phone call," he cracked.

"Lennie, darling! Why are you calling? Something wrong?"

That said a lot for their relationship. Not for Alice cozy mother-son chats. She came right to the point.

"I'm in L.A.," he said. "Nothing's wrong."

"Why are you here?"

Did he detect a note of alarm? Alice did not appreciate the fact that she had a thirty-year-old son. It made her feel ancient.

He juggled a cigarette from his shirt pocket and lit up. "I had a gig in Vegas, so I thought I'd visit."

Panic. "Me?"

"No. L.A."

Why would he visit *her?* She was only his mother.

"That's nice."

"Yeah. I thought I might get connected here."

"Well, darling, it's a good enough place to get connected here."

"And I thought I might throw in a visit to you at the same time."

There was a long silence. Oh, it was great to receive such a warm welcome!

He took her off the hook. "Unless it's not convenient."

"Darling! You're so understanding," she gushed. "Right now I have a new 'friend.' He thinks I'm forty. I don't want to surprise him. Not yet, anyway."

"When?"

"When what?"

"When will you surprise him?"

A shriek of laughter. "Never, I hope. He's a live one!"

"I'm glad you're happy."

"Ecstatic."

"Whatever happened to the schmuck with the false teeth?"

"Old news, Lennie, dear."

"I'll call you again."

"If a man answers—hang up."

"Wouldn't dream of doing anything else."

"You're such a good boy. And so talented." A flash of conscience. Maybe she should offer *some*thing; after all, he was her flesh and blood, and she loved him in her own special way. She just wished he didn't look his age. "Remember my friend Rainbow?" she said, not waiting to see if he did or did not. "Well, she married that *meshuggener* Foxie—you know—he owns the club on Hollywood Boulevard. Maybe they can use a funny person like you. Mention your father—she always had hot pants for him. I wouldn't be surprised if he *schtupped* her while my back was turned." Alice laughed gaily. "What the eye don't see the heart don't fret over. I should care. You think I wasn't having a good time myself? Lennie, I had every man in Vegas chasing after me. Every one!" A thoughtful pause. "Of course, that's when I was at my peak. I could twirl tassels like *no*body could twirl tassels!"

He had heard it all before. Alice the Swizzle. The toast of Las Vegas. And Jack Golden. What a comedian!

She never called Lennie a comedian. She referred to him as a funny person. In her eyes he didn't do much at all. Just stood there and talked a lot about life. When she had first seen him perform at a club in New York she had been shocked. "You use language like that—on stage? And they let you get away with it? Your father *never* used language. He could make them laugh just by being there."

Your father this, your father that. According to Alice, the sun shone out of Jack Golden's ass. And according to Alice, Lennie could *never ever* come anywhere near the dizzying heights his father had achieved.

Bull.

Shit.

He let her carry on for a while—she loved reminiscing. And when he said goodbye she did not even ask when she might hear from him again. He was not surprised. Alice was Alice. She didn't have a motherly bone in her carefully preserved body.

Leaving home at seventeen and taking off for New York had been one of the easiest moves he'd ever made. She had handed him a bus ticket, five hundred dollars and a kiss on the cheek. "Go for it, Lennie, darling," she had said, delighted to be rid of the responsibility of raising a son.

So he had done just that, even though his father had made a halfhearted attempt to persuade him to stay. Poor old Jack Golden. Alice had cut off his balls and used them for earrings.

He died six months after Lennie left. Alice didn't bother to inform him until two months after the funeral.

"I couldn't find you," was her lame excuse.

She hadn't tried too hard. He had sent her three postcards with his phone number and address. She claimed to have never received them.

Now he was in Los Angeles and she really didn't give a rat's ass. Why had he bothered calling?

"Remember my friend Rainbow?" his mother had said casually. Remember her? How could he ever forget her? For years she had reigned as queen of his adolescent fantasies. Rainbow. The most beautiful stripper in Las Vegas. She had made Alice Golden look like a cart-horse.

And Jack Golden was schtupping her? Really? Jack Golden. The mensch. His father. Schtupping beautiful Rainbow?

Lennie found it hard to believe, but Alice had said so . . .

He wished Jack was still alive. He imagined the conversation they might have had. *"Hey, Dad, did you ever get it on with Rainbow?"*

"Why, yes, son, as a matter of fact I did. Anything you want to know?"

"Yeah. Tell me about her tits, her pussy, her skin. Tell me everything, Dad, 'cause I jerked off just thinking about her a hundred and fifty times a day!"

He was twelve years old and out on a spree with Jess. They sneaked into the back of the Hot Banana strip club and caught the girls in action. When Rainbow came on, he thought he would faint.

Auntie Rainbow. She had been to their house on several occasions, Alice and she went shopping together. Auntie Rainbow with forty-three-inch tits, a sweet smile and cascades of red hair. Auntie Rainbow in a G-string that left little to the imagination, a couple of orange sequins, black net stockings with stiletto heels, and a long feather boa.

When Auntie Rainbow took it all off he had come in his pants.

"What's the matter with *you?*" Jess had said in disgust, and not spoken to him for a week.

After that, whenever Rainbow came to their house, he made sure he was around. Once he caught her in the downstairs toilet, sitting on the john, panties (black lace—he still remembered—oh, how he remembered!) around her ankles. She didn't bat an eyelash. Later he heard her say to his mother with a laugh, "The kid caught me taking a pee." His mother had laughed too.

Rumor had it Rainbow had arrived in Vegas many, many years before, at age fifteen. She had hooked up with a notorious gangster by the name of Jake the Boy. (Like Bugsy Siegel before him, he was handsome and a friend of the stars.) Jake had draped her in diamonds and furs, then dumped her when she turned seventeen. That was when she started her career. By the time Lennie first saw her she must have been at least forty—but even then she was devastating.

What did she look like today? Probably fat and ugly. Certainly old. Was it worthwhile destroying the fantasy? Would she even recall the kid who followed her around with lust and devotion shining from his teenage eyes?

Did he remember Rainbow? Ha!!

He decided he'd better find somewhere to stay. It was obvious camping at Alice's was out of the question.

He called Joey Firello, who advised him to book into the Chateau Marmont—an old hotel in the Hollywood Hills that catered to show business and would not cost him his balls. Joey sounded pleased to hear from him. "Check in and we'll get together later."

He wasn't sure he wanted to see Joey.

Joey Firello was on his way. Lennie Golden was stuck in the same old rut. Oh, yeah, he could always get work, but where was it taking him? All around him things were happening for other people: John Belushi, Dan Aykroyd, Chevy Chase, Joey Firello. They were on a roll.

Naively he had imagined Vegas as a springboard to bigger and better things. And he had ended up with shit on his face.

L.A. better have something exciting to offer, otherwise . . . Otherwise what?

12

Preparations for the gala evening to honor Francesca Fern were elaborate. The Magiriano's huge ballroom was festooned with exotic white orchids. An intimate touch supplied by Dimitri Stanislopoulos—his way of paying homage to Madame Fern.

Lucky dropped by during the day to see that everything was being set up smoothly. No problems. She had a terrific staff who rarely, if ever, put a foot wrong. And her catering manager was the best in town; the food would be magnificent.

Throughout the day celebrities arrived—by private plane, limousine and commercial jet. Naturally there were baskets of fruit, chilled champagne, caviar and a selection of expensive cheeses waiting in their suites, with a personal note from Lucky. No matter how rich or famous people were, they all adored getting something for nothing—a fact of life Gino had taught her.

She had never met Francesca Fern, but she sent her six bottles of Cristal champagne and a welcoming note.

Gino had already informed Lucky he would be bringing Susan Martino to the event.

"When is she leaving?" Lucky had been unable to keep from asking.

"Why?" Gino snapped. He wondered when Susan *was* leaving. Originally she had said she was in town for a few weeks. The subject had not arisen again. As far as he was concerned she could stay forever. She made him very comfortable indeed.

When he picked her up later that night to escort her to the Francesca Fern dinner, he broached the subject. "I kinda gotten used to havin' you around," he said. "You got no plans to leave, have you?"

Susan smiled wanly. "Life goes on," she said quietly. "Would that everything stopped at whim."

"Huh?"

She patted him lightly on the arm, the yellow diamond ring he had gifted her with sparkling brightly on her little finger. "I have a home to run, and many responsibilities. There's the charity work I'm involved with. My children . . . of course they're not children anymore. Nathan's at college and Gemma might be married in the fall. They still need my attention though, especially as Tiny is no longer with us."

"Yeh," Gino muttered uneasily. It was the first time she had mentioned her kids. Somehow he liked the thought of Susan with nobody in her life but him.

"I expect I shall leave this weekend," she continued. "I will need an excellent reason not to."

Wasn't he excellent reason enough? Jeez! How many women would kill to be in her place.

* * * * *

Dimitri glowered at his reflection as he adjusted his bow tie. Here he was, in Las Vegas, attending Francesca Fern's big event like an obedient puppy. She had insisted he be present. Naturally he had complied, had even arrived two days early so he would be rested and full of energy. Francesca admired ceaseless energy. She herself never stopped, and she expected—though never received—the same of the people around her. "Dimitri," she would purr in her deep, husky voice, "we are twins, the same star, the same destiny. Only *you* can keep up with me."

They were both Geminis.

Now Madame Fern had flown in with her entourage, including browbeaten Horace—and where was her phone call? Where was her presence in his suite? Where *was* the damn woman?

Dimitri knew exactly what time she had arrived—eleven-thirty in the morning. He had allowed her the courtesy of an hour to rest, and then he had called her suite and been told by her insolent male secretary that the great Miz Fern was in the middle of an interview with *Time* magazine and absolutely could not be disturbed.

"Disturb her!" Dimitri had bellowed, used to getting his own way.

"That's out of the question," replied the secretary.

"Disturb her!" Dimitri thundered a second time.

"I'm sure Miz Fern will return your call when she is able," retorted the secretary, and hung up.

Dimitri was so furious he called back immediately, only to reach Horace.

"Francesca's busy at the moment," said Horace in his usual worried whine. "I'll get her to phone you as soon as she can."

Dimitri had spent the day in his suite waiting for her call. It never came.

He was incensed. In all his dealings with women, nobody ever dared to treat him the way Francesca Fern did.

Now he was ready to attend her gala, and anger coursed through his veins. He was not some miserable fan. If Francesca thought she could treat him in this fashion and get away with it, she had better think again.

• • • • •

Lucky called Matt at the last minute. "You'll have to escort me to this thing tonight," she said with a sigh of annoyance. "Gino's taking Grace Kelly."

"Grace is in Monaco."

"Someone should tell dear old Susan. Maybe she'll stop the masquerade."

"Don't you like her?"

"Oh, Matt, you're so perceptive—right on the dime."

"She's a very nice lady."

"Hitler only had one ball, but he could charm 'em too."

"What are you talking about?"

"Forget it. Pick me up at six-thirty."

Matt decided he had a problem. Escorting Lucky Santangelo had never figured in his scheme of things. He had hoped to see Jess later. Not that she ever wanted to see *him* again. She had told him so, in no uncertain terms. Just because he had tried to jump her bones.

He shook his head. The sexual revolution seemed to have eluded poor Jess. Silly girl. But he was not prepared to give up yet. Now he was supposed to drop everything and be at Lucky Santangelo's beck and call. Why?

Because she's the boss, schmuck, that's why.

• • • • •

Francesca Fern clicked talon-red nails. "Emeralds," she commanded.

Horace sprang toward her traveling Vuitton jewel case and found the requested gems.

Francesca clicked again. "Jourdan diamanté shoes."

Horace raced for the closet and located the size ten evening shoes. Lovingly he placed them upon his wife's large feet.

Francesca arose, clipped a huge emerald to an outsize earlobe and snapped, "Perfume."

Horace obliged with a liberal spray of Joy.

"Let us go," sighed Francesca. "The peasants are waiting."

13

Mr. Wrong wore a white silk tuxedo, a plastic smile and several gold bracelets. He was a Spanish recording star, who—according to his PR—drove women crazy. His accent was enough to drive anyone crazy. Had he not been halfway famous, Olympia would have disregarded him totally. As it was, they were at adjoining tables in New York's Régine's on Park Avenue, and Olympia knew the platinum-blond Englishwoman he was with—a sort of international fixer-upper—who adored putting the right people together. So before long they all joined up—Olympia's group, Mr. Spanish Recording Star and his friend. His name was Vitos Felicidade, and by the time he rocked Olympia in his arms on the dance floor, he knew exactly who she was, thanks to his blond lady friend who excitedly filled him in, then told him in Spanish (good international fixer-uppers always speak more than one language) to go for it. Both he and Olympia sensed interesting but limited possibilities.

"You 'ave a wondeefool 'air," he murmured, pressing what appeared to be his idea of a hard-on between her thighs.

Olympia allowed desire to run rampant, hoped he was better equipped than he appeared, and said, "So do you." Although she wasn't quite sure whether he meant she had wonderful hair or a wonderful air about her. Since she had both, she didn't much care.

"I fluuuck yew beauuuutifully," he purred with a winning smile. Pure plastic.

I hope you fluuck better than you speak English, she thought as she discreetly slid her hand down and felt for his cock. An encouraging rub and they were away.

Outside the club the lurking paparazzi jumped to attention. Olympia Stanislopoulos and Vitos Felicidade. Together! More than together! The paparazzi jostled for position to capture the coupling of the two celebrities.

"This is so boring!" complained Olympia.

"Booooring," agreed Vitos, lifting his head so there was no chance of a bad angle. "We take my car or yours?"

Two chauffeurs stood by their respective limousines.

"Who cares?" sighed Olympia, throwing herself into the back of his. "Let's just get out of here."

14

"I hate these evenings," Lucky confided to Dimitri. "They make me want to scream and run naked down a beach someplace. Y'know what I mean?"

Dimitri regarded the black-eyed girl without a flicker of interest. He wished, quite frankly, that she would be quiet. He just wanted to concentrate on Francesca, holding court at the top table like the Queen of England.

And *he* was not seated at the top table. *He*, Dimitri Stanislopoulos, was sitting at the *next* table, the grandest insult of all.

Lucky waited for his reply, which was not forthcoming. Silence reigned. Screw him. If he didn't want to make conversation, she could take a hint. She was just trying to be polite because it was her hotel, he was a big gambler, and she could see he was pissed as hell about the seating arrangements. She wasn't exactly thrilled herself. Daddy and the widow at table *número uno* with the star, her seedy husband, and a clutch of major celebrities. Francesca's secretary had organized the seating arrangements. Badly, Lucky thought. She wished she hadn't come—who needed this shit?

Matt, sitting on her other side, seemed to be enjoying himself. He was surrounded by friends and acquaintances from Hollywood, where he had spent many happy working years. A fine escort *he* was. What had she expected—Al Pacino? She was trapped between the two dullest men in the room: Matt Traynor and Dimitri Stanislopoulos. Some winning combination.

Thanks a lot, Gino. Is this what my life has become?

She reached for her champagne glass and signaled for a waiter to refill it. Getting smashed was the only way to get through *this* evening.

• • • • •

Gino observed Susan in action. It was the first time he had seen her do her stuff surrounded by the elite of show business. She knew how to handle herself all right. Not one wrong move.

How would it be if he was married to a woman like Susan? He was too old to keep whoring around. One woman by his side and in his bed would suit him nicely.

He watched her chiseled profile as she chatted quietly to Horace Fern. After Maria, he had never thought he would marry again. Dear, sweet Maria . . . dead twenty-three years. . . .

Surely he had waited long enough?

He glanced across at Lucky, sitting at the next table. How would *she* take it? She would hate it. But she would get used to it. She would have to.

• • • • •

It was a long night. A night of speeches, performances, and tributes. The television cameras whirred and Francesca Fern blossomed. She played *grande dame* to the hilt. Francesca knew how to milk an evening.

Later, when the TV crew had left and the guests began to thin out, Francesca graciously did the rounds. She stopped next to Dimitri, bent to peck him on the cheek and husked, "So generous of you to be here tonight. Your gesture is much appreciated." Theatrically she posed next to him while her personal photographer captured the shot.

He gripped her wrist so hard she almost cried out. "What is this charade?" he demanded in a hoarse whisper. "How *dare* you treat me this way? What game are you playing?"

She managed a fixed smile, while hissing under her breath so that only he could hear, "Let go of me, you filthy animal. I know all about you and Norma Valentine. Don't think you can have us both, because you *cannot*. I *will not* be humiliated in such a way."

Norma Valentine. He almost laughed aloud. Norma Valentine was an English film star he had met in the south of France. She had been brought to his yacht a week previously by a

Greek business associate and she had stayed the night. One night only. She meant nothing to him. "I was in her company once," he explained. "I didn't even like her."

"Ah, but you liked her enough to fuck her. *And* to send her a Cartier bracelet the next day," Francesca said fiercely.

"A gambling debt. She won at cards."

"Please, Dimitri, credit me with superior intelligence. More than you—for I am telling you—if you can sleep with Norma Valentine, then, by God, you will *never* sleep with me again."

"You're married," Dimitri objected. "Since when do you forbid me to sleep with anyone else?"

"Sleep with whom you like," spat Francesca, her smile finally slipping. "Because you will no longer be sharing *my* bed." She wrenched her wrist free and stalked off.

"I guess the crunch is outta the cookie," commented Lucky, who could not help overhearing, and was feeling no pain due to several more glasses of champagne.

"I beg your pardon?" Dimitri glared at her.

She shrugged. "Francesca Fern and Norma Valentine were up for the lead in *Sirocco Sings* fifteen years ago. Norma went on to win an Oscar for the role *and* make it as a movie star. F.F. never did a flick. They are archenemies—it's Hollywood trivia. How come *you* don't know?"

He was outraged. "Were you eavesdropping on our entire conversation?"

"Couldn't help myself."

"Really!"

"Relax—you'll give yourself a hernia."

"You are a very vulgar young lady."

"Cut the crap, Dimitri. I'm not your daughter's little friend anymore. And I've had it with you ignoring me like I don't exist." She rose. "This is *my* hotel. You have been playing at *my* tables all week. Why don't you just loosen up and we'll go out and get drunk. Huh? How's that for a great idea? *I* need to, and you *certainly* do."

He saw her for the first time. And her smoldering beauty and vibrant youth struck him as the perfect way to erase Francesca from his thoughts. Lucky Santangelo was right. No more could he dismiss her as Olympia's little friend.

His penetrating eyes held hers. "So, you require a drinking partner, is that it?"

She returned his gaze, surprised to finally get his attention. "Yes. And *you* have been elected."

"Should I be flattered?"

She glanced over at Gino and caught him in a deep whisper with Susan. "Be what you like, but let's get out of here. And fast."

• • • • •

Gino and Susan were in Francesca's suite enjoying an after-the-event party.

"I had a busy life. Did a lotta things—some good, some bad. Y'know what I mean?" Gino rubbed the faint scar on his cheek.

"I realize you are not Billy Graham," Susan replied.

"When y'come from where I do, y'gotta learn to look after yourself. Nobody does it for you."

"I'm sure."

"I started out on the streets. Never had no formal education. Kinda picked up things as I went along."

"You're a true survivor. Look at where you are today."

"Yeh. I did okay. Like I made the great American dream come true. From nothin' I made it big."

"Quite an understatement."

"I know presidents, politicians, mayors, civic leaders. There's people owe me favors you wouldn't believe."

"Of course."

"Stick with me, kiddo. I'll show you one hell of a good life."

"Is this a proposal, Gino?"

"Y'know somethin? I think it is."

"I'm . . . surprised."

"*You're* surprised? How d'you figure *I* feel?"

"It's something I'll have to think about."

"So think. Who's stoppin' you? Think all you want. Only I'll need an answer before I go to sleep tonight on account of the fact that I might change my mind in the mornin'."

Susan laughed softly. "Gino, you're incorrigible!"

"Yeh? Make the most of it."

"I must talk to my family, my children. . . ."

"You see me askin' Lucky's permission?"

"It's not that easy."

"Make it easy—say yes."

"Yes," she whispered.

"What?"

"I said yes."

"Hey! I'll be damned!" He leaped to his feet. "I got an announcement to make!" The assorted group gave him their attention. "This lady and I—Susan Martino and I—Jeez! What can I tell you? We're gettin' married!"

• • • • •

Now she had his attention, Lucky found Dimitri an enjoyable drinking companion. He wasn't Gino, but he had that certain aura—and she liked the authority of an older man. He was also strangely attractive with his shock of thick white hair, prominent nose and penetrating eyes. The drunker she got, the more attractive he became.

Olympia's daddy. She was having erotic thoughts about Olympia's daddy!

He was very tall, a big man. Gino was much shorter, more wiry. Physically they couldn't be less alike.

"This is fun," Lucky said, as they roamed from bar to bar.

He was drinking ouzo, tossing it down like lemonade, but it did not seem to affect him.

He nodded. He didn't know why, but he was enjoying himself. Francesca Fern would regret tonight. He would personally see that she regretted it for the rest of her miserable life. Nobody spurned Dimitri Stanislopoulos, least of all a cheap whore actress.

At three o'clock in the morning they found themselves in a small Greek café, surrounded by waiters coming off their shifts, and other late-night workers. Dimitri bought drinks all around, while a thin boy played the mandolin—naturally the theme from *Zorba*. Dimitri danced, balancing a plate on his head, and he laughed so loud that for a moment Lucky thought he might choke. Then he smashed twenty-three plates in a row, gave the smiling proprietor a thousand-dollar bill, and with unspoken agreement they retired to Lucky's penthouse apartment.

For a moment, she was nervous, a kid again. She fluttered around, fixing him a drink, then going into her bathroom and holding a cold towel to her forehead.

I'm being ridiculous, she thought. *What the hell is going on here?*

She returned to the living room and faced him.

He said her name once, very quietly. Then without further ado he peeled the sensuous sheath of a black silk dress from her body with expert, strong hands.

She felt like a swimmer about to take the plunge. Expectant, excited, ready to excel.

His hands were big, his fingers long and firm. Slowly he explored her body, brushing her skin until he hooked into her bikini panties—the only other garment she wore—and drew them down past her thighs, her calves, her ankles.

She was naked, but he remained dressed, merely loosening his bow tie.

With great care he pushed her down onto the couch, took his brandy glass, dipped his index finger into the shimmering liquid, and brought it first to the nipple of her left breast, and then to the right one.

The liquor stung, but only for a second. With hardly a

pause, he started to suck it from her, making her sigh with pleasure. She threw her arms behind her head and stretched luxuriously. He cupped her breasts together and flicked his tongue across both nipples.

"Get your clothes off," she murmured urgently.

He laughed. "Such impatience!"

"Get 'em off, Dimitri. I mean *now*."

Keeping both hands on her breasts he traced his tongue down her body.

She writhed with excitement. Maybe I'm drunk, she thought, but this guy certainly has a great touch. Or maybe it's been too long between pit stops.

He opened her thighs by pushing his head between them.

"I . . . want . . . to . . . feel . . . your . . . body . . ." she murmured. "Please. I'm . . . asking . . . nicely. . . ."

His tongue, like his fingers, was thick, slow-moving and experienced.

"Ooooh . . . yes . . ." she moaned. "Oh, yes, yes, yes." Her legs parted even more as she felt the tenseness of the past months building up, preparing for release, getting ready to explode.

He paused to flavor his tongue with brandy while his hands continued to work on her breasts.

She felt the sting of the alcohol, the expertise of his fingers and the strength of his tongue.

"Oh, God, Dimitri! Oh, God! This is soooo great. So utterly fantastic. Ohhhhh . . ."

She hit the plateau. Hard. And it was worth waiting for.

He buried his head between her legs and enjoyed every hot, throbbing moment.

15

Jess found out nothing. Absolutely nothing.

Oh, yes. She had found out that Matt Traynor had a constant erection, talked a lot and thought he was God's gift.

Had he honestly believed she would fall for his very thin-on-the-ground charms? Had he really imagined she would jump between his brown-striped sheets like all the rest?

She actually had to fight him off. Do battle. And she was only five feet tall against his five eleven or more. It had been some struggle. If she hadn't resorted to slamming him in the balls with her elbow she would probably *still* be there.

And when she got home at some ungodly hour she found Wayland entertaining a group of scruffy friends who were eating *her* food, smoking *her* grass and messing up *her* house. She really let fly, and when roused she had some temper.

Wayland got excited—unusual for him—and left with his friends, only to return at seven A.M. so stoned he couldn't even speak.

They were all the same. And why hadn't Lennie phoned? Didn't he think she was worried about him? Didn't he think she *cared*?

In the morning she took the baby out beside the pool and lay with him in the long grass. Having Simon was the only positive thing she had done in her entire life. He gave her a reason to keep on going, to get through each day and make it to that weekly paycheck.

Wayland staggered outside. "There's no milk," he complained.

"Go to the market and get some," she said patiently.

"I don't have any money."

Reluctantly she fished a twenty from her jeans pocket and threw it at him.

He nodded wisely. "I'll stock up."

"Sure you will," she muttered. "Five bucks food and the rest on whatever you can score."

He didn't hear her. She couldn't care less. Quietly she rocked Simon in her arms and crooned a soothing lullaby. Soon it would be time to visit her mother in the hospital.

• • • • •

Foxie was eighty-five years old, small as an elf, bald, with sharp darting cross-eyes and ears that stuck up like something out of *Star Trek*.

Foxie was canny, cheap, insulting, a good friend and a mean enemy.

He was also a Hollywood legend—although only to people in the know.

Foxie had a keen ear, a cruel wit, limitless energy and no ailments.

For a man of eighty-five he was remarkable.

Lennie had never met him, in spite of Alice's suggestion he should go there. But the stories he had heard could fill volumes, and he was looking forward to the experience.

Foxie's (the place), named after the man himself, was located on Hollywood Boulevard and boasted a mixed clientele. People came to Foxie's to hang out and have fun. All kinds of people. From local pimps and hookers to Beverly Hills name-droppers to Sam Schmuck from the Valley and an occasional movie star or two, Foxie's was *the* place. The food was terrible, the drinks generous, and the entertainment hilarious. A mixture of new talent, strippers, working comics and a "discovery" night that was better than *The Gong Show*. Once a month was "Take-It-Off Night"—an evening where ordinary females leaped on the stage and couldn't wait to show everyone what they had. To get into Foxie's that night you had to book weeks in advance.

Joey Firello suggested they stop by. "It's where *I* started out here," he explained to Lennie. "Six weeks in and I got me the TV show. Now I'm signing autographs and turning down pussy."

Joey looked like a handsome monkey. He was thin, short and wiry, with Rod Stewart hair and Mick Jagger lips. He was, at twenty-six, four years younger than Lennie.

"Look," Joey said, "if Foxie don't like you we'll go to the Improv or the Comedy Store. You'll get connected."

"Sure. I know," Lennie said. He felt ridiculous. Joey the Kid giving *him* advice and help. Joey the Kid, who had arrived in New York three years earlier with twenty-eight bucks, some corny gags and a lot of hustle. For nine weeks he had slept on Lennie's floor. His hustle had paid off. Now he was wearing cashmere sweaters and driving a secondhand Jaguar. Foxie greeted him like a brother.

"I want you to meet a friend of mine," Joey said. "Lennie Golden. Remember the name. He's funny."

"As funny as you?" snapped Foxie.

"Give him a shot. See for yourself."

Foxie picked at his teeth with a wooden toothpick and cocked his head to one side. "You wanna try out tonight?"

"I wasn't planning on trying out," Lennie said quickly. "I've got a video of my work—I thought if you liked it we could do business."

"You East Coast momsers—you're all the same," Foxie snorted. "Don't want to try out. Want me to waste my time lookin' at tape shit." He bit the toothpick in half and began to eat it. "At Foxie's you either try out or get out. I can fit you in at ten o'clock. Take it or leave it."

Joey nodded. "He'll take it."

"Do I have a choice?" Lennie joked.

"No choice," said Joey. "Do it. He'll love you. I'm gonna get on the phone and summon up fans."

Lennie wondered if Joey might call Eden. They hadn't discussed her all night. The silence was killing him. Why didn't

Joey mention her? They must have seen each other. He was determined not to ask.

Christ! He was nervous.

Lennie Golden nervous. Christ!

He had played a thousand and one joints.

Foxie's was no different.

Except.

At Foxie's.

He had to be a smash.

16

Vitos Felicidade was not the most exciting lover Olympia had ever had. He was hot in a different way. He was a star, and therefore a worthwhile trophy to hang on to for a while.

Brigette took an immediate dislike to him. The child was becoming impossible. Since her display of temperament on Fifth Avenue she had discovered that being difficult resulted in plenty of attention, and if there was one thing Brigette craved it was attention. When she first met Vitos she kicked him in the ankle, called him a foreign pig and ran to her room screaming.

Olympia was humiliated. She took out her fury on Nanny Mabel, who promptly threatened to quit.

Vitos suggested that Brigette should be sent away to boarding school. Olympia was tempted, but the child was still so young, and she couldn't help remembering her own unfortunate experiences in such establishments.

On the day of her grandmother's wedding Brigette refused to get out of bed. Nanny Mabel came running to Olympia in a terrible state. Reluctantly Olympia stomped into her daughter's room to deal with the situation.

"Don't *want* to be the flower girl," Brigette kept on repeating stubbornly. "Don't *want* to wear a silly yucky dress. *Don't want to!*"

"You have to," Olympia admonished, trying to cajole the child into some form of obedience. "Your own grandmother is getting married. And if you are good—*very* good—I shall take you to Tiffany's—the big jewelry store on Fifth Avenue—and buy you anything you want."

Nanny Mabel, standing beside the bed, snorted her disapproval. Trying to bribe a nine-year-old child with jewelry—ridiculous!

"Anything, Mama?" questioned Brigette, her bright-blue eyes widening. "Anything at all in the wholewideworld?"

"Yes," agreed Olympia reluctantly.

"When?"

"Tomorrow."

"Okay." Brigette beamed and jumped out of bed.

Olympia glared at Nanny Mabel. "All right, Nanny? Do you think *you* can take over now?"

"Yes, madame," sniffed the disapproving woman.

Olympia swept from the room into the sanctuary of her bedroom. Vitos was arriving in two hours, and she had so much to do.

She regarded herself in a mirror. New York was not helping with her weight problem—her face looked positively round. Angrily she sucked in her cheeks. Why couldn't money buy great cheekbones? Why wasn't she six inches taller and twenty pounds lighter?

Hah! Vitos had no complaints. *He* thought she was perfect. Latin men liked a woman with flesh on her bones, not to mention millions in the bank. She scowled at her reflection.

Vitos arrived twenty minutes late, wearing a pink suit, dark glasses and his perpetual sneer.

Brigette, just about to depart early with Nanny, managed a quick "You look *soooo* dumb."

Vitos ignored her and helped himself to one of Dimitri's cigars.

When Olympia made her entrance ten minutes later, he was asleep in a chair, and the cigar had burned a hole in the polished top of a priceless antique table.

"Wake up!" Olympia screeched.

He did as she asked, and they snorted four lines of excellent coke to prepare themselves for the trip to her mother's wedding.

Olympia wore white. She knew it was incorrect, but so what? Her blond curls were frizzed and puffed out. A professional artiste had applied her makeup. She felt she looked her best, and Vitos seemed a suitable accessory.

The paparazzi, observing the couple so dressed at noon, decided *they* must be getting married, so they followed them in a variety of cars and motor scooters all the way to Long Island, where the wedding was to take place.

"How tiresome!" Olympia exclaimed, as the photographers drew alongside the limousine at every stoplight, clicking and snapping away.

Vitos raised his chin and smiled. "Tirrrrresome," he repeated, wondering if this extra blast of publicity would boost the U.S. sales of his new album, which was not doing quite as well as everyone had anticipated.

Olympia's mother was not pleased when the arrival of her daughter (always a handful—thank God she had decided to live with Dimitri) brought with her fifteen scurvy-looking photographers and a smiling but vacuous Spanish recording star. She took Olympia to one side. "You shouldn't wear white," she said sternly. "It makes you look fat. And exactly *who* is that person you have with you?"

"Vitos," said Olympia vaguely. "He sings. He's quite famous."

"I don't care *how* famous he is," admonished her mother. "He looks like a pimp."

Olympia giggled. "A pimp! Mother! Where did *you* learn words like that?"

"Please, Olympia. I am getting married today. I would appreciate it if you would refrain from upsetting me."

Charlotte's intended was a tall, thin man with mean eyes and a limp. Olympia took an instant dislike to him, and told anyone who would listen she thought he looked like a Nazi war criminal.

The wedding took place in the garden at 3 P.M. Brigette, as flower girl, was prettier than any of the bridesmaids. She looks angelic, Olympia thought with a proud smile, watching her daughter trail dutifully behind the bride. She caught Nanny Mabel's eye, and for once the two women were completely in tune—proud guardians of the exquisite little heiress.

This peaceful reverie was interrupted by three screaming paparazzi falling from the collapsing branch of an overhanging mimosa tree.

"Oh, God!" exclaimed Olympia as everyone panicked, thinking some sort of raid was taking place. "I'll get the blame for this, I know I will."

"You all *stink!*" yelled Brigette suddenly, jumping up and down with glee as she seized the perfect opportunity to cause trouble. "You all STINK STINK STINK!"

"Oh, *God!*" Olympia turned to Vitos for moral support.

He was asleep, a vacuous smile in permanent position. She kicked him sharply on the ankle. "Wake up!" she ordered. "What do you think this is—a rest camp?"

"Olympeea—" he began plaintively.

"Don't Olympia me. *Do* something!"

He leaped to his feet and waved an ineffectual fist at the photographers, who were now scrambling for their cameras and grabbing random shots.

"You all STINK!" Brigette continued to yell.

Olympia clutched Vitos by the arm and smiled—might as well look good if one was to be splashed across the front pages of the world. Vitos caught her message and also smiled.

All around them chaos reigned.

17

I want to talk to you," said Gino.

"I already heard," replied Lucky, trying to hide the hurt and rejection she felt.

"I've bin tryin' to find you all day."

"So you've found me." She shrugged. "Congratulations. What more can I say?"

They stood by the reception desk of the Magiriano. Lucky had just returned from a drive and wore jeans, a loose T-shirt and aviator shades. Her hair was wild and she was makeupless.

"Hey, kid, y'look about sixteen," Gino joked.

She pushed her hands through her hair and stared at him.

"You're mad at me," he stated.

"Why should I be mad?" she replied sarcastically. "I mean, you're only my *father*—that's all. So why should I be mad that you decide to get married and *I have to hear it from Matt Traynor*." Her voice rose. "Why the hell should I be mad at that?"

He fingered the scar on his cheek. "Circumstances, kid," he said. "I didn't plan it. Things just fell into position. I thought you were at the party when I told everyone."

"Thanks a lot. I guess my presence is really felt."

"C'mon, Lucky," he soothed. "I called you as soon as I got up this morning. It's not my fault you've bin out all day. Where were you anyway?"

"There's a whorehouse twenty miles outside town— sometimes I help out."

He frowned at her flippancy. "Let's go upstairs," he said. "I've bin hangin' around here for an hour. Does that show I care?"

"Big deal," she mumbled.

They walked to her private elevator, the sound of the slots jangling reassuringly in the background. She was frightened, truly frightened. If Gino got married again, where did that leave her?

She had driven through the desert for hours thinking about it. When Matt had phoned her early in the morning with the news, she had been utterly devastated. Dimitri had departed hours before and she was alone, hung over, and in no mood to digest such shocking information. Quickly she had dressed and slipped quietly from the hotel. In the underground garage she took possession of her Ferrari and drove out to the desert with Otis Redding on the tape deck and just her thoughts for company.

Now she was back, and Gino was there, and *how could he do it to her?*

Inside her penthouse there were incredible baskets of "Sterling Silver" roses everywhere. She looked around in amazement and turned to Gino. "Did you do this?"

His scowl deepened. "No, I didn't."

She reached for one of the white cards attached to the baskets. A simple signature, nothing else. *Dimitri.*

She crumpled the card in her hand.

"Who sent them?" asked Gino.

"Francesca Fern," she replied quickly, tossing the card into a corner.

"Nice of her."

"Why not? It was a great evening."

"Listen, kid." He sat down on the couch and sighed. "I made a mistake. I shoulda told you first—but I didn't, so let's not make a federal case out of it."

"Who's making a federal case? I just thought you might have discussed it with me before informing the world."

"You're my daughter, not my jailer. You think I need your permission?"

"I think you need my advice."

He was angry now. "Screw your advice," he said darkly. "Susan said you'd be jealous and she was right."

Lucky shared the Santangelo temper. She glared at her father. "I don't give a damn *what* Susan said. The widow Martino is your problem—and believe me, if you marry her you'll have more problems than you ever imagined."

"My daughter, the mouth. You don't even *know* Susan—so quit puttin' her down."

"I'm only trying to save you from making the mistake of your life."

"Kid, I made a lotta mistakes in my life—most of 'em before you were ever around. You know somethin'? I managed to survive *without* your advice—so stick it where the Pope don't go roller skatin', put a smile on your face an' wish me the best of luck."

She forced a stiff smile, hated him for being a stupid old fool, and nodded. "You're right. It's your life, and if it's what you want . . . well then . . . congratulations."

"That's more like it." He grinned, temper forgotten. "An' now I gotta get a move on." He headed jauntily for the door.

"Stop!" Lucky said urgently. "You can't keep me waiting any longer." The frustrations were building. "You've *got* to make a decision on Atlantic City."

He glanced at his watch impatiently. "Right now I gotta run. We can talk about it when I get back."

She glared at him. "Where are you going?"

"Didn't I tell you?"

She shook her head and waited for the bombshell.

He didn't disappoint. "Promised to fly to L.A. with Susan. She needs to tell her kids in person, doesn't want them reading about us in some newspaper."

It was starting. She was losing him. Gino . . . Daddy . . .

"What kids?" she asked calmly, although the last thing she felt was calm.

"I think she's got a matched pair, a boy and a girl."

Something icy clutched at her heart. "How old are they?"

"Who knows? Nineteen, twenty."

Susan was right. She *was* jealous. But not of the old bag—of the "kids" who might one day regard Gino as their stepfather.

Oh, God! She couldn't stand it. Why was this happening? Why had Susan Martino appeared in their lives and spoiled everything?

"When will you be back?" she asked, concealing her dismay.

"I shouldn't be gone more than a couple of days. I'll call you."

"But I need to know about Atlantic City *now*," she said desperately. "I've spent a tremendous amount of time and energy putting everything together. If we don't get a lock on it immediately all my work will have been for nothing."

He was anxious to be on his way. Susan was waiting, and right now she came first. "Everything'll hold," he said confidently. "When I get back we'll sit down together and work out the way to go. I promise. You can count on me."

Once she would have believed him. Now she wasn't sure. "I thought we wanted to build a hotel together more than anything else in the world," she said softly. "Surely you can give me a yes or a no so I can put the deal in motion?"

"Two days," he said, kissed her on the cheek and was gone.

She walked out to the terrace and stood for a long while gazing out at nothing in particular. The sun began to slide beneath a cloud, and a chill entered the warm air. Thoughtfully she bit her lower lip. Who *was* Susan Martino? What was her story? Married to the very famous Tiny for many years. But how about before that? Did Gino know anything about her at all?

On a hunch, Lucky picked up the phone and summoned Boogie. It took him only five minutes to arrive at her door.

"I want a full rundown on Susan Martino," she said. "Everything. Birth to now. You got it?"

He nodded. Over the years he had become used to Lucky's oddball requests. She always had a reason for everything she did. Lucky Santangelo had style. She was one of a kind, and his loyalty would never waver.

When Boogie departed she checked with the switchboard. Dimitri Stanislopoulos had called twice, and left a message for her to call him back.

Dimitri . . . she didn't know whether she wanted to see him or not.

Dimitri . . . Olympia's father.

Dimitri . . . an interesting lover.

She looked around the room full of flowers and decided she *would* see him again. Drunk or not, she had enjoyed his company *and* his lovemaking, although he was hardly the kind of man she was usually attracted to. For one thing, he was too old and too commanding. Lucky was used to calling the shots.

The thought of an evening alone while Gino flew to L.A. with his lady love drove her to the phone.

"I am leaving tomorrow," Dimitri informed her. "So tonight we will dine."

In a way he reminded her of Gino. A strong man who expected, and usually got, his own way.

For once she did not mind swimming with the tide.

• • • • •

Susan Martino lived in manicured luxury on Roxbury Drive. A large house, heavily mortgaged—although Susan did not reveal that to Gino.

A Swiss couple lived on the premises in a converted apartment above the four-car garage. The woman cooked and cleaned while the man looked after the garden and acted as general handyman. For these services they received two thousand dollars a month. Susan's business manager had told her she would not be able to afford to keep them much longer.

In the garage there was a yellow Rolls—leased. A brown Mercedes—leased. And a Toyota station wagon that belonged to the couple—courtesy of Tiny, who, when he was alive, spent money like it fell from the palm trees lining his drive-

way. Which was the reason Susan found herself in such dire
straits now.

Tiny had not left a will. He had left a mess.

A month after his unfortunate death, Susan had been
forced to face the grim reality. Within two years she would be
broke. In spite of the vast amounts of money Tiny had earned
during a wildly successful career, he had managed to dispose
of every red cent, one way or another.

When the accountant started going through the bills with
Susan, she shuddered. Tiny had done things with his money
she could hardly believe. Ten thousand dollars to this friend
in need, twenty thousand to that one. He kept a whole family
of relatives, and supported every hard-luck story that came his
way. Plus he seemed to have picked up every restaurant check
in the world—and thought nothing of spending a hundred
thousand dollars a month on gifts!

She ranted and raved for a while. Screamed, threw things,
sobbed uncontrollably. Then she sat up and took stock. She
was forty-nine years old, beautifully preserved (a touch of
surgery around the eyes and chin and a bust lift were all that
she'd had done), elegant, charming, a delightful companion,
and obliging in bed. What more could a man want? An older
man. *A much older man.* For she was smart enough to realize
that older men needed extreme youth—it propped up their
sagging hormones, not to mention their waistlines.

So Susan Martino made a list of suitable candidates and set
about snaring one of the men on it.

One by one she struck out for a variety of reasons. Somewhere down the list—way, way down—was the name Gino
Santangelo.

Susan had never imagined she would ever come close to
picking Gino Santangelo. He was a shady figure with an even
shadier past. A man of mystery, who lived in Las Vegas with
his pushy daughter. Some said a criminal who hid his activities
behind a million different companies.

Susan did not care. By this time she was desperate. There was hardly any money left, and something had to be done quickly. She rented a house in Las Vegas for a month, hopped on a plane, and within two days she was in business. *Voilà!*

Gino Santangelo had fallen neatly into her clutches. And her luck was in, for the pushy daughter was out of town, which gave her a clear runway for full thrust ahead.

Now she had him. And would she *ever* be able to introduce him to her friends?

Very very carefully. He was rough as a street hood in spite of the life he had led, and his impressive connections.

In bed he horrified her. He was so . . . crude. Even at his age he wanted to do so much. She was weary of his always trying to bring her to orgasm. As if she cared. For years Tiny had flung himself on top of her, heaved up and down a few times, and that was it. She really didn't want to be bothered by anything else. Sex. Ugh! It was so dirty. And Gino was especially dirty with his fingers and tongue and constant need to have proof he was giving her a wonderful time.

Nobody could say she wasn't a brilliant performer. She deserved an Oscar for Best Actress in Bed!

"Welcome home, Mrs. Martino," greeted the Swiss housekeeper.

"Thank you, Heidi, it's nice to be back," replied Susan with a warm smile. "This is Mr. Santangelo. He will be staying with us for a few days. Kindly make up the bed in the blue guest room."

Heidi nodded and went off to do as she was bade.

"Guest room!" exclaimed Gino, pinching Susan on the ass. "You gotta be kiddin'!"

"For show," she said. "The children will be here tomorrow."

He grinned. "Wassamatta? Don't they know Mama gets it on?"

Her smile remained in position. "Gino, dear," she said

briskly, "let us not create unnecessary problems. What we do is *our* business. I believe in setting an example in the home."

He whacked her behind. "Baby, when I'm in the home, we do what I say. Got it?"

Her lips tightened, but she didn't argue. For now, Gino was boss.

．　．　．　．　．

"I often fantasize about a man who is taller than me, richer than me and smarter than me!" Lucky hiccoughed delicately. "You know something, Dimi? I don't think he exists."

Dimitri smiled and stroked her breasts. "Perhaps you have found him," he said mildly.

She chuckled. "Well . . . you're sure as hell *older* than me. You are the oldest man I've ever been to bed with."

"And the richest, I presume."

She reached across him for a cigarette. "I guess."

"And I am tall."

"You sure are."

"And smart. Extraordinarily so."

"Except when it comes to Madame Fern."

He frowned. "We will not discuss Francesca."

She sat up abruptly. "Hey—I just had this great thought. You may—and this is only a thought, mind you—but you *may* be the perfect man!"

"I have been told that before," he said modestly.

She climbed off the bed and walked across the room naked.

Dimitri admired the strong symmetrical lines of her long lean body. She reminded him of a young French movie star he had once had. The confidence of her aggressive youth aroused him. She was not like other young women—there was something different about her. She had a dangerous edge to her personality—a certain aura of strength and power. He found himself intrigued and certainly aroused by her, even if she *was* the same age as his daughter. Usually a woman was not worth talking to—let alone bedding—until she was at least forty.

Lucky appeared to be the exception. She interested him in a new kind of way, *and* she managed to take his mind off Francesca—temporarily.

When he thought of Francesca he felt sweeping waves of rage. She had treated him inexcusably, and she would have to beg his forgiveness.

He knew her only too well. Francesca was a proud woman, and his indiscretion with Norma Valentine had bruised her ego. Now that he was aware of the enduring rivalry between the two actresses he could understand her fury. But there was no excuse for her dismissive rudeness. She would have to come crawling before he would even *dream* of taking her back. And she would. If he knew Francesca as well as he thought he did, she would.

Lucky selected a can of beer from her well-stocked bedroom fridge, and strolled back toward the bed. She offered the can to him. "Want some?"

He couldn't help being amused. "Your tastes are very plebian."

"My tastes suit me." She grinned. "For you it's the best Courvoisier. For me it's Coors!" With that she tipped the can, held a finger over the opening, and allowed a fine spray of liquid to cover his chest.

He was unamused. "Lucky—don't do that."

Laughingly she straddled him. "Why not, Dimi? Are *you* the only one allowed creative license?" Slowly she twirled his nipples with the tips of her fingers, then bent to lick the beer from them with quick flicks of her tongue. "Sometimes," she said wisely, "the cheap stuff works just as well as the expensive crap."

18

And he was.

A smash.

They loved him at Foxie's. Lennie had found a home.

Foxie offered him a three-month contract with time off to do any television spots that came his way. He was not really into committing for what he considered to be a lengthy amount of time, but the new agent he had signed with seemed to think it was the way to go. The agent's name was Isaac Luther. He was young, had plenty of enthusiasm and was a real pusher. He had done okay for Joey Firello—who had recommended him in the first place. Lennie liked Isaac's attitude. They both had the same long-term goal—stardom, big bucks and, hopefully, creative control.

"Take the gig," advised Isaac. "Everyone gets by Foxie's at least once a month. It's the place to be."

So he signed, settled in, and found it to be one of the best career moves he had ever made. Foxie's was not just a place, Foxie's was a way of life. The people who crowded in night after night were the most interesting, eccentric and exciting group Lennie had ever encountered. And they really liked what he did. The regulars especially, who never got tired of listening to the same old schtick, and were always on hand with encouragement and advice.

Foxie himself continually told Lennie what he thought. Do this. Do that. I like the hooker bit. Drop the burglar routine. He had a sharp ear for dialogue and a finely tuned sense of what would work and what wouldn't.

Any hecklers in the audience Foxie always dealt with personally, leaping up from his special table and showering them with abuse, or demanding that they be ejected by one of his two heavyset bouncers.

"I never take no shit in my place," he announced at least once a night. "People come to Foxie's, they gotta behave like human bein's. I don't stand for no trash in here."

Foxie was adored by the regulars. They traded insults and barbs, and once a week he took the microphone and gave them twenty-five minutes of his own particular brand of humor. He was like an old and feisty Don Rickles with flashes of Buddy Hackett and Charlie Callas.

At eighty-five, his timing was still impeccable.

Rainbow was away. "Visiting her sister in Arizona," Foxie said in staccato tones. "Do you know my Rainbow?"

Lennie explained the connection, something he hadn't wanted to do before.

Foxie laughed, a sound rather like several short trumpet blasts. "What a world! So you're Alice Golden's kid. *I* remember Alice the Swizzle." A wily grin produced a spread of tobacco-stained teeth—all his own. "I suppose she thinks I don't remember her. I *always* remember the good 'uns."

The grin spread into a leer, and Lennie received alarming visuals of Alice and this pint-sized lech in bed together. He tried to be understanding, but come on, Alice, really! Was there no end to her escapades?

Just watching Foxie was an education in itself. And watching the resident strippers was another fascinating pastime. There were three of them. A glorious-looking Mexican girl with blue-black hair down to her ass. A Swedish blonde with gravity-defying boobs. And a Chinese woman who performed with such delicate grace that "stripper" was hardly the word to describe her activities.

"My Rainbow trained every one of 'em," Foxie boasted proudly. "Knowin' how to take it off's a dyin' business. We're not sellin' pussy an' tits here, we're sellin' a *show*. You want pussy—go down the street to one of 'em porno places an' jerk off with the rest of the jerks. We're sellin' *art*."

Lennie would hardly call it art. But he had to admit that whatever the girls did, they did it with style.

Now that he was settled, he telephoned Jess a couple of times, always connecting with the monosyllabic Wayland. On the third try he left his number and instructions for her to return his call. "You'll remember to give her the message, won't you?"

"Sure, man," replied Wayland. By the time he replaced the receiver he had forgotten.

Lennie also called Eden again. Three times. On his first shot the same male voice picked up, so he didn't bother saying anything, just hung up. The second time the phone rang and rang. The third time an impersonal answering service asked him for his name and number. He passed. He had to talk to her direct.

Joey told him she had a new boyfriend.

So what? He didn't care. They were unfinished business, and she knew it as well as he did. It was only a matter of time before they would be together again.

• • • • •

There was always the routine to go through. Jess knew it by heart. Drive to the hospital, find a parking space, report to reception, take the elevator to the fourth floor. She could do it with her eyes closed. And sometimes, when she walked through the women's ward for the terminally ill, she wished her eyes *were* closed. Week after week the occupants of various beds changed. One down, another million to go. And the visiting relatives all with that same pained "why am I here" expression—an expression Jess knew only too well.

She summoned a smile as she approached her mother. She always took a little something—often only a new picture of the baby—but whatever it was, her mother seemed grateful.

She sat beside the austere hospital bed for forty-five minutes every day. The doctors had told her it was only a matter of time. Sometimes time passed so slowly.

When she left she was usually soaked with sweat and shaking. Sometimes she had to sit in the parking lot and smoke a joint before she could even think straight.

On Saturday, at two o'clock precisely, she arrived for her visit. Reception tried to detain her, but she went to the fourth floor anyway.

Her mother's bed was empty, the sheets stripped off.

A Black nurse put a kindly arm around her shoulder and said, "We called you late yesterday afternoon, honey. Didn't you get the message?"

She knew she shouldn't be shocked and sad. She knew it was something she had been preparing to happen for months.

"No, I didn't get any message," she mumbled, and her eyes filled with tears.

"Come outside," said the nurse sympathetically. "We keep some medicinal spirits for occasions like these."

"No, thank you," she replied politely, fighting to control her tears. "How can I make . . . arrangements?"

The nurse told her what to do, and she returned to reception, filled out various forms, made out a hefty check and left.

She sat in her car and gazed blankly ahead. Was it possible that the hospital had phoned to report the death of her mother and Wayland had been so stoned he'd forgotten to tell her? She knew he was in bad shape, but this was unforgivable. If it wasn't for Simon, she wouldn't even bother going home. Now that her mother was dead, she would have to try to put her life in some kind of order. Carrying on in the same old way was impossible; she was not the kind of woman who could allow a man to continue using her so blatantly.

She sighed. If only Lennie were around. She should have told him about her mother. If she had done so, he would have stayed, not gone running off with some bug up his ass.

Damn Matt Traynor. It was all his fault.

• • • • •

To celebrate his first week at Foxie's, Lennie took a group out to dinner. He rounded up the Barbie twins and Joey and Isaac and Isaac's pretty Black wife and the Swedish stripper with the great boobs. They partied all over town, and around about four in the morning he ended up in one of the twins' beds. He wasn't sure whether it was Suna or Shirlee, and these days it didn't really matter.

The next night he walked slowly into Foxie's, trying to take control of a monumental hangover. He felt like a ten-ton truck had bulldozed his brain.

Foxie greeted him at the door with a slap on the back and a wicked grin. "You'd better be hot tonight," he snapped. "Rainbow is back. An' if my Rainbow don't like you—you can be Bill Cosby and Carson rolled into one, but if she don't like you, *you're out!*"

19

Dimitri flew out of Las Vegas in his Lear Jet, and Lucky was relieved. She had no need of an involvement with a man old enough to be her father. A quick interlude was enough.

He sent her more baskets of "Sterling Silver" roses, an invitation to join him on his yacht and a list of his phone numbers across the world. She didn't miss him. But she did miss Gino, who had said he would be back in two days—and now a week had passed.

Boogie arrived with his report on Susan. It was interesting, but contained nothing earthshaking. So she was hot stuff before she married Tiny. So what? It would probably arouse Gino's interest further instead of dampening his ardor. The Widow Perfect *never* screwed around while she was married to Tiny. Gino would love *that*. Just spent money, hosted parties, gave great charity, bought jewelry and spent more money.

She had two offspring—Nathan, age nineteen, and Gemma, age twenty. There was no report on *their* activities. Lucky decided she needed one and sent Boogie back for further investigation.

The only news she could use was the fact that dear old Susan was broke, and if something didn't happen soon her Beverly Hills mansion would be snatched from right under her Beverly Hills ass. It *was* possible Gino was already paying the bills.

That was something she would have to find out, and soon.

• • • • •

The Martino children impressed Gino. They were so . . . upright. He had expected a few kinks here and there—that was only natural with teenagers. But these kids were perfect, just like their mother.

Nathan was the younger. He was of average height, with brownish hair, matching eyes and a polite manner. He attended USC, where he was studying law and philosophy. He was also on the football team, an excellent surfer, popular with the girls, and a straight A student.

Gemma had dropped out of college to pursue a career in interior design. She was an attractive girl with short honey-colored hair and a definite leaning toward anorexia. She was engaged to a boy she had been at school with.

Both children still lived at home.

"They like you," Susan announced after the first family dinner.

"And I like them," Gino replied, thinking, why couldn't Lucky and Dario have been like these two? Jeez! The troubles he'd had with his wild daughter and difficult son.

"It's not going to be easy for them to accept my getting married again," Susan explained. "So, if you don't mind, I think we should wait a few days before telling them. They'll get used to you in the meantime, and then it won't be quite such a blow."

"Hey—" he objected. "We *came* here to tell 'em."

"And we will," Susan soothed. "But there's no rush, is there? Since the press don't appear to know about us, I would sooner wait. Just a few days."

Waiting was no hardship. Susan treated him like a king. Nothing was too much trouble. He luxuriated in all the home comforts she provided. Living in a hotel with room service twenty-four hours a day was one thing. But living with a woman who catered to his every need was another. He basked in her constant attention. And although he knew Lucky was waiting for his decision on Atlantic City, he did nothing about it. Hey—surely he had his priorities straight if he put business second—for once.

• • • • •

"Honestly, Mother!" complained Nathan. "The man is a low-life."

"Yes," agreed Gemma hotly. "How could you bring him here? How *could* you?"

Susan gestured around her impeccable living room filled with objects d'art and expensive furniture. "This is the way we live. And I intend to maintain our style of living. Do you object to that?"

"But he's so crass and loud," said Gemma.

"Well," Susan replied calmly, "your father was hardly quiet."

"Daddy was a *star!*" steamed Gemma. "I hope you're not comparing him to . . . to . . . Gino Santwhateverhisnameis."

"Hood," said Nathan. "That's what we'll call him."

Susan flushed. "You will not."

"Hood." Gemma tried the word slowly. "Hmmm, not bad, brother."

"*Mr.* Santangelo is an American businessman," Susan said sternly. "He moves with the power brokers. He dines with presidents."

Gemma looked at Nathan. Nathan returned her stare. "Hood," they said in unison.

"Face it, Mother," Nathan added. "Because it's the truth."

• • • • •

When Gino had been away for ten days Lucky called. She had made up her mind she was not going to contact him, but the lawyers in New York were putting on the pressure. They insisted it was impossible to stall the involved parties any longer.

Furious, she placed a person-to-person call to Gino in L.A. "I think we've blown it," she said flatly. "The deal is off."

He hardly missed a beat. "Perhaps it's for the best," he replied. "At my age I don't know if it would've bin the right move."

Oh, Jesus! Suddenly Gino was *old*—and admitting it. What was the bitch doing to him? Putting bromide in his coffee?

"I don't believe what you're saying. We always wanted this, it was our . . . our . . . dream," she stammered.

"Yeh, kid, but dreams change. We'll talk about it when I get back."

"When will that be?" she asked, holding her breath, trying not to explode with fury. *When, Daddy, when?*

"Another day or two. Hang in there. We'll come up with another scheme—somethin' a little easier for an old man."

She flung the receiver down with such force that it smashed into two neat pieces. Old man indeed! This wasn't the Gino *she* knew.

What was she going to do? She was trapped in Las Vegas, trapped in a business partnership with a father who obviously had a bad case of senility. She couldn't make a fucking move without him. She had been better off when he was in exile and *she* called all the shots. If he was going to go through with this marriage, she wanted out.

That was a thought—and one that appealed.

Lucky Santangelo. On her own. With no one to answer to except herself.

She wondered how Gino would take the news. Especially when she told him he would have to buy her out.

Christ! He would never do that. It would mean selling the Magiriano and splitting the money down the middle. And there was a syndicate of investors to take care of, and no more freshly laundered cash coming in every week.

But . . . he would still have the Mirage, and all his holdings, companies, and other investments. It would hardly make any difference to him.

There was no way he would sell the Magiriano. And did she *really* want out?

Yes, she really did. There was no point in hanging around with Susan Martino in residence.

Besides, she was entitled to a life too. And a change of scene was exactly what she had in mind.

20

Rainbow did not look old, fat or ugly, even though her eyes were crinkled around the edges, deep laugh lines etched their way down each side of her mouth, and her use of makeup was excessive. A ruined beauty, true. But a spectacular ruin, with a statuesque body, magnificent breasts and a spread of pale-red hair.

Lennie figured she had to be in her late fifties at least. She made him feel like a teenager as she looked him up and down with a practiced eye and drawled, "Foxie tells me you're a pretty hot tamale. Gonna prove it to me tonight?"

Oh, the times he could have proved it to her!

"I'll try," he said, giving her the lopsided grin.

"If you're anything like your old man, you'll never stop trying."

So it was true—Jack Golden *had* indulged in the pleasures of Rainbow's fantasy-provoking flesh.

Fortunately she liked him. "Lennie," she told him magnanimously, "you're about as funny as your daddy. In a different way, of course. Jack Golden had 'em splittin' their pants. But I guess it's a whole new world today, and you seem to capture what's goin' on well enough." She swigged a glass of brandy and milk—her favorite drink—then continued, "Listen to Foxie—he *knows* what he's talkin' about. And in this business, knowledge is everythin'." She tossed her mane of hair, still thick and lustrous. "Me, I'm just an old broad who follows her gut instinct."

He wished the old broad would quit with the low-cut dresses. Every time he saw her ample breasts his imagination ran riot. It wasn't easy beating down the early memories.

She did have a great act. Hadn't changed a thing in all the years. Same smile, hair, hooker shoes and feather boas. Same sleight of hand that allowed you to see nothing while you thought you were seeing everything. Old-fashioned illusion. The girls took it all off, but Rainbow, thank God, stuck to her old routine. A peek here. A peek there. Nothing dirty. She was a relic from another age, and the audience went wild.

"She does it once a week," the Chinese stripper confided to Lennie. "And they love her."

"I can tell."

"Sometimes when Rainbow is on they line up around the block to get in."

He could believe it. Alice would be spitting blood if she knew Rainbow was still pulling them in. He phoned his mother on the off-chance that she might be wondering what was going on in his life.

She didn't ask what he was doing, where he was living or anything of a personal nature. She merely said, "Lennie, I have a twenty-five-year-old boy mad for my body. Should I let him?"

He took a deep breath, chose not to answer her question and said, "I'm working at Foxie's. Did you know your friend Rainbow is still taking it off?"

That stopped her in her tracks. "What?" she said at last. "At her age?"

"What age is she?"

"Better you shouldn't ask. Old enough to know she should have stopped doing that years ago."

"They love her."

"Who loves her?"

"The audience."

"They used to love me," Alice sighed wistfully. "And certain people still do. Lennie, darling, tell me—is twenty-five cradle pinching?"

"Snatching."

"Watch your language."

"Foxie remembers you."

A coquettish tone entered her voice. "That old *bubkes*. He was crazy for me. He had a *schnickel* like a ten-cent piece. Used to flash it at all the girls. But I never let him . . . *do* anything. You get what I'm saying, darling? *Never*."

Which meant, of course, that she had screwed his brains out.

"I thought you might like to see the show one night," he suggested. "I could drive out to get you and take you home later."

"I hate freeways."

"We don't have to go on the freeway."

"I hate driving."

"*I'll* drive."

"You know what I mean. Besides, who wants to see Rainbow and Foxie? I never liked either of 'em."

"Come *on,* she was your best friend. Besides, I was inviting you to see *me.*"

"You!" She laughed rudely. "You, with your filthy language and dirty talk. Once was enough, thank you. If your father was alive he'd disown you."

Disown him from what?

"Forget it," he said shortly, hanging up.

Why did he bother? Alice Golden did not give a damn about anyone except herself.

• • • • •

Hardly anyone came to the funeral. A couple of her mother's canasta-playing friends, an elderly cousin who lived in Tahoe, and three neighbors. Not a majestic turnout, but Jess did the best she could and invited them all back to the house for Kentucky Fried Chicken, potato chips and cheap red wine.

Wayland made a marvelous host. He greeted them with a casual wave, handed Jess the baby, then sat under a tree, cleaning his fingernails and staring blankly at the sky.

Jess curbed her anger, entertained her guests, fed Simon, cleaned up, put Simon to sleep for the night and headed for work. She had not requested time off. Who needed extra hours with Wayland for company?

Matt hit on her almost immediately. He sidled up to her empty blackjack table, sat himself down and said, "When is the most gorgeous chick in Vegas going to give me a second chance?"

"Go away," she said hollowly.

"Are you still mad about the other night?"

"Get lost."

"You should be *flattered* that I came on to you. What did you *think* we were going to do in my apartment—play tag?"

"I thought," she said slowly, "that we would have dinner and discuss why you fired Lennie Golden."

"Firing your friend was not my idea. If you want to meet me later I'll tell you exactly what happened."

"Sure, just like the last time."

He smoothed back a lock of silver hair escaping from an invisible cage of hair spray and tried to figure out what was so different about this one. Why did he want her so much—a lowly blackjack dealer, and short too?

"Jess," he said sincerely, "trust me. I'll take you *out* to dinner. How's that?"

Even dinner with Matt was better than going home to Wayland.

Two would-be gamblers climbed onto stools and thrust money at her. Big spenders. One proffered a twenty, the other slid across three ten-dollar bills. Automatically she stacked the chips and spun the neat piles in the right direction.

Matt stood up. "Same time. The parking lot," he said.

She nodded. She needed to talk. Like it or not, Matt Traynor would just have to listen.

• • • • •

"It's lovely," Eden said.

"I told ya I'd get ya the right place," Santino crowed, strutting around the marble terrace of the small empty house perched high on Blue Jay Way in the Hollywood Hills.

"I'll have to hire an interior designer," she mused.

"Sure." He puffed on a very large Cuban cigar. "I gotta decorator broad owes me a favor."

"It seems you have a lot of people who owe you favors."

"It's the only way t'go." He scattered ash on the ground.

Eden walked toward the gleaming blue pool with the fountain at one end, and the two stone cupids at the other. "I adore it!" she exclaimed.

Santino was pleased. The sooner he moved her in, the better. He wanted her under his control.

He took off his jacket and settled himself on a patio chair. This whole setup was going to work out fine.

"Why doncha take a swim?" he suggested. "Christen the joint."

She looked at him. He was sweating. He was always sweating. Well, anybody would sweat if they togged themselves out in a three-piece suit every day.

She remembered the first time they went to bed. Under the suit he wore patterned boxer shorts, socks with garters, and a shoulder holster with an ominous-looking gun nestled within. For one moment she had imagined he was a cop. A cop couldn't get her into the movies. She had almost dressed and left.

Her Swedish friend, Ulla, had told her that Santino Bonnatti had more money than brains. All her life Eden had been looking for a man with just such qualities. He would finance a movie for her to appear in. She would become a star. And then she would move on. In the meantime he was fortunate to have her.

"Go on, swim," he urged.

She knew what he wanted and she didn't mind one bit. His desire gave her power, and she liked the feeling. With studied sensuality she peeled off her dress. There was nothing underneath except pure perfection. Some men considered her on the slender side. Santino liked her that way. His wife, she had found out, was a heavy woman.

She kept her shoes on, strappy white sandals that emphasized her blood-red toenails.

Santino stood up. "Come here," he said thickly. "I just thought of another way to christen the joint."

•   •   •   •   •

"There's someone from *The Merv Griffin Show* out front," one of the strippers confided just before Lennie went on.

He didn't drop dead with excitement. There was always *someone* in the audience—an agent, a talent scout, a producer. Once it was rumored Burt Reynolds was sipping champagne at table number two. The Swedish stripper had been so unnerved by the rumor she ripped off her clothes five minutes before her grand finale.

Burt Reynolds turned out to be a look-alike fresh from a television contest. Miss Sweden was so furious she refused to talk to anyone for a week.

Lennie had been around long enough to know it didn't matter *who* was watching. When you went on you did your best. If your best wasn't good enough—fuck 'em.

He had some new material he wanted to try out. Some mother-son schtick, with Alice as the role model. Wouldn't *that* be a laugh if the Griffin show saw him, liked him, and insisted he use the new stuff on their show? Alice would *love* that. She probably wouldn't even recognize herself, although he was painting a ruthlessly cruel but truthful picture.

He was restless after the show. Nobody came running backstage to tell him how great he was. Nobody from the Griffin show materialized.

He had a drink at the bar and went home to the emptiness of his hotel room. It was after two in the morning, but fuck it, he needed her. Expecting the same male voice to pick up, or the answering service, he dialed Eden's number.

She answered the phone herself. That strange, throaty voice, which sounded like she had a bad case of bronchitis. "Hello." A sleepy pause, then stronger, "Hello."

He waited for the curse words. As if on cue, she let forth a volley of obscenities.

He timed her perfectly. You didn't live with a woman for three years without knowing every move she made.

Just before she was about to slam the phone down, he spoke. Softly. Slowly.

"Eden. This is Lennie. Prepare yourself. I'm back in your life."

21

Olympia knew the moment her father walked into his New York apartment that she had made a mistake staying there. Why should she, Olympia Stanislopoulos, one of the richest young women in the world, feel like a lodger? She immediately called a friend of her mother's who dabbled in real estate and requested she find her an apartment at once.

"Yes," the woman told her, "I know the perfect place."

"Show it to me at once," Olympia said. She had decided New York was very much to her liking and she should have her own home there. Hotels were so boring, and staying at her father's again was definitely out. It was acceptable to share his plane, his yacht, even his private island when the need arose, but in New York it was surely time to buy her own place.

Dimitri immediately spotted the cigar burn on one of his precious antique tables. He roared with fury and summoned his butler. Olympia allowed the stupid man to take the blame. It constantly amazed her that her father was so into his possessions. He was aware of everything. If one book was out of place in any of his homes, he knew it.

Brigette greeted Grandpop, as she called him, with a vigorous hug and a kiss on the lips.

He picked the child up in his arms. "How's my baby?" he sang.

"Very bad," said Olympia ominously. "She's been a *very bad* girl. She ruined Mama's wedding."

He ignored that piece of information and presented Brigette with several huge gift-wrapped boxes.

Olympia remembered when she was a child. Many presents—but gestures of affection were always reserved for his latest mistress. Perhaps he was mellowing. Or perhaps he liked Brigette better than he did his own daughter. She summoned Nanny Mabel and dispatched Brigette and the presents from the room.

"How was Las Vegas?" she asked her father dutifully. "I hear it's a dreadful place, full of terrible little people."

Dimitri regarded her critically. She was looking plump. Why didn't the girl take care of herself?

"You are right," he said. "But I was merely honoring Francesca Fern, hardly sightseeing."

"How *is* Francesca?" Olympia asked. She was always intrigued by his continuing infatuation with the horse-faced actress. Francesca was certainly lasting longer than any of the others.

"Very fine," snapped Dimitri. He had no intention of discussing his personal life with his gossipy daughter. If Olympia knew the affair was over, she would make sure it hit every society column in the world. "I saw an old friend of yours," he added quickly to get her off the scent.

"Who?"

"Lucky Santangelo."

Lucky Santangelo. Ex-best friend. Oh, the adventures they had shared! Once. A long time ago. Over fifteen years. They probably wouldn't even recognize each other now. And they certainly would have nothing in common.

"Where did you see *her?*" Olympia sniffed.

"She owns the Magiriano Hotel."

"Oh. Did her gangster father give it to her?"

"She built it herself while he was out of the country. She's a very clever businesswoman."

Olympia was silent. *She built it herself.* Oh, really? With her own two hands? Was he trying to make *her* feel guilty because she had never done anything except inherit money and marry a series of cretinous fortune hunters?

"How does she look?" Olympia asked curiously.

Dimitri changed the subject. It wouldn't do for his daughter to have knowledge of his latest affair. "Who notices such things?" he said dismissively. "I wish to leave for the airport at noon tomorrow. Please do not be late."

Olympia nodded vaguely as he left the room. She had no intention of leaving the next day, but she did plan to send Brigette and Nanny Mabel. The two of them were getting on her nerves; she needed a little time alone to recover from the trauma of her mother's wedding. Oh, the embarrassment of Brigette's outrageous behavior. The child was becoming a monster.

Yes, she would pack them off with Dimitri at noon. He could keep an eye on them in Paris while she purchased an apartment in New York and thought of herself for once.

Lucky Santangelo a very clever businesswoman indeed! Ha! Olympia remembered her as a raggle-taggle gypsy who couldn't even find a boyfriend. She, Olympia, had taught her about men and sex and clothes. And a fine lot of thanks she had received for her trouble. Not one word in fifteen years.

She remembered Lucky arriving at L'Evier, the boarding school they had both attended in Switzerland, a skinny dark-haired kid who had been registered under the name of Lucky Saint because no one was supposed to know who her father was.

As if anyone cared.

Gino Santangelo.

The first time Olympia set eyes on him from their window she had shuddered. He was so . . . sinister-looking. Dark like Lucky. On the short side, but very very sexy, with thick curly hair, a strutting walk and bad black eyes. It was the first time she had noticed the appeal of an older man.

For a long time she had fantasized about him. Sometimes, when she indulged herself, she had imagined Gino was in the room with her, sucking on her tits, sticking it to her with absolutely no finesse but a hell of a lot of brutal energy.

She had never confided to Lucky that she harbored a wish to fuck her father. Lucky would not have appreciated the thought.

Olympia sighed and recalled the time Gino got himself

engaged to Marabelle Blue, a famous blond movie star. He had informed Lucky on the telephone, and she had crawled into bed sobbing. At the time Olympia was not supposed to know who she was. She did, of course. She had found out by skimming Lucky's diary two days after she arrived at school. Lucky was sobbing, and Olympia couldn't sleep, so she went to her friend and comforted her, softly at first, but the softness had turned into passion, and before long the two schoolgirls were entwined like lovers.

One night of warm wet sweetness. The next morning things were back to normal. Neither of them had ever mentioned it. It was as if their lovemaking had never taken place. Sometimes Olympia thought of it. Over the years there had been a few women. Not one of them came close to the night of illicit passion with her school friend. . . .

"Mama!" Brigette entered her train of thought. "Look!" The child thrust an expensive Cartier watch at her.

Olympia glanced at the watch. It must have cost over a thousand dollars. Why did Dimitri buy such presents for a nine-year-old?

"Don't want it," Brigette whined. "Want a Snoopy watch, Mama. Want to go to Disneyland."

"Yes, dear," said Olympia, taking the watch and tossing it to one side. She would send the chauffeur out for a Snoopy watch and give it to Brigette just before the child departed the next day. That would circumvent a nasty scene, for Brigette would not be pleased when she discovered Olympia had no plans to accompany her.

22

Now Lucky found it was just a question of waiting for Gino to return so she could tell him she was moving on. The only problem was that he seemed to have no intention of doing so.

She steamed in the Las Vegas heat while the days passed slowly, and the nights even more so. Eventually she could stand it no longer. Atlantic City was over. Play the game or leave the field—she had been *forced* to leave the field.

Angrily she collected some of her favorite books, a tape machine and a stack of soul tapes. Then she got on a plane to Palm Springs and holed up in the Canyon Club Hotel, where she was given her own house and pool and complete privacy. "Call me the instant Gino returns," were her instructions.

The solitude was strangely welcome. She lay out by the pool all day with Bobby Womack and Teddy Pendergrass and Marvin Gaye for company. And at night she settled into bed with Mario Puzo, Joseph Wambaugh and early Harold Robbins (always a kick to reread *A Stone for Danny Fisher* and *The Adventurers*). She turned off completely. Ordered only healthy foods. Did not smoke or drink. Wore no makeup. And treated her bronzed body to a morning spa, half an hour of vigorous exercise and an evening sauna.

She was never lonely. She had learned at an early age to be satisfied with her own company. And although sometimes she thought about how pleasant it might be to have a sister or a brother—she could still remember the closeness she and Dario had shared as children—it was okay. She was reasonably content.

Waiting seemed interminable. But waiting *her* way was certainly more tolerable. Somehow she reveled in the peace and the quiet and the aloneness, because soon she knew everything would change. Soon she would be starting over.

• • • • •

"I gotta get back," Gino said often.

"Why?" Susan would reply. "You have people to run every-thing for you. Surely it is more pleasant to stay here with me?"

He had to admit it was. But he was beginning to feel guilty about Lucky. He knew she was angry at him; therefore he didn't even bother to call, reasoning that he would be better off to deal with her face to face.

Life in Beverly Hills was like one long vacation. Living in Susan's house, he found a freedom from responsibilities. For once the phone wasn't always ringing, people weren't bothering him with minor problems; he could relax and do what he wanted.

Long ago he had surrounded himself with the best lawyers, accountants and executives money could buy. It was called tak-ing care of business without actually having to do anything. He had learned that lesson while marooned in Israel for seven years: Delegate, but never lose touch. Besides, while he was away, Lucky would watch over everything. The kid was as smart as any man. He felt sorry about disappointing her on Atlantic City—but if he was going to get married, becoming involved in major new projects was out. For the time being, anyway.

Lucky would understand. She would have to.

Susan had still not mentioned to her children that they were planning to marry.

"C'mon," Gino complained. "Get it over with. Can'tcha see they love me?"

She told them over dinner at Chasen's with Gino present. The two of them made polite noises and kicked each other under the table.

"Y'see," Gino said later, "they think it's fine. Now I gotta get back to Vegas, tie up a few things. We'll leave tomorrow."

"*I* can't leave," Susan said quickly.

"Why not?"

She lowered her eyes. "It's just not possible. When Tiny passed away . . ." She paused. ". . . I didn't really want to mention this to you, but he left what my lawyers are beginning to call a financial nightmare. It's something I have to try and deal with myself, and since we've been together I haven't paid any attention to sordid business matters. If you return to Las Vegas, then I—"

He interrupted her, slamming his forehead with the palm of his hand. "Jeez! Why didn't you *tell* me? Christ! We're together, aren't we? We're gonna get married for crissakes. I should have asked you if everything was all right."

"It's not your problem, Gino," she said firmly. "Although I do appreciate your concern."

"Listen. From now on *your* problems are *my* problems. I'll fly back tomorrow an' send one of my best accountants to L.A. to meet with your lawyers. He'll get a handle on the situation, and then I'll put everything straight. How does that grab you?"

"You don't have to," she said, immediately agreeing.

He caught her in a tight hug. "Sure I have to. And next weekend you'll fly to Vegas an' we'll be together."

She had never thought it would be so easy. For a moment she tensed, not prepared for another of his vigorous lovemaking sessions. Then she relaxed and endured his suffocating embrace. After they were married he would not get within ten feet of her.

His hands began to reach for her breasts. "You're a sexy broad," he said, laughing. "Y'know that, don'tcha? You know that, Susie? You're one helluva gorgeous sexy broad!"

Inwardly she shuddered.

Outwardly she succumbed.

His rough touch did nothing for her. She couldn't wait until he left.

·   ·   ·   ·   ·

"Thank God the hood has gone!" announced Gemma, minutes after Gino departed for the airport. The three of them sat in the breakfast room picking at their food.

"Thank God is right," emphasized Nathan. "Mother, surely you're not serious about *marrying* that gangster?"

"Don't speak like that about Gino," snapped Susan. "And kindly accept the fact that now your father is gone I have to make a life for myself."

"Yes, but not with the hood," complained Gemma, crunching a piece of Crispbread.

"Certainly not," agreed Nathan, downing his orange juice.

Susan sighed. She had raised two tight-assed WASP snobs. Tiny would be horrified.

But of course, secretly she agreed with them. It was ludicrous that she was being forced to commit matrimony with a man like Gino Santangelo. Why hadn't Tiny taken care of his business affairs? Why hadn't he looked to the future? Thoughtless man.

She pulled her silk peignoir tightly across her breasts and eyed her two offspring. Gemma, so skinny and snippy-looking. And Nathan, a California boy with floppy hair and a surfer's body.

If she didn't have the two of them to support . . . And they expected every comfort. Children raised in Beverly Hills were different from the rest. Delicately she sipped her lemon tea. Thank God Gino had left. At least he would not be bothering her for a while. She had no intention of returning to Las Vegas on the weekend. There was a wedding to plan, and it would be a magnificent affair. At least she owed herself that.

If Gino wished to see her, *he* could return to Beverly Hills.

She hoped he wouldn't.

She knew he would.

· · · · ·

Lucky received the message out by the pool. Gino was back. She packed and was at the airport within an hour. A confrontation was long overdue.

23

They were to meet on the corner of La Brea and Sunset at Tiny Naylor's, a drive-in restaurant. Lennie got there first, and he sat in his rented car wondering anxiously if she would turn up. It was two-thirty in the morning, hardly time for a reunion. But when he had blurted "I've got to see you," over the phone, Eden had replied, "I'm busy tomorrow, but if you like I'll meet you now."

An uncharacteristic gesture. He had expected her to scream because he was calling so late. Instead, once she found out it was he, she had been surprisingly receptive, and now he sat waiting for her knowing it would be a typical Eden move for her to get him to come out, and then not turn up at all.

He lit a cigarette and ordered a burrito and a Coke from a tired waitress. Two hookers in matching purple hot pants and open-weave tops sauntered by.

"Wanna fuck or sumpin'?" demanded one, too exhausted from her night's activity to suspect he might be a cop.

"Not tonight, ladies," he replied civilly. That was a lie. He wanted to fuck Eden.

"Why not?" demanded the other hooker, a plump Mexican with a gold front tooth. "I give you a preview, honey, you shit your pants." She raised her open-weave top and flashed two globules of flesh at him.

He nodded approvingly and repeated, "Not tonight, ladies."

"Fag!" spat the Mexican.

"Shithead!" said her companion.

They spotted a motorcycle with two greasers astride and went on their way.

The waitress brought his burrito and Coke. He wolfed them, then glanced at his watch. She had said twenty minutes. Half an hour had passed. How long was he going to wait?

The hookers were doing business. The plump Mexican linked arms with one of the greasers and they vanished into the shadows. The other one leaned across the handlebars of the bike and whispered promises to the rider.

Eden wasn't going to come. Why should she? She hated him. She had told him so, that last night in New York.

"You're a loser," she had said. "A nothing, a lousy lay."

Eden had a way with words.

But he wasn't exactly blameless when it came to name-calling. He had called her everything from a stupid cunt to a talentless dumb bitch.

They had not parted on the best of terms.

And yet . . .

He could remember the good times.

When Eden wanted, she could be the sweetest female in the world. She could make a man feel like a king, top of the whole fucking heap. In the three years they were together the good times outweighed the bad. And the sex was great. Eden with her thin body, long silky hair, heart-shaped face and sly topaz eyes.

She was a killer. She had an exotic beauty that he just couldn't get enough of.

As if on cue, her pale-pink Thunderbird slid into the slot beside him. She lowered her window and smiled. Her eyes were obscured by Jacqueline Onassis sunglasses, her hair hidden beneath a silk scarf. "Hello, Lennie," she drawled in her best Lauren Bacall husky voice. "I bet you thought I wasn't coming."

•   •   •   •   •

Matt Traynor did not behave like a perfect gentleman. He met Jess in the parking lot as arranged. He took her to a Polynesian restaurant for dinner. He plied her with Scorpions and Navy grogs until she could hardly walk. And then he took her back to his apartment and tried to screw her.

She did not object.

She did not know.

As soon as they arrived she passed out on his couch. He

lifted her skirt, pulled down her panties and was just about to force himself aboard when his conscience got the better of him. What the hell was he *doing?*

Frantically he went into action, pulling her panties back up and rearranging her skirt. He felt like the world's worst heel. Groaning to himself, he poured a straight bourbon, and hoped to God she would never realize he had almost committed a dirty act. Then he threw a leopardskin rug over her and nervously paced the apartment.

She stayed unconscious until five-thirty in the morning, when she woke, swore loudly, demanded his car keys and rushed off into the early-morning light with a parting "I'll leave your keys under the front seat."

He was destroyed. He had expected, had even quite looked forward to the Doris Day–Rock Hudson scene.

Doris *(distraught)*: "Oh, dear! What happened? Tell me *now.* Did we . . . do anything?"

Rock *(with a manly, knowing smile)*: "Did we do what?"

Doris: "Don't torment me. You know what I mean."

Rock *(reassuringly)*: "Of course not. What kind of a man do you take me for?"

Doris *(relieved and grateful)*: "You're *my* kind of man."

Fade-out.

Now she was gone. And she hadn't even asked. Didn't she care?

He entered his stainless-steel kitchen and fixed instant coffee. His back hurt. All that bending over. His eyes ached. All that tension.

He wondered if she would ever talk to him again.

• • • • •

"I knew you'd come," Lennie said, although he hadn't known at all. He got out of his car and climbed into the passenger seat of the Thunderbird. Eden was wearing a skimpy sundress and high-heeled sandals. He reached over and took off her sunglasses. She wasn't wearing makeup but she still looked great.

"Hey." He reached over and touched her hair beneath the scarf. "Good t'see you."

She stared at him long and hard. "Hello, Lennie. You're a surprise, but a nice one."

She knew how to push his buttons—she always had.

"I thought we might drive to the beach," she suggested, "and you can tell me what you're doing out here."

Well, Eden, I came to the coast so that I could make love to you again. The hell with my career.

"Good idea. Shall I drive?" He hoped he sounded casual.

She nodded.

He got out of the car while Eden slid over.

The Mexican hooker was returning from the shadows with a triumphant leer. "Change your mind, cutie?" she yelled. "I can take us both to paradise for twenny bucks."

He ignored her and got behind the wheel.

Eden moved close to him. "I missed you, Big Man," she murmured softly, placing her hand on his thigh.

He developed an erection that wouldn't quit.

They roared down Sunset, made Brentwood in eight minutes, the Palisades in twelve, and within twenty they were cruising along the Pacific Coast Highway, searching for a suitable place to park.

She had been doing all the talking, telling him about her acting roles. "I never stop working," she confided. "I guess I'm a better actress than you thought."

He didn't want to get into *that*.

They parked on a bluff and made their way to the beach. It was a beautiful night. The moon was bright and the ocean at peace. They walked along the seashore, holding hands like new lovers and splashing in the surf. Then they fell on the sand like old lovers, and found every secret place with ferocious familiarity.

She wrapped her long legs around his neck and rocked with his rhythm as though she never wanted it to end.

He gave her what she wanted, what *he* wanted. Slowly. Fast. Very fast. Then slowly again, keeping his control by reciting the goddamn alphabet in his head, because he didn't want to come, didn't want it to end, wanted their lovemaking to go on forever.

"You . . . always . . . were . . . the . . . best," she said huskily. "Jesus . . . Lennie . . . my . . . big . . . man . . ."

He felt her spasms and let rip while she moaned with untamed pleasure. When they were finished, he stroked her silky hair and said, very quietly, "We belong together. You do know that, don't you?"

She didn't answer. The only sound was the sea lapping gently on the shore.

• • • • •

Jess raced Matt's ridiculous car to the hotel. She dumped it in the parking lot and leaped into her Camaro. Then she drove home in record time.

She could hear Simon crying as she parked. Her head throbbed. Too many fancy drinks, but getting plastered had taken her mind off the funeral, and that was something. The house looked disgusting. Wayland had obviously entertained again. Dirty cans and bottles, the lingering heavy stench of marijuana, empty McDonald's wrappers. And an unfamiliar male body asleep on the floor.

"Goddamnit!" she yelled, kicking at the sleeping form, who groaned and rolled over.

In the bedroom Wayland sprawled on the bed, fully dressed. Simon cried in his crib. There was the smell of urine and worse. She scooped him up and changed his filthy diaper. Wayland did not stir. Wearily she took Simon into the kitchen and fixed him a bottle. The crying was driving her nuts. The mess was driving her nuts. She shoved the bottle into Simon's mouth and enjoyed peace.

This week she would tell Wayland to get out.

24

Idon't give a fuck what you want to do!" screamed Gino.

"And I don't give a fuck what *you* think!" screamed Lucky.

They had been yelling at each other for an hour——one long hour of insults, recriminations and accusations. The harmony of their past year together had vanished, and it was back to the antagonism and ill will of former times.

"You don't run my life," Lucky stormed. "I'm not your sweet little girl who has to do what Daddy says. And I don't *work* for you either." She paused to catch her breath and glare at him. He wanted it all his own way. He wanted to marry Susan *and* keep daughter dear at his fingertips, some kind of surrogate boss who would take care of business while he pissed off to Beverly Hills.

Well, daughter dear was not standing for it. No way. No fucking way. Daughter dear was getting out.

"We're partners," she said coldly. "Half the Magiriano is mine——and I'm cashing in and going on to do other things. So we either sell or you buy me out. Which is it to be?"

He had to admit the kid had balls. Mad as he was, he could still admire her. She was a pain in the butt, but street smart and savvy and tough. One of life's natural winners.

"Hey." He threw his arms wide. "You want out, you got it. What're we fightin' over? I'm not gonna hold you back if you wanna do other things. I'll buy out your share. But you gotta remember, everythin' I own is gonna be yours one day anyway."

Who was he kidding? If he married Susan Martino, everything he had would be Susan's.

"That's settled then," she said evenly, weary from the argument.

"Yeh. An' if you're so sure it's what you want, I'll put it in motion right away," he said gruffly.

It's not what I want, it's what you want.

"There's one other thing," she said.

"What?"

"The house in East Hampton," she blurted. "I'd like to own it."

"Huh?" He stared at her—hard black eyes head-on with hard black eyes. "Why?"

"Because I don't want you taking another woman there. It was Mommy's house when we were all a family. It's the only real home I've ever known, and I want to have it."

He was angry again. First she wanted to sell the hotel, then she wanted him to give her the East Hampton house. What kind of shit *was* this?

"Okay, okay, it's yours," he said grudgingly.

She was very businesslike, aware of the fact that to protect herself, once he married Susan, she had to be. "I'll have a real estate agent put a price on it and I'll buy it from you. The money can come out of my share of the hotel."

He shook his head as if he couldn't quite believe what was happening. "Lucky," he asked softly, "why are we acting like a couple who's just gettin' a divorce? Before you know it we'll only be communicatin' through lawyers."

"Talking of lawyers," she said crisply, "I'm sure you've thought of asking Susan to sign a prenuptial agreement."

"What kind of smart-ass remark is that?" he shouted. "Jeez! You're somethin', you really are. You hardly even know Susan, an' now you got her walkin' off with all my money."

"I'm just behaving the way you taught me. This *is* California, and there are such things as community property laws."

"Jesus Christ!" he spat in disgust.

Quietly she left the room. She had pushed about as far as she could go.

• • • • •

Susan Martino, Gino discovered via the accountant he sent to L.A., was several hundred thousand in the hole.

He spoke to her on the phone. "How didja ever get in such a mess?" he demanded.

"Don't you mean how did *Tiny* get me into such a mess?" she replied logically.

"I'll take care of it." He was not exactly delighted, but it had to be done.

"I told you before, you don't have to," she reminded.

"Call it a weddin' present," he offered magnanimously.

"Thank you." Her tone was appreciative, but not overly so.

He admired the ladylike quality she brought to everything. She really was a class act. "You missing me yet?"

"Yes. But I have the wedding to plan, and it's keeping me extraordinarily busy."

"What's to plan? You'll hop on a plane an' we'll do it here. No big deal." He paused to light a cigar, in spite of the fact that after the heart attack his doctor had insisted he quit. "Hey— why don't we do it this weekend? Get it over an' done with."

She laughed pleasantly. "You *are* joking, aren't you? My God, Gino, 'get it over and done with'—you make it sound so trivial."

"You got other plans?"

"I most certainly do. A wedding is a sacred occasion. Surely you want to do it properly?"

"We can do it properly in Vegas."

"Not at all," she chided. "We must be married in Beverly Hills. I have so many friends here. It will be a joyous day— one to remember."

"*My* friends are *here*," he pointed out. "An' we'll be livin' here. I didn't want to tell you on the phone, but Lucky's leaving."

"She is?"

"Yeh. Gave me a whole speech about gettin' out an' movin' to New York. I gotta tell you, Susie, I'm sick about it."

He might be sick, but *she* was ecstatic. She had never thought it would be so easy to get rid of the pushy daughter.

"I'm sure it will be for the best, Gino, dear," she said comfortingly.

"You think so?"

"Oh, yes."

Susan did not tell him her plans for the weekend were to stay in L.A. She hung up with promises of love, and then she phoned her lawyers to find out when all the debts would be cleared. Obviously, Gino Santangelo had been an excellent choice. Old, rich and pliable. Oversexed for a man of his age, but she could put up with that for a while longer.

Putting up with men. The story of her life. From the age of fifteen, when she was deflowered by a swashbuckling movie star of the fifties while her hairdresser mother sat downstairs swigging vodka, to now, and Gino.

Putting up with men. A series of rich, important men. While Mother reaped the benefits of a pretty teenage daughter. No money ever actually changed hands, but something was always going on. A new white Cadillac for Mother to drive. Three televisions. Plenty of clothes. Hampers of food. Crates of champagne.

Susan felt revulsion whenever a man touched her.

Go upstairs with Mr. Whoever, Susan, he wants to show you something.

One wealthy man after another, until it became a way of life, and she played the game automatically, because *somebody* had to supply Mother with life's little luxuries and perpetual booze.

When she was twenty, her mother ran a light at Sunset and Fairfax and was killed instantly in a collision with a gardener's truck. The driver sued. Naturally Susan found someone to settle the case for her. Six months later she was smart enough to discover Tiny while doing extra work on one of his movies. He didn't stand a chance. She knew what she wanted, and she went for it with controlled dedication. He divorced his first wife with nary a protest, married Susan, and together they rose in the hierarchy of the Hollywood social scene. She became a perfect hostess, a warm confidante, and mother of his two children.

After a few years Tiny screwed anything that breathed in his direction—it wasn't easy being married to one of the queens of the Beverly Hills-Bel Air social set.

After a few years Susan met a beefy Russian masseuse named Gloria, who came to the house to ease her neck tension. It turned out Gloria knew plenty of other places where tension could be eased, and Susan succumbed. She had succumbed a few other times. But for the last three years she had been having a very satisfying affair with a producer's wife named Paige Wheeler. The women enjoyed discreet liaisons at various venues including each other's homes when they could get rid of the servants. Unfortunately Paige's husband, Ryder, had recently given birth to a huge hit movie, which meant Paige's time was taken up with a solid block of unavoidable social engagements. Plus the fact that she also dabbled in interior design. And of course Susan had been busy in Vegas snaring Gino. The two women hadn't seen each other in months.

Susan's hand hovered over the phone. She deserved a treat. One little treat.

* * * * *

The morning after her confrontation with Gino, Lucky awoke sick to her stomach. She threw up, felt only slightly better and crawled back to bed. This was not the right time to get sick. There was so much to do. She had to start packing, meet with her lawyers and get everything in order.

For a moment she wondered if she was doing the right thing. But in her heart she knew that if Gino married Susan she would be better off away from them. Maybe Susan *was* a wonderful human being. Maybe she *did* love Gino for himself.

Maybe . . .

On impulse she grabbed the phone and called Costa Zen-nocotti in Miami. He had retired there a year ago, and by all accounts was very happy to live the quiet life after forty years as Gino's lawyer and best friend. He was her friend too. After all, it was Costa who had nurtured her ambition and taught her everything about business while Gino languished in Israel.

"Uncle Costa," she greeted warmly when he picked up the phone, "how are you?"

"I am currently mastering the art of French toast," he replied, happy to hear from her. "At my advanced age I have finally decided I should cook."

She laughed happily. It was so good to speak to him. "I thought you had droves of women around you who did that sort of thing," she joked. She knew he was seeing a divorcee who apparently had caused him to gain fifteen pounds.

"Yes, yes," he said quickly. "But you know me, I hate to be dependent on anyone."

Indeed she did know him. Uncle Costa. A quiet, mild-mannered man. Married for over thirty years to Auntie Jen, who had passed away several years ago. One of those rare marriages where both partners grow together and remain content and in love. No screwing around for Uncle Costa. He had been the perfect husband.

"When did you last hear from Gino?" she asked.

"Not recently. Why? Is something the matter?"

"Oh, this and that. Nothing earth-shattering. I think I might be selling my share of the Magiriano."

"Nothing earth-shattering, she says! *That's* earth-shattering. What's the matter, Lucky?"

"Can I fly in and see you? I need to talk."

"When?"

"In a few days."

"Any time, my dear. You know I'm always here for you."

Yeh. Uncle Costa was always available. But what about Gino?

"I'll call you again."

"Make it soon."

"Yes, I will."

She hung up and thought that yes, it would be a nice idea to visit with Uncle Costa. Every time he talked, she managed to find out a little bit more about Gino's colorful past. Costa loved to reminisce and she loved to listen. Her mother, Maria, had been Uncle Costa's niece. And it was rumored that her grandmother, Maria's mother, had also been involved with Gino.

She shivered. Costa would never talk about *that*.

Feeling slightly better, she got up, dressed, and ventured downstairs. The casino was a hive of activity with early-morning gamblers out in full force. She bumped into Matt, who looked uncharacteristically harassed. She would have to call a meeting to let her key people know she was moving on. They all considered Gino their real boss anyway. She hadn't allowed that thought to surface before, but now she realized it was true.

You'll be out on your own, kid, for the first time in your life, she thought.

It was exciting.

It was very exciting.

She grinned. And suddenly she felt *much* better. Maybe she'd go for Atlantic City anyway. Without Gino. Find another property, new investors. Hey—she could do it. She *knew* she could do it—she just had to convince everyone else.

25

Lennie slept like he hadn't slept in a long time—one of those great dreamless sleeps where you feel cocooned by clouds and so comfortable and at peace you never want to wake up. But he did. And it was noon.

He leaped from bed, and threw himself under a hot shower where he sang "Staying Alive" at full volume.

In the bathroom mirror he observed the scars of battle. Eden and her lethal nails. His back looked like a road map criss-crossed with thin red trails.

So what? He had her again. What were a few scars between friends?

For a moment he stopped to think. They hadn't really talked, just enjoyed great sex and each other's bodies. She was as hungry for him as he was for her. On the drive back she had fallen asleep curled up against him. He had driven to his car and suggested he follow her home. "No," she had said. "I've got an early call."

So he had watched her drive off into the dawn, for it was five in the morning when they parted company.

Now all he had to do was get through the day without her. It occurred to him that he should have found out where she was working and met her for lunch. Come to think of it, he should have found out a lot of things. He didn't even know where she lived. All he had was her phone number.

Tonight he wanted her to accompany him to Foxie's. He would sit her at a front table and let her get a load of the feedback he was receiving from the audience. She had always criticized his work. Once she saw him in action in L.A., she would realize how wrong she had been.

It was just so right that they were back together. Sure, they had their fights, but who didn't? He and Eden were an unbeatable combination.

An inner voice mocked, *Who are you kiddin', Lennie Golden? She eats you up and spits you out. You and Eden together—forget it.*

He ignored the subliminal warning.

• • • • •

Eden had lied. Which she did a lot. Beautifully. There was no early call. The first item on her agenda was a one o'clock meeting with the interior designer who owed Santino Bonnatti a favor.

She rose late, luxuriated in a scented bath, dressed slowly, and arrived at the house on Blue Jay Way fifteen minutes late for her appointment. Punctuality was not one of her priorities.

The decorator was a woman, which annoyed her. She loathed dealing with women. They either hated her because of her beauty, or fawned over her because she was once one of the top photo models in America before she gave it all up for her acting.

This woman was different. She was short, in her forties, with a mass of copper-colored frizzy hair and a skirt split up to her crotch. She was also businesslike, with a gay assistant, a drawing board and a lot of sketches and ideas. Her name was Paige Wheeler. Idly Eden wondered what favor she owed Santino, but she wasn't about to ask.

"I want a lot of white," she said vaguely. "White couches and rugs and everything modern and clean-cut, with plenty of mirrors. I like chrome too. I want the place to look glamorous."

Paige nodded, made notes, showed her swatches of material and suggested certain ideas.

Eden agreed with most things. She was just as anxious to leave her apartment as Santino was to install her in the house. As long as the place looked sensational in *People* and *Us* layouts, what did she care? It would probably only be home for a short while anyway, because when stardom hit she was moving on. She had no intention of sleeping with Santino Bonnatti for the rest of her life—only as long as it took.

For a moment she thought of Lennie and their lovemaking. Oh, Lennie . . . he certainly hadn't lost his touch. The guy was a great lay. A *really* great lay. And she should know. Many men had made the trip to heaven and left without credentials.

It was a pity he was a loser. Always had been, always would be. Working at some dump on Hollywood Boulevard. Didn't he know Hollywood Boulevard was out of *town*, for crissakes? Nowhere City. Just like all the nothing gigs he had played in New York.

Nobody could say she hadn't given Lennie a chance. Three years' worth of a chance. But in the sex stakes he was still something, and after Santino's apelike attentions she needed a respite. So. She was glad he'd called. Glad she'd seen him. Just hoped he'd go away quietly.

"Peach wallpaper will look most effective in the bedroom," Paige said briskly. "Perhaps we could incorporate it into the total concept."

"Hmmm . . ." Eden agreed. "And I'd like a fur bedspread. Something wild and sexy . . . something . . . movie-starish."

"I know exactly what you mean." Paige nodded, exchanging an amused glance with her assistant.

"Good," said Eden. "Are we finished?" She had an appointment to have her nails done, and she was already twenty minutes late.

• • • • •

There was no getting rid of Matt Traynor. There he was again, hanging around her table, asking her how she felt, asking her out again. Jess couldn't stand him, and yet . . . at least he was there, and in his own peculiar way he seemed to care.

"I guess I made an idiot of myself last night," she mumbled.

She didn't know! Relief rushed through him. He had another chance. "Not at all. You told me about your mother. It did you good getting drunk."

"Anything would do me good lately."

"Let's do it again tonight."

"What, get drunk?"

"Just talk."

She had decided to tell Wayland to go. Why didn't she

delay it just one more night until she felt more able to deal
with it? Maybe she should ask Matt's advice. There were always legalities involved in things like this. Getting Wayland
out might not be as easy as she had assumed.

"Okay," she said, surprising both of them. "As long as it's
not dinner for two at Chez Traynor."

• • • • •

At three o'clock Lennie was paged beside the Chateau Marmont
pool, where he was working on a suntan. Well, not exactly paged
Beverly Hills Hotel style—more like the poolside phone ringing
and a pony-tailed blonde yelling, "Anybody named Golden here?"

He thought it was Eden and jumped.

It was not Eden. It was a researcher from *The Merv Griffin
Show*, who said one of the producers had seen him at Foxie's
the previous night, and that they had a spot open in three days'
time, and if he wanted it, it was his.

If he wanted it. Did Barbara Walters give Special? Was
Clint Eastwood Dirty Harry? If he wanted it. Ha!

"Yes," he said, "I think that fits into my schedule." And he
gave them his agent's number.

Eden was going to love this. She would come with him
to the taping, hold his hand, maybe slide to her knees in the
dressing room and give him a little bit of her special luck. At
last! He was on a roll.

Frantically he started thinking about what he could and
could not use. Television was different from playing clubs.
Television demanded great visuals, clean material, no bad
language and fresh, original routines. Not that all his routines
weren't fresh and original. He wrote his own material—nobody fucked with what Lennie Golden wanted to say.

He didn't know whether to work on his suntan or hurry to
his room. Eden had said he looked pale. "Like a New Yorker,"
she had husked.

So what was wrong with looking like a New Yorker?

Fuck it. He hurried inside. There was work to do.

• • • • •

"You went out last night," said Santino softly.

"I did not," lied Eden indignantly. She had no intention of answering to Santino. "I watched television all night, and it was extremely boring."

His voice was a cobra's whisper. "Where did you go?"

"Nowhere. I told you. I—"

His slap jerked her head back and left the red angry imprint of his hand on her face.

She was shocked and stunned. "How dare y—" she began.

A second slap stopped her. "Never lie to me, Eden," he said mildly. "Never. This time I'm gonna overlook it, but believe me—don't you *ever* do it again."

Santino strode from her apartment muttering to himself.

Blackie said, "Everything all right, boss?" as they rode down in the elevator.

Santino did not bother to reply to his bodyguard. He spoke when he wanted to speak, and only then.

He flexed his knuckles and studied the pointed toes of his handmade Italian shoes.

Women. Teach 'em up front who ran the show. The same applied to the people he employed.

Demonstrate strength and there would be no revolution.

• • • • •

Matt took Jess to an Italian restaurant. She found she was ravenous and ate her way through a pasta salad, a veal cutlet with a side order of spaghetti and clams, and a healthy piece of raspberry cheesecake. Tension and worry always affected her appetite, and she went on great eating binges.

She patted her lips with a napkin, stared piercingly at Matt, causing him to nearly choke on his salad, and said, "So go ahead, shoot."

"I thought you were a vegetarian," he stuttered, groping for something to say.

"Sometimes," she replied vaguely, and reached for her wineglass. It was empty.

He ordered another bottle, wondering if tonight was to be a repeat performance, and regretted the fact that they were not dining at the Magiriano, where he could have signed the check. But who knew the nondrinking vegetarian would change course with such a vengeance?

"Come on," she persisted. "Tell me about Lennie. It's time you opened up. If *you* didn't want to fire him, who did?"

He decided there was no harm in the truth. And there was also no reason why *he* should take the blame. He owed her something—he would give her the information. Perhaps she would be grateful enough to consummate their relationship properly.

"Lucky Santangelo wanted him out," he said smoothly. "Don't ask me why, because I don't know. She rousted me out of bed at two in the morning to fire him."

"Lucky Santangelo," Jess repeated slowly. "Why would *she* want to fire Lennie? I hear he opened great." She frowned. "I didn't think she even got involved in things like that. I don't understand."

"Nor do I. I'll tell you this though—I have all the clout in the world, but, honey, if either of the Santangelos wants something, I jump, just like everyone else." He toyed with one of his gold chains. Why was he telling her all this? He should be building himself up, not putting himself down.

Jess's mind was racing. Lucky Santangelo. The Lady Boss as she was known. What possible reason could *she* have to dump Lennie?

"Now you know the story," Matt continued. "And I don't think I have to tell you that it's strictly confidential."

"What do you think I'm going to do—put an ad in the trades?" He shrugged. "I just don't want to be quoted on it, that's all."

She nodded. Why hadn't Lennie called? She really missed him. And she needed him. And now she had something to tell him. "Matt," she said slowly, "do you have a lawyer? I think I want some advice."

"What kind of advice?" he asked quietly.

"The divorce kind."

She started to tell him about Wayland, and once she started she couldn't seem to stop—the drugs and the weird friends and the sleeping all the time. Everything came pouring out.

"*I* pay all the bills," she said. "He hasn't contributed one dollar since we've been married. If I tell him to go, will he?"

Matt listened carefully. And he didn't like what he heard. She was hooked up with some spaced-out drug addict, and they were always bad news, they *never* went quietly. He remembered one girl, a singer, who was living with a heroin user. When she told him to get out he had slit her throat with a razor. She lived, but her voice didn't.

"Is he violent?" Matt asked, questioning his own sanity in getting involved in this.

"No. Not at all. In fact he's quite gentle, especially with the baby." She sighed. "It's not going to be easy telling him to go. He's like a big kid. In a way I feel sorry for him."

"You have to see a lawyer," Matt urged. "I'll set you up an appointment. Why don't I get my man to fit you in tomorrow morning? He'll do me a favor. Call me at ten o'clock and I'll let you know what time."

She squeezed his hand gratefully. "Thank you," she said. "You're really a very nice man." *In spite of your silly hair, and your gold chains, and your dumb apartment,* she wanted to add, but she didn't. Slowly she was changing her opinion of Matt Traynor. He wasn't as bad as he looked.

● ● ● ● ●

The girl on the answering service was getting snippy. "Yes, Mr. Golden. I have passed on your *four* messages. And no, Mr. Golden, it is not my fault that Miss Antonio has not returned your calls."

"I'm at another number now," Lennie said edgily, giving her the number at Foxie's. "So this is message number five, and please tell her it's urgent."

"I'll certainly do that, Mr. Golden."

"Thank you."

"You're welcome."

He hung up, hating the operator more each time.

Why was Eden playing games? Why was she acting like a bitch before they were even back in gear? Goddamn her. Who needed it?

He went onstage and for the first time was lousy.

Foxie gave him the benefit of a stream of insults.

Isaac was there, and he announced it was a good job the Griffin show hadn't been in tonight.

Rainbow smiled. "Got your period, honey?"

He tried Eden's number again and again. The answering service picked up on all calls. They refused to supply him with her address. Joey Firello, who might have known it, was out of town. Suna and Shirlee were away for the week. Tomorrow he would find it. And he would also find out what kind of a game she thought she was playing.

He refused to fuck up his life because of Eden Antonio one more time.

* * * * *

At exactly ten in the morning Jess called Matt. He had kept his promise and arranged a twelve-thirty appointment with his lawyer. She was suitably grateful, and for once did not attempt to wake Wayland, who sprawled on the broken couch in the living room, out cold.

She fed Simon an early lunch and settled him for a nap. Then she crept quietly from the house.

Wayland awoke fifteen minutes later. He was groggy, still stoned. He looked around for Jess, and when he could not find her, realized she had gone to work early without leaving him any money.

He needed money. Edge was coming by the house later with some good dope, and he had promised him a hundred and fifty bucks. Jess would scream when he asked for money. If only she would get with it, she could sell some of the stuff he scored in the casino, and make them a solid profit. Had to talk to her about getting her act together. Had to—

He forgot what he was thinking, unzipped his pants and pissed against the living-room wall. Then he popped a few assorted pills, the last of his stash, and remembered again he needed money to replenish his supply. Jess was not treating him right. She shouldn't have sneaked off to work without leaving him money.

Sometimes she hid it.

He started a slapdash search, knocking things over, tipping coffee and sugar and flour out of their containers in the kitchen.

Sometimes she—

He couldn't quite grasp the thought. But he did know Edge was coming by soon and he needed to get connected.

In the bedroom the baby started to cry.

Sometimes she hid it—

He had the thought again.

Once she had hidden fifteen hundred dollars under the baby's mattress.

He staggered into the bedroom. Last night he had speed-balled with a few friends. They had come to the house. What else was he expected to do? He couldn't go anywhere when he was babysitting.

He lifted the kid from the crib and placed him carefully on the floor. Simon immediately started to crawl toward the open patio doors, but Wayland was too stoned to notice.

Frantically he began pulling at the sheets and covers. Then he lifted the small mattress and hurled it across the room.

Nothing.

Not a dime.

Not a dollar.

Not a cent.

Tiredness overcame him. He flopped across the bed and immediately fell into another deep sleep.

26

The Snoopy watch did not bring peace. Brigette screamed like a stuck pig when she discovered Olympia was not returning to Paris with her. It was almost as if the child sensed Olympia's withdrawal, and wanted nothing to do with it.

"I want my mommy!" she yelled, jerking away from Nanny Mabel, who was trying to secure her in a viselike grip, all the better to drag her into the limousine.

"Mama will follow you," Olympia sighed, hating the scene. "In a day or two."

"No, you *won't!*" screamed Brigette. "You won't! You won't!"

"I will," Olympia insisted.

"For God's sake—" Dimitri appeared, glaring thunder. "Why did you make this last-minute decision not to come, Olympia? It *is* irresponsible of you, telling the child now." He shifted his stern gaze to Brigette, who immediately shut up. "We will go now," he said. "Your mother will follow us in a few days. In the meantime you will stay with me."

Brigette's face brightened. As long as she wasn't left alone with Nanny Mabel.

"Thank you, Father," sighed Olympia, touching her blond curls.

He frowned. "No longer than a week," he said. "I have meetings in London and Rome, and I have no intention of taking Brigette with me."

"Certainly not, Father."

They exchanged dutiful kisses, and at last Dimitri, Brigette and Nanny Mabel were on their way.

Olympia threw herself into a soothing tub, ordered two bottles of Louis Roederer Cristal champagne and a healthy supply of caviar to be put out, then she summoned Vitos to spend the night.

He arrived with news of a party being given by a seedy English rock group called the Layabouts, contemporaries of the Beatles and the Stones.

Olympia decided she wanted to meet them, as the lead singer had always intrigued her although she had never met him face-to-face. His name was Flash, and he looked like a refugee from a gypsy encampment. Long dark curls, pock-marked skin, thin, cruel lips, rotting teeth, dangerous yellow eyes and a stringy body.

Vitos flashed his perfect, blank smile. "We shall go," he said, after she had told him that was exactly what they would do.

The limousine transported them to a huge loft in the Village where two burly security guards checked them out. This is what Olympia was learning to love about New York—there was always something unexpected going on.

Once inside, she smiled her way through the crush while Vitos guided her past the mass of seething freaks into the inner sanctum, where she set eyes on Flash for the first time.

She had seen him on television and in magazines for years. He was a cult figure, up there with Andy Warhol and Mick Jagger. He was also a reformed heroin addict, a dedicated cocksman, and possibly the best rock guitarist in the world. Meeting a passably pretty, plump Greek shipping heiress did nothing for his libido. He had no idea who she was. "'Ello, darlin'," he said. "Wanna snort?"

Olympia fell in love instantly.

Nobody had ever accused her of having perfect taste.

27

Now that she had made her decision, Lucky had no desire to spend any more time than was necessary with Gino. She didn't want to risk his trying to change her mind, because she knew what she was doing was right.

He was back in Vegas alone. No Susan. The Widow Perfect had remained in Los Angeles arranging the nuptials.

"You're comin' to the wedding, aren't you?" he asked.

She did not want to attend his wedding. Why should she be present when he committed an insane act?

"Well . . ." she began, searching for an excuse.

"I want you there," he said. An order, not a request.

"Sure," she agreed reluctantly, wondering why she still jumped.

There was no need for her to hang around while all the involved paperwork went ahead, so she planned to leave in one week's time. First she wanted to visit Costa in Miami, and then on to New York, which she had decided would be her base. Leaving the Vegas hotel business was going to be a wrench, no use kidding herself.

And leaving Gino . . .

They dined together one night. Conversation was stilted. Things just weren't the same. She told him when she was going, and he nodded resignedly.

Tell me it's all off between you and Susan and I won't budge, she thought.

He didn't say a word.

. . . . .

Matt heard about the tragedy on the early-evening news. Another backyard drowning—this time an eleven-month-old baby boy who had crawled out of an open patio door and fallen into the family swimming pool.

The newscaster, a woman who looked like she had just come from the Miss America contest, assumed a grave expression and informed her audience that although foul play was not suspected, the parents, Jess and Wayland Dolby, had been taken to the police station for further questioning.

For a moment Matt was stunned. *It was Jess. It was her kid. What the hell had happened?*

Galvanized into action, he grabbed his jacket and hurried from the office.

· · · · ·

Susan and Paige met at a Brentwood house that Paige was re-decorating. The owner, a macho superstar who had appeared in Paige's husband's hit movie, was in Hawaii with another macho superstar, also male.

Susan arrived at the house first and waited impatiently outside in her yellow Rolls. Paige kept her waiting only a few minutes before she arrived in her metallic gold Porsche. She hurried from her car and rushed over to Susan, who now stood beside her Rolls, allowing the affection she felt for Paige to envelop her. The two women embraced. They made an incongruous couple—Susan so elegantly groomed in a sleek silk suit, her blond hair upswept, and Paige, with her frizzy mass of hair and slit-to-the-limit skirt.

"Sorry I'm late," Paige said, exuding a mixture of strong perfume and musky body odors. "I just got a new house to decorate, a rush job. Some little starlet one of Ryder's investors is setting up. She wants the usual—Monroe white, mirrors and fur bedspreads—all the better to fuck on!"

Susan smiled. If Gino had made such a crass remark she would have reprimanded him with a look.

They entered the house. It was almost complete, a masculine fantasy of wood and leather.

"What do you think?" asked Paige, taking her through it room by room.

"Very impressive," enthused Susan, although it *was* a little overdone.

"Ted'll love it," said Paige. "So will his boyfriend."

They reached the bedroom and stood in front of the dark oak four-poster bed.

"King size," Paige said, "to match its owner."

"How would you know?" Susan asked quickly. She had her suspicions that Paige sometimes slept with her clients, although she never voiced such a thought.

"Because *every*one knows," Paige replied. "Just like everyone knows Tiny possessed one of the biggest cocks in Hollywood."

Susan frowned. Sometimes Paige went too far. Susan wished she would not mention Tiny. Now he was gone she would prefer to forget him *and* his hateful organ, which, as a matter of fact, *had* been one of the most awesome appendages she had ever seen. She looked at Paige meaningfully, and slipped the silk jacket from her shoulders. "Did you miss me?" she asked. "Because I missed you."

Paige smiled. "But of course," she said, stepping out of her skirt.

Susan hurriedly removed the rest of her clothes and waited for Paige's special touch. Sex with a woman was so natural. There was none of the underlying violence that always seemed to be present when sleeping with a man. Susan felt no threat or violation. It was so delightful to let herself go. To lie back and feel so totally and completely at ease.

Her orgasm, when it arrived, was the real thing. With a man she always faked it. Somehow it was easier that way.

She lay naked and content in the center of the big oak bed and began to tell Paige about Gino.

The other woman listened intently as the story unfolded.

Susan concluded with a sigh, "I'm marrying him," she said. "I'm afraid it's the only answer."

Paige nodded. Frankly she thought Gino Santangelo sounded like dynamite. The trouble with Susan was she didn't know a good thing when she saw it. After all, a fuck was a fuck—it didn't really matter what sex it was.

"I want you to know," Susan continued, "it won't make any difference to *our* relationship."

Paige rose from the bed. "Marriage agrees with you," she said. "You need a man around, if only to pay the bills."

Susan stretched luxuriously. "You, my dear one, are what I need." She parted her legs abandonedly. With Paige she could never get enough loving. With Gino it was always too much.

"I've got to rush," Paige said, beginning to dress. "I'm having twelve guests for dinner tonight. We're screening the new Bronson film. I would have asked you, but I know how you hate coming on your own. Never mind, soon you'll be a couple again."

"Yes," agreed Susan, a touch irritably. She had been ready to play some more, and now Paige was rushing off. It really was too bad, considering they hadn't seen each other in months. "Can we meet again soon?" she asked.

"We could," mused Paige, applying lipstick. "But I don't know if I'm ready to share a bed with my movie star client. He's coming back tomorrow. Which reminds me—I need fresh flowers, and more cushions, and . . ." She rushed to her purse and extracted a Gucci pad and pen. "Honestly, I don't know how I do it all. I'm like a juggler, keeping everyone's balls in the air. Ryder would fall to pieces without me, and the teenage monsters are *so* demanding. Bradford was thrown out of school last week for pushing pot. And Ricky smashed up his brand-new Corvette."

Later, driving home, Susan decided that her two uptight WASPs weren't so bad. And Gino . . . well, it *would* be nice to have a man by her side again. There was a time when Paige wouldn't have *dared* to have a dinner party without her. Now it was *I know how you hate coming on your own*—and that was that.

At home she called Gino. He sounded blue. She cheered him with soft words and decided to have the wedding as soon as possible.

· · · · ·

Over the years Gino had learned to appreciate a relationship as opposed to just getting laid. Any jerk could get laid; developing a closeness between two people was what really mattered.

He had married twice in his life. The first time to Cindy. She couldn't be trusted. The second time to Maria. The one true love of his life.

In between there had been few women who left their mark.

Clementine Duke—the wife of a Senator. A cool and classy lady who came upon him when he was twenty-two and guided him toward the good things in life.

Bee, who took him in when he needed her help, and waited for him while he spent seven years in jail.

Marabelle Blue, sex symbol supreme. She turned out to be a neurotic mess who tried suicide when he rejected her.

And the last permanent liaison was with an attractive widow, a woman not unlike Susan in the looks department. She had moved in with him in Israel and shared his exile. When he returned to America, he left her behind.

Now Susan.

Was he making a mistake? There was always that moment of doubt.

He didn't think so.

He lit a long thin Havana cigar and gazed thoughtfully into the future.

28

The detective had a few strands of carefully arranged greasy hair.

Jess couldn't help staring, even though she knew instinctively it was annoying him. Childishly she thought if she stared long enough this whole unbelievable nightmare would go away.

"Why didja leave him with your husband if y'knew he was zonked outta his skull?" the detective demanded. "Ain'tcha ever heard of child neglect? If y'ask me, you may as well've dumped the kid in the pool yourself. Mebbe y'did. Nothin' surprises me in this screwed-up world."

His cruel words did not get through to her. She refused to hear what he was saying. She knew they had to let her go. They couldn't keep her. She hadn't done anything. . . .

Except claw and scratch and kick and scream and if she'd had a gun she would have shot the sonofabitch.

Wayland.

Asleep.

As if he didn't have a care in the world.

And their baby . . .

Simon . . .

Floating . . .

Like a toy. . . .

The rush of horror. This wasn't happening, couldn't be happening.

Her breathing restricted. Reflexes slow.

She began to scream. And then she pulled her baby from the pool by his hair. A neighbor's son appeared and bent over the small bloated lifeless form.

Eventually Wayland staggered from the house, blank-eyed and shirtless. "Wassamatter?" he mumbled.

She flew at him, beating his chest with her fists, raking his vile face with her nails, until her screams brought more neighbors and finally the police.

It was all a blur from then on. A blur of hate, confusion and despair. Now she was waiting to wake up from the horrific nightmare, for she was sure this couldn't be reality.

And yet . . . she had held the cold, wet flesh of Simon, her only child, and she knew, without a doubt, that life was gone.

• • • • •

It was obvious Eden had no intention of returning his calls. Lennie could not believe she would casually come back into his life, screw up his head and then expect him to vanish as if nothing had taken place.

"Miss Antonio has received all your messages," the girl on her answering service told him when he called upon waking at noon. "And she will get back to you as soon as she is able."

So fuck off. That's what the message conveyed. *Fuck off and don't call again.*

He was angry. She had wanted him as much as he had wanted her. Goddammit. What *was* this crap?

He reached for the phone again and connected with Joey Firello's answering service. Didn't anyone pick up their own phone in California?

"Mr. Firello is out of town. I'll give him your message."

"I need to talk to him now," Lennie said quickly. "Don't you have a number where I can reach him?"

"I'll give him your message," the operator replied, ignoring his request.

Fucking zombie.

With difficulty he tracked down Suna and Shirlee in Palm Springs. Neither of them could remember where Eden lived, although they assured him it was near them.

"That's a big help," he said.

"You're not going to see her, are you?" questioned Suna.

"You and she together are poison," Shirlee added, on an extension phone.

He had not called for their advice. "Who's her agent?" he asked quickly.

"Nobody important," they said as one.

"I want a name, not a rating."

They supplied him with a name. He called and was informed by a secretary there was no way she could give him the home address of a client.

"It's urgent," he said sharply.

"Leave a message," she replied. Snitty broad.

He dropped the phone. It was happening already. Back in his life for one night and she was making him crazy.

He knew that if he was smart he would forget the whole thing. Dismiss her from his thoughts as she had probably dismissed him.

But who was smart? When it came to Eden he was the dumbest ass in town.

• • • • •

The imprint of Santino's hand burnt into the pale skin on her cheek. Eden stared into the mirror, her eyes cloudy with fury. Nobody had ever hit her before. Nobody would have dared.

Bastard.

Hairy bastard.

He looked like a bald ape. He should be worshipping at her feet, not lifting his hand to her.

It was all so unexpected. She had guessed Santino Bonnatti was hardly Mister Charm, but she had not been ready for such a vicious attack.

And how did he know she was out anyway? Was he having her followed?

She decided to dump him.

That decision lasted five minutes. Timing was everything, and with a new house, and his possible investment in a movie, now was not the right moment to say goodbye.

She leaned closer to the mirror and studied her face. Then she raised her hand and gently felt the marks of his jealousy.

She went into the kitchen, gathered ice in a towel and held it to her cheek.

The phone rang three times, and then the service picked up. She had no desire to speak to anyone. Lennie Golden had left countless messages. It was probably him again.

Screw Lennie. He was the cause of all her troubles.

And screw Santino Bonnatti.

Bastard.

He would not get away with such behavior. He would pay.

Eventually.

When the timing was right.

When *she* was ready.

· · · · ·

Scotch eased the rejection—half a bottle—and when Lennie hit the stage at Foxie's he was belligerent and mean, with a cruel edge to his humor.

Rainbow was standing at the side when he came off. She jerked her head toward the pay phone in the corner. "Somebody belled you from Las Vegas. I told them to call back in ten minutes."

"Who was it?" he slurred.

She wrapped her robe tightly around herself. "Do I look like a secretary?"

"You look like a hot piece of ass." He lurched in her direction.

"Aw, cut it out, Lennie." She gave him a disgusted shove. "If Foxie was around he'd skin your balls."

"At least I've still got 'em."

She laughed aloud. "Sonny, you'll *never* have balls like Foxie."

The pay phone rang, saving him from summoning up a smart retort.

He wondered who was calling him from Vegas and hoped it was Jess. He needed to talk. Once and for all, he had to get Eden Antonio out of his system.

29

Matt said, "I'd really like you to come to the funeral this afternoon. Jess is falling apart. You being there would mean a lot to her."

"I hardly know the girl," Lucky replied.

"She's worked for us for over two years. Can't you show her this kindness? I want her to know we care."

Lucky wondered at his involvement. Sophisticated, jaded Matt. When did he develop heart? "Okay," she said. "I'll come." And then she added with a sudden rush of sympathy for Jess, "Is there anything else I can do?"

"Just be there—that's enough."

She nodded. "Perhaps we can arrange for her to have three months' paid vacation. Send her away somewhere to think things out. It's going to take time...."

For a moment she remembered Marco. His smile, and the way his black hair curled over the back of his collar, and the way he used to look at her.

Oh, God. She still dreamed about him on nights when she was so lonely that only *he* could keep her company.

"I know," Matt said. "I was going to suggest that I take her to Europe." He paused hopefully. "You could manage without me for a few weeks, couldn't you?"

She wondered if now was the time to tell him she wasn't going to be around. Decided it wasn't.

"How involved are you?" she asked.

He shrugged. "I'm involved. She's not."

"Well . . . I hope it works out for you."

Matt wanted to talk. Quickly he said, "I know she's twenty years younger than me and we've got nothing in common. She's not even my type, but Jesus, when I look at her, it's all over. She could make me a very happy man."

Lucky stood up. She wasn't feeling great. "Why don't you tell *her,* not me?" She walked him toward the door, not wanting to appear rude, but also not inclined to hear the confessions of a reformed chauvinist. She almost had to push him out.

When he was gone she ordered tea and toast from room service and sat down at her desk to go over some papers.

She felt horribly nauseous. Just nerves. Once she was on her way, things would be different.

• • • • •

Matt hurried back to his apartment, where the maid was keeping an eye on Jess. She sat on the couch staring blankly into space.

"Guess what?" he said. "Lucky Santangelo wants to attend the funeral. That's really something. You must have made a big impression over the years." He walked to the bar and began pouring a hefty slug of brandy into a glass. "A lot of people are going to show up. Most of the croupiers, some of the showgirls, a couple of waitresses. Oh, and Manny—you know—your favorite pit boss. He's definitely coming." He handed her the glass.

"It's not a party," she said, her voice a whisper.

"Drink up, it'll make you feel better."

"It's not a party," she repeated sadly.

He held her hand. "I know that, sweetheart. But believe me, people care about you. They want to show their respect."

She took a gulp of brandy. "You turned out to be a very nice man," she murmured.

He was embarrassed, thinking that he wasn't so nice after all.

"I contacted your friend in Los Angeles," he said quickly. "It took me several phone calls, but I tracked him down at Foxie's. He's flying in today, and should be arriving about now. I've arranged a car to meet him and bring him straight here."

For a moment there was a flicker of a smile. "Lennie," she said quietly, "is my best friend in the world."

"I understand," Matt said reassuringly. "You told me yesterday. That's how I knew you'd want him here."

Since hearing the news, Matt had taken charge. It was he who had collected Jess from the police station, summoned a doctor, who had doped her up with sedatives, watched her as she slept restlessly in his bed, listened as she rambled on about her life.

It was he who had arranged for the funeral, organized cars and what he hoped would be a suitable turnout.

It was he who had fed her hot soup and held her as she sobbed the night away.

The day before, she had been hysterical. Now she was quiet, almost childlike.

"Lennie's my best friend," she repeated. "We grew up together, you know."

"Yes, I do know. You told me all about him."

He dared not ask whether that best-friendshipness had ever been sexual. What if she ran off with the guy? And if he, Matt Traynor, the jerk, had brought him back into town.

No time to worry now. He had too much to organize. The funeral was in three hours, and he wanted to make sure everything went smoothly.

• • • • •

Lucky decided a letter to her chief executives would be best. She drafted several, but ended up throwing them away.

Matt phoned to inform her that he had arranged for Boogie to pick her up at two o'clock. He was certainly concerned enough, making arrangements with *her* driver. Any other time she would have bawled him out.

The last thing she felt like doing was attending a funeral, especially when the normally blue desert sky was turning gray and the weather stations predicted thunderstorms. But she wouldn't let Matt down now.

She was just so *tired*, as if every ounce of energy had been drained from her body. All she wanted to do was sleep.

It occurred to her she should visit her doctor, have a physical, get a little vitamin therapy. It was no use running off to conquer New York feeling like a dead camel. She called her doctor and made a morning appointment.

Gino had returned to L.A. for a few days.

A few days. Sure. More like a few weeks.

Susan beckoned.

He came running.

How nice to have a permanent hard-on at his age. Maybe it ran in the family.

She laughed dryly. Sex was the last thing on her mind. She wanted to build an empire—her *own* empire—and then maybe think about her nonexistent sex life. There had been no one since Dimitri Stanislopoulos. Yet she didn't care.

Sex was important when she wanted it to be.

Only then.

30

The plane ride was bumpy, and by the time they prepared to land it was raining.

Nothing like a desert rainstorm, Lennie thought. Black clouds, tough, stinging hailstones and a humid heat that never quit. He had a hangover. And the memory of a fierce fight with Isaac Luther when he had told him he couldn't do the Griffin show.

"What do you mean, you *can't* do it?" Isaac had yelled.

"I can't do it because a friend needs me in Vegas, and I gotta go."

"Screw friends. This is the big break, man. If you blow this you're crazy."

Lennie shrugged. "Some things in life have to take priority. Maybe they can reschedule my spot."

"They're more likely to reschedule your ass," Isaac exploded. "You're letting them down at the last minute. Don't do it, Lennie."

He had gestured impatiently. "No choice."

Foxie had been more agreeable in his own inimitable way. "Go. Stay there. An' don't come back until you got yourself straight. I don't like drunks, an' I don't stand for no shit acts in my place. These last two nights you've given me both."

No arguing with that.

So here he was, back in Vegas, with the rain pissing down, and a lousy taste in his mouth.

In L.A. the sun was shining and he would have been preparing to go before the TV cameras.

He would also be getting no reply from the lovely Eden. A true cunt. As always. The hell with her. She was unimportant. What was going on in Jess's life was all he cared about.

Matt Traynor had called him the previous evening. The same Matt Traynor who had fired him. "Jess needs you here,"

Matt had said, and then given him a sketchy rundown on what had happened.

Jesus. Just looking at that freak Jess was married to had given him bad vibes. Wayland—a stoned creep scoring off the money she brought home. Why hadn't he, Lennie, said something to her? At least taken the time to find out what was going on.

But no. He hadn't done that. He had rushed out of town with a bug up his ass because he got canned, and only he, Lennie Golden, mattered.

Goddamn it.

She had needed him.

He never stayed around to care.

And now her baby was dead, and maybe he could have prevented the tragedy.

A car waited for him. An Oldsmobile driven by a retired showgirl in a purple-sequinned uniform. Ah . . . Las Vegas . . . city of bad taste.

The ex-showgirl drove like Paul Newman on the track, and by the time they arrived at Matt's apartment, Lennie was a nervous wreck. Thunder and lightning greeted him as he left the car. He pulled up the collar on his jacket and ran inside.

• • • • •

Matt glanced around the assorted gathering that huddled graveside and made a mental note to repay the favors of those who had turned up. It wasn't a huge group—maybe twenty people. But twenty was a respectable number, and he was pleased. Lucky—God bless her—was there. She hadn't let him down. She stood beneath a large black umbrella, her head bowed, as the pitifully small coffin was lowered into the ground.

Lennie stood to one side of Jess, supporting her, and Matt was on the other. He could feel her body shaking with silent sobs and he didn't know what to do. She made him feel helpless. He just wanted to protect her from the world. And if she would let him, that's exactly what he planned to do. As the second Mrs. Traynor, she would have more than enough protection.

Wayland was not present. Wayland was even now hitching a ride out of town, which Matt had assured him would be the healthiest thing he could possibly do.

The rain was relentless. It would have to rain, Matt thought, adding even more misery to the pathetic scene. After the ceremony he had arranged for refreshments in a nearby restaurant. It was a mistake. Everyone just wanted to get the hell out of there.

• • • • •

For a moment Lennie did not recognize the woman. Her jet hair was pulled back tightly, and dark shades covered her expressive eyes. Her body was concealed beneath a long black leather coat, tightly belted. She looked like a spy out of a Le Carré novel. Beautiful, mysterious and ice-cold hot.

Then he remembered. The girl from the casino. The nearly one-night stand. Why was she still in Vegas?

As soon as he could, he edged toward her. She stood at the bar gulping a Pernod on the rocks.

"Hey," he accused. "You stood me up."

She did not remove her black shades, so he could not tell if she was looking at him or not.

"Do I know you?" she asked coldly.

"We almost made history, only you wanted to start the course before I was ready. Lennie Golden. Remember?"

An imperceptible nod.

"So what happened? You were supposed to meet me in the bar."

"Maybe someone more willing to learn came along. Excuse me."

She brushed past him, went over to where Jess sat with Matt, said a few words and left.

First Eden, then this one. Was the famous Golden charm evaporating?

Christ, funerals were depressing. Poor little Jess seemed like a forlorn kid. He wished Matt Traynor would leave her alone, the old guy was a horny swinger, panting after her as if she were the only female in town. Hadn't he ever learned timing?

Lennie wondered what he could do to ease her pain, she looked so lost. He went over and squeezed her hand. "How're you feeling, monkey face?" He hoped to spur some sort of reaction.

She shook her head blankly.

There was nothing to say at a time like this. Maybe just being there was enough.

•　•　•　•　•

Santino returned at seven in the morning. Eden was asleep, but he had his own key to her apartment (when he had started to pay the rent and all the bills, he had insisted), so he let himself in, entered her bedroom and sat watching her for a while. She slept naked on chocolate-brown sheets, which contrasted nicely with the pallor of her skin and the blondness of her hair. Who did she think she was playing games with? One mistake was all he'd allow her. If she cheated on him again she wouldn't get away with a smack on the face.

She was a skinny broad.

After Donatella, his wife, Santino considered anyone under one hundred and fifty pounds skinny.

He could still see the mark of his hand on her cheek and it excited him. Broads like Eden Antonio needed constant watching. His father had taught him that. "Any cunt who thinks she's hot stuff is gonna need a sharp eye on her fanny," Enzio, his father, had announced one morning at breakfast to Santino and his elder brother, Carlo. "To keep 'em in line you gotta buy 'em plenty, fuck 'em regularly an' beat 'em occasionally."

Enzio had roared with laughter at his own wit and wisdom. But wit and wisdom had not been enough to protect him from cold, planned murder at the hands of a woman.

Santino scowled with fury when he thought of that fateful day a year ago. And he scowled even harder when he remembered the instructions he and Carlo received from his father's business associates. "No more killings," they were told. "No more revenge. The violence has to stop."

Just like that, they were forbidden to do anything.

As far as Santino was concerned it was like cutting off his balls. Although Carlo took it calm as a fucking priest.

Santino scratched his bald pate and thought about his brother. Carlo was a shithead, a nothing. Unfortunately they were partners and blood brothers, and as such had to stick together. But not in the same city.

With Enzio gone, Santino moved his end of their operation to L.A. And there he planned to stay. A wise decision. Without Carlo looking over his shoulder, he was able to expand and branch out. The family business had included a string of massage parlors. Santino found that the porno magazines sold in such establishments raked in a fortune. He investigated the publishers and distributors. Reasonable men. Before long, Santino was a part of the action—and with the imports he brought in from Denmark and Thailand, plus videos, he was rolling in profits. He had more money than Carlo. The shithead Carlo—what kind of man refused to act on his own father's murder?

Santino knew it was up to him to even the score with that bitch Lucky Santangelo. And he would do it one day. *For sure.*

Eden stirred, and threw her arms above her head.

Santino's small eyes bored into her pink-tipped breasts. Small but perfect. His wife filled a 42-D cup. It was like having sex with a pregnant cow. Quickly he rose and pulled down the jogging pants he wore. Then he allowed his erection to slip from the confines of patterned boxer shorts.

Eden sighed in her sleep.

Roughly Santino ripped the sheet from the bed, exposing all of her. She had blond hair on her snatch, which drove him crazy. He was partial to blondes. In one fast movement he straddled her chest and thrust his erection toward her mouth.

Her eyes were hardly open before he was rocking back and forth.

"Suck it," he demanded hoarsely. "Take it, baby. Take it all. You know you love it. You know Santino is King."

31

The drug culture had always appealed to Olympia, although she had never got into it in a major way. A lot of cocaine and plenty of pot was about as far as she had traveled. She did not want to become hooked like some of her so-called friends who couldn't get out of bed in the morning without a snort. She was smart. She was a social user. And if she wasn't going out, she could go days without indulging and not miss it at all. As far as she was concerned, a toot of coke was the modern-day equivalent of a Scotch on the rocks. Nothing wrong with *that*.

Dimitri had asked her once if she indulged. "Certainly not," she had replied, suitably shocked.

"Good," he had said, nodding thoughtfully. "Because a girl in your position has to be very, very careful. There are many people who would be only too pleased to discover you have a weakness. You would be exploited mercilessly."

What did he think she was? Dumb? She had married three men, all of whom had exploited her to the limit. Why hadn't he warned her about men? They were far more dangerous than drugs.

It completely slipped her mind that Dimitri *had* warned her. Constantly.

So . . . drugs were no problem. They made her feel good, allowed her to have a fantastic time at parties and did not give her a hangover or make her fat.

Conveniently she forgot the dawn cravings for chocolate cake, double-cream cheesecake and Häagen-Dazs rum-raisin ice cream.

She was sure Dimitri was into coke. Or at least some of his jet-set girlfriends were. How could one be part of the social circle without indulging?

Flash indulged. Heavily. He might be a former heroin addict, but that did not stop him from grabbing anything else going. Uppers, downers, sleepers, quacks, grass and, of course—cocaine. The rich man's drug. Only Flash never had to pay, because he was so famous—or maybe infamous—that the hangers-on and the gofers and the groupies and the starfucks always managed to get him everything he wanted for nothing.

Flash was looking for a place to crash in New York. He had a permanent residence in the Bahamas (for tax reasons) and in L.A. he stayed with a dissolute movie star (male) with stoned eyes and a grin like a sick cat. But Flash needed a New York base. And Olympia looked like she could provide it.

Enter Flash.

Exit Vitos.

Flash made a lot of money, but he was notoriously tight-fisted. Why spend when there were others to do it for you?

The first night he slept with Olympia he had no idea who she was. They whiled away a few hours rolling around on a water bed in an apartment he was borrowing. She wasn't really his type. Too chubby. His style was usually young, tall models with stringy hair and beautiful blank faces. But Olympia was there, coming on strong—and Flash needed to get laid. He *always* needed to get laid. So he had said goodbye to his entourage, and had taken her to his borrowed apartment.

Olympia told Vitos she had a very important business proposition she had to discuss with Flash. Vitos didn't seem to care. He was deep in conversation with Bianca Jagger—or was it Diane Von Furstenberg? Olympia never could tell them apart.

Flash proved his reputation to be true. And Olympia was happy. She left by cab while he slept. And at noon the next day she let him know she was not just another little groupie. He awoke to find six cases of Dom Pérignon, a healthy supply of Iranian caviar and a small gift from Tiffany's. The gift

was a solid-gold-and-diamond guitar pin. On it was engraved
OLYMPIA/FLASH NEW YORK 1978.

Even Flash knew that to get Tiffany's to engrave something in a couple of hours meant you had clout.

She had enclosed her card—*Olympia Stanislopoulos*—with an address and phone number. The surname was as well known as Onassis.

"Who is she?" he asked, handing the card to Como Rose, his manager.

Como looked at it, belched loudly and said, "She's Dimitri Stanislopolous's daughter, for crissakes. Richer than the Gettys."

Flash knew a good thing when it came his way. And she had come and come and come.

He grinned, revealing a full spread of dangerously loose, rotting teeth. Dentists were not an important part of his life.

"Call her," he said. "Have her here at five. I'm taking her to the concert."

She turned up at five-thirty, dressed in taffeta, lace and diamonds.

"You're friggin' late," Flash said. "Friggin' overdressed. And we're gonna need a couple more boxes of the fizzy stuff. Arrange it."

Nobody had ever spoken to Olympia like that before. She liked it. A lot. A refreshing change.

They snorted several lines of coke, swigged champagne on the way to the stadium where the Layabouts were giving their first New York concert in five years, and sent the paparazzi into a frenzy.

Within a week Olympia had purchased a huge apartment overlooking Central Park, and Flash took up residence on the same day she did.

That night they stood on the landscaped terrace and surveyed the city spread out before them.

"Not bad, gel," Flash announced, and lit a joint.

Olympia swigged from a bottle of Dom Pérignon she was holding (her new habit) and agreed. Why had she wasted so much of her life in Europe when New York was such *fun?*

She wondered what she was going to do about Brigette. So far she hadn't mentioned the existence of her daughter to Flash. Maybe she could just forget about her for another week or so. Why bring it up and ruin everything?

Flash dragged on the joint long and hard. Why hadn't he thought of shacking up with a rich bird before? It was definitely the way to go.

He wondered what he was going to do about his sixteen-year-old wife stashed somewhere in England. So far he hadn't mentioned her existence to Olympia. Well, it was a secret wedding—nobody knew. Maybe he could just forget about her for a while. She was used to his long absences. Why bring it up and ruin everything?

Olympia and Flash were perfectly suited.

32

The child's funeral depressed Lucky. It seemed so . . . pointless. It made her feel angry and helpless. If people brought children into the world, they should look after them. The infant's death was no accident. It had been caused by human error. She had heard all about Wayland from Matt. If he were her husband she would have strung him up by his balls.

Standing by the grave in the pouring rain was a downer. But later, in the restaurant, it was even worse. One fast drink and she was out of there. She had done Matt the favor he requested—it was enough.

She was alone at the bar drinking Pernod when the comedian materialized. He was tall and rangy, with green eyes and a killer smile. She remembered him instantly. She even remembered his name *before* he reintroduced himself. Lennie Golden. A comedian. And how.

She wanted to say, "What the hell are *you* doing here? I had you fired and I'm never supposed to set eyes on you again." Instead she said nothing, while he fumbled for words. And when he told her his name she pretended not to know who he was, brushed past him and made a fast exit.

The truth of the matter was she found him disturbingly attractive. He had turned her down once, and she did not plan to go for twice. What a nerve he had even speaking to her.

When she got back to the hotel she decided not to hang around any longer. There was no reason for her to stay; even Gino had left. She called Costa and told him she would be arriving in Miami the next day. Then she began to pack, urgently throwing things into several suitcases. Somehow she knew she had to get out at once.

· · · · ·

In Bel Air all was peaceful. The cook prepared sesame chicken, one of Gino's favorite dishes. There was an excellent baseball game on the Advent television, which he watched from a comfortable armchair while Susan, looking ladylike, yet sexy, in a pale-blue peignoir, attended to her needlepoint.

This is a long way from the streets of the Bronx, he thought—the long-ago far-away mean streets where he had started out without a dime to call his own.

He puffed contentedly on a thin Havana and dipped a silver spoon into a dish of ice cream.

Yeh. He was making the right move. This was the life for him.

Susan had set the date. He was ready.

• • • • •

Lucky took an early plane out of Vegas. She stopped at her doctor's on the way to the airport for a B_{12} vitamin shot. Her doctor, a woman—because male doctors seemed to treat female patients like backward children—insisted on running a few simple tests before giving it to her.

"I can never get you in here for your yearly physical," Dr. Liz Tierney complained with a smile. "So I'm grabbing you while I can."

"You'd better grab quickly," Lucky replied, surrendering her arm for a blood test, "because I'm on my way to the airport."

"Always in a rush. Have you ever thought of slowing down?"

"What for? I've got things to do."

"Well, find time to give me a urine sample, if you please."

"Just give me the shot, Doc. That's all I need."

Dr. Tierney handed her a small glass bottle and pointed her in the direction of the toilet. "*I'll* tell you what you need."

The flight to Miami took forever. The plane made two stops, adding even more hours to the journey. By the time Lucky arrived, she was tired out.

Costa was at the airport to greet her. Uncle Costa. She hadn't seen him for a year, and she marveled at how much better he looked. Last time they met he was gray-skinned and weary-eyed. Now he sported a healthy suntan, and his eyes were sharp and bright behind distinguished hornrims. He wore a snappy sports jacket, nicely creased pants and an open-neck white shirt. He presented the image of a respectable retired businessman. Which was exactly what he was.

"You look so well!" Lucky exclaimed, throwing her arms around him and hugging him hard.

He drew back and inspected her critically. "And you, Lucky, well . . . you look tired." One could always depend on the truth from Uncle Costa.

"Thanks a lot."

"Should I lie?"

"Yeh. Why not?"

"Because I never lied to Gino, and I'm not going to start with you. You'll have a good night's sleep and tomorrow you'll look as beautiful as ever."

"I didn't book a hotel."

"I should hope not. You're staying with me."

They walked toward a large Chrysler, followed by a porter with Lucky's three suitcases. She planned to have the rest of her things sent directly to the East Hampton house.

Happily she tucked her arm through his. "I was hoping you'd say that. I think I've had enough of hotels to last me forever. Staying with you will be wonderful."

He glanced at her shrewdly but said nothing. There was time to talk later and find out what was bothering her. He had always loved Lucky as if she were his own daughter, and anything she wanted she could have—even if it was only his time.

33

"You're comin' to L.A. with me," Lennie said firmly.

Jess thought of all the reasons she couldn't.

There weren't any.

"I'm going to L.A. with Lennie," she told Matt.

He didn't believe her. He was crushed. Making plans had kept him so busy he had forgotten to tell her about their future together. He wanted to look after her, provide for her, even *marry* her.

"You can't do that," he stuttered.

"It's the only thing I *can* do," she replied wanly. "I've had it in Vegas. Too many memories. Lennie is right, I have to get out of here."

"No, you don't," he protested.

"Yes, I do."

He wanted to tell her how he felt. Say all the right things, and by doing so, convince her she had to stay. But expressing himself, revealing his true feelings, was not an easy task for a man like Matt. He just didn't know how to begin.

"What'll you do in L.A.?" he asked blankly.

She shrugged. "I'll make out."

He was sure she would. Girls like Jess were a rarity. She was pretty and smart and vulnerable and wise. Some guy would grab her like picking peaches. Some schmuck. While he, Matt Traynor, that well-known man-about-town, couldn't even find the words to make her stay.

"Keep in touch," he said gruffly.

"Sure," she mumbled.

But he knew she wouldn't.

34

Being with Uncle Costa was almost as good as the last year with Gino—the year before Susan Martino had entered their lives.

Lucky talked to him long into the night. All her fears and frustrations, hopes and ambitions came tumbling out. He listened patiently, never interrupting, never criticizing.

"I love Gino so much," she concluded fiercely as the dawn light began to creep into the cozy living room of the oceanside apartment. "But I hate him too." She ran a hand through her unruly black curls, a gesture that immediately reminded Costa of Gino. "He can be so . . . so . . . stupid!" She jumped up and paced around the room. "Susan Martino is not his kind of woman. She's just a plastic, groomed-to-the-eyeballs ladylike bitch who's going to grab his money and make his life miserable. Any fool can see it. Why can't *he?*"

"Lucky," Costa said, choosing his words carefully, "Gino is just like you. He knows what he wants and he always gets it. If he decides to marry this Martino woman he will do so. Nothing you or I do or say will make the least bit of difference."

"I know *that.*"

"Besides, maybe you're wrong about her. Perhaps she will be good for him." He gave a long-drawn-out sigh. "A man needs the company of a woman. It is not good to be alone."

"He wasn't alone," Lucky blazed. "He had me."

"Did you share his bed at night?" Costa asked mildly.

"He could get laid any time he wanted," Lucky replied defiantly.

"And did it ever enter your head that a man of his age might need more than just a one-night adventure? When you get old, Lucky, companionship is what really matters. Someone who cares about you."

"*You're* alone. *You're* happy."

"If I could find the right woman I would marry her in a minute."

"Shit," Lucky muttered. She wasn't winning any wars.

"Accept it," Costa said. "You're doing the right thing by moving to New York. Now you can look around and do what *you* want—break the tie between yourself and Gino. Everything you've ever done has been for his approval. The time has come to live your life for *you*."

• • • • •

Lucky stayed in Miami for three days. The weather was nice, the lifestyle simple, and Uncle Costa an interesting and wise companion.

She flew into New York early on Saturday morning to find it was raining, the city hostile and alive. The streets were crowded. Oh, God! How she had missed the pace of the city. Immediately she felt great. There was a sense of excitement in the air. New York was a challenge. Costa was right, she had to start living her own life. If she didn't, she would regret it.

She checked into the Hotel Pierre and wondered how she was supposed to start.

There were a couple of messages waiting for her. One from Costa just to be sure she had arrived safely, and another from Dr. Liz Tierney. What the hell did *she* want?

Lucky felt a tingle of apprehension. All those stupid tests Liz had insisted on running . . . maybe there was something wrong with her. Oh, shit. She *had* been feeling tired.

Convinced she had some terrible ailment, she returned the call.

Liz Tierney was cheerful and to the point. "Lucky," she announced crisply, "I'm delighted to tell you that you're going to have to slow down."

"Why?" Lucky demanded suspiciously.

"Because, my dear, you are pregnant."

Book Two

THE SUMMER OF 1980

35

Carrie Berkeley anticipated her sixty-seventh birthday with mixed feelings. On the one hand, she looked great. Slim, athletic, her taut black skin hardly marked by the harsh march of time, her short dark hair, cut in the latest style, with only a sprinkling of silver streaks.

On the other hand, there was no escaping the fact that sixty-seven was sixty-seven, and *that* was getting up there. Dare she even think about it . . . that was definitely *old*.

Carrie shuddered at the very thought as she hurried around her Fire Island house straightening cushions and moving her collection of Art Deco silver frames to different positions.

The house was lovely. Comfortable and tasteful, a true reflection of her personal style. Every few months the editors of *Vogue* or *Harper's Bazaar* would phone begging yet again for a chance to photograph her at home. "Absolutely not," she would say firmly. "I no longer wish to be in the public eye."

And she meant what she said. Three years previously she had divorced her husband, prominent businessman and theater owner Elliott Berkeley. And by doing so, had given up all the trappings of being a rich man's socialite wife. *The* beautiful Mrs. Elliott Berkeley, perfect hostess, perfect fashion plate, perfect perfect perfect.

Oh, if they only knew the truth . . .

Carrie Jones, thirteen-year-old prostitute. Set on the streets by her grandma and uncle. Sent to Welfare Island. Hooked up with a pimp named Whitejack who fed her drugs while she plied her trade. At fifteen she was in a mental institution, out of her mind and completely alone in the world. Nobody cared if she lived or died.

She stayed locked up for nine long anguished years. And then came the jobs—everything from working as a maid to a dime-a-dance girl. Until she found herself pregnant and realized the only way to make enough money to survive when she had the baby was to return to the life she knew so well.

A whorehouse was better than working the streets.

A whorehouse meant her baby son, Steven, had a home, clean clothes and a nursemaid to look after him.

A whorehouse was her life until dear sweet Bernard Dimes rescued her and four-year-old Steven.

She would always be grateful to Bernard, always love him . . . even though he had been dead twenty-five years.

Bernard had introduced her to a different world. He was an elegant man with money and class. He was also a successful theatrical producer. When he married Carrie his friends and acquaintances were shocked. Who was she? Where had she come from? And how could he marry a *Black* woman?

It was Bernard's private joke—his boldest production yet—that he invented a background for Carrie which suddenly made her acceptable in their prejudiced eyes. According to Bernard's story, she was a beautiful African princess whom he had met on safari in Kenya and lured back to America with her baby son to marry him.

What an outrageous lie. Only someone like Bernard could carry it off.

Carrie lived the charade because it amused him. And by living it she became it—and was soon embraced by the media. Even her son, Steven, never knew the truth until 1977, when she was forced to reveal everything.

She had shattered his world, his security, his heritage. Disoriented and angry, he had given up his job as a respected public prosecutor and left America for Europe, where he wandered around for two years, finally returning at the end of 1979. He visited her once then to tell her that he understood. But she knew he didn't mean it. He was cold and distant. She hadn't heard from him since.

And then he had called her unexpectedly two days ago. "I have to see you," he'd announced.

And soon he would be there.

• • • • •

Steven Berkeley drove a black Porsche. It wasn't his. It belonged to his friend Jerry Myerson, who had lent it to him for the day. Jerry was one of New York's most successful lawyers. He deserved a Porsche if that was what turned him on. Frankly, Steven considered paying fifty thousand bucks for a car ridiculous. But, he had to admit, it *was* fun to drive.

He played with the accelerator, secretly pleased with the surge of power the pressure produced.

Jerry Myerson was a good friend. They had attended high school, college and law school together. Jerry had officiated as best man at Steven's 1966 wedding to an unsuitable dancer named Zizi. Bad news Zizi. Five feet two of dynamic trouble every inch of the way. He had stayed married to her for five years. The divorce was a relief. Carrie had always hated her.

Carrie.

His mother.

For a moment he felt the familiar surge of rejection and anger. Feelings he had hoped to conquer by now. Ever since she had told him . . . revealed herself . . .

All his life he had believed he had been born in Africa, that his father was dead and that Carrie had brought him to America as a baby.

The truth was a shock.

Born in America. Brought up in a brothel. And his father could be either of two men—both of them white.

He had forced their names out of her. One of them a brief one-night affair. The other a rape. Forty-one years ago he had been conceived, and Carrie couldn't tell him which one was his father. But he had to know. Then he could get on with his life.

Automatically his foot pressed down hard and his mouth tightened into a grim line. Steven was undeniably handsome. Over six feet tall, with the body of an athlete, very direct green eyes, black curly hair, and skin the color of rich milk chocolate. Age suited him. As each year passed he seemed to get

better-looking. Once he had been one of the hottest assistant
D.A.s in New York. A steely prosecutor, with an incorruptible
reputation. But Carrie's revelations had thrown him off track,
and for the last three years he had bummed around Europe,
taking transient jobs and trying to come to terms with the reality of his beginnings.

Carrie had brought him up believing in a dream. When she
shattered it, she broke his life in two. It was taking time to put
it back together again.

Now, finally, as he drove toward Fire Island, he knew what
he had to do. Three years ago she had given him two names,
Freddy Lester and Gino Santangelo. One of them was his father. And whether she liked it or not she was going to help him
discover which one.

36

The hot sun burned into Lucky's body as she stretched out on a mat beside a sea-water swimming pool shaped like a grotto. She wore only the bottom half of a minuscule bikini, and her skin glowed with oily bronzeness. Her jet hair was plaited into one thick roll, and a Sony Walkman rested beside her, the earphones firmly in place. She listened to the soulful sounds of Bobby Womack, a longtime favorite. And his voice enveloped her, leaving no room for thought as she lost herself to "Inherit the Wind." Only when the tape clicked off did she finally open her eyes.

It was a hot day. Blue skies, with little puffs of clouds so high they just drifted like decorations. A very slight breeze made the heat bearable.

Lucky stood up, stretched languorously, then dove into the pool. The water was cold, unheated, but invigorating and refreshing. Easily she began to do laps, cleaving the water with a stylish symmetry. She did not stop until the familiar white shoes of Dimitri appeared at the edge of the pool.

"Mr. Stanislopoulos," she said formally, treading water.

His piercing eyes met hers. She liked his eyes. They were deep, knowledgeable. He had the look of a man who had been many places and done many things.

"Lucky," he said, equally formal. "And how are you today?"

As if he didn't know. As if for nearly two years they had not been as close as two people could be.

Dimitri Stanislopoulos. Sixty-four years old. Old enough to be her father.

And like her father, he was a man of substance and power. A man with whom she had been able to find a comfortable companionship and a kind of love. Not the white heat of Marco, but a satisfactory relationship.

. . . . .

*When Lucky arrived in New York ready to start over and conquer the
world she had not planned on being pregnant. Hell, no! She had never
thought about having a baby. Not for her the maternal instinct. Babies
were for women who wanted to sit home, change diapers and vegetate.*

*Coolly she had thought about abortion. She had gone to sleep
thinking about abortion, and eight hours later she awoke knowing
it wasn't the answer.*

*Of course, she knew who the father was. No doubt about that.
Dimitri was the only man she'd slept with in months.*

Oh, God! Dimitri Stanislopoulos, father of Olympia. Oh, God!

*She hugged the secret to her for a week. She didn't have to
tell anyone, not even Gino. She could have the baby and bring it
up herself—she was more than capable and certainly financially
independent. Then other thoughts crowded her head. The child,
when it began to grow, would want to know who its father was. And
surely the child was entitled to that knowledge?*

The child.

Boy or girl?

She didn't care. Whatever it was, she wanted it.

Suddenly her life took on a whole new direction.

*She called Dimitri in Paris, choosing from the list of numbers
he had given her.*

*It was three o'clock in the morning there. He was asleep and
short-tempered about being disturbed. "Yes?" he snapped.*

*"This is Lucky Santangelo. You're going to be a father," she
announced. No point in playing games.*

"What?"

"I'm having a baby. And you are the fortunate daddy."

*Dimitri sat up in bed, relieved he was alone. "I don't
understand—" he began.*

*"It's easy. We played the game. We scored a goal. I'm de-
lighted, now that I've got used to the idea. How do you feel?"*

*He cleared his throat and squinted at his watch. "Have you any
idea what time it is?" he asked sternly.*

"What's the matter with you? I just told you you're going to be a daddy and you're worried about the time!"

He didn't know what to say. So he said what he always did when in doubt. "Do you want money?"

"Huh?"

He missed the ice that crept into her voice, and plunged ahead. "Call my secretary at a decent hour. She'll send you a check for an abortion and your expenses."

"You aaaaasshole!" Lucky screamed. "Do you honestly think I called you for money? *You fucking* creep. *Drop dead." And she slammed the phone down in a fury.*

Who did the man think he was? How dare he speak to her as if she was some little hooker looking to score. How dare he! Screw *Dimitri Stanislopoulos. And* his *stupid millions. She hadn't phoned wanting anything except his joy.*

Several months passed, during which time Lucky moved into the East Hampton house. Now she was pregnant, she didn't feel ready to conquer New York. And yet, sitting around for months on end was not for her either. She saw a top gynecologist who assured her the early-morning nausea and constant exhaustion would only last a short while. He prescribed vitamins, a healthy diet and rest.

She was fed up with rest. She needed action.

In the mail one morning she received an invitation to Gino's wedding. Immediately she called Costa. They talked it over and decided to go together. Not that she wished to attend. And yet she knew that she must. She refused to give Susan Martino the satisfaction of not *being there.*

The wedding was a circus. Layer upon layer of movie stars, studio executives, show-biz lawyers, agents, directors and producers. Gino's Vegas friends were lost in the shuffle.

Lucky felt like an outsider. Why did she feel she was at Gino's funeral rather than his wedding? She exchanged only a few words with him and sat quietly at a table with Costa, observing Beverly Hills social intercourse. She wore a simple white silk suit and emeralds she had bought for herself. Her four-month pregnancy did not show yet, but her constant exhaustion was causing faint circles beneath her eyes.

Gino did not comment on her appearance, but Costa was immediately concerned. He wanted to know what she was doing, and when she shrugged and said "nothing," he frowned, because knowing Lucky as well as he did he was aware something was wrong. She did not have the temperament for just sitting around. He put it down to the fact that Gino's marriage was upsetting her more than she cared to admit.

When Lucky met Susan's two offspring she loathed them immediately. A couple of snobbish rich kids with inflated ideas of their own importance.

And then she observed the entrance of English prima donna Francesca Fern with her entourage. Five minutes later Dimitri Stanislopoulos appeared.

"Oh, no!" Lucky muttered.

"What?" asked Costa.

"Nothing." She slouched in her seat on the tented patio, hoping he wouldn't see her. Better still, wouldn't remember her. Their baby was not for sharing. He'd had his chance and blown it.

He did notice her. Later. Fortunately they were surrounded by people when he came over to the table, kissed her hand, and mouthed a few inane sentences. She noticed that his eyes flicked over her, looking for a sign, wondering if he had imagined their Paris conversation.

She was coolly polite. Screw him.

A week later he turned up at the door of her East Hampton house. It was fall. She wore a white track suit, tennis shoes and no makeup. Her hair was piled untidily on top of her head.

"You look very young," he said, standing on the doorstep, his limousine and driver waiting in the driveway.

"What do you want?" she asked flatly.

His eyes dropped to the slight bulge around her waist she hadn't bothered to conceal. "I want to know if it's true. Are you having my baby?"

Voice like ice. "No."

He was very tall. A big man. Powerful-looking with his shock of white hair and piercing eyes. "I think you're lying."

"I don't give a damn what you think."

"If that's the case why did you phone me?"

"That was months ago," she said coldly. "I was testing you. You failed."

His eyes scorched hers. World-weary eyes filled with Greek fire. "I'll be back," he said.

And he was. There was no getting rid of him. As if to make up for his initial reaction he pursued her relentlessly. Silver-purple roses every day. Crates of champagne. Jars of caviar. Baskets of exotic fruits.

She finally allowed him to take her to dinner. He sent his helicopter to collect her, and they dined aboard a private yacht that circled Manhattan as they feasted on pâté and lobster.

Later they made love. His large hands traced her stomach gently. "I want a boy," he said.

"Don't be such a chauvinist," she replied.

On July second, 1979, in a private nursing home in Connecticut, Lucky gave birth to a son. Dimitri was present at the birth.

They named the child Roberto Stavros Gino Santangelo Stanislopoulos. He was their secret. And had remained so.

* * * * *

Lucky floated on her back and held her arms invitingly toward Dimitri. "Come on in," she called. "It's wonderful."

He did not need asking twice. He pulled off his white Lacoste tennis shirt. Unbuckled his black snakeskin belt, kicked off his shoes and removed his white linen pants. Dimitri Stanislopoulos did not believe in underwear. He had a firm, strong body, an excellent physique for a man of his age. He was a big man in every way, and took great pride in his physical strength and robust health. With a roar he jumped into the water, trying to grab Lucky, who wriggled from his grasp and kicked off down the pool.

He followed her with a powerful crawl until he cornered her in the deep end. A shadow lay over this end of the pool, and a rock-hewn waterfall took up one corner. Lucky swam to the waterfall and tried to shelter behind it out of his reach.

Dimitri pressed through the falling water and crushed her against the rough side. With one hand he tore the bottom of her bikini off and thrust himself upon her.

"You sneaky sonofabitch," she objected, half jokingly, as they began to sink beneath the cool green water.

He didn't relinquish his hold, merely gripped her tightly, his thighs like steel as they rocked together beneath the water. When they surfaced she was gasping for air, but her legs were wrapped tightly around his waist and her face was flushed with pleasure. Silently they finished the act, exploding with satisfaction at the same moment.

Dimitri let go of her. "I think it's time for lunch," he said.

"Jesus!" Lucky exclaimed. "Sex. Food. You certainly believe in catering to your appetites."

"Why not? Life is for living good. I worked hard for what I've got today. Now I enjoy myself. Surely you agree?" He hauled himself from the pool and wrapped himself in a terry-cloth robe.

She swam to the side. "I hope our son doesn't take after you."

Dimitri reached down to help her out. "I hope he does."

"Yeh. He'll be a fat stud. Great! Can't wait."

Dimitri roared with laughter. "Am I fat, Lucky? Am I a stud?"

"Given half a chance," she teased.

He smiled and passed her a robe. Then he scanned the horizon and said, "Let's hope there are no paparazzi hiding anywhere today. I don't enjoy giving exhibitions."

Lucky followed his gaze. The pool overlooked the sea. There were no craft in sight. Sometimes small vessels disguised as fishing boats bobbed about in the distance with hidden cameramen with long-lens cameras aboard. Dimitri's island was considered fair game. Today all was clear.

"Lunch," Dimitri said firmly.

"You go on up. I'll follow in five minutes."

"As you wish."

She was glad she had relented and allowed Dimitri to share their son. He was a great father when she let him be. But keeping their secret was becoming more complicated each day. She was sure the servants in the Greek villa knew. And CeeCee, the pretty Black girl who looked after Roberto. And the elderly couple who took care of the East Hampton house. And Dimitri's lawyer.

A secret is no longer a secret when shared by more than two people. Lucky sighed. Dimitri kept on mentioning marriage, but she shied away from the idea. She had tried it once and hated every moment.

Dimitri was becoming more insistent every day. He wanted to tell the world about his son. He wanted to be sure everyone knew Roberto was his rightful heir. "If anything happens to me," he warned Lucky constantly, "there will be nothing but problems."

"Why?" she asked. "You told me you've changed your will."

"It's not enough," he worried. "Olympia will want everything. She'll fight my instructions. I know her."

Lucky had not renewed her friendship with Olympia. Dimitri thought it best they did not meet. She also had not mentioned to Gino that he was a grandfather. He had married Susan and settled in Beverly Hills like a senile old fart. She heard he had people running the Vegas hotels and had liquidated a lot of his other business concerns. She had received more than her fair share of the Magiriano, banked it and forgotten it. Her career was on hold while she enjoyed her son. Why should she share him with Gino? He hardly ever called her. She hadn't seen him since his wedding.

Sometimes she awoke in the middle of the night thinking how she missed him. He was old. He had already suffered one heart attack. Why didn't she go to him, show him his grandson, mend broken bridges?

Because he didn't care about her.

Because he had chosen Susan Martino over her.

Lunch was served on a magnificent terrace overlooking the sea. Lucky could remember visiting Dimitri's private island as a teenager, with Olympia. She had never imagined she would be back as the mother of his child. Some of the servants remained the same. She wondered what they thought. Did they remember her? Would they tell Olympia?

"Olympia rarely comes here," Dimitri said dourly, when she mentioned it.

Lucky knew he did not approve of his daughter's high-profile romance with a drugged-out English rock star. They were constantly making headlines. It infuriated Dimitri. "The girl is a fool," he had commented. "She's married three fortune hunters. Now she's living with this . . . this . . . degenerate."

Lucky stifled a laugh. Sometimes Dimitri acted his age.

Not in bed. In bed he was a master. Sometimes too controlled and technically perfect. He knew everything there was to know, and used his skills accordingly.

She once asked him how many women he'd had. "Thousands," he'd replied without a trace of embarrassment.

Thousands. Hmmm . . . no wonder he knew every move to make.

She wondered if Gino had had thousands.

Probably. The two shared much in common.

After lunch CeeCee appeared carrying Roberto. He looked like Lucky—dark-haired and black-eyed, with an infectious grin. He also looked like Gino. She knew she was being unfair, keeping them apart.

Dimitri's face lit up. They had been on the island with him for a week, and he never tired of spending time with his son.

Usually he only saw him when he visited Lucky's East Hampton house.

When CeeCee took the baby away for his afternoon nap, Dimitri strode restlessly back and forth across the terrace. "Lucky," he said impatiently, cracking his knuckles irritatingly, "enough is enough. My son has to have my name. Legally. I insist. We must marry."

"How romantic," she murmured.

"For God's sake—you know I adore you."

Did he? They had been together on and off for a year and a half. During that time she knew he had seen Francesca Fern. She hadn't questioned him. It was not her style to cling.

"I don't know . . ." she began.

"What can I do to persuade you?"

What could he do? She had been thinking about Atlantic City again. She missed the hotel business. The excitement, the power . . .

She had money of her own, but not nearly enough. As Mrs. Dimitri Stanislopoulos she would be able to do whatever she wanted.

And Dimitri was right. Roberto deserved the protection of bearing his father's name legally.

"I want to build a hotel," she began slowly.

He nodded encouragingly. "Whatever you want, Lucky, you can have. Just tell me, and it will be yours."

37

No," said Jess into the phone cradled next to her ear. "Lennie Golden is booked solid for months. There's no way he can even read the script."

"Please," the person on the other end begged. "If he reads it, he'll love it, and then he'll want to do it."

"Sorry." She replaced the receiver and yelled out, "Vickie. Where the hell are you?"

Vickie teetered into the room on dangerously high stiletto heels. She wore them with black fishnet tights, Spandex shorts, and a Lurex boob tube. Her fine brown hair was teased to the limit, and her outstandingly ugly face was carefully made up. She looked like your friendly neighborhood hooker, not a personal secretary, which is what she was supposed to be. Jess wanted to fire her, but Lennie wouldn't hear of it.

"Sorry, Jess," Vickie squeaked. "I was in the john. I got a little bathroom problem this week."

"You've always got a little bathroom problem," Jess complained, and stood up from behind the old worn desk where she had been sitting. "I do not expect to have to answer phones. That's what we pay *you* for."

Vickie lowered two sets of false eyelashes. "Sorry, Jess."

Where did Lennie find them? The last one he had hired looked like a man in drag, but at least she/he answered phones. This one was always in the bathroom.

"I gotta go out," Jess said, reluctant to leave her in charge. "Can you hack it?"

Vickie grinned. She had never managed the money for a capping job, and her teeth were a mess. "Can I hack it? What a question!"

"Take messages," Jess admonished sternly.

Vickie nodded.

Jess left the small office in an unassuming building on Sunset, and knew without a doubt they needed larger space and two *decent* secretaries. Lennie was becoming big business, and they were running a penny-ante operation. Okay for six months ago, but not now. Not with Lennie rising like a meteor.

Jess rode the elevator to the underground garage and collected her car—a used Datsun. She kept on meaning to trade it in for something better, but who had the time? So much had happened, so many good things. Thank God she had listened to Lennie and left Vegas for L.A. At first it had been awful. She had sat in the hotel room Lennie put her in and stared at television day and night. He had allowed her to do that for a few weeks, and then one day he had said, "Okay, kid. That's it. You're out on the road again." And from that moment on he hadn't left her alone—he dragged her everywhere he went. She met all his friends—Suna, Shirlee, Joey Firello, Foxie and the statuesque Rainbow, Isaac and his pretty wife. They all accepted her immediately and went out of their way to rally round. The twins took her to the gym with them. Joey insisted she sit in on several tapings of his TV show. Rainbow escorted her to Frederick's, an outrageous lingerie shop on Hollywood Boulevard, and encouraged her to buy a slit-up-the-side purple satin nightgown. Isaac and his wife invited her to their house in the valley for Sunday barbecues. And Foxie, whose rudeness was legendary, developed a fast crush, and whenever she was around spent his entire time regaling her with stories of his colorful life. Since he was now eighty-six years old, they never ran out of conversation.

Lennie, of course, was always there for her. Supportive and understanding, a true friend. Without him she knew she would have fallen to pieces. But he pulled her through, and she owed him plenty.

Eventually the time had come for her to stop depending on other people. She was running out of money, and she had no intention of sponging off Lennie. But what to do? There was no way she was returning to Vegas, and jobs for croupiers were not exactly heavy on the ground in L.A. She turned to Foxie for advice.

He bit off the end of a stinking old stogie, spat on the floor and suggested something she had never even thought of. "Go into personal management," he said. "You're a smart little broad with a lotta moxie. Use it."

"Personal management of what?"

"Lennie, of course."

"Lennie's *got* an agent."

"Who's talkin' agenting?" He waved his cigar wildly in the air.

"If he has Isaac, why would he need a manager?"

Foxie shook his head in disbelief. "An' I thought you was smart. For a girl grew up in Vegas you don't know a lot."

"Sure I do," Jess bristled. "*Stars* have agents *and* managers. Then they can afford them."

"An' how do you think they got to be stars in the first place? You think some agent with thirty clients an' a mortgage to pay got 'em there?"

"I don't know."

Foxie nodded wisely. "Then listen." He talked fast, a jumble of words. And what he said made sense. Sure Lennie had an agent, and Isaac was okay—he had a stable of young comedians and did his best for all of them. But his best, split among all his clients, just wasn't good enough. Foxie cited *The Merv Griffin Show* as an example. "Lennie walked on account of wanting to be with you at your kid's funeral. You think Isaac's been back to 'em with the name Lennie Golden? Naw. He's shit scared—thinks it might affect his other clients an' *their* shots on the show. That's an agent for you. Now, a personal manager would be in there hustlin'. Get the difference?"

She got it. And it made sense. She also heard for the first time that Lennie had given up his chance of appearing on the Griffin show to be with her. She owed him more than she'd thought, and she was determined to pay him back.

"How do you become a manager?" she asked.

"You understand deals. You believe in your client two hundred percent. An' you go for it no holds barred. I coulda been the best manager in the business if I'd wanted to. I coulda sold shit to a stable of horses with dysentery!"

Jess giggled. Old Foxie certainly knew how to turn a phrase. "Teach me," she begged.

"You're a natural," he replied. "An' you got the right goods t'sell. Lennie's gonna be big. I picked it when he first auditioned."

Within a week she had rebooked Lennie on *The Merv Griffin Show*.

He was delighted. "How'd you do it, babe?"

She grinned. "Moxie and no mortgage."

"Huh?"

"Forget it."

And so his climb began. Jess was dedicated, and there was nothing else on her mind. She went for it, just as Foxie had told her to do. And Lennie was good, so everything she got him paid off and led to other things.

Isaac was pissed at first, but he soon got used to it—especially when Jess proved she knew what she was doing better than anyone else.

The Griffin show first. A repeat performance two weeks later because Merv liked him. A third shot a month after that because audience reaction was strong. Two guest appearances on Joey Firello's comedy hour. And then the offer of a weekly TV show in which he got to play a crazy doctor in charge of a health spa. The program, called *The Springs*, was a cross between *Soap* and *Hill Street Blues*. It started off with hardly any ratings at all, until gradually it built up a small cult following, then a large cult following, and suddenly it busted right to the top of the ratings and became a hit halfway through its second season. Lennie and the rest of the virtually unknown cast developed sensational TVQs overnight.

That had taken place six weeks ago. To say that Lennie was now hot was putting it mildly.

Jess steered the Datsun into the slow-moving afternoon traffic. There was so much going on, and hardly time to handle it all. She honked at an erratic driver who promptly gave her the V sign.

"Shove it up your ass, sailor," she mouthed, and shot past him.

The first thing she had to do was get Lennie straight. Rumor had it he was drinking, although not in front of her. But then, since the success of the show, she had hardly seen him. He was either doing interviews, working, or socializing with a series of willowy blondes who passed through his life like a dose of salts.

That was all they needed. A drinking problem, just when he was on the brink.

The erratic driver cut in front of her, forcing her to brake abruptly. She tried to control her temper but couldn't resist a massive blast on the horn.

Stay calm, she warned herself. She was on her way to lunch with Lennie and she didn't want to arrive flustered. It was important to maintain a cool, collected exterior. All the better to find out what he had been up to.

* * * * *

The blonde had said she was nineteen but Lennie wasn't betting on it. Seventeen, more like. A sexually experienced seventeen whom he couldn't wait to get rid of. One evening of lust was enough. He wished they didn't always want to stay the night.

She was dressing. Slowly. White pants, a cutaway top, lace-up shoes, dozens of bangles.

"Can you drop me in Westwood?" she asked.

"I'm not going that way. But I'll call you a cab."

"I don't have any cash."

"I'll pay the driver."

She tuned in to a soap opera on television while he phoned the taxi company and told them to send someone over fast. He wanted her out of his apartment. Not that there was anything wrong with her. She was pretty, with a California body, and she had a pleasant enough personality. But she was his third blonde this week, and he was overdosing on available pussy and not liking himself for it.

When the cab buzzed from downstairs he pressed twenty dollars into her hand, promised he would call soon and shut the door behind her with a sigh of relief.

Immediately she was gone he stripped the sheets off the bed, dumped them on the floor, opened all the windows and fixed himself a refreshing vodka and orange juice. It was eleven in the morning. Not too bad. His one day off, and nothing to do until a one o'clock lunch with Jess at Scandia.

He had been working nonstop. Not only was he rewriting his dialogue on "The Springs" as well as performing on the show most days, but he was putting together some new material for his act and also trying to work on a screenplay. Plus there was constant publicity to do, and a different party every night.

Well, why not? Didn't he deserve it at long last?

The phone rang. It was his mother. Dear old Alice had reentered his life with a vengeance. Amazing what a touch of fame could do.

"Lennie, dear," she said.

He reached for the vodka and gave himself a refill. "Yes?"

"I've been thinking."

"Yes?"

"Why can't you get *me* on *The Merv Griffin Show*?"

He was incredulous. "What?"

"Don't sound so surprised. I'd be marvelous."

"Doing what?"

"Doing what I do better than anyone. Telling about my life. Telling stories."

"What stories?"

"About Las Vegas. Your father. Me. I've had the most interesting life of anyone I know. Someone should write a book about me. Would they have a best-seller! I shiver to think."

"So do I."

"Don't be rude."

"Who's rude?"

"Since you got on television every week you're rude. I never hear from you, never see you. How do you think that makes me feel? I'm your mother, Lennie, and you've thrown me aside like old clothes."

All of a sudden Alice the swinger was his mother, a fact she would not have admitted six months ago. After his second Merv Griffin appearance she had written him a letter in care of the show. He had called and listened to her complain. It seemed she was put out because he hadn't invited her to the taping. Shortly after that he made the trek to Marina del Rey and spent a day in her company. She had fixed him a bacon sandwich, confided all about her new boyfriend—a twenty-six-year-old musician who was "out on the road"—and embarrassed him with an exhibition of six new exercises she claimed kept her fit, young and sexually active.

He hadn't seen her since, but she phoned him regularly—very regularly since "The Springs" had zoomed in the ratings.

He sent her money, which she never mentioned, and put up with her phone calls. What else could he do? She *was* his mother.

"Well?" demanded Alice.

"Very."

"What?"

"Very well."

There was a frosty silence while Alice considered what to say next. She came up with a humdinger. "I'm thinking of getting an agent."

Lennie reached for the vodka. "What the hell for?"

"Ha! You think you're the only one should have a career? If you cared about me at all you'd give me *your* agent. I sing, dance, tell funny stories. Why can't you get me a guest spot on your show?"

The thought of going to Isaac Luther and offering Alice as a client was too hilarious to contemplate. Lennie choked back laughter. "Gotta go. I'm running late."

"Think about introducing me to your agent. You won't be sorry. It's never too late to make it, you know."

"Yeah, Ma."

"Call me Alice—it sounds better. And lie about your age. Stick to twenty-five—you don't look any older. You can get away with it."

"Thanks for the advice."

He hung up, still laughing. If nothing else she was a character.

Harriet, the maid, arrived shortly after. She was extremely old and had trouble walking. Her cleaning left plenty to be desired, but he had inherited her when he rented the apartment—a one-bedroom penthouse in a service building on Doheny.

"Morning, Mr. Gold," she said.

"Golden," he corrected. She had only been working for him a year. She nodded absentmindedly and went into the kitchen where she took off her shoes and switched on the television.

Lennie returned to the bathroom. He stripped off his robe and stepped under a cold shower. He looked forward to lunch with Jess, and then at three o'clock he had an interview with *People* magazine. He hated giving interviews. They were an intrusion on his privacy, and he had nothing to say about his personal life.

What personal life?

Was getting laid a lot personal? He doubted it.

Toweling himself dry, he wondered what to wear. Most of

his clothes rested in a heap on the floor waiting for someone to take them to the cleaner's. From the pile he extracted black pants and a black shirt. Jess would probably complain. "You need to buy new clothes," she would say.

Now that he had the money, he didn't have the time.

What *did* he have time for?

Working.

Screwing.

Drinking.

Working.

Little Jess had really done it for him. She was a dynamo. She had taken over his static career and shoved him up the public's ass like a rocket. And not a moment too soon. She had saved both their lives. And now he was really on his way. TV series. Good money. Christ, if *People* magazine wanted him it meant he was somebody. They were going to take photos: a day in the life of Lennie Golden. He wondered if Eden would see them, and stepped on the thought.

Eden Antonio was old news.

Eden Antonio meant nothing to him.

He reviewed their relationship. Three years together in New York. Fought like tigers. She went West. He followed. One meeting. Great sex. And that was it. She had used him because she probably felt horny, and dumped him with about as much feeling as a sphinx. Christ, how he hated her.

Bull . . . shit.

What?

Bull . . . shit. If she came to you now you'd grab her.

Maybe.

Don't give me that maybe crap.

He loathed the conversations that took place in the privacy of his head because they were true.

He knew things about her.

She was living with some married hood. The guy had bought her a house, clothes, jewelry.

The twins gave him fragments. He tried to appear uninterested.

He knew where her house was. He knew her private phone number. He had driven past the house a few times. Phoned and hung up more than once.

But he refused to contact her. If she wanted him, let *her* come running.

And if she ever did.

Dressed in black, he prepared to leave the apartment.

Harriet lolled in the kitchen, varicose-veined legs stretched before her, a game show blaring on the television. "Just taking a lunch break, Mr. Gould," she said contentedly.

"Put clean sheets on the bed," he instructed, knowing she wouldn't and that he would have to do it himself. Feeling sorry for the old bag was one thing, but he needed a maid desperately.

In the underground garage he collected his new black BMW. What a car! He had walked into the showroom and bought it off the floor six weeks ago. His first extravagance. It felt good. He wished he had someone to share his success with. Jess was terrific, but she wasn't around when he really needed her in the cold, empty hours of the early morning when he desired the warmth of a lover, a companion, a soul mate.

Sometimes he would reach for the blonde asleep beside him, wake her gently and make love.

No. Not love. Sex. Just sex.

Success was great. Money was great. Recognition was great.

It just wasn't enough.

Something was missing in his life.

38

Driving back to New York, Steven Berkeley tried to decide how the meeting with his mother, Carrie, had gone.

She had been thrilled to see him, overly attentive. She had wanted him to stay the weekend, but he had declined, anxious to get to the point and out of there.

"Look," he had finally said. "I can't lie to you, and I don't intend to. I need to get my life straight, and to do that I have to know who my father is."

There had been a long pause while she got up, paced the room, sat down again and finally looked him in the eye. "I've told you everything I know—" her voice hardly more than a whisper.

"You gave me two names," he said harshly. "Two names, and that's supposed to satisfy me? Well, it doesn't. Not by a long way. I have to know *which one* is my father. And *you* have to help me."

It had not been easy. She didn't want to cooperate. She had no desire to sift through the ashes of her past. But gradually he convinced her that if she ever wanted to see him again she had no choice. Finally she had agreed to the plan he set before her.

Now, driving along the half-empty freeway, he wondered if he was doing right. Jerry Myerson had advised him against doing anything. "What do you think's going to happen?" Jerry had questioned. "You drag Carrie to see some guy who might—and I emphasize the 'might'—just be your old man. Then you tell him the facts—like forty-two years ago he went to bed with Carrie—and *then* you ask him to take a blood test. Are you *kidding?* If you were white, they'd kick your ass out the door. But when they take a look at you they're going to *laugh* you out. Why put yourself through it? And why humiliate Carrie?"

Jerry didn't understand. There were some things in life that had to be done.

He knew where Gino Santangelo was. Still alive. Seventy four years old. Married to Tiny Martino's widow and living in Beverly Hills. There was no doubt he was the same Gino Santangelo Carrie had had a one-night affair with back in 1938 when he owned a nightclub in New York called Clemmie's.

Tracking Freddy Lester had not been so easy. The only information Carrie could remember was that he was from a New York society family, his best friend was named Mel, and at the time she met him he had recently left college.

Steven had found three candidates: one a judge, one a publisher, and the third a retired doctor. All three were about the right age, lived in or near New York, and shared different versions of the same name. Judge Frederick Lester. Fred E. Lester. And Fredd Lesster, M.D. Of the three, Carrie would have to pick the right one

Jerry Myerson was correct. It was not going to be simple. But as a former D.A., Steven had tenacity and determination, and, even more important, he knew he could do it.

With a little help from Carrie. She at least owed him that.

39

Olympia had suspected for some time her father had a secret mistress. Not that she cared. Dimitri could do what he liked, and so could she. But her curiosity was aroused. Who was the mystery woman? And why the secrecy?

She ran into Francesca Fern in New York at "21."

"Dahling!" they both exclaimed. "You look divine! We must have lunch." Kisses brushed cheeks.

"How about tomorrow?" Olympia added, interested to find out if Francesca knew what was going on.

Francesca, who had no particular desire to lunch with Dimitri's petulant daughter, could think of no quick excuse.

"The Russian Tea Room, one o'clock," Olympia stated firmly.

Francesca nodded vaguely, planning to cancel at the last minute. But in the morning Horace annoyed her, she had a screaming argument with her agent on the phone, and lunch with Olympia seemed a welcome excuse to storm from the house.

Olympia awoke late in her luxurious Fifth Avenue apartment overlooking Central Park. Flash was in the south of France working on a new album with the Layabouts. She planned to join him in a few days, but quite frankly she was enjoying the peace and quiet. Life with Flash was a series of parties and peculiar people, late-night drug trips and kinky sex. Not that she minded any of it, but the break would do him good—make him appreciate her. Sometimes she felt he took her too much for granted. He had money, but never spent a dime. He always expected her to pay for everything—which she did. "The rich bint'll get it," he'd say to anyone who asked. "She's got more loot than the friggin' Queen of bleedin' Blighty."

Olympia, remembering her lunch appointment with Francesca, hurried to dress. She put on a cream leather miniskirt, which refused to zip. She discarded that and wriggled into a silk Chloé dress, which made her look fat. She finally settled on a blue linen suit that hid a multitude of sins. Lately Flash had taken to calling her Tubs, which infuriated her. She, in turn, had nicknamed him Bones, which made him snigger.

Tubs and Bones. The current darlings of the gossip columns. Oh, if the public only knew!

The two women arrived simultaneously, kissed each other vaguely on the cheek, and settled into a lefthand booth, whereupon Olympia ordered a Bloody Mary and Francesca decided on Perrier. Olympia immediately regretted her decision to invite Francesca to lunch. What were they going to talk about for two hours? They had nothing in common except Dimitri, and five minutes would dispose of him.

"I have a two o'clock appointment with my couturier," Francesca announced briskly, as if thinking the same thoughts.

"Good," replied Olympia swiftly. "I have a manicure at two."

Francesca reached into her purse and produced a thin black cheroot. She placed it between brightly carmined lips, and two waiters leaped forward. She accepted their attentions with the attitude of a star and, tossing her flame-red hair, announced to Olympia, "I leave for Paris in the morning. I never stop traveling."

Olympia plunged right in. "Have you seen Dimitri recently?" she asked.

"Isn't he in Greece?" Francesca replied offhandedly.

"Yes." Olympia paused mysteriously. "Again."

Francesca did not jump to the bait. Her hooded eyes surveyed the room and her husky voice summoned the captain. "Menu," she commanded. She looked bored.

Olympia persevered. "This is his third trip to the island this year."

Francesca turned toward her. "So?"

"So . . . don't you think it's a little . . . strange?"

Francesca shrugged, snatched the menu from the hovering captain, and studied it intently. "Nothing strange. It's *his* island."

"Hmm," said Olympia. "*I* think it's strange that he hands out explicit instructions *nobody* is to visit while he's there. And that includes me. I wanted to send my daughter to him and I was informed I couldn't."

Francesca dragged deeply on her cheroot and waved to a passing producer. "Why are you telling *me? I* have no wish to go there."

"You and Dimitri are such good . . . friends. I thought you might know why he's acting like this. Does he have a new girlfriend?"

Francesca turned her brilliant gaze on the captain. "An herb omelet," she requested. "And a green salad. No dressing."

Olympia frowned. Francesca didn't seem at all concerned that Dimitri might be shacked up with a secret new love.

"For you, Miz Stanislopoulos?" the captain asked respectfully.

"Blinis, sour cream, caviar, apple pancakes and a dish of strawberries on the side."

Francesca's look said it all. "Don't you watch your diet?" she murmured.

"No," Olympia replied defiantly. "It goes straight to my tits—and Flash watches those."

Lunch, after that, was all downhill—stilted conversation, and a rush to be the first to leave.

"Goodbye," said Francesca graciously. "I expect we shall see each other as usual in August."

"I don't know about that," replied Olympia. "Dimitri might be otherwise engaged. He could cancel the cruise."

"I don't think so," said Francesca with a knowing smile, and swept out.

Olympia could not stand the woman. She decided to stay and order another portion of strawberries, a fresh Bloody Mary and maybe just the tiniest piece of cheesecake.

She was glad she did, for who should appear a few minutes later but Vitos Felicidade, her short-term lover before Flash.

"Vitos," she cried out, waving vigorously.

He stopped, glanced in her direction. It took him a moment to remember her, but when he did the smile was perfect, the hand-kissing beautifully executed. "Oleeempeea! So loooovlee."

Vitos had been the focus of a huge media blitz in the past

year, and was now far more famous than when they first met. He was dressed impeccably. A Savile Row blue silk suit, a custom-made shirt, gold cufflinks and a not-so-discreet diamond identity bracelet. He was accompanied by two women. One of them was his personal PR and the other a fat female carrying a tape recorder and a file of clippings.

"Thees ees *The New York Times*," he announced, indicating the large woman. "Ana thees—Pamela." The PR nodded curtly as Vitos elaborately gestured toward Olympia. "Ladeez, may I presenta you, Senorita Ole*ee*mpeea Stane*ee*zlopoulos."

Both women jumped to attention and stared at the voluptuous puffy-faced blonde. Her affair with rock cult figure Flash had been making headlines for two years.

Olympia nodded dismissively—she hated the press unless it was *Vogue* or *Baçaar*—even *Architectural Digest* passed muster.

She scribbled her phone number on a book of matches and handed it to Vitos. "Call me," she instructed with a knowing look. "Later."

His smile was still perfection. He clicked his heels in an old world fashion, saluted and departed, the two women close behind him.

Olympia pursed her lips. He might provide a relaxing interlude. The afternoon stretched endlessly before her. She did not have an appointment with her manicurist. In fact, she had nothing to do at all except return to her apartment (dull without the electric presence of Flash) and her child. Brigette, now eleven, was even more of a monster. She and Flash had experienced instant hate, and a month after their meeting Olympia had arranged for Brigette to continue her education in England. Flash's manager had suggested a suitable school in Oxfordshire, and Olympia packed Nanny Mabel and Brigette straight off. Brigette attended boarding school during the week, and Nanny Mabel was installed in a house nearby so that Brigette would have somewhere to spend the weekends. It was all working out well enough—if one chose to ignore the dreadful report cards.

The major problem was vacations. Naturally Olympia had to spend *some* time with her child, and there was no escaping vacations. She had hoped she could send Brigette and Nanny to Dimitri's island, but he, surprisingly, had said no. That was when Olympia realized something was up. She had thought Francesca might have provided answers, but no such luck.

It was not easy being a mother. Awesome responsibilities. And Brigette did not appreciate a thing. The older she got, the more difficult she became. Did she realize that right now Olympia was giving up precious time with Flash?

No, of course she didn't.

Leaving the restaurant, Olympia dismissed her limousine and strolled along the street to Bendel's, one of her favorite department stores. She browsed for a while, picking a pale-beige suede outfit, and an eight-hundred-dollar pair of se-quinned shoes. She ordered them to be sent.

It was a pleasant summer day, not too humid, so she headed for Bergdorf's and dropped another two thousand dollars there. As she proceeded across Fifth Avenue on her way home, she no-ticed a newsstand on the corner. She observed the stand, because displayed amidst a bunch of girlie magazines, right next to the *Enquirer* and the *Star,* was a rag called *Pointer.* And on the cover of said rag was a large picture of Flash, leering, naked from the waist up except for a long, ragged scarf, with his scrawny arm around a couldn't-be-more-than-seventeen, skinny, flaxen-haired doll. And the headline read: SECRET FLASH MARRIAGE WITH TEENAGER.

Olympia stopped and stared. She narrowed her small blue eyes. She reached into her Hermès bag and thrust a ten-dollar bill at the news vendor while snatching a copy of the offending paper. And as the old man groped for change, she scanned the caption beneath the picture. It was brief and to the point:

Legendary Rock Superstar Flash Revealed in the south of France, where he is working on a new album with The Layabouts, that he has been secretly married to eighteen-year-old Kipp Hartley for three years. Kipp, a schoolgirl when they met, is expecting their first baby early in the New Year.

40

The decision was made. Lucky was getting married. For the second time.

"No big ceremony. Let's do it here with just the staff for witnesses," she told Dimitri.

He agreed. That way people would have no idea when they were married, and Roberto would not have to go through life with even a shadowy stigma of illegitimacy.

They decided to have the ceremony the day before leaving the island. Dimitri's lawyer flew in forty-eight hours beforehand. He carried with him a briefcase stuffed with papers. Most of them were for Lucky to sign. She didn't mind, as long as the most important paper of all was included. This was an agreement between her and Dimitri stating he would be entirely responsible for purchasing the land, building and financing an Atlantic City hotel which would belong to her free and clear. And on her death it would pass into the hands of their son, Roberto.

"Your wedding present," Dimitri said, signing the document with a flourish.

She added her own signature. Other than that, she relinquished most of his fortune. What did she care? Roberto would receive half of everything anyway, and the hotel was a multimillion-dollar investment which would be all hers.

The day of their wedding was perfect. Lucky wore a simple white dress with flowers in her hair. Dimitri chose a lightweight suit—nothing too formal.

A Greek Orthodox priest was flown from the mainland for the ceremony. The wedding guests were the staff and Roberto, who spent most of the day balanced on CeeCee's hip, not understanding at all what was going on, but enjoying the excitement in the air.

Lucky remembered her first wedding at sixteen. Las Vegas. Five hundred guests. A big gaudy circus she had been a part of. Unwillingly.

Gino's fault. Gino's way of getting rid of her.

The sun cooled, Roberto was put to bed, and Dimitri and Lucky dined on the terrace alone. They feasted on thinly sliced roast lamb smothered in herbs, roast potatoes flavored with garlic, small fresh peas sautéed in butter. And for dessert a miniature wedding cake made of strawberries and meringue.

They toasted each other with ouzo, Dimitri's favorite liquor, and later swam naked in the pool.

In bed he made love to her slowly, and she gave herself up to the ritual of his experienced, talented lovemaking.

How different from her wedding night with Craven in the Bahamas. He had burned himself to a crisp in the hot tropical sun and had spent the night bitching and whining. What a wimp!

Tomorrow we will leave the island, she thought.

Tomorrow I must telephone Gino and Costa.

Tomorrow . . . tomorrow . . . tomorrow . . .

She drifted off to sleep, one arm flung casually across her new husband.

* * * * *

Gino raised his hand and bid five thousand dollars toward yet another needy cause. Susan had needy causes coming out her ass. One thing after another. You couldn't fault Susan Santangelo. She gave great charity. With *his* money.

Susan tossed him a bountiful smile. "Thank you, darling," she whispered.

They were at a function at the Century Plaza Hotel. Table for twelve. His table. No, her table. He paid. She invited.

He was seated between Susan and her good friend Paige Wheeler. He liked Paige. She had a sense of humor, which was more than could be said for most of Susan's "good friends."

The other guests included Paige's husband, Ryder, a film

producer who had no conversation except "the industry." And
an assortment of Susan's attendants. Her hairdresser, her couturier and her dentist. And of course her children. Gemma,
Miss High and Mighty. And Nathan—"mustn't-soil-my-
hands-with-a-day's-work-now-that-I've-graduated-from-
college."

Once he had thought them charming, a credit to their
mother. But two years in their company had taught him otherwise. They were convinced the world owed them a living—
both victims of Too much, too soon, and What's in it for
me? Two Beverly Hills brats in designer sports clothes and
matching convertibles.

Sadly Gino had to admit he could not warm to either of
them, although he had tried many times.

He knew they didn't like or even approve of him.

Fuck 'em. What did he care? He had married Susan, not
her kids.

Susan was determined they should all be one big happy
family, and she never stopped shoving them together.

They called him Gino.

Susan wanted them to call him Father.

They tried to stay out of his way.

Susan wanted him to adopt them legally.

Jeez! He had laughed in her face when she first suggested
it. "*C'mon.* They're grownups, adults. What's all this adoption
crap?"

"They're children at heart. They need a proper father. Unless you adopt them, Gino, show them you *really* care—then
I'm not sure if you'll *ever* get along."

"Horseshit."

"No, dear. Face the truth."

She had already discussed it with her lawyer, who, according to Susan, thought it an excellent idea.

Whenever she brought the subject up, which was often,
Gino changed the conversation. "Wouldn't it be nice," Susan

was fond of saying, "to have children who really care about you?"

Her way of getting in a dig at Lucky.

It *was* true. He never heard from her. She attended his wedding with an uptight expression, and he didn't think she had called more than twice since.

When he first married Susan he had never really given much thought to how Lucky must have felt. *He* was getting married. What did *she* have to do with it? But, in retrospect, maybe he should have shown her more consideration—after all, they had been inseparable for a year, after a lifetime of misunderstandings and fights—and he had enjoyed their closeness as much as she had.

The Santangelos. Father and daughter. An unbeatable combination. He missed her. Maybe the time had come to mend bridges.

"Methinks your mind is elsewhere," Paige whispered in his ear. "And who can blame you? These events suck."

He turned to regard Susan's friend. She was an attractive woman with her unkempt frizzy hair and what in his day had been known as "bedroom eyes."

She rested her hand lightly on his thigh. "Charity balls have always bored the pants off me. Send a check is my motto. Don't you agree?"

He could feel the warmth of her hand through the material of his trousers, and he could also feel his cock begin to grow hard. Susan, for a variety of reasons, had not slept with him for six weeks. He might be old, but he wasn't buried. He needed regular sex.

Paige's hand did not budge. If she moved it up a couple of inches she would feel the strength of his reaction.

She didn't have to move it. She knew.

"You're a very sexy man, Gino," she said, making sure her words were for his ears only.

"An' you're not a bad-lookin' broad," he replied, playing the game and enjoying it.

"Don't you think," she said, very softly indeed, "it's high time we did something about it?"

He hadn't played around on Susan. He had been faithful.

Screw faithful. He felt hotter than he had in a long while. To tell the truth, Susan was not the greatest in bed. Too damn ladylike. She was a fantastic wife if you liked tasteful parties and needlepoint and weekends in Palm Springs knocking a dumb golf ball around.

Paige, unobserved by the rest of the table, and cloaked by a long tablecloth, was moving her hand up and rubbing his hard-on. He almost groaned aloud.

"Yeh," he encouraged gruffly.

"Call me at my office," she responded with one final squeeze. "Soon. Very soon."

41

Lennie had not expected the cover. Not the goddamn cover of *People* magazine.

Everyone was impressed.

Except Alice.

Naturally.

She had called in a fury. "I'm hardly mentioned," she screamed. "There's no picture of me. Are you trying to sabotage my chance of a career too?"

He just didn't believe her. "C'mon—" he began.

"No. *You* come on," she yelled. "I've written them a letter. I want an apology. I want them to do a piece on *me*."

There was no satisfying Alice. Instead of being proud of his success she was jealous. His own mother jealous! It was ridiculous.

The twins insisted on throwing a party for him. They were flourishing, having landed a series of highly lucrative toothpaste commercials which had made them into visible personalities. Suna was going out with a plastic surgeon, and he allowed the party to take place in his Coldwater Canyon house complete with Jacuzzi and tennis court.

A hundred people were invited.

Two hundred turned up.

The plastic surgeon served Mexican food. A raucous rock group played loud music (courtesy of Shirlee—she was going out with the drummer). And a wild time was had by all.

Lennie found himself, at four in the morning, bombed out of his mind and naked in the Jacuzzi with three girls and an assortment of drugs supplied by kindly well-wishers. He dragged on a joint, as two of the girls snorted coke and the third nearly drowned while trying to go down on him.

Was this stardom?

Was this having it all?

Free drugs and too much pussy. There had to be more than this.

He was glad Jess had left. He knew her feelings on "letting things get out of control."

"Whatever you do, Lennie," she had told him earlier in the evening, "don't turn into an asshole."

He knew exactly what she meant. But couldn't he be an asshole for just one night? How many times in life did you get to be naked in a Jacuzzi with three hot females and as many drugs as you could handle?

One of the girls had enormous boobs. She straddled him against the side of a jet and dangled them near his face. He caught a nipple in his mouth and went for it.

One of the other girls, equally well endowed, decided to get into the act. She crammed the tip of her right boob into his mouth.

Now he was sucking on the two of them, and the aqua baby was sucking on him.

He felt lift-off.

The zoom.

The peaking.

The throb.

The landing.

Jeeeeesus!

Nothing like being a star.

He wanted to go home. He pushed away female flesh and leaped from the pool. People were littered around in various stages of undress. He picked his way over bodies, found his clothes and dressed.

His car waited in the driveway. Jess had stuck a note on the windshield. "Asshole," she had written. "Drive carefully."

He did. All the way to her apartment, which was one block away from his.

She ushered him in without complaining, fed him black

coffee, and they sat around talking until the morning sun was bright in the sky. He let it all out. His high at finally making it. The constant nagging feeling in his gut that it was just temporary, that maybe he shouldn't get too excited—it wasn't going to last.

"You'll last," she assured him. "This is just the start."

"From your lips . . ."

They hugged tightly. He started to say something about Eden, then changed his mind.

Jess fixed him bacon and eggs and put him to sleep in her bed. Fortunately it was Sunday. No work. No grind.

She went into the other room and called Matt. They had kept in touch. When Gino Santangelo got married and left Vegas he had promoted Matt to general overseer of everything concerning the Magiriano. The only person Matt had to answer to was Gino himself.

He was always delighted to hear from her. Even more delighted that in a few days she would be returning to Vegas with Lennie. Only for a week, but it was better than nothing.

Six months previously, before Lennie was really hot, he had booked him to appear in the main room of the Magiriano, sharing top billing with Vitos Felicidade. What a coup! When he had booked them, neither had been a big star. Now they both were.

"Want to release us from our contract?" Jess joked, as she had been doing for the last couple of months.

"You're cute."

"Thank you."

"What can I do for you today?"

"Just wanted to check details."

"You've checked them a hundred times."

"I'm meticulous."

She liked her talks with Matt. In a funny sort of way she almost missed him. She wondered if he still weighed himself down with gold chains, blow-dried his hair and hit on every showgirl in town. Somehow she had thought he might visit her in L.A., but he never had. "Too busy," he'd explained when she'd asked him once.

She knew about busy. Lennie's career kept her on the go. No time for anything else—not even a personal life. In two years she had indulged in only one affair. A sometime actor with spectacular pectorals, amazing thighs, rock-hard everything else, and the brain of a retarded teenager. Their affair lasted exactly six weeks. It was all she could take of fantastic sex and nothing much else. When they parted, he suggested she become his manager. His manager! Sleeping with him was ordeal enough.

After talking to Matt she pulled on shorts and a T-shirt, checked that Lennie was asleep and drove down the hill to Carl's Market, where she picked up groceries and the papers. She couldn't help worrying about Lennie. Eden Antonio still had a hold on him. He wasn't going to feel really good about anything until he put her behind him once and for all. And how was he going to do that when he wasn't even seeing her?

Jess frowned. She had never met Eden, but she had heard enough stories to know the woman was a spoiled bitch living with some rich mafioso hood, and ambitious as hell. A few days in her company would surely allow Lennie to see her for what she really was?

Wishful thinking.

He was hooked.

The only way he could get unhooked was to do it himself.

$\bullet \quad \bullet \quad \bullet \quad \bullet \quad \bullet$

Eden stared at the cover of *People* and bit down hard on her lower lip. Sonofabitch! The bastard had actually made it. Who would have thought Lennie Golden would ever get himself on the cover of *People*? Not her, for one. As far as she was concerned Lennie had limited talent. Oh, sure, he was a great lay. But fine cocksmanship did not a cover make.

She narrowed her topaz eyes and glared at his picture. He

was grinning. At her? Like—*Listen, baby, I told you I'd make it. Now what the fuck are you doing?*

What *was* she doing?

Not enough.

Not nearly enough.

She was living in the house Santino Bonnatti had bought her, virtually a prisoner. He kept her locked up on Blue Jay Way with a chauffeur-bodyguard to take care of her every need. That's what Santino had said when he installed the goon as if he were doing her a favor. "This is Zeko. He's gonna look after ya an' drive ya around. He's gonna take care of your every need. Okay, bunny rabbit?"

What was she supposed to say? No? It was either put up with what Santino wanted or get out of the relationship fast. And she was too smart to get out before the moment was right. Santino was the key to her future, and, while it was taking time, she knew it would happen—eventually.

Now, at last, there was a decent script, an interesting director and a legitimate producer—Ryder Wheeler. The film was titled *My Life as a Call Girl*, and she was to star in it. Santino was putting up most of the money, and he was also executive producer.

Eden was excited. It had taken a long time coming.

Zeko entered the room without knocking and stared at her. He had one real eye and one glass. This gave him a crazed look. He was six feet four inches tall and bald as a baby's ass. She was sure he spied on her when she took a bath in her beautiful marble bathroom with the glass wall and thick foliage outside. She could imagine him crawling through the prickly cactus to catch a peek. Perversely, she did not install window shades. Let him look if that's what turned him on. Occasionally she would part her legs and stroke her golden pussy, give him a real show.

"Yes?" she asked haughtily.

"I'm gonna get Mr. Bonnatti now," he said.

"Go ahead," she said dismissively.

It was past noon and she was not dressed. She wore silk pajamas and high-heeled mules. Santino always visited after Sunday lunch with his family, an event that seemed to make him exceptionally horny. In a perverse way she had grown to enjoy his attentions. He was everything the other men in her life had *not* been. He had an attitude of being able to get anything he wanted—and this seemed to make up for his lack of physical attributes. Sometimes he was a little kinky, and a couple of times he had gotten carried away and hurt her. But ultimately she felt she was still calling the shots. Santino obviously adored her—and so he should. Where else would a man like him find a woman like her?

She had found out how he made his money, and it wasn't from importing olive oil and coffee. Santino Bonnatti dealt in pornography and drugs. She shivered and glanced once more at Lennie's picture, then discarded the magazine and went into the bathroom to shower and dress. Santino liked her squeaky clean, in contrast to his wife, who, according to him, took only one bath a week.

After showering, she inspected her closet. So many clothes, and so little opportunity to wear them. Santino only took her out in public once in a while, although he had mentioned that soon they might be having dinner with Ryder Wheeler and the new director at Chasen's. She looked forward to the occasion and planned what to wear. The sensational red Halston, with the ruby necklace he had given her on her birthday. At times he was very generous. There had to be *some* compensations for putting up with a man like Santino Bonnatti.

42

Vitos called. Not a moment too soon.

"Let's party," Olympia said.

"Lasta time we party you go offa weeth Flash, you leava Vitos alone. No nice for Vitos."

"Did *I* do that? I didn't mean to."

"Now Vitos beeg star you want heem again. Why I shoulda?"

"Because you'll get your dick sucked just the way you like it."

"Oleeempeea!"

He collected her in a white stretch limo, and they partied all over town. For once, Olympia did not snub the lurking paparazzi. Instead she posed for them, one arm around Vitos's neck.

He responded nicely. In America, publicity was the name of the game. And who better to play it with than one of the richest women in the world?

Not that he considered Olympia a woman. She was girlish, like an excitable puppy. She was also a lot plumper than the last time they had been together. In bed it didn't bother him. He had always liked females with meat on their bones. Olympia had more than meat, she had potatoes and vegetables too. Undressed she was roly-poly.

He enjoyed making love to her. He sank his teeth into rolls of sweet-smelling flesh. Buried his head between suffocating thighs. Grazed among the wonders of her very large breasts.

She liked to climax several times. She was not easy to please, and at the end of two hours they were both bathed in sweat and exhausted.

"Why don't we get married?" Olympia suggested, bunching a pillow behind her and sitting up in bed.

Vitos smiled. Wonderful teeth. A matinee-idol smile. It was a shame his hair was thinning.

"Whatta you mean, Ol*eee*mpeea?"

She squinted at him. He was handsome but dumb. Flash, with all his drug problems, was ten times the man Vitos was.

"Married. M-A-R-R-I-E-D. You understand what I'm saying?"

She had figured it out. Marry Vitos. Piss Flash off—serve the scummy bastard right. When Flash had learned his lesson she would simply divorce Vitos. So it would cost a couple of million to pay Vitos off. Cheap at the price.

"You lika the idea marriage?" Vitos asked, stroking her thigh and thinking what marriage to Olympia Stanislopoulos would do for his PR rating.

"I think we make a beautiful couple. Don't you?"

"Mebee we do."

"Is that a yes?"

"Tomorrow I go Vegas. One week the Magiriano Hotel. You come with. We talk."

"That's a *hell* of an answer," she snapped. "I don't ask people to marry me every day of the week.'

"Ol*eee*mpeea," he said soothingly, "I beega star now. The American wimmen they lova me. I taka time, we do it. Whatta you say to *that?*"

She swallowed what she really wanted to say, and nodded understandingly. "Sure, Vitos, I'll come with you. I'll wait, and we'll see what happens. Right?"

He smiled happily. "Right, Ol*eee*mpeea. Right, my darling."

43

They sat in Judge Frederick Lester's courtroom for two days. During the luncheon recess on the second day, Carrie turned to Steven and said, "It's not him. I'm sure now."

Steven felt a chill of disappointment. Of all the candidates, Judge Frederick Lester was the one he had hoped would turn out to be his father.

"How can you be so sure," he asked in a low angry voice. "It's been over forty years."

"I *am* sure. I've stared at the man for two days." She was near tears, but she held them in check, not wanting Steven to see her distress.

They left the courthouse and stood on the steps outside.

Carrie gazed straight ahead and wondered what the result of Steven's quest for his past would be. She did not want to remember . . . but it was impossible to forget.

• • • • •

It was her friend Goldie's twenty-first birthday. She had a date with her boyfriend, Mel, and he was bringing along Freddy Lester. It was after show time, and the girl who had agreed to be Freddy's date had turned her ankle and was hobbling around in agony. Goldie looked beseechingly at Carrie. "Please!" she begged.

Carrie did not see how she could say no. After all, it was Goldie's birthday. Anyway, she had to learn to trust herself sometime; she couldn't be a recluse for the rest of her life. Nine years locked in an institution was enough. "Okay," she agreed reluctantly.

When they emerged from the theater, Mel and Freddy—who was quite good-looking and knew it—were waiting outside the stage door. They greeted the girls with enthusiasm.

"Hiya, fellas," said Goldie in her best Mae West voice.

"Happy birthday, gorgeous," replied Mel, grabbing her in a bear hug and kissing her full on the mouth.

Carrie and Freddy stared warily at each other.

"Whoops-a-daisy!" exclaimed Goldie, pushing him away. "You're spoiling my lipstick, you big oaf." She grinned at Freddy. "Hello, I'm Goldie, as if you didn't know. And this is Carrie— your dream date for the night. Aren't you *the lucky one!"*

Freddy's expression did not indicate that he was the lucky one at all. He nodded curtly at Carrie as the four of them set off down the alley to Mel's car. Once there, Mel opened the doors. Goldie climbed into the front, and Carrie got into the back while Mel and Freddy stood outside.

"What's the matter with you?" Carrie heard Mel ask his friend.

"Je-sus!" Freddy replied, in what was supposed to be a whisper. "She's a fucking dinge!"

"So?" replied Mel matter-of-factly. "Haven't you ever heard of black pudding?"

"Sure," replied Freddy, "but I've never taken it out in public."

"Aw, c'mon," laughed Mel. "Let's get this show on the road." They climbed into the car.

In the back, Carrie gazed miserably out the window. Their hateful words hung in her ears: Fucking dinge. Black pudding.

Her eyes filled with salty tears which slid silently down her cheeks. She kept her head determinedly turned toward the window so that no one would observe her misery.

They started the evening off in a small jazz joint on Fifty-second Street. Neat little combo playing, champagne flowing. Goldie was in high spirits, rarin' to go. And when Carrie stated she wanted to stick to fruit juice, she let her have it full blast. "Hey, listen, chickie. It's my birthday an' *I plan to have* fun. *If you're gonna moon around with a long face it's gonna spoil everything. Now have some champagne, for God's sake, an' put a smile on your face!"*

Carrie obliged. She had forgotten the potent taste of champagne, although when Whitejack, her former pimp, was flush, he had bought it by the bucket.

One glass turned into two, then three, and on to another club, and frothy white daiquiris which were so delicious she had at least four. After all, they were such little drinks, what harm could they do?

By the time the four of them piled into Clemmie's nightclub they were feeling no pain. Carrie and Freddy were the best of friends, giggling, laughing, dancing. And when his hands accidentally on purpose kept brushing against her breasts she didn't mind one bit. She felt free and alive. It was the first time in years she could honestly say she was living.

"You are sim'ly great, y'know that?" Freddy slurred.

She responded by locking her hands around his neck and gazing into his eyes. *Fucking dinge* no longer reverberated in her mind. "Thank you," she murmured sincerely. It had been a long time since anyone had told her that.

"No, I mean it," Freddy insisted, as if he was expecting her to argue.

"Hey," said Goldie, nudging Carrie. "You see that guy over there. That's *the* Gino Santangelo. He owns the joint. I met him once. He's a real *bad* boy."

Carrie's eyes swiveled to check him out. "I've taken on a lotta bad boys in my time," she boasted.

"Carrie!" exclaimed Goldie, giggling. "I've never seen you like this."

"Yeah. You don't know nothin'!"

Goldie nudged Mel. "She's really bombed."

Mel grinned. "How'd you like to make yourself fifty bucks. Carrie?"

"What didja have in mind, big boy?"

"I betcha fifty bucks y'can't make it with the great Mr. Santangelo."

"Yeah?" Her eyes gleamed. "You just lost yourself a bet."

Before any of them could stop her, she was on her feet and sashaying across the crowded club.

Goldie clapped her hand to her mouth in amazement. "Oh, my God, Mel. What have you done? This isn't like her at all."

He laughed nastily. "C'mon, doll, she ain't gonna do anything she hasn't done a hundred times before."

Freddy grimaced drunkenly. "Thanks a lot, old buddy," he complained.

Gino sat at his usual table. Cock of the walk. A constant stream of customers trailed over to pay homage.

He wore his customary dark three-piece suit, white silk shirt tasteful tie. His black hair was slicked down. The huge diamond ring on his pinky caught the light occasionally and gleamed expensively. The scar on his face gave him a slightly sinister look—that and his hard black eyes, which one woman had recently compared to Rudolph Valentino's.

He sipped his Scotch and inspected the female heading his way. Black. Exotic. And breasts that would stop traffic.

She reached his table and smiled. "Mr. Santangelo?"

"Yes."

"I hear you own this place. I just thought I'd stop by and tell you what a classy spot I think it is."

He smiled. He liked bold women. Sometimes. "Sit down, have a drink."

Carrie sat. She felt marvelous. Just drunk enough to believe she could own the world if she wanted to.

"Champagne?" he questioned.

"Naturally."

He clicked his fingers and a waiter was instantly by his side.

"A bottle of the best champagne."

Gino studied her. A rare, unusual beauty. One glass and he would take her home.

One more glass and she would go.

Later they were together in his apartment and the lovemaking was good. When it was over, he wanted her to leave. He got up from the bed. "Hey, hey, hey," he said, "betcha didn't learn to do that in school."

The champagne was still coloring Carrie's mind. She felt powerful and in control and oh, so good. Gino Santangelo had not used her. She had not used him. It was a mutually enjoyable experience.

Lazily she stretched. Her body felt reborn, as if someone had come along and hammered out all the tenseness.

"My car's downstairs. The driver'll take you home whenever you're ready," Gino said easily. "Oh—and here's a little present for you. Buy yourself something pretty."

He handed her a hundred dollars. He always gave the women he took to bed money for a gift. It was an idiosyncrasy of his, and no one ever objected.

"You sonofabitch!" she screamed, leaping up from the bed. "You think I'm a whore?"

"Hey, of course not . . ."

"How dare you! How *dare* you!" She struggled into her clothes, glaring at him and screaming like a wildcat.

"Hey, listen, if I thought you was a whore I'd have given you the going rate. This money's a present."

"Fuck you!" she screamed. "If I was a whore it would have cost you a hell of a lot more." And throwing the money in his face she stormed out of his apartment.

She ignored Gino's car and driver waiting downstairs, and began to walk along Park Avenue. She was sobering up in a hurry. Fucking dinge *was coming back to haunt her. And a red-hot fury was building inside her.*

What had she been thinking of, approaching Gino Santangelo like that? Who else but a whore would go over to a man's table, sit down and half an hour later share his bed?

Fucking Dinge. Whore. *The words flew through her head. She had tried so hard to be decent, and now—after one night— she was back where she had started.*

She walked seven blocks before she got a cab, and then the driver gave her a dubious look and said, "I ain't goin' to Harlem, honey."

"Nor am I, honey."

He didn't like that. He maintained a frosty silence all the way to the Village.

She paid him off and climbed the three flights of stairs to the roomy loft she shared with Goldie. Once inside, she was dismayed to find Freddy Lester in bed. Her bed. *She could not believe her eyes.*

Angrily she shook him awake. "Get out of here," *she said in a furious whisper.*

"Aw, c'mon, toots," *he mumbled, bleary-eyed and still drunk. He had no intention of getting up and going home.*

"Will you get out of my bed?" *she insisted.*

"Whyn't you come in an' join me? I've been waitin' all night," *he slurred.*

"Whyn't you drop dead?"

He gripped her wrist. "C'mon, sweetie pie, be a sport."

"Let go of me."

He was surprisingly strong. With ease he pulled her onto the bed.

"I'll scream if you don't stop," *she raged.*

"Don't you do that, sweetie." *And he placed the heavy palm of his hand over her mouth, stopping her from screaming and holding her down all at the same time. With his other hand he pulled up her skirt and ripped off her panties.*

She went numb. The strength just drained right out of her.

He took this as a sign of acquiescence, and somehow got out his penis and began jamming it into her.

She made little choking noises in her throat. His hand prevented her sobs of anguish from emerging. She willed her mind to go blank, and when he took his hand away she did not scream. She waited until he finished, and then said calmly, "That'll be thirty bucks, mister. Thirty big ones."

"What?" *he mumbled.*

"You screw a whore, you pay," *she said in a cold, unruffled manner.* "Especially when you screw a fucking dinge."

"But—"

"Pay or I holler rape."

He paid.

Six weeks later she realized with a dull shock that she was preg-

*nant. It was a bombshell, because she had always thought she was
unable to conceive. "You just ain't fertile," Whitejack had assured
her on many occasions.*

Now she was pregnant and she had no idea who the father was.

Gino Santangelo. Freddy Lester. It could be either.

She didn't know what to do or where to turn.

• • • • •

"Well," Steven said tightly. "I guess we go see the publisher
next. I'll arrange an appointment—you can say you want to
do a book on your life."

Carrie nodded numbly. Why was Steven torturing her like
this? She had been a good mother. He had never suffered because of the life she once lived. Even when she ran a brothel
and sold drugs for the notorious Enzio Bonnatti, she had always seen to it that he was never involved.

"When?" she asked listlessly.

"I'll arrange it as quickly as possible."

She nodded again, and for one brief moment hated her
good-looking, unfeeling son. What did he know about her
suffering? What did he even care?

44

They spoke on the telephone. Lucky and Costa.

"Uncle Costa?"

"Yes."

"I'm married."

"You're what?"

"I'm married again. To a very nice person, you'll like him."

"Do I have a choice?"

"Trust me."

"Ah, Lucky, I've always done that. Does your father know?"

"Uh . . . not yet. I'll tell him."

"When?"

"Soon."

A grunt of disapproval. "Who's the boy?"

A nervous laugh. "Well . . . er . . . he's not exactly a boy."

The phone rattled while Costa moved his position. "Who is he?"

She quickly changed the subject. "I've got another surprise for you."

"Isn't one enough?"

"You're a great-uncle."

"Thank you."

"No, no. A *great-uncle*."

"I don't think I understand. . . ."

"Yes, you do. I have a baby."

"Whose baby?"

"*My* baby."

She could hear the shock in his voice. Costa had always been old-fashioned. "*Yours*, Lucky? What does this mean?"

"It means," she said patiently, "that sixteen months ago I gave birth to a fantastic little boy named Roberto, and two days ago I married his father."

Silence.

A long silence.

Then: "Does Gino know?"

"Not yet."

A drawn-out sigh. "Not yet."

"Don't repeat me like that, I hate it!"

"What *should* I say?"

"Congratulations. Tell me it's wonderful, and that you can't wait to fly in and see me and Roberto. Because we're dying to see you."

"Sixteen months ago you had a baby, and now you're dying to see me. Hah!"

"Don't be mad," she pleaded. "You know I love you."

"What a way to show it! *I* feel bad enough. How do you think Gino is going to take it?"

"He won't care—he has his own life with Superwoman. She'll *hate* him being a grandpa. It'll remove the curl from her hair for a week!"

"Lucky—I think you'd better visit Gino. I don't recommend you tell him on the phone."

"I'm hardly a child," she said stubbornly. "I don't have to ask his permission to do anything."

"Who's talking permission?" Costa replied gently. "You can do whatever you want, but I think it would be a nice gesture, don't you? Gino's first grandchild, his only one . . . He's not so young . . . his heart's not in such great shape. . . ."

"Did something happen?" she asked quickly, frantically.

"No, no, nothing happened. But I spoke to him a few weeks ago and he sounded fed up and bored. He said he missed you."

"Did he really?"

"I don't make things up."

She was thoughtful for a moment. Why not visit Gino in California? Take Roberto. Oh, she couldn't wait to see his face when he saw such a gorgeous baby. *Her* baby. *Her* accomplishment. And she could tell him about the hotel and casino she was going to build in Atlantic City. At last. Without his help.

"I'll go," she decided impulsively. "Will you come too, Costa? I'd like that a lot."

He hesitated. "I don't know if it would be a good idea. There'll be you, the baby, your husband——"

"Oh, he won't come. He's off on a business trip, and won't be back for a week."

"I thought you said you only got married two days ago."

"So what? That doesn't make us joined at the hip. We both lead our own lives."

Costa sighed. "You young people . . ."

"Uh . . . he's not so young. . . ."

"How not so young?"

"I'll tell you when I see you."

. . . . .

Paige Wheeler screamed aloud. Several times. Gino Santangelo might be old. But he was dynamite.

Susan never made her scream. Nor did Ryder. But then, of course, Ryder was completely disinterested in sex. Only business turned him on—one of the reasons Paige enjoyed so many lovers.

She and Gino shared a large double bed in the Beverly Wilshire Hotel. Paige had booked the suite for a client two days earlier. The Beverly Wilshire was the perfect place for an assignation. Central. Luxurious. And if one was spotted in the lobby or thereabouts, well, one was merely visiting Tiffany's (located right next door) or lunching in the very fashionable El Padrino restaurant, or browsing Brentano's bookstore. Perfect alibis, all of them.

"Hmmm . . ." said Paige, sitting up in bed and stretching for a cigarette. "Now I know why Susan's always complaining."

"What's she got to complain about?" asked Gino, reaching across her full breasts for the matches and lighting her up.

Paige drew deeply on her cigarette. "Your . . . er . . . enthusiasm, stamina, and staying power."

"You gonna tell me you broads discuss sex?"

"What else is there to discuss?"

"An' she *complains?*"

"Foolish woman."

"Jeez!"

"Susan never did know how to enjoy herself. Poor Tiny had to go elsewhere all the time."

Gino felt like he was getting an education. Since marrying Susan, she had grown less and less willing in the bedroom. The more she pushed him away, the more he tried to please. Christ! He had thought there was something wrong with *him.* Like age had finally caught him with his pants down and he no longer had what it took. He had been knocking himself out, and now her best friend calmly informs him Susan doesn't like sex. Some act she must have put on in the beginning. Jeez!

"Is this a revelation, Gino?"

"A what?"

"Didn't you know?"

He felt ridiculous—a position he very rarely found himself in. "I guess I knew," he said guardedly, "otherwise I wouldn't be here with you today."

And he had to admit that being with a woman like Paige was a relief after two years of Susan. Paige stripped off all her inhibitions with her clothes. She was no great beauty, but she was an enormously sexy lady.

"Maybe I shouldn't have said anything," Paige said delicately.

"What would have stopped you?" Gino replied. "A tank?"

She lifted one leg from beneath the sheet and trailed her toes down his chest. "You . . ." she murmured huskily, "are a very raunchy man. And I . . . am a very raunchy woman. Do we have to waste our time talking about Susan?"

He lifted her toes to his mouth and sucked on them one by one. "Who's talkin'?" he growled.

45

Lennie, Jess, Isaac and his pretty wife, plus a reporter from *Rolling Stone*, flew to Vegas in a private plane, courtesy of Matt Traynor and the Magiriano Hotel. For about ten minutes they tried to hide the fact that they were impressed.

Lennie was the first to break. "I gotta tell you—if Alice could see me now she'd shit a brick!"

Isaac began to laugh. "How about *my* mother, man? She used to wash other people's floors, an' now her son's flyin' high. Wait until I tell *her!*"

His wife, Irena, shyly pulled out a camera and started to take snaps. "Nothing like a little proof," she murmured.

The reporter from *Rolling Stone* was not at all impressed. He flew in private jets with rock stars all the time. He was amused by their excitement and promised not to write about it.

"Sure," muttered Jess, the cynic of the group. "He'll make us out to be a bunch of hicks just off the bus."

"Who cares?" laughed Lennie. "All the reader remembers is seeing your name. That's what you're always telling me."

"Just so long as they spell it right," added Isaac, king of clichés.

Jess had negotiated the Magiriano appearance. She negotiated the money on most of Lennie's deals, but he still kept Isaac on and paid him ten percent commission.

"We don't need him anymore," she had pointed out to Lennie months ago. "He's taking a free ride."

"Let him ride," Lennie had said easily. "He was there for me when nobody wanted to know. We can afford it."

When Matt sweetened the Vegas deal with the private plane and other trimmings, Lennie had immediately suggested they take Isaac and Irena along. Jess agreed. She had nothing against them personally; they were a nice couple. It was only businesswise she got angry.

"I think," Lennie said, "tonight I am going to blow a thousand dollars at the tables. I always wanted to do that."

"How much are they paying you for this gig?" asked the *Rolling Stone* reporter.

"He never discusses his money or his sex life—just makes funny about other people's," interrupted Jess quickly.

Lennie fixed her with a look. Lately she was coming on a little too heavy. He could answer his own questions, and fully intended to. He needed no wet nurse.

• • • • •

"You look so . . . so different!" Jess exclaimed. "You lost weight. You look . . . great."

Matt smiled. "I dumped fifteen pounds. Cut my hair. And I jog—two hours a day. It keeps me sane."

Gone was the Matt Traynor of old. In his place was a thin, fit-looking man, with gray crew-cut hair and a flat stomach. Instead of the fancy clothes he used to favor, he wore plain dark slacks and a white open-neck shirt.

"No gold chains." Jess grinned.

"Had 'em melted down and sent to Sammy Davis, Jr."

"I bet he was thrilled."

"Hasn't stopped calling me since."

They exchanged smiles.

"And you?" he asked. "Miss Success Story. When are they writing you up in *Forbes?*"

"When I let 'em."

"Seriously, Jess. I'm very pleased for you."

"Thanks."

She had dressed especially carefully. He hadn't said a word about how *she* looked.

While minions were frothing about showing Lennie and the others to their suites, he offered her a drink.

"In your apartment?" she asked jokingly.

"I gave it up. I live here now."

"Lead the way."

• • • • •

Lennie's penthouse suite left nothing to be desired. Water bed. Mirrored ceiling. Jacuzzi. Thick pile carpet. Color televisions everywhere—including the john. A magnificent terrace with breathtaking views.

Everything

Except

Eden.

He had thought—only for a moment—what if Eden were here, waiting for him?

Who needed her?

There was a fully stocked bar and plenty of beautiful, available showgirls downstairs. He was a star now. He could choose anyone he desired.

• • • • •

Not an initialed glass in sight. No fake marble, ornamental gilt or dimmed pink lighting either. Just a modern functional penthouse with clean lines and a masculine feel.

"Drink?" Matt asked.

"Anything cold and nonalcoholic," Jess replied, looking around appreciatively. "You've changed your style of living," she commented.

"It was about time," he replied, fixing her a tall glass of grapefruit juice with shaved ice from behind a high-tech bar.

She accepted the drink and sipped it slowly. "Ummm, delicious."

"I'll tell room service."

"Is that how you live now? All room service and never having to do anything for yourself?"

"I run the hotel, Jess. I'm on call twenty-four hours a day. I never have *time* to do anything else."

"Nothing?" she joked.

"Well . . . this and that."

They laughed, and neither could think of anything else to say. So, naturally, they both spoke at once.

"Do you think—?" Jess started.

"I thought that later—" Matt began.

A buzzer sounded on one of the three phones located on the bar.

"Excuse me," he said.

"Sure." She sipped her drink and watched him as he took the call. They were being so polite to each other. It was as if they were vague acquaintances, not two people who had shared the tragedy of her life. She scarcely ever allowed herself to think about the nightmare of losing Simon. But she would always be aware that it was Matt who got her through the first forty-eight hours. If he hadn't been there for her she would probably have gulped down the nearest bottle of pills and ended it all.

He put the phone down with a grimace.

"What's up?" she asked.

"Vitos Felicidade has added to his entourage. He's on his way from New York, and he's bringing Olympia Stanislopoulos, her child and nanny. I'm running out of penthouse suites."

"Oh, shame!"

"Still a smart-ass."

"Yes. And look where it's got me."

"I have to meet with my reservations manager."

"I understand."

"He's on his way up."

She set her glass down and walked to the door. "I was finished anyway."

He hurried after her. "Tonight I want to host a dinner for Lennie and his friends."

"I'll check with him."

"Call me soon. Let me know how many."

She nodded and departed.

Once the door was shut behind her, Matt sighed with relief. He had been determined not to make a fool of himself, and he thought he had handled it pretty well. It was obvious from past experience that Jess was never going to regard him as anything more than a good friend, and even though he still wanted her as much as ever, he had decided to cool it. He was too old to start chasing after someone who didn't want him. Too old and too wise.

Jess checked her reflection in the mirrored wall of the elevator. She thought she looked pretty good. L.A. suntan. Jose Eber short haircut. A green cotton jumpsuit that complemented her orange hair. High-heeled shoes that added inches and made her into a grownup.

Hmmmm . . . he hadn't said one thing about the way she looked.

Not that she cared.

Why the hell *should* she?

But she *had* enjoyed his having the hots for her. Oh, yes, she remembered how his hands used to shake when he was near her, the way he looked at her all the time—and quite frankly, for two years she had missed that ardent attention.

Now he was Mister Businesslike. Charming and nice, but where were the shaking hands and the lingering looks?

Maybe he had only liked her when she was Little Miss Nobody.

He *did* look good. Was it possible that now he wasn't hot for her, *she* had an itch for him?

Nonsense.

•　•　•　•　•

Being back in his hometown as a star was very pleasing to Lennie. And the timing was perfect. Cover of *People*. Local boy makes good. Jack Golden's kid—Lennie. Bigger than his father ever dreamed of being.

Briefly he thought of Alice. She would have loved coming back like a big shot. But she was so busy bitching about her own career (what career?) that he hadn't even bothered to tell her about his return appearance at the Magiriano.

Two years before, he had roared out of town busted out and pissed off. He would have gladly strangled Matt Traynor then. But time passes . . . things happen. . . . Jess had explained it wasn't Matt's fault. Some bitch upstairs had ordered him axed. Lucky Santangelo—whoever she might be. "The lady boss," Jess had whispered.

Screw *her*. Apparently she had nothing more to do with the hotel—he had made sure of that before agreeing to return.

Now he was back. And they were giving him all the home comforts a star grows to love and expect. Private plane. Twenty-four-hour limo and driver. A bodyguard (did he really *need* a bodyguard?). And the pencil.

Ah . . . the famed Las Vegas pencil. It was not an actual pencil—just permission to sign for anything he wanted and never having to pay. Food, drink, room service . . . whatever. Oh, the times he and Jess had dreamed of having that power. Only high rollers and big stars were given the privilege. He was more pleased about the pencil than anything else.

Jess arrived in great spirits. He had been a little worried about her returning to Vegas and the memories, but she genuinely appeared to have put it all behind her. Not a mention of Wayland or the baby.

"Well, well, well!" she exclaimed, looking around at the baskets of flowers, the champagne cooling on ice, and the huge dish of exotic fruit sliced and laid out on a buffet table. "I see they welcomed you properly."

"Hey"—he grinned—"they're lucky to have me. If I'd held a grudge they'd *never* have gotten me back."

Jess picked at a slice of papaya. "Matt wants to have a dinner for you tonight, and whoever you want to invite."

"How *is* your boyfriend?"

"Don't say that," she snapped, a little too quickly, causing Lennie to raise an eyebrow.

"Where's your sense of humor, monkey face?" he asked.

"Don't *call* me that!" she yelled.

He held up his hands, making a peaceful gesture. "I come as a friend. Have mercy."

She couldn't help laughing.

"Hey," he said, "I want to use the fucking pencil, only I've got everything I need."

"It's tough bein' a star," she commented dryly.

"Let's go to the drugstore. I have this insane urge to sign."

"Call down. Stars have things sent."

"You're so full of shit. Let's go."

He pulled her by the hand and they left the suite.

The drugstore, located at swimming-pool level, sold everything from paper panties to three-thousand-dollar mink bikinis. Lennie grabbed a wire basket and started throwing things in: toothpaste, toothbrushes, after-shave, shampoo.

Jess trailed patiently behind him. "Do you really need all this?" she asked.

"Kid—it's free," he mumbled, filling one basket and starting on another.

"Lennie," she suggested, "if we're going for freebees let's go for the good stuff." She dragged him over to the cosmetics counter. "Stock me up with Estée Lauder," she commanded, getting into the spirit of it all. "And Dior. And Clinique."

They filled the second wire basket, and a third.

"I think that's enough," Jess said, when he started piling in a month's supply of candy.

"But I don't have everything I need," he objected, grabbing three boxes of Tampax and a handful of tastefully wrapped Durex.

Jess began to break up, and when Jess laughed, everybody noticed. Her laugh still sounded like that of a crazed hyena.

"Oh, shit!" said Lennie, as a few stares came his way.

"Aren't you on the cover of *People* magazine?" asked a bronzed woman in shorts that displayed large cellulite-dimpled thighs.

"Oh. You're Leonard Goldman," announced a tall brunette—as if he didn't know.

He grinned engagingly. A crowd began to form.

"Who's de jerk?" snapped a red-faced New Yorker.

"Nobody," replied his Spandexed girlfriend.

Lennie turned to Jess for help. She was bent double by the magazines.

"Can I have your autograph?" sighed a winsome little thing. "I watch you every week. I'm your favorite."

They were moving in on him—a wall of people. He was being crowded into a corner, and suddenly he felt vulnerable and under attack. Pens and slips of paper were shoved at him. He scribbled his name a few times. Shit! If this was what stardom was all about, you could shove it.

A pregnant girl touched his face. "For luck," she giggled; while an older woman hissed out of the corner of her drooping lips, "God is watching you. You'd better be careful. God doesn't forgive."

He wanted out. He needed rescuing. Fortunately Jess got herself together and grabbed a security guard. Together they hustled Lennie through the throng and rushed him to the nearest elevator.

"That crowd weren't nothin'," the elderly guard sneered. "Once I hadda rescue Elvis. They tore his pants off. They woulda killed him with love. Took eight of us to get him in a limo. *Those* were the good old days."

Back in the suite Lennie said ruefully, "I never did get to sign."

Jess grinned. "What were you going to do with eight packets of Durex anyway?"

"Fuck a lot."

"So what else is new?"

46

Vitos had not expected Olympia to insist on bringing her child and nanny to Vegas. But insist she did. "Brigette will be my bridesmaid," she said. "I cannot get married without her. What kind of a mother do you think I am?"

The truth of the matter was, Olympia did not want Nanny Mabel and Brigette in New York answering the phone and telling tales. She wanted them with her, where she could keep an eye on them. Now, when Flash called, he would get the answering service, and they wouldn't know where she was. Let the scumbag suffer. He wasn't winning *her* back so easily.

It never occurred to Olympia that he might not want her back. She sailed through life filled with supreme confidence— easy when you could buy and sell most people.

Before leaving New York she contacted her lawyer. "Courier me a marriage document," she demanded. "You know what I mean—a prenuptial agreement."

"You're not getting married again, are you?" he groaned incredulously.

"I might be."

"Please, can't you wait until we can discuss this properly? Your financial affairs are complicated. It'll take time to work out."

"I want it now. Immediately."

She had never been to Las Vegas before, and it both fascinated and repelled her. "All these dreadful people," she complained to Vitos, as they were whisked through the lobby with their accompanying entourages.

He nodded like a puppet, blazing the perfect Felicidade smile at his fans.

"Everyone looks so . . . so . . . cheap," she said in the elevator.

"These pipples buy my records," he remarked sagely.

"They would!" she muttered under her breath.

They were placed in adjoining suites. Vitos had the more lavish one, which infuriated Olympia. She decided to call Lucky Santangelo and complain. Dimitri had mentioned that Lucky owned the Magiriano. It would be interesting to see her again. . . .

What did she look like? Was she married? Did she have kids?

Once settled, Olympia sent Nanny Mabel off with Brigette to explore, and then she called the front desk. "This is Olympia Stanislopoulos," she announced imperiously. "Kindly tell Lucky Santangelo I wish to see her."

"Miz Santangelo's no longer with us," said the operator.

"Where is she?"

"I'm afraid I can't help you, ma'am."

"Who can?"

"Perhaps the manager, or Mr. Traynor."

"Have either of them call me. Immediately."

She felt strangely disappointed. It would have been interesting to see Lucky again. Or would it? They had shared so many memories of a carefree summer once, long ago. Lucky had been her best friend. But who needed friends? They always let you down eventually.

• • • • •

Vitos spoke heatedly to his manager in Spanish. The gist of the conversation was his marital situation. He had been married at eighteen to a local girl in his Spanish hometown. When his star began to rise in America, the marriage was annulled. Now he wished to marry Olympia. How legal was the annulment? There were no children. And where were the documents?

His manager grimaced. This was a great opportunity. Big as Vitos was becoming, marriage to Olympia Stanislopoulos could only mean more fame and acceptance in America—the Promised Land. It was not something to be rushed into and blown.

"We must obtain the best legal advice," he warned. "And I will order a search for the papers."

"Quickly," Vitos cautioned. He had a hunch Olympia was not the most patient of women.

• • • • •

Brigette eyed the busy gambling tables, the scurrying crowds, the scantily clad cocktail waitresses, the over-made-up hookers. "This place *stinks!*" she informed Nanny Mabel loudly.

"Shhh," Nanny admonished.

"Stinks!" yelled Brigette. "Stinks! Stinks! Stinks! I hate it."

Privately Nanny Mabel agreed, but she wasn't about to hear it from her precocious charge. The child became more like her mother every day.

"Be quiet," scolded Nanny Mabel.

"Won't!" screamed Brigette. "Can't make me. This place is *stiiiinking!!*"

"If you misbehave here I'll be forced to tell your mother. And she'll—"

Before she could continue further, a grim-faced security woman packing a gun appeared. "Shut the kid up," she commanded.

Nanny Mabel shot Brigette a warning look.

"I'm not going to shut up," Brigette yelled. "*I'm* going to do whatever *I* like. So there, you stupid fat pig!"

"Oh no you're not," said the guard.

"Oh yes I am," said Brigette.

"Oh dear," said Nanny Mabel.

• • • • •

Matt Traynor presented himself at Olympia's door.

"Who are you?" she demanded, pulling a Chinese robe tightly around her.

"I run the hotel, Miss Stanislopoulos."

"You got my message I presume?"

"What message?"

"About Lucky Santangelo."

"No, I'm afraid I didn't."

"Well, where is she?"

"Miss Santangelo is no longer connected with the Magiriano."

Olympia frowned. "Too bad."

Matt did not appreciate being kept at the door like a delivery boy. "May I come in?"

"What for?"

Matt decided he did not like the plump blond heiress with the petulant expression and all the charm of a bad-tempered shopgirl. "We have a slight problem with your daughter. . . ."

"How boring! What's she done?"

"Kicked a security woman, tried to dismantle a blackjack table and—"

"Where is she?" Olympia interrupted.

"We have her downstairs in an office. She's creating a considerable disturbance. She refuses to er . . . be quiet . . . until you collect her."

"God!" Olympia was visibly irritated. "What about her nanny? Why doesn't *she* deal with her?"

"She seems to have no control of the situation."

Olympia rolled her eyes heavenward. "This is most inconvenient," she said testily, as if it were Matt's personal fault. "Wait. I'll have to dress."

She slammed the door in his face and left him angrily marching up and down the corridor for ten minutes. Eventually she emerged and they proceeded downstairs in silence.

Brigette sat moodily in a small office chanting "Las Vegas stinks! Las Vegas stinks!" at the top of her voice.

Nanny Mabel, red in the face, hovered outside, while the grim-looking female security guard stood at attention.

Olympia fixed her daughter with an icy-blue stare, and she shut up.

"What's been going on?" Olympia demanded.

Brigette produced a full flood of ever-ready tears. "Mama,

Mama," she cried, "these people have been *so* mean to me. Really really *mean*."

"Excuse *me*," said the security woman. "This child needs a good spanking. She's rude and spoiled and—"

"I'm not interested in your opinion," Olympia said dismissively. "Come along, Brigette. It's time for bed." She glared at Matt. "My daughter is tired, it's been a long day."

With that she took Brigette by the hand and swept out, a nervous Nanny Mabel trailing in her wake.

47

Carrie Berkeley had immense style. For many years, while married first to Bernard Dimes, and then to Elliott Berkeley, she had been a celebrity—the sort of celebrity who never really does anything but is always mentioned in gossip and society columns and is often photographed for the fashion magazines. Several years in a row she had appeared in *Harper's Bazaar* as one of the "Ten Most Beautiful Women in America."

When she divorced Elliott and went to live permanently on Fire Island, she retired from public life. But hers was still a well-known name, and it was no problem to arrange an appointment with Fred E. Lester of Lester and Wellington, Publishers.

Steven wanted to accompany her but she refused to let him. "I'm quite capable of deciding whether it's him or not," she said coldly.

Lately that was how she felt about Steven. Cold, withdrawn. He was her son, but she would never forgive him for what he was putting her through. Never.

What did it *matter* which one his father was? They were both bastards. Who cared?

Fred E. Lester sat behind an oak desk in a large, comfortable office. He was tall and broad-shouldered, bald with encircling flurries of white hair, and a healthy weekend tan. He was in his late sixties. He rose when Carrie was ushered into his office by a solicitous secretary, walked around his desk, and with outstretched hands said, "I don't suppose you remember me, it was a long time ago, but . . ."

She felt a moment of sheer panic. *It was him.*

The blood drained from her face and a sickness filled the pit of her stomach.

". . . a charity ball," he was saying. "It must have been some twenty years ago. You still look exactly the same. Lovely as ever."

Thankfully she slumped into a chair. *It wasn't him.* Fred E. Lester looked nothing like the college boy of so many years ago. How was it going to be possible to recognize a man she had only spent one night with forty-two years ago? Damn Steven. Why was he putting her through this?

"Coffee? Tea? Perhaps a drink?" Fred Lester asked.

His secretary stood by the door expectantly.

"Tea," Carrie said quietly. "With lemon."

"Make that two," Fred said, sitting down behind his desk, and playing with a silver pen.

Carrie tried to recover her composure. She glanced around the office. There were framed covers of books on all the walls.

"My successes," Fred said with a modest smile. "In this business you boast about your successes and try to hide your failures."

She smiled politely.

"Now then," Fred said, clasping his hands together. "Let's hope that you and I are going to have a big success."

"I beg your pardon?"

"You *do* want to write a book for us, don't you?"

She remembered that it *was* the reason she was sitting in his office. Steven had called and made the appointment. "Mrs. Carrie Berkeley has an interesting idea for a book," he had said, and an appointment was immediately forthcoming.

"I have a few ideas," she faltered.

"That's where it all begins." He beamed.

She stared at his bald head. It shone, as though someone had polished it with a soft cloth. Whitejack's head had shone. Black and shiny. Sometimes he oiled it. "Makes all the pretty ladies cum," he used to say with a wicked grin, flashing his large white teeth.

"My hunch is that you would like to write a beauty book," Fred Lester said. "Am I right?"

"Beauty and . . . uh . . . maybe fashion, style," she replied, picking up on his idea.

"Couldn't be better. The timing is just right."

He had very nice eyes. Kindly brown eyes. On his desk there were three silver frames containing family pictures.

She felt secure with him. In a funny way he reminded her of Bernard, her first husband.

"Now then," he said, "why don't you tell me what you have in mind, and we can proceed from there. Does that sound reasonable?"

She nodded, and racked her brain for ideas.

48

Costa met Lucky at the L.A. airport. He fussed over Roberto as if *he* was the proud grandpa.

"You haven't told Gino, have you?" she demanded.

"I arrived late last night," Costa said. "He doesn't even know *I'm* here."

"Good. We'll really surprise him."

She checked into a bungalow at the Beverly Hills Hotel, and immediately called Gino.

To her disappointment he was out. Now that she had decided to tell him, she was too impatient for roadblocks. It was only a matter of time before Dimitri would make an announcement, and she really did not want Gino reading about her marriage in a newspaper.

"When will he be back?" she asked the maid.

"Later," the woman said unhelpfully.

Later could mean any time. She wondered where he was. What did a person who wasn't in the movie business *do* in L.A.? Gino had always been so active. Didn't he miss the hustle of Vegas? Surely he couldn't spend his days strolling up and down Rodeo Drive.

She and Costa lunched out by the pool, while Roberto napped.

"Well, Lucky," Costa asked, "when are you going to tell me? Who is this man you have married?"

She took a deep breath. "Dimitri Stanislopoulos," she announced.

"No, really, who?" he persisted.

She shrugged. "Dimitri."

Costa shook his head and looked grim.

"It's not a crime for crissakes," Lucky said quickly. "So he's a few years older than me. Big deal."

"I wish your Aunt Jennifer were alive," he said dourly.

"We *all* wish she were alive. But she's not, and even if she were, she wouldn't be telling me what to do."

"You've been on your own too long," Costa said. "You've never had anyone to turn to. When you were growing up you should have had a mother. Someone to confide in. A—"

"Will you quit with the dirge? I *like* being on my own."

"Dimitri Stanislopoulos is an old man."

"So are you. Does that make you a terrible person?"

"Lucky, Dimitri Stanislopoulos is a father figure. Don't you see what you've done? You've—"

"Fuck you, Costa." Her black eyes blazed anger. "I expected a lecture from Gino, but I don't have to take this crap from you. I am nearly thirty years old. Will everyone stop telling me what to do?"

She stormed from the table.

• • • • •

Paige Wheeler had this little trick of holding him inside her like a vise. "I used to go with a snatch quack," she informed Gino when he asked her where she'd learned it.

"A what?"

"A gynecologist. He taught me everything I know. The man was an expert. Well, he was looking at it all day, I guess he picked up a thing or two."

Gino liked her little trick. It meant he could go for as long as he wanted, and then she would take over, holding him, keeping him hard, until he was ready to make it again. Gino never liked to rush. He genuinely loved pleasing women. It gave him a real charge to observe their abandonment and pure lustful pleasure. That's why marriage to Susan was such a deep disappointment. Paige was right—Susan did not like sex. Why hadn't he noticed the signals *before* marrying her? Now he was stuck in a marriage he really didn't want.

Every day he thought about getting out, calling Lucky and saying, "Hey—kid. I was wrong. Let's go take over Atlantic

City, an' build our own hotel. Let's set the fuckin' world on fire!"

It wasn't as simple as that. Susan never set a foot wrong. She was solicitous and attentive. She watched his diet. Made sure he exercised. Had the cook prepare all his favorite meals.

And she looked good, too. Attractive, groomed, gowned to perfection. They attended all the best social events, including every A-rated party.

Apart from sex, Susan was the perfect wife. She was also suffocatingly boring.

He hated Beverly Hills. He hated the whole phony social bit. He hated the A-parties filled with senile geriatrics. Same people. Same conversation. Same fucking bullshit.

Gino Santangelo wanted out. He just had to figure a way to do it.

• • • • •

"Oh, hi, Susan," Lucky said. She *would* have to get stuck with Grace Kelly. "Is Gino around?"

"Are you here? In California?"

No. I'm at the north fucking pole. Where does it sound like I'm calling from? "Yes. As a matter of fact I am."

"How nice."

"Isn't it?" Beat of three. "Can I speak to Gino?"

"Sorry, dear. He's out."

"Will he be back soon?"

"One never knows with Gino."

"Very true." At least she knew that much about him. "I'll call back later."

"Good."

Sure. You're really pleased I'm here. Not even a "Where are you staying?" Or "We must get together."

She prowled the bungalow. Roberto was out with CeeCee by the pool. She didn't know where Costa was. She didn't care.

Oh, yes, she did. He was concerned about her. How could

she fault him for that? Dimitri *was* thirty-five years older than she. Costa would just have to see them together, and then he would realize the relationship worked.

. . . . .

Paige dressed. She wore delightfully whorish clothes and drove a gold Porsche, which Ryder had bought her for Christmas. Sometimes Gino puzzled about Susan's friendship with her. She was so unlike Susan's other friends—the polished Hollywood wives with their designer clothes, flawless facelifts and narrow code of ethics.

"Susie likes me because I'm outrageous and fun," Paige confided. She didn't add that Susan liked her because they had been having a hot and heavy affair for several years.

Paige realized she might be playing a dangerous game, bedding both the wife *and* the husband. She wouldn't mind giving up Susan. But Gino was irresistible, and great in bed.

It seemed unlikely they would confide in each other, so she saw no pressing reason to surrender either.

"Tomorrow," Gino said. "Same place. Same time."

"Impossible. I promised Ryder I would go with him to Las Vegas. He has to entertain one of his investors."

Gino threw her an incredulous look. "You're goin' to Vegas an' you didn't tell me? You gotta be kiddin'. I used to *own* that friggin' town. I coulda got you the finest reservations, the best tables, anything you wanted."

Paige applied a bright red lipstick to her full lips. "Ryder spent his erstwhile youth ferrying young ladies to Vegas for dirty weekends. I don't think he'd appreciate any suggestions about where we should stay and what we should do."

Gino shrugged. "You're missin' out. There's only one way go to Vegas, an' that's with me."

"Would we take your wife and my husband, or leave them behind?"

He ignored the dig. "When d'you get back?" he asked.

"Wednesday."

"We'll meet Thursday. Same place. Same time."

"I can't. I'm working."

"So cancel."

"I'm doing a Bel Air estate for a bisexual movie star, and he's *very* demanding."

He grabbed her around the waist and rocked against her.

"So am I."

She laughed. God! He must have been the horniest man alive when he was young. As it was, he was sexier and had more staying power than a lot of men half his age.

"Yes, I know. That's why I need a few days off from your amorous attentions."

He narrowed his eyes. "Who else're you screwin'?"

She fluffed out her frizzed hair. "Whoever drops their pants for me. Just like you."

He grinned. "You're some broad. You don't jump. I like that."

"Thank you. I do love compliments."

• • • • •

Rodeo Drive was not her scene, but Lucky gave it a shot anyway. She wandered into Lina Lee and bought a deep purple leather jacket with huge shoulders. She studied the windows of Fred the jeweler's, and then strolled down the street to Giorgio's, where she purchased several drop-dead dresses. Shopping was not one of her great passions—she preferred to live in jeans and shirts—but occasionally she indulged. When she did dress up, she loved extravagant outfits. The way rock stars dressed appealed to her. They had a certain style, a freedom, a knockout approach. Recently she had watched Flash on television. He wore black leather, trailing white scarves and gold earrings. He looked sensational.

Dimitri had mentioned that Olympia was living with Flash. What a couple they must be!

Lucky was quite looking forward to seeing her again. Growing up she had had no other girlfriends, only Olympia, and for a while, they had been so very close. . . .

What if Olympia was furious that she'd married Dimitri? What if—

Oh, shit. She hated playing "What if?" It was a stupid game. When Dimitri returned from his business trip, they would announce their marriage. Olympia would either like it or not. Whatever.

• • • • •

"Lucky telephoned you," Susan said.

Gino had been home for an hour. "Why didn't you tell me before?" he asked angrily.

Susan gestured vaguely. "I didn't think it was important."

"Did she say?"

"Did she say what?"

He tried to hold his temper. "Whether it was important or not?"

"No."

He started toward his study.

"She's not in New York," Susan added.

"Where is she?"

"I think she said something about being out here."

"What's her number?"

"I don't know."

Now he was really furious. "Why didn't you get it?"

Two bright red spots appeared on Susan's porcelain cheeks. "I'm *not* your secretary, Gino."

"Then don't take my friggin' calls."

He stamped into his study. Lucky was in town and he didn't know where to reach her. What was the matter with his wife?

• • • • •

Lucky apologized to Costa when she returned from her shopping trip. He hugged her and told her he was concerned only for her well-being. They sat in the Polo Lounge and she started to confide in him about her plans.

He watched her intently. She was so like her father. Ah . . . he could remember the good old days as if they were only last week. Gino—with the same enthusiasm and bright-eyed optimism. They were both go-getters. But Lucky had grabbed what she had wanted in a man's world. It wasn't easy. Being married to a man as rich and powerful as Dimitri Stanislopoulos could only help.

At five o'clock Lucky looked at her watch and said, "Let's call Gino." A waiter brought a phone to their table and she requested the number. A maid answered. "Mr. Santangelo" Lucky said.

"One moment, please."

She held her breath. It was several months since they had spoken. She loved him. She hated him. Goddamn it, she *missed* him.

His greeting was deceptively casual. "Hey—kid."

"Hey—Gino."

"Where are you?"

"L.A."

"Where?"

"The Beverly Hills Hotel."

"So, you don't let anyone know you're comin'?"

"Why? Would you have sent a brass band to the airport?"

"Smart mouth."

She sensed a warmth that had been missing. She knew him well enough. He was genuinely delighted to hear from her. "I've got a surprise for you," she said quickly.

"Y'know I don't like surprises."

"This one you'll like—love."

"Yeh?"

"Yeh."

"How y'bin, kid?"

"Pretty good. And you?"

"Makin' out."

"Costa's with me."

"Costa! Jeez! Whyn't you both come over?"

"We'd love to."

• • • • •

Susan was sitting at her dressing table removing the day's makeup with cold cream.

Gino bounced in. "Lucky an' Costa are comin' for dinner Tell the cook."

"We're eating out tonight," she informed him.

"Change it."

"I can't do that. We're going to a sit-down dinner for twenty at April Crawford's."

"Call her. Tell the old bag we can't make it."

Susan continued to tissue off her makeup. "April Crawford is *not* an old bag," she said calmly. "April Crawford is a fine and respected actress, a *real* movie star of the old school. We can't possibly cancel, it's her birthday." She crumpled the used tissue and leaned back. "I wrote this engagement in your appointment book three weeks ago. It's on your desk."

"Hey—my daughter's in town. She's comin' over. *That's* what we're doin' tonight."

"Is that the same daughter you haven't heard from in months? The same daughter who never calls or writes?"

He didn't need Susan's criticism of Lucky. His eyes were hard. "Hey—big mouth," he said. "*You* go to April Crawford's. I'll stay here. Tell the cook to fix something."

A moment's pause. Susan knew exactly how far she could go. She got up, went to him and placed an affectionate kiss on his cheek. "Sorry, darling," she whispered. "I wouldn't think of going without you. I'll have Cook prepare something delicious. *Of course* we must be here for Lucky and Costa. Excuse my sarcasm, it's just that sometimes I get so . . . hurt for you. A proper daughter would—. Oh, forget I said anything."

"Yeh. Why don't I just forget it."

49

Dinner was a noisy affair which took place in the Rio restaurant at the hotel. There was Lennie, high on too many shots of vodka. There were Isaac and Irena. There was the *Rolling Stone* reporter with a young female photographer mysteriously known as Mouth. There was Matt, with an attractive thirtyish divorcee. And there was Jess. Alone. Sober. And suffering from a double dose of anger.

First, she was angry because Matt had a date.

Second, she was angry at herself for *being* angry.

"Why don't you loosen up?" Lennie hissed. "You're acting like an old maid at a wedding."

"Why don't you butt out?" Jess suggested.

Mouth busied herself with a string of cameras. She was intelligently pretty, with spiked hair, sharp eyes, and pointed breasts bra-less beneath a loose T-shirt.

Isaac and Lennie swapped stories while Irena listened admiringly.

Matt's date looked out of place in a cocktail dress and mink wrap.

The *Rolling Stone* reporter watched everyone and everything.

Matt played genial host.

Jess tried to be pleasant and did not succeed.

From the restaurant they all went up to Lennie's suite. Isaac produced some good grass, which made Matt uncomfortable and he left, his date hanging onto his arm.

Everyone turned on except Jess. She wasn't in the mood.

They played music, drank a little, smoked a little. And later Lennie found out why the photographer was nicknamed Mouth. She left his suite at five in the morning with a smile and some great photos.

He couldn't sleep. He went down to the pool and did laps. Walked outside the hotel and inspected his billboard. Lennie Golden. In twenty-foot letters. Lennie Golden. Thousands of twinkling lights. It felt unreal. He handed a passing drunk ten bucks for luck and breakfasted in the coffee shop. It was too early for the fans. Only a few die-hard all-night gamblers and some ragged-looking hookers.

Opening night tonight. Sharing the limelight with Vitos Felicidade. He wasn't nervous. Performing never gave him the jitters. In fact, being onstage, communicating with an audience, was the only place he felt really secure and in charge. When he was a kid at school he could grab attention any time he wanted by telling dirty jokes—the dirtier the better. Jess used to feed him material. Jess had the filthiest mouth of anyone he knew. He loved her. She was his only real family. Count Alice out.

He finished breakfast and returned to his suite. He had a busy schedule. There was an early-morning rehearsal. Lunch with the *Rolling Stone* reporter for an "in depth" talk. Two scripts of "The Springs" to check out. And another photo session with Mouth.

He was sorry he'd allowed her to do the things to him she did so well. Jesus! If he was a female he'd have the reputation of being the easiest lay in town. What he really needed with a woman was a solid relationship. He'd had it with one-night stands. How about someone to care for him and share his success? Someone who didn't just jump into bed with him because he had some half-assed name.

Eden.

Fuck Eden.

Wouldn't you just love to?

No.

For a moment she was on his mind.

But only for a moment.

Things were getting better.

• • • • •

Olympia was bored. Acutely. She had come to Vegas to spite Flash and marry Vitos. But Vitos seemed more concerned with his stupid opening night, rehearsing and constantly gargling with some disgusting honey concoction. Now she was stuck out by the pool with a disapproving nanny and a truculent daughter, and she had nothing to do except sulk.

Clad in a white one-piece swimsuit, rolls of excess flesh peeping out everywhere, she lay on a striped chaise under a protective umbrella. She had purchased piles of magazines, but watching the passing parade was definitely more interesting. It had been a long time since Olympia had sat beside a public swimming pool. She could have stayed upstairs on her private terrace, but it was so hot, and besides, Brigette had asked her to come with her to the pool, and it was one of Olympia's "I am a perfect mother" days.

"Let's take a swim, Mama," Brigette suggested. She was indeed a lovely-looking little girl—it was a shame her personality did not match her looks.

"Not right now, dear," said Olympia. "I need to rest. Nanny will take you."

Nanny Mabel, awkward in an old-fashioned bathing suit, glared at her boss.

Olympia was oblivious to the baleful stare. She was too busy eying the bikini-clad lifeguards, whose bulging crotches received her full attention.

· · · · ·

Lunchtime. And Lennie was safely settled with the *Rolling Stone* reporter.

Walking through the lobby, Jess bumped into Matt.

"How's everything?" he asked.

She smiled brightly. "Fine."

"Nothing you need?"

"Can't think of anything."

"Is Lennie happy?"

"He seems to be."

"What time did the party end?"

It slipped out before she could help it. "I thought *you* were the one having a party."

He laughed easily and said, referring to his date of the night before, "Tina's an old friend."

Again she couldn't help herself. "*Old* being the operative word."

He laughed again. "How about a snack?" He took her arm, assuming she would say yes.

"I'm too busy."

"You've got to eat."

"I'll have something sent up. I have calls coming in from L.A."

"Diligent lady."

"I enjoy my work."

"You've certainly done all right for Lennie."

"He would have done it without me. He's brilliant. You should have spotted that when you first had him here."

Matt frowned. Sure Lennie Golden was good. But why did Jess gleam when she talked about him? Why did her whole face light up?

She was sleeping with him. He knew it for sure. And that meant he, Matt Traynor, didn't stand a chance.

He had known it all along. When she had left Vegas with Lennie he knew it. That was why he'd never pursued her.

"I'll see you later," he said. "Are you sure there's nothing you need?"

"Nothing."

He's not interested in me anymore, she thought. He couldn't give a damn.

Why should she care?

She only knew she did.

• • • • •

"Tell me about your mother," the *Rolling Stone* reporter said.

Lennie had a mouthful of hamburger. He chewed slowly. "What do you want to know?"

"Well . . . your father was a comedian—you told me that. You don't have any brothers or sisters. You arrived in New York at seventeen, and we've got the story from there. But you never mention your mother. Is she still alive?"

How tempting to do away with Alice. Kill her off in print and never have to deal with her again. But Alice would hardly stand for that. Now that he was famous she found it perfectly acceptable to have a thirty-two-year-old son.

"Yeah, she's alive," he said.

"How does she feel about your material? Your mother-son comedy routines hit a nerve in all of us. Does she love it? Get upset? What?"

Lennie hunched his shoulders. He had had enough of being interviewed. Who gave a shit *what* Alice thought! She had never offered an opinion. He had never asked. The only comment she had ever made about his act was that he should clean it up.

He grinned, stretched. "Hey—you wanna know stuff like that, you'll have to ask her." Quick glance at his watch. "I have to move it. See you later. You'll be at the show, right?"

The reporter nodded and clicked off a small tape recorder.

Lennie rose, winked at a hovering waitress who had asked for his autograph earlier, and strode out of the restaurant.

• • • • •

At three o'clock Olympia left the pool so she could begin readying herself for the evening ahead. Vitos was in his suite, stretched out on a slant board, practicing scales. "Oleeem-peea!" he exclaimed. "So lovleeee."

"Vitos," she said sharply, "I did not come to this tacky gambling palace in the sky to sit around. What's happening?"

"Tomorrow I weel know," Vitos said, sitting up with a big smile. He had told Olympia he needed certain papers from Spain. It was true. He had to get his annulment papers and nobody seemed able to locate them.

She picked a grape from a table laden with fruit, and pouted. "How long do we have to stay here?" she asked.

"One week."

"Thank God that's all. This place sucks."

• • • • •

Lennie wore a black leather jacket, tight black pants, a white shirt open at the neck with a narrow black leather tie and white tennis shoes. His dirty-blond hair was artfully tousled.

Jess stood on tiptoe and kissed him on the cheek. "You look gorgeous," she whispered.

And then he was on.

Deep breath.

Get the adrenaline pumping.

Go for it!

• • • • •

Sitting in the audience Eden wondered if he would spot her. He could hardly help doing so. She was at the best table, center front. She was with Paige and Ryder Wheeler. Quinn Leech, the director of the soon-to-be movie, and his contemptuous, plain girlfriend. Santino, of course. And two of his Las Vegas acquaintances. "They could be investors," he had told her earlier. "Be nice to 'em."

Both men were repellent. One short and squat, with a wild abundance of hair sprouting from his ears, nose, neck, hands— Eden got the creeps just looking at him. The other, big and paunchy, with small, mean eyes and slicked-back greasy hair. Neither had dates, which meant that after cursory glances at Paige Wheeler (at forty plus, too old for their jaded tastes) and Quinn Leech's girlfriend (too plain for their *Playboy* mentalities), they concentrated all their attentions on Eden.

She responded with frosty looks and flat conversation. Living with a man like Santino Bonnatti was bad enough. Why should she be nice to a couple of gorillas who only *might* invest in the movie? Santino didn't need investors anyway—he had enough money to do it himself.

She stared at Lennie, center stage. He looked great. Well, he always was a handsome son-of-a-bitch. Fortunately she knew she looked great too. A silver dress cut low and slinky. And she was wearing her ruby necklace and earrings—Santino's gift. Her hair, parted in the middle, brushed her shoulders—a pale curtain to frame her chiseled features.

When Santino had said they were going to Las Vegas for a few days she was delighted. It was so boring sitting in the house on Blue Jay Way, a virtual prisoner. She couldn't wait for the movie to start so she could get out and resume some kind of a normal life. When filming began, Santino would just have to leave her alone. There would be costume fittings, script conferences, rehearsals—she hoped. Some directors liked to work with their actors for weeks before production began.

Naturally Santino had not given her any notice. "We're goin' to Vegas," he'd announced, and an hour later they were on their way by car, with Zeko driving. It would have been nice if she'd had time to go to the hairdresser's, get her nails done, maybe do some shopping.

But no. Santino did things his way. Eden had learned to go along with it.

Once they arrived, Santino settled her in a suite at the Sands Hotel, with Zeko in attendance; then he left, returning an hour later. "Get dressed," he said. "We're goin' to an openin'."

"What opening?" she asked.

"That Spanish singing pimp—Vitos somethin'. Here." He thrust a wad of bills in her hand. "Go an' buy somethin' that'll give me a stiff prick. Take Zeko."

She had no idea Lennie Golden was sharing the bill with Vitos Felicidade. It wasn't until they were driving up to the Magiriano that she saw the huge billboards.

Paige leaned across the table and whispered something.

Eden didn't hear her. "What?"

"Hot, isn't he?" repeated Paige. "Reminds me of a horny Redford with a touch of Newman's heat."

It occurred to Eden that nobody knew about her three-year affair with Lennie Golden. For some obscure reason she found that aggravating. He hadn't even mentioned her in the *People* article—just vaguely stated that he'd dated a lot of models in New York.

Wasn't she part of his past? A big part.

It infuriated her to think he had made it first. *She* should be the one getting all the attention. *She* should be on the cover of *People*.

Paige was obviously waiting for an answer to her comment. "Not bad," she managed.

"Not bad!" exclaimed Paige. "He is *hot*, honey. When *I* say someone's hot you'd better believe it."

Eden quite liked Paige Wheeler, although she hadn't spent much time with her. A couple of dinners, two or three lunches, with Santino's permission. Paige was fun. She enjoyed life, and it came across. Oh! Wouldn't it be interesting to see her face if Eden confided just how hot Lennie Golden really was?

And she missed him.

For a moment.

Only for a moment.

And only in bed.

· · · · ·

The audience loved him. They were the real power; they could make or break a star.

He knew he had them the minute he walked onstage. He could feel the vibes—feel that they wanted to share this evening's success with him.

His humor was deadpan, ironic, cutting.

They went for it immediately, picking up on every little nuance.

He told truths. It broke them up.

He trashed television. They loved it.

He started on family relationships. People were crying with mirth.

He hit his stride. Confident, in charge, his timing impeccable.

And then he saw her.

50

Where the *hell* do you think it's getting you?" Jerry Myerson shouted.

Steven and he stood at opposite ends of the living room in Jerry's New York townhouse. They were both angry. Steven because he wished Jerry would butt out. And Jerry because when he was a very young man he had once harbored a secret crush on Carrie, and he hated to see what this was doing to her.

Steven gestured impatiently. "I'll let you know when I get results."

"And when will *that* be?" Jerry asked sarcastically.

"Don't you think I wish I knew?" Steven turned his back and stared out of the window at the snarled traffic on Fifty-fourth Street. A cabdriver was making obscene signals at the driver of a large delivery truck blocking traffic. Soon a fistfight would erupt.

"The best thing you can do is get back to work," Jerry stated bluntly. "I've told you there's a job for you with my firm any time you like."

Steven turned around. "That's what I *want* to do. And as soon as this thing is settled, that's what I *will* do."

"Good. Then you can pay me back the money I've loaned you."

Steven's eyes blazed. "Are you worried about your money, Jerry?"

"No. Asshole. I'm worried about *you* and your state of mind."

They argued some more, but both of them knew it wouldn't make any difference. Steven had something to do. Nothing was going to stop him.

The next day Jerry took Carrie to lunch at Le Cirque. She

looked tired, but she was pleased to see him and hugged him tightly. He was the only other person to know the truth about her past, and he seemed to understand a lot better than Steven.

"He's taking me to see the retired doctor tomorrow," she said wearily. "Who knows? Maybe the face will fit the name."

"I hope so," Jerry said, "for both your sakes."

She toyed with her Martini glass, and lowered her eyes. "Jerry," she began hesitantly, "I just don't know what to do anymore. When I'm with Steven I feel he hates me. It's as if he's put a steel cage around himself, and there's no penetrating it. I only did what any mother would have done—I protected him from the truth."

"I know," said Jerry sympathetically. "You can't blame yourself. He's caught up in an identity crisis. There's only one way he can work it out, and that's by himself. It's not just you—neither of us can help him."

"I'm glad you understand."

"That's what friends are for."

"Thank you, Jerry." She put her hand over his and squeezed. "And how's everything with you?"

He grinned. "I am managing to stay single in spite of overwhelming odds. It's not easy being rich, straight and successful in New York. The ladies go right for the good old wedding ring."

Carrie smiled and felt relaxed for the first time in weeks.

• • • • •

Fredd Lesster, M.D., lived halfway between New York and Philadelphia. He turned out to be eighty-five years old and half Lebanese. One glance was enough to rule him out.

Steven, once again borrowing Jerry's Porsche, drove Carrie back to the city in silence. She was staying in a friend's apartment. Her friend had gone to Europe for six months, and it seemed more sensible to be there than at her house on Fire Island.

"Why don't you come up? I'll fix you some eggs or something," she offered.

He shook his head.

She wanted to reach out and touch him, he looked so miserable. Why couldn't he just accept things the way they were?

"I'm sorry about today," he said, staring straight ahead. "It was a wasted trip."

"It doesn't matter."

"Yes it does. It won't happen again."

She wondered if that meant he was giving up on Freddy Lester. Maybe he didn't need him after all. Maybe Gino Santangelo was his father. Steven knew where Gino was. Why didn't he just fly to California and persuade him to take a blood test?

She almost laughed aloud. Gino Santangelo would never remember her. He would think Steven was a madman, a mental patient. He would spit in his face.

"What now?" she asked quietly.

Steven leaned across and opened the passenger door. "I'll speak to you in a day or so," he said brusquely.

Thank you very much. Shall I just put my life on hold while I wait for your next move?

"Goodnight," she said, getting out of Jerry's car.

He roared off into the night with not a backward glance. He didn't even bother to see that she got into the building safely. So much for love and concern, of which he had once had an abundance. He made her very sad.

She couldn't sleep, and sat for a while by the window watching nighttime shadows and listening to the perpetual whine of the police sirens. Memories invaded her head, and when she did finally fall asleep, it was an uneasy rest.

51

Susan was no slouch when it came to doing things her way. Within three-quarters of an hour she had phoned April Crawford and pleaded a dreadful migraine; phoned Chasen's and ordered a supply of their wonderful chili; applied an understated makeup and dressed in a simple peach caftan. When Lucky and Costa arrived she was ready.

Gino was also ready. He was delighted to be greeting the daughter he found he had really missed. "Kid!" He threw open his arms.

"Daddy!" She fell into them. Too bad if he didn't like the title—she felt like using it for once.

Susan smiled graciously at Costa. "Welcome. Do come in."

They all trooped into the house. A casual California four-million-dollar mansion. Nothing pretentious.

"Well, well, well," exclaimed Gino, surveying Lucky with a grin. "Lookin' as good as ever." He turned to Costa, poked him playfully around the middle. "An' you my friend, gettin' a little gutty. Too much home cookin', huh? Too many Miami widows handin' you somethin' hot?"

"Yes," Lucky joined in. "I've been meaning to talk to you about your weight, Costa. They're turning you into a fatso!"

They all roared with laughter except Susan, who failed to see the humor in someone's not watching his diet. She was meticulous about everything she put into her mouth, which was one of the reasons she had stopped performing fellatio on Gino a month after marrying him. He hadn't been pleased, but too bad—there was nothing he could do about it.

"What'll you have to drink?" Gino asked, putting one arm around Lucky and the other around Costa as he guided them toward the bar.

"Pernod on the rocks," requested Lucky.

"Something soft," said Costa.

"Something soft! The story of your life!" joked Gino, preparing to fix the drinks.

"Hans will do that, dear," intoned Susan smoothly, gliding over.

"Forget it. I'll do it," replied Gino, already putting chunks of ice in the glasses.

Susan motioned Hans, the houseman, away. Then she turned to Lucky with a pleasant smile. "And how are you, my dear? It's been quite some time."

Phony broad, thought Lucky. *You haven't changed. Still doing your Grace Kelly number.*

"I'm in good shape, Susan." *Ha! Wait until she hears I've married Dimitri Stanislopoulos. She'll wet her panties!*

"You certainly look very well," said Susan. "A touch tired, but I expect it's the time difference. I'm always wretched when I do that trip. Three hours' difference may not seem a lot, but believe me—"

"Hey, Gino," Lucky said, ignoring her. "You missing Vegas yet?"

He grinned. "Are you?"

"Me? I've got a lot of other things to keep me busy."

"Like what?"

"Like Atlantic City. I'm going in, before it's too late."

"You are?"

"Why not? It's what I want. And now I've got the financing."

"Yeh?"

"Yeh."

"Who from?"

"I'll tell you later."

Susan's smile was fixed. She had no idea what they were talking about. "I've ordered chili from Chasen's," she announced. "I do hope you both like chili, but Gino gave me such short notice, I really—"

"Why can't you tell me now?" demanded Gino, following Lucky's lead and ignoring Susan.

"Because," she replied, "it's a long story."

"I got all night."

Her black eyes gleamed. "Why are you so anxious to know? You want to come in with me?"

"Hey"—he laughed—"I know what your game is. You don't have all the money, and you want me in for a slice of the action. Right?"

"Wrong."

"Yeh?"

"Yeh. *I* am finally building *my* hotel. I don't need any partners."

"And how have you managed that?"

"Wouldn't *you* like to know?"

"I'll know 'cause you're gonna tell me."

"Yeh? Don't bet on it."

They were both smiling broadly, playing games, batting words back and forth just like they used to when things were good and togetherness was the name of the game.

"Dinner will be here in a minute," Susan said stiffly.

"Did I hear you mention chili?" Costa asked politely.

"Yes," Susan replied, favoring him with a glance and not particularly liking what she saw. Why did Gino have to burden her with his dull friends as well as his difficult daughter?

"Perhaps—if it's no trouble—I could have something else," Costa requested quietly. "A can of soup, some eggs." He patted his stomach. "Chili's too spicy for me. Doctor's orders."

"I'll see what I can do," Susan said frigidly. Gino and Lucky had moved to the end of the bar and were deep in conversation. Gino was withdrawing from her—she had sensed it for months. Now, seeing him talking to his daughter, so animated and alive, she realized she had better be careful. It was possible she could lose him. And she wasn't ready for that. Not yet.

Quickly she moved to his side and took his arm propri-
etarily. "Now, Lucky, we want to hear all about what you've
been doing, dear. Everything." Her voice was honey, her tight
smile, sugar. "You know, this household really misses you. We
miss her, Gino, don't we darling?"

• • • • •

Gino insisted that dinner be served in the kitchen. "It's chili
for crissakes. Whatta ya wanna make a big deal for?"

So dinner in the kitchen it was, much to the servants' annoyance. The kitchen was their domain; they did not appreciate being banished.

Susan kept her smile in place all night, but it wasn't easy.
Gino, Lucky and Costa formed a group. All Gino wanted to
talk about was the good old New York days, and Costa was the
perfect foil, Lucky the perfect listener.

Susan had no desire to hear any of it. The good old days
sounded sordid and disgusting.

Halfway through dinner Gemma arrived home with several friends. "I thought you were going out," she said rudely.
"And what the hell are you doing in the kitchen?"

Susan delicately patted her lips with a napkin. "A change
of plans, dear. Gemma, you remember Lucky, don't you? And
this is Costa . . ." She paused, trying to think of his surname.
"Zennacot."

"Zennocotti," Gino corrected.

"Ah, yes," Susan said quickly. "Zennocotti."

"Hi," Gemma said, but her heart wasn't in it. She had
hoped to have the house to herself so she and her friends
could relax and do a little coke. Now they would have to go
elsewhere. She had no intention of sitting around with this
over-the-hill group. Sulkily she left the room.

Lucky pushed her half-eaten plate of chili away. She wished
that she, Gino and Costa were alone. There was something
stifling about Susan. Her glassy smile, and the way she tried
to join in. And the house was oppressive, not homey, more like

something out of a magazine. And now Gemma, the uptight daughter. Gino seemed so like his old self—surely he didn't enjoy living with these people?

"Why don't you come by the hotel?" she said to him quietly. "I have a surprise for you."

"What is it?"

"Come with me and you shall see," she teased.

He didn't need much persuading. "Let's go."

Susan was not pleased when they left immediately after dinner. She wanted to accompany them, but Gino said, "No, I'll be right back. You stay here."

They piled into Lucky's rented car and raced to the hotel, laughing all the way like kids playing truant.

As she parked the car on Crescent Drive, Lucky thought of the enormity of the surprise she was just about to spring on Gino. She hadn't even told him she was married. She took a deep breath. He had to be thrilled. What other reaction could he possibly have when he first set eyes on Roberto? *His* grandson. *His* flesh and blood. Oh, God! Why did she feel so nervous?

They made their way carefully along the foliage-lined paths to her bungalow. She put the key in the door, opened up and sprung the lights.

"Where's my surprise?" Gino asked genially, looking around.

"What did you expect? A Ferrari?" she jested.

"I kinda thought you'd have my portrait waiting. I always fancied hangin' on somebody's wall."

She laughed softly. "Wait!" she commanded. "Fix him a drink, Costa."

Hurriedly she went in her bedroom, shutting the door behind her. Roberto was asleep in a cot beside her bed. CeeCee was watching television in the other bedroom.

She stared at her baby, her little boy. Sixteen months old and totally sensational.

He slept face down. Santangelo black hair. Jet eyes with their long curling lashes hidden.

She loved him so very much. Gino had to feel the same way. He had to.

Gently she picked him up. He was warm and damp and smelled of talcum powder and soap. "Roberto," she whispered. "Mommy's home." The child's eyes flickered open. "Hey— this is a really big day," she crooned. "You, my fantastic little boy, are just about to meet your grandpop." She hugged him. "Now you *are* going to be a good boy, aren't you?" Roberto displayed a three-toothed grin. He had the greatest disposition in the world.

She hugged him even tighter. "Let's move it, baby kid," she said. "Let us go and make a good impression."

52

Lennie felt like someone had delivered a blow to his stomach. *Pow.* Right in the solar plexus. *Take that, you sonofabitch.*

For a split second his eyes met Eden's. She did not nod or indicate in any way that she knew him. She merely turned to the man seated beside her and requested a cigarette. He knew she did it purposely. It was a "don't care" gesture. A shrug of indifference, as if to say, The rest of the audience might think you're hot stuff, but frankly, *I* don't give a damn.

Thin-faced bitch.

She looked knockout.

While all these thoughts were churning through his head he maintained a cool exterior. Did not blow a line. Just kept right on doing what he was so good at doing, while the bitch drew on her cigarette and sipped her wine and pretended she didn't know who he was.

She spurred him on. Made him soar. Made him hotter than a whore on payday. He went beyond what he had planned and rehearsed. He ad-libbed, played with the audience, ran ten minutes over and received a tumultuous ovation.

Lennie Golden. Star. If she hadn't known it before, she knew it now. He leaped offstage, high on adulation and applause, ready to do it all over again.

"You were senfuckingsational!" enthused Jess, bright-eyed and filled with delight.

The thunderous applause wouldn't quit. He went back three or four times to take a bow, until Vitos Felicidade's theme music cut into the noise, and it was on with the second half of the show.

"Good Golly Miss Molly," raved Jess. "You sure gave 'em Great Balls of Fire tonight."

Everybody was crowding his dressing room. Isaac and Irena, Matt Traynor, Mouth with her cameras, the ever-present reporter from *Rolling Stone*.

He wanted to be alone. He needed just a few moments of peace and quiet. Jess caught the message and emptied the room while he shut himself in the bathroom, stripped off his clothes and stood under the icy needles of a cold shower.

Eden was here.

Maybe she had come specially. Unlikely, but a thought.

He turned off the shower, wrapped a towel around his waist and reentered his dressing room.

Jess sat on the couch hugging her knees and balancing a glass of champagne. She raised the glass in his direction. *"Salute."*

"Eden's here," he said. "Find out who the fuck she's with."

• • • • •

Vitos Felicidade was gazing straight at her. She knew it, but she refused to react. Since every other female in the audience was swooning with joy, she was not about to join the club. She was Olympia Stanislopoulos. And she could have any man she wanted. Any time. Any place.

Unfortunately, after the rather unkempt but adventurous attentions of Flash, Vitos, with his limp-wristed delivery and sickly smile, presented no challenge. But he would do. For now.

He was warbling on about lost love and passion and starlit summer nights. Frankly, Olympia decided that the comedian, Lennie something, had far more going for him than Vitos ever would. Now *he* was sexy in the same way Flash was. Streetwise—a phrase Flash had taught her, which she loved.

Streetwise. It conjured up visions of someone who knew what life was all about. Vitos appeared to exist in a vacuum of perfection. He was also lousy in bed. A limp wrist was not his only problem.

She fidgeted uncomfortably. All dressed up, and another half hour of Vitos's dreary melodies. She wasn't at all sure she could sit through it.

• • • • •

Lennie played the room. The dressing room. Easier than being onstage, but a game all the same. He was getting pretty adept at fielding questions. There were two local reporters present as well as the *Rolling Stone* regular. They all wanted to know the same things. How did he start? Where was he born? When did he decide to take up comedy?

Why the hell didn't they read the neatly typed bios Jess handed out?

Dumb questions. Boring questions. Another couple of months and he would give up interviews altogether. This, of course, would make him even hotter.

Jess came back into the room. He made his way over to her, dogged by Mouth, who must have taken at least ten thousand pictures of him by this time.

"Well?"

"Bad news."

"What?"

"She's with a couple of Vegas hoods and a compadre of theirs from L.A."

"How do you know?"

"Straight from the captain's mouth. We're old friends—he knows everything and everybody. Believe me, Lennie, these guys are headlines, not a tiny item on the back page—so stay away. Am I reaching you?"

He nodded.

But they both knew she wasn't.

• • • • •

Eden admired Vitos Felicidade's style. He was smooth, assured, probably a thoughtful and sensuous lover.

Making love with Santino was like being in bed with a slobbering baboon. He had no idea how to please a woman. More than likely he wasn't aware that women *could* climax. All he was interested in was getting his rocks off, and a little cruelty and violence if the urge came over him.

"Whattaya think of the Spanish pimp?" he asked, as if reading her thoughts.

"Why?" she asked guardedly.

"Quinn an' Ryder thought he might be okay for the movie."

Eden tried not to react. She knew Santino well enough to realize that if she showed one flicker of enthusiasm, Vitos Felicidade would no longer be a contender. "What makes you think he can act?" she asked offhandedly.

"The same reasons y'think you can." He guffawed and was promptly *sshhed* by a woman at the next table.

Eden burned. "I went to acting classes in New York," she hissed. "And I've appeared in a number of TV shows. Don't compare *me* with your singing Spanish pimp."

Excellent. Now he would think she hated Vitos. And maybe they would hire him. And if they did, she would have an affair with him. A discreet affair. Not so discreet if the movie was a hit. If it was she would leave Santino immediately.

• • • • •

Vitos was nearing the end of his act. Resplendent in black tie and tails, he blew a kiss to Olympia and introduced her to the audience. Then he dedicated his latest single, "The One Love of My Life," to her, and proceeded to sing it on one knee, gazing into her eyes.

She thoroughly enjoyed the charade. Once people realized who she was, they stared at her more than they did at Vitos. She was a newsworthy rich heiress, with a string of husbands and a wild headline-grabbing affair with the legendary Flash.

She pulled her shoulders back and smiled prettily.

• • • • •

Matt had a new date for the gala party taking place in the private ballroom—a party to honor Lennie Golden and Vitos Felicidade. She was a retired showgirl: forty, still beautiful, and six feet tall.

Jess took one look and backed away. Tall, haughty, *tall*, elegant, *tall*, sophisticated, *tall*.

Goddamn Matt Traynor. Back to his showgirls. He was a jerk anyway.

• • • • •

Both stars had their entourages, Vitos's larger than Lennie's. Managers, agents, photographers, gofers, reporters, hangers-on. And Vitos had Olympia. But Lennie had the current cover of *People*. So they attracted equal attention as they arrived within five minutes of each other at the party.

Santino and his group were already ensconced at one of the best tables. Santino's father, Enzio Bonnatti, had taught him at an early age, "You go to a friggin' fancy party, get there early, take the best friggin' table and don't move ass for nobody."

Santino missed the wit and wisdom of Enzio. What a man he had been. A real capo. He knew how to do business, pull people's strings and break their fucking balls if they didn't do things his way. Sitting in the ballroom of the Magiriano Hotel brought back memories. In 1975 Enzio had taken over the Magiriano. Looked after the whole Santangelo Vegas operation as a favor for Gino Santangelo—out of the country on some tax scam—and Lucky Santangelo, who ran from town when her boyfriend Marco got himself killed.

Fuck the Santangelos. They had paid Enzio back with threats, not gratitude. And one hot September day in 1977, Lucky Santangelo—Enzio's *goddaughter* for crissakes—had arrived at his Long Island mansion and shot him. *Shot him in the stomach, the neck and the balls. Three fucking times.*

Self-defense, she had claimed. He was attacking me, trying to rape me. And the authorities believed the cunt! The case never even came to court. She was free as a fucking 747. The final straw was being forbidden retribution. The Family said no. Carlos had no balls, but Santino still brooded about it.

Fuck Carlos.

Fuck the Family.

The Santangelos had not heard the last of Santino Bonatti. No way.

53

For a moment Gino said nothing. He stared at Lucky and the baby, then he turned to Costa for an explanation.

Costa cleared his throat and was silent.

"This is Roberto," Lucky said, with pride in her voice. "Your grandson."

Another long moment of silence.

Lucky held her breath. She wanted Gino to be thrilled, delighted, ecstatic!

"Hey," he said at last, sitting down. "Some surprise."

"Better than a portrait, huh?" She grinned.

"What didja do, adopt a kid?" he asked.

"No. This is Roberto," she said indignantly. "*My* baby. *Our* flesh and blood. *Your* grandson. He's sixteen months old and he's been looking forward to meeting you."

Once again Gino looked to Costa, but Costa felt that this was a matter he shouldn't be involved in. "I'm going to bed," he said. "I'll phone you in the morning, Gino. Goodnight." He let himself out.

"Well?" Lucky laughed nervously. "What do you think?"

"I think," Gino replied slowly, "that if the kid's bin waitin' to meet me, you could have arranged somethin' before this." He held out his arms for the baby. "Maybe I should hold him." She placed Roberto carefully on his lap. "Haven't held a kid for quite a while," he said, shifting awkwardly.

"Roberto's tough. He won't break." God! She sounded like one of those dumb new mothers. But she felt terrific. She had finally brought the two most important people in her life together.

"So"—Gino bounced the baby a little—"you wanna tell me about it?"

"He looks like a Santangelo, doesn't he?" she asked excitedly.

"He looks like you when you were his age."

She was thrilled. "Really? Honestly?"

"Spittin' image."

"I wish I had some baby pictures of *you*."

"Hey—I was fortunate if I got a meal a day. There was no money for pictures."

"You know something?" She bent to kiss him. "I love you, I really do." The last time she had uttered those words, he had been close to death after the heart attack. Now she was saying them again, and their estrangement of the last two years felt like it had never happened.

"I feel the same way about you, kid. I may not have always shown it—but y'know, after your mother was murdered I—"

The phone rang, cutting into his softly spoken words. He clammed up immediately.

Lucky was furious. Just when he was about to open up for the first time. He had never discussed Maria's murder with her, or even mentioned the fateful day when she was five years old and had come upon her mother's body floating in the swimming pool. Now that he was about to, the goddamn phone had to interrupt. She could have screamed with frustration as she snatched up the receiver. "Yes?"

"Lucky, dear—" Susan's well-modulated tones. "Is Gino still there?"

She handed him the phone. "It's your keeper," she said, hoping he would get rid of her quickly.

He threw her a look. She lifted Roberto from his knee and took him back to his cot. When she returned, Gino had hung up. *Well?* she wanted to ask. *When the Widow Perfect calls do you still run?* Instead she said, "I guess you've got to go."

"There's a problem with Gemma and her friends," he sighed.

"Only you can solve it, huh?"

"Yeh. Well I'm the only one they'll listen to when I throw 'em out."

"I'll drive you."

"Don't worry, kid—I called the front desk, they've got a car for me."

She opened the door, trying to hide the letdown she felt.

"Breakfast tomorrow?" he suggested. "We can talk then."

She nodded. But she knew it wouldn't be the same in the morning.

"Goodnight, kiddo."

"Goodnight, Gino."

He hugged her; but he was already on his way home.

She sat in the darkness and brooded for a while. Then she picked up the phone and dialed his number.

Susan answered.

When he came on the line he sounded harassed. "What's up?"

"Just a postscript. I *am* married, you know."

"I didn't know that. I kinda thought you kept the baby quiet because you weren't."

"How archaic!" she scoffed. "It's 1980 for goodness' sake."

"So . . . where's your husband?"

"Traveling. He's a businessman." She paused, then added, "You might remember him."

"Do I know him?"

"You sure do. Dimitri. Dimitri Stanislopoulos. Olympia's father."

54

There were fire-eaters at the party. And jugglers dressed as white-faced clowns. And a handsome Black singer. And an excellent band. There was also a sumptuous buffet, scads of gorgeous showgirls, and many celebrities in addition to the two stars for whom the party was being held.

Press abounded. Pretty girls in neat dresses with notepads and pencils. Sweaty photographers with bulky flash cameras. A few network people with TV cameras balanced on their shoulders.

Vitos and Lennie formed separate camps with their various entourages.

Lennie found himself surrounded by women, and since he had spotted Eden sitting at a table with a group who looked straight out of *The Valachi Papers,* he didn't mind at all.

Vitos also had women fawning all over him. He responded with charm. Olympia responded with a ferocious scowl as she found herself shoved to one side.

Jess scouted the room on the lookout for someone she might have fun with. She was fed up with always being on her own—good old Jess—Girl Friday, fixer of everything. Maybe she would have a go at fixing her love life.

Matt divided himself between the two camps. His girlfriend-for-the-night fell deeply in lust with Vitos, settled herself at his table and refused to budge.

No great loss, Matt decided. He observed Jess chatting with a member of Vitos's band, and wondered what she had to talk to *him* about. When the conversation had gone on for more than ten minutes he went over to them.

"Time for a business discussion," he said briskly, taking her arm.

"What business?" she asked, as he steered her toward the bar.

"Lennie was such a hit tonight I thought we should start negotiations for next year."

"Now?"

"Why not?"

"Because this is a party."

"It doesn't suit you."

"Huh?"

"Partying."

"You're crazy."

"Are you and Lennie sleeping together?"

"That's none of your business." She stalked away. It is difficult stalking when you are only five feet tall, but Jess managed it.

• • • • •

Ryder Wheeler introduced Paige to Vitos. He bowed. Clicked his heels together. Murmured *"Enchanté."*

Paige thought he was full of shit.

Eden danced with the tallest of Santino's friends, the one with the small mean eyes and the greasy hair. Add BO, bad breath and sweaty palms to his list of accomplishments.

She hoped Lennie wasn't watching her.

In spite of the fact that he was surrounded by girls, she knew he was. She could have him back any time she wanted. One sign of encouragement from her and he'd come running.

It made her feel good, in spite of Sweaty Palms grinding his semi-hard-on into her thigh.

Lennie got up, relieved Mouth of her cameras and whirled her around the dance floor, ignoring her protestations that she was not dressed for dancing.

"You're the best-looking girl here," he said, as soon as he was close enough for Eden to overhear.

"I've got to work," Mouth insisted. "Take me back to my cameras."

He noticed Eden smirking. She had an infuriating way of curling her mouth at one corner.

Their eyes met, and they practiced mutual nonrecognition.

Olympia announced she wished to meet the comedian. Matt arranged it on neutral territory between the two camps.

"You're very very funny," Olympia said in her most charming fashion. "I must watch your television show. I hear it's hilarious."

Lennie smiled his thanks, and was just about to move on when he spotted Eden watching him. This time there was no curled lip. This time she was jealous.

What does it take to make Eden Antonio jealous?
One of the richest women in the world.

He gave Olympia Stanislopoulos the benefit of his ocean-green eyes and a lopsided grin. "Wanna dance?" he asked.

She smiled. Lovely smile. Lovely hair. Lovely boobs. It was a shame she was thirty pounds overweight.

"Yes," she said.

And they hit the dance floor to the strains of "Street Life."

• • • • •

The evening progressed.

Dessert was giant bowls of ice cream in ten different flavors with various toppings. The handsome Black singer gave his all to interesting imitations of Stevie Wonder and Smokey Robinson.

Vitos Felicidade enjoyed the attentions of every woman in the place. He failed to notice that Olympia had settled in a corner with Lennie Golden and that their conversation appeared more than casual.

Eden noticed. She danced with Santino's lousy friends and noticed a whole lot.

Jess resumed friendship with the member of Vitos's band she had been talking to earlier. He played guitar, spoke passable English and had very expressive eyes and hands.

Matt watched from afar. He wasn't pleased. It was obvious Jess was coming on to the guitar player because Lennie was making out with the rich broad.

Santino decided he wanted his picture taken with Vitos Felicidade. He liked being photographed with celebrities—he had quite a collection. Eden was summoned from the dance floor where she was struggling with Santino's short hairy friend. He was even shorter and hairier than Santino himself, and she was delighted to be relieved of duty.

Ryder Wheeler took them over to Vitos's table and introduced them. Vitos dazzled her with his teeth, took her hand, squeezed it imperceptibly, brought it to his lips and kissed it. His eyes were pools of desire. *"Enchanté,"* he murmured.

She thought she read a definite message—a message that said, *"I want to make love to you. Soon. Very soon. You won't regret it."*

Santino shoved her between them for the photo. Vitos's touch made her shiver.

Santino decided he didn't like that pose, so he put himself in the middle and made the house photographer take it again.

Vitos was most cooperative. His manager had filled him in on Santino Bonnatti. They had been negotiating for weeks with Ryder Wheeler about the movie he wanted Vitos to star in. Money seemed to be the only stumbling block, and Ryder had explained that Bonnatti was the chief investor, and as such made the final decision. Vitos wanted to do the movie. He oozed charm.

Lennie observed Eden. She had the hots for the Spanish singer. Her body language was eloquent. At the same time, he managed to catch every word Olympia Stanislopoulos was saying. She had overdosed on champagne and was regaling him with tales of her life. Poor little rich girl. Too much too soon. It wasn't easy being one of the richest girls in the world. People used you for who you were. They wanted your money, or notoriety, or they just wanted to be seen with you.

He started to feel sorry for her. Everyone expected the image—the rich spoiled bitch. But this was a rather sad, insecure woman, who, if she lost some weight, would be very attractive.

Not his type, of course.

Spectacular boobs.

Not his type.

Of course.

Eden was watching them.

"Why don't we get out of here?" Olympia whispered forlornly. "I need to be with someone who cares."

Eden was watching them.

He hesitated. "I thought you were with Vitos."

She shrugged. "He's not a man, he's a puppet. Pull his string and he sings. Pull again and he smiles for the cameras."

Eden was *definitely* watching them.

What sweet revenge to exit with Olympia Stanislopoulos while Eden was stuck with her gangster boyfriend.

He stood up. "Let's go," he said decisively. "I'll buy you a drink at my place."

55

Lucky did not linger in L.A. She had told Gino about his grandchild and her marriage before he read about it in the newspapers, and that fulfilled her obligations. Fortunately Dimitri had the power to keep the news from breaking in the press until he was ready to make the announcement.

The morning after, she ordered a limo, booked an early flight and set off for New York with Roberto and CeeCee.

She wasn't angry at Gino. Their evening together had been wonderful until Susan broke the spell. But she had to be realistic. Things were different now. It wasn't father and daughter against the world. It was father with a wife, stepchildren and a new kind of lifestyle. And it was daughter with a husband and son. She had other priorities, too.

She left a message at the desk for Costa. To Gino, she wrote a short note, explaining that Dimitri had returned early from Europe and she had to get back to New York immediately.

Dimitri . . . when she had told Gino to whom she was married, there had been an ominous silence. He was too smart to criticize, and a muttered "We'll talk tomorrow morning over breakfast" was all that he'd said.

Well, *she* was having breakfast aboard a 747. She wondered what *he* was doing.

· · · · ·

"More toast?" Susan asked.

He shook his head.

"Tea?"

Again negative.

"How about a Danish? Prune. Your favorite."

He got up from the table and paced the breakfast room. Lucky's note had arrived while he was dressing. It had upset him. Why was she running off?

It was Susan's fault. Susan and her goddamn phone call. Interrupting him just when he felt the time was right to speak to Lucky about her mother's murder. He had wanted to talk to her for so long. . . . And then there was the subject of her marriage to Dimitri Stanislopoulos. Was she crazy? The man was old enough to be her *grandfather*. And he had a lousy reputation. The world knew he had been sleeping with Francesca Fern for years, and *she* was a barracuda.

Jeez! What Lucky needed was a little fatherly advice. Not that she'd appreciate it—she'd probably tell him where he could shove it.

But he was her father. He had to try, didn't he?

"How about some fresh grapefruit?" Susan asked cheerily.

He wanted to scream at her. Tell her to shut the fuck up.

But then he reasoned it wasn't her fault she had started to bore the shit out of him. *She* hadn't changed. *He* had. Not for Gino Santangelo the sedentary life of luxury Beverly Hills offered. Not for Gino Santangelo the openings and events, the small talk and the gossip. He was a street kid, used to a fast life. Right now he was seventy-four and feeling it.

Back in Vegas, where he belonged, he knew he'd regain his energy and drive.

·   ·   ·   ·   ·

Dimitri's New York apartment was old-fashioned, stuffy, and filled with priceless antiques. Two servants and a butler lived in, and two more in help came in daily to attend to the more menial tasks.

Lucky arrived the day before Dimitri, and hated it. She had been to the apartment before—but living there was another thing.

Total redecoration had to take place, or she was returning to her house in the Hamptons, which she loved. It was so white and airy and peaceful. The only thing she had changed about it was the swimming pool. The ground had been filled in and a rose garden planted.

Sometimes, in recurring nightmares, she could still see the floating raft . . . her mother's body spread-eagled . . . dead. . . .

Dimitri phoned from Paris. "How is Roberto?" were the first words he uttered.

"Fine. He wants a new room."

"I beg your pardon?"

"Your apartment is *depressing.* Can I do something with it?"

"Do you object to my furnishings? The finest interior designer in New York worked with me on it."

He hardly thought he should reveal that when he decorated the apartment five years before, Francesca Fern had been promising to leave her husband. It was she who had worked with the designer with a view to moving in, but by the time it was completed she had changed her mind and reconciled with Horace.

Dimitri had been furious. However, he loved the way she had decorated the apartment. He had no wish to change it.

"It's so old-fashioned and stuffy," Lucky complained.

"We'll discuss it," Dimitri replied.

"You've *got* to be kidding. No discussions. It's dull and I'm changing it."

They talked a while longer, and when Dimitri replaced the receiver he was thoughtful. Lucky Santangelo was young and strong-willed. Her language was sometimes startling, and she did what she wanted. He was used to a different kind of woman. Expensive jet-set beauties with a knowledge of all the finer things in life. Lucky was a gypsy. Had he done the right thing marrying her?

Yes. She was the mother of his son and heir. And as such she deserved his name.

In Paris, Francesca Fern had reentered his life with a vengeance. Francesca with her red hair, wide crimson lips and husky dramatic voice. She had been cool to him for two years, ever since their confrontation in Las Vegas at the gala honoring her. But Francesca had uncanny timing. She knew he was no longer available, so she wanted him again. She called him in Paris. "I had a feeling you'd be here," she murmured, her tone warmer than it had been for years. "I'm alone. When shall we see each other? Tonight?"

Francesca was not a woman to turn down. She throbbed with sexual passion. She had been his mistress for many years, and Dimitri saw nothing wrong in continuing the affair. It certainly would not affect his relationship with Lucky. "Tonight," he promised.

"I've missed you," she purred.

And she was back in his life.

56

Fred Lester, the publisher, called Carrie several times. He wanted to take her to lunch and discuss the book she was supposed to be thinking about. After the third call she decided that maybe it wasn't such a bad idea. Fate had brought her into the office of Fred Lester, why shouldn't she take advantage of it?

She agreed to lunch with him. They went to the Four Seasons and talked about her nonexistent book.

"I've found the ideal ghostwriter for you," he said enthusiastically. "Her name is Anna Robb. She works fast, and I think you'll approve of her style." He named two well-known television stars whose beauty-and-exercise books she had worked on.

"Didn't they write the books themselves?" Carrie asked naively.

Fred laughed and said briskly, "They had neither the time nor the talent. Not that I'm casting any aspersions on *your* talent," he added quickly. "Maybe you don't want or need help. But believe me, if you've never done it before, it's easier this way. No worries about grammar or punctuation or putting sentences together. Just a free-thought flow, which Anna will capture on a tape recorder. How does that sound to you?"

Carrie had to admit it sounded pretty easy.

"Do you have an agent?" he asked.

"Do I need one?" she countered.

"If I was to lie, I'd say no. But an agent does look after your best interests—although I'm prepared to offer you a very fair deal, and you can trust me. You do know that, don't you?"

She nodded. It was ridiculous, really. She had been in his company only once before, but he seemed honest, and she liked him.

"I don't think I need an agent," she decided.

"Let's barter," he replied, a spark of amusement in his kindly brown eyes.

. . . . .

"You're doing *what?*" Steven snapped.

"Writing a book," Carrie replied calmly.

He gave her a withering look. "*You're* writing a book?"

"Why shouldn't I? You sent me to the publisher in the first place. And they're supplying me with a ghostwriter and paying me excellent money." She paused, hoping his reaction would be a little more positive. It wasn't. "I *do* know a lot about fashion and beauty and entertaining," she continued. "It will be a book on style."

Steven snorted his disapproval and moved right along. "I came to tell you we're flying to California next week," he said flatly.

She was almost afraid to ask. "Why?" she managed.

"Because I've hit a dead end on Freddy Lesters. Maybe that wasn't even his name."

"It was."

"He could have lied to you."

She gestured hopelessly. How could she convince him it didn't matter? "I just don't know anymore."

"I guess it doesn't affect you at all, does it?" he observed coldly. "Why should it? You made a new life for yourself. You lived the charade pretty well."

"I wanted to protect you," she said in a low voice.

"Then why did you ever tell me the truth?" he blazed.

"You know why," she whispered. "You were working on the Bonnatti case. Enzio Bonnatti was once my boss. I sold drugs for him . . . supplied girls . . . ran his brothel. . . ." She choked back sobs. "Steven, I was warned by an old friend— *Enzio knew who you were.* He followed my life after I escaped and *he knew who you were.* Can you imagine what he would have done to you if you'd ever got him in court? He would have exposed both of us."

"But I never did bring him into court, did I?" Steven said harshly. "Lucky Santangelo got to him first. I'd been on his case for over a year, and she just walked in and blew his balls off."

Nervously Carrie reached for a cigarette. "He deserved it," she said in a shaky voice. "Enzio Bonnatti was a monster." She had never told Steven the real truth about that day in 1977. Early in the morning she had rented a car, taken a gun from Elliott's collection and driven to Bonnatti's Long Island mansion. Once there, she had sat outside his gates all day, waiting . . . trying to summon up her courage. But then she had seen reason, driven back to the city, and rushed to Steven's office. He was just leaving and had no time to talk. She did not know he was on his way to arrest Bonnatti. She did not know that by the time he reached his house, Bonnatti would have been shot to death by Lucky Santangelo.

When Steven returned home in the evening, she revealed everything about her past and his low beginnings. If she had known Bonnatti was dead, she might not have done so. But now it was too late to think that way. She had told Steven, and it seemed to have destroyed him.

Now, three years later, how could she give him back his pride?

"Why are we going back to California?" she asked quietly, although she knew only too well.

"We're going to pay a visit to Gino Santangelo," Steven said evenly. "We're going to find out if we have to continue the search for the real Freddy Lester."

57

They fell into bed together for all the wrong reasons—
Olympia Stanislopoulos and Lennie Golden.

Ensconced in his penthouse suite, they demolished two
more bottles of champagne, smoked a little grass and threw
off their clothes with stoned abandon. Then they got down to
some serious fucking.

Olympia closed her eyes and thought of Flash.

Lennie closed his eyes and thought of Eden.

The result was a fantastic orgasm for both of them.

They took a shower together, did a large amount of coke
Olympia just happened to have in her possession, and discussed what a great time they were having.

Lennie was not into drugs, but tonight he felt like it. The
hell with everything.

What would Alice the Swizzle say if she could see him
now? Here he was, Lennie Golden, back in his hometown.
Only now he was king of the whole fucking heap.

He was a star.

He was in bed with one of the richest women in the world.

And he was loving every minute.

"We should do something wild," Olympia decided. Her blue
eyes shone brighter than diamonds. "Something *really* wild."

"I thought we just did," he joked.

Olympia jumped from the bed. She looked very Rubenesque
with her ripe curves and huge breasts. "Let's get married," she
said. It came out easily—she was becoming used to saying it.

"Let's get *what?*" He was stoned, but not *that* stoned.

"That'd give 'em *all* something to think about," she giggled. "Can you imagine? We'd make every front page."

"Hey . . . slow down. *I* am not even remotely interested in
getting married."

She was genuinely surprised. "Why not?"

"Because . . . uh . . . well, it's just not something I've ever thought about."

"I've done it three times," she observed solemnly. "With three losers." She moved back to the bed and sat beside him, stroking his chest. Her eyes were wide and serious and cobalt blue. "What have you got to lose? It would be an adventure, and who knows, you might even like it."

He began to laugh. It was such a crazy idea. "C'mon . . ."

She put her arms around his neck and nuzzled her luscious breasts against his naked chest. "I'm not Little Miss Nobody, Lennie. You know who I am. You know the kind of life we could have. And if it doesn't work out . . . no strings, no alimony, none of the usual crap. Who else could offer you a sweetheart deal like that?"

He thought about it.

Seriously.

Well, as seriously as he could after overdosing on champagne, grass and coke. Not to mention half a bottle of vodka earlier in the evening.

If Lennie Golden married Olympia Stanislopoulos, Eden would freak. The ultimate revenge. Christ! He could do it if he wanted to. Olympia was right. What *did* he have to lose?

One-night stands. A mother who never cared. Star-fuck groupies. An apartment in L.A. with a senile maid. Lonely nights thinking of Eden.

"Look," he said, trying to get his thoughts straight, "we don't know each other. We're a couple of strangers who just had a good time in bed."

"That makes it particularly exciting, doesn't it?" She sighed dreamily. "A real magical mystery trip. What more could one ask?"

• • • • •

"I'm not going to do it, you bastard," Eden hissed. "You can't make me."

Santino picked at his teeth with a fingernail and regarded

her stonily. They faced each other in the bedroom of their hotel room. Outside in the living room sat his two greasy Vegas friends.

"Y'would think I was askin' ya to run naked down the friggin' Strip," complained Santino, his left eye twitching—a signal Eden knew meant trouble. "All I wancha t'do is take off your clothes an' parade through the other room in ya high heels. Is that such a big friggin' deal?"

"You want me to put on a show for your lousy cheap friends," she said tightly. "And I *will not* do it."

"Like hell ya won't," snapped Santino. "If ya wanna be in the friggin' movie, ya better." In one swift movement his pudgy hand reached into the bodice of her new gown and tore downward. The silver material ripped.

"You bastard!" Her voice was low.

He slapped her lightly across the face. "For openers," he said calmly. "You want more—then just keep up the dumb-cunt act." He walked to the door, and turned to stare at her. His eyes were the smallest, meanest eyes she had ever seen. "I wancha to parade through the other room, ass-naked, like ya don't know nothin's goin' on. Fix yerself a drink an' walk back in here. Ya got it?"

"*Then* what do you want me to do? Sleep with them?" she blazed.

"Honey—you fuck anyone else an' I'll kill you." He left the room.

She bit down on her lower lip trying to control a surge of anger. Who did he think he was?

She swept into the bathroom and stepped out of her ruined dress. The mirror showed her Santino's hand had left only a slight imprint on her pale skin. She added more powder, covering the redness. Then she applied blusher and lip gloss and smoothed down her fine blond hair.

Santino Bonnatti wanted a show.

She would *give* the bastard a show.

With great care she rouged the nipples of her small breasts so that they stood out bright red and erect. Then she removed her panty hose and fluffed out the golden triangle between her legs. Next she took an atomizer of baby oil and sprayed herself all over until her body gleamed. Several spritzes of Shalimar completed the effect. All she had to add were stiletto-heeled silver sandals and a thin silver chain around her waist.

When she considered herself ready she stood back and surveyed the result. *You're playing a role*, she told herself. *Go for it. Make it work. Don't let the sonofabitch get to you.* With haughty dignity she threw open the door to the living room and sauntered in.

Santino and his two cronies were talking. They all stopped and stared.

She ignored them and strolled to the bar.

Santino started speaking again as if nothing was going on, but he had completely lost his companions' attention.

Coolly Eden fixed herself a glass of white wine with ice. Then just as coolly she walked back to the bedroom door, where she paused for a moment. "Goodnight, guys," she murmured huskily.

What an exit! In a funny way the whole thing was a turn-on. She had *enjoyed* giving them a free show. God, talk about drooling!

She wished she was with Lennie now. She was hot and ready and. . . .

Santino flung open the door. He was in a hurry, dropping his pants as he came toward her. He didn't say a word as he forced her to her knees in front of him.

* * * * *

His manager informed Vitos that Olympia Stanislopoulos had retired to her suite. Vitos was hardly sorry. It had been a long day and he was not up to Olympia's aggressive demands in bed. He left the party smiling all the way. Several women tried to leave with him—one of the hazards of being an international sex symbol. But he managed to extract himself with charm and good grace and lousy English, which seemed only to enhance his appeal.

Alone at last, he let the smile drop. Thankfully. Without

it he was a dour-looking man in his thirties with melancholy eyes and a weak mouth.

Alone at last, he was able to unglue the small hairpiece that covered the tiny but alarming bald spot on the back of his scalp.

Alone at last, he undressed, and happily did not have to hold his stomach in and shoulders erect.

Alone at last, he was not obliged to create a hard-on and prove his manhood.

For once the sex symbol could relax. And he did.

• • • • •

"Breakfast?" Matt suggested.

"Why not?" Jess shrugged. Vitos's guitar player had turned out to be a crazy gambler, and after trailing him around the tables for a while she had given up and returned to the party to find it breaking up. Matt caught her at the door. There was no sign of his girlfriend.

"Nice evening," Jess said.

"Not bad," Matt agreed.

They both wanted to say more, but the moment wasn't right.

• • • • •

"I do," said Olympia. She was still stoned, but knew exactly what she was doing.

"I do," said Lennie, slipping a cheap plastic ring on the third finger of her left hand. He had bought it at the door of the Wee Wedding Chapel of Love and Honor. WE WILL SERVE YOUR NEEDS 24 HOURS. He was still *very* stoned, and feeling no pain.

"I pronounce you man and wife," said the female preacher, a vision in hair curlers and a thick velour robe. "You may kiss the bride."

Lennie grabbed Olympia, bent her backward in an exaggerated tango stance and laid one on her.

Both collapsed in gales of laughter. The female preacher was unamused. It was five o'clock in the morning and she wanted to get back to bed.

58

Dinner was being served in the Stanislopouloses' New York apartment. Three servants attended to Lucky and Dimitri's every need.

"I can't find Olympia," Dimitri said with a grunt of disapproval. "She's departed from New York with Brigette and left no word where she is."

"Olympia's a big girl," Lucky commented, picking at her salad. "You don't want her to check in every time she makes a move, do you?"

"I expect to be able to reach her if I need to," he grumbled indignantly.

"She'll be in touch. You said she always comes on your summer cruise, and that's only a couple of weeks off."

"Yes." Dimitri reached for a glass of red wine. He had arrived from Paris the day before and had yet to inform Lucky that Francesca and Horace Fern would be joining them on the cruise. This was the perfect opportunity. He cleared his throat and presented her with a list of guests. These included Francesca and Horace, Olympia and Flash, with Brigette and her nanny. A Texas oil tycoon and his wife. And a billionaire Arab fixer with his well-known socialite girlfriend.

Lucky grimaced. "Sounds like a fun group," she said with more than a hint of sarcasm.

"My summer cruise is a social highlight," Dimitri said pompously. "An invitation is a coveted prize."

Lucky burst out laughing. "Sometimes you're so full of crap!"

"Why don't *you* invite some friends?" he asked, anxious to keep her happy.

"Do I have to come?" she inquired earnestly. "Social highlights are not exactly my scene, and I have so much to do. I'm viewing sites in Atlantic City tomorrow, and if I see the right space, I need to get right on it. You know, meet with builders, architects. Start things moving."

"Naturally you must come. You are my wife now, and I want to introduce you to my friends. Even if you found the right site tomorrow, negotiations take time. My lawyers can handle everything." He paused. "Olympia will be on the cruise. We must tell her our news together."

"I wonder how she's going to take it." Lucky sighed reflectively as two servants cleared the salad dishes and refilled the wineglasses.

"You were close once. You can be so again," he stated. "Perhaps you can be a positive influence on her. This ridiculous affair with Flash is headed for disaster. You can advise her."

"Oh, great. Old friend Lucky reappears and immediately tells her how to run her life. That'll go down big."

"Olympia needs guidance."

"Well she's not getting it from me."

A uniformed maid appeared with a platter of thinly sliced roast beef, and Lucky helped herself. She would have to do something about these formal little dinners for two. A pizza in front of the TV was more her style.

"I have an idea," Dimitri said. "Why not invite your father and his charming wife on the cruise? I feel this should be a family affair."

Lucky almost choked. Gino. On a society cruise. No way. Mind you, the charming wife would probably love it. Lucky could just imagine Susan frolicking with a clutch of fun-loving elderly billionaires. "I don't think so," she said.

"Why not?" Dimitri persevered. "Shall I have my secretary telephone and issue an invitation?"

She shrugged. "Okay," she said, knowing full well Gino would never come.

• • • • •

"Yes," gushed Susan. "Tell Mr. Stanislopoulos we would be delighted to join him on his yacht."

She hung up the phone and immediately thought of clothes. What did she need? What should she take? A full shopping trip had to take place at once. How fortunate that Lucky Santangelo had done *one* intelligent thing in her life and married Dimitri Stanislopoulos. Although how she had landed *him*, Susan would never know. What could a man like Dimitri possibly see in an uncouth girl like Lucky? She must have tricked him with the baby.

Susan remembered meeting Dimitri in Las Vegas. For one brief moment she had considered him as a prospective husband, at the time she was shopping for one. But it soon became obvious that all the stories about Francesca Fern were true— he talked of the woman all night. How had Lucky removed the formidable Francesca from his life? Maybe she would find out on the boat trip.

Why was she wasting time? Neiman-Marcus was waiting. Saks, Magnin, Bonwit . . . Hurriedly she left the house.

59

"I can't believe you did this!" screamed Jess. "Are you crazy? Insane? What?"

"A simple 'congratulations' would be enough," Lennie groaned.

"You," Jess yelled, "are positioned to be the next big star—and I mean we're talking fucking stupendous, man."

He was lying on a couch in his suite, watching Jess bounce angrily up and down the thickly carpeted length of his room. His head ached. His eyes ached. His body ached. Even his teeth were giving him trouble.

"And what do you do? *What do you do?* You marry some nympho moneybags who'll use you to carry her *luggage.* You are certifiably *insane.*"

Lennie moved the cold washcloth from his forehead and requested, ever so politely, that she lower her voice.

Jess responded with a malevolent glare. "Asshole!" she muttered.

"Rich asshole," he responded wearily.

"*Dumb* rich asshole," she shot back. "Marrying Olympia Staniswhateverhername is just a bad joke. How many husbands has she had? How many famous boyfriends? Join the list, Lennie. You are now one of a *very* big crowd. She's the female Warren Beatty of the jet set *without* the talent. How does it feel to be one of many?"

"Jess," he said quietly, "do me a favor and piss off."

"I only wish I could."

"Force yourself. There's an army of gorillas stamping through my head and I think we need to be alone together."

"Oh, Lennie." She sat down beside him and took his hand. "I suppose you were stoned and in heat. Why didn't you just fuck her instead of *marrying* her?"

"I think we did that too."

Jess shook her head despairingly. Lennie. Best friend. Always capable of falling in the mire when it came to women.

She had arrived in his suite an hour earlier to find him sprawled on the couch, asleep, fully dressed, with the washcloth dripping on his forehead. It was eleven o'clock in the morning and she had attempted to move him into the bedroom. He had pried open his bloodshot eyes and said, "I think I've done something I'm not going to like." Then he confessed, and there was the marriage certificate on the floor to prove it.

Now the screaming was over she tried to collect her thoughts and look at the situation logically. "Where is Olympia?" she asked, sounding far calmer than she felt.

"I dunno," he moaned, getting up and staggering into the bathroom. He peed, took one look at himself in the mirror, and lurched into the bedroom, where he threw himself face down on the bed. No more drugs. Never again.

Jess followed him in. "I've ordered breakfast," she said. "You'll feel better when you eat."

"Don't *mention* food."

"Get up. Take a shower. We've got to sort this mess out."

"Piss off, Jess."

"Don't keep on saying that. I'm here to help you."

He scratched his head, sat up and reached for a cigarette. "I think you're a little late."

• • • • •

Olympia did not sleep. She had learned a useful secret from Flash. After an all-night session of drinking and dope, the only way to face the new day was with a little help from a couple of large white pills. Quaaludes.

She took two on returning to the hotel, and by the time she had bathed and changed her clothes she was ready to set things in motion. First she called her lawyer in New York. Then the Magiriano's publicist. And—because she was not lacking in good manners—Vitos.

"Mr. Felicidade is accepting no calls before twelve noon," the operator twanged.

Tough. Mr. Felicidade would just have to find out the hard way.

• • • • •

Eden awoke early and slid from bed like a conspirator. Santino slept on his back, snoring loudly.

Quietly she took some clothes from the closet, crept into the bathroom and closed the door.

Why hadn't she spoken to Lennie at the party?

Why hadn't *he* spoken to her?

She rinsed her face with cold water. The mark of Santino's slap was gone. She looked as beautiful as ever with her porcelain skin, topaz eyes and exotic cheekbones.

She applied a touch of brown shadow, blusher and a dash of lip gloss. Then she tied her fine blond hair back in a ponytail. The young unsophisticated look. Lennie loved it.

She dressed in white cotton pants and a silky T-shirt.

Almost holding her breath, she slid back into the bedroom. Santino still slept. On a table beside the bed lay a wad of bills, several items of gold jewelry, and a snubnosed revolver. Carefully she ignored the gun and jewelry, and took several hundred-dollar bills from the stack. Then, going over to the desk, she scribbled a short note: "Gone shopping. Back soon." He wouldn't like it, she knew that. But she needed to get out without being followed. And, hopefully, Zeko was not sleeping outside their door.

Santino was a dangerous man. Obsessive and unpredictable. She had put up with him for two years, and she was prepared to continue to do so until the movie was made. But obviously, after last night's performance, she needed insurance. And what better insurance than Lennie Golden? Especially now he was riding high.

• • • • •

"Who are *you?*" Olympia demanded imperiously as she swept past Jess into Lennie's suite.

The blond heiress was dressed for business in a white lace dress with pink flowers festooned in her hair. She was trailed by several salespeople carrying suits hidden beneath protective polyethylene, an array of shirts on hangers and an assortment of boxes.

"I'm Lennie's manager," Jess said. "And what is——?"

"Hmmm . . ." Olympia destroyed her with a sweeping look. "I expect you've heard our news then."

"Yes, and——"

Olympia ignored her and turned her attention to the minions with the clothes. "Leave everything on the couch and go," she commanded.

They did as they were bade.

When they had departed, Olympia once again directed her cool gaze at Jess. "Now," she said crisply, "there are several arrangements I want you to double-check. The reception is arranged for three this afternoon. The hotel is supposed to be taking care of the food and flowers—but make sure it's done properly. And *triple-check* the press attendance. I want to be certain this is covered by the best. Several journalists are flying in from L.A. I need a limo to meet their plane, and they must be taken care of while they're here." She paused for breath. "You don't *look* like a manager," she added disparagingly. "Anyhow, I suppose Lennie knows what he's doing. Where is he?"

Jess was almost speechless. Was *this* what Lennie had married? This shrill, bossy Kewpie doll with fat legs and enormous boobs? Lennie, who had always had the cream. Class A ladies only.

She gestured helplessly toward the bedroom. "In there," she said. Let *him* deal with it. He was the one who had married it.

• • • • •

Vitos awoke to the sound of his own voice. It soothed him to reenter the world listening to his soft, caressing tones. The tape-alarm clock did its duty at twelve noon precisely.

He rolled over in bed and drifted in and out of sleep for a while, then he arose, exercised, showered, shaved, glued his hairpiece into place, and summoned room service and his manager. They arrived simultaneously.

While Vitos tackled fresh grapefruit, scrambled eggs and lemon tea (he had to watch his diet at all times) his manager nervously paced the room. He had discovered Vitos when he had caught his Mexican maid drooling over the singer on a Spanish TV station several years earlier.

"These wimmen in America, they lova me so much," Vitos crooned, reflectively sipping his tea.

"Yes," agreed his manager, wondering how to break the news that was buzzing all over the hotel.

"Sometimes is so difficull maka the universal language offa lova. I thinka everyones, they unnerstanda me so well."

"Yes."

"Ah . . ." Vitos sighed. "Wimmen. They lova me."

"Where is Olympia?" his manager asked quickly, seizing the opportunity.

"You hava my papers from Spain?" Vitos inquired, rising from the table and admiring himself in a nearby mirror. He practiced his smile, liked what he saw, and proceeded to do a few facial exercises guaranteed to get rid of any lurking double chins. Not that he had any—but you could *never* be too careful.

"The papers haven't arrived yet."

"Too bad." Vitos thrust his chin forward and back. "Maybe nota *too* bad. Thisa marriage, you really thinks I should do it? The wimmen be—how you say?—broken in six."

"Two."

"What?"

"Forget it."

"Good morning!" Olympia flung open the shower door. "And how are *you* this morning?"

Lennie regarded his bride, who seemed to be feeling no

pain. She looked fresh, bright and exceptionally pretty, if a little plump.

"I feel like camel dung," he said dourly. "Did we really do what I think we did?"

She selected a large towel and held it open for him to step into. "We did."

"Shit!"

"You're not sorry, are you?" She widened her blue eyes and managed to look hurt and vulnerable at the same time.

"Jesus! I don't know." He knotted the towel around his waist and tried to review the situation. Here he was in the bathroom of a Las Vegas hotel with one of the richest women in the world, whom he had known for less than twenty-four hours, and they were married! Any moment he expected to wake up. This wasn't real life, as Jess had so eloquently pointed out—this was insane.

"We've got to talk," he said, walking into the bedroom and searching for a cigarette. "Uh . . . I don't know about you, but I was stoned last night. I mean *really* out of it. And . . . well . . . Jesus, in the cold light of day it's not so funny, is it?"

He fixed her with a hopeful look. He was hopeful she would agree with him, say, "What a mistake! I came to tell you I've taken care of the whole thing—had the ceremony reversed. We are no longer legal."

What she actually said was, "I've planned the reception for three o'clock today. Not that we need another party, but we want to have photographs and a cake." She laughed gaily. "What kind of a wedding would it be without that? Oh, and my daughter, Brigette, will be *so* disappointed if we don't *do* anything. She's adorable, you'll love her. She's out with her nanny now, choosing a dress."

"I didn't know you had a kid," he said blankly.

"There are a lot of things we don't know about each other, aren't there?" She caressed him with an innocent smile. Olympia could play innocent—when it suited her—to the hilt. "But that's going to be half the fun, isn't it? Finding out." She hugged him warmly. "I've bought you a selection of clothes. They're in the other room with your . . . er . . . manager girl. I thought you'd want a new outfit for our wedding party. Oh, Lennie, I'm so excited. In one night you've changed my life. I was really depressed. I can't begin to tell you how unhappy I was." She lowered her lashes and her voice. "Almost suicidal," she whispered. "But you've changed everything. It's as if we found each other just in time."

He had things to say. He couldn't get them out. How could he tell her it was all a mistake? How could he back out now? *Thanks, Eden, look what you got me into this time.* He was married to a total stranger, and there was nothing he could do about it.

60

Happiness was getting back into action. And Atlantic City was exactly where Lucky wanted to be. She left Roberto in New York with CeeCee and departed for Atlantic City in high spirits.

She knew what she was looking for, and the real estate agents were eagerly awaiting her arrival. Unfortunately, the location she had been after with Gino was long gone. And prices had zoomed. Atlantic City was taking off in a way nobody had quite imagined. She had known it would be that way. Damn Gino. They could have enjoyed the excitement of being in at the beginning. But the hell with it. She would build the finest hotel ever. She would create a legendary palace, a shimmering tower. And she would call it "The Santangelo."

• • • • •

For two days Susan and Gino argued back and forth. He refused to entertain the idea of going on the cruise unless Lucky called him personally. And Susan insisted it was an opportunity she absolutely could not miss.

Gino had yet to admit it to anyone except himself, but his marriage was over. Susan, the warm and wonderful woman he married, had turned out to be an empty shell.

Wind her up and she dresses the part.

Press her button and she gives a great dinner party.

Shove her in the right direction and she spends money like it's going out of style.

Lucky had been right about her all along. Why hadn't he seen it? She'd taken him for a schmuck.

He thought about Lucky a lot. And he missed her. But there was no going back. She had married Dimitri, given birth to a baby. And not once had she consulted him.

He called Costa in Miami and complained.

"You get what you give in life," Costa said philosophically. "What have you ever given Lucky that makes her feel she should turn to *you* for advice?"

Gino hung up, furious. Costa was getting senile.

"We'll *go* on the goddamn cruise," he told Susan. "I want to spend some time with my grandson, and this seems to be the only way I can do it."

Susan smiled. "Yes, dear," she replied calmly. And rushed out to spend another few thousand dollars.

• • • • •

Dimitri had just put down the phone after speaking with Francesca when his secretary announced that Olympia was on the line.

"Where have you been?" he roared. "I've been trying to reach you."

"I'm in—"

"It's not good enough, Olympia. You *must not* vanish for days on end. For all I know you and Brigette could be in the hands of kidnappers. You are a Stanislopoulos and you must always—"

"I got married again."

"Christ, girl!" he thundered. "Live with that degenerate rock person if you must. But marriage is *out of the question.*"

"I didn't marry *him.*"

She had always been impossible. Spoiled and thoughtless. "Who then?" he demanded furiously.

"Look on the cover of *People* magazine. Lennie Golden. He's a comedian."

"A *comedian!*"

"Stop screaming. He's better than the other three. I've got to go now, we're having a reception. Can you do me a favor and tell Mommy for me?"

"Your mother doesn't know?"

"She will when you tell her."

"Olympia—"

"Bye, Papa, we'll see you on the cruise."

Dimitri paced his office. Olympia was the stupidest girl in the world.

He communicated with his ex-wife, who did not seem unduly perturbed.

He sent his secretary out for a copy of *People* and studied the latest fortune hunter leering at him from the front page.

He phoned Francesca in Munich and she laughed.

Olympia, Olympia. He had not been blessed with a smart daughter.

* * * * *

Lucky returned full of excitement later that evening. Dimitri had just finished a solitary dinner and he was not in a happy frame of mind.

"I've found *exactly* the right site," she enthused. "Multi-fantastic, and no way can we lose it. You've got to put your lawyers on it *at once*." She clasped her arms around his neck. "I feel so great. Let's go in the bedroom and celebrate. Making deals *really* turns me on."

"Don't talk like a cheap whore," he said abruptly, disengaging himself from her grasp.

"What?" She stared at him in amazement.

"You are my *wife* now. Kindly try to remember that."

She backed away. "I don't think I'm hearing you right."

"I've had an extremely tiresome day," he said. "And I have no need of further aggravation."

He missed the danger in her eyes. The sudden storm.

"Olympia got married again," he said shortly. "She's irresponsible. She deserves to lose every penny of her inheritance."

"Hey, man," Lucky said rudely, affecting a tough New York street accent. "Dintja hear me? I feel *hooorny*. Wanna get it on?"

His face was carved in granite. "I beg your pardon?"

"Yeh, man. An' y'can kiss my ass too."

She slammed into the bedroom without a backward glance. No way could he talk to her like that and get away with it.

He followed her, unused to being answered back.

"Stay out of my way," she burned.

"What's the matter with you?" he demanded.

"Think about it."

"There is nothing to think about. I corrected you on your behavior."

"Corrected me? Corrected me? Who the *fuck* do you think you're talking to?"

"My wife, the mother of my child. And you *will not* use language like an alley cat."

"Jesus H. Christ! What the fuck is going *on* here?"

He slapped her face. She sprang at him, clawing with her nails. They raked his skin, drawing blood.

He was a big man, powerful. He pinned her arms and they fell together heavily on the bed.

Lucky could not believe what was happening. She had known Dimitri for two years and he had never revealed this side of his character before. She had married an equal, not a fucking father figure who told her how to speak and behave.

He gripped her wrists and forced them backward.

She tried to bring her knee up to his balls, but he was too strong for her. She was athletic, certainly no weakling, but the strength faded from her as he concentrated on holding her down.

And then it happened. She felt his excitement and she didn't want it. Not this way. Not as the result of their violent scene.

He attempted to keep her captive while he fumbled with the zipper on his pants.

She managed to bring her arm up sharply and smash him under the chin.

He yelled in pain.

The brief moment was enough for her to roll out from under and lock herself in the bathroom. She was shaking with anger.

He did not pursue her further.

61

There were good days and there were bad. Now that California was a definite yes, Steven felt slightly better. He was living in a one-room apartment on Third Avenue, having rented out his very nice brownstone when he went to Europe.

His life was a mess and he knew it. Once he had been full of ambition, but Carrie had ruined everything with her sordid revelations. Since returning to America he had done nothing except think about himself and his problems. He slept late, didn't eat properly, and hung around his one-room dump watching television. The only friend he had contacted was Jerry Myerson. And then only because he needed to borrow money.

Women he picked up at random. Once so particular about his female companions, he now favored any girl he didn't have to make conversation with. What a difference from his past life. Fine upstanding Steven Berkeley. Hardworking, an assistant D.A., with nowhere to go but up. Life was strange. He remembered with bitterness arriving at Enzio Bonnatti's Long Island mansion that fateful afternoon in 1977, set for action.

But Lucky Santangelo got there first.

The same Lucky Santangelo he had been trapped in an elevator with only days before during the great power blackout.

The same Lucky Santangelo who might—just might—be his half sister.

Lucky.

She was difficult to forget, with her smart mouth and dark gypsy looks.

Lucky.

Thank God they hadn't—

He didn't even want to think about what had nearly happened between them.

He wondered how she would feel if it turned out they *were* brother and sister. Would she even remember him?

Oh, yes, she'd remember him—his pride told him that.

What pride?

He looked terrible. He had to get himself together, back to work, and put the past behind him.

Soon.

62

All things considered, Vitos Felicidade took the news well enough. Really, there was nothing he could do but smile for the cameras (of which there were many) and pretend it was he who had encouraged the "instant love" match.

In private, he brooded. What was wrong with him? Why had Olympia spurned him? Twice. Did she perhaps see behind the facade? Did she alone know that beneath the throbbing sex symbol hovered an insecure, plain and ordinary man?

He did not wish to think about it. He attended the wedding reception for an hour and then retired to his suite where he sat and sulked.

Jess did not take it so well. She sought Matt out and complained hotly. He agreed with her and pointed out that nothing could be done.

Back at the Sands Hotel, Eden stared numbly out the window, while Zeko played solitaire nearby. She had crept out in the morning fully intending to see Lennie, but just as she was about to enter a cab, Zeko had appeared from nowhere and announced that the boss had said he was to accompany her everywhere she went. She had almost screamed with frustration. Instead she had smiled glassily and allowed the dumb ox to trail her around a parade of tawdry shops. Las Vegas was the pits. She couldn't wait to leave.

Paige had invited her to lunch, and she was allowed to go. But while digesting a tuna salad, the news had spread about Olympia Stanislopoulos and Lennie Golden.

Hot gossip.

She had wanted to throw up. Now she was gazing out at neon and desert, wondering if she had made the right choice.

Santino Bonnatti.

Lennie Golden.

She hoped she had backed the winner.

She had a horrible suspicion she might not have.

• • • • •

"You stink," sneered Brigette.

"You're kidding. I took a shower specially," replied Lennie, deadpan.

"I said, 'You stink,' " Brigette repeated.

"You sound like a broken record."

She gazed up at him. Sapphire blue eyes (her mother's) in a heart-shaped face. "I hate you," she uttered spitefully.

He grimaced. "Can't win 'em all," he said with an engaging smile.

Nanny Mabel, embarrassed, said, "I'm so sorry, Mr. Golden. She's tired, it's late, and—"

"C'mon," Lennie interrupted mildly. "It's four-thirty in the afternoon. If the kid wants to hate me—no excuses, let her do her thing." He bent to speak to the child. "Y'know something? Brigette is a *very* pretty name, and you are a *very* pretty young lady."

Brigette blinked several times. Why was this one talking to her? Usually when she told them they stunk, they glared at her, then ignored her, and she never had to talk to them again—which was the way she liked it. Mama's boyfriends were pigs. She hated them all.

Lennie didn't wait around for a response. He was off and running. Olympia had assembled enough press to launch a hit movie, and she was loving every minute, posing for pictures like a professional. But then, in a way, she was. She had grown up with photographers on her doorstep. Olympia Stanislopoulos. Heiress. Fair game for the paparazzi and gossip columnists of the world.

Somehow she had managed to make their wedding into a special event. The cake was a fantasy, with a miniature dancing couple on top. The Magiriano ballroom was transformed into a fairyland of flowers. And the Louis Roederer Cristal champagne flowed.

He shuddered to think how much it was all going to cost. Was he supposed to pay? Or was this a gift from the Magiriano?

A grim-faced Jess shrugged when he asked her. "I don't know," she said tartly.

She wasn't happy about the whole scene. He wasn't exactly ecstatic either, but what was done was done—and who knew? Maybe it would work out. Stranger things had happened.

Sure.

63

Compromise was not Lucky's style. She had no intention of sitting around waiting for Dimitri to apologize. He had to learn, and fast, that she was nobody's doormat.

The morning after their fight she took off for the East Hampton house with Roberto and CeeCee. The truth of the matter was, she was more than a little disturbed by his behavior. She wanted an equal partnership. Not an uneven relationship with a man who felt he could call every shot. Chillingly she knew that marrying Dimitri had been a mistake. There was an age gap that could never be bridged, and no way was she ready to play the role he had in mind for her.

It did not bother her at all that he made no attempt to contact her for three days. Coolly she called his lawyers and gave them instructions to negotiate on the piece of land she wished to purchase in Atlantic City. Then she double-checked with her own lawyers to make sure everything went ahead. Dimitri had signed a legal document. The hotel would proceed, whatever happened.

He arrived at the house three days later. "Forgive me," he said, standing on her doorstep with her favorite 'Sterling Silver' roses, and a Tiffany box.

She knew apologies were difficult for him. She could have made him sweat, but she let him in, and they walked in the garden and talked it out—as much as one could talk it out with a man like Dimitri. He was of his generation and did not believe in long, analytical discussions.

She opened the Tiffany box. It contained an opulent diamond choker, at its center a huge heart. Dimitri fastened the clasp around her neck and considered everything to be all right. He kissed her chastely and informed her that Susan and Gino had accepted his invitation to join them on his yacht.

Oh, God! She had never in a million years expected Gino to say yes. She didn't know why she was so upset. Her feelings about her father were confused. Sometimes she loved him more than anyone in the world, and other times she couldn't care less if she never saw him again. It had always been that way.

"You're pleased, aren't you?" Dimitri inquired.

She swallowed her real feelings. "Sure," she replied casually.

She wasn't looking forward to the cruise at all. Dimitri's friends. Francesca Fern and her bumbling husband. Now Susan and Gino. And they would all be trapped on a boat together. However large and luxurious Dimitri's yacht was, it was still close quarters. An inescapable round of lunches and dinners.

Maybe Olympia and her new husband, whoever he might be, would save the day. Lucky had forgotten to ask who he was, and now Dimitri had returned to New York leaving her to prepare for the two-week cruise. She did so reluctantly.

• • • • •

It seemed to Gino that the only days he got out of bed in the morning with enthusiasm were the days he was seeing Paige. She put a little zing in his life. She was bawdy and uninhibited, but most of all, she was fun.

He looked forward to her return from Las Vegas, and he arrived at the Beverly Wilshire an hour early for their Friday assignation. Paige turned up half an hour late. She smelled of her usual musky scent and wore a white skirt split almost to the crotch.

"Did anyone ever tell you that you dress like a hooker?" he asked with an amused grin, sitting on the end of the bed.

"Yes." She fluffed her frizzy hair. "And don't you just love it!"

With one quick movement she unhooked her skirt at the waist and it fell to the floor. She wore no panties.

"Hey—" He began to laugh.

"Quick service. With a smile," said Paige, walking toward him. "And please leave fifty dollars on the table."

"Kinda cheap," Gino joked, enjoying the game.

"That's because you're a favored client," said Paige, pressing her wiry bush of pubic hair against his face.

He responded accordingly. Sex kept him young—he was sure of that. Not for Gino Santangelo the aches and pains of old age. Sex kept the vital juices flowing. As long as he could get it up he felt invincible, and Paige Wheeler gave him the best hard-on he had had in years.

What would life be like if he were married to a woman like Paige? A great deal more exciting than being with Susan day in and day out, that was for sure.

Their lovemaking took time. Paige required more than one orgasm, unlike Susan, who considered the moment she climaxed it was all over and shoved him off.

Paige enjoyed experimenting. Sometimes he wished he were younger, more athletic. But she didn't seem to mind. Anyway, he knew he pleased her.

"How was Vegas?" he asked, when Paige was finally satisfied.

She lay spread-eagled on the bed, totally nude. "Interesting," she replied.

"How interesting?"

"Well . . . I went to Vitos Felicidade's and Lennie Golden's opening night at your hotel."

"How was it?"

"The service or the show?"

"Both."

"Excellent. Lennie Golden is really something special. And Vitos has a certain European charm. Naturally, everyone was talking about Olympia Stanislopoulos and Lennie Golden getting married the next day. She came there with Vitos, you know."

"Yeh?"

"Don't you read the gossip columns?"

"Only when I'm in 'em."

"There were parties every night. And I played a little blackjack."

"Did you win?"

"Lost."

"You shoulda bin with me. I'd never let you lose."

He touched the hair on her crotch. It was damp. She stretched languorously.

"I'm gonna be away for a coupla weeks," he said. "Think y'can manage without me?"

"I'll try," she said teasingly. "Where are you going?"

"I don't know if I told you, but my daughter, Lucky—she's kinda crazy like me—married the other Stanislopoulos—the father, Dimitri. Can you believe it? He's nearly as old as me. Lucky used to go to school with Olympia." He sighed. "She's nuts."

"What's so nuts about marrying one of the richest men in the world?"

"Lucky doesn't need his money," Gino said shortly, removing his hand.

"Put that back!" scolded Paige.

Gino did as she requested.

"Hmmmm . . ." Paige surrendered herself to sensual feelings.

Gino sensed her further need and bent his head to her. Within seconds she was moaning loudly and climaxing yet again.

In all his experience with women, Gino could not remember a woman as insatiable as Paige.

She sat up, kissed him and said, "Thank you. Now, tell me about your daughter."

He shrugged. "Nothin' to tell. She married the guy an' they've invited us on this cruise they're havin'. Susan wants to go."

"I can imagine."

"An I'm goin' because it'll give me a chance to see the kid."

"What kid?"

"I'm a grandfather."

"Oh, no!" Paige jumped from the bed, her face a mask of mock horror. "I'm sleeping with a *grandfather!*"

"Hey—" He grinned. "You ain't no spring chicken."

"I'm in my forties. I am not yet ready to be bedding grandfathers."

"Fuck you."

"Anytime, pops."

They both started to laugh. He got up, put his arms around her, and they rocked with mirth.

"You know somethin'?" he said. "You're my kind of broad."

"We're a few decades apart," she mused, "but we both grew up on the streets of New York."

"You never told me that."

"You never asked. Besides, it's not something I care to broadcast."

He reached for a robe. "So—tell me your life history."

"One of these days. Right now I'm late for an appointment."

"Jeez! I thought we'd be able to sit around an' bullshit. Don't make other appointments when you're seein' me."

She hurried into the bathroom. "When do you leave?" she called out.

"In a few days."

"I'll miss you."

"Not as much as I'm gonna miss you."

• • • • •

Susan looked impatiently at her gold Patek Philippe watch as she sat on the outdoor terrace of the Bel Air Hotel. Paige was late. Again. She was always late—that is when she had time to see Susan at all. For the past few months their meetings had been impossibly brief, and Susan was beginning to suspect Paige had someone else.

She frowned, and realized she wouldn't be able to stand it if Paige told her it was over between them. It wasn't fair. She couldn't take it. Paige meant everything to her.

The waiter at her elbow asked her if she would care for another drink. She ordered her third Martini, and sat back to wait.

Within minutes Paige arrived, looking flustered, her hair a mess and her outfit ridiculous.

The two women kissed.

"I am *so* busy!" Paige exclaimed. "It seems *everyone* is into new decor. Ever since they featured the house I did for Ramo Kaliffe in *Architectural Digest* my life is not my own."

Susan smiled politely. Paige smelled of musk and sex—she always did. Two men across the terrace were staring. Paige attracted attention wherever she went. She was not beautiful, not even pretty, but her allure spoke volumes.

"I thought you weren't coming," Susan said reproachfully.

"You know I'm always late."

"We're going on a cruise through the Greek Islands with Dimitri Stanislopoulos. I had to see you before we left." Susan lowered her voice to a whisper. "It's been two months since we've . . . been together. I can't stand it any longer."

Paige gazed restlessly across the terrace. Her eyes met one of the men who had been staring. He raised his glass to her. She wondered if she knew him, decided it was probably a friend of Ryder's and acknowledged him with a wave.

"Well?" Susan questioned insistently. "Don't *you* think two months is a long time? Don't *you* miss *me* as much as I miss you?"

Paige took a deep breath. How did one tell a woman it was over? If Susan had been a man, it would have been a cinch.

She picked some nuts from a dish on the table. "Ryder has never been an easy man to live with," she began.

"I know that," Susan interrupted. "Do you think Gino is easy? He's old and difficult and sex-crazed. I just don't know how I stand him. If it wasn't for you I—"

"Listen to me," said Paige forcefully. She didn't want to hear about how terrible Gino was. She happened to think Gino was pretty special, and for just that reason she planned to give up all her other lovers—including Susan. "Ryder has changed. I don't know what's come over him, but he has certainly changed—and it's for the better."

Susan stared at her blankly. "What?"

"I want to give our marriage a fair chance," Paige said with false conviction.

"What?" Susan repeated numbly.

"Excuse me, ladies." The man whose eye Paige had caught earlier was at their table. He was middle-aged and L.A. casual. "I have taken the liberty of ordering champagne."

The waiter deposited an ice bucket with a bottle of Dom Pérignon next to the table.

"My friend and I decided that two beautiful women such as yourselves deserve only the best," said the man. At which point his friend, short, with a beard, joined him, and they stood there expectantly, waiting to be asked to join the party.

"Thank you," Paige said graciously, crossing her legs.

They caught her scent and stood ramrod-straight—two hounds ready for the chase.

"I *would* ask you to join us," she continued, "but Mrs. Santangelo has just suffered a death in the family—so I am sure you can understand this is not the right time for us to become . . . social."

"*Sure,*" the first man said emphatically. "Wouldn't dream of troubling you and Mrs. Santer—um, maybe *you* might be free for dinner later?"

"What a tempting offer," Paige sighed. "But quite impossible. So nice meeting you." She recrossed her legs, giving them another whiff of paradise, and dismissed them by turning her back.

They got the message and walked reluctantly off.

"What do you mean—you're giving your marriage a fair chance?" Susan asked in a furious whisper.

"Exactly what it sounds like," Paige replied calmly. "I'm going to be faithful."

"You!" exclaimed Susan scornfully. *"Never!"*

The waiter poured champagne.

"Please don't underestimate me," Paige murmured. "If I want to do something, *I do it.*"

Susan's eyes filled with tears. "What about us?" she asked mournfully.

"We'll put what we had on hold and see what happens."

64

Alice Golden arrived in Las Vegas two days after her son's wedding made worldwide headlines. She was not exactly what he needed in his life at that particular moment. He had a wife and a stepdaughter, and he was busy trying to get used to *them*. An instant mother was unnecessary luggage. However, to hear Alice tell it, mother and son had been inseparable. She had taught him everything he knew. And while Olympia's entering their tightly knit relationship was a shock, Alice was prepared to accept her with open arms. She had given three "exclusive" interviews to that effect before she even saw Lennie.

He greeted her warily as she was ushered into his suite by a bemused Jess.

"I found her kicking up a fuss in the lobby," Jess whispered, "demanding God knows what, so I thought I'd better bring her up. I don't think she remembers me."

"My darling!" Alice exclaimed, throwing open her spidery arms. Dieting had caused her flesh to become scrawny, and her hair was bleached a too-white blond. She hugged Lennie tightly.

"Alice," he said, "what are *you* doing here?"

"What am *I* doing here?" She gazed around the suite as if there was an attentive audience, when in fact there were only Jess and Lennie. "What am *I* doing here? Your mother. Your flesh and blood. What am *I* doing here? Hah! A funny kind of question from a boy who just got married without a word to his caring, worrying, *lonely* mother."

Finally she was doing Jewish mother schtick. Lennie didn't know whether to laugh or cry.

"Cut it out, Alice," he said.

Jess hovered. She couldn't make up her mind if she should

stay or go. Lennie made it up for her. "Order tea," he said brusquely, "for the three of us."

Alice was clutching a battered carpetbag which had obviously seen better days. She placed it on the floor and looked around. "Where's the hairness?" she asked.

"The what?" questioned Lennie.

"I think she means heiress," said Jess, trying to stifle a giggle. "Isn't that what you mean, Mrs. Golden? Heiress?"

Alice peered at her through three sets of stiff false eyelashes. "Who are you?" she asked crossly. "You look familiar."

"Lennie's old school friend, Jess Skolsky."

Alice stared. "The shrimp," she said at last, bringing back every painful memory Jess had of growing up.

Alice sat down on the couch. She was wearing a cheap polyester dress, cut low to exhibit tired breasts, and short to exhibit still-spectacular legs. "I flew here," she announced. "The men on the plane wouldn't leave me alone. When I told everyone I was your mother, Lennie, the women wouldn't leave me alone. I have four numbers for you, but I don't expect you'll want them now you're married."

"My wife wouldn't be thrilled," he commented dryly.

"Where is she? I came to see for myself this"—she paused, determined to get the word right—"hairess."

"Her name's Olympia."

"Fancy name." She favored him with an accusing look. "You could have phoned me. You could have *invited* me to the wedding. You could have told me you were headlining in Vegas—my home, my town. I was a star here too, once, you know. Not *that* long ago. Alice the Swizzle. I'm *still* famous in this town. You should only know how famous. *You* should be as famous as I once was—maybe still am. Who knows if they remember . . ." she trailed off.

"Where are you staying, Mrs. Golden?" Jess asked politely, thinking the time had come to ease her out. Lennie liked to be alone before the evening show.

"Here, of course," Alice snapped waspishly. "Arrange it for me. I *am* the star's mother, you know. I deserve recognition. Without me he wouldn't be here, would he?"

"And how long will you be staying?"

"As long as my boy wants me to."

Lennie shrugged helplessly. "I just got married, y'know."

"That's why I'm here."

He didn't have the heart to tell her to get lost. Who needed a mother after thirty-two years?

Whether he needed her or not, she was very much present. Olympia and Alice together should be a riot. He couldn't wait.

• • • • •

The day after the reception—as soon as she was sure her wedding pictures covered the world press—Olympia phoned Flash in the south of France. A girlish voice answered.

"Get me Flash," Olympia demanded imperiously. "And hurry up, I'm calling from America."

She then had an eleven-minute wait before his rich cockney tones crackled down the line. "I s'pose it's you," he remarked rudely. "Fuckin' marvelous! I waited at the airport two bleedin' hours last week, an' I don't usually give airport."

"Did you honestly expect me to come?"

"Why not? You said you was comin'."

"I didn't come," she said icily, "because I don't think *your wife* would have liked it."

"Aw, shit! Is *that* what you're on about?"

"*Your wife,* Flash. *Your wife,* whom you *somehow neglected to* mention to me. Your *pregnant teenage* wife. God, you're a prick!"

He gave a whiskey-soaked laugh. "You been readin' those supermarket rags? Didn't think rich bints like you ever went near a bleedin' supermarket."

"Real life does have a habit of catching up with one—rich or not. I've had all your things from the New York apartment packed up and sent to the Goodwill."

Outrage. "Yer *what?*"

"You heard."

"Jesus Christ!"

"And talking of newspapers, have you read yours today?"

"You're a really stupid cow."

"To put up with you, I must have been."

"Get your fat arse over here an' I'll explain everything."

"Shall I bring my husband?"

"Yer what?"

"Read the papers."

"Aw, c'mon—yer silly bitch. You didn't go an' do it?"

"It seemed to be all the fashion."

"Who'd you do it *with?* Not that Spanish asshole with the wig."

"I resisted the temptation."

"Thank Christ for that."

"I married Lennie Golden."

"Who's he?"

This conversation was not proceeding as Olympia had hoped. First of all she had confidently expected Flash to know all about her wedding. And she had certainly expected him to know who Lennie was.

"I really hate you," she snapped irrationally.

"Are you comin' or not?"

"Haven't you been listening to me? I'm *married*—just like you. It's over."

He was clearly bored. "Suit yerself, Tubs."

She could almost see him twitch his skinny shoulders, the way he did when he was aggravated or fed up. He didn't give a damn! Furiously she slammed the phone down. Her father had been right all along. Flash was a selfish, depraved user, and she was well rid of him.

So why did she feel so blue? She was a bride again. She should be singing and laughing—at least have a smile on her face.

She visited her stash and snorted some coke. Who was Lennie Golden anyway? And *why* had she married him? To spite Flash? Kind of a dumb reason to tie oneself up.

God! What had she done? Lennie seemed nice enough, and he was attractive and great in bed—but nice guys had never been her scene. She had made another mistake. In a few weeks, after the cruise, she would instruct her lawyer to get her out of it. No big deal. Another payoff. She could afford it. There had to be *some* compensations for being rich.

65

Lucky planned to take only sports clothes on the cruise, but Dimitri informed her, rather late in the day, that dinner each evening was a formal affair.

"You dress for dinner?" she asked, amazed.

"Tradition," he replied.

"Whose tradition?"

"Mine."

She searched his granite face for any sign of humor. There was none. Now that she was his wife she realized she didn't know him very well at all. In the eighteen months they had been together it had been an intermittent affair—with short blocks of time spent on his island—where they had been alone and wonderfully relaxed. Now a new Dimitri seemed to be emerging—a stuffy man with rigid tastes and old world codes of behavior. She wasn't sure she liked the new Dimitri at all. She *was* sure she should have kept the relationship the way it was before. Why had she given in to his pressure?

The property deal in Atlantic City was almost set, and she was elated about that. But she dreaded the cruise. She hoped she would be able to find a quiet corner and flake out.

Dimitri had decided that this year it would take place in the south of France. He didn't mention to anyone, especially to Lucky, that this was to accommodate Francesca—who had a gala dinner being given for her in Monte Carlo she did not wish to miss.

They flew by Concorde from New York to Paris, and from there a private Lear Jet transported them to Nice airport, where a chauffeured Rolls waited to take them to *The Greek*, as Dimitri had modestly named his yacht.

Roberto took the journey well. He was an extremely active, happy child, nothing seemed to upset him, and Lucky felt fortunate to have found someone like CeeCee to look after him. She was a pretty Black girl of twenty, with a double helping of large white teeth, a ready grin and tightly corn-rowed hair. Lucky had discovered her working as a waitress in a hamburger joint six weeks before she gave birth.

"I'm *sooo* envious!" the smiling girl had remarked, gazing at Lucky's huge stomach while she served her forbidden French fries, a milkshake and a large juicy burger. "I just love babies. I've got six younger brothers and sisters back in Jamaica, and I miss the little ones so."

They got to talking, and before she knew it, Lucky had offered her the job and CeeCee had accepted immediately.

Dimitri had been disapproving. He wanted a trained English nanny for his son, not some inexperienced Jamaican waitress. But Lucky always went with her gut instinct, and CeeCee had turned out to be a gem. She loved Roberto almost as much as they did.

It was Lucky's first visit to *The Greek*. It was huge. She had expected luxury, but the sheer opulence of it surpassed her expectations. A three-hundred-foot white palace with a full crew, eight magnificent staterooms, each decorated by a different famous designer, an Art Deco cinema with black silk walls and state-of-the-art equipment to show either videos or the latest movies, a gold-and-white mosaic swimming pool, and numerous decks and other areas for entertainment and recreation.

The captain greeted them. He was an Englishman with a ruddy complexion, a handlebar mustache and a falsely jovial attitude. His wife, a horse-faced woman with a skin like leather, stood by his side. She was in charge of the kitchen. They had worked for Dimitri for fifteen years, and regarded Lucky with ill-concealed suspicion. Captain and Mrs. Pratt ran riot with creative financing—they did not wish the interfering presence of a wife.

"Have any of my guests arrived?" Dimitri boomed.

"Not yet, Mr. Stanislopoulos," replied Captain Pratt, welcoming them aboard. "But we're all ready and prepared." His flat eyes stripped the clothes from Lucky as he pumped her by the hand and said how delighted and happy they all were that the boss had found himself a wife.

I'll bet, she thought. She knew automatically they were on the take. Years running a hotel in Las Vegas had taught her many things about human nature. She had a nose for the swindlers and cheaters of the world. Automatically she smiled. How good she was getting at displaying social graces. She hoped she could keep it up throughout the cruise. And then she would be off. Atlantic City beckoned.

Dimitri took her arm and escorted her to their living quarters. A very masculine stateroom awaited her—all dark browns and earth tones. The king-size bed featured a leather headboard and polished leather-and-brass bedside tables. The walls were padded with leather. On one wall hung a large portrait of a nude woman.

"Picasso," Dimitri pointed out, noticing her staring at it.

She moved through to the bathroom. Caviar marble. Cold and impersonal.

"Well?" he asked. "Do you like it?"

"It's . . . severe," she replied.

"I think you mean cleancut. I commissioned it three years ago from one of the finest designers in Italy."

"It's still severe. I would have preferred something more relaxing." She looked around again. "Where are the books? The magazines? Even more important—where is the music?"

"What music?" he asked, frowning slightly.

He had yet to discover her passion for soul music. She felt lost without an available stereo. How could anyone design a bedroom without incorporating a great sound system?

Roberto and CeeCee's quarters were certainly more cheerful. Planned originally for Brigette and her nanny, there were nursery animals climbing the walls, a mural on the ceiling depicting sky and sun, and a sunny yellow bathroom. Lucky knew she would be spending more time there than in Dimitri's austere sanctuary.

* * * * *

"God!" screamed Francesca Fern. "Be careful with my luggage, you dolts!"

The French porters exchanged looks. They didn't understand what she said, but she was English or American—no difference—and all English-speaking tourists were to be looked down upon and treated with as much insolence as they could muster on this hot and windy day. By accident on purpose one of her Vuitton suitcases (there were twelve in varying sizes) fell from the top of the cart on which they were being wheeled to a waiting car.

"Horace!" Francesca yelled. "How dare you allow this to happen!"

Horace, who was certainly not to blame for the fall, said, "I'm sorry, dear. It won't happen again."

"I should think not," snorted Francesca, as she marched regally toward the car, ignoring the gawking tourists, who all recognized her, and the waiting chauffeur, who bowed respectfully.

Horace thrust some money at the two disdainful porters. "Please," he begged. "More careful. Yes?"

The men pocketed the money and ignored his plea, allowing the suitcases to slide from the cart onto the dusty sidewalk as soon as they reached the car. They had already been tipped, so they did not bother to help the elderly chauffeur load them into the trunk, but merely slouched away, searching for their next victim.

Fortunately Francesca was in the limousine by that time, fanning herself and complaining about the heat. She always had something to complain about, and Horace was always around to take the blast. He loved his large, volatile wife desperately, and knew that as a great talent she had to have *someone* to vent her frustrations on. Through eighteen years of marriage he had been the perfect target for her whiplash tongue. Mopping his brow, he got into the back seat beside her.

"Hmmm," sighed Francesca, in her famous deep-mahogany voice. "I am utterly exhausted. I could sleep for a week."

Horace agreed with her. He always agreed with her. He thought she was the most striking woman he had ever set eyes on, and it never failed to astound him that she had chosen *him* to be her husband.

"Perhaps that's what you'll do, dearest," he said, knowing full well it wasn't what she would do at all. When she and Dimitri Stanislopoulos were in each other's company, they were up all night, drinking, laughing, dancing. Horace did not allow his mind to wonder what else they might be doing, and he didn't venture to ask. Once he had attempted an inquiry. "How *dare you* spy on me?" Francesca had raged. "Dimitri is my best friend in the world, and I *will not* be questioned by you."

After that, Horace shut up. The cruise was a yearly event, and even if Francesca did sometimes slip into bed at six in the morning, he knew it was only a temporary aberration, and soon she would be all his again.

This year, anyway, things might be different. Dimitri had taken another wife. "A Las Vegas slut," Francesca had exclaimed in disgust when she heard. Horace had visions of a busty blond showgirl.

"Driver—" Francesca leaned forward and tapped sharply on the glass partition. "Slow down, for God's sake. You drive like a maniac."

The chauffeur, overexerted from his bout with her suitcases (six had had to be put in a following taxi) and driving no more than forty miles an hour, said a stoic *"Oui, madame"* and wished he was home with his new young wife who kept him up far too late every night.

The journey toward Cannes progressed uneventfully for ten more minutes, until for no apparent reason the car started to weave back and forth crazily across the highway, missing other shrieking motorists by inches.

"My God!" screamed Francesca in horror. "Horace! *Do something!*"

With a shuddering lurch the car turned inward toward the sidewalk, smashed into a lamppost and came to an abrupt halt. Francesca was hurled to the floor, and Horace fell on top of her. Miraculously, neither of them was hurt.

"Get off me, you fool!" shrieked Francesca, removing a spike-heeled shoe and hitting him randomly.

Horace raised his voice to her—the first time he had ever done so. "Stop that," he barked.

"Don't you tell *me* to stop *anything*," she shouted, incensed, as she continued to hit him.

The cabdriver who had been following them with the rest of the luggage ripped open the back door and, with the help of several passers-by, pulled them from the car. French exclamations abounded. *"Mon dieu!" "Merde!"* and other such phrases were bandied about.

The driver was dragged from his seat. He had a small cut on his forehead—other than that, he was quite dead.

"Horace!" screamed Francesca. "This is all your fault! You'll do anything to ruin my holiday!"

66

A week in Vegas was hardly the right setting to embark on married life. Especially with good-time Alice along for the ride. In the great tradition of mothers and daughters-in-law, Alice loathed Olympia, and Olympia returned the compliment.

"She's fat," Alice said.

"She's a witch," Olympia said.

"She's rude," Alice said.

"She's embarrassing," Olympia said.

And so it went. Lennie received a litany of complaints from both of them. And to tell the truth, he didn't much care. Olympia *was* a little overweight—he made her promise to lose ten pounds. Alice *could* be a witch. He told her to behave herself or ship out. Olympia treated staff badly, Lennie noticed, and called her on it. Alice was always an embarrassment. He couldn't do anything about *that*. She had been that way all her life.

The big surprise was Alice and Brigette. They loved each other! The blond child took one look at the faded stripper and a bond was formed. Brigette had never liked a grownup in her life. Alice had always hated kids. Together they were the odd couple—chatting about television programs, food and clothes as if they were equals. Neither Olympia nor Lennie could believe it. Secretly Lennie had always suspected his mother's mentality was in the low-teenage range—but Brigette was only eleven. Yet you would think she and Alice had been lifelong friends. Their relationship saved the day. Olympia accepted Alice because of it. Suddenly Brigette was behaving like a human being—a new phenomenon.

Marriage, Lennie found, had certain advantages. No more one-night stands was one of them.

He certainly did not kid himself that he and Olympia were madly in love, but they had plenty of time. They'd done it, and he, for one, was prepared to give it his best shot.

He pushed Eden to the back of his mind.

Olympia, too, found that marriage (for the fourth time) was advantageous. Especially to someone like Lennie. He was not like her other three husbands—she knew that immediately. He was smarter and sexier and not obsessed with her money as the others had been. In fact, he didn't seem to even care about money. When she thrust the prenuptial agreement at him three days into their marriage he had signed the back-dated document with hardly a glance. "I didn't marry that part of you," he said dismissively.

He had electric eyes, persistent lips, gentle hands and an awe-inspiring cock.

He wasn't Flash. But he was something.

She put Flash on hold. He could wait.

• • • • •

Jess was well aware she was hardly witnessing love's young dream, but it wasn't as bad as she'd thought it would be after her initial encounter with the Greek Princess—as she had christened Olympia—even though she looked more Californian than Greek.

"Lennie," she commented, "I don't know what you said to her, but whatever it was, keep repeating it—she's *almost* bearable."

He laughed. "You've got to understand Olympia," he stated patiently. "Sure, she's spoiled. Wouldn't you be if your old man owned half the world and you grew up expecting to own the other half?"

Jess tried to put herself in that position and couldn't quite make it.

"Olympia is *very* insecure," Lennie the analyst continued. "That's why she treats people the way she does."

Oh yeah? Insecure about what? Now the picture was becoming clear. Lennie Golden. Champion of the underdog. He had married the richest girl in the world to save her from herself. Hah!

"When you get to know her," he added, "you'll really like her."

An acquired taste, like eels on toast. "If you say so," Jess agreed amiably. She didn't feel like arguing. He would learn in his own sweet time.

Meanwhile Matt was driving her nuts. Now that she had decided she really liked him—a lot—he had become Mister Best Friend who will never lay a hand on you. She wanted more than his hand, and she hinted this to him.

"You were always right about us, Jess," he said, not getting the hint at all. "I must have seemed like a real jerk to you when I wouldn't leave you alone."

"No, you didn't," she replied hopefully.

"Yes. I was a jerk," he repeated. And he had no intention of making a fool of himself again.

• • • • •

Olympia had discussed Dimitri's upcoming cruise with Lennie. He consulted Jess and found he would be able to make it for a week; after that he had a firm commitment to do *The Tonight Show*, his first shot, and he was looking forward to it although he was also nervous. Appearing with Carson was like receiving an audience with the Pope.

"They've promised you a seven-minute spot," Jess said eagerly. "Freddie de Cordova said he couldn't understand why you haven't been on before. I didn't want to tell him we've been bombarding them for two years."

Lennie decided he and Olympia would leave immediately after the last show on Saturday night, take a car to L.A., the polar flight to London, where they would stay overnight, and then another plane the next day to the south of France. He was enthusiastic about the trip, having never been abroad, although fortunately he had acquired a passport years before when he and Eden once planned a trip to Venice—which never came off because she ran away to L.A. with her actor boyfriend. Whatever happened to *him?*

Olympia enjoyed his enthusiasm. What fun it would be to show him around. She only wished they had more time.

Nanny Mabel and Brigette were due to leave two days before they did, and then Olympia came up with a brilliant idea. Why not send Alice with them? At least the child would behave herself with Alice along.

She told Lennie her plan, and he quickly said, "Forget it."

But somewhere along the way, word leaked out, Alice got to hear about it, and she confronted Lennie immediately with bright-red cheeks and shaking hands. "You *can't* deny me this chance," she stated dramatically. "You've kept me off the Griffin show—I know that. I'm not some *schlump* you can push in the background, I'm your mother, Lennie, your mother!"

As if she didn't tell him ten times a day. Reluctantly he agreed that she could make the trip, although he had a horrible suspicion they would all live to regret it—especially him.

The rest of the week in Vegas passed quickly. He and Vitos Felicidade were doing sellout business, and the reviews that came out sounded as if he'd written them himself. *Variety* was particularly flattering. They described him as having a multitude of talents, with the timing of Carlin, the irreverence of Bruce, and the comic madness of Chevy Chase. Not bad. Jess clipped it out and put it with the stack of newspaper stuff she was saving for scrapbooks.

Matt threw a small dinner party the night before they left. He didn't have a date and neither did Jess. They sat sedately beside each other, both thinking private thoughts that remained unsaid.

Vitos attended with a svelte brunette who licked his ear throughout dinner.

Make the most of his ear, Olympia thought, *there's not much else.*

Vitos was scrupulously charming to all and sundry; one would never have imagined Olympia had jilted him less than a week before.

Lennie got drunk, and Olympia got stoned.

In the morning he decided to give up drinking. He didn't like what it did to him or the hangovers he endured.

Olympia was busy packing. Jess came by for lunch; she was all set to return to L.A. the next morning.

"Why don't you drive back with us tonight?" Lennie asked.

She shook her head. She wanted one more night in Vegas. All the better to give Matt one last chance.

• • • • •

Olympia received special treatment wherever she went; it didn't take Lennie long to discover that fact of life. In America he was starting to get VIP treatment, too—how potent fame, not to mention the power of television. In Europe nobody had heard of him, and all of a sudden he was *Mr.* Stanislopoulos. The first time he was called that he laughed. The second time wasn't so funny. And the third time he failed to see the humor in it at all.

Olympia tossed blond curls and told him to get used to it.

"I'll *never* get used to it, lady," he replied angrily.

London was just like he'd imagined, although it was warmer than he'd expected. A steamy heat rose from the asphalt streets. A white Bentley met them at the airport and a matching white-haired chauffeur drove them to the Connaught Hotel.

"My father always stays here," Olympia announced. "It has the best restaurant in town."

Best restaurant or not, they ventured out for dinner to an exclusive club, Annabel's, in Berkeley Square, where Olympia met up with some English friends. They were a strange group, with even stranger names like Muffy, Pinko, Nigel and Poopsie.

"The English country set," Olympia whispered.

The men had braying accents and the girls, although delicately pretty, looked untouchable with their perfect pink-and-white skin and artfully styled Princess Di hair. He danced with one of them to a record playing Sinatra's "Come Fly With Me," and everyone seemed to be having a wonderful time. The girl smelled of stale roses as she pressed her bony body hard against his.

"Let's move on," Olympia suggested after a delicious dinner of crab cocktail, steak Diane and bitter chocolate ice cream.

"Aren't you tired?" he asked. Jet lag was catching up with him.

"Not at all," she replied, and wondered if she should have offered him some of the great coke she had snorted before coming out. No—it was *her* supply, and she wasn't about to share it. Once they were on the yacht she didn't know where she could get hold of any more—so hanging on to what she had seemed important. Besides, Lennie had told her he wasn't into drugs, so why waste it on him?

Briefly she thought of Flash. Now with Flash there was never any problem. He was a doper supreme. Who knew— maybe they'd run into him in the south of France. He was lurking in a villa above Cannes with his teenage pregnant wife, both probably stoned out of their heads.

From Annabel's they proceeded on to Tramp in Jermyn Street, another private club, but more laid back and fun than the sedate Annabel's.

Tramp was run by an affable Englishman called Johnny Gold. He greeted Olympia like a long-lost friend, although she had only been in the club once before with Flash. And he was equally friendly to Lennie—in fact, he even seemed to know who Lennie was, which pleased him. Instinctively Lennie knew Tramp was his kind of hangout. He took off his tie, loosened the top buttons of his shirt and felt instantly better.

Johnny led them into the jammed discotheque and squeezed them around an already full table. He introduced them to his wife, Jan, a striking ex-model. And some of the other people sitting along the comfortable banquettes included Ringo Starr, Jack Nicholson and British football star George Best.

Lennie shifted into second gear—suddenly he wasn't tired at all.

He and Olympia staggered from the club at four in the morning, tried to dodge hovering paparazzi, collapsed into the waiting car and slept all the way back to the Connaught.

It was a memorable evening, and by noon the next day they were on yet another plane, this time to the south of France and Dimitri's summer cruise.

67

Lucky established attitude and position from day one. She sat back quietly and watched, feeling like a reluctant but accurate observer of life's great charade.

Actually, she was quite used to observing people and situations, having spent four long years in Washington when married to the annihilatingly boring Craven Richmond.

Now she was Mrs. Dimitri Stanislopoulos, and sometimes she found herself wondering if this one would be any better. Maybe married life was not for her. Being free and single seemed a more appealing prospect every day—because every day she felt she knew Dimitri less. He had become arrogant and overbearing, a tyrant to his minions. Once he had been an exciting and skilled lover, but since they were married he seemed to have lost all interest in sex.

Francesca Fern arrived amid a blaze of theatrics. The driver bringing her to the yacht had had the bad manners to suffer a stroke and *die* mid-journey. She was suitably outraged. She blamed her unhappy husband, Horace, for the entire incident.

Horace accepted her wrath as his due.

Dimitri consoled her with champagne and roses and a great deal of solicitous attention.

Lucky, who knew of his longtime affair with Madame Fern, found herself wondering if it was indeed over, as he had assured her when they were discussing the guest list. "Francesca was once my passion," he had openly confessed. "But now she is merely my good friend, and I want to invite her."

"Sure," Lucky had said, not being of a jealous nature. And, quite frankly, she hardly saw Francesca as any kind of threat—just a very famous middle-aged woman with a face like a horse.

After the Ferns were installed, Saud Omar, an extraordinarily wealthy Arab, and his socialite girlfriend, Contessa Tania Zebrowski, came aboard. One look and Lucky inwardly groaned. The short fat man with the soaked-in-oil brown eyes was a definite lech, and his girlfriend, dripping diamonds and gold, was a hard, face-lifted woman whose beauty had seen better days.

Next came Jenkins Wilder, the Texas oil tycoon, a flamboyant man in his fifties, with Fluff, his eighteen-year-old wife, who called him "daddy-pie" and "bumpkins."

That was the first day.

The next morning brought Nanny Mabel, Brigette and an outlandishly dressed Alice, who threw her arms around a chagrined Dimitri, kissed him lasciviously and announced, "I feel I've known you all my life. We're family now. Let's get acquainted properly."

Gino and Susan arrived at noon, and the yacht set sail shortly after.

The cruise had begun.

• • • • •

Friendships were formed.

The Contessa and Susan hit it off immediately.

Fluff and the Arab lech found they had snorkeling in common.

Francesca and Dimitri parried words and lingering looks.

Alice took a shine to Horace.

Jenkins Wilder spent most of his time on the phone.

Which left Lucky and Gino.

"How're you doing?" she asked.

"Why'd you run off from L.A.?" he asked.

"Susan looks well," she said, for the sake of something to say.

"This guy—Dimitri—he's too old for you," he grumbled.

What the hell are we doing here? she wanted to ask. *We don't fit in at all.*

"Hey, kid, what are we doing here?" He spoke the words aloud. Good old Gino, always ready to say what was on his mind.

She shrugged and gazed out to sea. The yacht was moving smoothly through the azure water as they headed for Saint-Tropez, where they were due to pick up Olympia and her latest husband. She and Gino lay on a top deck sunning themselves. Below them, on another level, Dimitri and Francesca played a boisterous game of gin rummy.

"I've no idea," she said at last.

"You know something?" Gino reflected. "I think we both made mistakes this last couple of years."

She looked at him intently. What was he trying to tell her? That he, too, was having second thoughts about his marriage?

She wanted to ask him, but before she could, a servant appeared and announced that lunch was served. Whenever she and Gino were due to embark on a serious conversation, something interrupted. She hoped he would hang back, let the others go to lunch. But he didn't. He arose, pulled on a polo shirt and offered her his hand.

"Let's go, kid," he said. "The more meals we eat, the sooner we can get off this floating crap shoot, and I, for one, can't wait!"

· · · · ·

The Stanislopoulos yacht arrived in Saint-Tropez harbor at seven. Dimitri made the decision that as most of his guests were probably suffering jet lag, they would remain on the yacht for dinner.

Lucky was restless as she changed into a long white dress and fastened her new diamond choker around her neck, brushed her hair vigorously and shook it into a cloud of jet curls. Next she applied a light makeup.

Dimitri changed into a dark suit, white shirt and silk tie, then preened in front of the full-length mirror, dousing himself with cologne.

"This is really ridiculous," Lucky commented. "We're in Saint-Tropez, on a boat, on vacation—and we're dressing up as if we're going to the first night of the opera!"

"It may seem ridiculous to you," he replied pompously. "However, my dear, this is the way I do things."

"What about me?" she blazed. "Don't *I* have a say in how things are done?"

He looked her up and down. "That dress is excessively low-cut," he remarked. "And you have on too much eye shadow."

It was the first time he had ever criticized her appearance. "Screw you!" she replied heatedly.

Dimitri stared at her and realized with deep regret that they should never have married. Lucky was too young, too wild, and certainly too outspoken. He had hoped that when she became his wife she would accept his authority, guidance and superior knowledge of life. This was obviously not to be.

They were hardly on the best of terms when they sat down for dinner in the grand dining room. Dimitri was seated at one end of the table with Francesca on his left and Susan on his right. Lucky found herself at the other end with Saud Omar and Horace Fern. Gino was somewhere in the middle next to Fluff. Lucky was not pleased. Who had arranged the seating?

She picked up a silver place-card holder and discovered Dimitri's scrawl on the white card.

Damn him. She was getting good and tired of his calling every shot. As Mrs. Stanislopoulos, wasn't she supposed to have some clout too?

Dinner conversation was stilted, to say the least. Lucky loathed Saud, with his lecherous eyes and greasy hair, Horace was a nonentity, and the women were all boring, their conversation concerned only with clothes, designers, jewelry, gossip and servant problems.

What am I doing here? she thought. *Have I flipped out or what? Because this is just not my scene.*

Francesca had a laugh like a buzz saw. She used it often; she and Dimitri seemed to be having a wonderful time together. Susan was all but ignored. Gino was unusually silent.

Dinner passed slowly. Caviar to begin with. Then chateaubriand with pureed potatoes and a choice of vegetables. All this served by three Filipino maids in starched white uniforms.

This is archaic, Lucky thought, picking at her food.

By dessert she was bored out of her mind. And so was Gino, in spite of the fact that Fluff was doing her best to keep him entertained. He had given up on eighteen-year-olds many decades ago.

They looked at each other across the table. He shook his head as if to say, *What is this crap?* She pantomimed a *How the hell would I know?* They grinned conspiratorially. God, she had missed him!

Dessert was richly coated chocolate *profiteroles,* and as Lucky made desultory conversation with Horace, she noticed Francesca feeding the round cream-filled delicacies to Dimitri, one at a time, while their eyes exchanged heated looks and Francesca laughed throatily and licked her darkly painted lips with a snake tongue.

That sonofabitch is still sleeping with her.

Lucky knew it for sure, and she was furious.

Of course she had known it from the moment Francesca arrived on board. It was glaringly obvious. The long, intimate looks, the hand-touching, the attention he paid her. All conclusive evidence. Lucky was no idiot. She was also not in love with him—in fact, she never had been. Oh, sure, for a moment she had fooled herself that maybe he was the man for her. But looking at things clearly, she had married Dimitri because it seemed the right thing to do for Roberto's sake, and also—she couldn't shirk facts—because she wanted to build her hotel more than anything in the world.

Damn! Whatever happened to love? After Marco she was certain she could never love again. Not that white-hot all-consuming passion. And she was right.

Damn! Damn! Damn!

Horace was repeating some inane question. She wished he would shut up. What kind of man was he anyway? He must know what was going on.

Jackie Collins

She narrowed her eyes and tried to form a plan of action. First of all, she decided, she was not going to humiliate herself and make a scene. That was probably what they were all waiting for, this illustrious group.

No, she would bide her time and wait for the right moment to strike.

Why couldn't Marco have lived?

Her eyes threatened to fill with tears. She blinked them away. Crying was a weakness, and above all else, Lucky Santangelo was strong.

68

Carrie and Steven arrived in L.A. late in the afternoon. As usual, Steven was silent, allowing his resentment and fury to bubble beneath the surface. After checking into the hotel, he turned to Carrie and said, "I'll see you at ten in the morning." And that was it. She was on her own. He didn't care that a long, lonely evening loomed ahead for her.

"Very well, Steven," she replied quietly, walking toward the elevator.

He went to his room, eyed the phone for a while, shaved, showered, ordered a half bottle of Scotch from room service, stared at the phone.

At a quarter of seven he picked it up and dialed. A woman answered.

"This is an emergency," he said, his voice controlled. "I have to speak to Gino Santangelo at once."

"Oh, dear." The woman sounded flustered. "What kind of emergency? Mr. and Mrs. Santangelo left the country yesterday. They will be in Europe for two weeks."

"Europe?" he questioned blankly.

"France," the woman said. "I can try to contact—"

She was still speaking as he hung up.

Later that night he rented a car and drove past the Santangelo residence. That was when he became aware of what a protected life these people led, and realization dawned—there was no way Gino Santangelo would listen to him even if he *was* in town. Why was he fooling himself?

Dejected, he drove around for a while, headed back to Sunset and finally pulled into the parking lot of a bar. He had no idea it was a strip joint until he got inside, and by that time he felt like having a drink and really didn't care what kind of a dump he got it in.

The place was full of men staring at a regal-looking Scandinavian woman who took it off suggestively on a scuffed runway snaking between the chipped tables. Red satin stripped away to reveal smooth flesh, jutting breasts and a thick bush.

Steven ordered a double Scotch from a topless waitress in a grass skirt. She had stringy hair and perky breasts. She couldn't have been more than seventeen. He felt sorry for her, and when she returned with his drink he dropped her a big tip.

She looked at him with stoned eyes and whispered, "I take a break at nine-thirty. I can give you a blow job in the parking lot for twenty bucks."

Her offer offended him. Was he starting to look like a john? "No, thanks," he said shortly.

"Fifteen," she whispered hopefully.

"No."

"Ten," she pleaded. "I've got a kid. He needs things."

"What kind of things?" he asked quickly.

"Oh," she looked around furtively. "Food, clothes. You name it."

"Bull."

"I'm not shittin' you."

"Eh—Desiree," the barman yelled. "What's goin' on over there? You takin' another order or what?"

She froze like a cornered rat.

"That's okay," Steven said, "bring me another drink."

Onstage, the Scandinavian made way for an action-packed Puerto Rican with startlingly white teased hair. She was clad in a cowboy outfit, which stayed on her nubile body for exactly three and a half minutes. Then she stripped until all that remained were tassels on her nipples and crotch. She squatted down and began to twirl, while the audience of men shouted ribald encouragement.

Desiree returned with his second drink.

"How old is your kid?" he asked.

"Nearly two."

"And you?"

"How old do you want me to be?" she replied coquettishly. "I can play schoolgirl or whore. You wanna come back to my place later an' find out? It'll cost you fifty—but it'll be worth every dollar. If you wanna pay me sixty, I can quit now. I'll tell 'em I'm sick."

"Desiree!" screamed the bartender.

"Well?" she asked anxiously.

His curiosity was aroused. "Quit now," he decided.

"The parking lot in five minutes," she mumbled, and scurried away.

He sat through a few more minutes of twirling nipples. But when the woman onstage began to pick up rolled dollar bills with her crotch, he got up and went outside.

The air was balmy and rich. He stood by his rented car and waited.

Desiree eventually appeared, wearing jeans and a T-shirt, her stringy hair tied back in a ponytail. Now she looked twelve. She walked toward an old Pontiac. "Hand over the money and follow me in your car," she instructed.

He did not have a large bankroll by any means, but he was caught up in the game. "Half now, half later," he bargained.

"You're not gonna stiff me?" she pleaded.

"You're not going to run off on me?"

"No way, man. I like you. I'll make you feel real satisfied."

He didn't want to tell her he had no intention of having sex with her. She would consider him a weirdo and run.

Maybe that's what he was turning into: a fucked-up weirdo who spent his time cruising hooker bars and searching for a father it was too late to find.

Desiree lived in a rundown apartment on a street off Santa Monica. She double-parked her car and told him it was okay for him to do the same. "You'll hear 'em holler when they wanna get out," she stated.

He followed her up rickety stairs to a small room that contained her life—including a toddler asleep in a battered cot pushed into one corner, and a ragged-looking cat dozing in another.

She switched on a lamp and said matter-of-factly, "You're not a cop, are you?" And when he shook his head she recited, "Straight sex only for sixty. Anything else will cost you extra."

He indicated the baby. "What about him?"

"No kiddie porn," she answered quickly, her blank eyes alarmed.

Steven felt helpless. And very very angry.

"I meant," he said slowly, "does he stay in the room? What if he wakes up?"

"He won't."

"How do you know that?"

"Because he just won't," she replied stubbornly.

"Who looks after him while you're out working?"

"He sleeps all the time."

"Are you telling me you simply walk out of here and leave him *alone?*"

"He never wakes up."

"How are you so sure?"

"Because I give him a sleeper—it knocks him out cold." She glared at him. "Does that satisfy you?"

He sat down on the side of the bed. "Jesus!"

She took this as a sign and began to pull her T-shirt over her head.

"Don't undress," he said quickly.

She pulled her T-shirt back down. "I gotta take off my jeans," she complained, fiddling with the zipper.

"I just want to talk," he said. "Nothing else."

Restlessly she picked up the scraggy cat, opened the door and threw it out. She was uncomfortable with talk—at least with sex she knew what she was dealing with. "I want the rest of my money," she whined.

He handed it over and said quietly, "Do you know that giving a small child sleeping pills is very dangerous?"

"What are you—a social worker?"

"It could be fatal. And so could leaving him alone in this firetrap."

"Don't jinx me, man."

"Who is his father?"

She laughed aloud. "I don't know. I don't even care. Who gives a shit anyway?"

"Maybe *he* will when he's old enough to ask. Have you thought about that?"

"Listen, man." Suddenly her dull eyes were alive. "I *look after* my kid. *You* may not think it's much—but it's the best I can do. When he's old enough to ask, I'll tell him the truth. I'll tell him that I kept him with me, paid his way, and he has *nobody* to thank but me—because if it wasn't for *me* he'd be in some stupid state orphanage without anyone caring."

Steven didn't stay around to talk or anything else. He left, her shrill words ringing in his ears . . . *If it wasn't for me he'd be in some orphanage without anyone caring.* . . .

If it wasn't for Carrie, that would have been his fate. And how was he repaying her? By dragging her around the country, searching for a dream or a nightmare. And she was beginning to hate him for it—he knew it—and who could blame her? He was subjecting her to an ordeal that would alienate her, perhaps forever. For the first time he began to realize just how much she meant to him, and how he was making her suffer. He had shut her out. Maybe the time was right to start opening doors. This chase—this quest for the truth—was heading nowhere.

Early in the morning he called Jerry in New York. "I need help," he said.

"What's happened now?" sighed Jerry wearily.

"We're here in L.A. Gino Santangelo's not. I called his house and found out he's away for two weeks. And you know something? I guess I finally realized you're right—if I turn up at his front door with my story, he's going to call the cops and bust my ass. Why shouldn't he?"

"You had to go all the way to California to find that out?" Jerry commented dryly.

"I drove by his house. There are gates, closed-circuit TV and armed patrol."

"Which means you, with your black face, are not going to get near the sonofabitch."

"Right."

"So you're calling me for help."

"Right."

There was a long silence, broken finally by Jerry. "Steven," he said harshly. "I'm getting sick and tired of lending you money, handing out free advice and listening to you bitch."

"I agree with you."

"What?"

"I said, I agree with you. If I were you, I'd have given up on me a long time ago."

"Am I about to hear that you are abandoning this cockama-mie search and regaining your senses?"

"I still need to find out who my father is," Steven replied seriously. "But I'm releasing Carrie from the responsibility. I'm through dragging her around the country. And—if the offer is still open—I'm coming to work for you. It's time I started paying my debts."

"I don't believe this!" Jerry exclaimed. "One day on the West Coast and you found God!"

"Cut it out. I need support, not wisecracks."

"Have you told Carrie?"

"Not yet."

"Do so. At once. And get your ass back here pronto."

•   •   •   •   •

They were staying at the Hyatt Hotel on Sunset. The California sun was blazing and the lobby was full of tourists. Steven had arranged to meet Carrie by the front entrance at ten. He spotted her from a distance. Aloof and erect, forever stylish and ageless, she stood apart from the crowd.

She thought they were going to visit Gino Santangelo—a humiliation she was prepared to go through with for him.

He approached her from behind and hugged her. She was startled.

"We're going home," he said. "Back to New York."

She searched his face, knew something had changed, and didn't ask questions.

"I've missed you, Steven," she said softly.

"I know," he replied. "I *do* know."

69

From the moment they left the Connaught and set off for Heathrow airport, Olympia was insufferable to everyone, including Lennie. When they reached the plane he had had enough. The first thing she did was insult the stewardess.

"For Christ's sake, cut out the rich girl act," he said in a low, angry voice. "What are you aiming for? Cunt of the year?"

"I've got a hangover," she replied sulkily.

"So live with it and stop taking it out on everyone else."

She liked forceful men. It was a shame there weren't more around. "Sorry," she answered contritely. "I'll behave."

But she didn't, and by the time they arrived at Nice airport he was fuming. A helicopter was waiting to take them on to Saint-Tropez and the yacht. Olympia climbed aboard, and promptly fell asleep.

Lennie brooded about the wisdom of what he had done. Jess—who rarely called a shot wrong—had said he was insane. If this was a taste of things to come, she was right.

The luxury and opulence of the Stanislopoulos yacht amazed Lennie. Only in movies had he seen anything like it. *The Greek* was a floating palace.

Alice ruined everything. She was the first to greet them as they came aboard—a bizarre picture in a red striped romper suit worn with stiletto heels, fishnet tights, and an abundance of makeup including false eyelashes. "Welcome," she said graciously, as if it were *her* yacht. "Make yourselves at home."

Olympia threw her a withering look. "Alice, dear," she said, "this *has* been my home for most of my life. I don't need you to welcome me. Where is Brigette? And why aren't you with her? She *is* the only reason you're here. I'm sure you're aware of that."

Olympia did not believe in holding back—she wanted Alice to get the message up front.

Lennie couldn't care less. He looked around. Servants seemed to be appearing from everywhere, taking their luggage, offering cold champagne on silver trays.

"Where is my father?" Olympia demanded of a man in a white uniform.

"He's gone ashore, Miss Olympia," replied Captain Pratt. "For lunch. He's due back shortly. He said you should meet him in the upstairs bar at three o'clock."

"He's taken Brigette," added Alice. "I wanted to go with them, but your daddy said I should stay here."

"Wise man," murmured Olympia. She turned to the captain and said haughtily, "And where are the rest of the guests?"

"Most of them are ashore, Miss Olympia." Captain Pratt gave Lennie a quick once-over while Olympia yawned and complained about the trip. "Will you be wanting lunch, miss?" he added.

"No," she replied, not even consulting Lennie. "I need to rest."

Alice laughed gaily. "Well, Lennie, well, my *boychick*, what do *you* think of all this?"

"I think I want to take a piss and change my clothes," he replied dourly. She had not caught him at the right moment.

• • • • •

Saint-Tropez was at the height of the season. Tourists mixed with the natives on the cobbled harbor streets lined with fashionable boutiques and open-air restaurants. Yachts jostled for position along the small harbor, and their occupants sat out on deck sipping margaritas and watching the passing crowds. By noon there was a lunchtime parade of nubile bodies clad in the latest fashions.

Dimitri strolled with his pretty blond granddaughter accompanied by Saud Omar and Jenkins Wilder. Between them the three men could buy and sell France—easily. Several paces behind hovered various bodyguards trying to appear unobtrusive in city clothes with hidden shoulder holsters.

All three men eyed the passing female parade with a mixture of boredom and halfhearted lust. Money had taught them most women were available, for a price. Whether the price be a new dress or a fleet of Mercedeses was up for discussion. But the fact remained that the excitement of the chase was never really there because the prize was always a foregone conclusion.

Brigette skipped happily along, holding on to her grandfather's hand. She loved being with Dimitri. He called her his little Diamond Princess and bought her anything she wanted. Anything at all. She was glad to be off the yacht. Things were different this year. Dimitri had married again and had a disgusting baby called Roberto.

Stupid name.

Stupid baby.

Brigette hated them both, and wondered why her mother hadn't told her about them. After all, the dumb baby had taken over her old room with his stupid Black nanny. But that was okay, really, because she had a new room, a grown-up room with blue wallpaper and a bubble-jet tub. *And,* best of all, she didn't have Nanny Mabel sharing it with her—she had her new friend, Alice, and Alice was lots and lots of fun and stayed up all night long talking. Brigette didn't understand half of the talk, but that didn't matter. Alice was fun even if she did look a little screwy, smelled kind of odd, never stopped talking and wore more makeup than Miss Piggy.

"We'll stop for lunch here," Dimitri decided, pausing in front of a fashionable restaurant. Quickly a front table was cleared for them while the bodyguards settled nearby.

Brigette had spotted an Aladdin's cave of trinkets next door. "I want to go shopping, Grandpapa," she announced sweetly.

"Tomorrow," Dimitri said dismissively. "One of the women will take you."

"I want to go *now*." She managed to make her bottom lip quiver. "I can go by myself. The store's right there. Look. *See?*" She pointed.

"All right, if you're quick."

"I don't have any money, Grandpapa."

Dimitri groped in the pocket of his sports shirt, but like most very rich people, he carried no cash.

"Here you go, honey," boomed Jenkins Wilder, reaching into a Gucci clutch he carried everywhere and producing a stack of hundred-dollar bills. "How many will make you happy? Two? Three?"

She grabbed three hundred dollars.

"Too much," grumbled Dimitri.

"I'm buying presents, Grandpapa," Brigette explained patiently, and skipped off.

Dimitri nodded at one of the bodyguards to follow her.

Jenkins Wilder sat back and grinned. "Crrrazee-lookin' broads here," he remarked. "If'n I wasn't a marrried man, I might have myself a time."

"Frenchwomen expect too much attention," Saud said, his oily eyes watchful. "And usually they are not worth the trouble."

"I agree," said Dimitri. "Englishwomen are the most sensual."

"God darn—you just got yourself hitched to an American gal," Jenkins pointed out.

This was true, Dimitri reflected, and Lucky was certainly an unsual beauty. But she was not Francesca, and he still harbored a deep passion for Madame Fern—a passion that never seemed to cool.

He was beginning to think that inviting her on the cruise was not such a good idea. Now he and Lucky were married, it was impossible to spend private time with Francesca. Before, with only Horace to contend with, it had never been a problem. Horace had not dared to interfere.

Dimitri half hoped Lucky would tire of the cruise and fly back to New York. He had preferred their relationship when it was not quite so permanent. But of course he had to marry her because of Roberto. No son of his was going to go through life without the protection of the Stanislopoulos name.

"I have also found in life," Saud Omar contemplated, "that Englishwomen are indeed the most erotic in the bedroom, when you penetrate their natural reserve." He lingered over the word "penetrate," while his olive-oil eyes surveyed the bouncing breasts of two teenage girls passing by, wearing thin knit tank tops and minuscule bikini bottoms.

"Ah never had myself a limey chick," ruminated Jenkins Wilder. "Ah was stationed outside of London with the Army way back in fifty-one—but I was too doggawned scared of catching the clap!"

- - - - -

Lennie showered and changed into Levi's cutoffs and a faded denim shirt, while Olympia lay on the bed and complained.

She complained about her father's not being there to greet her.

She complained about Alice.

She complained about Captain Pratt. "I've told Papa to get rid of him for years. He's got nasty little eyes."

She complained about Captain Pratt's wife. "A terrible cook. Why do you think I refused lunch?"

"C'mon," said Lennie, trying to ignore her bad mood. "Loosen up. We're supposed to be on vacation. Let's hit the streets and explore."

"Explore?" she sneered derisively. "I hate Saint-Tropez, it's full of boring tourists and hookers."

"I want to explore," he said stubbornly.

"Go ahead. I'm not stopping you. But I do expect you to wait until after you've met Dimitri."

He looked at the time. It was a quarter to three. "That's the reason I'm here, isn't it?"

She got off the bed and started to primp in front of the mirror. She wanted to snort some coke, but once again she didn't care to share it. Casually she smuggled her supply into the bathroom, locked the door and laid down two lines.

Relief was immediate. She had been feeling lousy all day with just a few Valiums to keep her going. Like a fool she had packed her supply of coke, and had only now been able to get her hands on it.

She snorted first one nostril, then the other. Clouds lifted. Her head was clear. She felt ready to take on the world.

Lennie banged on the door. "What are you doing in there?" he yelled.

"Just fixing my hair," she called back.

"Hurry up." He was strangely disoriented. London had been great. But maybe agreeing to come on this cruise was a mistake. Taking on Olympia was one thing—he could handle her, even if she was turning out to be a prize pain in the ass. But the father was going to think he was after her money, and the rest of the group did not exactly sound like fun city. Plus he had Alice to put up with. And all he really wanted to do was work on his material for the Carson show.

Olympia finally emerged and took his hand. She seemed in a better humor. "Let's go meet Daddyoh!" she said brightly. "He looks a bit forbidding, but take no notice of that, he's really easy. Just answer his questions, don't get pissed off, and I promise you we'll only have to do this once a year."

They made their way to the upstairs deck. Greek music was playing through stereo speakers, and Dimitri was demonstrating some intricate steps to Brigette. The child was sunny-faced and laughing, while Alice stood to one side clapping her hands joyfully.

"A perfect family scene," whispered Olympia gleefully. And then she threw herself into the whole greeting routine.

"My baby!" to a disinterested Brigette. Kiss kiss.

"Papa!" to Dimitri, who waved her away while he finished his dance.

When he was ready, and only then, did he return her greeting.

Lennie hung back, watching from the sidelines, willing Alice to keep quiet. And for once she did.

"Papa, I want you to meet Lennie Golden," Olympia announced. "My new husband."

Christ! She made him sound like a possession. He extended his hand and wondered for a moment what he was doing on a huge yacht in the south of France meeting a man like Dimitri Stanislopoulos and married to his daughter. It was crazy time.

Dimitri glared at him with piercing eyes, his expression rock-hard. "So," he said loudly, "*you're* the latest one."

A remark Lennie did not like, especially as his extended hand was ignored. He formulated something insulting to say. Nobody was going to get away with treating *him* like shit— Olympia's father or not.

Before he could do or say something Dimitri suddenly enveloped him in a bear hug. "Welcome to our family," he boomed. "If you are good enough for Olympia, then you are good enough for me." A brisk wave at the barman. "Champagne for everyone. We have much to celebrate."

Olympia grinned and hugged Lennie's arm. "I know," she said. "It's wonderful, isn't it?"

"Wonderful. Excellent," agreed Dimitri, beaming. "And I have a surprise for you, too."

"What?" demanded Olympia, thinking perhaps a new diamond necklace—Dimitri was always generous when she married.

"Grandpop got married too!" chirped Brigette excitedly. "And you have a *brother*, Mama. And I'm his *aunt*. Really. Truthfully. Honestly. I'm an auntie!"

Olympia's smile stiffened. Was the limelight to be stolen from her? She looked at her father for confirmation that Brigette was lying as usual.

He nodded. "It is true. I also am married again. And I have been blessed with a son."

For a moment Olympia felt faint. Too much traveling and

not enough coke to ward off the effect of this latest bombshell. "I don't believe it," she said vaguely.

"It's true! It's true! It's true!" chanted Brigette.

"Yes, it is," said Alice, grabbing a glass of champagne from a silver tray and joining in what she perceived as a riotous celebration.

Olympia took a deep breath. His getting married again wasn't too bad. But having a *kid*—at *his* age. She was the only Stanislopoulos heir, and that's the way it had to stay. Rich as she was, she had no intention of sharing the vast inheritance she would come into when Dimitri died. It was all hers. This just wasn't fair!

Lennie handed her a glass of champagne and took one for himself. "Congratulations, Mr. Stanislopoulos," he said, happy to relinquish being the center of attention.

"I love weddings," sighed Alice. "Such happy times. I remember my wedding day as if it was a week ago. I wore a white cocktail dress—so smart—with a cinched waist." She turned to Olympia who couldn't care less. "Do you know, my dear, I had an eighteen-inch waist. Eighteen inches!"

"Really?" asked Brigette.

"Yes, really. I had—"

"Alice, take Brigette for a nap," Olympia said shortly, her tone brooking no argument.

"But Mama—" Brigette began.

"Now!"

"Come along, pretty-puss," Alice crooned, shepherding the child from the room.

"Who did you marry, Papa?" Olympia asked sweetly, knowing it couldn't possibly be Francesca, and wondering if it was that Brazilian whore who had nearly captured him a few years before. Or maybe the English socialite with the stately home and faint connections to the royal family. Dimitri always *had* liked culture.

"Ah . . ." he said. "Now you'll *really* be surprised."

Lennie felt this was between them, and a perfect time to

make his escape. "Would you excuse me if I took a walk?" he asked.

"Go ahead," said Olympia, with hardly a glance.

He left quickly.

"Who?" Olympia persisted.

"Well," said Dimitri, stringing it out. "Do you remember quite a while ago I told you I had bumped into an old school friend of yours, Lucky Santangelo?"

"Yes."

"We renewed our acquaintanceship in New York, and"—he shrugged expansively—"things happened."

"Things happened!" shrieked Olympia, louder than she intended. "You didn't marry *Lucky?*"

"That's exactly what I did."

70

Now that Lucky knew—was certain—that Dimitri was continuing his affair with the flamboyant Madame Fern, she decided to see as little of him as possible. Roberto appeared to be happy in the excellent hands of loving CeeCee, so it was easy for her to slip away in the morning and wander around the picturesque streets. She left Dimitri a note saying she had gone on a sight-seeing tour. Why should she suffer on the yacht when she could be out on her own, free to sort out her feelings?

Being alone had never bothered Lucky. It was the story of her life. But now she had Roberto, which was the main reason she hadn't taken a plane back to New York and the nearest lawyer. She wanted a divorce. But she didn't want to lose the opportunity to build her hotel, and she had to make quite sure that everything was locked up before she made a move.

After wandering through the many boutiques and other small shops, she took a cab to Tahiti Beach, which she had heard was the place to go. She was wearing an oversize T-shirt, with a small scarlet bikini underneath and thong-toed sandals on her feet. Her jet hair hung down her back in a thick plait, and dark shades covered her eyes.

Armed with a Sony Walkman, a bottle of Ambre Solaire suntan oil and a good book, she approached the fashionable crowded beach with confidence. She spoke a smattering of French, picked up in her youth, and she requested and paid for the hire of a striped chaise, towel and large umbrella.

The bronzed attendant settled her in a row near the water's edge, and she lay back to relax and observe.

One of life's greatest pleasures was watching the world pass by. And on Tahiti Beach, in Saint-Tropez, you certainly saw some sights. Many of the women went topless, and there were breasts of all shapes and sizes and ages. Nobody seemed to object—in fact everybody was remarkably unself-conscious.

The French men favored very small, tight bikini bottoms, and thrust their cocks out as if parading for first prize. There were some interesting contenders.

Lucky grinned. She liked their attitude. Being married to an older man she had forgotten the sheer pleasure of a perfect male body—that sweet combination of gleaming muscles and beautiful youth. She allowed her eyes, still under cover of the dark shades, to sweep over their bodies, checking them out as men had always checked out women. It was an enjoyable pastime.

• • • • •

Lennie did not speak one word of French. He could say "Fuck you" in Italian, curse in German and utter words of love in Swedish, but French eluded him. Perhaps it was because he had never slept with a French girl, and it was always his short-term lovers who taught him fragments of a language.

It didn't matter. In Saint-Tropez everyone spoke English—sometimes fluently, most times brokenly—but they all made an attempt.

He fell in love with the place immediately. It had a laid-back ambiance that grabbed him. He was not yet rich enough or jaded enough to see it as a dirty, overcrowded tourist trap. He merely observed a lot of young people out to have a good time—and it appealed to him. He grabbed a seat in a sidewalk café, ordered a Cinzano on the rocks and sat for a while. It would have been nice, he mused, to have been here with a group. Jess, Isaac, Joey, the twins, Eden . . .

How had *she* slipped into his thoughts? She had looked like a five-hundred-dollar-a-night hooker, sitting at a front table on his opening night in her silver-sequinned dress with her gangster friends.

Eden Antonio.

I thought you were going to become a movie star. Whatever happened?

He imagined her face when she read about his marriage to Olympia Stanislopoulos. Slanty eyes. Thin lips. Elegant nose. It must have given her a jolt. He hoped.

Or did he?

The torch was dimming. This was the first time he had thought about her since leaving America. Things were looking up.

A young couple sitting at the next table were eying him with more than casual interest. The girl, pretty in an outdoorsy way, caught his eye and smiled. Politely he smiled back, causing her to nudge her companion, a long-haired greaser in a studded denim vest and dirty jeans. Before Lennie could even think about moving, they were at his table.

"You *are* Lennie Golden, aren't you?" the girl asked excitedly. She had a bold suntan, with American teeth and an accent to match.

"Guilty."

"I *told* you!" the girl exclaimed. Her companion didn't crack a smile. He had a skull and crossbones tattooed on his arm and a brooding expression. Not exactly James Dean— more the young James Coburn. He hung behind his girlfriend and scowled.

"We're Americans," she announced, still dazzling with her teeth. "We've been here a month."

"What do you want—a medal?" deadpanned Lennie.

"I never expected to see *you!*" Dazzle, dazzle. "I'm crazy for your TV show. I *love* it. Never miss it. When I'm there, of course."

"Of course."

"Yeah, man, it's okay," said Mister Scowl, joining in at last.

"Glad you approve."

They sat down uninvited, but not exactly unwelcome. Lennie felt like company, and they seemed to be okay kids.

A conversation took place. The usual. *What are you doing here? How long are you staying? Do you like it? Wanna score some great dope?*

Lennie had a feeling a few ace joints might help the trip no end. And Olympia would be delighted if he returned bearing gifts.

"Our stash is at the beach with my sister," explained the girl. "It's only a few minutes away. Come on, we'll take you."

They offered him a ride in a decrepit old Renault, which choked and spluttered all the way. He was hunched in the back, bent double. Nothing like getting back among the people. In a perverse way he enjoyed it. Limos, Lear Jets, penthouse suites and private yachts were still a touch rich for his plebian blood. He was already working on a monologue in his head about the way the very wealthy lived. So much material! And untouched, like a virgin oil well. If he could get it together in time it would be great to use on *The Tonight Show*.

The girl with the dazzling smile had a sister who disdained clothes and wore only a native suntan, plenty of Indian beads and a suede G-string. Where was she hiding the famous stash? Clearly not on her person.

Her French boyfriend was clad in a black jockstrap which he patted affectionately most of the time. Between them they shared a large canvas bag filled with goodies.

"You name it, we got it," announced the greaser, taking over and pulling out a small package of hash which he expertly rolled into a joint. He handed it to Lennie. "Compliments of the casa. Try it. Like it. Buy it."

Lennie tried it, liked it and ordered two dozen joints— "Rolled, please."

The greaser was only too happy to oblige, and he set about his task with insouciant ease.

"I'll be back," Lennie said, and wandered off down the beach admiring the scenery. Most of the women wore only the bottom half of scanty bikinis and acted as if they were fully clothed—jogging along the shore, running after escaping children, licking ice-cream cones, lying back with open thighs—all the better to obtain the perfect tan.

For fifteen minutes Lennie thought he had died and gone to

tit paradise. And then . . . so what? Big deal. Nipples could get boring too and unless they were *really* special . . .

And then he spotted the girl with the jet hair and black eyes who had come on to him in Las Vegas. Here she was, two years later, lying on the beach in Saint-Tropez looking as sensual and wild as ever. Naturally she was not topless. Why give a free show? She wore a dangerous red bikini, earphones, and her eyes were closed. He recognized her immediately. Somehow she had made an indelible impression.

Proceed with caution, a voice in his head warned. *Remember—she has an acid tongue.*

And one of the horniest bodies he had ever seen. Tall, slim and supple, with long legs, a small waist, great breasts and broad shoulders.

He remembered her walk. Pantherlike, graceful.

He remembered their one kiss before he had called a halt to the proceedings. Schmuck of the year.

How was he to approach her now?

Why was he to approach her now?

You are a married man, said his conscience sternly.

So what? replied his libido.

Don't do it, said his conscience.

Go ahead, replied his prick.

She must have sensed someone staring at her. Without warning she suddenly sat up, removed the earphones, took off her shades and returned his quizzical stare.

He was not close enough to say anything. Fortunately. Because whenever he opened his mouth she shot him down.

Did she remember him? Was she going to come over?

He stood by the seashore, waiting.

Slowly she got up. Stretched languorously, and headed toward him.

He held his breath. He might be married, but he wasn't dead. This was one opportunity he wasn't going to miss. Not the second time around.

Their eyes locked. As she got closer he was mesmerized by the blackness of hers, the long lashes that surrounded them, her glowing skin and full, lush lips.

He started to say something, he wasn't sure what— "Hello," "You again"—something innocuous. It didn't matter. She walked straight past him into the sea.

For a moment he was stunned, but recovery was rapid. He turned around and watched her strike out toward a floating wooden platform. Without another thought he stripped off his shirt, threw it on the sand and plunged into the sea after her.

She was a powerful swimmer and had a good lead on him. But with his highly personal erratic crawl he set off like a piston and caught up before she was even halfway there. He swam alongside her. She didn't say anything. Neither did he.

It was late in the afternoon and the raft ahead of them looked deserted.

He noticed her ears were pierced as her head rose and vanished beneath the surface of the sea. She wore small diamond studs.

He noticed her arms, strong and powerful, as they cleaved the water.

He sensed adventure, knew anything was possible, and didn't draw back. How many times in his life was he going to come across a woman like this?

Eden.

Eden who?

• • • • •

Lucky was enjoying the game. She had watched Lennie approach through hooded eyes. Remembered him from their abortive meeting in Vegas, and immediately wondered if maybe this was what she needed—a purely physical encounter with no entanglements. If he didn't back off like the last time.

Lennie Golden. She even remembered his name. A horny-looking guy. Why not put him to the test? After all, fate had placed them both on the same Saint-Tropez beach and getting even had always appealed. He would be the perfect person to use to equal the score with Dimitri—who was probably still fawning all over that awful Fern woman.

She rose and strolled casually toward him. He mumbled something as she passed. She ignored him and plunged into the sea, knowing he would follow. *Don't talk. Don't spoil it,* she willed.

There was a wooden raft some way from the shore, and she struck off toward it.

He was behind her.

If Dimitri thought she was the kind of woman he could screw around on and get away with it—then he lived in a dream world. Lucky Santangelo could give as good as she got. And let nobody forget it.

The raft lay ahead, empty and inviting. What must it be like to be shipwrecked, cut off, alone in the world? She often felt alone in the world. Dimitri had done nothing to change that feeling.

They reached the raft together and hauled themselves aboard. He had caught her silent message and didn't say a word. The sun was low in the sky, and people on the beach were beginning to pack up and go home. A lone water-skier passed in the distance, causing the raft to rock as the waves hit. Their eyes met, and as if by unspoken agreement they moved closer. She was staring at him with those crazy gypsy eyes, black and wildly sensuous—the signal was clear.

He wanted to know who she was. What she was doing here. Everything about her intrigued him. But the timing was wrong and he knew it. Which didn't mean he couldn't go along with the game.

He reached out and pulled her to him. She moved into his embrace as naturally as if they had known each other for years. Electricity sparked as they began to kiss, long, lingering kisses, tongues entwined.

Their bodies were wet. Salty flesh crushed against salty

flesh. He pressed his hands into the small of her back and let her feel his hardness.

She didn't draw away, but moved her hips slowly, suggestively. He ran his hands leisurely up her spine, felt for the end of her thick plait of hair, removed the rubber band and unplaited the luxuriant mane until it tumbled damply around her shoulders.

And all the while their lips were together, tantalizingly hot.

A motorboat passed nearby, causing the raft to rock again. He held her tightly, expertly flicked open the clasp on her bikini top, let it drop, and felt the excitement of her bare breasts against his chest.

.She trailed her hands very, very slowly down his back, tracing patterns with her fingers, and when she reached the waistband of his shorts she drew her hands to the front and caressed his hardness through the material.

He groaned involuntarily, stepped back for a moment and struggled out of his shorts, not caring if he was seen from the beach. Not caring about anything at all except this crazy real-life fantasy.

Her hands were on him, caressing, stroking, driving him nuts.

Control, a voice screamed in his head. *Don't blow it.*

He reached for her breasts. Hard nipples, soft firm contours. Beautiful. Perfect.

He peeled the bottom of her bikini down and she stepped out of it.

They sank onto the cold wet surface of the raft, neither of them noticing the discomfort. There was nothing awkward about their lovemaking. He entered her smoothly, and she wrapped her long legs tightly around his waist and moved with him as if they had been together many times before. Instinctively she knew his rhythm and he knew hers.

He was iron-hard, but surfing only. The perfect wave was yet to arrive, and when it did, he wanted them to ride it together.

An elderly Frenchman in a bathing cap swam toward the raft. He paused to catch his breath before climbing up, saw the entwined couple and swam away again, thankful his disapproving wife was not with him.

Lucky closed her eyes and gave herself up to the moment. She had known when she first set eyes on Lennie Golden that he would be a sensational lover. And he was. And it frightened her—because this was supposed to be a mindless revenge move—just something to get her own back on Dimitri. And yet . . . it was more, much more. It was body talk at its most eloquent, and the last thing she needed in her life was another relationship.

She felt the roller-coaster ride beginning. And she knew without a doubt that this was not just another two-dollar trip. This was the big one, the double-dipper, the whirl, the cartwheel twice over.

"Oh, God!" she heard herself cry out. "Oh, *Jeeeesus!*"

And she was lost in sensation. Floating in paradise. Taken over by a throbbing release which sent her into spasms of delight.

Lennie felt the same way. The intensity and depth of his orgasm took him by surprise, leaving him shaken and drained. He lay on top of her for a moment, still joined, and stared into her eyes, so deep and full of secrets.

Who was she?

He had to know.

And yet . . . maybe her way was best. She was a woman of mystery, and she obviously planned to stay that way. What was he going to say anyway? *I'd like to see you again?* Sure. *And I'll bring my wife.*

He rolled off her and groped for his shorts, thankful they hadn't fallen into the sea.

She sat up, reached for her bikini and put it on.

The sun was setting, and a chill pervaded the air. Two beachboys were stacking mattresses on the nearly deserted beach, and in the distance a blond girl jogged along the seashore with a white police dog.

Lucky bent forward, shook out her hair and casually knotted it on top of her head. She looked at Lennie once, briefly, and in the softest of voices murmured, "*Sayonara*, friend." Then she dived gracefully from the side of the raft, and the last he saw of her were her strong brown arms flashing from the sea as she swam toward the shore.

He waited ten minutes before he followed. By the time he reached the beach she was gone, and he realized he would probably never see her again.

One afternoon's fantasy . . . and he didn't even know her name.

71

We're havin' dinner with the Spanish pimp an' Quinn.
I think we got a deal."

"When?" Eden asked quickly.

"Tonight," Santino replied, belching and scratching his
stomach.

Eden bit back a sharp complaint. Why did he always tell
her these things at the last minute? It was a quarter to six—
how the hell could she look her best when they were probably
meeting in an hour?

She got out of bed and hurried into her marble bathroom.
"What time and where?" she called out, turning on the shower.

"I'm takin' ya to Chasen's," Santino announced. "Look
hot—but not too hot, it's a classy joint."

She gritted her teeth. He talked to her like she was some
two-bit whore off the streets.

"Be ready by seven-fifteen. Zeko will drive ya. I gotta go
home now—I'll see ya there."

She didn't bother to reply. She was already under the
shower, washing off his smell, shampooing her hair, feeling
for the golden triangle and bringing herself to the climax he
never managed to give her.

She didn't need a lot of time to get ready. As a former
model she had the drill down pat. Out of the shower, towel-
dry, plug in the heated rollers, splurge with the Estée body
cream, spray on the Estée scent. Naked, she sat in front of her
dressing table mirror, cleansed her face with cottonwool and
astringent, applied moisturizer, skin-tone base, shading, powder, blusher, eye shadow, eyeliner, mascara, eyebrow pencil,
lipliner, lipstick and lip gloss.

The whole routine took her fifteen minutes, and the effect
was dynamite.

Next she blow-dried her fine hair and placed long coils of it in the heated rollers.

All she had left to do was decide what to wear, and that always took time. A large walk-in closet led off from the bathroom, and it was filled with clothes. She strolled up and down, trying to select the perfect outfit—something that would suit Santino, Quinn (a weirdo if she'd ever seen one), Vitos, and, of course, Chasen's. Choosing the right ensemble for a restaurant was of paramount importance.

Outside her bathroom window, hidden among the dense foliage, Zeko finished jerking off. He had practically given up normal sex. Getting off on his boss's girlfriend was the biggest kick of all.

He zipped up and returned to the house, where he picked up a copy of *Auto Mechanic* and took it into the kitchen to read.

Eden selected a narrow black dress with a wide gold cinch belt. She pulled on patterned black panty hose, stiletto heels, and a lacy bra. Then she removed the rollers from her hair and styled it.

She was ready at five after seven, and decided to arrive at Chasen's early—hopefully, before Santino. Even five or ten minutes of freedom was worth *something*

Zeko, the big ox, was in the kitchen, reading. She was surprised he *could* read.

"Let's go," she announced impatiently.

"The boss says we leave at quarter past."

"And *I* say we go now."

She stared coldly at the hateful man, daring him to argue. He didn't.

• • • • •

Home for Santino Bonnatti was a gated mansion in Bel Air. Once the residence of a silent screen star, it now housed the Santino chapter of the Bonnatti family. Donatella, Santino's wife, was a plain, grossly fat woman. She was a bride imported from Sicily eighteen years before, and her heart remained in the small village she had been plucked from.

There were four Bonnatti children ranging in age from seven to seventeen, three girls (all, unfortunately, fat like their mother) and one boy (a replica of his father, with the added advantage of a full head of hair). The boy, named Santino, Junior, was the youngest child and the spoiled favorite of both his mother and father, who vied with each other to give him the most attention.

"Santino!" Donatella greeted him at the door of the mansion wringing her hands, her expressive eyes full of distress. "Santino, Junior—he sick. He gotta da fever. He *very* sick." She accused him with a look. "Where you been, huh? I try calla your business—nothin'. Where you been?"

Santino nearly slipped on the polished wood floor in his haste to rush upstairs and view his "very sick" son for himself. Donatella did have a tendency to melodramatize.

"I had a meetin'," he explained—although explanations were not really necessary. He could do as he liked, and they both knew it—so long as he sent money to her relatives, kept her and the children in the style they had grown accustomed to, and fucked her every couple of months. She was not demanding, but she did expect it every once in a while, and six times a year was not too bad.

She followed him upstairs and was right behind him as he flung open the door to his son's bedroom.

"You see!" she crowed triumphantly.

Santino, Junior, lay in the center of his bed, pajama'd and flushed. A large-screen television offered a Charles Bronson movie, and the room was extremely hot.

"Son!" exclaimed Santino, rushing to his bedside and placing a clammy hand on the boy's forehead.

"You see!" repeated Donatella. "He gotta da fever!"

•   •   •   •   •

Eden entered Chasen's like a star. She asked the maitre d' for Mr. Bonnatti's table. He had no knowledge of a reservation for Mr. Bonnatti. She suggested the table might be under Mr. Quinn Leech's name, or maybe Vitos Felicidade's.

"Ah, Mr. Felicidade," sighed the maitre d', impressed at last. "This way, please."

She didn't have to follow him far, because Vitos was seated at a booth in the front room with his manager—no sign yet of either Quinn or Santino.

"Good evening," Eden said graciously, as both men struggled to stand. "Am I early? Or is everyone else late?"

"It seems you are on time, my lady," crooned Vitos in his best English, executing a small formal bow. "And you are . . . ?"

Didn't he remember her?

She certainly remembered *him*.

"Eden Antonio," she said smoothly, not allowing her aggravation to show. "We met in Las Vegas."

"Yes, of course," sighed Vitos, not remembering at all. He took her hand and bestowed a kiss. *"Enchanté,"* he murmured.

She fluttered her eyelashes, a move she would not have dared make with Santino present. "Thank you," she said demurely.

Vitos's manager thrust a hand in her direction. "You're Quinn's lady, right?"

"No. I am not Quinn's lady," she said shortly, furious at being mistaken for Quinn Leech's dull-looking girlfriend. "I was in Vegas with Mr. Bonnatti discussing my role in *My Life as a Call Girl*. I'm to star in the film, you know."

She slid into the booth next to Vitos and ordered a Martini, not noticing that he and his manager were exchanging puzzled looks.

"I understand Mr. Bonnatti is negotiating with you about co-starring with me," she said, determined that this time they would remember her. And how.

"We speak 'bout movie," said Vitos apologetically, "but no call wimmen's title."

"What?" He was not easy to understand, but his broken English sounded charming.

"Vitos means that we *are* discussing a film for him to star in. It's called *The Singer,*" said his manager.

"The Singer?" she asked blankly.

They were saved from answering by the arrival of Quinn Leech, alone and reeking of garlic and whiskey. "Hiya all," he said and slid into the booth beside Eden, imprisoning her between himself and Vitos. "Where's Santino?"

"He hasn't arrived," replied Eden, stating the obvious. "And what's all this about a film called *The Singer?* I thought we were talking to Mr. Felicidade about *My Life as a Call Girl.*"

"Rewrite," said Quinn blithely.

"Rewrite?" screeched Eden.

Quinn nodded. "I take it the sonofabitch didn't tell you?"

She shook her head while anger flooded her body.

"Listen," said Quinn, whispering confidentially into her ear. "You think Vitos Felicidade is gonna star in a movie with 'Call Girl' in the title? We changed the concept. You'll read it. You'll love it."

"Yes, but am I still in it?" she asked bitterly.

Quinn threw up his hands. "That's not for me to know. I'm only the director."

"Did Santino ever tell you this was supposed to be a star-ring vehicle for me?" she hissed.

"Never heard that," said Quinn honestly, ordering a double shot of Jack Daniel's.

Eden slumped into silence. The bastard! The bald, hairy, horny bastard! No wonder he told her never to discuss the movie with anyone but him. No wonder he told her the time was not right for her to talk to Quinn or Ryder or Paige or *anyone* about the project. He was stringing her along. He was fucking her with empty promises. She felt like primal scream-ing in the middle of Chasen's. She felt like *killing* him.

A waiter brought a phone to the table. "There's a call for Miss Antonio," he said.

She took the phone, held it to her ear.

"What the frig didja leave the house early for?" com-plained Santino.

"Where are you?" she asked, her voice constricted.

"My boy is sick," he said. "He's got a fever. I can't leave him. If you hadn't left the house before I told you, I coulda stopped you from goin'."

"I'm here now," she said.

"I friggin' *know* that. An' I want ya outta there. Pronto. Tell 'em I can't make it, an' why. Lay it on thick—I don't want 'em thinkin' I'm backin' off the deal. An' then ya split, an' get the fuck home. Ya hear me?"

"I hear you."

"Make an excuse. Ya got the rag on, a headache, anythin'. But I wancha outta there in five minutes. Got it?"

"Yes."

"Notheeng wrong, I hope," said Vitos, as the waiter whisked the phone away.

"Mr. Bonnatti cannot be with us tonight." Eden toyed with her Martini glass. "His son has a temperature and he doesn't want to leave him. He hopes you will all understand."

Everybody assured her they understood.

"He's such a loyal family man," she added.

"Yeah!" agreed Quinn, and under the table his hand did exploratory surgery on her thigh.

She removed it. "Mr. Bonnatti requested that someone instruct his driver, Zeko, to take the rest of the evening off. Could we send that *personal* message from Mr. Bonnatti out front?"

"No problem," said Quinn.

"You, beautiful lady, weel stays?" inquired Vitos, his liquid eyes melting with hers.

"Absolutely," she replied briskly. "Mr. Bonnatti insisted that I should."

72

Lucky raced back to the yacht. Dimitri and Francesca sat on an upper deck engrossed in each other and a game of backgammon. There was no one else around. Francesca wore a green sundress and a matching bandana that almost hid her flaming red hair. Dimitri was still in khaki shorts and a sports shirt.

"I thought I was late for dinner," Lucky said, out of breath.

Francesca ignored her. Dimitri glanced up briefly, said "Dinner is at eight," and returned his attention to the game. No *Where have you been all day? Why are you late?* Not even a *How are you?* Any guilt she might have felt was washed away immediately.

"Where is everybody?" she asked.

"Aha . . . got you!" husked Francesca, making a key move on the backgammon board.

"You think so, woman?" roared Dimitri, countering with his own clever move. Their laughs intermingled.

Lucky felt the sharp stab of rejection she had known all her life. Fuck 'em. If they wanted each other so badly, they were welcome.

"I'm going to shower," she said stiffly.

Dimitri waved her away—a gesture that plainly stated, *Don't bother me, I'm busy.* "Dinner is at eight," he repeated.

"Can't wait," Lucky murmured sarcastically.

She visited Roberto, who was playing in his yellow bathtub, content and happy, watched over by the ever-smiling CeeCee.

She hugged his wet body close to her. "Hiya, baby gorgeous," she sang. "How's my boy? How's my kid?"

"Mama," he chirped happily. "Nice nice Mama."

"He's been so good today," beamed CeeCee. "This is one kid who *never* cries."

"Just like Mommy," sighed Lucky softly.

"Huh?"

"Nothing."

Back in Dimitri's masculine stateroom she stripped off her clothes and stood under a hot shower, closing her eyes as the water beat a soothing rhythm on her skin. For a moment she allowed herself to think of Lennie and their incredibly erotic and satisfying encounter.

This time he had gone along with her game. No corny lines or bullshit. Just wonderfully uninhibited silent sex.

She shivered. Sex hadn't felt that good since Marco.

· · · · ·

Alice wanted to complain to Olympia. She knocked on her stateroom door late in the afternoon and caught her flinging things around the room in a fury.

"What's the matter, dear?" she asked, forgetting her own problems.

"Nothing," scowled Olympia. "What do *you* want?"

"A nice way to talk to your mother-in-law," clucked Alice. "I thought we were friends."

"What?" snapped Olympia. She was in no mood to humor Lennie's eccentric mother.

Alice came right to the point. "I'm very insulted," she stated, picking at her nail polish.

"Why?"

"Am I, Alice Golden, former *star* of Las Vegas—Lennie inherited everything he knows from me—not good enough to sit at the dinner table with the likes of the hoi polloi?"

"Is that a question?"

"It's a statement, my dear. A statement." She paused dramatically. "I have shared meals with kings, danced for princes. What do you think I am—a *shluhb* with no feelings?"

"Please, Alice. I have a hangover and a headache. What do you want?"

"To eat dinner with my own son."

"You're here to be with Brigette," Olympia pointed out.

"Does that mean I can't sit with Lennie? Brigette goes to bed at eight. Am I supposed to stay below deck with the help?"

Olympia frowned. Where *was* Lennie when she needed him? "I don't know," she said irritably. "Do what you like."

A gleam of triumph filled Alice's watery eyes. "Thank you, dear," she said, already thinking up stories she could entrance the dinner guests with.

* * * * *

Gino did not like France. He did not understand the language. He found the people rude. It was too hot. He hated being confined on a boat. And he missed Paige.

Susan, social as ever, insisted they spend the day with friends of hers who owned a summer villa in the hills. The man was a film star. He had a rugged profile, yellowing teeth and badly dyed black hair. His wife was a sharp-tongued European, who, in the course of an afternoon, trashed everyone she knew, including all her dearest friends.

Gino hated every minute. He told Susan so on the way back to the yacht.

"*I* had an amusing time," she said.

"You wouldn't be so amused if y'could hear what that bitch is sayin' about you now," he replied.

"What are you talking about?"

"Forget it."

He knew there was no way he was going to last two weeks on *this* trip.

* * * * *

"My game," husked Francesca.

"You always win," laughed Dimitri.

"How true."

"We must get ready for dinner."

"Yes." She snaked a white hand to his cheek, her nails blood-red and inches long. "Why did you marry her, Dimitri? Why did you humiliate me?"

"Francesca—*you're* married," he pointed out.

"It's nothing. Horace looks after things for me. It's a marriage of convenience."

"Divorce him."

"I can't. It would break his heart."

"Then what are we discussing?"

"Your disloyalty."

"Never."

"Yes."

"I married Lucky to give my son his rightful name."

Lightly Francesca scratched her nails where she knew it would have the most effect. "Now you can divorce her," she suggested.

· · · · ·

Having got rid of Alice, Olympia threw another fit. Where the hell was Lennie? She needed someone to scream at. What good was a husband if he wasn't around when you needed him?

She had a blinding, throbbing headache. Who wouldn't when the news of a half brother was thrust upon her? Not to mention the fact that Dimitri had married Lucky Santangelo.

Lucky and Dimitri! Unbelievable! Ridiculous! Obscene!

She marched into the bathroom, went straight to her stash and snorted the rest of her coke supply. Then she gulped a couple of Quaaludes and tried to decide what to wear to confront her latest stepmother.

Stepmother!

What a joke!

Lucky Santangelo.

Friend.

Some friend.

73

Dimitri was an excellent host. His summer cruises were legendary. No expense was spared to make sure all his guests had a marvelous time.

Finishing his game of backgammon, he hurried to shower and change his clothes, and was ready to greet his guests as they arrived on the upper deck for predinner drinks. Lucky accompanied him. She looked particularly stunning in a St. Laurent white tuxedo, her hair loose and wild. Gino stood alone at the bar. Lucky went over to him immediately.

"I gotta get outta here," he announced.

"So do I," she agreed.

"Hey—maybe I can come up with some family business that takes us both to New York. Y'know somethin', kid? I really miss the city."

"I thought you loved Beverly Hills."

"It's too slow for me. I've had it."

"Really?"

"I need more action."

"What about Susan?"

"I haven't told her, but I'm thinkin' of buyin' a place in New York."

"And dividing your time?"

"Why not?"

"Sounds good to me."

• • • • •

"We spent such an interesting day," said Susan to the Contessa, scooping a healthy amount of Petrossian beluga caviar onto a cracker and disposing of it in one mouthful.

"Did you?" replied the Contessa. "*I* was frightfully bored. I like to play baccarat. I can't wait until we arrive in Monte Carlo. I am simply desperate for the tables."

"When my late husband, Tiny Martino, was alive, we used to visit Monte Carlo all the time," enthused Susan, trying to impress. "Tiny was a friend of the Rainiers, you know. He and Grace were *very* close."

The Contessa raised a penciled eyebrow. "*You* were married to Tiny?" she questioned.

"For twenty-five years," Susan said proudly. And then she added coyly, "I was a child bride, you know."

The Contessa smiled and patted her hand. "Weren't we all, darling."

Susan waited for her to remove the pressure of her rather warm hand, each finger loaded with impressive diamonds.

She didn't.

* * * * *

Olympia was angry because Lennie appeared to have vanished. She had no intention of sitting around. If he missed dinner, it was his loss. Besides, she couldn't *wait* to see Lucky. Skinny, naive little Lucky Santangelo. Former best friend. Former confidante. Ha! It never paid to be nice to people. They always took advantage of kindness and shafted you whenever the opportunity arose.

The very thought of Dimitri and Lucky in bed together was disgusting to her. She, Olympia, had taught Lucky everything she knew. When Lucky had arrived in Switzerland fifteen years ago she had never even been *kissed!* Olympia had educated her about men and life and how to have *fun*. Just look at the thanks she received.

She dressed in an expensive gold Ungaro outfit that would have looked sensational on a tall, flat-chested model. It did not suit Olympia at all. She applied heavy-duty diamonds to her ears, fingers and throat. Then she fluffed out her long blond curls and set off for a face-to-face confrontation.

* * * * *

"I've never been to Paris," Alice confided to Horace, a faraway look in her eyes.

"Haven't you?" He kept glancing over to see when Francesca would appear. She had forced him to go on ahead of her, claiming that he got in her way while she was trying to dress.

"Gay Paree," sighed Alice. "Oo la la!" She snatched a hot canapé from a passing waiter. "I shall probably go there with my son. He's very proud of me. It takes talent to know talent, and he knows." She nodded. "Ah, yes, he certainly knows."

"I'm sure," agreed Horace.

"Shortly I will be appearing on *The Merv Griffin Show*." She munched contentedly on a stuffed olive. "I love Merv. He's such a *warm* man."

"Good."

She leaned intimately toward him. "*Very* good," she said, winking slyly. "Very, very good."

"Excellent."

"Yes."

"Yes."

• • • • •

Olympia entered the bar. Paused. Looked around. Spotted Lucky immediately. Did a double take. Could not believe her skinny little nothing friend had grown into such a beauty. And not an ounce of fat on the entire package.

Lucky saw her look, and for a moment their eyes met and they were kids again, playing hooky, smuggling boys into their dorm and indulging in "almost"—a game they thought they had invented.

Most of her life Lucky had been a loner. No girlfriends, no mother, no one to giggle or chatter with—except once there had been Olympia.

She rushed across the room, arms outstretched.

Olympia backed off.

Instinctively Lucky knew she was not thrilled about the marriage, and who could blame her? It *was* kind of a crazy co-incidence. She turned her outstretched arms into a pat on the shoulder. "Olympia! God, it's been a long time. You look great."

Olympia was at a loss for words. Too much coke was clogging her brain. She wanted to be cool and act as if she didn't care, but she *did* care very much that Lucky had dumped her and never tried to contact her, even when they reached adulthood and could have seen anyone they pleased.

"Little Lucky Saint," she said coolly, using the name Lucky had been known by at school. "You certainly grew up."

"I should hope so."

"You were always such a dumb jerk."

"Thanks."

"Does the truth hurt?"

Lucky lowered her voice. "Let's not start off being hostile, huh?"

Olympia bridled. "Who's hostile? Certainly not *me*. Why should *I* be hostile?"

Lucky was saved from answering by Francesca's entrance. She wore a red ball gown that matched her hair. Around her neck was a magnificent ruby necklace.

Horace cringed. He had never seen the necklace before. He knew it must be a gift from Dimitri—therefore it signaled the affair was still going strong.

"Damn!" he muttered.

"Has anyone ever told you that you look like Burgess Meredith?" Alice fluttered her false eyelashes. "I always thought he was such an *attractive* man."

• • • • •

Lennie hitched a ride back to the port in a convertible with two sunburned German homosexuals. They didn't speak English. He didn't speak German. But a lot of polite nodding and smiling went on.

He skipped aboard the yacht and encountered Captain Pratt. "Did you have a pleasant look around, sir?" asked the captain.

Lennie didn't know if it was his imagination or not, but he could have sworn the man gave him a lewd wink. "Thanks. Yes," he replied.

"You *are* a bit late, sir," the captain added. "They're just sitting down for dinner."

"It'll take me five minutes to change. Can you get a message to my wife?"

"Certainly, sir." Was that another conspirational wink? "I must say, sir, your mother is a very fine woman."

Oh, shit. The captain wanted to *schtupp* Alice. Sorry, my friend, you're about twenty years too old for the likes of Alice the Swizzle.

"Yeah," said Lennie vaguely, and made a dash for it.

•　•　•　•　•

Polite conversations took place as servants tended table and fine wine was poured into silver goblets. Olympia found herself seated next to Gino Santangelo. She thrust her chest forward and flirted with him outrageously. He might be an old man, but if Lucky could have Dimitri, why couldn't she give Gino a tumble?

She leaned close to him. "Betcha don't remember the last time we met," she whispered.

He did remember. Only too well. It was a picture fixed firmly in his mind forever. Sixteen-year-old Olympia Stanislopoulos, her bare pink ass stuck in the air as she concentrated on giving her boyfriend of the moment a blow job.

"You know somethin'—you're right, I *don't* remember."

She pouted. "Come *on*. How could you ever forget?"

He knew what he *did* want to forget. This trip. These people. Tomorrow he would arrange a cable summoning him urgently to New York.

•　•　•　•　•

Olympia had said, "We dress for dinner," whatever that meant. Reluctantly Lennie put on a suit. What bullshit. Why was he going along with it? One night was enough. From here on he planned to take Olympia off the boat to explore. There must be so many great restaurants around, and he had no intention of spending his vacation playing stuffed shirt with the rich folk.

He checked himself out in the mirror and wondered if he

had time for a joint. Reflected beside him he imagined he saw the girl from the beach. Dark, mysterious, sexy . . . He had always gone for blondes, but she made him forget every blonde he had ever known—even Eden.

Free at last?

Yeah.

Why hadn't he found out her name, at least?

He loosened his tie, ran his hands through his hair, lit up a joint, took a couple of deep drags and set off for dinner.

• • • • •

"Business is business," Saud Omar said. "And women are women. And never the two shall meet."

"What antiquated crap!" exclaimed Lucky. "Where have *you* been for the last fifty years?"

Saud blinked, unused to women answering back. Besides, he had not been talking to Lucky; he had been making a general remark.

"I agree with *you*, Saud," Fluff squeaked. "I *never* want to work. Never, ever! Ugh!"

"And you'll never have to, pumpkin tush," Jenkins Wilder joined in. "Smart girlies never have to lift a finger."

"Only their ass," murmured Lucky.

Alice cackled.

Francesca threw Dimitri a simmering look.

Susan said, "I think females should all learn domestic arts in school. Cooking, sewing and general housekeeping."

"How about screwing?" Lucky suggested. "I mean, shit, Susan, if you go to school to learn how to take care of a guy, you may as well learn to do it properly, don't you think?"

Dimitri gave Lucky a warning glare, which she ignored.

Susan blushed beet-red.

Gino said, "Hey, kid . . ."

The Contessa laughed.

Olympia scowled. Skinny little Lucky had developed a mouth.

Lennie entered the room, saw Olympia and headed straight for her.

"Where have you been?" she demanded crossly.

"Sorry I'm late. I couldn't get a ride back from the beach," he explained.

"The beach!" Olympia sneered, as if it were a dirty word.

"Yeah, y'know. That's the place where the peasants hang out—not everyone has a yacht to throw themselves about on."

"Very funny. Why don't you sit down?" She addressed herself to the table. "I'd like you all to meet my husband—Lennie Golden."

He saw an array of jewels and old men. He also saw Alice, which filled him with dismay.

"Now, let me see," continued Olympia, playing the perfect hostess. "This is Contessa Zebrowski and Saud Omar. Mr. and Mrs. Jenkins Wilder, Susan and Gino Santangelo, Francesca and Horace Fern, and you met my father earlier." She paused, wondering if she could get away with snubbing Lucky. Too obvious. "Oh, yes, and this is Lucky." She refused to give her billing.

"My wife," Dimitri said.

"Your wife," Lennie repeated.

He stared at her. She stared back. It was as if time stood still.

74

Returning to the real world was just what Steven needed. He had always resisted the temptation of working in a big, expensive law firm, preferring to do time as an assistant D.A. and public prosecutor, where the money was by no means great. But he was getting older and wiser by the moment, and now security and making it seemed a whole new challenge. It wasn't as if he had to grab anything that came his way—Jerry assured him he could take his pick of the many rich clients who needed help.

"Just because they've got bread doesn't mean they're all bad," Jerry explained amiably. "Why don't I give you the Mary Lou Moore case? She's the cute Black actress on TV with the large family image. She's suing some porn magazine that just printed naughty photos of her taken before her big success. We go into depositions this week."

Mary Lou Moore. Steven had watched her show a few times. A funny sitcom set in Connecticut in which Mary Lou played the adopted daughter of a white family. She was a kid, eighteen or nineteen, and very pretty.

"Am I going to get all the Black clients?" he asked bitingly.

"Only if you want 'em. This is a juicy case. The put-upon heroine against the bad guys. Your kind of action. She signed nothing. In fact, she says the pix were taken by her boyfriend when she was fifteen, as a lark. You think we've got a case?"

"I would say we can't lose."

"Go for the big bucks. These guys can afford it."

After getting settled at the office, Steven informed the tenants who were renting his brownstone basement apartment that he planned to move back. His luck was in—the man, an engineer, had just landed a job in the Middle East and was prepared to vacate at once. An adjustment on the rent took place (more borrowed money from Jerry, but it would soon be payoff time) and Steven moved in.

He really was coming home after three lost years. It felt wonderful.

· · · · ·

Carrie met with Anna Robb, the ghostwriter Fred Lester had recommended. She was a small, precise woman of forty, who wore sensible shoes and big woolly sweaters. She appeared to be physically attached to her Sony tape recorder, which she switched on the moment she entered Carrie's life.

"Just talk," she said reassuringly, "about anything you like. I'll be able to extract exactly what we want."

So Carrie talked. At first about clothes, then about style, and on to the subject of entertaining. Soon she was reliving her life with her first husband, Bernard Dimes "We had such interesting parties," she recalled with pleasure. "People from the arts, ballet stars, writers. Bernard knew everyone. He was a fascinating man."

"How did you two meet?" Anna asked, sipping the lemon tea Carrie had prepared for her.

"I don't think I want to speak about that," Carrie replied quickly.

Anna was a skillful enough interrogator to move on to something else immediately.

They did three taped sessions within a week, each one of four hours' duration. By the end of that time Carrie felt at ease in Anna's company and had told her all she could possibly dredge up on fashion, style, beauty, and diet. Anna said she had everything she needed.

"But it was easy!" Carrie exclaimed.

"For you," Anna said. "For me the real work comes now. First I write the book, then divide it into sections. We go over what I have written to make sure you approve. Then we begin to choose the pictures and decide what new ones are to be taken."

"It's so exciting!" Carrie said.

"If the book is a best-seller it's the most exciting feeling in the world." Anna smiled. "If it flops, it's the worst."

"How do we make it a best-seller?" Carrie asked naively.

"If I knew that, Fred Lester would be working for me."

"Tell me about him," Carrie said. "He seems such a nice man. Is he married?"

"Are you interested?" Anna teased.

Carrie was taken aback. Why on earth would she be interested? She had given up on men when she divorced Elliott Berkeley, and now she was too old and set in her ways to start thinking of another relationship. Besides, if she did become involved with a man again, she would have to be truthful about her past. And who would want her when they heard the truth?

No. Involvements were out. She had Steven back, thank God. She had a few friends. What more could she possibly want?

"Certainly not," she said primly.

"He's a widower," Anna volunteered, packing up her tape machine. "But I think I should warn you that he's living with a woman."

Carrie was longing to ask who the woman was, but she didn't pursue it. How embarrassing if Anna thought she desired her boss. Quickly she began to talk about something else.

75

Lucky had no idea how she got through dinner. She tried to avoid looking at Lennie, and she knew he was attempting to do the same with her, but it was impossible. Their eyes met constantly and when they did the electricity they generated seemed to ignite the entire room.

Over the course of dinner they both found out a few things.

Lucky, who rarely read anything besides books other than *Newsweek*, *The Wall Street Journal*, and *Blues & Soul*, and never watched television, learned, mostly from Alice—who couldn't seem to stop talking—that Lennie had hit the big time and was now a personality and television star.

"Didn't you read about our wedding?" Olympia asked belligerently. "We made worldwide headlines."

"No. I didn't see it," Lucky replied politely, causing Olympia to pout.

"What about my Lennie on the cover of *People*? Surely you saw that?" scolded Alice.

"Sorry," apologized Lucky.

"*He* should have been sorry," remarked Alice darkly. "He left me out. But they'll be writing a piece about me soon. Probably not a cover, but you can't have everything in this life can you, darling?"

Lennie learned just exactly who Lucky was. Not only was she married to Olympia's father, but she was Lucky Santangelo—*the* Lucky Santangelo who had canned his ass two years before at the Magiriano Hotel.

Suddenly everything fell into place. Now he knew why he had been fired so abruptly and run out of town like bad eggs.

She had wanted to get laid.

He hadn't obliged.

Get rid of the sonofabitch. He could just imagine her giving Matt his orders.

With good reason, he was furious.

"Are you the same Lennie Golden who just headlined at my hotel?" Gino asked.

"Yeah," Lennie replied. What was this? Family week? Lucky with her father. Alice sitting at the table—the original proud parent. Christ! He felt like he was in the middle of a bad dream.

"You broke house records," Gino said. "I told Matt I want you back whenever you can make it. In fact, I asked him to work out a deal with your agent—like you do a week for us every couple of months. Exclusive."

Lucky had not realized Gino still kept an eye on things—she had thought he collected the money and that was it.

Lennie Golden headlined *her* hotel, and she hadn't even known. She felt like a fool.

It's not your hotel anymore, an inner voice reminded her. *You sold out, ran out. Why should you have known? Why should you even care?*

Yes, goddamn it. Why should she care? Who was Lennie Golden in her life anyway? So she had balled him—big deal. Sex was sex, and it was unfortunate that she had ever set eyes on him again.

Oh, yeh?

Yeh.

· · · · ·

After dinner several of the guests wished to go nightclubbing ashore.

"I want to go," Olympia announced to Lennie. She was nicely coked up and ready to fly all night.

He, on the other hand, was beginning to feel the effects of nonstop traveling, not to mention the tension of sitting through dinner with Lucky just across the table. "I'm gonna check out," he said.

"Like hell you are," Olympia replied crossly. "You've been checked out all day while *I've* been stuck here. We are going nightclubbing, so jump to it."

"Don't talk to me like that," he said angrily.

"I'll talk to you any way I like," she sneered.

He stared at the woman he had married. She had small blue eyes in a puffy pink face. Her painted lips curled derisively, and her blond curls were drooping. Yes. Jess was definitely right. Insanity had struck.

"Listen," he said, his voice low and even. "Talk to who the fuck you want that way—but don't *ever* talk to me like shit. You got it?"

She refused to be intimidated. She tossed her hair back. "I take it you don't wish to come," she said haughtily. "Well, *I'm* going, with or without you."

"Have a wonderful time."

"Don't think I won't," she said, flouncing off.

Across the room, Lucky pleaded a headache to Dimitri, who was only too delighted.

Francesca, of course, was ready, willing and able. She did not consult Horace on his preference. "You'll stay here," she informed him. "You know how you hate nightclubs."

Since no one was inviting Alice, she put on a brave front. "I'll look after Horace," she volunteered.

Francesca ignored her—Francesca had a habit of ignoring most people, with the exception of Dimitri.

Jenkins and Fluff Wilder elected to go. So did Saud and his Contessa. Susan said yes. Gino said no. She was tempted to take off without him, but he didn't suggest it, so she stayed—reluctantly. The Contessa was such an interesting woman—she wanted to find out more about her.

As soon as the nightclubbers departed, Gino said good-night, and he and Susan retired. Lucky felt her eyes drawn toward Lennie. He returned her gaze. Alice was regaling Horace with stories of Las Vegas. She was in her element with a captive audience of one and limitless supplies of Grand Marnier—her favorite tipple. Lennie gestured toward the door.

Lucky nodded her agreement. "Goodnight, all," she said quietly, and was gone.

Lennie waited a beat of ten; then he too rose.

"Oh, dear!" exclaimed Alice with a girlish giggle. "Are you leaving us alone? I'm not sure I can be responsible for my actions if I'm left alone with such an *attractive* man!"

Lennie did not know which he hated most—the cloying mother or the flirtatious ingenue.

Out on deck he looked for Lucky. She was leaning against the rail smoking a cigarette, her eyes dark and watchful as he approached.

"It's a smaller world than we think," she said in a low voice. "We should have left it the way it was in Vegas. Less complicated."

He had plenty to say to her—like: Why did you have me fired? for starters. But words were elusive. He just wanted to hold her.

She dragged deeply on her cigarette, then flicked it over the edge. Without another word, as if by mutual agreement, they fell into each other's arms as though it was the most natural thing in the world. He was ready for her at once, all thoughts of tiredness and tension gone.

She kissed him with her lips, her tongue, her hands caressing his face, then moving down his body with indecent haste.

He returned her kisses, slipped his hands beneath her white tuxedo, and freed her breasts from the confines of the scant silk top. "I want you," he muttered. "All the time, everywhere. I want you."

Weakly she tried to push him away. She had no desire to tell him to get lost. He awakened feelings in her that had been long dormant. Sexually he turned her on to a degree she had forgotten existed. He was a dangerous ride, and she couldn't seem to stop herself from taking it.

Silently they kissed and caressed until it was his turn to push her away. His voice was strangled. "What are we playing here, cocktease?"

"I never tease," she said, unzipping his pants and sinking to her knees. "Never." And her mouth was on him, taking him to heaven and back and swallowing the evidence.

"Oh, Jesus!" he exclaimed. He had experienced good sex, bad sex, mediocre sex. He had *never* experienced sex as erotic and exciting as Lucky Santangelo.

"I thought about doing that to you all through dinner." Her eyes gleamed. "Sort of like a farewell present."

"Hey, lady—if that was goodbye, I can't wait to see the way you say hello!"

She didn't laugh. "It *was* goodbye. Neither of us is looking for trouble. Today was a dream . . . a fantasy. Now we go back to real life."

"Are you kidding?" He gripped her by the arms. "Do you love the old guy you're married to, or did you marry him for his money?"

"That's not your concern," she said sharply. "And while we're asking questions, why did *you* do the deed with Olympia? Was it her sunny personality that hooked you? Or her astronomical bank balance?"

He grabbed her urgently, bending her backward while bringing his head down to her breasts.

"No!" she commanded.

"Yes," he insisted. "Oh, yes."

She lost herself in his arms. Something was happening. A passion she hadn't felt since Marco. And Marco had been dead five years. . . .

She was strangely frightened and yet exhilarated at the same time. All reason deserted her as he crushed her to him. And she wanted him again.

Captain Pratt, crouched on all fours on an upper deck, nearly fell over the edge. The rich! They were no different from anyone else. He wondered what Mr. Stanislopoulos would have to say about this little lark?

What *could* he say? That very afternoon Dimitri Stanislopoulos had taken the ugly Fern woman to his study and stayed in there for over an hour with the shades pulled down and a DO NOT DISTURB sign on the door. No wonder his wife was randy. She probably never got anything from the old Greek—he was too busy giving it all to his girlfriend.

Captain Pratt stood up and brushed himself off. He wondered how much he could sell his story for. The English newspapers loved scandal and gossip—especially about the super rich. *News of the World* or the *Sunday Mirror* would pay a fortune for some of his stories. Not to mention the *Enquirer* or the *Star*.

Yes. Captain Pratt reckoned that when he was ready to retire he had his nest egg waiting.

· · · · ·

"We're crazy," Lucky said, finding her abandoned clothes and struggling into them. "Absolutely crazy. Anyone could have stumbled across us. This yacht is crawling with servants. We're *crazy*. I mean it."

"You don't have to keep on saying it. I'm convinced."

She turned to face Lennie defiantly. "This is sex, just sex. You *do* know that, don't you?"

He returned her gaze. "I don't know about you, but my marriage was over before it began. I married Olympia one wild night in Vegas at the Wee Wedding Chapel of Love and Honor—can you believe it?"

She nodded. "I know it well. It's the place chorus girls drag out-of-town mustangs who've scored more than a hundred grand on the crap tables."

"You *could* say that I scored, but for all the wrong reasons. I was stoned out of my head, recovering from bitch-of-the-century, and anxious to destroy myself. You get the picture?"

"I'm beginning to."

"You—are probably the woman I've been looking for all my life. Only I got sidetracked by a million blondes."

"Great sex does not a relationship make," she observed wisely.

"But it sure beats the hell out of lousy sex."

"True."

"I only speak the truth."

"When it suits you."

"What do you mean by that?"

"C'mon, Lennie. You're a lady-killer, a hotshot lover boy. You're not even my type."

"And what makes you think you're mine?"

They both burst out laughing.

She touched his cheek lightly and couldn't stop herself from saying, "Lennie Golden, I don't know what's going on here, but I think something's happening."

"Like a thunderbolt," he responded.

"A flash of lightning."

"Not just sex."

"Nope."

"More."

"Right."

"Much, much more."

"You said it."

"And we don't even know each other."

She stared at him. So many feelings all at once.

Before she could think of what to do or say next, Alice and Horace stumbled upon them.

"Oh!" exclaimed a startled Alice, adding a delicate hiccough. "What are you two doing out here?"

Horace shuffled uncomfortably.

"Playing tennis," Lennie said dryly.

Alice giggled. "Saint Troopo is a lovely place," she trilled, and hiccoughed again. "So very . . . tropical."

"Saint-Tropez," murmured Lucky.

"Horace is showing me the boat," Alice offered, staggering slightly and clutching the railing for support.

"How nice," said Lennie sarcastically.

"Come along, Horace," flirted Alice. "I want to see the lifeboats. I can't swim, y'know, so I must make sure everything is shipshape and ready for action." Shrieking with laughter, she dragged a reluctant Horace off.

"My mother!" Lennie said dourly. "The last of the all-time great swingers."

"Does she embarrass you?"

"I'm too old to be embarrassed."

"How old *are* you?"

"Thirty. And you?"

"I'm going to join you at that illustrious milestone in two days. It's the official beginning of being a grownup, isn't it? The end of the frivolous twenties."

"No more outdoor fucking, huh?"

"It's not something I make a habit of."

He gripped her by the shoulders. "What are we going to do, Lucky?"

"About my birthday?"

"Don't be flippant."

She shrugged impatiently. "I don't plan to screw up anything because of you. I've told you what I think. We say goodbye and pretend nothing happened."

"Just like that, huh?"

"I can do it if you can. Easily."

"Oh," he said acidly. "Your solution to everything, right? Just blank it out. Is that why I had my ass run out of Vegas— so you could pretend our little scene never happened?"

"What was I supposed to do? Keep you around to remind me of our one night of nothing?"

"You don't can somebody just because they won't sleep with you."

"I can do without the lecture, thank you."

"I'm trying to teach you something."

"Teach *me*." She raised her voice. "Teach *me*. Ha!"

"Don't yell."

"Who's yelling?" she yelled.

The low throb of a motorboat announced the return of the nightclubbers.

"Christ!" Lennie exclaimed in disgust. "When am I going to see you again?"

"Tomorrow. At breakfast, lunch *and* dinner. Unless one of us takes off, there's going to be no avoiding each other."

"You know what I mean."

She was already moving toward the stairway. "I gave you my goodbye present, Lennie. Let's just leave it that way."

They both had a feeling it was impossible.

76

Eden had every intention of ending up in the sensuous embrace of Vitos Felicidade. If she was going to stray, it might as well be into the arms of the popular Spanish lover. However, sometimes the best-laid plans go astray, and as the evening wore on she found herself increasingly drawn to Quinn Leech. He was a heavily bearded man in his fifties, cadaverously thin, with lecherous eyes and pawing hands. But he was a film director, and therefore he had the edge. She had seen several of his movies. Strange commercial thrillers, with more than a healthy dose of sex and violence. He liked ripping women to pieces—on screen. Feminists enjoyed ripping him to pieces—in print. His last two movies had been box-office disasters. Once he had been "a young, hot director." Now he was just marking time until his next big hit. The studios were off him, so when his old friend Ryder Wheeler had approached him about doing a movie financed by "connected" money, he had agreed immediately. What did he care where the money came from?

Ryder had warned him up front. "Stay away from Bonnatti's girlfriend," he had said. "Don't fuck with the paid help."

But Quinn never had liked being told what to do.

They rolled out of Chasen's before midnight. Vitos climbed into his limousine with his manager and bid Eden and Quinn a polite goodnight.

"Schmuck!" Quinn muttered as the limo slid off along Beverly Boulevard.

"Don't you like him?" Eden asked.

"What's to like or dislike? He's an empty canvas."

She tapped her long nails against the small gold purse she was carrying and waited for him to proposition her. She had already decided to say yes.

"Where's your car?" he asked.

"Don't you remember? We sent the driver home."

"*You* sent the driver home."

The doorman appeared with a black Porsche.

"Can you give me a ride?" she asked quickly.

"The best you ever *had*, baby!" Quinn boasted.

He lived in the Hollywood Hills, on Laurel Canyon. A black leather house in a jungle of plants.

He drank Chivas Regal from the bottle, ripped off his clothes, requested that she strip very, very slowly, and then couldn't get it up.

He suggested an alternative—a black high-tech vibrator kept lovingly in a black leather case. And the company of his resident girlfriend who was asleep upstairs.

"Count me out," said an offended Eden, and called a cab.

When she left, he was snoring on the couch. She couldn't understand why she had chosen him over Vitos.

Zeko was waiting for her when she arrived home. "The boss is gonna bust ya ass," he crowed, rubbing his bald head.

"Only if you tell him," she said shortly. "And *if* you tell him, I shall be forced to mention how you crouch out in the bushes watching me and jerking off when I bathe and dress."

Her threat worked. Zeko never said a word.

When Santino appeared at the house the next day, Eden told him she had stayed for dinner at Chasen's.

"Why'd ya do that?" he demanded, a muscle in his cheek twitching uncontrollably, "when I told ya not to?"

"For you," she replied calmly, thinking to herself that if the sonofabitch didn't come through with the movie soon, she was leaving. "It would have looked bad if I'd left. As if we didn't care."

Santino's eyes bulged angrily. "When I tell ya to do somethin', ya *do* it, get me? Whaddya think ya are, a partner?"

"Quinn Leech told me there's been a rewrite, and that the film is now called *The Singer*," she said tightly.

"He told ya that, did he?"

"Yes he did."

"Friggin' asshole. He's got a big mouth."

"Why didn't *you* tell me?" She glared at him accusingly.

"I gotta keep tellin' ya every little thing?"

"Rewriting the film and giving it a new title are hardly little things."

Santino paced the room. "Dumb cooze," he spat. "I need naggin', I can get it at home. I come over here t'relax."

Eden was not sure how far she could push it. But she had caught him off guard so why not go all the way? "I want to see the new script," she said insistently. "I want to see what's happened to my part. You promised me this was *my* film, *my* vehicle. Quinn Leech doesn't even know I'm supposed to be the star."

His first blow struck her on the cheek.

"You bas—" she began.

His second blow knocked her to the ground. "Doncha go givin' *me* orders," he growled. "I told ya to shift your ass outta there last night. But no, y'couldn't do *that*. Y'had t'stay around askin' questions—makin' me look like some stupid shithead with a ball-breakin' girlfriend. Y'do that again an' ya out."

She began to cry, more out of frustration and anger than anything else. "Maybe that's what I want," she sobbed. "To get away from you."

He glared at her with small, mean eyes. "When I'm ready," he said slowly. "Only when *I'm* ready."

77

Dimitri was planning a party. A big one. Lucky didn't know if it was out of a sense of guilt or what, but there was no deterring him from celebrating her birthday in style. She decided there was nothing to do except go along with it—and then she would leave. Gino had already arranged for a cable to summon him to New York for a business meeting.

"You'll come with me," he told Lucky. "You can say we have to meet with lawyers on Vegas stuff."

She wanted to get away. It was bad enough before, but now, with the added complication of Lennie, it was impossible. Why weren't things simple anymore? Why did she look at Lennie and want to fly? Why did she look at him five minutes later and never want to set eyes on him again? She didn't understand what was going on. Lennie Golden was not her type. It was just sex. And yet . . .

She thought about Marco. They had spent one glorious, unforgettable night together. Then he was gunned down. She never wanted to experience that kind of heartbreak and loss again.

Lennie belonged to Olympia anyway. Plump, petulant Olympia, who treated her as if she was one of Dimitri's temporary girlfriends instead of his wife. She had tried to talk to her in private. Olympia brushed her aside with a caustic "How would you feel if I went to bed with *your* father?"

Lucky had to admit the idea was repellent.

It did not escape her attention that Olympia flirted outrageously with Gino at every given opportunity. He appeared not to notice.

The yacht sailed for Cannes, where the party was to take place. Lucky lay out by the pool watching CeeCee teach Roberto to swim. Brigette kept jumping in and splashing him in the face. CeeCee told her off, and the child yelled insults. "Dirty Black pig," she chanted. "Dirty! Dirty! Dirty!"

Lucky jumped up and whacked the little girl on her bottom.

Brigette looked at her for one horrified moment and then burst into loud, phony tears.

"Cut it out, kid," said Lucky. "You don't have an audience."

Brigette stopped crying abruptly. "I hate dirty Black people," she said spitefully.

"Why?" asked Lucky calmly.

"Because, because, because . . ." She screwed up her pretty little face. "Because Mama does!" she ended triumphantly.

"Not a good enough reason."

The child stuck a thumb into her mouth.

"You're too old for that!" Lucky exclaimed.

"I'm not! I can do what I want."

"Dirty baby pig!" Lucky chanted jokingly. "Dirty! Dirty! Dirty!"

Brigette scowled. "I hate you," she said.

"No you don't," replied Lucky briskly. "You simply do not understand me."

Brigette retreated to the other end of the pool, where Nanny Mabel sat knitting.

"Spoiled brat!" muttered CeeCee.

"Neglected brat, more like," observed Lucky. "I have not seen her mother pay one bit of attention to her. She just pats her occasionally like a puppy. The kid is screaming out for attention."

"I'll give her attention," grumbled the usually smiling CeeCee. "I'll whip her butt!"

"I already did. It won't make any difference. She needs love."

For a moment Lucky recalled her own childhood. She knew what it was like to be alone and unloved.

She had survived. No analysts for Lucky Santangelo—but she could see that, if Brigette didn't get help, the kid was in trouble.

Lennie appeared at lunchtime. They scorched each other with searing looks, but Olympia was right behind him. It was as if she sensed the electricity in the air and was not about to let it spark. She threw Lucky a vague hello, blew a kiss in Brigette's direction and headed for the upper deck. "Come on," she called to Lennie.

"I'm taking a swim before lunch," he said.

"Take it afterwards," she ordered impatiently.

"I'm taking it now."

"Oh, very well. Hurry up." She vanished from sight.

He looked at Lucky. "How are you today?"

She returned his gaze and was almost lost in his lazy green eyes. "I'm okay."

He quickly checked out the pool activity. Two nannies and two kids.

"I think I miss you," he said, very quietly.

Brigette clambered from the pool and ran over to him. She flung her wet body possessively against his. "Do you like *Black* people?" she asked loudly.

CeeCee glared at her.

Lennie assessed the situation at a glance. "I like green people, orange people, fat people, thin people. Sure I like Black people. How about you?"

"I dunno." Her mouth drooped. She had hoped he would take her side. "Can you swim underwater? Can you teach me?" she begged.

He glanced at Lucky. She was playing with Roberto in the shallow end. "Come on, pretty girl," he said, swinging Brigette in the air. "I'll teach you to be a fish. How's that?"

She squealed with excitement, wriggled free and jumped into the pool with a splash. "Hurry up!" she commanded. "Hurryup! Hurryup!"

He made a racing dive from the side, churned the length underwater, and surfaced next to Brigette. She climbed aboard his shoulders, giggling, and he transported her around the pool.

"Me!" yelled Roberto. "Me! Me!"

Lennie dropped Brigette off and placed Roberto on his back.

"Careful!" Lucky admonished.

"Hey, lady." He winked. "I'm an expert with kids."

She met his eyes, and warmth flowed between them.

For once Lucky felt unsure about what was happening. Her thing with Lennie was sex—pure sex. And yet, why did she thrill to see him? Why was she shivering—ever so slightly?

He wasn't even her type. He wasn't Marco. His hair was dirty blond, his looks more Redford than Pacino. His eyes were green—killer green.

She watched him play with the kids. They screamed with laughter as he shared his attention between them. Roberto giggled uncontrollably as Lennie tossed him in the air. Dimitri, Lucky noticed, had little time to play with his son. Plenty of time for Madame Fern though.

She frowned. Of all the mistakes she had made in her life, marrying Dimitri was probably the biggest.

· · · · ·

The night of the party was perfect. A clear sky filled with stars, no breeze, no humidity. The yacht, decorated with a thousand fairy lights, looked incredibly lovely. Round tables festooned with fresh flowers were set on the lower deck for a hundred guests, and on the upper deck a five-piece combo played romantic ballads and soft rock.

Ceremoniously Dimitri presented Lucky with her birthday present just before the outside guests were due to arrive. A square leather box lined with plush velvet. A Van Cleef and Arpels insignia. And in the middle of the box a magnificent necklace of perfect diamonds and glittering emeralds set in white gold, with matching pendant earrings.

"Gorgeous," purred the Contessa, who knew a thing or two about jewels.

"So lovely!" sighed Susan, thinking Gino's gifts seemed paltry by comparison.

"*Wowee!* Heavy duty!" from Fluff.

"It's beautiful," Lucky exclaimed, lifting the necklace from the box. "Thank you, darling." She kissed Dimitri chastely on the cheek. He smiled at the assorted gathering.

Francesca glared.

Olympia pouted.

Then there were other presents to open. A pair of heavy silver frames from the Contessa and Saud. A solid-gold traveling clock from Jenkins and Fluff. An ugly silk shirt, several sizes too large, from the Ferns. Nothing from Olympia. A cashmere sweater from Susan, and a small leather box from Gino. "Somethin' I picked out—on my own," he said in an embarrassed voice. "If y'don't like it, y'don't have to wear it."

She opened the box slowly. Gino hadn't remembered her birthday in years. Inside was a pavé diamond panther brooch studded with cabochon rubies and emeralds. It was the most exquisite piece of jewelry she had ever seen. Totally original, and absolutely her style. "I *love* it," she said softly, thrilled that he had chosen it himself. "It's just great! I *really* love it!" She grabbed him in a hug.

"I love *you*, kid," he said, very quietly. "Happy birthday."

Soon the outside guests began to arrive, most of them bearing gifts, which were placed in a huge pile to be opened later.

Lucky was wearing a scarlet silk jersey dress that touched the ground, skimmed her body and was slit at the front. She put on her new necklace and earrings and pinned the panther brooch to the flimsy material. She looked darkly exotic with her hair piled on top of her head and her deep suntan. She circled the party. She played the role. She was Mrs. Stanislopoulos to the hilt—aware it was only a temporary position.

Lennie hung back and watched. The fantasy had become a reality, and she was under his skin with a vengeance.

He caught up with her at the bar and eased himself into a boring conversation she was having with a soignée blonde in a million dollars' worth of diamonds. "I miss you," he whispered.

She felt a shiver of anticipation. The blonde moved off.

"I'm horny, lonely and screwed up," he continued. "And this you are *not* going to believe, but I think I'm in love."

She kept her tone light. "Anyone I know?"

He touched her arm. "How do *you* feel?"

"Married," she replied flatly. "And so are you."

"I'm leaving Olympia," he said quickly, "as soon as I get back. How about you and Dimitri?"

"I don't know," she replied honestly.

"What do you mean, you don't know? You *are* going to divorce him, aren't you?"

She resented the question. What business was it of his? "I don't think I mentioned I was planning on doing any such thing," she said coldly.

He touched her necklace contemptuously. "I guess that kind of little bauble *would* make it difficult to come up with an answer."

She was suddenly furious. "Are you implying I'm staying with him for his *money?*"

"Give me a better reason."

"Fuck you!" she exploded.

He wanted to defuse her anger. "I wish you would."

She refused to become any further involved. "Get lost, asshole."

Olympia walked into their conversation. Her cheeks were flushed, her breasts bulging from a low-cut yellow dress that made her look like an overripe banana. She was also stoned— but not mellow. And drunk—but not happy.

"You two really seem to have hit it off," she slurred. "What are you talking about?"

"Nothing much," Lennie said.

"She called you an asshole." Olympia's small eyes glinted with jealousy. "It must have been *something.*"

"I told her a bad joke."

"*All* your jokes are bad."

"Thanks a lot."

"You're a lousy comedian. You ever seen him do anything, Lucky? He stinks." She giggled.

"As a matter of fact"—for some unknown reason Lucky found herself springing to his defense—"I've seen Lennie onstage and I think he's brilliantly innovative."

"*Where* have you seen him?" Olympia demanded hotly.

"I owned a hotel in Vegas once, the Magiriano. Lennie appeared in the lounge."

"So you two met before?"

They both replied at once.

"Yes," said Lucky.

"Not really," said Lennie.

"What did you do, screw each other?" Olympia sneered with drunken insight.

"You're bombed," Lennie said quickly, putting his arm around her shoulders.

She shrugged him away. "Don't give me that solicitous-husband crap just because I hit pay dirt. You probably *did* screw her. I understand if it wore pants and moved, she fucked it."

"I thought that was you," said Lucky icily.

"*I* never had to search it out," said Olympia. "I can remember when you and I were in the south of France—on the run from school. Nobody even *looked* at you. You couldn't find a boyfriend if you stood on your head."

"I didn't know you two were at school together," Lennie said, trying to change the subject.

"Shut up, asshole," Olympia said fiercely. "I *am* allowed to call you asshole, aren't I?" she added sarcastically. "Or is that a privilege reserved only for little Lucky Saint?"

He fixed her with a look which said more than words and walked away.

"Well?" Olympia demanded belligerently of Lucky, "*did* you fuck him?"

"Hey," Lucky replied coolly, "if I had, I wouldn't tell you.

And if I hadn't, the same applies." She turned her back and vanished into the heat of the party.

"Uptight bitch!" Olympia screamed after her. "I know all about you. I know where you're coming from. Don't think you fool me with your airs and graces. You're street scum, just like your gangster father!"

"Olympia!" A harsh voice, a heavy hand. "Do not disgrace yourself this way. Go to your stateroom until you are fit to be seen." Dimitri's face was a thunder mask. He summoned a servant. "Take Miss Stanislopoulos to her room. Feed her coffee until she is sober. I will not tolerate this behavior."

Olympia went meekly. She needed more than a joint and a few glasses of champagne—she needed cocaine, and she needed it badly.

78

It was hot in New York, the streets were awash with tourists, and the residents survived only because of air-conditioning. The offices of Myerson, Laker and Brandon were on Park Avenue in a tony building. Steven was allocated a large corner office with all home comforts: a fridge, a television and video recorder, a stereo set and a tape machine. "Why not be able to relax?" Jerry said affably. "I think a good working environment makes for good workers." His own office was like an apartment, with a small seductive bedroom leading off it in case he wished to spend the night.

"You know Jerry," Sam Laker, one of the partners, confided. "He wants it just in case."

"In case of what?" Steven inquired.

Sam winked knowingly. "In case he needs to entertain a client."

Steven reflected on how different it was from the working space he was used to as an assistant D.A. Well, things were different now. He was in business to make money, just like Jerry. To hell with being a do-gooder.

His first client was Mary Lou Moore. She was prettier than she appeared to be on television. She had waist-length black hair, widely spaced brown eyes and a devastating smile. She traveled with an entourage that consisted of her mother, her aunt—who was also her manager—and her boyfriend, a white kid with frizzy hair and a tendency to pop bubble gum.

After an initial chat Steven got the distinct impression Mary Lou would have nothing to say while her entourage was present.

"I'd like to speak to Mary Lou alone," he said.

The mother looked at the aunt. The aunt looked at the boyfriend. They all looked at Mary Lou, who nodded her permission. When they had departed, Steven said, "Tell me about it."

She shrugged, trying to act cool. But when she began to speak about the outrage, the humiliation and the fury the publication of the nude pictures had caused her, she seemed nothing so much as a gauche teenager. "These scummy guys who put out these magazines shouldn't be allowed to get away with this kind of rip-off," she said. "Okay, so it wasn't too bright of me to pose for the pictures in the first place, but I was only fifteen—and foolin' around with my boyfriend. Did I know he was gonna keep them—and *sell* them?" She set her pretty chin at a determined angle. "I want to sue."

"It'll take time."

"I don't care."

"Their lawyers will defend the case. They'll try to discredit you in any way they can."

"I'm ready."

"You'll be involved in depositions, postponements—and finally you'll have your day in court."

"That's what I want."

"We're embarking on a journey. Once we get on the train, there's no getting off."

"Go for it, man!"

After she left, he picked up the offending magazine—a glossy porno rag called *Comer*. Mary Lou was featured on six pages. The pictures were clearly not the work of a professional, but whoever had captured the fifteen-year-old had done a thorough job.

Steven had the names of the boyfriend from her past, the publishers of the magazine and the distributors. As far as he could tell, she had a good case against all of them.

• • • • •

Anna Robb diligently worked at her typewriter. She had already completed four chapters of *The Carrie Berkeley Book of Beauty and Style*. It was going well.

She yawned and stretched. A break was most definitely in order, she decided, as she walked into the living room of the Manhattan apartment she shared with her lover. He was asleep on the couch, glasses on the end of his nose, pages from a manuscript scattered on the floor.

She gathered them together and woke him gently.

"I fell asleep," he explained superfluously.

She glanced at the Cartier watch he had bought her for Christmas and was surprised to find it was past twelve.

"It's late," she said. "Shall I make us some cocoa?"

He rose from the couch. "I can't think of anything I'd like better."

"You go to bed, I'll bring it in."

"Don't forget the chocolate biscuits."

"As if I would."

He was watching the end of *The Tonight Show* when she entered the bedroom carrying a tray with two steaming cups of cocoa and a box of English biscuits.

"I've been working on the Carrie Berkeley book," she said.

He broke open the biscuits. "How's it going?"

She perched on the end of the bed—a small birdlike woman with plain features and a warm smile. "Very well. I think it will be a winner."

"I certainly hope so."

"I'll tell you something, though."

"What?"

"There's another story under all the gloss and glitter."

He stared at the television. "There is?"

"Oh, yes. Definitely." Anna nodded. "Carrie Berkeley has a *real* story to tell. You know how I can sense these things."

He nibbled on a chocolate biscuit. "You're a regular Sherlock Holmes," he commented.

"No. I just have good instincts. Plus I read between the lines and fill in the gaps." She paused and allowed her attention to be caught by an animal trainer showing Johnny Carson a small but frisky animal. "I'd like to discuss an autobiography with her. What do you think?"

"Let's see how the beauty book does first."

"Do you think she'll go out on the road to promote it?"

"I don't know."

Anna smiled a secret smile. "*You* could persuade her," she said. "She likes you."

"What do you mean?"

"My famous instincts again. She asked me if you were married. I told her you're living with a woman." She laughed softly. "I didn't tell her it was me."

"That's ridiculous. What makes you think she likes me?"

Anna raised an amused eyebrow. "Have I stumbled on a mutual attraction?"

He was flustered. "You can be such a stupid woman. She must be in her late sixties."

"And so are you," Anna pointed out.

"Such nonsense," he grumbled.

"I'm glad you think so." Anna finished her cocoa and went into the bathroom to prepare for bed.

Fred E. Lester gazed blankly at the television and failed to appreciate the comic antics of Mr. Carson and an excitable monkey. His thoughts were drifting back in time to many, many years ago.

• • • • •

Freddy was a fresh-faced college boy with a smart mouth and a drunken disposition. He was on vacation, and his friend Mel Webster fixed him up with a blind date. The girl, Carrie, was beautiful—and Black. He was shocked at being fixed up with a Black girl. His family was originally from the South. "Je—sus!" he muttered to Mel. "She's a fucking dinge!"

"So," Mel replied, "haven't you ever heard of black pudding?"

Why not? Freddy thought. Why not?

He didn't remember much else. A series of nightclubs and booze. The anticipation of laying a colored girl. The champagne flowing and everyone getting high.

Next memory . . . He and Mel and Mel's date driving back to an apartment. It was a big roomy loft with a bed on each side. Mel and his girl started going at it on one of the beds, and he had stumbled over to the other one and fallen asleep. It seemed only minutes later that Carrie was shaking him awake. She looked so pretty, and he felt so randy. Why weren't they doing the same as Mel and his girl?

She put up a fierce fight, but he was stronger and he overpowered her until she lay helpless beneath him. He knew he was raping her but he didn't stop. Who cared? She was getting what she really wanted—what all women wanted.

After it was over, she demanded money. He was angry, he threw what he had at her, took the keys to the sleeping Mel's car and staggered out of the place.

The streets were deserted and he was anxious to get home and shower the smell of the Black bitch off him. He drove recklessly, with no thought for anyone else, and as he swerved the car around a corner, it ended up on the wrong side of the street and smashed headlong into an oncoming truck.

The next thing he remembered was waking up from a coma in a hospital, months later, with a face that resembled a complicated road map. His scars were horrifying, but his parents could afford the finest plastic surgeons. He spent many months in and out of hospitals—and all through that desolate period he kept on seeing Carrie's face. He had raped her—that was why he had been punished.

It changed his life.

Years passed. He married a good woman who bore him two fine children. He started his own small publishing firm, and over the years built it into one of the most successful houses in New York. One night, in 1960, he was at a charity ball and he saw her. Carrie. Even though she was gowned and groomed, her hair swept up and diamonds at her ears and throat, he recognized her immediately. She brought back every guilty memory. He prayed that she wouldn't remember him. She didn't.

Relief was immense. She had no idea he was the same callow youth who had treated her so badly all those years before. When he thought about it later, he realized there was no way she could have recognized him. Plastic surgery had changed his appearance considerably, and twenty years had passed. He remembered her, because her face was burned into his memory.

He found out who she was and couldn't help himself from following her life in Vogue *and* Harper's Bazaar *and* Women's Wear Daily. *Carrie was a personality. He was glad for her.*

His wife succumbed to cancer in 1973. His children, both grown, chose suitable partners and went off to pursue their own lives. He was alone and lonely until Anna Robb came into the office for an interview one day. They had lived together for two years. It was no passionate love affair—not that he expected passion at his age. But they were compatible.

When Carrie reentered his life, he was shocked. He had never thought he would see her again. Over the years her name had faded from the columns, and the last mention he could remember was news of her divorce. Then nothing.

· · · · ·

He thought back forty-two years. "She's a fucking dinge," he had once said—that stupid, prejudiced, bigoted young man How things had changed.

Anna had said, "She likes you." Was it true? Did she?

If she ever knew who he really was, she would damn him to hell.

79

Gino was the first to leave. He bid his farewells the morning after Lucky's birthday party, pleading urgent business commitments.

Susan elected to stay. "You don't mind?" she asked in a concerned wifely voice.

"Go ahead—enjoy yourself," he replied, looking forward to his freedom. They arranged to meet in Los Angeles in ten days' time.

He took a plane to Paris and the Concorde to New York, where he had booked his usual suite at the Pierre. The first thing he did was call Paige in L.A.

"Get on the next flight here," he commanded.

"Don't be ridiculous."

"I've got a present for you."

"What?"

"Something you're gonna eat up!"

"Has anyone ever told you that you're nothing but a dirty old man?"

He chuckled. "Be on the next flight."

"Gino—"

"Don't give me a hard time."

"Only if you promise to give me one!"

"You have my word."

She called him back an hour later. "I'll be there on Wednesday."

"Not soon enough."

"Don't complain. I have a business to run, not to mention a husband and family."

He contacted Costa in Miami. "Let's have a reunion," he suggested.

"What's going on?" Costa inquired.

"I'm in New York. I feel good. I thought we'd look up some of the old faces."

"Where's Susan?"

"I left her on the Stanislopoulos yacht. She's happy."

"And Lucky?"

"She's due in tomorrow. Just a minute." He put the phone down to let in room service bearing him a thick juicy steak, French fries, chocolate cake and ice cream—food forbidden by Susan, who was always carrying on about cholesterol and diet. He picked up the phone again and continued his conversation with Costa. "Come on, old friend. We'll have a good time."

Costa had a litany of complaints. "I've got arthritis, my joints are killing me, my gums need work—"

"Fall to pieces on your own time. How often am I in New York?"

"Maybe a few days would be a change," Costa mused, and then decisively, "Yes, I'll come. Why not?"

Gino ate the steak, every one of the French fries, the ice cream and the cake. Then he belched with contentment and fell asleep on the couch.

* * * * *

Another day of long meaningful looks between Lennie and her, and Lucky knew she had to move on. Perhaps when she wasn't facing him every day, the strong attraction would cease. God! Was this what happened when you didn't get laid for a while?

She knew, although she wasn't prepared to admit it, that it wasn't just sex. With plenty of opportunity to observe, she found him to be funny and warm and great with both Roberto and Brigette. She remembered from his original stint at the Magiriano that he was also an extremely talented and clever comedian.

How did he and Olympia ever get together? He was too smart to put up with her shit. But even smart people get caught on occasion, and he was savvy enough to get out fast.

Lucky knew she must do the same.

"I have some family business matters to attend to with my father," she told Dimitri. "Papers to sign, things like that," she added vaguely. "I must go to New York at once."

He nodded. His mind was elsewhere. Francesca was jealous of the diamond necklace and earrings he had gifted Lucky with, and he had to arrange for a present of equal, if not more, value to be discreetly delivered to the temperamental actress.

"Do what you have to do," he said.

"Roberto will stay here with CeeCee," Lucky decided. "Perhaps I'll fly back in a few days."

She had no intention of doing so. Cruising the Mediterranean on board a floating palace was not her idea of a good time—especially with people like Saud Omar and Jenkins Wilder aboard. She hated that kind of man. Rich powerful sexist chauvinists. She could smell 'em a mile away.

So how come you married one?

Dimitri had seemed different. Unfortunately he was not.

She didn't bother with goodbyes. She doubted she would be missed by anyone other than Roberto and CeeCee. And Lennie—but that was a relationship she did not care to pursue. Dangerous territory. Olympia hated her as it was. She didn't want to make things worse.

• • • • •

"Where's Lucky?" Lennie asked at dinner.

"What do you care?" Olympia snapped. She had been bad-tempered and impossible since her outburst at the party.

He shrugged. "Who cares? I just wondered."

"She had business in New York," Dimitri explained.

"What kind of business?" Olympia sneered. "Shopping for a new dress?"

Dimitri silenced her with a look.

After dinner there was the usual discussion of who wanted to do what. "Let's go dancing," Olympia suggested restlessly, gulping brandy and wishing she had some coke to take the edge off her nerves.

"I'd like to gamble," the Contessa announced.

So they split into two camps. Saud, the Contessa, Jenkins Wilder, Dimitri, Francesca and Susan elected to go to the casino. And Lennie found himself saddled with Olympia and Fluff, who wished to discotheque. Alice and Horace were invited with neither group. "You're tired," Francesca told her timid husband. "Get some rest."

"We'll have a nightcap, Horace," Alice said with a lewd wink.

"You look after my little tootsie roll," Jenkins said to Lennie, pressing several thousand-franc bills into his young wife's eager hands. "In case you need to powder your nose, doll."

"Thank you, Big Daddy," she squeaked.

A fleet of Cadillacs waited to take them wherever they wished to go.

"Regine's," said Olympia.

So Regine's it was—an elegant private club perched next to the sea.

"Miss Stanislopoulos," the maitre d' purred. "Welcome back. So nice to see you again."

They were given what Lennie presumed to be the best table.

"Let's dance," said Olympia, bouncing toward the dance floor.

"Go ahead," encouraged Fluff, a teenage vision in skin-tight satin pants and a boob tube—more boob than tube.

They hit the floor to the strains of Stevie Wonder. Lennie made all the right moves while his mind wandered and he thought of Lucky and how much he wanted her. He had to tell Olympia that their marriage was a mistake. She must know. They had about as much in common as a Harley-Davidson and a Rolls-Royce. Maybe the best way to handle it was to say nothing—simply fly to L.A. for *The Tonight Show*, and not come back.

Stevie Wonder was followed by a rasping Rod Stewart, after which they sat down.

Fluff was being hit upon by two leering Italians. She didn't seem to mind at all—in fact, she was encouraging them with moist-lipped smiles and high-pitched giggles. One of them invited her to dance, and she took off for the dance floor like a bird let loose from its cage.

"At least *somebody's* having a good time," Olympia said pointedly and went off to share a snort with one of her friends, an angular-looking beauty in a fishnet dress. "Where can I buy some coke?" she asked the girl, an English socialite.

"Search me, darling. I got *my* little bit of snuff from a rather peculiar type outside the casino yesterday. Ask McGuiness, he's always up on that sort of thing."

McGuiness was an upper-crust English creep with an unfortunate stutter. He led her to his source, a young English dress manufacturer with wiry hair, pinpoint eyes and a thick cockney accent. They did business in a quiet corner—and that was where she was when Flash made his entrance.

Ah . . . the aura of a rock star. Not for them the ordinary entrance. They like attention, people, and plenty of noise. Flash was no exception. He was dressed in black leather and flowing, if rather ragged-looking, white silk scarves. His hair was long and dyed a very stern black (gray was not a color rock stars cultivated). He wore the customary gold hoop earring—only one—and his teeth looked worse than ever.

Olympia took one peek and her heart gave a little leap.

Flash paused at the entrance to the discotheque just long enough to let the peasants know he was honoring them with his presence.

The disc jockey, no slouch in the "I can recognize a celebrity at twenty feet" stakes, immediately abandoned the Pointer Sisters and slyly changed over to Flash's most famous hit, "Raunchy Lady," written in the mid-sixties when he was living with a former nun.

"Flash!" exclaimed Olympia.

But she was not alone. Half the females in the club breathed an excited "Flash!"

"Yeah—yeah—yeah—there's my man!" recited the cockney dress manufacturer, who would sooner have been a full-time drug dealer any day. He pocketed Olympia's money and raced toward his hero, who he knew would spend—spend—spend!

Olympia frowned. Flash was not alone. He had a blonde on one arm and a brunette on the other, both jet set groupies whom Olympia knew and loathed. No wife in sight.

She stuck out her chest (Flash was a tit man), waited until he was seated, and made her way over to his table. "Well!" she steamed. "We meet again."

His eyes were bloodshot and wary as he squinted up at her.

"'Ello darlin'," he mumbled at last, not sure who she was for a moment.

"How's married life?" she demanded sarcastically. "Miserable, I hope."

"Cor blimey! It's you! Tubs!" he cackled. "Put on a pound or two, 'ave we?"

Automatically she pulled her stomach in. "Trust you to be rude," she spat. "*You* look like the walking dead."

"Hello, Olympia," said the blonde, clinging to Flash's arm as if he were a lifeboat.

Olympia favored her with a cursory nod.

The brunette, taking care of his other arm, said nothing. She had spotted her reflection in a mirrored wall and was admiring her own sultry beauty.

"Thought you was gonna be 'ere sooner than this," remarked Flash cheerily. "Thought we was gonna go on yer old man's fishin' boat."

"You missed the boat," said Olympia grandly. "My husband and I are on it."

"Yer sound like the bloomin' queen!" cackled Flash.

"Where's teenage wifey?" asked Olympia, her bosom straining the silk of a red Givenchy creation.

"Leave it out, babe," said Flash easily. "I don't like to be reminded."

"You *have* got one, haven't you?" she questioned insistently.

"Yeah. An' now you've got an old man, so we're even. Right?"

"Let's dance, Flash," begged the blonde, tripping dainty scarlet fingernails up his leather-clad thigh.

"Not 'ere, love," he replied in a "don't you know Rock Stars do not put on shows in public places unless they are getting paid" voice.

"Where then?" she replied logically.

"Wanna score, Flash?" asked the cockney dress manufacturer, overcome with joy at being close to his hero. "It's on the house." He tried to elbow Olympia out of the way, but she stood her ground.

Flash got up. "If it's free, it's for me. 'Scuse us, chicks, we're gonna see a man about a dog." He put his arm expansively around his new friend, who almost hyperventilated with excitement, and the two of them repaired to the men's room.

"Shit!" said Olympia.

•   •   •   •   •

Across the room, Lennie watched it all. And he didn't care. Why should he? Soon he and Miss Stanislopoulos would be just a memory. The sooner the better.

80

The first thing Lucky did when she arrived back in New York was call Gino. "I've got a surprise for you, kid," he told her. "Be at the Pierre by five-thirty."

The second thing she did was call her lawyers about the land deal in Atlantic City. It was a go situation—a few signatures, and the piece of real estate she had been after was hers.

She was excited. Now the fun would start. Creating a hotel from the ground up was a challenging, exhausting, but ultimately rewarding job. She should know—she had done it once with the Magiriano.

Ah . . . but the work!

She was ready. She had been idle too long. To immerse herself fully in the project was just what she needed. It would take her mind off Dimitri and his hardly subtle affair. And stop her thinking about Lennie—who was *definitely* off-limits. Now that she was away from the yacht and could look at things clearly, becoming involved with Lennie was sheer madness. He was married to Olympia—reason enough to stay away from him. But he was also more than a one-night stand. She had a feeling he was the man who could make her forget Marco. . . .

And what if he could?

No, thank you. She did not want that kind of involvement ever again. It was just too painful. The best thing she could do was forget Lennie Golden. Which is exactly what she intended to do.

Three hours later she arrived at the Pierre. The last time she had visited Gino in his favorite suite at the New York hotel was the night her brother, Dario, was brutally gunned down in the street.

In the elevator a man in a dark-gray suit asked her if she

was a model. She gave him a long, cool look. Raked him from head to toe. "No," she said slowly. "Are you?"

This confused him. He was fifty-two years old, with teen-age children. Where did *she* get off asking him if he was a model? Goddamn nerve. He got out of the elevator on the fourth floor without another word.

Gino greeted her with a hug and a wink. "Just like old times, huh?" He grinned. "Look who I got for you."

"Uncle Costa!" she exclaimed in delight. "What are *you* doing here?"

While they embraced, Costa explained how persuasive Gino could be. "A visit to the big city is not such a bad idea," he allowed. "And how could I resist seeing you?"

She laughed happily. "Uncle Costa, you're a *wonderful* surprise."

There was more to come. Gino had arranged dinner with old friends in an Italian family restaurant in Queens. Present were Aldo and Barbara Dinunzio—she a frail little woman, and he as fat and contented as a lazy cat. Then there were their grown children and the children's various spouses, plus a smattering of grandchildren. Altogether sixteen people sat around the table drinking cheap red wine, enjoying delicious pasta which Barbara had personally supervised in the restaurant kitchen (the place was owned by her cousin), and finishing off with spumoni, Gino's favorite ice cream.

Lucky hadn't seen these people in years, nor had Gino, and the warmth and joy at the table were contagious.

"I can't wait until you meet my son, Roberto," Lucky told Barbara proudly. "He's gorgeous—eighteen months old and totally gorgeous! Just *wait* until you see him!"

The old woman, who had known and loved Lucky's mother many years before, clutched Lucky by the hand and squeezed tightly. "Maria should be here today," she said regretfully. "She was a beauty. A gentle sweetheart. We all miss her still."

"Hey," interrupted Gino, as he noticed Lucky's expression.

"We talk about the present, not the past. When you get a peek at Roberto, you'll see a true Santangelo. He looks just like me."

Lucky swept away the sad memories and grinned. She liked to hear her father boast about Roberto.

"He's got my eyes, my hair," Gino continued. "Right, Lucky? Right, kid?"

She fingered the panther pin he had given her. She had worn it ever since her birthday, while Dimitri's diamonds languished in a safe. "Yes, Daddy," she replied softly. "Just like you."

• • • • •

Later, on the drive back to the hotel, Gino said, "You wanna come up for a nightcap, kid?"

She couldn't think of anything she'd like better.

After Costa had retired to his room, they ordered Brandy Alexanders and sat together on the comfortable couch in the living room of Gino's suite.

"This is nice," he said. "We gotta get around to doin' it more often."

She nodded her agreement and tentatively touched his arm. "You know, earlier, when Barbara was talking about Maria . . . my mother . . ." She trailed off, her voice filled with emotion.

Gino picked up the message. "We never talked about it, huh, kid?"

She shook her head and whispered, "Never."

He got up and walked to the window. Then he turned and stared at her. "Your mother was the kindest and most beautiful woman in the world," he said gruffly. "She loved you an' me an' your brother. She loved us all too much. When they laid a hit on Maria they cut out my heart. Y'know what I'm sayin', kid?"

Gino's explanation for all the years of running away from his children. Putting them in the charge of nannies and guardians and boarding schools. He had always figured if he didn't love them too much, he would never lose them.

Wrong.

But it was over now.

She arose from the couch, went to her father and hugged him tightly. "Tell me about Mommy. I want to know everything. Please. Make her a part of my life again." Gino needed no further urging. He had bottled up his feelings for years, and the joy of finally talking about Maria and the happy times was wonderful.

The hours sped by, and it was almost dawn when Lucky left the hotel. She felt lightheaded and very, very happy. Since she was five years old her mother had been missing from her life. Now she felt she really knew her. Gino had handed over priceless memories. Maria might be gone, but she was certainly not forgotten.

•   •   •   •   •

"Welcome home to the City of Angels," Jess said formally. She met Lennie at LAX with a limousine and a travel representative who whisked him through customs as if it didn't exist.

"Nice being a star, huh?" she asked, as they settled into the back of the limo. "Was your trip okay?"

"I think I'm in love," he said, reaching for a sweet roll and a glass of orange juice—it was a well-stocked limo.

"Hmmm," replied Jess briskly. "A usual reaction when returning from one's honeymoon."

"Not with Olympia, schmuck."

"Oh, I see. You're *not* in love with your wife, and that makes *me* a schmuck. So what else is new, Mr. Charm?"

He fumbled for a cigarette and grinned disarmingly. "Don't get mad at me. I need comfort and advice."

"Not that you'll take it."

"How well you know me." He reached forward and switched on the built-in TV. "You're never gonna believe me, but I met the one and only lady I think I can spend the rest of my life with."

"Don't tell me," Jess said dramatically. "Eden snuck onto the yacht and whisked you right out from under the Greek princess's cute little nose."

"Eden!" he laughed derisively. "Who's *she?*"

Jess sighed. "The love of your life. Remember?"

"Didn't I tell you? I'm just about to start a new life."

"With or without the Greek princess?" She paused meaningfully. "Remember her? *She's* the one you just got married to."

"Can I get it annulled?" he asked hopefully.

"Did you sleep with her?"

"Of course I did."

"Then unless she wants to say you didn't, I don't think you have a chance in hell."

He changed channels on the TV and reached for another sweet roll.

"True love does not seem to have diminished your appetite," Jess remarked dryly.

"I'm nervous."

"About *The Tonight Show?* I can't wait to hear your new material. Isaac's coming over to the apartment later. I thought you might want to run it by us."

"No new material."

"Whaaat?"

He wolfed the roll, oblivious to her consternation. "You don't seem to understand," he explained gravely. "I want *out* of my marriage. It's over—finito—kaput. How you ever let me do it I'll never know. You must have—"

"Hang *on* a moment," she spluttered indignantly. "How *I* ever let you do it? *I* went to bed—you were getting laid. *I* woke up—you were married. I was not exactly around to stop you."

He leaned over and kissed her on the cheek. "I love you, Jess. How's everything with you? Did you and Matt ever get together? What's been happenin' in L.A.?"

She glared at him. "You're strange, you know that?"

"Secret of my success."

They fell into silence. Sometimes Jess thought she knew Lennie better than anyone in the world. Sometimes she felt she didn't know him at all. He had asked about Matt. But did he

really care? Not at all. It didn't matter. There was nothing to
tell anyway. Matt treated her like a sister—she no longer cast
a spell on him. Her last night in Vegas she had spent with an
old boyfriend. Boring. Boring.

At least Lennie looked great, but he was unsettled and restless. Better keep him away from the booze.

"Does the bride know she's redundant?" she asked.

"I haven't told her."

"Is she going to be pissed?"

"I don't think she's gonna light candles and shout Halle-
lujah!" He paused. "On the other hand, I will not be breaking
her heart—just bruising her ego. She's still got a thing for
Flash."

Jess's face lit up. "You met Flash?" she asked excitedly.

"Met him, smelled his bad breath, admired his even worse
teeth and got stoned out of my skull just breathing the air
around him."

"Oh, boy! You met Flash."

"I'm telling you—he's no big deal."

"Sure he's not. Like we didn't get off on his music a hundred times a day when we were in school."

"*You* got off on him," Lennie pointed out. "I just liked the
way he played guitar and held a tune."

Jess began to giggle.

Lennie couldn't help joining in.

"Who'd you fall in love with this time, schmuck?" she
asked affectionately.

"Lucky Santangelo," he replied, suddenly serious.

She widened her eyes in amazement. "Are you kidding
me?"

He grabbed another sweet roll. "Never been more serious
in my life."

81

With the departure of Gino, Lucky and Lennie, life aboard *The Greek* underwent certain subtle changes. Susan did not make a move without the Contessa's approval and consent.

Dimitri, who considered the renewal of his affair with Francesca had been conducted most discreetly, relaxed his strict code of behavior and spent virtually every waking hour with the volatile actress. Most of the sleeping ones, too.

Horace was an embarrassing presence whom they both tried to ignore. Alice consoled him all the way to her cabin, where he had sex for the first time in four years. Francesca didn't do that sort of thing with him. Horace was just around to organize her life and handle her business affairs.

Olympia stayed on the yacht for an hour after Lennie left. Then she called Flash at his villa.

"Get your stupid knickers over 'ere," he commanded. "An' bring some bread, we'll 'ave a party."

The party lasted three days, and so did Olympia. She wondered how to tell Lennie it was over between them. Perhaps she wouldn't bother. Let her lawyer do it—she paid him enough.

Fluff went on a shopping trip, then secretly ran off to Portofino with one of the Italians she had met at Regine's. Jenkins hired detectives to find her, and when they did, he sent his bodyguard to bring her back. She returned, a sulky, pouting teenager. Shortly after, they left for Texas.

Brigette tried to drown Roberto in his bath. CeeCee caught her in the act and spanked her until she wept.

Two days later Brigette went to her grandfather and complained that Roberto's nasty Black nanny had touched her "down there."

Dimitri, too caught up in his passionate affair to bother with matters domestic, instructed Nanny Mabel to deal with the situation. Nanny Mabel, drunk with power at last, spanked Brigette for twenty blissful minutes. "And if you run to your granddaddy and tell him," she threatened, "I'll spank you again."

CeeCee thought the punishment excessive but kept her mouth shut and an eagle eye on Roberto at all times.

One long hot afternoon when everyone except the Contessa was ashore, Susan went to her stateroom and lay naked on her bed. Within minutes the Contessa entered and indulged her as only Paige Wheeler had indulged her before.

Susan shut her eyes and cherished every minute. The female touch was so . . . delicate. She wondered if she could ever stand Gino near her again.

Captain and Mrs. Pratt saw all, heard all, and pretended nothing was going on.

The weather in the south of France was delightful. Dimitri Stanislopoulos's summer cruise was a triumph—as usual.

82

It was not easy for Paige to arrange a sudden and unexpected trip to New York, but she managed it. Ryder had never been a possessive husband, thank God—just a man completely caught up in his work. Putting a deal together meant everything else came second. So when Paige told him she had to go to New York to meet an important furniture designer from Italy, his only concern was the dinner party they were supposed to be having for Vitos Felicidade. The Spanish singing star was causing problems with the contract he had been offered. He wanted script approval, co-star approval, billing approval. "I think he wants to approve the way I take a crap in the morning," Ryder announced glumly.

The movie Bonnatti was financing seemed to be taking more time to put together than a bishop getting laid. Any producer would be getting edgy. Ryder saw the dinner party as a social occasion to soothe ruffled egos and get the goddamn show on the road.

"Postpone your trip," he told Paige.

"I wish I could," she lied. "But don't you worry about a thing. I'll make sure every last detail is taken care of."

At the office a dozen appointments had to be juggled. Business was better than ever. Paige had a distinct style, and right now she was hot. She called Irwin Stroll, a very dear designer friend of hers, and asked if he could possibly take over a Brazilian couple who were on their way into town with nothing but money to spend. Irwin happily agreed to help her out.

Fortunately her two teenage sons were in Europe, backpacking across France. It would do them both good. Let them find out that life was not all new convertibles and Beverly Hills glitz.

She left on a Wednesday morning, and couldn't quite understand why the prospect of seeing Gino Santangelo excited her so much.

On the plane she sat next to a young actor with a new TV

series and one of the best bodies she had ever seen. Once he might have presented a challenge—how long would it take for her to get into *his* pants? But now it didn't seem important. All she wanted to do was be with Gino.

You're getting old, she scolded herself. And somehow she didn't mind one bit.

• • • • •

Lucky and Paige hit it off instantly. Gino brought her to dinner and said, "Paige is an old friend of Susan's an' mine from California."

Oh, yeh? thought Lucky. *I bet.* She remembered Gino the womanizer. Susan had put a stop to all that. Now he had that look in his eyes again.

They ate at Elaine's, one of the great New York restaurants for seeing people and having fun. Elaine, a dark and interesting woman who knew *everyone*, escorted them personally to a table in the back.

Paige waved at some writer friends, while Bobby Zarem, the legendary PR whiz, stopped by their table to say hello.

It turned out to be one of those evenings where helpless laughter is only a breath away, and everyone had a wonderful time.

"Who is she?" Lucky asked Gino, when Paige vanished to the ladies' room.

"Kinda Susan's best friend," he answered sheepishly.

"Can you do a swap?"

He almost grinned. "Don't get smart-ass, kid."

"I don't think it's smart-ass, I think it's one of the best suggestions I've ever come up with! What do *you* think, Uncle Costa?"

Costa nodded, enjoying the game.

They stayed at Elaine's until 1:30 A.M. and then it was time for home and bed.

Lucky observed her father's hand on Paige's thigh before they all rose from the table. He was still going strong. She loved him for it. She loved the whole week in New York. Things were signed and sealed in Atlantic City. Meetings were arranged with architects and builders. She was back in business with a vengeance, and it was a sensational feeling.

Waiting at the apartment were three messages from Lennie, written out in the butler's spidery script. "Please return Mr. Golden's call," the messages read, and there was a number in L.A.

She crumpled the pieces of paper and dropped them in the wastebasket. Olympia had found him first. She, Lucky, was not about to become involved.

You are involved.

I am not.

Really? What do you call it?

A transient lay.

Bullshit.

She pulled the crumpled messages from the basket and smoothed them out. Just as her hand hovered over the phone, it rang.

She knew it was he and hesitated before picking up the receiver.

You are involved.

I am not.

"Hello."

"Lucky?"

"Who is this?"

"Don't give me that Who is this? crap. I'm in L.A. I'm doing the Carson show tomorrow. Can you fly out?"

She reached for a cigarette and noticed her hand was trembling ever so slightly. "Stop living in a dream world, Lennie. What we had was . . ." She searched for the right word, couldn't find it and settled for ". . . momentarily exciting. Now it's over. Just forget it. I have."

He ignored her speech. "I'm contacting a lawyer. If Olympia agrees, I'll go for an annulment."

Lucky thought for a moment of Olympia. There was no way they could ever be friends again.

"Did you hear me?" he demanded.

She sighed. "Do what you have to do."

"I intend to. How about you?"

She took a deep breath. "Right now I am embarking on a project. I'm building a hotel in Atlantic City. It's going to take all my time and energy."

"You're not answering my question."

"I didn't know you'd asked one."

"Let me spell it out. Are you going to divorce Dimitri?"

She didn't want to be placed in this position. Who was he to question her?

"Why don't you leave me alone," she said wearily. "You're a complication I don't need in my life right now. Just leave me alone."

She put the phone down, drew deeply on her cigarette and took no notice as it began to ring again.

• • • • •

Back at the Pierre, Gino and Paige were getting reacquainted.

"Higher," instructed Paige.

Gino raised his tongue a fraction.

"Softer," she begged.

He relaxed the pressure.

"More," she pleaded.

He buried his face in her juices and felt thoroughly at home.

• • • • •

Lennie had no new material to use on *The Tonight Show*, much to Jess's and Isaac's disgust.

"What the hell were you *doing* on that goddamn boat?" Jess complained. Then she remembered the name of his latest passion, and shut up. Lucky Santangelo. Holy shit! Lucky Santangelo. The Lady Boss. Lennie might be a star, but he was way out of his league with that one. Way way out.

"She's the girl I met in the casino that time," he confided. "Remember? I told you about her. She stood me up."

"And had you fired."

"So what?"

"Are you *kidding?*" Jess screeched. "You went *ape shit* about being canned."

"It didn't do me any harm, did it?"

Jess shook her head. "Jesus! What can I tell you? Lucky Santangelo is . . . connected. She plays games with the big boys. Her father is notorious. He's Gino Santangelo—one of the mob."

"How many years ago?"

"Who gives a shit?"

"No, come on," he persisted. "You're such an expert on the Santangelos. How many years ago? 'Cause right now he's just a feisty old guy married to a movie star's widow."

Jess was sullen. "Believe me, Lennie. Trust me. A few years ago Lucky Santangelo was involved in a shooting."

"What kind of shooting?"

"Oh, it was all hushed up. The rumor was she'd shot this man who was her godfather."

"Don't give me rumors, give me facts."

"She shot him in the balls with his own gun, if you really want to know—something like that. The story was he tried to rape her—but the gossip around town was that it was a revenge move. He'd had her brother killed *and* her boyfriend."

"What boyfriend?"

"Another charmer. Marco. He looked like he walked straight out of a gangster movie."

"What happened to him?"

"He got his head blown off in the parking lot of the Magiriano. I remember it well. I'd only been working there six months. It was frightening—like everyone was talking about some big gang war taking place, but it never happened. Lucky took off for a while, and everything quieted down. Enzio Bonnatti came in to run the hotel—he's the guy she shot."

Lennie was silent while he digested the information. He wasn't sure whether he believed Jess or not. She had a vivid imagination.

"Matt knows the real story," Jess added. "Not that he's likely to tell it. The whole mob scene in Vegas is a gray area—nobody talks."

"Thanks for the guided tour of Lucky Santangelo's life. It doesn't make any difference. I still feel the same way about her."

"Christ! You sound like some naive jerk up from the sticks. What *is it* with you and these dumb stupid obsessions you get? I can remember the Lennie Golden who could get laid without giving a damn. What happened?"

"You know something, Jess? You're my manager, not my fucking keeper."

They glared at each other, neither giving an inch.

The Tonight Show came and went. He was good—not as good as he could have been, but Johnny seemed to like him— in fact, he asked him to sit with the other guests after he'd done his bit, and they chatted, and Johnny was charming, and when it was over he got invited back.

"You were great. They loved you," Jess enthused in the limo on the way home. "When Johnny asks you over to sit with him, you *know* you've got it made."

He wasn't really listening. He was wondering if Lucky had watched the show, and hoped she had.

They were only hours apart, but he missed her.

· · · · ·

Lucky utilized Dimitri's desk and worked on ideas for the Santangelo. She put on her Sony earphones and listened to Isaac Hayes, one of her favorite soul singers. He really let it all hang out, his deep sensuous voice expressing everything she felt.

At eleven-thirty she glanced at the television and automatically switched it on.

"*Heeeeere's* Johnny!" said the familiar voice of Ed McMahon introducing Johnny Carson.

The most famous man on American television strolled in front of the camera and indulged in light banter with his excited audience.

Lucky fixed herself a drink and stared at the set. Halfway through Johnny's monologue she turned it off.

Five minutes later she switched it on again.

Why watch Lennie Golden?

Why not?

When he finally appeared, he received a wild ovation from the audience. Obviously, as Alice had said, he was hot.

And he was. His cutting, ironic wit hit home with everyone. And he looked great, too.

She lit a cigarette and blew contemplative smoke rings.

Lennie Golden.

More than just a casual encounter.

$$\bullet \quad \bullet \quad \bullet \quad \bullet \quad \bullet$$

The day after the Carson show, Lennie canceled a club engagement, much to Jess's fury, and flew to New York. He checked into the Regency Hotel and called Lucky. "I'm here, and we have to talk," he announced.

"Forget it. Nothing's going to happen," she replied.

"Don't give me a hard time. Just have dinner with me."

"What for? It won't do any good."

"Because I want you to tell me, face to face, nothing more can happen between us, and then I'll leave you alone. That's a promise."

She hesitated.

He persisted. "Is it a deal?"

"I don't know . . ."

"Hey, you want to get left alone, don't you? I mean I can really drive you nuts with phone calls and letters and flowers. I can hang around outside your apartment, complicate your life—you know what I mean?" He paused, then, "If I was you, lady, I would *grab* this magnificent offer and run like crazy." He waited a beat, giving her just enough time to make a decision. "So—what time shall I pick you up?"

"It won't do . . ."

". . . any good," he finished the sentence for her. "Expect me at eight-thirty."

She started to object, but he hung up before she could argue further.

Lucky Santangelo was going to be his, and nothing was going to stop him.

83

Francesca Fern considered Dimitri Stanislopoulos's marrying again a direct insult. She brought the subject up at every opportunity, becoming progressively agitated as the cruise drew to an end.

"It is humiliating!" she complained, as they faced each other over the ever-present backgammon board. "The *world* knows it is *me* you love. And now you have married this . . . this . . . person. How do you think I feel? You have made a public fool of me."

He leaned over and touched her coarse red hair. Then he let his hand stray down the neckline of her low-cut dress reaching for her prominent nipples. "Magnificent!" he murmured. The jut of her breasts reminded him of a native African woman he had once seen pictured in *National Geographic*. To chew on her nipples was the greatest aphrodisiac a man could know.

She slapped his hand away. "Good God, Dimitri!" She glared at him. "Wasn't *my* love enough?"

Quickly he defended himself. "I married Lucky because of the boy," he explained for the hundredth time.

"Yes. And now you must divorce her," Francesca replied imperiously, her tone brooking no argument.

"I don't think so," Dimitri said. "She doesn't bother us. She's very independent, and, quite frankly, my dear, when you are not around I need a woman by my side."

"She's no woman!" Francesca spat viciously. "She's a slut! I don't know how you can have touched her in the first place. She's a Romany—a Gypsy. She looks dirty to me."

Francesca was not happy when denied her own way.

"Enough!" said Dimitri sharply. "I never criticize that miserable dog *you're* married to."

"Why should you? Horace has been very . . . understanding over the years."

"Understanding indeed! He's nothing but a cuckold with no balls. A joke, my dear, hardly worth mentioning."

She pursed her thin lips slashed with carmine. "Goddamn you to hell," she snarled. "All you want is my body. You use me. You care nothing for my feelings."

Dimitri laughed harshly. "Nobody uses *you*, Francesca."

She rose from the table. Tall, big-boned and sinewy. "True," she said haughtily. "Nobody uses Francesca Fern— not even the big bad Greek." Her voice began to mock. "Dimitri Stanislopoulos, with all his money and power. Dimitri Stanislopoulos, who would *die* to be near me but who refuses to obey my one tiny request."

"And what about *my* request?" he bellowed loudly. "For too many years I have been asking you to free yourself from Horace and marry me. I have begged and threatened, done everything a man can possibly do. You *dare* to talk of humiliation? *I'm* the one who has been humiliated. That you should choose to stay with such a pathetic creature when you could have been Mrs. Stanislopoulos. My God, Francesca!"

"Divorce the Gypsy and we shall see," she murmured mysteriously.

"No," Dimitri replied, pushing the backgammon board away and getting up. "*You* divorce Horace and we shall see."

"Don't blackmail me," she raged. "Don't you *dare* to blackmail Francesca Fern!"

"This is not blackmail, this is survival," he countered sternly.

She swept her lover with a look. "Very well," she decided dramatically. "The time has come."

"For what?"

"For us to be together as you have always wished."

"You will divorce Horace?"

"I will think about it."

Dimitri thumped the table with his fist. "God*damn* you, woman! Make up your mind."

Her eyes flashed as she tossed back her mane of red hair. "Yes," she said. "I will do it!"

* * * * *

The Contessa clasped Susan's hand. "Goodbye, my dear," she said. "Or should I say *Au revoir*, for surely we shall meet again."

The Contessa smelled of Chanel. She had leathery skin and a downturned, discontented mouth. Her beauty must have been exceptional when she was young. Now she was merely chic. She made Susan feel like a naive girl—a feeling she hadn't had for thirty-five years.

"Please phone if you ever get to Beverly Hills," Susan urged politely, and hoped she wouldn't.

"Beverly Hills," the Contessa said with an amused smile. "Rodeo Drive and film people." She made both sound like dirty words.

"And Arabs," Susan added tartly. The Contessa was a snob. And as far as Susan was concerned, she was also a pervert. After their first delicious sexual encounter the Contessa had suggested that her oily Arab boyfriend join in the fun. Susan had been appalled. "Certainly not," she had said, and the Contessa had treated her with irritating condescension ever since.

Susan thought about Paige. She couldn't wait to see her. Paige would never suggest a threesome.

* * * * *

Olympia returned to the yacht, happy and coked up to the eyeballs. Dimitri was too busy to notice. Francesca had agreed to visit his lawyer in Paris and work out the details of getting rid of Horace. Then they would tell him. Together.

Olympia kissed Brigette on the cheek and counted the days before the child returned to boarding school in England. Having a daughter was such a burdensome responsibility. If it wasn't for Brigette, she would be free to do whatever she wanted. It never occurred to her that she did do *exactly* whatever she wanted at all times.

Flash had flown off to Germany for a recording session. They were to meet in her New York apartment in a week's time. Life would be normal again. Sex, drugs and rock 'n' roll.

Olympia was pleased with the way things had worked out. Flash never mentioned his teenage wife except to wave his hand airily and say, "A mistake, gel. She'll never bother us."

Olympia felt the same way about Lennie—a mistake also. Now she had Flash back, she would get rid of Lennie. He was in California, far, far away. No problem.

"Francesca's going to Paris for the day, later in the week," Dimitri announced casually over dinner. "My plane will take her." Horace busied himself with his cracked crab, determined to ignore the fact that his world was about to crumble. There were only the Ferns and Olympia left on the cruise, and the two children and their respective nannies.

"Wonderful!" Olympia exclaimed. "I'll go too. I need a day's shopping."

"Can I come, Mama?" begged Brigette, who had been allowed to eat with the grownups as a special treat.

"Don't be so silly, darling," trilled Olympia.

"Why not?" demanded Brigette.

"Because . . ." replied Olympia vaguely.

Brigette chewed on her thumb. "Please, Mama!" she whined.

"No," snapped Olympia. "Absolutely not."

Brigette glared. "I hate you!" she yelled suddenly, taking everyone by surprise. "I really hate you. You're a big fat cow!"

"Brigette!" thundered Dimitri. "How dare you talk to your mother like that. Go to your room immediately."

Brigette weighed the chances of taking on her grandfather and decided against it. "But Grandpapa, it's just that I never *see* Mama," she whined pathetically. "I'm sorry, really I am. But why *can't* I go?"

Dimitri turned to his daughter.

"Ridiculous!" sniffed Olympia. "I am not dragging a child with me."

Brigette decided a few sobs might come in handy. She began to snivel.

"God!" huffed Olympia, and rang for Nanny Mabel, who removed the crying child immediately.

84

A date. Lucky didn't go on dates—it had never been part of her lifestyle. "I'll pick you up at eight-thirty," Lennie had said. She hadn't agreed. He had merely stated what he was going to do and she had accepted it.

Now she wished she hadn't. What good would it do? Theirs was a relationship headed nowhere. She realized that. Why didn't he?

At seven o'clock she instructed the butler to say she was out of town. Then she spent the next half-hour worrying about what Lennie would do. Maybe it was best to see him and sort things out once and for all.

She changed her instructions and tried to decide what to wear. Dimitri liked her to dress up, but she preferred casual clothes, so she settled for soft black leather pants and an oversize white silk shirt, which she belted tightly. Black boots, gold hoop earrings and her panther brooch completed the outfit. She wore her hair loose.

By eight o'clock she had changed her mind again. *Why* see him? He obviously didn't understand what a delicate situation they were caught in. Like most men he probably thought he was on to a good thing—an available piece of ass had presented itself and he had gone for it. Shit! He had suckered her. He was chasing an easy lay. That's all she was to him. Men couldn't seem to understand that women could be as sexually free as the male sex. Screw Lennie Golden. Why *should* she see him?

"I'm going out," she informed the butler. "When Mr. Golden gets here tell him I won't be back tonight."

"Yes, madame," said the butler, his Englishness betraying not a flicker of interest.

Where was she going to go? Gino was with Paige, and Costa had returned to Miami.

Maybe she wouldn't go out. The hell with it. Just have the butler *tell* him she was out.

Frightened of facing him?

Absolutely not.

She fixed herself a Pernod and water and chain-smoked two cigarettes.

"I've changed my mind," she told the imperturbable butler. "When Mr. Golden gets here, show him in."

"Yes, madame."

She paced the sumptuous living room. Sumptuous and perfect and expensive and boring. If Dimitri expected her to live in this apartment, he had better agree to redecorate. She felt stifled, period. Why had she married him? Why had *he* married *her?* It was obvious his heart belonged to the horse-faced Madame Fern, and quite frankly she didn't care. No jealous pangs. Dimitri and she had married each other for reasons that did not include love and passion. Was this to be the story of her life? Two husbands, neither of them lovers in the true sense.

She felt lonely and restless, as if her life was one big void.

The hotel will fill it, she thought. *My hotel . . . Mine . . . and Roberto. My wonderful little boy.*

The butler presented himself at the door. "Mr. Golden, madame," he said with a slight bow.

She stubbed out her cigarette, took a deep breath, and turned to greet him with a falsely polite smile. "Lennie!"

Their eyes locked and she was lost.

"Hiya, beautiful lady," he said, walking to her and taking her hands in his.

His touch made her weak. What was going on here?

"Can I get you a drink, sir?" inquired the butler, hovering solicitously.

"Vodka. On the rocks," Lennie replied, glancing around.

"Yes, sir."

Lennie grinned. "I feel like I'm in a museum!"

Lucky couldn't help smiling back. "You are," she said softly.

Silently they waited while the butler poured, cubed and stirred. Then he handed over the lead-crystal glass and exited discreetly.

Lennie stared directly at her, raised his glass in a salute and said, "To us. To our life together. To the way it's going to be."

85

Susan returned to Beverly Hills to find Gino missing and her daughter Gemma in residence. "Why are you here, dear?" she asked, trying to conceal lurking resentment. Gemma was such an untidy girl. It had been quite a relief when she had set up house with her boyfriend.

"We had a fight," Gemma explained, biting into an apple.

"Nothing serious, I hope," fussed Susan.

"It depends on what you consider serious," replied Gemma, discarding the apple she had been eating and placing it on a polished tabletop. "I caught the jerk with his hand up my best friend's skirt, *and* she wasn't wearing panties. What category would you place *that* little bit of business in?"

"Are you sure, dear?"

Gemma regarded her mother with amusement. The woman was unreal. She lived in a dream world. "I'm sure," she said calmly. "How was your trip?"

Susan rearranged a vase of flowers, carefully removing a dying rose with a touch of annoyance. "Very nice," she said. "A charming group of people."

"Who?" questioned Gemma, not really caring, but feeling she should make conversation, as she had moved back home and she didn't want her mother complaining about *that*.

"Oh, Francesca Fern and her husband. Saud Omar." An imperceptible pause. "The Contessa Zebrowski. Lennie Golden."

Gemma snapped to attention. "Lennie Golden!" she exclaimed. "Really?"

Susan finished with the flowers and began straightening ornaments. "He's married to Dimitri's daughter," she explained.

"He's hot," sighed Gemma.

"Hot is a very vulgar expression," Susan chided.

"Hot is where Lennie Golden's at," enthused Gemma.

"Can I meet him? Can you throw one of your dinner parties or something?"

"No," snapped Susan. "Gino's still in New York, and I'm tired. I need to rest. It's been an arduous trip."

Gemma reached into a silver dish for another apple and took a large bite. "I didn't mean tomorrow," she sniffed. "Next week maybe."

"Will you still be here next week?" asked Susan, hoping the answer was no.

"If the jerk doesn't come crawling to me on his knees and apologize, I could still be here next year!" Gemma smiled. She had very small, very even, very white teeth. "I'm home, Mother. To stay."

• • • • •

Gino saw Paige off with regret. Their few days in New York together were memorable. She was his kind of woman.

He sent her off with a contented smile on her face. She enjoyed being with him as much as he enjoyed his time with her.

"I'll be back in L.A. in a few days," he promised.

"Then I shall book our suite in the Beverly Wilshire," she said warmly. "Just let me know when." Neither of them had any idea where their affair was going, but they were both on for the full ride.

Paige arrived home to find a depressed Ryder. "You can shove Bonnatti, Vitos, Quinn fucking Leech and the whole goddamn movie up your ass," he announced.

Paige summoned wifely concern. "Wasn't the dinner a success?" she asked.

"We haven't *had* the fucking dinner yet," Ryder snarled. "I had to cancel your goddamn caterers, who are trying to stick me with the bill anyway. Vitos got sick, Bonnatti got called out of town, and Quinn got temperamental. I've arranged another dinner for Monday."

"The same caterers?"

"Are you kidding? Chasen's this time."

Paige nodded. "Wise choice." Then she waited for Ryder to ask about her trip. He didn't. Why should she feel guilty when he didn't even care?

Susan Martino Santangelo had left three messages. Reluctantly Paige called her back. She wasn't sure she could go along with the "I'm screwing your husband but we can still be best friends" game.

"I must see you," Susan said.

"I'm inundated with work," Paige replied briskly.

"It's vitally important," Susan insisted, lowering her voice to a whisper.

Had she found out? Paige hesitated. "Well . . ."

"Come for tea tomorrow. Four o'clock at my house."

"You're so English!"

"Please come."

Paige sighed. Best to face up to things immediately. "I'll be there."

* * * * *

Gino had thought that with Paige returned to L.A. he would spend a couple of days with Lucky before returning to the coast. But Lucky informed him breathlessly on the phone, when he tracked her down, that she was incredibly busy, that she would love to see him, but that right now it was impossible.

To say Gino was put out was an understatement. He was hurt and angry. He had stayed in New York to spend time with his daughter, and she didn't seem to care.

Kids. Appreciation. What did they know? You gave up your life for them and they couldn't even be bothered to give you the time of day. Conveniently he forgot that for the past few days he had been closeted with Paige and had had no time to bother with anyone—including Lucky.

"Not even dinner tonight?" he demanded on the phone.

"I'm *really* tied up," Lucky explained apologetically, sounding remarkably happy for someone too busy to find time to have dinner with her father.

"Sure," said Gino. "I understand, kid."

But he didn't. And he decided to leave for L.A. early—surprise Susan *and* Paige.

86

Falling in love is like getting hit by a large truck and yet not being mortally wounded. Just sick to your stomach, high one minute, low the next. Starving hungry but unable to eat. Hot, cold, forever horny, full of hope and enthusiasm, with momentary depressions that wipe you out.

It is also not being able to remove the smile from your face, loving life with a mad, passionate intensity, and feeling ten years younger.

Love does not appear with any warning signs. You fall into it as if pushed from a high diving board. No time to think about what's happening. It's inevitable. An event you can't control. A crazy, heart-stopping, roller-coaster ride that just has to take its course.

Neither Lucky nor Lennie was expecting it. Oh, sure, they were attracted to each other, the whole sexual bit was in full swing. But love?

Come *on*.

They were two strong-minded, independent, smart people who had been around the track a time or two. They were career-oriented, with definite goals in mind. Lucky had her hotel to build, and Lennie was set to soar as high as he wanted to go.

Theirs was an impossible relationship.

And yet . . . They were two soul mates who had found each other—two reckless, passionate people filled with a sensual zest for living.

"What are we going to do?" Lucky asked after forty-eight hours of togetherness. The most exciting, incredible forty-eight hours of her life.

"We are going to extract ourselves from the craziness we're caught up in—and then we'll do something *really* stupid like get married, grow old, have a dozen kids. Whatever," Lennie joked. But he was serious.

Lucky was in a daze. No longer in control. And it didn't disturb her at all. She felt wonderful.

"We will?"

He grinned. "Whatever."

"Stop saying that."

"Why? Does it turn you on?"

She leaped upon him. "*You* turn me on. You really do."

Giggling, they rolled around the bed in her East Hampton house—the house that had once been Gino and Maria's when Lucky was just a little girl with wide eyes and an inquisitive nature.

Lennie pinned her down and lay across her. "Hey, lady— why are you always fighting me?" he demanded.

She put out her tongue and rolled it suggestively. "So's you can win," she said huskily. "I like winners."

He crushed her with a kiss and she reveled in his strength, the feel of his body and the smell of his skin. Her reserves had crumbled. Lennie, with his rangy good looks, light banter, admirable talent, gentleness with kids, not to mention bedroom performance, had won her over. He was the sort of man she had never known before, and he was special.

One date was all it had taken. He had collected her at the New York apartment and taken her to a Chinese restaurant where they had shared spring rolls, spicy shredded beef and a bottle of vodka. Polite conversation lasted exactly ten minutes. After that they were into exploring each other's lives, trading experiences, listening, telling, revealing. When the restaurant closed at 1 A.M. they were still talking, so they went on to a Greenwich Village jazz joint that accommodated them until four in the morning.

"I don't want to go home," Lucky remembered saying.

"Who's talking home?" Lennie had replied.

He took her to a place frequented by waiters and night workers that didn't even open until dawn. There they sat in a corner and drank coffee endlessly, while Billie Holiday belted blues on the old jukebox and an overpainted whore danced gaily around the tiny dance floor.

Lucky told him things she had never told anybody. Discovering the mutilated body of her mother when she was only five. The withdrawal of her father. Running away from school with Olympia when they were both teenagers. And the marriage Gino had forced her into at sixteen. "I hated him for years," she explained. "But you know something? I think I always loved him."

"I can understand the whole love-hate trip," Lennie sympathized.

And they began to talk about Alice, and how it was to grow up with a mother who truly didn't give a damn.

At eight in the morning they stopped by the basement garage where Lucky kept her Ferrari. She threw Lennie the keys and directed him to the East Hampton house.

With Otis Redding on the tape deck and light morning traffic, it was an easy drive. At a local supermarket they bought French bread, butter, bacon and eggs.

"I can't cook," Lucky confessed.

"I can," Lennie assured her, adding mushrooms and tomatoes to their haul.

The East Hampton house was locked up. The housekeeper had returned to her family in Finland for a month's vacation.

"No problem," Lucky announced, springing a downstairs bathroom window and gaining an undignified entrance.

Neither of them was sleepy, but after breakfast, cooked quite professionally by Lennie, they retired upstairs to the large white-wicker master bedroom and made slow, leisurely love as if it were their first time together. And then they slept, entwined in each other's arms.

Lucky awoke at dusk. Lennie sprawled asleep beside her. Quietly she went downstairs to the kitchen, opened a can and fixed two large mugs of steaming-hot potato soup. Then she switched some slow soul music on the stereo and returned upstairs.

She kissed him awake and handed him his soup. "Suste-

nance," she explained with a grin. "You're going to need all
the strength you can get."

"Hey!" He sipped the hot soup. "You certainly know how
to open a can."

She laughed softly. "For you I'll learn to cook."

"You will?"

"Not really. But it sounds good."

He abandoned the mug and reached for her. "C'mere."

She didn't argue. She yearned for his touch. He made her
skin electric and every caress gave her small exquisite shocks.

They experimented with each other's bodies, teasing,
holding back, testing to see who could last the longest before
dissolving into orgasmic ecstasy.

"*You* are really something," Lennie said, meaning every
word.

"And you are not exactly a slouch yourself," Lucky replied, smiling.

They talked deep into the night. She told him about Gino's
tax exile and how she had taken over the family business. "I
built the Magiriano," she said proudly. "I was twenty-five
years old and female. It wasn't easy."

"I can imagine."

"No, you can't. Not really."

"I'll try."

"Try this."

She wanted him in her mouth. She wanted to feel his hardness, the beat of his maleness. She wanted him in her power,
under her spell.

He groaned his pleasure.

She smiled her triumph.

He confessed his once passionate obsession for Eden. How
trivial it seemed now.

"What did she look like?" Lucky wanted to know.

"Skinny, blond, predatory."

"She sounds like a bird."

"She was very beautiful."

"Who cares?"

"I don't."

He spread her olive thighs and buried his head between them. Her jet pubic hair felt like silk. She tasted of musky crushed flowers. Bittersweet.

She threw her arms above her head and murmured his name over and over until she came in heavy throbs of abandonment as he sucked her dry with feverish desire.

They slept through the rest of the night.

In the morning Gino called. She couldn't remember what she said to him. She didn't want real life invading her time with Lennie. Soon Dimitri would be back and things would have to be settled.

87

Francesca dragged on a long thin black cheroot as Dimitri's plane flew her and Olympia toward Paris. "Did you ever think about having a series of slimming injections?" she asked Olympia with harsh directness. "There is a clinic in Switzerland—they specialize in weight problems."

"Oh," said Olympia brightly. "Is that the place where you had your face lifted?"

Francesca frowned. "I have never had a face-lift," she lied.

"No?" said Olympia innocently.

"No," stated Francesca firmly.

Conversation lapsed. Olympia wished Flash had come with her. She could just imagine him with Francesca. What a collision!

She summoned the stewardess, a tall Swedish woman with tanned skin and an icy smile. When Dimitri traveled she gave him massages. Olympia imagined that was not all she gave him.

"I need a chocolate fix," she told the Swede. "What do we have?"

"Parfait, sundae, fresh berries."

"Strawberries?"

"Blueberries."

"Dip them in chocolate sauce for me. I suppose they'll have to do."

The Swede flashed her icy smile and retreated to the galley.

"Blueberries in chocolate sauce," admonished Francesca, fanning her horsey countenance with a copy of French *Vogue*. "You must be desperate."

Olympia, secure on coke, smiled. "Not half as desperate as *some* of the people I know," she said, and reached for a set of headphones.

· · · · ·

"How civilized," observed Paige, gazing at the English tea Susan had set out. There were wafer-thin cucumber sandwiches, light scones with a touch of cream and jam, a ginger cake, Earl Grey tea, and fine bone-china plates, cups and saucers to put it all on.

"Tea was served on the Stanislopoulos yacht every afternoon at four." Susan announced proudly.

"What a cozy little get-together *that* must have been," replied Paige, unimpressed.

"It was wonderful," Susan sighed. She *had* enjoyed the trip. She just wished she hadn't succumbed to the Contessa's perverted advances. "I wish you had been there," she added, fixing Paige with an intimate look.

Paige wolfed a sandwich. Hadn't she told Susan it was all over before her trip? Surely the woman had understood her?

"I missed you," Susan said, drawing closer on the pale-beige damask couch. She put her hand on Paige's shoulder. "Very much."

The sound of a bee droning broke the afternoon silence. Paige shifted uncomfortably. Why were affairs so difficult to end? Male, female, there was always the final struggle.

She took a deep breath and stood up. "Susan, dear," she said, facing her perfectly groomed blond friend, "I know we had something good together—once." She emphasized the "once." "But time passes, and things change. I told you the last time we saw each other that Ryder and I were giving our marriage a second chance."

Susan's clear blue eyes, beautifully tucked and stitched, filled with tears. "I know, I know," she said, trying to control herself. "But I *need* you, Paige. You mean *so much* to me. We've meant so much to each other."

Paige glanced anxiously at the door. It wouldn't do to have the housekeeper eavesdrop on this little scene.

Susan followed her glance and rose from the couch. "I gave the couple the rest of the day off," she said. "They won't be back until late. And Gemma has gone to San Francisco. We are quite alone," she added meaningfully.

Paige nodded. One more time with Susan. A proper goodbye. It wasn't the way she wanted it, but it would work.

88

Reality invaded. Lennie had a career on hold. And commitments.

He called Jess in L.A. and listened to her yell like she was deranged. "Where *are* you?" she screamed. "You told me you'd be back in twenty-four hours for crissakes. And then you fucking vanish. You start taping the new series in two days. The network is going bananas, and so am I. Where *are* you, Lennie? Christ, don't you have *any* sense of responsibility?"

"Calm down," he admonished. "You'll have a heart attack."

"I'm too young for a heart attack," she replied dourly. "And *you're* too young to screw up your career on account of the fact that your dick is out of control again. What happened to the stud I once knew and loved?"

"You're a princess with words."

"And you're a major asshole."

"Now that we both know what we are, I called to tell you I'll be back tomorrow."

"Great. Marvelous." She snorted her disgust. "What'll you do? Go straight to the studio from the airport?"

"I thought you said I had two days."

"That's right. Today and tomorrow. There's a script waiting at your hotel—read it on the plane back. Your studio call is eight A.M. on Monday." She paused, then said, "Lennie."

"Yeah?"

"I just want you to know that I hate you."

He laughed. "And I love you."

"Big fuckin' deal," she said grudgingly.

He hung up. Lucky sat cross-legged on the bed beside him, clad in a huge sweatshirt, with knee socks and her hair in braids. Without makeup she looked like a glowingly beautiful sixteen.

"I guess the world is creeping in on us," he said.

She shrugged. "It had to happen."

He held her with his eyes. "I wish you could come with me."

She nodded, seriously, wishing the same thing, but they both knew it was impossible. Dimitri was due back with Roberto, and there was much to sort out before they could be together for the rest of their lives. They had spent hours discussing their future, and a short separation was the only way to handle it. She was going to tell Dimitri it was over. And Lennie would contact Olympia.

"I don't want to leave you," he said, stroking her leg.

"You think I want you to go?" she replied. And she meant it.

He took her in his arms and cradled her gently.

She breathed his special smell and was content.

"You're shaking," he said with concern.

She snuggled closer. "I'm cold."

"We won't be apart too long."

"I know that."

"I can fly back Friday after taping. I'll take the Red Eye— meet you here. We'll have all day Saturday and most of Sunday."

She laughed softly. "Then I shall cook you great meals."

"Yeah. Stock up on cans. Your potato soup wins prizes."

"Wait until you taste my wild mushroom. Mister, you ain't had nothin' yet."

"Hey—lady—I've had the best time of my life. I want you to know that."

She touched his cheek lightly. "I do know."

They made love again, and it was more tender, more caring than either of them had ever experienced before.

Lucky slept the night wrapped in the protection of his arms, and in the morning they awoke early and drove silently back to New York.

The idyll was over.

Marco had left her once. . . .

She had never seen him alive again. . . .

89

Gino did not like getting older. In one way, he didn't mind, because only the fortunate were still around to tell their tale. On the other hand, getting older sucked. Suddenly, at seventy-four, he could see the light at the end of the tunnel, and it seemed to be coming closer every day.

Unlike Costa, he was not falling to pieces. He still had his hair—mostly gray now, but thick and strong. And his teeth—all his own. And since the heart attack, no real problems. Indigestion sometimes, a recurring ulcer, an aching shoulder now and then—but nothing to get alarmed about.

While he was in New York he went to his doctor for a full checkup.

"You're in marvelous shape," his physician assured him. "You've got the heart and lungs of a man of fifty."

Screw fifty. He wanted the heart and lungs of a twenty-year-old. One's own mortality was a frightening thing.

He flirted with the stewardess on the flight back to L.A. She had copper hair, which reminded him of Paige, and a pertly pretty face, which reminded him of Cindy, his first wife, all those years ago.

She responded nicely. He didn't know if it was because she found him irresistibly attractive or because she sensed he was rich. The latter was not difficult to know. His suit was custom tailored, his shirt, silk. His gold Rolex watch cost six thousand dollars. He knew if he invited her out she'd say yes in a minute. Women. Easy. The story of his life.

But he didn't come on to her. He felt a certain sense of loyalty to Paige. Right now she had his full attention. Every inch. And there were still plenty of inches in that department. *Plenty.*

Susan had disappointed him. Underneath all the grooming she was a cold one, and somehow he had never gotten through to her.

At the airport he took a cab into Beverly Hills. He should have phoned Susan and told her to send the car and driver, but he had left in a hurry, due to Lucky's unavailability, and besides, he liked the idea of surprising Susan. She wanted every move plotted and planned—a little unexpectedness would do her good.

The cabdriver was foreign. He talked nonstop in broken English about every subject that took his fancy. Gino just grunted occasionally and told him to slow down when he jumped two red lights.

The man grinned and waved stubby fingers in the air. "I no kill you, meester!" he joked, just missing a poor old lady who was crossing the street. "Jaywalker!" the cabbie screeched from his window.

"Prick!" the old lady yelled back, giving both Gino and the driver pause for thought.

Beverly Hills was manicured, peaceful and perfect. Just like my wife, Gino thought, as he paid the driver, adding a hefty tip.

"You a real gentlemans!" the cabbie said, screeching off.

Two squirrels ran across the front lawn as Gino approached the house. Susan's Rolls was parked in the front drive, and behind it was Paige's gold Porsche.

Two for the price of one. He would get to see Paige sooner than expected.

He quickened his step and reached for his keys.

* * * * *

Once rid of Francesca—who Olympia decided was the pain of the century—even worse than Lucky, if that was possible—Olympia settled down to some serious shopping. She wished to return to New York with an entire new wardrobe, and Flash on her arm. The party season began in September, and she did not plan to miss one festivity.

Lennie never even entered her thoughts. He was old news. As good as divorced. The moment she returned to New York she would instruct her lawyer to terminate the marriage.

* * * * *

Susan lay naked and aquiver. Her smooth alabaster skin had not been exposed to the southern sun of France. She was pale perfection, with just a small appendix scar marking the flesh-scape.

Paige had stripped to aubergine bikini panties and a lacy matching bra from which her generous bosom bulged. She gazed down at Susan and felt no stirring passion whatsoever. The thrill is gone, she thought.

Susan's breasts were flaccid, the nipples inverted, waiting to be brought to attention. She always *had* expected Paige to do all the work. Once the challenge had been enjoyable. Now Paige didn't know where to start. A tweak here, a feel there. It did not take much to turn Susan on.

Paige gritted her teeth and bent to the task ahead.

* * * * *

Dimitri's lawyer in Paris ushered Francesca Fern into his office with great solicitousness. He had been warned by the man himself to handle her with great care. "Whatever she wants—do it," Dimitri had commanded. "Her divorce must be expedited immediately. No holdups. When it is done I shall decide what to do about my present wife."

"Dimitri," his lawyer groaned, "if you are thinking of divorcing Lucky it will cost you a fortune."

"Are you forgetting she signed a marriage contract?" Dimitri reminded him.

"No. But you also put your signature to a paper allowing her to build a hotel in Atlantic City at your expense. It could cost you many millions."

"She'll never do it," Dimitri said dismissively. "And if she doesn't handle it personally, the document becomes null and void. There is also a time limit involved. I am not a fool."

His lawyer said, "No, you are not." But privately he thought any man who would prefer Francesca Fern to Lucky Santangelo had to be racing toward senility.

Francesca sat before him in a short silk dress, black stockings and very high-heeled shoes. She smelled of Calèche, smoked disgusting cheroots, and every so often indulged in a coughing fit. Her legs were heavy, and when she crossed and uncrossed them, which was often, he couldn't help noticing she wore no panties.

"If I *do* decide to divorce my husband, Horace, at Mr. Stanislopoulos's request," she said huskily, "Horace is to be compensated handsomely from Mr. Stanislopoulos's pocket, *not* from mine. Is that clear?"

"Yes, Madame Fern," the lawyer agreed pleasantly. "Dimitri made that clear to me on the telephone yesterday."

She ignored his use of Dimitri's first name, signaling a closer relationship than she wished to acknowledge. To Francesca, anyone you paid was an employee, and that was the way she treated them.

"Should I proceed with this divorce," she mused, "papers must be prepared for both myself and Mr. Stanislopoulos to sign."

"Naturally," replied the lawyer. A marriage between these two without a financial contract was unthinkable.

"I have many needs," continued Francesca, blowing smoke in his face and crossing her heavy legs yet again.

"I'm sure that you have, Madame Fern," soothed the lawyer, hating this horse-faced woman who talked down to him as if he were an office boy.

And then she told him of her needs, and he loathed her even more. Not only was she a bitch. She was a calculating one. Her requirements were outrageous. When he relayed them to Dimitri he hoped he would be equally outraged.

She wanted a huge cash settlement on the day of her divorce. A further fortune when she and Dimitri were married. More lump sums of money for each year they were together. A massive monthly expense allowance. An apartment in Paris and a duplex in New York. A weekly clothes budget that would feed a family of four for a lifetime. *And* a special clause stipulating that over the period of a year she and Dimitri had to spend only six months in each other's company. The rest of the time they were free to travel wherever they so desired.

The lawyer tried to remain expressionless as she relayed her requests, but a nerve in his cheek began to jump uncontrollably.

"I hope you have made a full list of my requirements," she said, standing up and smoothing down her skirt.

The lawyer rose also. "Yes, madame," he said politely.

"Good," she replied haughtily. And without so much as a goodbye she stalked from his office.

Immediately he reached for the phone.

· · · · ·

The Beverly Hills house was hardly a welcoming place to return to. It was less home than showplace.

Late afternoon, and the only sound was a bee buzzing.

Gino walked into the living room and found a half-eaten English tea set out on the coffee table. He helped himself to a cucumber sandwich and wandered into the kitchen, which was also deserted. Then he made his way upstairs, prepared to find Susan showing Paige some new couturier creation. Women and clothes. The two went together like money and power. They spent fortunes on various expensive outfits and then wore them only once. Who could figure it?

He smelled Paige's perfume in the air. Musk oil. She drenched herself in it. Better than the sickly-sweet Joy that Susan favored.

He smiled to himself. Gino Santangelo—the scent expert. The street kid with a nose!

He threw open the bedroom door and stood quite still. A tableau greeted him. Two women frozen in shock.

The blonde, not so young, but well preserved. Whiter-than-white skin and unexciting breasts.

The copperhead, buxom and raunchy.

They were playing games. *You show me yours . . . I'll show you mine.*

The only sound in the entire house was the roaring in his head.

Lucky tried to concentrate. It was not easy. She kept thinking of Lennie, and when she did a stupid grin would spread itself across her face and she felt a complete fool.

"What's the joke?" one of the architects she was meeting with repeatedly asked. He was an attractive guy in his early thirties. Once she might have whiled away an evening with him—but things were different now.

"No joke," she said, still grinning.

He flirted with his eyes. "In that case you've got a great disposition."

She didn't want to encourage him, but obviously her permanent smile was doing so. "Try telling that to my husband," she said offhandedly, and turned away.

Dimitri. What was she going to do about him? Since she had left the yacht a series of pictures had cropped up in various publications taken by lurking paparazzi. All were of Dimitri with Francesca. Getting on the yacht . . . off the yacht . . . running from a nightclub . . . entering a restaurant. Arms around each other, teeth flashing. The irrepressible pair—Dimitri Stanislopoulos and Francesca Fern.

How the newspapers and magazines loved them, the aging billionaire and the prima donna. Both married, flamboyant and great newspaper fodder.

Lucky was delighted that his interest in Francesca seemed not to have been dimmed by his marriage. It would make it all the easier for her to tell him it was over. The perfect excuse. She wished she could drop him a short note: "Dear Dimitri. I am releasing you from our marriage for obvious reasons. Let's stay friends. Lucky."

How clean and simple it would be.

Instinctively she knew it would not turn out to be that civilized.

• • • • •

Olympia had purchased three hundred thousand dollars' worth of clothes in Paris. Plus a new sable coat and a selection of extravagant jewelry. She had also scored an excellent supply of top-grade cocaine, a substance she now needed daily if she was to function at all. How fortunate she had been born an heiress. There was no way she could imagine a man spending that kind of money on her. Men were cheap, however much money they had. She had observed her father over the years. He rarely dipped into his pocket unless it was for himself or Francesca.

She glanced at the aging actress sitting across the aisle of Dimitri's private plane. What *did* he see in the old cow? And why hadn't he done something about it after all these years?

She wondered why Francesca had made the sudden trip to Paris. Maybe she would ask Dimitri upon their return. He might tell her, then again he might not.

She leaned across the aisle. "Did you do any shopping?" she asked.

Francesca favored her with a look. Deep-set brooding eyes decorated with sweeping fake lashes. "Shopping bores me," she said.

"It doesn't bore *me*," Olympia replied, flashing a gaudy ruby-and-diamond bracelet. "Beautiful things turn me on."

Francesca smiled condescendingly. "Perhaps if you had worked a day in your life you would realize that shopping is merely mind fodder for the idle rich," she commented.

"What utter balls!" Olympia responded. She would have said more, but the plane was entering a summer storm and the sudden turbulence shut her up.

• • • • •

And in the south of France Dimitri waited patiently for the return of his mistress. He watched Roberto and Brigette splash and play in the pool. He tried to ignore tentative remarks from Horace. He listened to his lawyer on the telephone from Paris and roared with laughter when he heard Francesca's demands. "Give her whatever she wants," he boomed. And he meant it.

Francesca was finally going to belong to him. He didn't care *what* it cost.

• • • • •

Lennie flew back to L.A., an angry Jess and an empty apartment. The producers of "The Springs" were not exactly wild with happiness either, especially when he complained about the script he had been sent in New York and had read on the plane.

"It's shit," said Lennie.

"Fuck you," said the producers. "We start shooting tomorrow. You want changes? You should have been here."

Lennie sat up all night rewriting, trying to keep his concentration, thinking of Lucky.

He called her every hour until she said, "This is ridiculous." And still they continued talking.

"I've got to get some sleep," she finally said. "Dimitri's coming in tomorrow and I have to be clearheaded."

"You'll call me," Lennie instructed. "I'll be back from the studio around eight, L.A. time."

They had planned the scenario. Lucky wasn't going to hesitate. She was to tell Dimitri it was over as soon as possible. Then she was to move out of the New York apartment with Roberto and CeeCee and resume residence in her East Hampton house. Lawyers would then take over.

It all sounded trouble-free. With acute intuition Lucky knew it would not be.

• • • • •

Olympia sensed something was wrong immediately. She had flown long enough and far enough to observe trouble when it happened. They had been preparing to land for far too long.

The Swedish stewardess was pale beneath her tan, and it had nothing to do with the storm and the turbulence they had traveled through.

"What's the matter?" Olympia demanded, grabbing her arm as she attempted to rush past.

The woman gave a sickly smile. "Nothing," she said, falsely jovial.

"Don't give me that," replied Olympia, strangely calm.

"Just a problem with the landing gear."

"What kind of problem?"

"It's stuck."

"Oh, wonderful!"

"Nice Airport has been alerted. But the captain feels it will right itself before we have to use emergency procedures."

For a moment Olympia felt panic, but only for a moment. She glanced at Francesca—the prima donna slept. "Don't wake her until you have to," she ordered.

The stewardess nodded, visibly shaking beneath her Swedish cool.

"How long before we have to land?" Olympia asked.

"Twenty minutes."

Twenty minutes to get the landing gear to work.

And if it didn't?

Olympia reached for her stash.

91

Dimitri Stanislopoulos's private plane crash-landed at 7:45 P.M. on Friday evening.

There were nine people aboard——seven crew and two passengers.

Upon landing on a sea of foam, the plane careened down the runway and burst into flames. Two members of the crew and one of the passengers managed to escape the fiery furnace. All three were severely burned.

The rest of the people aboard perished.

Book Three

THE SUMMER OF 1983

92

Carrie Berkeley smiled at Bryant Gumbel as the two of them entertained America on "The Today Show." It was early in the morning and a steaming heat wave was searing the streets of New York. But inside the air-conditioned NBC studio in Rockefeller Center, Carrie Berkeley, a very well-preserved and stylish sixty-nine, and Bryant Gumbel, one of the best interviewers on television, exchanged words and looks, creating an easygoing banter.

Carrie was promoting the paperback of her book, written in conjunction with Anna Robb, entitled *The Carrie Berkeley Book of Style*. Already the book was climbing the paperback best-seller lists. The hardcover had hovered on *The New York Times* list for seven weeks.

Bryant Gumbel grinned—he had an irresistible grin—and concluded the interview.

He is a most attractive young man, Carrie decided, the kind of man she would like to have introduced to her daughter—if she had ever had one.

In the Green Room she rejoined the skinny publicity man assigned her by her publishers. He was admittedly gay, with carrot-colored hair and an engaging smile. "You were dandy!" he enthused. "You always are."

"You'd say that, whatever I did," she teased him.

"Naturally. I'm no fool."

He took her arm and they left the building.

Outside there were a few autograph hunters. One of them presented a dog-eared copy of her book to be signed. She did so with a flourish.

A limousine waited curbside to take her on to her next appointment. She sank back into luxurious leather and marveled, as she did several times a day, at what her life had become. She,

Carrie Berkeley, was a published author! With a lot of help from Anna Robb. The two women had become close friends. So close, in fact, that Carrie had allowed Anna to pry the secrets of her life from her. And for the last year they had been collaborating on Carrie's biography, an explosive manuscript, recently completed and now ready to show to a publisher.

"We could be looking at a half-million-dollar advance," Anna had said calmly at their last meeting. "Your story is dynamite."

Carrie wondered if it was worth revealing her life for half a million dollars. But then again, she had not become involved with the book for monetary gain. It was a story Anna had convinced her *should* be told. And reading the pages, at times so painful she could hardly keep going, she realized Anna was right.

So far, nobody knew about the book. Not Steven, not even Fred Lester. It was a project the two women had kept to themselves.

"We have to show the manuscript to Fred first," Anna fretted. "I don't think he'll pay the price, but he has the option and, besides, he deserves first look."

Carrie agreed. She knew of Anna's and Fred Lester's relationship. For months Anna had kept it to herself, but one day she had let it slip. "You're very lucky," Carrie said. "He seems like a nice man."

"He is," Anna agreed.

"Do you think you'll marry?" Carrie asked, wondering why she felt so let down.

"No," said Anna, and never discussed their relationship again.

Carrie was nervous about anyone's reading the thousand-page manuscript. It was all there in neat typescript. Her life, her shame, every innermost secret.

Ah, but the relief of letting it all out—it had been a cathartic experience.

She worried about Steven's reaction. Anna quite rightly pointed out that Steven was a big boy. "You must do what you think is right," she said. "And Steven has to accept your decision."

Carrie knew this was so. However, it didn't stop her from worrying.

• • • • •

"I'm ready," Mary Lou Moore said, her large brown eyes wide and determined. "I'll go in fighting and I'll come out a winner."

"You're absolutely sure?" Steven Berkeley asked. "It won't be easy. They're really out to get you."

"I'm *more* than sure," Mary Lou replied fiercely.

"Then we shall have our day in court," Steven said evenly, satisfied she could handle it. "The date is set. No more postponements."

"And no more depositions either." Mary Lou sighed with relief. "I *hate* those things. All those crummy lawyers digging into your past like dirty little maggots."

Steven laughed. "You turn an interesting phrase."

She caught his eye. "And so do you, counselor."

He glanced away and busied himself with a stack of papers on his desk. Lately Mary Lou had been throwing some very hot looks in his direction. He didn't want to read anything into them. They were lawyer and client, that was all—even though he did find her extremely attractive. In three years he had watched her grow from gauche teenager to a warm young woman. It had been an interesting transition. When they first met, she wouldn't move without her mother, her manager, and a series of spaced-out boyfriends. Now she was on her own, with a legitimate agent and manager and no visible entanglements. She came to his office unaccompanied, and had conducted herself with dignity throughout the long and tedious steps needed to get them to court.

"How about lunch?" Mary Lou asked brightly. "We should

celebrate, now that we're finally going to court, shouldn't we?"

He found her very appealing—but she was so young, just twenty. Besides, he never *had* believed in mixing business with pleasure. "I have a lunch appointment with a client," he lied apologetically.

"*I'm* a client," she pointed out, tilting her head to one side.

"I know. And we'll be having plenty of lunches together when we're in court."

"Can't wait."

When she left his office he sat silently for a moment. Would it be wrong to take her out?

Yes.

Why?

Because she's still a baby.

He was forty-five, old enough to be her father. And she was an actress, a television star.

So what?

Maybe when the case was over, he would take her out.

Maybe when the case was over, she wouldn't want to go out with him.

He thought about her case for a moment. They had started off suing some half-assed magazine publisher, Vista Publications. But during the course of depositions and discovery, it had come to light that the publishing company was actually owned by Bonnatti Publications, and although the offending magazine had been distributed by Ravier Distribution, Inc., it turned out that Ravier was merely a subsidiary of Bonnatti. So, their case was against Bonnatti Publications and Bonnatti Distribution. And the main shareholder of both companies was a man named Santino Bonnatti. And Steven knew plenty about Santino Bonnatti. He was the son of the notorious Enzio Bonnatti, whom Steven had once almost arrested and brought before a grand jury. Until fate intervened, and Lucky Santangelo had killed the sonofabitch. Supposedly in self-defense.

Now he had a crack at the son. He wouldn't be able to put him away, even though he was a known dealer in prostitution, drugs and pornography on the West Coast, but he could hit him where it hurt. In the wallet.

Mary Lou was suing for ten million dollars. And Steven planned to collect every penny.

Jerry Myerson entered his office. "What's happening, Steven? I just had a cancellation. Are you free for lunch?"

"If you're paying, I'm free."

They went to the Four Seasons because Jerry felt like it. And there they bumped into Carrie, lunching with Anna Robb and Fred Lester. She radiated style and chic.

"Your mother is something else," Jerry said admiringly, after they were seated. "What she's done with her life is quite remarkable."

Steven agreed. And he was glad that three years before he had dropped his quest to find out who his father was and had concentrated on getting his own life back on track. He was doing extremely well. So well, Jerry wished to make him a full partner, and that was something to think about.

He was living in his own house again and dating several interesting women. Things were good.

So why wasn't he happy?

Because deep down he still needed to know who his father was.

And one day he would have to find out.

One day.

93

Lennie!" A sharp, whining command. Then louder. *"Len-neee!"*

He was in his study but he heard her. Christ! He could be at the beach and he'd still hear her.

He picked up the phone and pressed the intercom. His voice conveyed irritation. "What is it?"

"I'm lonely."

"I'm working."

"I know. But I'm still lonely. Come and talk to me."

"Give me ten minutes."

He put down the phone and stared out the window. There was an incredible view. Lush manmade waterfalls, tropical foliage, palm trees and greenery as far as the eye could see.

His study was leather-paneled, with the latest state-of-the-art stereo equipment, video recorders and a TV set that could tune in all over the world.

The mansion he lived in was high up in Bel Air. It had fourteen bedrooms, fourteen matching bathrooms, and living rooms that went on forever. There were indoor and outdoor swimming pools, two tennis courts, a cozy Jacuzzi large enough for twelve, and a roller-skating rink.

In the basement there was a large mirrored discotheque complete with flashing strobe lights and a rare collection of classic rock albums. Another room housed two pool tables. And there was also a private cinema that seated thirty.

Not that they ever had anyone over. Olympia was paranoid about being seen, even though her burn scars were long healed and the wonders of plastic surgery had restored her face to its former prettiness. She didn't want people over because of her weight. Once pleasantly plump, Olympia Stanislopoulos now weighed over two hundred pounds. She was a fat, blond,

bad-tempered rich heiress, who hid her blubber beneath volu-
minous caftans, promised Lennie she was dieting, and had one
of the maids smuggle in Twinkies, chocolate cakes and candies
from Godiva to See's—in fact, anything sweet she could lay
her hands on.

"Lennie!" She screeched for him again.

He stood up and reluctantly went to find her.

She was in the large kitchen gazing mournfully into a
well-stocked restaurant-style fridge. A nervous maid hovered
nearby.

"There's never anything decent to eat here," Olympia
complained.

"We had lunch an hour ago," he commented.

"You call carrots and celery lunch?" she sneered. "I've
heard of dieting, but this is ridiculous."

"You should go to a clinic," he remarked. "It would make
it a lot easier for you."

Her blue eyes were vindictive pinpoints. "And for you,
huh? Send the wife off to a fat farm while the star gets laid."

Here it came. The usual argument. How long could he take
this shit?

"I don't know why you keep on fighting it," he said evenly.
"The only way you'll get rid of the weight is with professional
help."

"Screw you," she spat. "All *you're* interested in is getting
rid of me so you can turn this house into Bimbette City."

She had never caught him. But she suspected every move
he made. Quite rightly so. He was hardly celibate. Getting laid
was one way of killing the pain.

What was he supposed to do? The news of the plane crash
three years ago still reverberated in his head. An urgent phone
call. A distressed voice. Fragments of what had taken place
*"Your wife . . . terrible inferno . . . Francesca Fern dead . . . a
tragedy . . ."*

At first he had thought Olympia had been killed too. But

no. She was alive and in a coma. Severely burned. Hanging on in intensive care. A flight was arranged for him immediately. Before he knew it he was back in Europe, standing beside her hospital bed.

Olympia. Her blond hair shaved, one side of her face and her right arm a mass of horrifying burns.

"She'll live," one of the doctors assured him. "But she has to be given the *desire* to live."

Dimitri appeared at the hospital with Lucky. He was white and drawn, a strange expression on his face—a kind of pent-up madness waiting to explode.

Lucky hid behind huge black shades, preventing any glimpse of her eyes. While Dimitri stood by Olympia's bed, Lennie managed to take her to one side. "We have to talk," he said urgently, gripping her arm.

She did not remove her shades. In an expressionless voice she said, "Things are different now."

"Just a temporary setback—" he began.

She cut him off sharply. "No. It's fate. We weren't meant to be together. I knew what we had was too special to last."

"When Olympia gets out of the hospital—"

Her voice was devoid of emotion. "She'll need you," she said flatly. "And you must be there for her."

"Lucky—"

"It's not just Olympia," she continued calmly. "Dimitri needs me too. In fact"—an imperceptible pause—"he won't let me go."

They were unable to speak any further, and shortly after, she and Dimitri departed. The concerned father obviously did not plan to hang around.

Lennie was angry. It seemed Dimitri's visit was merely a courtesy call. Didn't he care about his only daughter?

As for the situation with Lucky . . . well, it was early days. Once Olympia was out of the hospital and Dimitri was over his shock . . . everything would work out. Reluctantly Lennie decided he had to stay with Olympia, at least for a while. He had married the girl—he could hardly desert her now.

He spent every day at the hospital, a witness to her unbearable agony. In America, the producers of his television show demanded his immediate return or a lawsuit. "Forget it," he told Jess long distance. "There's no way I can leave her now."

Jess flew in to convince him he was committing professional suicide. She was brutally frank. "You don't love her," she pointed out. "And you don't need her money. So what the hell are you hanging around for?"

He looked at her long and hard. "Because she's in a coma, and she doesn't *have* anyone else," he explained. "I'm not going to run out on her. Don't expect me to."

Jess nodded. She understood. Show Lennie someone in trouble and he was there. It had always been that way.

Dimitri did not return to visit his daughter. According to one of his minions he had gone into seclusion on his island, mourning Francesca Fern.

"Where's Lucky?" Lennie had asked, trying to keep his voice casual.

"She's with him," the man had said.

She's with him.

The words haunted Lennie.

Was she with him in every way? Were their lips touching? Their bodies entwining? Were they making love? *She's with him.*

And why not? *He* was with Olympia.

Oh, God! Both he and Lucky were busy doing the right thing when they should have been together. It wasn't fair.

After several weeks, Olympia came out of the coma. The first thing she did was ask for a mirror. When she got it her screams could be heard throughout the hospital. Lennie attempted to reassure her. Only one side of her face was burned—the other was perfect. "I've talked to the doctors," he said confidently. "With plastic surgery, skin grafts, you're going to look as good as new."

"You stupid fool," she yelled, tears streaming down her face. "What do *you* know?"

He contemplated leaving. But she was his wife, and it seemed she had nobody—only him.

"Get me some coke," she demanded, the next day.

"Are you crazy?" he replied. "You're on all kinds of medication. Do you want to kill yourself?"

"I don't care," she replied blankly. "Maybe that's what I *should* do."

Dimitri still did not come back to visit, although he sent flowers daily, and one of his personal secretaries arrived to report to him on Olympia's progress.

"Where is Dimitri?" Lennie demanded angrily.

"Mr. Stanislopoulos is not well," the secretary replied in hushed tones. "He's unable to leave his island."

"What's the matter with him?"

"I'm not allowed to divulge that information," she replied primly. But she did divulge that his wife and child were still with him.

Lucky was back with Dimitri with a vengeance.

Lennie slumped into a depression. He tried to phone the island, but Lucky was always unreachable and never returned his calls.

Another week passed. Olympia's mother, Charlotte, turned up, slightly late in the day. She arrived from New York, a tense woman, well dressed and tight-lipped. "I would have come before," she explained airily. "But it was impossible."

Why? Lennie wanted to ask. *It's your daughter lying there, you cold bitch. Why was it impossible?*

Charlotte stayed twenty-four hours.

"I want to see Flash," Olympia mumbled one day. "Has he sent flowers? Has he called?"

There were banks of flowers, too many to deal with. The cards were kept in a box, and Dimitri's secretary typed neat thank-you notes. Lennie asked the woman if Flash had sent anything. He was not jealous, merely relieved that there might be a way out.

"No," she replied, consulting a file of names in a leather book.

Lennie tracked the rock star to London and phoned him. "Olympia wants to see you," he said, hoping Flash would jump at the opportunity, thereby taking him off the hook.

"Listen, man," Flash confided, "that was over long ago—she's too effing rich for my blood. I hope she's awright an' everyfing—but it was never any big deal."

Olympia swore that Lennie was keeping them apart.

Eventually the day came when she was ready to leave the hospital. A series of operations were planned, but they could not take place immediately, as her skin had to heal first.

"I'll take you to your father's island," Lennie suggested, with the thought of seeing Lucky.

"No," Olympia replied quickly, well aware of Dimitri's lack of concern. "I want to go to California." She had just read that Flash had bought a house there, and she was determined to see him. Without Lennie's knowledge, she purchased the Bel Air mansion for ten million dollars over the phone. She didn't tell him until they arrived.

Once back in America, he had no idea what to do. He had planned to stay with her until she left the hospital, but dumping her now seemed cruel. At times she was okay. It wasn't all screaming and name-calling. So, much as he wanted to tell her it was over, timing was everything, and the moment was not right. Maybe after the first operation, when she began to look normal again and regain her confidence.

The producers of his TV series were suing him for millions.

Rolling Stone ran the cover story they had been working on. It made him look like egomaniac of the year.

Jess finally quit bugging him about when he was going back to work.

Alice was giving eccentric interviews to anyone who asked.

Add asshole of the year to his list of credits, for that's what she was making him look like.

Olympia and he moved into the house with an army of servants in attendance. Shortly after, Brigette and Nanny Mabel arrived for the Christmas vacation.

"Mama, you are so ugly!" Brigette crowed. "I can't stand to look at you."

The moment Christmas was over she was sent to stay with her grandfather, still closeted on his island.

"I hate that child," Olympia complained bitterly. "I plan to see as little of her as possible."

Early one morning, a few days after Brigette left, Olympia ordered the car and chauffeur and mysteriously went out, her face shrouded by a long scarf.

When Lennie heard, he was delighted. It was the first time she had left the house. He was not so delighted when she returned an hour later, hysterical. She never told him, but he soon found out she had been to see Flash, and the rock star had taken one look at her and said, "Cor blimey! No offense, love, but I can't take fucking disfigurement. Makes me sick to me stomach, know what I mean?"

Lennie got the news from Flash's manager, who phoned to request that she stay out of his client's life.

"Tell your shithead client to go fuck himself," Lennie fumed, and slammed down the phone.

Shortly after that Olympia began to cling, something she had never done before. And she wanted sex—a subject which had not come up since the accident.

Lennie tried, but his desire level was zero.

Olympia was surprisingly understanding. Matter-of-factly she blamed it on the way she looked.

He had no excuse except the one he couldn't tell her. Lucky was in his head, his heart, his whole being. She was the only woman he ever wanted. And now, because of a tragic set of circumstances, they were apart.

Once again he tried to contact her, but to no avail. It was clear she was avoiding him. He was angry and rejected. He was also trapped. And going crazy.

The time had come to get back to work, but Jess informed him offers were sparse. Once so hot, he was now not even lukewarm. Bad publicity and a lawsuit did not help.

He had been toying with the idea of writing an original screenplay. "Maybe we can get the financing and produce it ourselves," he suggested to Jess.

"Why not have your wife put up the money?" she replied tartly. "She's buying you everything else."

It was true. Olympia sat in a chair all day and ordered things over the phone. So far she had bought him a Mercedes, a Porsche, a portable gym, legions of electronic equipment, a boat, tapes, books, clothes. She had turned into a catalogue freak. She ordered and ate, ate and ordered. And so her days passed.

The first operation on her face was a success. She and Lennie flew to Brazil, where she spent several weeks in a private clinic being attended to by the world's finest plastic surgeons. Lennie stayed with her all the time. He worked on his screenplay and visited her daily. She needed all the support she could get.

Dimitri sent a flower shop of roses. It was nearly a year since she'd seen him.

It was nearly a year since Lennie had seen Lucky, although he still thought of her all the time. She obviously didn't give a damn about him—otherwise she would have tried to contact him, as he had her. He felt a heavy sadness, but he still refused to believe it was over.

By the time Olympia was allowed to go home her spirits had lifted considerably. She was still putting on weight, but it didn't seem to bother her. She spent hours studying her face in the mirror and waiting for the day when it would be completely healed.

Lennie finished his screenplay and turned it over to Jess. "This is what I want to do," he said. "No more clubs or TV. And no, I am not asking my wife to put up the money."

Jess raised a cynical eyebrow. Lennie was a comic, a TV star. Nobody was running to finance him in a movie. After she had read the script she changed her mind. It was a hilarious comedy about crime called *Private Dick*—with all the ingredients it took to become an excellent little sleeper.

She started looking into financing, and every studio turned her down. At a party she met a producer named Ryder Wheeler. He had recently scored a mild hit with a low-budget movie starring the singer Vitos Felicidade. She told him of Lennie's project and he was interested. She sent him the script, and within three weeks a deal was set.

The rest was history. *Private Dick* was the most financially successful film of 1981. And Lennie became an instant movie star—with a megabucks contract from one of the biggest studios to write, produce and star in three more movies.

Now, professionally he was the hottest property around.

But personally his life was a void.

For three years it had been that way.

94

Opening nights always scared the hell out of Lucky, and this was her second one. Her first was the Magiriano Hotel in 1975, eight years before. If she closed her eyes she could still summon back the feeling. Hot-and-cold anticipation. Crazy excitement. It was like having a tiger by the tail and waiting for it to take off. Ah . . . the trip . . . the incredible high . . .

And now the Santangelo Hotel, in Atlantic City, was ready to be launched. She couldn't wait.

Slowly she went through the ritual of preparation. A long, warm shower, which she switched to icy at the end. The tingle of the cold water was almost a sexual thrill. And then the luxury of giant fluffy bath towels, towels made specially for the Santangelo Hotel in wonderful colors matching the particular bathrooms they were assigned to. Not for Lucky Santangelo boring white bathrobes. At her hotel the bathrobes were made of silk in Hong Kong and were to be given to the guests as gifts, not added onto the bill.

After her shower, wearing a cinnamon silk chemise, she sat in front of her dressing-room mirror and applied glamour. Usually she did not wear a lot of makeup, but on a night such as this she felt the need to go all the way. Dark gold eyeshadow, black kohl pencil, burnished bronze blusher and sensual gloss.

She looked, at thirty-three, sensational. The years had only heightened her darkly exotic beauty—made her more intriguing and mysterious. She was staggeringly beautiful in an erotic and unusual way.

She slipped off her chemise and, quite naked, stepped into a long dress made of black satin, snakeskin and lace. The dress fitted her like a second skin, skimming every curve of her supple body and plunging daringly between her breasts.

Her hairstyle was always the same. Wild jet shoulder-length curls, thick and shiny.

Satisfied with her appearance, she added her favorite jeweled panther pin, diamond drop earrings and matching diamond cuff bracelets. On the wedding finger of her right hand she wore a huge pear-shaped diamond. Dimitri showered her with gifts. It was his way of saying Thank you.

Thank you for what?

Three years previously, Francesca Fern had perished in a plane crash. He had never recovered. He was thanking Lucky for staying with him, remaining his wife, and for giving him the only reason to stay alive—his son, Roberto.

Thoughtfully Lucky stared at her reflection in the mirrored wall of her penthouse apartment atop the Santangelo. She knew that when people looked at her they saw a strong, confident, sexy woman. What they didn't see was the heartbreak beneath the cool exterior. For she would never get over losing Lennie. And she must never allow herself to be caught in the lethal clutches of love again.

First Marco . . .

Then Lennie . . . Both taken from her by circumstances beyond her control.

Often she wondered how he felt. In the beginning he had tried to reach her constantly. Phone calls, messages, even a letter insisting that they speak.

Didn't he understand? The plane crash was a warning. If she ever saw him again something terrible would happen. She knew it.

One deep breath and she was ready to go. She licked her lips, threw back her head, and strode to her private elevator.

• • • • •

"It's really something," said Costa.

"Stupendous!" exclaimed Costa's wife.

"An achievement," allowed Gino.

Their roles were reversed as they waited in the Art Deco bar for Lucky. Costa was now married, and Gino divorced.

Costa's wife was a retired call girl of forty. Her name was Ria, and she was fond of gardening and bridge. They had met at a bridge club in Miami a year ago and had hit it off immediately, in spite of a thirty-five-year age difference. Then they set up house together. Ria was truthful about her past, and Costa didn't seem to mind. They lived together for a while, and then, very unexpectedly, Ria became pregnant. Naturally Costa did the right thing and married her, even though he wasn't 100 percent sure the baby was his. She had confessed to a short fling with an old love. Costa had experienced over thirty years of a wonderful marriage to his first wife, but sadly, it was childless. He didn't care who had fathered the baby. At seventy-five he was about to become a papa for the first time, and he was the happiest man in the world.

At first Gino had been more than cynical. Lucky also. But once they met Ria and got to know her, they both changed their minds. She seemed to adore Costa—and besides, she had faithfully promised him she would never play around again.

Gino glanced at his watch. "Where's Lucky?" he asked. "I didn't fly in from Vegas to sit around waitin'."

"Be patient," Costa admonished. "It's her big night." He sighed with nostalgia. "Ah . . . how I remember the opening of the Magiriano. What an evening!"

"Yeh. With me stuck in Israel," Gino complained. "Schmuck of the year!"

He was now divorced.

Susan had demanded his balls.

And everything else she could lay her hands on.

California law.

You could stick California law up the Holland Tunnel and block both ends!

He had caught *her*—and she was the one with the million-dollar demands.

Ladylike cunt.

Into broads all the time.

He would *never* forget the expression on both their faces when he caught them in the act.

Susan and Paige.

His wife and his lover.

Two dumb tramps.

He would never admit it, but he missed Paige. *She* was the real disappointment. Naturally he had never spoken to her again.

"Here she comes," said Costa, admiringly. "And look what she looks like!"

"Stupendous!" sighed Ria.

Yeh. Gino had to admit it. His daughter was an absolute stunner.

• • • • •

Brigette Stanislopoulos removed the heated rollers from her long blond hair. She was fourteen years old, but she could easily pass for eighteen or nineteen. People told her that all the time. People who didn't know came on to her like crazy, and she loved every minute of it.

Brigette now attended school in Switzerland. L'Evier, a strict private girls' school, which both her mother, boring, fat Olympia, and her grandfather's wife, Lucky, whom she had grown to adore, had been expelled from. Sometimes Brigette wondered why her mother had sent her there. And then she figured it out—it was far away and it was easy.

She also figured out, exactly like her mother before her, how to leave school after lights out. So simple. Hundreds of rich little schoolgirls had followed the path to freedom and the nearest village. The name of the game was not getting caught.

Brigette could play the game expertly. And she didn't need any help. She had no desire to pal up with any of the other girls; they were all stupid babies, whereas Brigette liked to consider herself a woman of sophistication and experience. After all, she had been around. Her grandfather was one of the richest men in the world. Her mother was a famous (unfortunately fat) heiress. And her stepfather was a movie star. (She liked Lennie, even though she rarely saw him. Most of her vacations were spent on her grandfather's island.)

She had quite a pedigree, and didn't mind boasting about it. And a temper—which was why people did not go out of their way to make friends with her.

Except the boys in the village. For they didn't care how bad-tempered she was as long as she allowed them liberties the other girls were not prepared to grant.

Brigette Stanislopoulos had never gone all the way.

But she planned to.

Soon. As soon as she found the right boy.

Brigette smiled to herself. She was remarkably pretty. She had all her mother's good features, and none of her bad ones. She had great boobs. Big ones. Boys loved big ones, and she loved having them. "Playing titty," as she called being fondled, was her favorite part of sex. Sucking the boy's "thing" was her least favorite. Although she did it. Had to. They loved it *soooo* much. And once she had a boy in her mouth, she had him under her spell. This was a good thing to know in life.

Brigette smoothed down the bodice of the white dress Lucky had brought her specially for the opening of the Santangelo. It was an okay dress, not spectacular, but kind of funky in a youngish way. She would have preferred something black and slinky. Black was boss. Especially with blond hair.

Boys loved her long blond hair. They loved to run their hands through it and drape it over their "things." They loved to jerk off in her hair. Ugh! Sometimes boys were disgusting creatures.

Brigette often wondered what Lennie did to Olympia in bed.

Then she wondered what Dimitri did to Lucky.

He probably didn't do anything. He was too old. His "thing" must have withered and fallen off by now.

Was that what happened? She decided to ask someone. Although who would know? After all, it wasn't exactly something you could look up in the reference books. What would one look under? *Prick, the decline of.*

She giggled aloud and hoped Lucky wouldn't complain about her makeup. She did have a lot on, but she *looooved* makeup so.

· · · · ·

Lucky strode regally toward her father. She moved like a leopard—graceful, surefooted and dangerous.

"Kid!" He rose to greet her.

"Old man!" She grinned.

"Enough with the smart mouth." They hugged and kissed. "I'm proud of you, kid," he mumbled in her ear.

"It wasn't easy," she replied.

"Nothing worth having ever is."

What a cliché. But true.

She flashed onto thoughts of Lennie. She had seen *Private Dick* four times, and his follow-up movie, *Piece of Class* three.

Pure torture. Just seeing him up on the screen her body cried out for his touch. Fortunately she never had to face him. He stayed in California with Olympia. They were still married. Things must have worked out after all.

Yes, and you're still married to Dimitri, an inner voice reminded. *Has your marriage worked out?*

Nooooo, she wanted to scream. She was married to a recluse. Dimitri was a poor excuse for the man he once was. He mourned Francesca. He had no intention or desire ever to leave his island again.

For a while Lucky had comforted him. Why not? He was old and alone, and he needed Roberto around just to get through the day. Eventually she announced the time had come for her to move on. The plans for her hotel were ready and she wanted to get started.

"You can go," Dimitri stated. "But I'll never allow you to take Roberto. *Never.*"

"I can take him any time I want," she had retorted angrily.

His smile was a death mask. "Try it and you will lose. There will be no hotel, and, believe me, Lucky, one way or another you will never see Roberto again." He paused. "You may come and go as you please. You may build your hotel, travel, do whatever you want. But you must leave Roberto here with me. He is my son until I die. Then he is your son. Roberto will inherit everything."

Dimitri was not a man to issue idle threats. Lucky thought about what he had said, and knew it would be a vicious battle if she decided to take the boy. And a fight for what? If she was able to come and go as she pleased, why *not* leave Roberto with Dimitri? He was safe on the island with his father—for kidnapping threats were not uncommon. And he was certainly happy. He had CeeCee to watch over him, and CeeCee loved him almost as much as she did.

After a lot of thought she decided to accept Dimitri's proposal. She would divide her life. Spend part of her time on the island and part in Atlantic City building her hotel. There was no reason for her *not* to accept. Lennie was with Olympia. And if she couldn't have Lennie she did not want anyone. Relationships were out. Caring, needing, loving—they were all out.

Maybe an occasional one-nighter, if she so desired. No commitments. Nothing personal. Just sex.

"You have done a magnificent job, my dear," Costa praised, also rising to greet her.

"Yes, it's unbelievably stupendous!" gushed Ria. Stupendous was her favorite word.

Lucky imagined Ria in her hooker days. She probably said things to her clients like "And you have a stupendous cock!"

Fancy old Uncle Costa marrying a retired call girl.

Lucky controlled mirth and said, "I'm glad you all like it."

She tried not to think mean thoughts about Ria, for she certainly made Uncle Costa happy. Since divorcing Susan, Gino had returned to Vegas and all his old ways. Not that Lucky saw that much of him. She had visited him in Vegas a

few times and he had come to the island on three occasions to
see his grandson. Twice he arrived on his own, and once he
brought a twenty-five-year-old starlet who talked about her
career and her one moment of *real* fame as Centerfold of the
Year in some dumb men's magazine.

"Please," Lucky had said, "find another Susan. But don't
subject me to one of those again."

Gino had grinned. What a grin! "Hey, kid, I thought you
hated Susan."

"I did," she agreed. "It was Paige I liked. Whatever happened to her?"

"The broad was a fake," Gino growled. He did not explain
further.

Lucky really felt that by building the Santangelo Hotel
herself and not turning to Gino for help, she had finally come
to terms with her father and their relationship. She loved him
very much. But she no longer believed that his approval was
the most important thing in the world.

He lived in Vegas.

She lived between Atlantic City and Dimitri's island.

It would have been easy to run back to him when his
marriage failed, or when all the problems happened as she
was building the hotel. And there were *major* problems. She
couldn't prove it, but somebody had made things extremely
tough for her. It was one long uphill battle, with union dis-
putes, strikes, picket lines, fights and constant trouble.

When she investigated, the name of Santino Bonnatti kept
cropping up.

Ah . . . Santino . . . A long time ago they had been uneasy
friends. And then she had been forced to shoot Enzio, his father, and she knew that Santino waited, like a deadly cobra, to
strike and take his revenge.

Once she found out it was Santino who was sabotaging her
progress on the Santangelo, she acted.

One phone call. Without Gino to back her up.

One meeting with a very old man in New York.

A simple request.

After that, the troubles had stopped.

She had been ready to take it a step further if need be. But Santino was basically a coward—she knew him of old. When he received instructions to lay off, he did so—and fast.

Gino looked around, his eyes filled with admiration and pride. "You really did it, kid," he said with warmth. "The place is spectacular. Makes the Magiriano look like a toilet."

Lucky laughed happily. "Not quite." She linked her arm through his. "Hey, let's party. I feel like having fun with my old man."

"Cut the 'old,' kid."

"You got it."

95

The sun streamed through the huge plate-glass windows of the house on Blue Jay Way, but Eden Antonio did not care to remove herself from the king-size bed. She lay beneath the patterned sheets and silently cursed Santino Bonnatti. He had ruined her life.

Oh, God! She should never have hooked up with him in the first place. One look at the hairy-bodied, baldheaded pervert should have warned her. He was scum, the lowest. And steadily, year by year, he was dragging her down to his level. Why hadn't she realized right from the beginning what kind of evil man he was? She was no fool, she had been around. And yet Santino Bonnatti sucked her in. He let her believe she called the shots, and in the long run he would do what *she* wanted.

The truth of the matter was that Santino was in charge. He always had been.

She knew, without a doubt, that she should have got out a long time ago, for slowly and surely he was getting worse all the time. When he reneged on his promise to star her in the movie he financed for Vitos Felicidade, she should have made her move then.

But no. She just sat in the house on Blue Jay Way, guarded by Zeko the baboon, and went along with everything Santino wanted. When she *did* finally get up the courage to split, he refused to let her. "Ya'll go when *I* friggin' wancha to," he had told her ominously. "An' don't worry, I'll let y'know when that day is. Only don't count on it bein' too soon."

So far, the moment had not arrived. She was weak, and she knew it. The longer she put off her escape, the more difficult it would be. And she wasn't getting any younger. . . .

She turned over beneath the sheets and lay flat on her stomach. Nobody would believe her if she told them what was going on. Nobody would believe that in Los Angeles, in 1983, a woman could be kept a sexual prisoner by someone like Santino Bonnatti.

Of course, she could go to the police if she ever got the opportunity—which she didn't—Zeko was on her case all the time. And even if she *did* go to the cops, what then? She had no proof that Santino threatened her constantly, made her do things she found repulsive and obscene, and swore he would carve her face up if she ever ran out on him.

"What about my career?" she demanded as often as possible. "You promised me a movie. You *know* you promised me."

He let the bait dangle, never withdrew it completely. "Ya gotta play the right part," he promised. "When that comes along, it's yours, honey puss."

The right part had not existed in the final script of the Felicidade movie. An established actress had been cast as the love interest. Then Santino had put up the money for *Private Dick,* Lennie Golden's first film. Eden had seen the script and *known* the girl's role was for her. "I want to do it," she had told Santino breathlessly. God! If she could get to Lennie and tell him what was happening to her, he would help her, she knew it.

"I got no input on this one," Santino spat. "I'm just puttin' up the friggin' green stuff on account of the fact I think it'll be a moneymaker."

He was right. *Private Dick* broke records. Lennie Golden became a star. Eden never even got to go to the opening. Santino took his fat wife, while she sat home staring at television, with Zeko lurking in a corner picking his nose.

What a horrible trap she was caught in. She lived in a beautiful house. She had gorgeous clothes, for when Santino took her out he wanted her to knock his friends' eyes out. And what else?

Nothing.

Her life was nothing.

She was nothing.

Restlessly she kicked off the sheets. A Mexican gardener working on the foliage outside nearly dropped his hose.

She reached for the phone. She knew Santino taped all her calls, but she was allowed a couple of girlfriends to have lunch with occasionally. Ulla, and Paige Wheeler—not exactly a girl, but a sympathetic friend. She was tempted to tell Paige everything in the hope that she could help.

Sure. She could really help when Eden hit the hospital with her face carved up and her looks gone forever.

• • • • •

"Faster," ordered Santino to his driver as they sped along the freeway heading for L.A. after a business meeting in San Diego.

"Everything okay, boss?" asked Blackie, seated next to the driver.

"Y'know what I'm gonna put on your tombstone?" Santino growled. "'Everythin' okay, boss?' Ya sound like a fuckin' record."

"Sorry, boss."

"Forget it."

Santino struggled out of his jacket and folded it carefully. The slight aroma of his own sweat twitched at his nostrils. It bothered him. Goddamn deodorants. They never worked. He should go into the deodorant business—he'd own the world. Santino was not in a good mood. It had been a bad week. Lucky Santangelo had finally opened her lousy hotel in Atlantic City and it burned the shit out of him. He had done everything in his power to stop it from happening—put up roadblocks everywhere—and then, just like that, his fucking brother Carlo had called him from New York. "The word is out you're to cease bothering the lady."

The lady! What fucking lady? Lucky Santangelo was a cunt, and one of these days he was going to get her good.

"What word?" Santino screamed. "Who from?"

"There was a meeting yesterday. A vote was taken. You are to stop harassing her."

Santino stopped. He knew who to listen to.

That didn't mean it was over. One of these days he would get the bitch. One of these days . . .

96

Like all good Californians Lennie learned to play tennis. When he wasn't filming he awoke at seven. No need to worry about disturbing Olympia—they had separate bedrooms. Then, after showering and shaving, he sometimes drove over to Ryder Wheeler's house, where they played three punishing sets. Occasionally Paige was around. He enjoyed seeing Ryder's wife. She was a lot of fun and he liked hearing all the latest "trash"—her word for gossip.

When he left there, he went home and worked. Six or seven hours locked in his study with his new toy—a word processor—was not unusual. Sometimes he would break for lunch, sometimes he wouldn't.

He had a few women dotted around the city he could call at any time—usually attractive working females, who were delighted to see him and made no demands. They knew he was married—he could hardly hide it—and they accepted that fact. Occasionally he would visit one of them and just end up talking the afternoon away. Sex was no big deal since Lucky had exited his life. Sex was just . . . getting laid.

He knew he had to leave Olympia. Their marriage meant nothing. He had only stayed to see her through the series of operations which had restored her looks. Besides, he had no pressing reason to make the move. Lucky was not waiting. She didn't give a damn. For three years she had ignored him, not responding to any of his attempts to contact her. She was still with Dimitri—and it burned the hell out of him.

However, enough was *more* than enough. Olympia's looks were finally regained. So was her personality. She was the same rich spoiled heiress, and when he wasn't locked away working—which was most of the time—they fought constantly.

"I think we should get a divorce," he told her one day, as they skidded out of yet another fight.

She stopped mid-sentence and stared at him. Pained blue eyes in a piggy face. "I don't want a divorce," she said quickly.

"Hey—listen." He walked to the bar and fixed himself a bourbon. "We were never a match made in heaven."

"How can you say that?"

"Maybe because it's true."

"Just because I'm slightly overweight—"

"It has nothing to do with your weight."

"Oh, yes, it does," she yelled. "You hate me because you think I'm fat, you lousy bastard. It wasn't *my* fault I was in a plane crash. It wasn't *my* fault—"

Oh, shit. Freedom was not going to be easy. Every time he brought it up it was the same old story.

"Sonofabitch," she mumbled. "Why don't *you* desert me too? Everyone else has. Big fucking movie star. Take off, Lennie. You think I care? Shit. I don't care. Maybe I'll kill myself—would that be more convenient for you? Would you like that?" She began to sob theatrically.

"Cut it out, Olympia," he said grimly. "You know I'm not going to leave until you're ready."

He meant what he said. After all, he had nowhere to go. And her suicide threats, which she made often, bothered him. He didn't want to feel responsible if anything happened to her.

He knew Lucky was about to open the hotel she had built in Atlantic City. Some PR had sent them an invitation to the opening. For one wild moment he had contemplated attending. But what good would it do? Screw Lucky Santangelo.

He hated her.

No he didn't.

Yes he did.

Lucky . . . Lucky . . . she was with him every day.

Once a month Dimitri telephoned and spoke dutifully to

his daughter. It was always the same conversation. The "How are you?" speech, Lennie called it. The duty call.

"I can't stand him!" Olympia always shrieked when she slammed down the phone. "I don't know why he bothers. He treated me as if I didn't exist when I was in the hospital practically dead. And I hate that bitch he's married to as well. Lucky fucking Santangelo. You know something? He wishes *I* was the one who died in the crash, not his precious Francesca."

Although he didn't voice an opinion, Lennie was inclined to agree with her. Dimitri obviously couldn't care less if he ever saw his daughter again. She was a sorry reminder of his lost love. But his granddaughter, Brigette, was another matter. She spent most of her vacations with Dimitri, and that suited Olympia just fine. In fact, Brigette had not visited them for over a year, although she was due to arrive within days, shortly after attending the opening of Lucky's new hotel.

The last time she had been at the house was with dear old Alice, who turned up with an out-of-work actor of twenty and a raving queen of fifty. The three of them got drunk and very disorderly, and Lennie had never invited her back. Alice complained at first, but he discovered that if he sent her money— lots of it—she shut up and left him alone. He hadn't seen her in over a year.

Thank Christ he had his work. It was all-consuming. He didn't think about much else. Writing and starring in movies was a twenty-five-hour-a-day occupation. No time to worry about real life and what might have been. Just get on out there and do it.

• • • • •

Jess loved lunching with Paige Wheeler. Paige was the only person she could be seen in public with and not feel short, for Paige was only inches taller than she. And Paige talked dirty. None of the Hollywood bullshit for her. She said what was on her mind, and it was usually outrageous and funny.

"Did you ever go to bed with Lennie?" Paige asked, as soon as they were settled at a table in the Bistro Garden.

"What kind of a question is that?" Jess giggled. "He's my friend. You don't go to bed with your best friend."

"Oh, no?" Paige winked.

"You're terrible!" Jess said, laughing.

The women had become friendly when Ryder started producing Lennie's movies.

"I can ask, can't I?" chided Paige. "I think he's very hot-looking. Sometimes the hot ones turn out to be duds in bed."

"Not Lennie."

"I thought you said—"

"His reputation goes before him. Don't forget, I've known him since we were kids."

They consulted the menu and ordered a light lunch.

"I'm going to Atlantic City this weekend," Jess confided over the chopped salad.

"Anything or anyone I should know about?" Paige asked, twirling her fingers around the stem of a wineglass.

Jess's eyes were sparkling. "There's this guy—an older man—"

"The best kind," Paige murmured.

"He sort of liked me—once," Jess continued. "But, you know, he was one of those guys that had it on offer all the time—so I didn't jump."

"Good for you. Although *I'm* always wondering what I might have missed!"

"When I went back to Vegas a few years ago with Lennie, he was different. Like he didn't come on, he was very cool and—"

Paige finished the sentence for her. "—naturally you wanted him at once."

"How did you know?"

"Simple. It's always that way. They want you—you don't want *them*. You want them—they don't want you." She leaned forward with interest. "What's happened now?"

Jess grinned. "He wants *me*. I think."

"And do you——?"

"Yes!"

Paige nodded with satisfaction. "That's wonderful. Who is he? And does he deserve you?"

"His name is Matt Traynor. He used to run the Magiriano Hotel in Vegas for Gino Santangelo. Now he's running Lucky Santangelo's new hotel in Atlantic City. He's kind of fiftyish, and——"

Paige tuned out as Jess gave a full description of Matt. The sound of Gino's name evoked embarrassing memories. He never *had* allowed her to explain——and what could she have said anyway?

"——and so he called and invited me for the weekend. Says he *has* to talk to me and can't do it on the phone."

"Sounds good to me," said Paige encouragingly.

Jess grinned. "I hope so. To tell you the truth, if I have to go out on *one more* date and make stupid conversation, I'll ace myself!"

• • • • •

Olympia called one of her drug dealers. She had several. They knew her well and trusted her. Dealing by mail was usually out. But for Olympia Stanislopoulos, anything was possible.

She hoarded drugs. She had a formidable supply. And she had the best place in the world to keep her stash——a secret room shown her by the realtor on the day they moved into the Bel Air mansion. While Lennie was downstairs the realtor had led Olympia to the back of her dressing area, pressed a hidden button, and there, revealed by a sliding panel, was a small windowless room. "To keep your dope in," the realtor had joked.

Ha ha. Some joke.

"Don't tell my husband," she had said quickly. "It's a great place to hide Christmas presents."

Never again would she be without drugs. Never. Never. Never.

Being in the plane crash was bad enough——she had ongoing nightmares about *that*. But when they deprived her of cocaine and grass and pills—all the things that kept life worth living—she was outraged.

Now she had a hoard of everything. The hidden room looked like a hospital storeroom.

After she'd called her dealer and put in an order, she examined her face in the mirror and fingered her soft new skin. She was pretty again, perhaps even prettier than before the accident.

She sucked in her cheeks and imagined herself thin. Ah . . . when she was thin she would conquer the world. She would emerge from hiding and surprise everyone with her beauty.

She would surprise Flash.

That bum.

She would have him again. For sure.

97

Y ou have too much makeup on," scolded Lucky. "But you look great anyway—so don't sweat it."

"Too much makeup?" squealed Brigette. "Like I usually wear twice this amount!"

"Where? In class?"

"No. Out of class. My favorite place!"

Lucky hugged her. The young girl reminded her so much of Olympia at the same age. She was very fond of the child— although Brigette was hardly a child anymore. She was almost as tall as Lucky and looked eighteen.

"I'm glad you're here," Lucky said warmly. "And the dress we picked is just right."

"Nice and virginal." Brigette winked.

Lucky smiled. "If you say so." She put her arm around the girl's shoulder. "Come along, I want you to sit with Gino and Costa."

Brigette gazed around the crowded ballroom. She was excited to be at the opening of the Santangelo. But it wasn't cool to be excited, and above all, tonight of all nights, she wanted to radiate cool.

As they walked toward their table she thought she spotted John Travolta, and wasn't that Cheryl Tiegs? And . . . holy shit . . . it couldn't be, but it was, actor Tim Wealth. He was twenty-six and *fantastic!* Like she could *die* for him, and here she was right in the same room!

Gino greeted her with a kiss on the hand. "Quite a young lady now," he said. "And a very pretty one too."

She liked Lucky's father. He was old, but he was more fun than Dimitri, who sat in a rocking chair all day gazing out to sea with a mournful expression on his craggy face. Brigette knew she was fortunate to be at the opening. She had been begging Lucky for months, via letter and phone from Switzerland, to allow her to come.

"Just for a couple of days," Lucky had finally said. "Then you have to go straight to California to see your mother. She's expecting you."

Brigette wished she didn't have to leave at all. Spending the summer with Olympia was a depressing thought. Her mother was so weird and fat and uncool. Brigette would have been perfectly happy spending the whole vacation with Lucky. Now *she* was cool.

*   *   *   *   *

It was a marvelous evening, and all seemed to be enjoying themselves. Lucky had put together an experienced and innovative management team headed by Matt Traynor, whom Gino had allowed her to steal.

Matt, looking dapper in a new tuxedo, his gray hair cropped close to his head, seemed to have acquired a new girlfriend. She was short, with curly hair and a great body. Lucky knew she had seen her somewhere before, but she couldn't quite remember where, until Matt introduced them. Then it all fell into place. Jess. The croupier from Las Vegas whose baby had drowned. Lennie's friend. Lennie's manager.

Lucky smiled at her. "It's good to see you, and congratulations on all your success with Lennie Golden." *How is he? Does he ever talk about me? Is he happy?*

"Your hotel's incredible," Jess exclaimed. "It must have been some project to put together."

"It was," Lucky replied. Did Jess know about her and Lennie? No. Nobody knew. It was their secret.

"Anyway . . ." Jess gestured around the magnificent ballroom filled with a glittering array of first-night guests. "It's really something."

"Thank you." *Does Lennie miss me? I miss him.*

"Hi, Brigette." Jess leaned across the table. "I haven't seen you in ages. I hardly recognized you. You look so adult!"

"Oh. Hi."

"I hear you're coming out to visit."

"Yes." Brigette fidgeted uncomfortably. She was fed up with being polite to everyone. Sweet little Brigette in the virginal white dress. My! Hasn't she grown up! They should only know.

Across the room she watched Tim Wealth get up from his table and wander off. He was probably as bored as she was. Quickly she stood up. "I've got to go to the bathroom," she whispered to Lucky.

Without hesitation Brigette set off in the same direction as the young actor.

• • • • •

There were stars from every field at the opening. Lucky moved from table to table, smiling, greeting, welcoming. It wasn't her job, but she knew how to do it better than anyone.

It was a high-profile party. Vitos Felicidade entertained, the champagne flowed, there were silver bowls of caviar on every table and all the food was gourmet.

Lucky had invited Dimitri, and for one moment she had thought he would accept. But no, he decided against leaving his island. In three years she had watched him grow into an old man. It seemed that when Francesca went, his will to live went with her. All he wanted to do was stay on his island and vegetate, handing his business affairs over to minions and taking no interest in anything or anyone except Roberto and Brigette. His son and his grandchild kept him alive.

Lucky came and went as she pleased, and while she was building the Santangelo it suited her fine. Now that the hotel was finished and Roberto was reaching school age, she wasn't sure if she wanted to continue this arrangement. Roberto was four and a half, a sturdy, quiet little boy. Was he to grow up in isolation with Dimitri looming over him? As it was now, the only friends he had were the children of servants on the island.

Brigette was another matter. She arrived for vacations,

swam, sunbathed and water-skied. Then she returned to the real world—if you could call an expensive private girls' school in Switzerland the real world.

Lucky had enjoyed watching her change from an impossible whining brat into a pretty young teenager. And it was especially pleasing that she treated Roberto as if he was her younger brother.

Brigette *never* wanted to visit Olympia, who appeared not to care at all. In a way Lucky felt like the child's surrogate mother. She didn't mind the responsibility, which had been hers ever since Nanny Mabel was dismissed at Brigette's insistence when she was twelve. Lucky took over willingly. She had tried to teach Brigette certain values and a sense of independence. She had also given her advice on everything from drugs to boys.

Brigette was not looking forward to spending the summer with Olympia, but Lucky persuaded Dimitri to make sure she would. "Maybe now that Brigette is growing up, the two of them will get along," she urged. "If they don't do it now, they never will."

As a consolation prize Lucky had allowed Brigette to attend the opening of the Santangelo, and the young girl certainly seemed to be loving every minute.

• • • • •

"I thought we might get married," Matt said formally. "It seems ridiculous for you to come all this way without us doing *something* to commemorate the occasion."

Jess could not believe what she was hearing. Several years of silence, then this.

"What do you think?" he continued matter-of-factly.

"Uh—" she stared at him dumbly. "I . . . uh . . . *married?*"

"Yes. Unless you think it's the worst idea you've ever heard in your life."

She shook her head. "Why?" she asked blankly.

"Why not?"

She recovered her composure. "Shall I give you a list?"

He backed away. "Forget I suggested it."

"Why?"

"Will you stop saying 'Why'?"

"Matt."

"Yes."

"I don't think it's such a weird idea."

• • • • •

Brigette was outside the men's room when Tim Wealth emerged. "Hi," she said brightly, as if they were old friends.

He looked around to see if she was addressing someone else.

"I'm speaking to you," she said boldly. "We met. Remember?"

Tim Wealth was tall and gangly, with a thin face, intense eyes and longish brown hair. He wore a rented tuxedo, black shirt and a small gold stud in one ear. He had made one movie two years before and had been hailed as the hottest newcomer of the year. Since that—nothing. Not one single script came his way.

Who could explain the vagaries of the film industry? Certainly not Tim Wealth.

After holding out for eighteen months he was finally reduced to guesting on bad TV shows. After that it was all downhill. Now he was in Atlantic City with a gay producer who promised him more than a crack at his skinny ass.

"Where did we meet?" he asked, looking her over. "I think I've got Alzheimer's, and I'm too young to die."

Brigette blinked. "What?"

"Forget it."

She couldn't believe she was actually talking to him. "I saw your movie six times," she said excitedly. "Why haven't you made any more?"

"Good question," he said dourly.

"My stepfather's an actor."

"That's exciting."

"His name's Lennie Golden. Do you know him?"

"Do bears shit in the woods?"

"Pardon?"

"Forget it."

Brigette soldiered on. "My sort of aunt owns this hotel."

"And who is your sort of aunt?"

"Lucky Santangelo. Have you seen her?"

"Could I miss her?"

"Are you with a girl?"

"Are you offering your services for the night?"

Brigette felt a tingle of excitement. Tim Wealth was even better in the flesh than on the screen. "Yes," she said quickly.

He stared at her quizzically. "How old are you?"

She didn't hesitate. "Eighteen," she lied. "And you?"

"I'm twenty-six pushing fifty. And if this evening goes on much longer, I'll be pushing sixty."

She giggled. "You're bored."

He raised an eyebrow. "You're smart."

"Where do you live?" she asked enthusiastically.

"L.A.," he replied.

"I'm going there tomorrow," she announced proudly.

"What d'you want, a medal?"

She giggled again and thrust her bosom to the limit in the virginal white dress Lucky had chosen.

He could not help but notice. And although Tim Wealth swung both ways, a magnificent pair of boobs always intrigued him. And his producer friend wouldn't come up to the suite for hours. "Want to see my feet?" he questioned.

"Your *feet?*"

"My toes are famous."

"Honestly?"

"Are you for real?"

"What?"

"Follow me, little girl."

· · · · ·

"Where's Brigette?" Lucky asked.

"Never mind about Brigette. When am I gonna see my grandson again?" Gino responded.

"Soon," Lucky promised.

"Why don't you bring him back to America where he belongs?" Gino asked testily.

Yes. Why didn't she? The time had come.

But how? Dimitri would never agree.

"I'm going to," she said firmly.

"Good, good." He leaned back and looked around. The place was jumping. He couldn't have done it better himself. A lot of the party guests had already drifted out to the tables, and the satisfying whirl of roulette wheels filled the air.

"Where *is* Brigette?" Lucky asked again, but her attention was taken by Vitos Felicidade, who came by the table, trailed by his entourage, to tell her what a magnificent party it was.

She smiled. "Thank you, Vitos." He was costing her a fortune, but the way the audience loved the Spanish singer made him worth every cent.

He had hangdog melancholy brown eyes. "Would you care for a drink?" he asked. His English was much improved.

"I have a drink," she replied.

His eyes signaled an invitation. "Weeth me."

Vitos Felicidade was a heartthrob. Millions of women worldwide bought his records and desired his body. For Lucky he did nothing.

"I'm just too busy tonight," she replied with charm. "Maybe some other time."

He rather liked being turned down; it was a refreshing change. "Mebee." He winked roguishly. "Mebee not."

What *was* she going to do later when the party was finished? She was on a high, the adrenaline pumping. There was no way she would want to be alone.

Sex.

Why not?

With a stranger. Someone she would never have to see again.

• • • • •

"Drink it."

"Suck it."

"Snort it."

Tim Wealth issued a list of instructions, and Brigette obeyed because she was overawed to be in his presence.

He made her drink neat vodka, and it was disgusting, like medicine. But she drank it all down anyway because she didn't want to look like a baby.

Then he unzipped his fly, told her to kneel in front of him, and thrust his "thing" into her mouth. Only *his* "thing" wasn't like those of the boys from the village near her school. His was limp and wobbly, like a soft rubber toy.

She did her best but nothing happened, and she didn't really mind. How she hated that moment when the warm salty liquid exploded in her mouth. *She* hated it, but boys loved it. Tim Wealth seemed different.

Pushing her away, he stuffed himself back into his trousers and walked across the room. Fumbling in a drawer, he came up with a small packet of white powder which he carefully arranged in two straight lines on a marble table top. Then he handed her a rolled banknote and issued his third command. "Snort it."

She knew what it was. Cocaine. One of the girls at school— a rich Arab's daughter—did it all the time.

Brigette had smoked grass, but this was her first time with coke. She sniffed gingerly, spluttered and choked, and the two neat lines of white powder scattered everywhere.

"Shit!" exclaimed Tim. "What are you, a fucking novice?"

"I'm sorry," she gasped.

"You should be," he complained, laying out more of his precious supply. "Now snort it. Properly."

Her second attempt was more successful, and suddenly she felt *soooo* good.

"Undress," Tim Wealth commanded.

She hesitated for only a moment. Usually boys undressed *her,* and it was in a dark field or the back of someone's car. This was different. *He* was different.

She did as he requested, shedding her white dress, bra and panties with feverish abandon. She felt funny—sort of excited and strange and expectant.

When she was fully undressed he produced his "thing" again, and this time it was big and hard and red. And he made her kneel on the floor doggy style. He entered her from this position fast and furious.

She stifled a frantic yell. He was hurting her, but at the same time waves of feeling washed over her, and she felt a loss of control. *Wonderful* waves of feeling.

Something was happening to her and she didn't understand what.

He slapped her on the ass, hard, and began to thrust like a madman.

The good feelings combined with the bad, and she cried out, begging him to stop.

He didn't do so until he was ready. Then he exploded with a sigh, and rolled away from her across the floor.

She shivered and tried to get up. When she did, her legs were weak and shaking and she felt the stickiness of blood.

"Get dressed, little girl, and go home," he mumbled sleepily from his position on the floor. "I'll see you around."

Didn't he realize he had taken her virginity?

Obviously not.

She didn't know what else to do, so she gathered her clothes together and dressed quickly. Then she wrote her name and the phone number of Olympia and Lennie's house in L.A. on a message pad, which she then propped against the phone.

Tim Wealth was asleep.

His satisfied snores followed her out the door.

• • • • •

"I want to phone Lennie," Jess said.

Matt smiled. "You know, I used to think you were having an affair with him. I tried to like him, but I was jealous as hell."

"Idiot!" She grinned. "Why has it taken you all this time to tell me how you feel?"

He threw up his arms. "Listen to you. Anyone would think that you *welcomed* me when I first came on to you. Your attitude was a killer, my dear."

"Well, you were a jerk." Hastily she added, "Then."

"Thanks."

"You're welcome."

"I wish we were in Vegas now, we could do it tonight."

Her grin widened. "Oh, we'll do it tonight."

"We will?"

"You betcha ass, Mr. Traynor."

• • • • •

"There you are!" exclaimed Lucky. "Where have you been?"

"Exploring," replied Brigette innocently, her cheeks flushed, but other than that her appearance quite normal.

"I don't like you disappearing," Lucky admonished. "If you want to go off exploring, tell me, and I'll arrange for someone to go with you."

"I'm not a baby," Brigette objected, thinking to herself that at last she was fully grown up, for surely the sensations she had recently experienced with Tim Wealth made her a real woman. He had taken her virginity, and she was glad it was him and not some creepy village boy.

"I know you're not," Lucky said patiently. "But you *are* a very important young lady, who one day is going to inherit a great deal of money. And you can't just wander off without telling me where you're going. Your grandfather would throw a fit."

"I understand," said Brigette, although she didn't at all.

Sometimes Lucky could be as dumb as all the other adults. "Actually, I'm kind of tired. Is it okay if I go to bed now?"

"Certainly," agreed Lucky, relieved to have the responsibility of Brigette off her hands for the night.

• • • • •

"I'm getting married," Jess announced, long distance.

"To Matt?" Lennie replied, delighted for her.

"No! The bellman at the hotel, asshole!"

"When?"

"Soon."

"Hey—are we having a big wedding?" he joked.

"I don't know what we're having, but whatever it is I want you to be my best man."

"The groom has a best man—you have a maid of honor."

"Screw tradition. I want a best man," she said stubbornly.

"Then you shall have me."

"*Now* you offer yourself!"

He tried to keep his voice casual. "What's the hotel like?"

"Amazing."

"Have you seen Lucky?"

"Sure."

"How does she look?"

"Amazing."

"You really are a mine of information."

"I'll tell you all when I return."

• • • • •

By 3:30 A.M. the last stragglers left the party. Lucky sat at a table with Matt and Jess, Gino, and a pretty showgirl he had charmed.

The indefatigable Gino. Was there no stopping him?

Obviously not. He rose to leave, the showgirl in tow. "This is a late night for me," he said, putting his arm around the girl. "I'm an old man. I'm not used to all this activity."

"Oh, yes you are." Lucky grinned.

Gino winked and kissed his daughter. "You're one of life's winners, kid," he whispered affectionately. "Don't ever forget it."

"He's really something, my old man," she sighed as he departed.

"We should all have such . . . uh . . . energy at his age," Matt said admiringly.

"Is that what they call it?" said Lucky jauntily.

Jess sipped the remnants of champagne from a glass on the table. "When I worked at the Magiriano," she said, "*all* the girls lusted for a night in Mr. Santangelo's company."

"Really?" Lucky smiled. She wasn't surprised.

"And the ones who made the trip *never* returned disappointed."

"I don't know if I should be hearing this," Lucky laughed.

"I thought *I* was the resident stud," interjected Matt.

"You were the resident joke!" teased Jess.

Lucky feigned a yawn. She wanted to be alone. Much as she liked Matt—and Jess, who she was gradually getting to know—it had been a long night and she needed tranquility or anonymous sex. Either would do.

"I'm going to bed," she said. "And may I suggest you two do the same?"

"Good suggestion," said Matt.

"Yes," agreed Jess, feeling shy for the first time in years.

Lucky stood up, and so did they. "I'm very pleased for you both," she said warmly. "Very pleased."

Jess gazed up at Matt—so far from the type of man she usually went for she couldn't even believe it. "So am I," she murmured.

As they walked from the ballroom Lucky turned casually to Jess. "And how is Lennie?" she asked in a throwaway manner.

Jess, who of course knew everything, picked her words carefully.

"He's well," she said slowly. "Working hard. Sometimes I think his only pleasure in life is work."

Lucky digested *that* piece of information while they said their goodnights at the elevator.

Once upstairs in her penthouse she couldn't sleep. She thought about what Jess had said. *Sometimes I think his only pleasure in life is work. . . .* How true. If she didn't have Roberto, she would feel the same way.

Lennie . . . Lennie . . . Lennie . . . He haunted her thoughts.

She decided to change clothes and go out. There was an all-night Western bar she knew of where the action never stopped. With haste she stepped from her dress, and as she reached for jeans and a shirt, her phone rang. For one wild moment she imagined it might be Lennie. Quickly she picked up.

"Meesis Stanislopoulos." A foreign accent, the line long distance.

She had a sudden premonition of bad news, and her heart began to beat much too fast. Roberto. *Please God, let nothing have happened to Roberto.*

Her voice was tremulous when she spoke. "Yes?"

"I'm so sorry . . ."

"What?" she screamed, fearing for her son.

"Meester Stanislopoulos . . . a massive stroke . . . no time to summon you . . . he died an hour ago."

98

Jury selection took days. Every time Steven approved a juror, the opposing counsel would object. And vice versa. But at last a jury was settled upon, and things could begin.

Mary Lou appeared in court from day one. She sat on the front bench and watched intently as the case unfolded.

It took a week. Moore versus Bonnatti. And at the end of that time Steven felt pretty confident they were going to win. As a witness, Mary Lou had conducted herself impeccably, whereas the opposition had presented nothing but men in three-piece suits with weak excuses, shifty eyes and slicked-back hair.

Bonnatti himself did not appear. Steven wished he had. He would have liked to have seen his face when the jury returned a verdict of sixteen million dollars in Mary Lou's favor.

She was ecstatic. "It's not the money! It's not the money!" she kept on repeating excitedly. "I feel like Clint Eastwood. I stood up for something on principle, and I won!"

"They'll appeal," Steven warned. "With an award this large, it could be drastically reduced."

"I don't care," she shouted. "This is my victory, and nobody can take it away from me!"

He took her out to celebrate. They celebrated all night, and he found himself in bed with a twenty-year-old television star with whom he had no intention of getting involved. She was disarmingly young and pretty and sweet.

"What am I doing here?" Steven groaned, after they made love.

"Didn't you enjoy it?" Mary Lou asked, her brown eyes wide and innocent. She knew only too well he had enjoyed himself every inch of the way.

"What a question!" he exclaimed, eying her gorgeously

compact body, the color of milk chocolate—perhaps a shade lighter than his own skin.

"I had a perfectly fantastic time." She grinned. "I guess it's true what they say about lawyers."

"And *what* do they say about lawyers?"

She giggled. "That if you get a good one he'll be on your case forever! Steven, you sure do have stamina!"

He couldn't help laughing. God, she was pretty. But of course he must never let this happen again.

He spent the night, and in the morning he informed her sternly that it was not going to work.

She smiled happily and said, "I absolutely agree with you." Then she wrapped herself around him and he was lost in her sweetness.

Making love to Mary Lou was special, and he knew it, and so did she.

When he finally left her apartment she said, "I'll cook you dinner tonight."

"I told you," he replied, "this relationship is not going to work."

"Sure." She grinned. "Let's not make it work together. Be here at seven. I give great Chinese food."

Within a week she had moved from her apartment into his house.

"God help you," cautioned Jerry.

"Isn't she a little young for you?" ventured Carrie.

Steven agreed with both of them. But Mary Lou took the bitterness out of him.

He had never been happier in his life.

• • • • •

"We have a great offer. A firm offer," Anna Robb said. "I want you to guess who it's from."

Carrie shook her head. "I have no idea."

"That's good," said Anna smugly. "Because you'd never guess."

"Who?"

"Do you really want to know?"

It was unlike Anna to be so playful. Carrie was beginning to get aggravated. "Yes," she said shortly. "Kindly tell me."

Anna took a deep breath. "A half-million dollars. A quarter on signing. A quarter on publication. A quarter on paperback publication. And the rest six months later."

"Who bought it?" demanded Carrie.

"Fred!" exclaimed Anna. "Can you believe it? Fred Lester. The original tightwad."

"Fred," repeated Carrie.

"Yes, my dear. And he bought it because it's the best biography he's read in years, and he thinks it will be a giant smash. He says, and I quote, 'The honesty in this book made me want to cry.' Now for Fred Lester to say something like that—"

Anna continued talking, but Carrie stopped listening. She was on the road to revealing her story to the world. And it wasn't just her story, it was Steven's too, and she should have asked him.

". . . Fred wants to see you. Tomorrow if possible." Anna beamed. Carrie had never seen her so happy. "He has big plans."

Big plans. Oh, God. Perhaps she had made a mistake. Sharing her life's secrets with Anna was one thing, but spreading them across the country was something else entirely.

"I don't know—" she began.

"You don't know what?" shouted Anna, quite out of character. "Smile, for goodness' sake. Smile, Carrie. You are going to be the most famous Black woman in America!"

99

Cocksuckers!" screamed Santino Bonnatti. "Whadda they think I am? A dummy? A mark? If they think they'll ever see two fuckin' cents of sixteen mill, they're pissin' in a high fuckin' wind. Donatella!" He yelled for his wife.

She took her time coming into the room. And then she glared at him and his henchmen. "Your language. You gotta filthy language problem," she said. "You thinka the kids they no hear?"

Some dumb spade was hitting him for sixteen million big ones and Donatella was worried about the kids. "Fuck the children!" he yelled.

"Fucka you!" responded Donatella. She crossed herself and gazed ceilingward. "Ah, God, you shoulda forgive me. I'ma married to a pig!"

"The pig who pays the bills," growled Santino.

"Whata you want?" demanded Donatella, placing large hands on ample hips. "You want I kissa your ass?"

He glared at her. "I'm going out," he said grimly. "If any reporters call, tell them no comment."

"Whatsa no comment?"

"Just say it. You don't have to understand it." With that, he stamped from the house. Goddamn it! He bought her everything she wanted, she lived in a fucking palace, and the fat bitch couldn't even speak proper English. Was it any wonder he ran to Eden for a little class—and a little ass?

He almost guffawed at his own wit. And then he scowled as he remembered the bad news. His lawyer in New York was a prick. He should have defended the case himself. This was America—you could goddamn well print what you liked— and if the stupid cooze had posed with no clothes on, then he was entitled to print the pictures. And anything else he wanted.

No shithead judge was going to tell Santino Bonnatti what to do.

· · · · ·

Eden had just finished working out when Santino arrived. He stomped into the living room like Little Caesar, sweating in his silk shirt and three-piece suit. With a grunt he threw himself into an armchair, spread his legs, unzipped his fly and commanded, "Give me a blow job."

Eden was outraged. Zeko was in the corner of the room playing solitaire. The maid was vacuuming out in the hall. A pool man worked outside.

"I've had it with you," she said bravely. There was nothing he could do to her with all these people around.

Before she even realized it he was up from the chair and upon her, short arms flailing wildly.

Slap. Slap. Shove. Slap.

She fought back. "You *bastard!*"

The diamond pinky ring on his little finger ripped into the smooth skin of her cheek and drew blood.

"I *hate* you!" she cried in a fury, clutching her cheek.

Zeko did not look up from his game. The maid continued to vacuum. The pool man shook solution into the pool.

Eden rushed into the bathroom and stared into the mirror in horror. Her face was ruined.

Santino followed her, a plaintive whine in his voice. "Why'dja always gotta give me a hard time?" he questioned. "Ya ask for trouble. I got other things on my mind."

She soaked cotton wool in witch hazel and carefully bathed her cheek.

"I gotta put up with shit at home. I come here t'get my rocks off and relax."

She ignored him.

He caught sight of his reflection in the mirror beside her and straightened his tie. It pissed him off that he was practically bald. But what was it they said? Bald head, big prick.

Talking of which:

"Get down on ya knees, honey."

Honey? He was calling her honey. He was asking her to suck him off after what he'd done.

No way.

She was through.

Somehow she had to get out.

•   •   •   •   •

Two days later Santino informed her the perfect part had finally arrived. He threw a script at her.

She had not forgiven him for messing up her face, but she read the script anyway and cringed.

Pure pornography.

"Tits 'n' ass," he argued. "*Soft* porn. There's a big difference. Ya don' wanna do it, I'll find someone else."

She read the script again. Maybe with a few changes here and there, cut out the rape scene, work on the girl's *character*. It *was* a starring role.

"Who's the director?" she demanded.

"Ryder wants to take a shot."

"He's a producer."

"Reagan was a fuckin' actor. Look at him today."

"Who's my co-star?"

"A kid by the name of Tim Wealth."

She tried to keep her face impassive. Tim Wealth. The young actor she had run away to L.A. with when she dumped Lennie in New York five years ago.

"Ya ever heard of him?" he asked.

"No," she lied.

"Nor have I," spat Santino. "But they say he's good. Ya wanna do it or what?"

She sighed.

And said yes.

Tits 'n' ass was better than nothing.

100

The funeral of Dimitri Stanislopoulos, held on his private island, was a somber affair. The day was overcast and foggy in a week filled with sunshine. His friends and business associates came from all across the world to pay their respects. Lucky, dressed in black, held the hand of Roberto, who really didn't understand what was going on. Brigette, denied a trip to visit her mother, stood nearby as the coffin was lowered into the ground. Gino had insisted on accompanying Lucky to the island to lend his support. And so had Costa and his wife. Olympia had failed to show up—a sign of disrespect that would have horrified Dimitri.

"I understand that Mrs. Golden is sick," the family lawyer informed Lucky.

"What's the matter with her?"

The lawyer cleared his throat. "I don't believe she has fully recovered from her accident."

"That was three years ago," Lucky pointed out.

"I know," the lawyer replied sagely. "But I understand that she plans to be well enough to attend the reading of Mr. Stanislopoulos's will."

Sarcasm scorched her voice. "Naturally."

Burying Dimitri was a strange sensation for Lucky. She did not feel like a bereaved widow. She felt as if she had lost a friend—for, once she had accepted Dimitri's terms concerning Roberto, they had gotten along pretty well. Since Francesca's death he had been neither husband nor lover. But he had been a wise adviser and an excellent father to his son. She would miss him.

What now? She had her freedom *and* Roberto. She could take him wherever she wanted. The world was wide open.

Only now that she had it, she didn't know what to do with it.

. . . . .

Olympia would have attended her father's funeral; she wanted to. But how could she when she looked like a baby elephant?

When she received the news, she did not believe Dimitri had died. He couldn't do such a thing to her. They had been having a cold war. Eventually Dimitri would apologize for his blatant neglect, she would forgive him, and things would return to normal.

But that couldn't happen now that he had died on her.

First she was frustrated, then angry, and finally she broke down and sobbed bitter tears. All her life Dimitri had been the rock in the background waiting to save her from her escapades. When she was a child he had rescued her from an unloving mother and allowed her to live with him. When she was a teenager he had dealt with furious teachers who wished to expel her from every school she attended. And when she was a woman he had paid off her husbands and seen to it that her life ran smoothly. With Dimitri Stanislopoulos as a father she had never had to worry about anything.

Now he was gone.

And it was all Lucky's fault.

"That bitch killed him," she informed Lennie. "The hotel isn't enough for her. That bitch wants all his money."

"What are you talking about?" She was driving him nuts. Three years of penal servitude was enough—he could not take any more.

"It all started when he married her," Olympia ranted. "*She's* the one who prevented him from coming to see me in the hospital. She was always jealous of me."

"He *came* to the hospital."

"Once!" Olympia spat. "And then somehow she got him to stay on the island." She nodded her head. "I don't know how she did it, but she killed him."

"You're talking crap."

"Am I?" Olympia fixed him with baleful blue eyes. "What is it with you and that bitch? Why do you always defend her?" It was not the first time they had discussed Lucky and Olympia had roared with fury and hate. "I should know her better than you do," she continued. "When we were in school together I *thought* she was a friend. But believe me, she's evil, and she killed Dimitri. I know she did."

There was no arguing with Olympia once she had made up her mind.

• • • • •

As soon as Jess arrived back in L.A. she called Lennie.

"Can I see you at once?" she asked.

"Meet me in the Polo Lounge," he said. "I feel like getting out of the house."

They met at lunchtime, and Jess couldn't wait to flash her sapphire-and-diamond engagement ring at him.

He kissed her and wished her the best, then said, "I suppose this is where we go our own way."

She waved at an agent lunching with two blond clients. "Are you kidding?" she exclaimed. "I'm not giving up ten percent of you. Absolutely not." She ordered a Bloody Mary and a Neil McCarthy salad, while Lennie opted for a screwdriver and scrambled eggs. "Matt and I have discussed it," she continued earnestly. "And I'm going to commute."

"Between here and Atlantic City?"

"No. I thought Leningrad and Paris might be more fun!"

"Ha ha. Another comedian."

"It'll work out fine. I have the office here, and the accountant and the secretaries. Instead of putting in an everyday appearance, I'll do three days a week. The rest of the time I'm only a phone call away. Does that suit you?"

He shrugged. "Whatever you want. I thought you were going to give it all up and iron shirts."

She giggled. "Fuck you!"

He leaned closer. "Promises, promises!"

She took a healthy gulp of her Bloody Mary. "Listen, star. Thank God we never did."

A statuesque brunette in a sweeping red outfit stopped by the table. She was no juvenile, but she was remarkably striking. "Hi, Lennie," she rasped.

He had no idea who she was. "Hey—how're you doin'?"

"My agent tells me you're casting. Any roles for a ballsy old broad?"

Bingo! She was a movie star from the sixties who hadn't worked in ten years. Once, in his teens, he had lusted after her body. "Why don't I write one in?" he deadpanned.

"Why don't you?" She licked her lips and slipped him her card. "Call any time," she murmured as she undulated out.

"Pulling older ladies?" teased Jess.

"Anything that comes my way, pal."

The Polo Lounge was in action. A male movie star, suffering from one face-lift too many, paused at the entrance to make sure everyone got a good look at him. Two would-be starlets in tighter-than-tight toreador pants and second-skin sweaters giggled their way in.

"Did I tell you I saw Lucky?" Jess remarked casually.

Lennie observed the starlet duo. They swayed in the breeze, while a tall dude with a mustache whisked them to his table.

Lennie took a hefty swig of his screwdriver. "How is she?" he asked, just as casual as Jess.

"Not as icy as I used to think she was. In fact, she was great to me. And the hotel is a mind-blower. If you ever want to play a room again . . ."

Jess began describing the hotel, while Lennie considered what might have been. Yeah. What might have been if Lucky had wanted him as much as he had wanted her.

But obviously she hadn't. Staying with Dimitri and building her hotel had taken top priority.

He wondered what she would do now Dimitri was dead.

Olympia had asked him to accompany her to New York for the reading of the will. He didn't start shooting the new movie for several months, and for once he was blocked on writing, so he thought he might.

Sure.

Be casual about it.

He was going to see Lucky again after three years.

He couldn't wait.

101

Becoming the widow of one of the richest men in the world was an awesome experience. As Dimitri Stanislopoulos's wife Lucky had been treated with a certain amount of respect by his business associates. As his widow, she was fawned over.

It occurred to her that she was now in a position of power she had never dreamed of. Olympia and Roberto would inherit the lion's share of Dimitri's vast wealth, but that did not exactly leave her a pauper. She owned the Santangelo free and clear. She had money in the bank from the sale of her Magiriano shares. And the East Hampton house was all hers.

She did not need any of Dimitri's money, and she did not expect to get any. She had signed an agreement before their marriage relinquishing all rights to his vast estates and fortunes. The hotel was enough for her. She had realized her dream. Still, she had to attend the reading of the will. Roberto's interests must be protected. Not that she anticipated any problems. Dimitri had doted on the boy.

Gino was returning to Vegas, and Costa and Ria were accompanying him for a visit. Lucky decided it might be a good idea to send Roberto and CeeCee with them. She didn't want to leave Roberto on the island—too many sad memories. And she didn't want to take him to New York with her. She trusted CeeCee implicitly. Besides, it would be good for him to spend some time with Gino.

Arrangements were duly made. Brigette was to go with them as well and be dropped off in Los Angeles. Lucky didn't want her traveling alone. "I really should have a bodyguard go with you," she worried.

Brigette giggled at the very thought. "Nobody knows who *I* am."

"As long as we don't put Stanislopoulos on your ticket. In public you are Brigette Standing. Remember that."

Memories drifted back. When Lucky was a girl at school, Gino had insisted that she not use the notorious Santangelo name. She had been known as Lucky Saint. What a name to be stuck with! Olympia had soon uncovered her secret and they had become friends.

Once.

Long ago . . .

* * * * *

Brigette got to sit next to Gino on the plane. She was glad. Costa was so dull, and his wife, Ria, talked too much. CeeCee she had never gotten along with. And Roberto—or Bobby, as she called him—was just a stupid little kid.

Brigette was sorry Grandpapa Dimitri had died. But it opened up a whole new and exciting life for her. Now she couldn't be dumped on the boring old Greek island every time she had a vacation. There was only so much swimming and sunbathing one could do. Perhaps Lucky would allow her to visit Atlantic City often. The Santangelo Hotel was a blast—oh, the times she could have there! And then maybe she could go and see Gino in Vegas—after all, they *were* sort of related, and they got along fine. Then there was Grandma Charlotte in New York. She was a pain, but an occasional weekend in New York might be fun. And there was always L.A. And Mommy. And Lennie.

Mommy was a big drag.

Lennie was terrific.

And Tim Wealth lived in L.A.

She shivered with anticipation.

The stewardess walked along the aisle. She had on a tight skirt, too tight, Brigette thought. It made her bottom look huge.

"Want a drink, kid?" Gino asked.

"Scotch on the rocks, please," joked Brigette.

"Smack on the ass," grinned Gino.

The stewardess smiled superciliously. She had very big white teeth. Brigette wondered if she had ever thought of doing a toothpaste commercial.

"How about a nice glass of milk, dear?" beamed Big Teeth.

Brigette scowled. Talking to her like a baby. She *hated* it when grownups spoke down to her. Didn't they realize how dumb it made them look? She was fourteen, not four.

• • • • •

Olympia was finally spurred to go on a crash diet—not that the loss of a few pounds made any difference in her mammoth proportions, but she pretended it did. Lately she felt paranoid and unable to sleep. Somehow her never-ending supply of cocaine was not giving her the kick she needed. She had complained to one of her dealers on the phone that he was shipping her inferior stuff.

"Meet with me, pretty lady," he had crooned. "I gotta way to prolong that old coke high gonna see you fly!"

"I want something that'll make me feel good and stop me from eating. I need to lose a pound or two," she said, as if conversing with a respected doctor.

"I got just what you want, pretty lady. But I have to show you how to do your thing."

They arranged to meet in a Hollywood hotel the next day. Olympia wasn't nervous. She had never been nervous about anything in her life.

The dealer was a sallow-faced man in his forties with peroxide hair and missing front teeth. Olympia had found him through a dealer of Flash's in New York. The man had an alarming facial tic and smelled of stale smoke. When Olympia entered the hotel room he switched on the television set and locked the door.

"What have you got for me?" she asked restlessly.

The man squinted at the fat blond heiress and saw dollar signs.

"What haven't I got for you, pretty lady," he said.

An hour later she left, a spring in her step and a mellow, satisfied expression on her face. She had a purseful of goodies. Snorting heroin beat coke any day.

Lennie was working in his study when she arrived home.

"Where'd you go?" he asked, delighted that she'd ventured out.

She smiled dreamily. "Shopping," she said. "The pounds are dropping from me. I have to buy new clothes for New York."

"That's good news."

"Oh, and Lennie," she added imperiously, "hire a plane. I'm not going to New York on an ordinary airline." She swept from his study.

Only *he* would end up married to a woman who said "Hire a plane" as if she was ordering dog food.

He tried to work for another hour but it wasn't happening for him, so he went upstairs. Olympia was in her bedroom, clothes spread around everywhere.

"Brigette's arriving this evening," he reminded her. "And we're leaving on Monday. Shouldn't we have someone in the house with her other than the servants?"

"Who did you have in mind?" she asked, inspecting a selection of silk caftans.

He paced around the room. "Maybe Jess."

"Isn't she rushing back to Atlantic City and that hood she's engaged to?"

"Oh, yeah." He had forgotten Jess was now commuting.

Olympia held blue silk in front of her. The color complemented her eyes. If she were only a few pounds thinner—well, more than a few, she had to admit—she would be the prettiest girl in the world. And pretty girls got laid. She was tired of Lennie and his feeble excuses.

"I've made a decision," she stated dramatically.

"Yeah?" Olympia's decisions usually lasted ten minutes.

"I'm going to take a sleep cure and really lose weight."

When they returned from New York she would cease to be his problem. He had given enough. One divorce coming up. "That's great," he said, hoping she meant it for her own sake.

"That's great," she mimicked. "I wonder if you'll think it's so great when I start taking charge of my own life again."

"*Hey*—that's exactly what I want you to do."

She glared. "What?"

He smelled the beginning of a fight, and who needed it? Brigette was arriving soon. They hadn't seen her in over a year, and it would be nice if they were both talking to each other and not at each other's throats.

"Listen, how about Alice?" he suggested, changing the subject with a quick idea which, if he had thought it through, was madness. He was desperately trying to keep Alice *out* of the house, not bring her in.

Olympia decided she didn't feel like a fight either. "Hmmm, they get along, Brigette likes her, and she drives. She can take her to Disneyland and Magic Mountain and all those kiddie places. Shall we have one of the secretaries phone her?"

"Yeah, good idea." He stretched. "I'm going over to Ryder's for a meeting."

She frowned. "Why do you always go to him? Why doesn't he ever come to you?"

"Because *you* never want anyone in the house."

She narrowed her eyes. "And it suits you fine, doesn't it? That way your freedom is assured. Yes?" She threw the blue caftan on the floor. "Well, make the most of it, husband, dear. Because things are going to be very different in the future. You've kept me shut up here long enough."

"*I've* kept you shut up?" he snorted angrily. "Me? Getting you out to see your plastic surgeon is a major fucking coup."

She was too mellow for a fight. "Goodbye," she said crisply.

"Forever," he muttered.

"What?"

He strode from the house, threw himself behind the wheel of his Porsche and zoomed off.

• • • • •

Ryder Wheeler was on the tennis court pinging balls that bounced out at him from a machine.

Lennie settled himself in a chair next to the outside bar and watched.

Ryder managed a couple of great shots, spotted Lennie and walked over.

"Do you always play with yourself?" Lennie asked sarcastically.

Ryder grabbed a towel from the back of the chair and swung it around his neck. "Only when Paige is out of town."

As if on cue, Paige emerged from the house. She wore a short scarlet dress, very high heels, and her legs were bare. She looked like a Marseilles hooker.

"Hiya, sexy," greeted Lennie.

"I didn't know you two had a meeting planned," she said, bestowing a kiss on his forehead.

"We didn't," Lennie replied. "But I sure as hell needed a shot of fresh air."

Like everyone else, Paige had often wondered about his marriage. They had all heard of Olympia Stanislopoulos, but nobody ever saw her. She never appeared in public and Lennie offered no explanations to anyone, including the press—who speculated constantly. According to Jess the marriage endured. That was all Paige could find out.

"You'll get plenty of fresh air here. I'm off to the work dungeon." She pecked Ryder on the cheek. "Bye bye, sweetheart." For a moment she paused, looked from one man to the other, and added mischievously, "Tell Lennie about your new project. Talk dirty. Who knows? Maybe you can get him to put in a guest appearance."

"What new project?" Lennie asked, watching Paige out of sight.

Ryder plucked a prune danish from a plate on the table, picked up the intercom and ordered hot coffee, then leaned back in his chair. "I'm doing a porno," he said.

"What?" Lennie was not sure he'd heard correctly. Since making his last two pictures, Ryder Wheeler was one of the most successful producers in town.

"Soft porn, of course," Ryder added quickly. "Beautifully done. I'm directing."

Lennie started to laugh. "I don't believe what I'm hearing."

Ryder shrugged. "I've got everything I want. All the money I'll ever need. So I decided to indulge myself and do something I've always hankered after."

"You *are* kidding me?"

"No. I'm serious."

"*You're* not a director. You're a great producer—but a director—come on!"

Ryder picked his teeth with a matchstick. "There is no great mystique to directing a film," he said. "If you surround yourself with the right crew and a clever cinematographer, then you're ninety percent of the way. *And* if you can talk to actors and pick a perfect cast, you're all the way. Besides, if anyone's going to be in the front line for pussy, it better be me."

"You don't even *chase* pussy. You're the only guy I know who doesn't screw around."

"I'm not doing it to get my rocks off," Ryder explained patiently. "If I wanted to get laid, this is climax city." He paused. "I am doing it, Lennie, because directing a porno is my one unfulfilled ambition. Plus one of my investors is putting up all the money, and I have a large piece of the action, which—if we want to talk video sales—is going to be tremendous."

"What about your reputation?"

Ryder laughed heartily. "A reputation in this town is how much money you make. Shit, Lennie, for a hip guy you sure sound like a Boy Scout at times."

"Fuck you, asshole."

Ryder beamed. "Come by the set sometime. It beats out a game of tennis any day."

102

Coffee was served in fine china teacups with large ungainly spoons. Carrie decided she would buy him a set of delicate silver spoons for Christmas, but, knowing Fred Lester, he probably wouldn't use them.

Fred cleared his throat for the second time and stroked the palm of his hand across his bald pate.

Carrie crossed and uncrossed her legs. She still had beautiful legs. The wrinkles of time had not reached them—yet. Sometimes, when she looked in the mirror, she was dismayed to notice age catching up with her. But she was alive, so surely she was one of the lucky ones? She often wondered about the companions of her youth, the hookers and the strippers, the pimps and the con men. Were they still around today? She sincerely doubted it. Life was harsh back then, and only the fittest survived.

"Your book is a gem," Fred Lester said at last. "A shining piece of honesty in a dishonest world."

"Thank you," Carrie murmured gratefully. Fred's comment was the first reaction she had received on her book. She still had not mentioned it to Steven.

Fred placed the tips of his fingers together and made a funnel. He gazed across the room, not meeting Carrie's eyes. "There might be legal problems with some of the names you've used. It may not be possible to . . . uh . . . use all the real names." He laughed hollowly. "Especially Freddy Lester."

She laughed with him. "I never told you this, but his name brought me to you."

He studied his fingernails. "Did it?"

"Absolutely. You see, when I finally told Steven the truth, he became obsessed with finding out who his real father was: Gino Santangelo or Freddy Lester."

"Did you go to Gino Santangelo?"

"Almost. We flew to California, but something stopped Steven from pursuing the search. Thank God."

It was raining on the streets of New York, and the relentless drops pounded on the office window.

"How many Freddy Lesters did you find?" Fred asked. "And what eliminated me?"

She sipped her coffee. It was strong and too hot. "Why?" she joked. "Are you telling me it *was* you?"

There was a moment of silence before Fred's hearty laugh filled the room. "I wish," he said.

"No you don't." Her tone was suddenly harsh. "That man was an animal, with no regard for anyone except himself." Her voice shook. "He raped me. Even if I was once a whore, I had *some* rights, didn't I?"

He calmed her. "Of course you did, my dear. Of course you did."

She arose and walked to the window. "I still remember," she said bitterly, "the pain I had to endure." She stared unseeingly at the stream of traffic crawling along the rain-soaked streets below. "I was alone, with no money, no job, and a baby growing inside me. There was no other way. I had to go back to the only profession I knew to make a living. I had no choice. *He* gave me no choice."

Fred rose and stood behind her. "But you have a fine son. Out of the pain came *some* good."

She had never thought of it that way before. She nodded wearily, and was assailed by a flash of doubt. "Steven doesn't know about the book. I don't want to upset him."

"If your life upsets him, surely that's *his* problem."

"I know. But—"

"Would you like *me* to tell him?"

She shook her head. "It's my responsibility. I'll talk to him tomorrow."

"Maybe I should be with you."

There was something in his tone that alerted her. She moved from the window and stared at him. Slowly realization dawned. "It's you, isn't it?" she whispered at last. "*It is you*. And that's why you're paying half a million dollars. Guilt money. It is you!"

"Yes," he said, and a heavy weight fell from his shoulders.

103

"Hi," said Brigette chirpily, trying to conceal the shock she felt on seeing the size of her mother.

"You're all grown up!" Olympia exclaimed. "Oh, God! You make me feel so *old*. Which I'm not," she added quickly.

"Why didn't you come to Grandpapa's funeral?" Brigette asked accusingly, not wasting any time.

"I hate funerals," Olympia said petulantly.

"Your mother was sick," Lennie cut in.

"She looks fine to me," said Brigette, cobalt-blue eyes shining.

"So tell her," said Lennie gently. "She's had skin grafts and plastic surgery and God knows what. Tell your mother she looks pretty again."

"You do look pretty, Mama," said Brigette reluctantly. "Did anyone call me?"

"Who were you expecting?" Olympia asked, hating the fact that her daughter looked so mature and well developed for a fourteen-year-old.

"I have friends here," Brigette said vaguely. "Like from school and stuff."

"Good," said Olympia.

"Great," said Lennie.

"We have to go to New York," Olympia said quickly. "Alice is going to come here and stay with you."

"Who?"

"Alice. You remember her. Lennie's mother. You used to adore her."

Brigette yawned and stretched. "Oh, yeah." *That old bat,* she thought. *Well, I'll certainly get as much freedom as I want with her around.* "How long will you be gone, Mama?" she asked innocently.

"Just as long as it takes," said Olympia. And she added silently to herself, *Just as long as it takes me to make sure that bitch Lucky gets no more than she deserves. Which, if I have anything to do with it, is—nothing.*

• • • • •

Tim Wealth moved out on his lover the day he started shooting Ryder Wheeler's movie *Heat*. He moved out because his lover was beginning to treat him like something less than dog shit, and who needed it? The man was only a lousy movie producer, not the second coming of Clark Gable.

Tim was working again, he could pay his own bills, and while starring in *Heat* was hardly the lead in *Gatsby*, it was still a hot movie. In every way.

The first day on the set he came face to face with his co-star. He took one look and double-taked. Eden Antonio.

"Do you know each other?" asked Ryder, noting Tim's expression.

"No," said Eden, turning away.

Lying bitch, thought Tim. But then she had always been a liar *and* a bitch.

• • • • •

Tim Wealth arrived in New York from Detroit at the age of nineteen. He quite expected theater doors to open up for him. He was an actor, and a good one. The only doors that opened up were the doors of cars cruising Times Square looking for a fast score. He became a male hustler—not from choice, but because it paid well and enabled him to attend acting classes during the day.

One of the other students was a girl named Eden. She was the most beautiful female he had ever seen. Not only was she beautiful, but she was sophisticated and worldly—and just listening to her talk was a thrill. He hung on her every word, for Eden was classy and stylish—all the things lacking in Tim's life.

Occasionally they got to do scenes together. She wasn't a very good actress, but her exotic beauty compensated. Even though she was several years older than he, they became good friends, and even though he knew she was living with a guy, they became lovers.

One day she arrived in class with a determined look on her face. "Listen," she said. "I don't know about you, but I've had it with this town. I want to head for L.A. and break into movies. Why don't we go together?"

"What about your boyfriend?" he asked.

"What about him?" she replied.

Once they decided to do it, she left all the arrangements to him. He had managed to save some money. The one good thing about hustling was that it paid well—cash, no taxes. And Eden expected him to pay for everything. Which he did.

Two first-class tickets. "I want to do it properly," Eden said.

Reservations in the Beverly Hilton.

Several new outfits for Eden to storm the casting agents with.

Four weeks into hotel life and no jobs, Tim realized he was busted out.

"Too bad," said Eden, and moved out of his life one L.A. rainy morning when he was away from the room buying the trades—leaving him with a three-thousand-dollar hotel tab and no way of paying it.

He was devastated. But it gave him a fast education on classy, stylish women.

He skipped without settling the bill and resumed the only sure way of making a living he knew.

Hustling Santa Monica Boulevard was not that different from Times Square.

Age twenty-one, he was picked up one day by a well-known male superstar, whose private life was firmly in the closet. The man was married, with children, but that didn't stop him from setting Tim up in an apartment with a generous clothes allow-

ance and all expenses paid. The arrangement suited Tim fine. It kept him off the streets, allowed him to entertain girls when his benefactor wasn't around, and to concentrate on his acting studies.

His diligence paid off, and in 1980 he landed the lead role in a movie, much to his boyfriend's chagrin. They parted company acrimoniously.

Smash reviews and good box office led to exactly nothing. The rejected superstar had clout, and he used it to make sure Tim Wealth's career went right down the toilet.

Which is where it stayed until the offer of the Ryder Wheeler flick came his way. "It's kinda close to the bone," his agent warned him. "But it's gonna be done with class and plenty of the green stuff."

Tim said yes. He had nothing to lose—only his modesty, and that had never counted for much. The script read porno. But with Ryder Wheeler in charge, Tim hoped it would be something more. He had once had a taste of stardom; he was desperately hungry for more.

• • • • •

Eden Antonio. She was as hot as the movie. Icy cool was how Tim would describe the lady. He had never forgotten her. But now he was older, and a hell of a lot wiser. There was no way Eden could walk all over him this time around.

She radiated style and sex, even though her figure bordered on the anorexic. Kind of a strange choice for the leading lady in a flick that promised to reveal a lot of flesh.

"It's okay," the makeup man told him. "The rest of the bunnies make Dolly Parton look like she got steamrolled!"

Tim couldn't wait. Tits and fags. The story of his life.

He never *had* been able to choose.

Now they were shooting the movie, and he was glad he'd said yes. Hell, if Richard Gere could show it all, why couldn't he? Although he was doing a lot more than just showing it.

Ryder Wheeler said that the kind of film they were doing

was the movie of the future. "The public wants t'see it all," he assured his actors. "Today it's you—tomorrow it'll be Burt Reynolds and Jessica Lange."

Tim had his doubts. But at least—true to his agent's words—everything was being done with class and money.

The first time they found themselves alone together Eden said, "So you didn't make it either, huh?"

"You're one ace bitch," he replied.

"One of my main attractions," she retorted.

They were in her dressing room. He kicked the door shut and had her for old times' sake.

"My boyfriend will kill you for this," she whispered, "if he ever finds out."

"Are you going to tell him?"

That throaty, husky laugh. "What do *you* think?"

The second week on the set Tim met the "money man," Santino Bonnatti. He strutted around like he owned the world and everyone in it. He quite obviously owned Eden—whom he affectionately called "cunt" in front of the entire crew.

"Your boyfriend?" Tim asked unnecessarily.

"Unfortunately," she replied.

On the screen together they created sparks. Eden Antonio and Tim Wealth. And they hadn't even gotten to any of the hot stuff yet.

Ryder knew it immediately he saw the first dailies. He called Paige and told her to get right over to the screening room.

She saw Tim and Eden together and agreed with him at once.

"We've got to keep this film at a level," Ryder said. "I want it to be a *Last Tango* of the eighties—not a return of *Deep Throat*."

"You have no problem with that, do you?" asked Paige.

"*I* have no problem, but Bonnatti will give me a hard time. Wait and see."

Sure enough, several weeks into shooting, Santino demanded more. "I want more tits. I want more ass. I want more sucking and I want more fucking."

"Don't hang back," Ryder urged. "Tell me what's on your mind."

Santino glared. He was putting up money for porno, and all he was getting were long shots and clever lighting and artistic shit.

"Do it," he warned. "Or get your ass off my movie."

Two days later Ryder Wheeler did exactly that.

Tim Wealth and Eden Antonio were appalled. Especially when Santino brought in a well-known sleaze director who lost no time in going right for the bone—in more ways than one.

Between setups, when Santino wasn't hovering, and the ever-present Zeko was chasing extras, Tim consoled Eden in the privacy of one or the other's dressing room. They came together urgently. Eden, nervous and edgy and hungry. Tim, surprised that he could summon up feelings he thought were long dead.

It didn't take long before Santino became suspicious. He watched them in front of the camera and didn't mind what went on there—because he was in control and Eden was his property. But off camera he didn't even want them to speak.

"You've got to get away from him," Tim cautioned.

"I know," Eden agreed.

Tim Wealth couldn't figure out why he was getting involved. Shoot the flick and run. Santino Bonnatti was bad news—the serious kind.

"If I came up with a big score, we could go to Mexico and hide out," Tim suggested.

Eden nodded. Where was Tim Wealth going to come up with enough money to assure their safe flight?

That evening he dug in his suitcase—the one he had carried to Atlantic City on his last trip with his lover. Scrunched in one corner was a slip of paper. On it was written BRIGETTE STANISLOPOULOS, and a phone number.

Tim did not hesitate.

104

Brigette was bored. Being stuck in the Bel Air mansion for weeks with an army of servants and crazy Alice for company was the pits. She had come to visit her mother and Lennie, and practically the moment she arrived they had raced off to New York with hardly a hello-goodbye. Wow—they really wanted to see her, didn't they?

She amused herself for a while by going through Olympia's closet, all of her drawers and her desk. Then she explored Lennie's study, but he had a habit of locking things up, so she didn't get very far there.

Alice said, "Do you want to go to Disneyland, dear?"

Disneyland! Brigette gave her a filthy look.

Alice got the message. Disneyland was out. Instead they went to an R-rated movie on Hollywood Boulevard and later cruised along in the back of Olympia's white Rolls-Royce with a uniformed chauffeur at the wheel, watching the hookers parade Sunset.

Brigette was fascinated. "Do they really get paid for it?" she inquired, filled with curiosity.

"Naturellement, ma chérie," replied Alice. She had been picking up French phrases from a well-developed foreign midget she had met in a bar. His name was Claudio, and he came from circus stock.

"What do they *do?*" demanded Brigette.

"What *don't* they do," replied Alice mysteriously. *"Oo la la!"*

They returned to the mansion and played cards. Every day Brigette waited for the phone to ring because she was quite sure Tim Wealth would call, while Alice wondered if she dare invite Claudio to the house. Lennie had been very specific with his instructions. "I don't want *any* of your friends here, male, female, straight or gay. Not one of them."

Poor little Claudio. He was gentle and quiet. And certainly very sexy for a small person. Surely Lennie would not bar Claudio from coming to the house?

"I'm bummed out," Brigette complained constantly. "Can't we do something funky for a change? Don't you know any *people?*"

Alice did not understand what either bummed out or funky meant—both sounded rude to her. She sighed. Youngsters today were different. Brigette seemed such an advanced teenager. Or maybe she was normal. On impulse she phoned Claudio and invited him over.

"I've got a friend coming," she informed Brigette.

"Nice for them," the girl muttered to herself.

"He'll take us out." Alice nodded to herself. She had had enough of playing baby-sitter. When Lennie had called and asked her to stay, she had been thrilled. She wanted to be close to her famous son, not cut out of his life forever. But keeping an eye on a restless fourteen-year-old was not exactly what she'd had in mind. Claudio would definitely liven things up.

"It'll be nice to see *someone,*" grumbled Brigette. She was pissed at Tim Wealth. Weeks had passed and he hadn't even called. Soon she would have to leave L.A. and return to school. Who did he think he was?

"Yes," Alice mused happily. "We'll have ourselves some fun with Claudio."

"Brilliant," said Brigette.

Alice simpered coyly. "We'll get down and get funky!"

Brigette giggled. Alice had always made her laugh with her birdlike movements, dyed hair and rouged cheeks. "Right on, Grandma!"

The smile vanished from Alice's face. "Don't call me that, dear. It makes me feel ancient."

• • • • •

In New York the battle was on. Dimitri Stanislopoulos's will was a lengthy and complicated document. To everyone's surprise, he left the bulk of his money, business interests and estates to Lucky—to be held in trust for Roberto until he reached twenty-five.

Olympia was not exactly left out. She was to receive a lifetime allowance of a million dollars a year, which she considered an out-and-out insult. Brigette was to get double that amount, and also a twenty-five-million-dollar inheritance when she reached twenty-one.

"How dared he!" Olympia screamed, as they left the lawyer's office. "How dared that senile sonofabitch do this to me!"

Lennie was not really interested in Olympia's hysterical complaints. He had just come face to face with Lucky for the first time in three years, and he felt as if someone had kicked him in the stomach with a steel-toed boot. She was as wildly beautiful as ever in a simple black suit, her jet curls pulled severely back from her face.

She had walked toward them and offered a hug of sympathy to Olympia, who had shrugged her off with a cold glare.

He didn't know what to say. Everything seemed inappropriate. Hey—the big movie star was speechless. "How are you?" he managed to mumble.

She barely glanced in his direction. "Fine, thank you," in clipped tones.

And that was it—the full extent of their conversation, followed by hours of boredom while the will was read.

He had tried to catch her eye, but she was aloof, and very remote, which destroyed him. It seemed that as far as Lucky was concerned it was over. And there was no way he could convince her otherwise while he remained married to Olympia.

"It's all that bitch's fault," Olympia ranted on. "She brainwashed him. She coerced him. But she needn't think for one moment that she's getting away with it, because she's not. My lawyers will fight it every inch of the way—every goddamn inch."

. . . . .

The newspapers descended like a plague of ants, and Lucky, who had always managed to keep a fairly low profile, suddenly found herself the center of attention. As Mrs. Stanislopoulos, she had kept in the background. But as the widow Stanislopoulos, and the inheritor of most of Dimitri's fortune, she was suddenly thrust unwillingly into the limelight. Unwanted headlines began to appear. Pictures were dug up from her days as Senator Richmond's daughter-in-law, the opening of the Magiriano, and more recent ones from the Hotel Santangelo opening night.

DAUGHTER OF FORMER MOBSTER HITS THE JACKPOT, screamed one tabloid. SANTANGELO KID GETS RICH QUICK, offered another.

It wasn't long before industrious digging produced the story of her attempted rape at the hands of Enzio Bonnatti, and the subsequent shooting. It had taken six years to make the headlines, but now it was hot news. STANISLOPOULOS HEIRESS KILLED RAPIST.

She was outraged by the sudden loss of privacy, and when they printed a picture of Roberto playing in the pool at the Magiriano, where he was staying with Gino, she really freaked out and called Gino immediately. "What the hell is going on?" she demanded. "Why are you letting them photograph Roberto?"

"I'm not," he replied grimly. He too was upset by the unwelcome thrust of publicity. "I got security guards throwin' the newspaper bums on their asses, but I can't control the tourists with their cameras," he complained.

"I want Roberto out of there," Lucky said urgently. "At once."

"I know," Gino agreed. "I was thinkin' along the same lines."

He told her his plans. Costa and Ria had rented a house in Beverly Hills for the month. They were flying to L.A. that evening, and he planned to take Roberto and CeeCee and go with them. "I can't put up with the shit goin' on here," he said. "This way nobody will know where we are, an' we'll get some peace."

"Sounds good to me," said Lucky. "I'll join you as soon as I can."

"No rush," Gino assured her. "Roberto's safe with me."

"I know," she replied quietly. "But I miss him." And she did. Desperately. A hotel was no substitute for a son.

They talked some more, and at the end of the conversation she felt better. She could finally turn to Gino in times of trouble. He understood and was always there for her. Right now she needed someone.

Lennie.

Still married to Olympia.

Why had she ever thought they had something going?

105

If only she could get to Lennie, Eden knew he would lend her the money to free herself from the deadly clutches of Santino Bonnatti. With Ryder Wheeler off the movie, things deteriorated day by day. Her scenes with Tim presented no problem. They were steamy, but she could handle them because she was with him. However, when Santino insisted the rape scene go back in, she knew she was in trouble.

A hulking actor from hard-core movies appeared on the set to play her assailant. And she sensed, without a doubt, that Santino had told the director to run the scene to its limit.

Tim slipped her some pills before he was ordered to leave the set. "Take 'em," he commanded. "They'll get you through."

She did as he said, and felt better immediately.

Santino was sitting ringside when she was called to start the scene. He sat in a director's chair behind the camera, a leer on his face, and the stub of a stinking cigar stuck between his teeth. "Lotsa luck, honey," he said, the concerned boyfriend.

She smiled vaguely. The pills had taken her to another place where nothing mattered.

The director, a New Yorker with dyed hair and slit eyes, said, "Let's go with the flow, sweetie. Live it. Feel it. I'm going for one take in long shot, then we'll move in for the close-ups."

"Do I look beautiful?" she murmured.

"Hot stuff, sweet ass. You'll have every *schlong* in the theatre at full mast."

She licked her thin lips and waited for the magic word "Action!"

The director called it, and they were away.

She moved into the scene like the pro she was.

Eden Antonio.

Great screen beauty.

She wore a satin nightgown and not much else.

The hulking actor lurked behind a curtain waiting for his moment. At a signal from the director he moved into shot, huge and sinister. He grabbed her quickly. She was like a helpless doll in his vicious grip.

She relaxed and went limp in his arms.

"Struggle!" the director hissed.

"Yeah, struggle," Santino repeated, leaning forward, sweat beading his brow.

Why did she have to fight? Whatever happened now was inevitable, all the struggling in the world wouldn't stop it.

Feebly she attempted resistance.

The hulk loved that. He ripped at satin, lifted her bodily, and threw her down on the bed.

The pills had an anesthetizing effect. She was glad. Getting raped on camera had never been a career goal.

•　•　•　•　•

"Hello, little girl."

"Tim!"

"What a memory!"

"Why haven't you phoned me before?"

"I thought rich little girls like you wouldn't want to be bothered with broke actors."

"Are you broke?"

"Nearly. But I think I can rustle up enough change to take you to dinner tonight."

"Honestly?"

"Why not? You're free, aren't you?"

"Oh, yes."

"I'll meet you in the bar at Trader Vic's, eight o'clock."

Brigette replaced the receiver and squealed with joy. She had known Tim Wealth would phone, and now he had. Brilliant!

He had asked her on a date and she would go.

Except . . .

How was she going to get out of the house?

Alice was taking a nap in front of a giant TV.

She snored delicately.

Brigette shook her vigorously awake.

"Where am I?" mumbled Alice, lost for a moment.

"My girlfriend from school is here," Brigette announced.

"Where?" panicked Alice, sitting up in a hurry and looking around.

"Not here, silly. In L.A. She's visiting."

Alice had been dreaming of John Travolta. She had read somewhere once that he preferred older women, and she knew if he ever clapped eyes on her it would be love at first sight. Mrs. Alice Travolta. That would make Lennie sit up and take notice. "How nice, dear," she said vaguely.

"She wants me to stay overnight with her," Brigette lied.

Alice was delighted. "That'll be nice for you," she said, patting her hair. Claudio was coming over and this would give them an opportunity to be alone. Looking after Brigette was one thing—but neglecting her sex life was another. Claudio was an extremely *talented* short person, and she missed his ardent attentions.

"I don't want to go to my friend's house in the Rolls," Brigette announced. "It's so embarrassing!"

If Alice had her way, she herself would never go anywhere except in a Rolls-Royce—ever again. What a peculiar child Brigette was.

"How will you get there?" she asked.

"I'll call a cab."

"Lennie said—"

"Please, Ali. Pretty please! I won't tell Lennie if you won't."

Alice failed to see the harm in allowing the girl to go by cab. "Oh, very well. But don't talk to the driver. They're all illegals, you know."

Brigette grinned slyly. What she planned to do was also illegal, but who cared?

She raced to Olympia's closet and scanned her clothes. Sweaters and blouses, dresses and skirts, scarves and belts, jackets and pants. Browsing through Olympia's closet was like being in a store. Her mother's taste was gross, and Brigette couldn't find anything worth wearing except a ragged-looking leopardskin scarf hanging in the back. She could have bet it once belonged to Flash.

Excitedly she reached for it. Tight jeans, one of Lennie's jackets, and the scarf—especially if it really had once belonged to Flash—would be a cool outfit.

As she tugged at the scarf, there was a whirring noise, and part of the wall in the closet slid away, revealing a hidden room.

Brigette was startled, but only for a moment. She figured she had stumbled across the hiding place for her mother's jewels.

Inquisitively she pushed past clothes and entered the tiny room. Shelves lined the walls. And on the shelves were stacked bottles and bottles of different-colored pills, glass phials, boxes of smelly brown tobacco stuff, and packets of white powder.

Brigette frowned.

Drugs?

Whose?

Lennie's? He was a movie star. Weren't all movie stars supposed to be bombed out of their minds? She had read it in the *Enquirer* or somewhere.

Curiously she picked up a packet of white powder. It looked like powdered sugar, but she guessed it was cocaine. With a rush of excitement she remembered her last meeting with Tim Wealth. He had snorted coke and had been cross with her when she sneezed and blew most of it away. What would he say if she took him a gift? He would *have* to be pleased. And she wanted to please him more than anything else in the world.

· · · · ·

"Hiya, little girl," Tim Wealth said, rising to greet her.

"I'm eighteen," Brigette lied. "Fade-out on the 'little girl.' "

He leaned toward her. "I always get horny in Polynesian restaurants. How about you?"

She was weak in the knees, but she didn't want *him* to know.

"What are you drinking?" she asked, looking at his glass.

"Whiskey sour."

"I'll have the same," she said, and hoped and prayed they wouldn't ask for her I.D.

As if reading her mind, he said, "You're only eighteen— you can't be a legal drinking partner until you hit twenty-one. You want to get me arrested?"

If he only knew!

"I'll order you a Mickey Mouse drink and you can share my whiskey sour on the sly. How's that?"

She nodded happily. He was so fantastic! And understanding.

Dinner was wonderful. At least it looked wonderful. Brigette was too excited to eat. It was difficult to believe she was actually sitting in a restaurant with Tim Wealth.

"Tell me about yourself," he encouraged over chicken chow mein. "Are you really the granddaughter of Dimitri Stanislopoulos?"

She nodded. "He died, you know."

"Yeah, I read about it," he said casually. He had read *all* about it. "A rich old dude, huh?"

"I guess."

She guessed. He stared at the pretty little blond girl and wondered how best to use her. He felt no remorse that he had to do so. She was using him. Fourteen years old and pretending to be eighteen. Jail bait. Rich jail bait. *Dangerous* jail bait. She couldn't care less that because of her deception he could have got his ass slung in the can. Why should she? Everything had been handed her on a silver platter all her life, and always would be. Slightly different from *his* humble beginnings. At fourteen he was fighting off his stepfather in the outside john. Miss Stanislopoulos, with her big blue eyes and golden curls, probably didn't even know what an outside john was.

He wondered what kind of access she had to all the money that was supposedly hers. Fourteen was kind of young. No doubt she was surrounded by trustees and guardians and was watched all the time.

If she was watched all the time, how come she was out with him, guzzling his whiskey sour and waiting impatiently to get laid?

He asked her a few questions about who she was staying with in L.A., and heard all about crazy Alice, Lennie Golden's mother.

"How'd you get here? he asked curiously.

"Uh . . . I took a cab." She hesitated. "I would have driven, but my car is in the shop being fixed."

"Oh, yeah, what's wrong with it?"

"Engine trouble." She took a quick sip of his drink and hoped he wouldn't ask any more questions.

"What do you drive?" he persisted.

She thought of Lennie's Porsche sitting in the garage. "A Porsche," she said quickly.

He was playing with her. "What model?"

She struggled to get up. "I gotta go to the bathroom."

He stood politely. "Be my guest."

106

Jerry Myerson threw the glossy magazine on Steven's desk with a resounding thud. The Bonnatti publication, titled *Comer*, featured Mary Lou Moore in black stockings, garter belt and little else. She gazed at the camera, lips moist, expression sulky and position precarious.

"Get a load of this," said Jerry, pointing to the caption alongside the near-naked girl. MARY LOU OPENS UP . . . SEE ALL HEAR ALL . . . FIVE GLORIOUS PAGES.

Steven looked. And swore. And flipped the magazine open, searching for the other photos.

"Did you know about this?" Jerry asked.

"Hell, *no*," Steven replied through clenched teeth as he studied the rest of the pictures.

"She should have told you," Jerry grumbled. "This is going to blow our victory right out the window. The decision'll be reversed and she'll end up paying Bonnatti's costs."

Steven was silent as he stared at the offensive shots. There was Mary Lou in an empty bathtub, one leg thrown casually over the side. There was Mary Lou lying on a chaise lounge, legs apart, with just a feather boa for company. And more of the same. Each shot portrayed—as known in the wonderful world of men's magazines—split beaver.

"Damn!" said Steven harshly.

Jerry was sympathetic. "I know, I know. It's a shock. You thought she was a sweet kid, and all that. But believe me— women—you never can tell what they're going to get up to next. I—"

"Spare me your half-baked philosophies," interrupted Steven angrily, still staring at the photos. "This is *not* Mary Lou."

"Steven. I know you like the girl, but—"

"This is *not* Mary Lou," he repeated angrily. "These pictures are fakes."

"What are you talking about?"

"Fakes. Composites," Steven said excitedly. "Her face. Somebody else's body superimposed. Jesus! I'm talking English, aren't I?"

"Are you sure they're not the real thing?"

"Jerry. Please. I'm *living* with the girl. I should know what she looks like without her clothes on." He waved the magazine in the air. "This is definitely *not* Mary Lou."

"So all we have to do is prove it," said Jerry logically. "And then it's back to court for a *real* payoff. If what you say is true, my friend, this one's a piece of pie with double-whipped cream. We are looking at a *massive* settlement."

"That's three, four years down the line," Steven pointed out. "It's more depositions and papers and meetings and postponements. All the legal machinations."

"Why are you telling me something I already know?"

"Because I'm not sure Mary Lou is willing to go through it again. She's going to want these pictures never to appear."

"Impossible. The magazine's hitting the stands any moment."

"How would you like it if somebody did this to you?" Steven said furiously.

Jerry laughed. "I don't think I'd sell as many magazines!"

"You asshole. Everything's a joke to you, isn't it?"

"There are certain things one cannot control. We have a legal system to take care of such things—which, I might point out, you are part of. So either you go with it or you have a nervous breakdown."

"Screw you!" Steven exploded. "This one I'm not going to sit back on."

Jerry shrugged. "There's nothing you can do."

"Just try me," Steven said grimly.

107

The thrill was in doing it. Now that she had achieved that feat, Lucky needed to move on to something else. She had built the Santangelo. It was everything she wanted it to be. Her hotel. Her pride. But she had no intention of sitting in Atlantic City counting the money. She wanted a new challenge, another adventure.

A business consortium wanted to buy her out. They were offering a huge profit on the two hundred million the hotel had cost to build.

Sell, she decided. Take the money and run, as Gino would say. Not that she needed the money—she was rich beyond her wildest dreams. What she *did* need was the freedom. Being tied to Atlantic City for the rest of her life was not her idea of heaven. Quietly she instructed her lawyers to proceed with the deal.

"Olympia Stanislopoulos is challenging the will," her legal advisers informed her.

It came as no surprise.

"Tell her I'll double what her father left her," Lucky generously decided. "And she can have the yacht as a gift."

Olympia's answer was swift and to the point. "No."

Lucky tried again. "I'll treble what Dimitri wanted her to have, and I'll throw in the New York apartment. If she doesn't accept my offer within ten days, I shall withdraw it and all previous offers."

Olympia's reply was, "Why wait ten days? When I get that bitch in court and prove she killed my father and forced him to change his will, *everything* will be mine."

The lawyers rubbed their hands together gleefully. And so did the press.

• • • • •

"I'm leaving," Lennie said.

Olympia favored him with a glare. "You don't mean it,"

she said. "You wouldn't walk out on me and all the things I can give you."

They had been fighting for weeks, ever since the reading of the will. In the Bel Air house he could escape. But in their New York apartment there was no such luxury. Lennie knew he couldn't take it anymore. Why was he hanging around anyway? Olympia's looks were restored—plastic surgery had taken care of every one of her scars. So she was fat. Was that his problem? Was he supposed to feel sorry for her and stay with her forever?

"I don't *want* anything from you," he said wearily. "You can have every single thing you've ever given me. The cars, the house, the furniture. I'm going to walk away from this marriage empty-handed."

"Empty-handed, my ass," she yelled. "What about all the money *you've* made?"

"I made it, didn't I? It's mine, isn't it?"

"Not when I've finished with you," she ranted. "California law. Half of everything you have is mine."

"And vice versa. But I don't want anything from you. So leave me alone, and I'll show you the same courtesy."

"You fuckhead!"

"Such a lady."

"Piss off. You're only leaving me now because I'm not as rich as you thought I was going to be."

"Money has nothing to do with it, and you know it."

"Sure," she jeered. "But you'll be sorry, just you wait. The will'll be reversed and I'll be the richest fucking woman in the world. Then you'll be *really* sorry."

He threw clothes in a suitcase, snapped it shut and walked to the door. "Goodbye, Olympia."

She followed him and hurled a lead-crystal ashtray. It missed his head by inches.

He opened the door and stepped into freedom.

He should have made the move a long time ago.

108

How was it, dear?" asked Alice gaily, as a taxi delivered Brigette to the door of the mansion just before noon. "Was your girlfriend delighted to see you?" She didn't wait for an answer, just fluttered on with, "Gino telephoned. He's here in Beverly Hills with Roberto—and your little uncle wants to see you." She snickered. "Fancy having an uncle of four and a half! Gino's sending him and CeeCee over this afternoon."

"Why are *they* here?" Brigette mumbled truculently.

"I don't know," trilled Alice, happy after a night with her tiny lover. *"Je ne sais pas."*

Brigette frowned. She had been looking forward to a nice quiet day thinking about Tim. What an evening they had spent together! The most exciting night of her entire life. Tim Wealth was the biggest babe ever.

She loved him.

She would do anything for him.

He was absolutely boss.

· · · · ·

Tim's dressing room was their only escape. "How did it go?" he asked Eden.

There were deep circles under her eyes and bruises on her body. "Once for the camera, and once for Santino when he got me home," she complained bitterly. "If I'd had a gun I would've killed him."

"You don't have to go that far. I'm working on a plan to get us out of here first class. How would you like to spend the winter in Acapulco?"

"I've *got* to get away from him," she said urgently. "I can't take any more."

"Don't worry. It's in the works."

She put her thin arms around his neck and kissed him with

her thin lips. So different from the baby girl he had spent the night with. But much more of a turn-on. Eden Antonio pressed all the right buttons. She was one woman he knew he could spend time with and not get bored shitless.

A knock on the dressing-room door made them leap apart.

"Who is it?" Tim shouted.

"You're wanted on the set."

"Be right there."

* * * * *

Gino, Costa, Ria and CeeCee, with Roberto, lunched in the Polo Lounge of the Beverly Hills Hotel. Gino enjoyed the scrambled eggs and smoked salmon. He also enjoyed the passing parade.

People stopped by his table. A Senator with steel-gray hair and a young secretary on his arm. A large woman dripping in daytime diamonds who had once sold him a house. A stoned entrepreneur with darting nervous eyes. And finally, Paige Wheeler.

She entered, spoke with the maitre d', saw Gino, wanted to walk past his table, but good manners overcame her. Not to mention Costa, who waved and called out her name.

Paige wore one of her famous split-to-the-crotch skirts, and a linen jacket with a polka-dot blouse underneath. Her full breasts pushed aggressively against the fabric of the blouse. She wasn't wearing a bra, and Gino could make out the firm swell of her nipples.

"Gino!" Warm smile. "Long time."

They hadn't seen each other since he had caught her with Susan, and his subsequent divorce.

He rose, always the gentleman, and kissed her on both cheeks. She smelled the same. Musky and sexy. But she looked a little older. So did he. Big deal. Neither of them were spring lambs. She was heading toward fifty, and he was racing out of his seventies full speed ahead.

"And Costa," she beamed. "How nice to see you."

Costa introduced Ria and mentioned the fact that he was about to become a father. Paige was duly impressed.

"And this is Roberto, Gino's grandson," Costa continued. "Don't they look alike?"

Paige smiled at the little boy. "Exactly," she said.

Roberto stared at her with his huge long-lashed Santangelo eyes, and nibbled on a roll.

"How about joining us for a drink?" Costa asked. He knew nothing of the circumstances which had forced Gino to stop seeing her. Nobody did.

She glanced at Gino fleetingly. He didn't react.

"I can't," she apologized. "I'm meeting a client for lunch. Maybe some other time."

"Call us," urged Costa, writing their phone number on a book of matches. "We're here for a month."

She stared straight at Gino as she murmured, "Maybe I will."

He still didn't react.

"Well, it was nice to see you all again," she said cordially, and left to join her client.

"I like her. She's a very classy woman," Costa said. "How come you let her go, Gino?"

Gino didn't say anything. He was too busy remembering.

• • • • •

In front of the camera Eden ran her hands down Tim Wealth's chest. She kissed him passionately and felt his sharp response as he peeled the dress from her shoulders and bent her back across a table.

"Cut!" the director shouted.

Santino hunched forward in his usual ringside seat. He did not like the amount of time it took for them to separate. He mumbled curses under his breath.

They broke the clinch and Eden walked over to her hairdresser, who began to fuss with her hair.

"Hey—cunt," Santino called out loudly. "C'mere."

She ignored him.

"I said, *Come here*, movie star cunt," Santino repeated.

The hairdresser's hand began to shake. Eden was cool. Inside she was raging. The entire crew was on full alert. Tim had vanished into his dressing room.

Slowly she walked toward her keeper. He was a monster. A short, bald, hairy pig. And he was getting crazier every day.

"What?" she hissed.

He stood up and pulled her roughly by the arm. "Ya got a few minutes, movie star?" he questioned.

Her voice was strained. "Yes."

Everyone was listening, even though they pretended they weren't.

"I feel like a blow job," Santino announced lazily. "Let's go to your dressin' room, movie star, I'm gonna let you suck me off."

She froze inside. It wasn't enough she was his. He had to publicly humiliate her. He had to show the world he could treat her how he liked. If she'd had a gun she would have shot him right between his beady little balls.

Lennie needed time to be alone and think things out. So he told no one he was returning to L.A., not even Jess. He flew in and took a cab from the airport to his old apartment, which he had kept for sentimental reasons.

The one-bedroom penthouse on Doheny smelled musty and unused. He opened up the shutters. It felt like home. More home than the multiroomed mansion in Bel Air had ever been.

Harriet, the old crusty maid who had looked after him when he lived there, was supposed to come in and clean once a week—she was still on the payroll—but it was obvious she never did. He fingered a shelf, and thick dust ran riot.

He looked around. The bed was unmade—fond memories of a thousand little blondes. The living room was untidy. He found half a bottle of vodka and a stack of yellow legal pads he had been writing on. Once. A long time ago.

The apartment was peaceful. No servants padding around, no telephones ringing, no secretaries and, most of all—no Olympia.

He had made the move.

He was free.

Almost.

· · · · ·

After lunch break, Santino left the set.

Eden held her head high, although deep down she was mortified. He had forced her to her knees and threatened her when she tried to object. He was definitely becoming unhinged. Escape had to be soon. She was convinced that eventually he would threaten her life, not just her face.

Tim held her close in front of the camera, and then later, in his dressing room between setups, he held her for real, and they made love urgently. She did things to Tim Wealth willingly. Things Santino had to force from her.

"I'm working on getting us out as soon as possible," Tim assured her. "Maybe tomorrow. I want you to be ready for my call."

"We can't go anyplace where Santino can reach me," she said anxiously.

"Money'll take us a long way, and I'm scoring us plenty."

He had figured out a scam—of sorts. It involved Brigette. So what? She was a spoiled, rich brat. It was about time she learned the ways of the world.

• • • • •

The last thing Brigette felt like doing was playing with a four-and-a-half-year-old boy. And she had always loathed CeeCee.

They sat around the pool like one big happy family. Alice in a cutaway swimsuit revealing gnarled flesh and an alarming growth of pubic hair straggling from the crotch. Alice's friend, Claudio, perfectly formed in every way, but hardly taller than Roberto, who played happily in the pool. CeeCee, watchful as ever. And Brigette in a white bikini, looking at least nineteen.

Brigette sunbathed enthusiastically, knowing that a tan went well with her long blond hair. She wanted to look her best for Tim. The summer was ending, and soon it would be time to return to hateful school. She couldn't bear it. Her thoughts were all of Tim Wealth. He was unlike anyone she had ever met before. He was so moody and smart and sexy. . . .

After dinner at Trader Vic's he had taken her to his apartment in Hollywood. One room. One bed. Oh! Was he sexy!

He had undressed her, made love to her, caused her to shiver and shake, and then, as a joke, he had said, "Let's take some pictures, little girl."

She had giggled with embarrassment when he told her how to pose in front of his Polaroid camera. "Do this. Do that. Smile. Look happy."

At first she was shy—but after he told her the photos were for her to keep, she had relaxed and enjoyed the game. He presented her with the pictures. She presented him with the bag of white powder she had taken from Olympia's dressing room. He was really pleased.

What a brilliant adventure, spending the night with Tim Wealth. She wished she could spend every night with him.

In the morning he called her a cab, said he would phone her later, and sent her on her way.

She waited eagerly to hear from him.

• • • • •

After delivering Roberto to spend the afternoon with Brigette, Gino was at a loss. Ria had taken Costa shopping along Rodeo Drive—and the afternoon stretched emptily before him.

Since divorcing Susan, he had no order to his life. He did whatever he wanted whenever he wanted. It was good, but there was something missing. He liked the companionship of a steady woman. He liked to be able to wake up in the morning and find someone there. He was too old for the quick lay— and most of the women he went to bed with now failed to hold his interest.

Finally, Gino had to admit, he was getting old.

With Paige Wheeler he had never felt old. Seeing her again had rekindled all the memories, and they were pretty good memories.

He thought he had noticed a gleam in her eye when she looked at him today. Was he mistaken, or did she miss him too?

Impulsively he drove to the Beverly Wilshire Hotel and checked into a suite.

"No luggage, Mr. Santangelo?" questioned the desk clerk.

"It'll be over later. Send up a bottle of Dom Pérignon and a dish of your best caviar."

"Yes sir."

Once upstairs he paced the suite.

So—he had caught Paige with Susan. Well, she had never professed to be a virgin.

So—was he going to call her or what?

• • • • •

Outside Lina Lee, on Rodeo Drive, at four o'clock in the afternoon, Ria broke her water.

"Omigod!" she squawked. "Get me to the hospital—quick!"

Costa, a calm man all his life, panicked completely.

A tourist from Minnesota and a concerned salesgirl took charge of the situation. If it wasn't for them, Ria might have started labor on the sidewalk.

• • • • •

"I need an estimate on a decorating job," Gino said formally into the telephone.

Paige recognized his voice immediately. She waved an assistant from her office and leaned back in her comfortable leather chair. "What kind of a job?" she inquired, equally formal.

"Urgent."

"Urgent?"

"Very."

"Hmmmm . . ." She paused as if consulting a full appointment book. "I'm afraid I have no free time until next week."

"Fit me in."

She propped her legs on the desk. "I don't know if I can."

"You can."

"Where?"

"The Beverly Wilshire. Where else?" He gave her the suite number.

"Have you any idea what you require?" She asked in a businesslike tone.

"You. And fast."

Smiles suffused both their faces as they hung up.

• • • • •

"Have a piece of fruitcake, I made it myself," trilled Alice, offering it around. "All pure ingredients. Oo la la! It's so good!"

She had covered her swimsuit with a garment that resembled a flowered tablecloth and was trying to impress Claudio with her skill as a homemaker. Last night he had confided that he came from a titled French family. He was secretly a count. Countess Claudio! Ha! That would *really* impress everyone.

CeeCee took a bite, and promptly broke the cap of her front tooth on a stale walnut. Clutching the offending cap, CeeCee glared.

"I suppose we'll have to get you to a dentist," Alice said reluctantly. "What a nuisance!"

CeeCee nodded. She had no choice. The cold air was hitting a nerve, and she could feel the onslaught of a nagging toothache.

"I have a dentist in Marina del Rey," Alice said with a martyred sigh. "I'd better call him." She huffed with the inconvenience of it all, and picked up the telephone.

• • • • •

"Hello, little girl."

Brigette almost jumped with delight. "I was waiting for your call," she said. "I didn't think I'd hear from you this early."

"Wanna come over to my place and play?"

"Oh, no! I can't. I'm looking after my stupid uncle."

"Your *uncle?*"

"He's four and a half years old. And dumb."

She missed the catch of excitement in Tim's voice as he said, "Roberto?"

"How'd you know his name?"

"I'm not just a beautiful actor."

Brigette giggled.

"Where is everybody?" he asked curiously. "How come you're looking after the kid?"

"Roberto's nanny broke her tooth, and Alice and her boyfriend—he's a freak—like they all went off in the limo to get it fixed. Alice's dentist is in Marina del Rey, and Alice wanted to take her friend—you should *see* him—to look at her apartment. So . . . like I got stuck, didn't I?"

"I'm fond of kids," Tim said quickly, his mind reorganizing the scam he had planned.

"You wouldn't like this one," Brigette said grimly. "He's a geek."

"Bring him. I'll let you know."

She giggled. "I can't do that."

"Sure you can. Take a cab to the corner of Fairfax and Sunset, and I'll meet you there. We'll buy the kid an ice cream and I'll drive him home. Then we can have the whole evening alone together. How's that?"

Brigette was tempted. She wanted to see Tim more than anything. But if she took Roberto anywhere CeeCee would go bananas. CeeCee was very protective. As soon as she realized she had to go to the dentist she had tried to get Gino or Costa to come and collect Roberto, but they were both unreachable. And she didn't trust the maids. Reluctantly she had left the child in Brigette's care. "Don't let him out of your sight," she had admonished. "I'll be back as soon as I can."

CeeCee was so bossy. All she cared about was stupid Roberto. It would serve her right to come back and find him gone.

"Well?" Tim demanded. "What's happening?"

"We're coming for ice cream," Brigette giggled. "Can't wait!"

. . . . .

Things were working out better than Tim expected.

He picked up the tabloid newspaper on the table in front of him and stared at the heading above a picture of a small dark-haired child climbing out of a swimming pool. THE RICHEST BOY IN THE WORLD.

He reread the small print underneath:

Is Roberto Stanislopoulos the richest boy in the world? Close friends of the late billionaire, Dimitri Stanislopoulos, say that he soon will be. It was reported in New York today . . .

Slowly Tim put the paper down. Brigette Stanislo-poulos was catch enough, but now he would have both of them.

It was a piece of good fortune he could scarcely have dreamed of.

Steven didn't know whether to tell Mary Lou or not. He agonized over what he should do, and then he realized there was only one way to go. He had to tell her. The offending magazine was just about to hit the stands. The press would be bugging her, waiting for her comments. *He* knew it wasn't Mary Lou in the pornographic photo spread, but they were going to have to prove it to the rest of the world.

"Goddamn it!" he muttered to himself. And he wondered how slime like Santino Bonnatti could even exist.

Lucky Santangelo had eliminated Santino's father, the notorious Enzio. She had had her reasons. According to the word on the street, Enzio had been responsible for the murder of her lover, Marco, *and* her brother, Dario. At the time Steven had been disapproving. The law was adequate. The law would have dealt with the likes of Enzio Bonnatti.

Now he wasn't so sure. The law was a long, shaky process. People could be bribed to see that justice never took place.

He canceled an appointment and hurried home. The sooner he told Mary Lou, the better. She would have to speak to the network and the sponsors of her show. The best thing to do was to have her release a statement before the press besieged their brownstone.

He planned how to handle the situation. Dignity and denial, that was the only way.

The strong smell of gas hit him as he opened the front door. He gagged and almost choked—the air was thick with it.

Jesus Christ! Had Mary Lou left the oven on? She hated to cook; they usually sent out for food.

He held his breath and rushed into the kitchen.

Mary Lou was on the floor slumped by the open oven.

Next to her lay a copy of *Comer* magazine.

111

Lucky wandered into Matt's office and perched on the ledge of his desk. "I've had it," she told him with an exhausted sigh. "I'm taking off for L.A. in the morning. I'll spend the weekend and be back on Tuesday. Can you manage without me?"

"I think we'll get by," Matt said dryly. "As long as calling you day or night is in order."

The Santangelo had opened to capacity business—but there were the usual problems with chefs, managers and general staff. All controllable.

Lucky smiled ruefully. "You know I never sleep. And you also know I like to be the first to hear everything that goes on."

Matt said, "So go—relax—have a rest and enjoy yourself. You deserve it."

She picked a pencil off his desk and played with it. "I can't wait to see Roberto. That's what I really need—a massive fix of baby love."

"Sounds good to me."

"Well, who knows, maybe when you and Jess do the deed you'll have one of your own."

He laughed self-consciously. "I don't know about that."

They discussed several business matters. Matt knew of Lucky's plans to sell. She had included him in for a piece of the action. He hadn't made up his mind what he would do next. The potential buyers had offered him a firm management contract with points—but he needed to discuss it with Jess before deciding.

Business concluded, Lucky pecked him on the cheek and went off to pack. She hadn't called to tell Gino she was coming. She wanted to surprise everyone.

The sound of the shower filtered through to the bedroom. Gino, clad in a bathrobe, sat on the edge of the rumpled bed and plucked a bottle of Dom Pérignon from the ice bucket on the side table. Empty. Every drop gone. And he couldn't remember drinking that much.

"Hey—" he called out. "We finished the champagne."

"Live dangerously," Paige called back. "Order another bottle. There must be *some* compensations for sleeping with a rich old man."

He chuckled as he picked up the phone. She always made him laugh. "More champagne on the way," he said as he walked into the bathroom, opened the shower door and watched her soap herself. She had full, real breasts (how he hated silicone—whoever invented silicone tits should be shot), a firmly packed body, soft thighs, and an unmanageable thatch of pubic hair, copper—like the hair on her head. "Y'know what I want," he said.

She massaged her breasts vigorously. "What?"

"I want you to stay the night. Just like in New York. Remember? We had some good times there, didn't we?"

She put the soap down and allowed the water to wash over her. Then she stepped from the stall and enveloped herself in a fluffy towel.

"You know I can't stay," she said briskly.

"Why not?" he demanded.

"Because," she replied patiently, "I am a married woman, and I have a husband at home who will be extremely concerned if I just decide to stay out all night."

"Will he?"

She began to towel herself dry. "Yes, he will."

"He doesn't mind you spending the day gettin' laid, but an all-nighter is out of line, huh?"

She refused to let him get to her. "You got it." She dropped the towel and reached for a bathrobe.

He sat on the side of the tub. "I missed you, kiddo," he said. "I tried a selection—but you're the only one can do it for me."

She began to laugh. "I don't believe *that*, Gino. You'll go to your grave with a hard-on!"

He grabbed her around the waist and pressed his face against her stomach.

She parted the bathrobe. "While you're down there . . ." she murmured.

He didn't need any more encouragement.

·   ·   ·   ·   ·

Alice lingered with Claudio in Marina del Rey. She showed him her old photo albums and carefully preserved silver-tasseled G-strings. He was duly impressed. Especially when she produced the candid snaps she had taken of everyone on the famous Stanislopoulos cruise.

They sipped Martinis, admired the view from Alice's waterfront apartment and made out on the couch. Alice smiled to herself. Claudio might be short, but he had the biggest *schlong* she'd ever seen.

It wasn't until an irate CeeCee phoned from the dentist's waiting room that Alice realized they were running two hours late. "Oo la la!" she exclaimed in mock horror. "The *schvartze* is mad—we'd better be running."

·   ·   ·   ·   ·

The harsh slap sent Eden reeling across the room.

"You're a cunt, that's all y'are. An' an *old* cunt at that."

"I'm thirty-one," Eden sobbed, out of control. "That's not old. . . ." She crouched in the corner waiting for his next move. *"That's not old,"* she shrieked.

"In this town it's friggin' pushin' up daisies—for a woman," Santino spat out disdainfully. He had removed his jacket and vest and rolled up the sleeves of his striped shirt—beating up a woman took it out of you. He was sweating more than usual.

Eden pulled herself into the fetal position, knees up to her chest, arms clutched around them. She was a mess. One eye was blackened and half-closed, her jaw was swollen and bruised purple, blood dripped from a cut lip.

Santino bore down on her. "If ya fuck around on Santino Bonnatti, ya gotta pay the price. Understand, cunt?"

"I haven't done anything," she whimpered.

He raised his arm to strike another blow but thought better of it. She had learned her lesson. She wouldn't open her legs for anyone else in a hurry. She *knew* who she belonged to.

Now all he had to do was deal with Tim Wealth. Teach *him* the score.

Nobody fucked Santino Bonnatti's woman off camera.

Nobody.

Not unless he said so.

113

S o this is the kid?" Tim Wealth asked.

"This is the geek," Brigette agreed.

"Not a geek. Not," Roberto asserted.

"Hold my hand, brat, and shut up." Brigette grabbed the small boy's hand. Traffic was racing past on Sunset. All she needed was for Roberto to wander under a car. Lucky would never speak to her again.

Tim bent to talk to the child. "Hello there," he said.

"Ice cream?" the boy asked eagerly.

"If you're good," replied Tim.

Brigette giggled. "I bet people passing by think we're a family," she said. "I'm Mommy, and you're Daddy, and this is our little one." She exploded with mirth.

Tim looked quickly around. He didn't want anyone noticing anything. Brigette was not exactly low profile in a red T-shirt with HOT STUFF emblazoned on the front, skin-hugging white jeans and cascades of long blond hair.

"Let's go to my place," he suggested.

"Ice cream," repeated Roberto, trying to wriggle out of Brigette's grasp.

"Shut up, Bobby," she snapped, thinking to herself that she should have left the kid at home. What was the *point* in bringing him along? CeeCee would be furious.

So what? She was only a stupid nanny. Who cared *what* her reaction was? In fact, it would do her good to worry. Brigette would never forget the spanking she had received because of her when she was eleven. The humiliation still stung.

"You promised the geek ice cream," she pointed out. "Let's get it over with and send him home."

There was no way she could let Tim drive Roberto back to the house. She had already decided to put him in a cab and then call Alice and say he was on his way. Alice would believe anything. "Hi, Ali," she would say. "I'm over at my girlfriend's house and we're going to a movie. Bobby's in a cab—he should be there any minute. And I'll probably stay at my friend's tonight." That way CeeCee couldn't say a word to her. Yeah—the brat would be okay, it was only a ten-minute ride. She couldn't wait to get rid of him and be alone with Tim.

"I've got ice cream at my place," Tim said.

"You have?"

"Häagen-Dazs. Chocolate-Chocolate Chip."

Brigette linked her arm happily through his. "What are we waiting for?" She grinned, pulling Roberto along with her other hand. "Let's go."

114

Information.

Carrie had the information her son required. And once Fred Lester confessed the truth, it was all so simple.

Gino Santangelo was Steven's father.

Gino. A memory from so long ago . . .

He had fathered her child and had no idea he had done so.

Gino Santangelo.

Over the years, she had occasionally read about him in the newspapers. Once a gangster, he was a big man now, and old—as she was. And respected. Only last week she had seen a picture of him in the newspaper at a charity function in Las Vegas with an ex-President. The two men had faced the camera with their arms around each other. Good friends.

Steven's father.

She couldn't care less. But Steven needed to know.

Carrie hurried along Lexington heading toward Steven's brownstone on Fifty-eighth Street. Her head was filled with thoughts. She was confused . . . so very confused. For forty-five years she had remembered Freddy Lester as nothing less than scum. And now he had reentered her life. A perfectly respectable man. A good-humored man with excellent manners and a kindly face.

It was so difficult to believe he had once been the drunken pig who had raped her. The unfeeling lout who had called her *"a fucking dinge."*

He had told her his story while she stared at him, contempt written across her face.

He told her about his accident and his family and his life.

She listened in stony silence.

Finally he had said, "If I *was* Steven's father I would want to know so that I could begin to make up for all the lost years."

Her voice was cold. "I don't know and I don't care."

"But I *do* know," he had said very quietly. "Once I was in possession of all the facts, I made it my business to find out."

"How could you possibly do that?" she asked.

"If you are positive that Gino Santangelo and I were the only two candidates, then there is no doubt."

"My book is the truth," Carrie said icily. "I don't lie."

"Well, then, Gino is Steven's father. I have an extremely rare blood type. I checked Steven's medical records—the laws of genetics prove I could not have fathered him." He paused, then continued, "I took the liberty of investigating Gino Santangelo's past. He was in jail between 1940 and 1947. They have a complete medical history. His blood type matches Steven's exactly."

Fred had continued further with confirming facts. He also had full documentation of all the evidence he had collected, which he handed to her.

Eventually he stopped speaking and she gathered herself together.

"Mr. Lester," she said coldly, "I don't wish to proceed with the plans for my book to be published."

"But—"

She raised her hand to stop his protestations. "Please. I need time to think. Maybe I'll feel different next week, next year. I simply don't know."

"I hope so," he said anxiously. "I can't tell you how important it is to me that we publish this book. It is a—"

"Ah, as long as the names are changed," she interrupted dryly, "to protect the not-so-innocent."

He gestured helplessly. "Carrie—it all happened a long long time ago. . . ."

"Not long enough, Mr. Lester. Not nearly long enough."

She left his office and walked unseeingly down Fifth Avenue. Now it was late afternoon and she was approaching Steven's house. He had to know the truth at once.

There was an ambulance parked outside, and a small crowd had gathered to gawk.

Carrie pushed her way through. "What's going on?" she asked a well-dressed woman.

"Suicide, I think," the woman said, eyes agleam. "Don't light a cigarette, the whole neighborhood'll blow up. Gas, I think. Can't you smell it?"

For one heart-stopping moment Carrie thought the victim might be Steven. But, thank God, before she could panic he came rushing out of the building, and behind him hurried two ambulance attendants carrying a stretcher.

"Steven," she called out desperately. "What happened?"

115

A very pleasant nurse kept Costa sane while Ria spent hours in delivery.

He continually tried to phone Gino but a stupid machine kept on answering the phone, and Costa had no intention of speaking to a machine. Finally he called Olympia's mansion to speak with CeeCee and Roberto, but a maid informed him everyone was out.

Was there no one he could give the good news to? He, Costa Zennocotti, was, at the age of seventy-five, about to become a father.

· · · · ·

CeeCee had bad feelings, she didn't know why, but they were powerful bad feelings. The day Dimitri Stanislopoulos died she had suffered from the same thing. Woke in the morning. Brushed her teeth and washed. Got Roberto up and fed him his favorite hash and sunny-side-up eggs. Then together they had gone to visit his father, as they always did.

Mr. Stanislopoulos was sitting in his usual place. He looked weak and tired.

"Good morning, CeeCee. Good morning, Roberto," he had said. Just as usual. And she had known at once that he wouldn't last the day through. Now she was racked with those ominous forebodings again.

She glared at Mr. Golden's foolish mother and her foreign companion, for they were responsible for Roberto's being left with Brigette longer than he should have been.

Brigette was irresponsible. She had no idea how to look after a four-and-a-half-year-old child. She was spoiled, selfish and jealous of Roberto—she always had been.

CeeCee sighed loudly. She had not known Marina del Rey was such a long drive. If she had been aware of the distance, she would have ignored her tooth, stuck the cap back with chewing gum or something. On top of everything else, Alice had left her sitting in the dentist's waiting room for nearly two hours. CeeCee was silently fuming.

Finally they were on their way back to Bel Air in Olympia's white Rolls-Royce.

"How long before we're there?" CeeCee asked the chauffeur.

He was a dour-faced Englishman in full uniform. "About half an hour, madam, depending on the traffic," he said sonorously.

"Thank you." She wished the bad feelings would go away.

116

Do you like me?" Tim Wealth asked.

Brigette didn't know what to say. Roberto sat at the kitchen counter slopping chocolate ice cream all over himself, and Tim was asking her the most important question of her life. *I don't like you, I love you,* she wanted to shout out loud, but maybe it was a bit too soon. After all, he hadn't mentioned love to her.

"You know I do," she said at last. "I don't do the things we do with anyone else. I *more* than like you." Hint, hint, maybe he would take it.

"I like you too," he said, very seriously. "But I know something about you that's bothering me."

"What?" she asked quickly.

"More ice cream," demanded Roberto.

Oh, God! She could smack the dumb little geek!

Tim moved to the fridge and took out another carton, which he placed in front of the child.

Brigette fidgeted impatiently and waited to find out what it was that bothered him.

He did not keep her in suspense. "I know how old you are," he said.

She felt herself begin to blush. "I'm eighteen," she bluffed.

"You're fourteen," he countered.

"I'm not," she lied desperately, feeling humiliated.

"You are," he said grimly. "And have you got any idea what that makes me guilty of?"

"What?" Her tone was sulky.

"Statutory rape."

The only sound in the room was Roberto slurping his ice cream. Brigette wished he wasn't there. She wished the floor would open up and swallow her. Tim Wealth was just about to tell her he couldn't see her anymore and she wanted to die.

"How did you find out?" she muttered, red-faced.

"You're not exactly a state secret," he said. "I was reading about your grandfather and his will."

"It's all lies."

"What is?"

"My mother says that everything the newspapers print is lies."

"Maybe so. But I checked, little girl, and you *are* fourteen. Your fifteenth birthday isn't until December."

"Happy birthday to me," she mumbled.

Roberto had spotted a television in the corner of the one-room apartment. "Wanta watch," he said, pointing.

Brigette flopped on the end of the couch that converted into Tim's bed.

Tim switched on the television for Roberto, and the child climbed down from the counter, took his carton of ice cream and sat on the floor a few inches in front of it, totally absorbed.

"I don't want to be fourteen," Brigette sulked. "I hate it. I really hate it!" Tears filled her big blue eyes. "And now you hate me too."

"No I don't," Tim said soothingly, putting his arm around her.

"Yes you do," she whimpered.

"No I *don't*. But we've got a big problem, and you have to help me find a solution."

She wished Roberto wasn't there. He was getting on her nerves just being in the same room.

"Don't worry," she said truculently. "I'm going back to school in Switzerland in a week, so I won't be such a big problem anymore."

"Do you want to go?" he asked quickly. "Or would you like to stay with me?"

The possibility of staying with him had never even entered her mind. But now he'd mentioned it, it was *exactly* what she'd like to do.

"How can I do that?" she asked hopefully.

"Listen to me, little girl, and listen carefully. I've got a plan."

117

Paige Wheeler called home at five-thirty. An urgent business trip to San Francisco had come up—she wouldn't return until the next day.

"Aren't you even going to pick up an overnight bag?" Ryder asked.

She explained about the Arab client with the private plane impatiently waiting to leave.

Ryder understood. Business was business.

Gino called the rented Beverly Hills house. There was nobody home, just the answering machine.

"This is an adventure," Paige purred, with a wicked smile. "I haven't had an adventure in a long time." She lay back on the bed and stretched contentedly. "You're so persuasive, Gino."

"Story of my life," he grinned. "I've had it pretty easy when it comes to gettin' my own way."

"I bet!"

· · · · ·

Lennie worked on a new script all afternoon. He finished the half bottle of vodka, put Bruce Springsteen on the stereo, and watched the sunset from his Hollywood apartment with the unmade bed and the thick layers of dust.

Christ! He felt terrific. Better than he had in a long time. And the material he had written was good, sharp-edged and full of caustic wit. He was on a roll after being blocked for months.

He was going to be free again.

No more mansions and servants.

No more Olympia.

It was as if he were starting over, and there was nobody to think about but himself.

Of course. He was rich in his own right now. He was hot. A movie star.

Shit! He was just a comic who got the right breaks at the right time. No movie star he.

There were things to be settled. Before Olympia returned to L.A. he had to collect his personal possessions from Bel Air. Clear out his study, take only what he had paid for. And then he would have to explain to Alice. She was up at the mansion looking after Brigette. Gently he would give the two of them the news. Brigette was basically a good kid—if she wanted to keep in contact, he'd be happy. She didn't have much of a life. Being stuck with Olympia for a mother was no smooth ride.

Tomorrow he would deal with them.

Tonight he would enjoy himself.

With that thought in mind he called Jess and asked her if she wanted to go with him to Foxie's.

She was leaving on an early-morning plane to spend the weekend with Matt, but she jumped at his offer, anxious to hear everything.

"Pick me up around eight," he said. "I'm the guy without a car."

"You've got four cars, Lennie," she pointed out.

"Not anymore," he said, without one note of regret.

• • • • •

The moment the Rolls-Royce pulled into the driveway of the Bel Air house, CeeCee leaped out.

"You'll break your neck, dear," warned Alice.

CeeCee moved fast. It was past six. If Lucky ever found out she had left Roberto for this length of time she would be furious, and rightly so. CeeCee knew she was trusted implicitly, and she was very proud of that fact.

"Roberto," she called, as she rushed into the house, trailed by Alice and Claudio, who seemed to have taken up residence. "Roberto!"

No response.

"They're probably up in Brigette's room," said Alice, leading Claudio into one of the vast living rooms.

CeeCee hurried up the majestic marble staircase, along a never-ending hallway. The house was ridiculously large. Six families could live in it and never bump into each other.

"Roberto," she called out anxiously.

Brigette's room was empty. There were clothes and records and magazines scattered everywhere. But no Brigette and no Roberto.

CeeCee wished the bad feelings would leave her. They were getting worse every moment. Without a doubt she knew something was wrong.

"Roberto!" she shouted. "Roberto. Where are you? *Roberto!*"

They searched the house, Alice complaining every inch of the way.

Two Mexican maids, who spoke very little English, professed to know nothing. Then a third maid appeared and mumbled something about a taxi.

"Did Roberto go in the taxi with Brigette?" CeeCee demanded, spacing her words to make sure the woman understood.

"*Sí, sí,*" the woman nodded.

"All this fuss." Alice shook her head wisely. "When Brigette realized we were late, she decided to take Roberto home."

A phone call to the rented house received no reply.

"Gino's taken them out for dinner," Alice suggested.

CeeCee nodded, hoping this was so. But the bad feelings would not leave her, and until they did, she could not be sure about anything.

118

The paparazzi sprang into action when Olympia Stanislopoulos put in an appearance at Studio 54 in New York. A bountiful princess, she emerged from a sleek gray limousine with black-tinted windows.

She wore a huge sable coat over her ample figure, and her long blond hair flowed across her shoulders.

Accompanying her was a short, snappish hairdresser, male, dressed from head to toe in studded leather; a Black secretary, female, who was six feet tall; and a long-haired makeup artist, transvestite.

Olympia beamed at the paparazzi. "Hi, guys." Her voice was slurred, and the pupils of her blue eyes piercing pinpoints of light. She draped herself provocatively against the front of her limo. "Wanna take my picture?"

Flashbulbs exploded as they jostled for position. Olympia Stanislopoulos looked like a pretty, blond baby elephant. These photos would front-page worldwide.

"Where's Lennie?" one of the photographers shouted.

Olympia frowned. "Lennie?" she asked, as if she honestly didn't know what they were talking about. "Lennie who?"

A spiffy young girl, camera at the ready, and shorthand going on in her head, made a good guess and said, "Is it true you two have split?"

Olympia wrapped her sable around her bulk and headed for the entrance of the club. "Lennie Golden," she announced grandly, "is a lousy husband—correction—*was* a lousy husband—*and* a lousy lay. Print that."

She swept inside, followed closely by her adoring entourage.

• • • • •

The Santangelo casino sparkled with activity. Lucky was all packed and ready to leave. She planned to drive to New

York, spend the night at the Pierre and catch the early flight to L.A.

Before leaving, she strolled through the casino. It always gave her a thrill to know she had created such excitement.

Vitos Felicidade was headlining, and the crowds were pouring out of the Diamond Room, having just sat through his first show. The women were all aflutter, clutching programs with Vitos's picture on the front and chattering about how gorgeous and *virile* he was.

They should only know! Lucky had spent one night in his company. He had achieved a two-minute erection and poured out all his troubles. She felt sorry for him. They had not consummated the act, merely talked the night away.

She waved to one of her pit bosses and pointed out a dealer getting too friendly with a plump brunette at a blackjack table. A stickman at the craps table called out a winner, and the crowd cheered. Two hookers discussing a tightfisted john careened past in low-cut clinging dresses.

Lucky's dark eyes swept the room. Everything was going smoothly. She was satisfied.

* * * * *

"'Ello, 'ello, 'ello. It's Tubs in full bloom, ain't it?"

Olympia peered at the skinny figure standing before her in the noisy club. Lately she was having a little trouble focusing. "Hello," she said vaguely.

"It's *me,* yer silly bint. Flash."

"I *loooove* your work," sighed the transvestite, leaning forward.

"So do I," agreed the hairdresser, not to be left out.

"Piss off, yer two old queens," Flash said good-naturedly. He sat down beside Olympia, who finally realized who he was.

"Yer lookin' all right," Flash said, peering at her face. "Bit of added flesh, but yer really got it together, dint you?"

"I feel sensational."

He slipped his hand beneath folds of sable and squeezed

her waist. "I always liked fat chicks. Turns me on, y'know what I mean?"

"I am not fat. Merely a few pounds overweight."

"And some."

"Where do you get your scarves? I *looooove* your scarves," crooned the transvestite, stroking the stream of dirty white silk hanging around Flash's neck.

Flash grimaced. "Ere, leave it out, will ya. What kinda bums yer travelin' with, Tubs?"

She had him fully in focus now. Flash. Rock star. Lover. Prick.

"You treated me like nothing when I really needed you," she steamed, staring at his pockmarked face. "And from what I hear, things are not too good for you lately. What a *shame*," she added sarcastically.

"I told yer," he said slyly. "I just wasn't inter fuckin' disfigurements. But yer lookin' good now, Tubs. Just like new."

"What do you want?" she asked grandly.

"Whatever he wants—give it to him!" shrieked the hairdresser.

"Ooooh, yes," sighed the transvestite. "*Sooo* macho!"

"Just bein' friendly," Flash said.

"You've never been friendly in your life," Olympia pointed out.

He stuck his tongue in her ear. "Wanna fly?" he whispered.

His breath was tinged with garlic and tobacco. His clothes smelled of old smoke. His teeth, when he opened his mouth, were as rotten as ever.

She remembered old times. Sex, drugs, and rock 'n' roll.

Why not one more fling with a faded rock star?

119

All of her life Brigette had been waiting for something wonderful to happen. She had grown up in a world of thoughtless adults who gave her a superabundance of material possessions but nothing much else. When she was little she could get everyone's attention by screaming, and she would carefully pick her moments. This infuriated her mother, who was so pretty . . . always dressed up in furs and jewels with her blond hair curling softly around her face. But her mother was always busy with her latest boyfriend. Forever distracted by other people.

Brigette had *loved* spoiling her mother's perfect day. It always made Olympia so mad when she screamed and yelled, but at least it forced her to notice she had a daughter.

For the last few years Brigette hadn't cared whether she noticed or not. And when her mother was in the plane crash, she had been secretly pleased. If Olympia died, she wouldn't have to force her to notice anymore.

However, Olympia didn't die. She just got fat. And Brigette grew up. And learned there was more to life than grabbing Mommy's attention.

Now Tim Wealth had entered her life. And Brigette knew the wonderful moment she had been waiting for had finally arrived. Forget school and lessons and everything else. Tim Wealth was her future. Tim Wealth wanted to be with her forever. He explained his plan while she listened responsively and Roberto stuck his hand in the empty ice-cream carton and edged closer and closer to the television until he was only inches away.

Tim kept on emphasizing the fact that she was only fourteen. "If you were eighteen we'd have no problem," he explained patiently. "We could skip off to Nevada or somewhere, get married, and there's nothing anyone could do about it. But because you're under age, we've got to go into hiding. And to do that we need plenty of money. And to do it *successfully*, I'm talking *a lot* of bread. Multibucks."

"I'm *very* rich," Brigette announced matter-of-factly. "My grandfather just left me a fortune."

"Sure. But it's all tied up until you're eighteen or twenty-one. Something like that, huh?"

"Yes, but it's still mine."

"*I* know that and *you* know that, but try telling *them*." He paused, then reeled her in nice and easy. "I want to be with you all the time, little girl. You're very very special, and I don't want to risk losing you. Understand?"

She nodded, enthralled. Every dream she had ever had was coming true.

Tim roamed the room, balling his fists, talking fast, getting her involved and enthusiastic. "Whether your mother cares about you or not, she'd try to split us up," he said. "And so would Lennie Golden. *And* Lucky. They'd all say you're too young. We'd have no chance. They'd lock you up somewhere and we'd never see each other again."

"I'd escape," Brigette said fiercely.

"Yeah, well, I don't want to put you in that position," he said quickly. "We've got to strike before they do."

She was completely caught up in what he was saying. "Yes, yes," she agreed, blue eyes shining brightly.

"This is what we have to do," he said, keeping his voice low and moving very close to her. "We have to get *your* money from them. It's *your* money, and you're entitled to every red cent."

She nodded excitedly.

"But they're not going to want to give it to you," Tim continued. "So we've got to trick 'em."

"How do we do that?"

"By playing a game."

"What game?"

"Let's call it 'kidnap-and-ransom.' "

She shivered. "Is it dangerous?"

He laughed. "Would I involve you in anything dangerous? You've got to trust me."

"What about *him?*"

They both turned to stare at Roberto.

"He's a bonus," Tim said. "Kind of like insurance to make sure they pay up quickly. Like tomorrow."

Brigette felt a twinge of conscience—only a twinge.

"After they've paid, they'll get both of you back," Tim continued.

"*I'm* not going back!" Brigette wailed.

"Only for a couple of days while I get our escape organized," he said hurriedly. "Then you meet me at a prearranged spot, and we skip. In the meantime you describe your kidnappers as a couple of Mexicans who kept you in Santa Monica— make up whatever you like."

"Hmmm . . . and how do I explain taking Bobby off in a cab?"

"You got an urgent phone call. A message from your mother to meet her and bring the boy."

She giggled. "You've thought of everything."

"I sure have." God! She was naive. Couldn't she see the scam he was pulling? By the time she realized he wasn't going to meet her, he'd be long gone with Eden, and she'd be sent back to Switzerland in disgrace.

If they ever did track him, he had two Polaroid pictures of sweet little Brigette at play. She thought she'd kept all the prints, but it had been easy to slip a couple to one side. Those photos alone should be worth a million bucks to her family to suppress. Yeah. A million dollars meant nothing to those kinds of people. Once he had the money, it was a clear run ahead.

"How much are we going to ask for?" Brigette ventured.

"A million dollars," Tim replied seriously. "A million buckeroos."

120

By nine o'clock at night CeeCee was frantic, yet nobody else seemed to give a damn. She had been running back and forth between the rented house and the Bel Air mansion, hoping for news. The rented house was empty. No Gino or Costa.

"Don't be such a worrywart," Alice said, totally unconcerned. "Brigette's with Roberto, so he's quite safe. They're either out with Gino or maybe at her girlfriend's house."

"Who *is* her girlfriend, Mrs. Golden?" CeeCee asked desperately. She was probably worrying unnecessarily—they were more than likely with Mr. Santangelo, as Alice said.

Alice shrugged. "I don't know . . . a school friend. Brigette stayed with her last night."

If they *were* with Gino, CeeCee thought, then why hasn't he left a message? "Do you have a phone number?" she asked, still concerned.

Alice shook her head.

"How about Brigette's friend? What's her name?"

"Je ne sais pas."

CeeCee was at boiling point. "Mrs. Golden!" she exploded. "You're a disgrace. You're supposed to be in charge of Brigette, and you don't even know where she spent the night."

"Don't you speak to *me* in that tone of voice," Alice said haughtily. "I was once a star, y'know. Everyone thinks my son is the big shot in the family, but *I* was famous before he was born. So stick that in your thinking cap and don't be so rude, young woman."

CeeCee glared. Roberto's safety was at stake, not to mention her job, and this old crone was giving a speech about stardom. "I just want Roberto home," she said through clenched teeth. "How can we find out who Brigette's friend is?"

"I don't know," snapped Alice. "And I wish you'd stop fussing so. They'll be back in a minute, just you wait and see."

• • • • •

"I don't believe it!" Rainbow exclaimed. "The man himself."

Lennie swept her into a hug.

"Foxie!" she called. "Come an' see what I got for you!"

Foxie came scurrying out from his office, took one look at Jess and grabbed her.

"Not her!" Rainbow laughed. She kissed Lennie jammily on the mouth. "*This* hunk."

"A hunk, a skunk, who cares?" said Foxie, rolling his cross-eyes. "When my sweet Jess is around, nobody else counts."

"Charming!" Rainbow smiled. "He loves another woman!"

"And I love him, too," Jess said firmly, cuddling the little man.

Lennie smiled and relaxed. He had neglected his friends since hitting it big. Well, Olympia would hardly have fitted in—he could just imagine her with the lecherous Foxie. Or making conversation with raunchy Rainbow.

Lucky would fit in. Lucky would fit in anywhere.

Give it a couple of months, and he would call her.

Yeah.

Maybe they could start over.

Maybe.

• • • • •

Costa became a proud father at 9:40 P.M. He was ecstatic. He had a seven-pound, two-ounce baby daughter.

He marched along the hospital corridor handing out cigars to strangers. Then he rushed to the telephone to inform Gino of the marvelous news.

CeeCee answered the phone. "Oh, Mr. Zennocotti, where are you?" she wailed. "Is Roberto with you?"

"Why would he be with me?" said Costa, puzzled. "Put Gino on the line, quickly."

"He's not here. Roberto's not here." And she launched into a jumbled explanation.

Costa said exactly what Alice had said. "They must be with Gino. Don't worry. I'm sure they'll be home any time now. And when they get there, have Gino call me. Pronto. I have magnificent news."

• • • • •

At ten o'clock exactly the telephone rang in the Bel Air mansion.

"Hello," Alice said gaily. She was quite merry on several glasses of Grand Marnier, and Claudio was feeling no pain after imbibing a half bottle of Delamain Cognac.

"A million bucks," said a muffled voice.

"What?"

"Roberto. Brigette. A million bucks for the two of them."

"I can't *hear* you. Speak up."

"Don't call the police, just think about getting the money together. Cash. Fifty-dollar bills. Unmarked."

"I don't understand. Who *is* this?"

"Farmers Market. Four o'clock tomorrow afternoon. Go into the bookstore with a bag containing the money. Go over to the diet book section in the back—put the bag in the corner and leave the store by the other entrance. Don't look back. Got it?"

"Oh, dear!" Alice fluttered.

"If you want to see either of them alive again you'd better follow my instructions. A million bucks. No cops. No fuckups. No second chances. If you do exactly as I say, the kids will be returned to the house within an hour."

The line clicked dead.

121

Kennedy airport was crowded with people determined to get an early start on the weekend rush.

Lucky strode straight through to the Pan Am lounge. She just had time for a cup of coffee before her flight was called.

Steven arrived at the airport fifteen minutes later. His expression was grim as he bought a ticket for the next Pan Am flight to L.A. He was unshaven and unkempt, having spent all night at Mary Lou's bedside.

Sometimes in life there are things you have to do. And sometimes staying on the right side of the law means these things never get accomplished.

Steven, for once in his life, planned to take the law into his own hands.

Steven, personally, planned to beat the shit out of Santino Bonnatti.

122

I'm uncomfortable," Brigette whined. She had been whining on and off all night long. A list of complaints spewed forth from her rosebud lips.

"For crissakes," Tim said, "go back to sleep."

She sat up. "Gotta go to the bathroom," she mumbled.

"Well, go," he said bad-temperedly.

She climbed off the couch bed, stepped over Roberto, who was sleeping on a makeshift pile of cushions, and shut herself in the tiny bathroom. It was no fun sleeping next to Tim squashed up together like sardines in a can. It might have been fun if the stupid kid wasn't with them. She couldn't stand dumb little Bobby. Why did they have to keep him?

She imagined CeeCee freaking out. Oh, the panic she must be in!

Tim was up when she emerged from the bathroom, and so was Roberto. "I'm hungry," the boy said, rubbing his eyes.

Lucky would freak too. Brigette felt a bit bad about that— but it wasn't like they weren't looking after Bobby. "I'll make breakfast," she said cheerily.

"There's nothing to make," Tim replied. Now that the wheels were in motion, he wanted it to be over and done with. Timing was everything.

Collect the money.

Dump Brigette and the kid.

Grab Eden.

And run.

There was a late-afternoon flight to Mexico City and he had booked two seats. From there they would hire a car and drive into oblivion.

"Wanta go home," Roberto said. "Want CeeCee. Want Mama."

Brigette opened the fridge. There was nothing in it.

"Don't you ever eat?" she asked Tim. "I'm starving."

He had sent out for pizza the night before. There was some left in the box. "Feast on that," he said.

"Ugh!" she exclaimed. "I'll go out to the market."

"No, you won't," he said quickly. "I'll do it—write down what you want."

The last thing he needed was Brigette wandering around the neighborhood getting seen and remembered. He thought about what must be going on at the Bel Air mansion. They were probably amassing the money and keeping quiet. Rich people didn't like publicity. His hunch was they would pay and shut up—as long as they got their kids back.

He had quizzed Brigette relentlessly about whether she had ever mentioned him to any of them.

"No way," she had assured him. "Like they'd freak out if they thought I was seeing anyone."

He dressed in a hurry while Brigette scribbled out a list of her requirements. Could he trust her? She seemed happy enough, but just in case, he warned her not to pick up the phone if it rang, and to double-lock the front door behind him when he left.

Once on the street he phoned Eden. "Can you talk?" he questioned.

"No." Her voice was tremulous. "I think you have the wrong number."

He kept his voice low and spoke fast, "Meet me outside the front of the May Company on Wilshire just after four today. Everything's in motion. We're on our way."

• • • • •

"Who was that?" Santino asked.

"Wrong number," Eden replied.

"Did they talk dirty?"

"No."

"Then why'dja hang on an' listen?"

"They repeated the number, just to see if they dialed correctly."

"You think I'm fuckin' stupid or what?"

She was sick of his abuse, physical and mental. There was no letup. He had stayed the night to torment her. Now she had to plan her escape. It would not be easy to get out. "I think you should leave me alone," she said wearily.

"Yeah. I think so too. You're not gettin' any younger. *You* are an old broad—you know that? Kinda sad—but I got a heart of gold hangin' around, fuckin' ya, lettin' ya live here. Doncha think?"

"I appreciate everything you've done for me, Santino." He had trained her to behave like a lapdog, to roll over and play dead.

"I even starred ya in a movie," he continued. "Just what ya wanted. Right, honey?"

She nodded. "It was very kind of you."

The moment he left the house, she was going. Zeko would be easy to lose in Beverly Hills while she supposedly shopped. There was one store she knew where the fitting rooms led onto a back alleyway. If she took a pile of clothes and left Zeko waiting in front, it would be hours before he even realized she'd gone.

"Sure, sure, sure," Santino said expansively. He sat up in bed and stroked his hairy chest with loving care. "I starred ya in a movie—pretty generous of me considerin' you're over the hill."

"Thank you," she murmured.

"Ya paid me back though."

She had no idea where he was heading. Silence was safest.

"Yeah," Santino said reflectively. "Ya certainly paid me back. An' how."

Her face felt terrible. She could hardly see out of her left eye and her lip was swollen and sore. What a mess she must look.

"I got a head for revenge," he said vindictively. "Cross Santino Bonnatti an' you'd better not walk down any one-way streets on a dark night. Not even ten years later. Ya gettin' my drift?"

"I've never crossed you."

"Whaddya call fuckin' your co-star?"

"I didn't."

A smash across the face.

She felt her teeth rattle. "I *didn't,* you bastard!"

"Maybe ya did an' maybe ya didn't," he said mildly. "I figured it might be a gag t' find out."

He had opened the cut on her lip. Blood dripped slowly onto satin sheets.

Where was Gino? A message from him turned up on the answering machine saying he would be out all night, but leaving no clue to his whereabouts.

Alice, when she received what she considered to be a garbled phone call about kidnapping and ransom, sat in shocked silence for a few moments and then had hysterics.

Claudio sent for CeeCee. She immediately located Costa at the hospital, then collapsed in a chair, shaking and muttering to herself. Shortly after, Costa arrived at the house, and tried to take charge. "No police," he kept on saying. "No outside help until we hear from Gino."

"What about Lucky?" wailed CeeCee. "She'll go crazy. She'll blame me, and it *is* my fault."

"It's nobody's fault," Costa said wearily. This was turning out to be the worst night of his life as well as the best. He attempted to reach Lucky at the Hotel Santangelo and spoke to Matt, who told him she was flying into L.A. on the early-morning flight. "You can reach her at the Pierre if it's important," Matt added.

Costa didn't know what to do. If she was coming in anyway, why worry her? He decided to meet her at the airport. In the meantime, he tried to reach Olympia and Lennie.

A maid informed him that Miss Stanislopoulos was out, and that Mr. Golden no longer lived there.

"Where is he?" Costa asked.

The maid, who had been awakened from her sleep, was uncooperative and professed not to know.

Costa spent a restless night. He ordered a still-hysterical Alice upstairs, with Claudio to comfort her. And he sent CeeCee back to the rented house to wait for Gino. Meanwhile, he sat up in Lennie's study all night, counting the minutes and trying to figure out who could possibly have snatched the kids. They wanted—whoever they were—a million dollars in cash. An impossible task to get it together by four o'clock in the afternoon, although if anyone could do it, Gino and Lucky could.

Costa just wished he could contact one or the other. He had made a bad decision by not trying to reach Lucky before she left New York, but when he did finally decide to call her she was already on her way to the airport.

He checked with the hospital. His wife and baby were doing fine.

He didn't feel so fine himself. He felt like an old old man.

• • • • •

"Gotta tell you—you make me feel sixteen again!" Gino beamed, in the morning. "Well . . . maybe twenty."

Paige stretched luxuriously. "God, Gino. You *really* must have been something when you were young."

"Horny, hotheaded—they used t'call me Gino the Ram."

Paige laughed aloud. "The Ram! I love it. Tell me more."

"Well, I kinda lived between foster homes, an' there was this one woman—she had the biggest bazookas I'd ever seen—an' she expected me t'call her Mom."

Paige sat up in bed. She looked good in the morning, not washed out like a lot of women her age. "What *did* you call her?" she asked eagerly.

"Anything except Mom. I was thirteen—an' she kinda showed me the way t'go."

She nodded knowingly. "Ah . . . so you received your sexual education from an older woman.

"Yeh. An' I learned how t'fuck, too."

"Gino!"

"Don't tell me I finally shocked you?"

"Never."

"What are you? Unshockable?"

"Yup."

"Tough broad."

"Tougher than you."

"Yeh?"

"Yes."

He reached for her, but she evaded his move. "It shocked you when you discovered me in bed with Susan, didn't it?" she asked quietly.

Silence hung heavy. He had been prepared to forget that little incident. Now she was dragging it up.

"As a matter of fact," she continued, determined to get it out in the open, "Susan and I were having an affair long before she met you. We were—"

"I don't want to know about it," he interrupted roughly.

"I think you should. When you and I got together I realized that I wanted you a great deal more than I did her. Susan was reluctant to let go—the day you found us together was my goodbye."

"Some goodbye," he snorted.

"Haven't *you* ever taken a lover to bed to let them down easily when it's over?"

"I'd sooner see you in the sack with a young stud than with my wife," he said tightly.

"Next time I'll try and oblige."

"Hey—" He pulled her down close to him. "Has anyone ever told you that you got a big smart mouth?"

"Not lately."

He rolled on top of her, groaned and rolled off.

"What's the matter?" she asked, concerned.

"Why should I do all the work? I'm an over-the-hill stud—you're the sex maniac. Go to it, Mrs. Wheeler."

She sighed. "My oh my," she said, shaking her head. "Whoever your teacher was, she certainly did a thorough job!"

• • • • •

Lennie slept, cocooned in good feelings. He was working again, the creative juices flowing. He was back among his friends—an evening with Jess and Foxie and Rainbow was pure enjoyment. And he was free.

He got up in the morning and went straight back to work with a stack of yellow legal pads, a ballpoint pen and just his mind for company.

Later he would call Alice and give her the news of the impending divorce. She would probably have a nervous breakdown when she realized he would no longer be married to one of the richest women in the world. She had liked having a Stanislopoulos for a daughter-in-law.

Oh, well . . .

Too bad.

Poor old Alice.

124

Tim whistled as he headed back to his apartment carrying a paper sack containing milk, orange juice, bread, jam, and ice cream to keep the kid quiet. The hustle was going to work like a dream. He had been thinking that perhaps after Mexico he and Eden might head down to Brazil.

Ah . . . Rio. Ipanema Beach. Copacabana. With a million bucks to keep them company, they could do anything they wanted. Maybe he'd give up his acting career that wasn't going anywhere in a hurry and become a songwriter or a beach bum. He would soon be able to afford to do whatever he wanted. Anything at all.

He balanced the paper sack and groped for his keys as he walked up the outside stairs to his apartment, calling out, "It's me," as he turned the key in the lock.

And then he didn't know what hit him. Someone came up behind him and hurled him to the ground, shoving him inside the apartment with brutal force.

The paper sack of groceries went flying—milk spilled, ice cream splattered the walls, orange juice dribbled onto the floor.

"What the fu—" he began to say. But a sharp kick in the guts shut him up.

Both Brigette and Roberto started to scream.

"What we got *here?*" said Santino Bonnatti, stepping over Tim, nodding to the two hoods who had gained entry for him, and staring at Brigette and Roberto. "Family fuckin' circle?"

"Who are you? What do you want?" Brigette gasped. And then she sprang at one of the hoods who was casually and methodically kicking Tim as he tried to curl up in a ball to protect himself.

"Leave him alone!" she yelled.

"Leave him alone," copied Roberto, running to her side and clinging to her leg.

Santino's lip curled in disgust. Where did Tim Wealth inherit kids, for crissakes?

125

A very friendly Chinese man received no conversation at all from Steven on the five-hour flight to L.A. Up in first class, Lucky gave the same treatment to an elderly businessman with bad breath.

Neither of them ate. Neither of them watched the movie. Upon landing at LAX they hurried from the plane and managed to disembark at the same time, coming face to face at the point where first class meets tourist.

"Lucky Santangelo," Steven said.

She hesitated for only a moment, and then remembered. "Mister D.A.," she said with a wry grin.

He grimaced. "No more."

"You gave it up? I felt for sure you'd end up Mayor of New York City."

They walked together down the corridor linking the plane to the airport. He felt so strange seeing her again, now that he knew there was a wild possibility they shared the same father.

"Last time we met I was just about to be arrested." She turned to look at him. "Remember?"

"Oh, I could never forget that," he said. "You shot the guy I'd been working two years to indict."

"Self-defense."

"Sure."

"Really."

She recalled their meeting six years ago. The long, sticky New York blackout of 1977. And she had been trapped in an elevator with Mr. Steven Berkeley for a whole night—nine long hours. They had become friends—of sorts. They had almost become lovers.

A day later she had discovered he was the D.A. working on a case against Enzio Bonnatti. She hadn't seen him since.

"Do you live here?" he inquired politely.

She shook her head. "Do you?"

"Just visiting."

"What do you do, now you're not a D.A. anymore?" she asked curiously.

"I sold out. I'm a lawyer."

They stepped aboard the moving runway. She remembered going to his apartment that hot and humid morning because she had lost the keys to hers. He let her take a bath and borrow some of his clothes. God, he was so straight! But he had been tempted until his girlfriend invaded the mood that was starting to take place.

"Did you ever marry that girl—Ellen, wasn't that her name?"

"Aileen. No, I never married her."

Lucky grinned. "Good. She ruined the start of what could have been a beautiful relationship."

He forgot his anger for a moment and took her by the arm. "Many years ago your father, Gino, knew my mother."

She stared at him. He was startlingly handsome with his tight black curls, chocolate-cream skin, and deep-green eyes. "Really?"

"He owned a nightclub, Clemmie's, in the thirties, I think."

"That's right."

"Well—"

"Lucky!" Costa was at the end of the runway, waving frantically.

She waved back, wondering how he knew of her arrival.

"My uncle," she explained to Steven. "It was . . . nice seeing you again. Take care."

Was it his imagination or did he see a flash of himself in her goodbye smile?

He watched her out of sight and knew, once and for all, he had to find out who his father was.

• • • • •

There were drugs everywhere in Flash's hotel room, and Olympia was floating in heaven. She and Flash had soared through the night on a trail of good times, and she never wanted to leave his side again. He was no longer a reformed heroin addict—he had been back on the stuff for a while—and seeing Olympia in Studio 54 had sent dollar signs doing neon dances before his eyes.

The truth was that Flash was broke, busted, and a bum. His former group refused to have anything to do with him, and his teenage wife had thrown him out.

Olympia appeared at the right moment.

Olympia was cool to get high with.

Olympia could buy him anything he damn well wanted.

They started off on coke, switched to freebasing, and ended up doing speedballs—a mixture of cocaine and heroin.

It was a long night, interrupted only by a series of drug dealers who came and went with their variety of wares whenever Flash summoned them.

Levine, a former groupie turned addict and pusher, had serviced the happy couple at six in the morning.

"Come back in a few hours," Flash instructed her. "Bring me everything you got—grade A."

Levine promised she would.

Flash promised that if she delivered what he wanted he might strum her a few notes on his guitar.

Levine said, "Yeah!"

Olympia just smiled.

Levine returned at ten-fifteen in the morning with a whole bunch of goodies. She had stopped off at her apartment and collected a small Sony tape recorder. If Flash was going to play, she was going to get it down. Yeah!

The hotel was a dump, but it was a comfortable dump, and Flash liked the bohemian atmosphere of the place.

Levine knocked and then opened the door with the room key Flash had given her.

She took one horrified look, turned around and ran.

126

Santino Bonnatti strutted around Tim Wealth's one-room apartment. "Ya got a dump here," he remarked, picking up a framed picture of Tim and smashing it viciously to the floor.

"Wanta go home," screamed Roberto, clinging tightly to Brigette.

Tim attempted to get up, but Santino's hood kept a heavy foot on his stomach.

"Wanta go home!" yelled Roberto.

"Shut the fuck up," Santino said, glaring.

Brigette shivered. She wanted to go home too. She had no idea what was going on, but whatever it was, she was scared.

She spoke up in a shaky voice. "I'm taking Bobby home, Tim." Nervously she edged toward the door.

Tim saw a million dollars taking off. He also saw a lot of trouble in store for him if he didn't do something about it.

One of Santino's hoods blocked the door.

"Let 'em out," Santino said. "An' don't go runnin' for help or your little brother'll be missin' an arm."

"We won't," said Brigette gratefully. She gripped Roberto's hand tightly. "Come on, Bobby."

The hood stood to one side.

Santino walked over to Tim. "Pretty-boy shithead actor," he snarled. "Ya really think ya gonna fuck my woman an' get away with it?"

Brigette hustled Roberto from the apartment.

"Ya really think that?" Santino continued incredulously. "'Cause if ya do, you're a bigger prick than I thought ya was." He kicked Tim in the neck with the tip of his shiny pointed Italian shoe.

Tim began to gag.

"I'm gonna break your fuckin' arms an' your legs. An' I'm gonna smash that pretty-boy face outta action for a while."

"I can pay you not to," Tim gasped, grabbing for survival. Better to share than to have nothing at all. "I can split a million bucks with you if you get those kids back."

Santino poked at Tim's throat with his shoe. "What kinda shit ya talkin'?"

"Those kids are special," Tim choked. "She's a Stanislopoulos, and so is the boy. He inherits the whole goddamn fortune. His mother is Lucky Santangelo and Dimitri Stanislopoulos was his father. I've got a million-dollar scam going."

"Are you shittin' me?" Santino's beady eyes were ablaze.

"I wouldn't do that," Tim said desperately.

"Naw, ya wouldn't do that," Santino mused. He nodded to one of his henchmen. "Get 'em back, Blackie. Now."

The man raced from the apartment.

Tim rubbed his throat where a purplish lump was forming. "Can I get up?"

Santino wasn't listening. He was remembering.

No retribution, huh? That's what *they* thought. That's what they all thought. Even that chickenshit Carlo. But now . . . with the kid in his possession . . . *her* kid . . .

Jesus Christ! It was manna from heaven.

127

On the drive to the Bel Air house Costa told Lucky the whole story. As she listened she went white. Her black eyes shone with fury.

"Where's Gino?" she demanded, when he had finished.

"I don't know. He left a message on the machine saying he wouldn't be back all night, and he hasn't called this morning."

"Does he have a girlfriend here?"

"No one I know of." He hesitated. "We did bump into Paige Wheeler yesterday at lunch. You don't think—"

"Call her home and her office."

"Good idea."

Lucky's tone was fast and businesslike, although inside she was burning with horror and frustration. The one thing she had always dreaded was happening, and she was out of control. "Has anyone checked the cab companies? Found out what driver picked Brigette up, and where he took her and Roberto?"

Costa shook his head. "No," he replied sheepishly. Why hadn't *he* thought of that?

She didn't want to look at him. He was just a tired old man who didn't know what to do. But how could she blame him?

She glanced at her watch. It was near noon. "God, Costa!" she couldn't help exploding. "Why didn't you phone me the minute this happened? And how come Matt wasn't alerted? You know we can trust him. We should have started getting the money the moment Alice received the call."

He bowed his head. "I know. It was an error in judgment. You were on your way here anyway . . . so I thought . . ." He trailed off miserably.

Don't scream at Costa, she warned herself. *Stay calm. Work things out. Roberto's going to be fine. He's with Brigette. She'll look after him.*

How come Brigette left the house with Roberto in the first place? And why hadn't Costa checked the cab companies immediately?

Oh, God! Where was Gino? He would have taken care of things by now.

Thinking aloud she said, "I'll contact Boogie. I can arrange to raise the cash in Vegas, and I'll charter a plane for him to fly in with the money. Once we get to the house I'm going to have to call in some favors."

Alice, with an attentive Claudio and a red-eyed CeeCee, waited at the Bel Air mansion.

"Who's he?" Lucky demanded at once, staring straight at Claudio.

"My gentleman friend," Alice replied tremulously. "I don't know what I would have done without him."

Lucky immediately decided he needed investigating. It was impossible to decide who was involved in this. Alice could have engineered the whole thing with the help of her tiny friend and some outside accomplices.

"Has anyone contacted Olympia?" she asked.

"Olympia's not home," Costa said quickly. "I've left messages."

"How about Lennie. Isn't he there?"

"Apparently not. According to the maid, he's moved out. They don't have a number for him."

Lucky paced restlessly around the room. "I need to be alone," she said.

They left, and she sat by the phone thinking. After a few moments she made a private call to an old business associate of Gino's. "This is Lucky Santangelo," she said guardedly. "I'm calling in a favor you owe my father. I need a car with an experienced driver. And two armed men. I also want a surveillance van, and a two-way tracking system. I want the best, and I want them within an hour."

Immediately after that, she put everything in motion as far as raising the cash was concerned. Thank God for Vegas,

Gino's friends and Boogie. She could have gone to a bank, but most of her assets were not liquid, and although she was able to come up with the money, it would have taken time and hassles. The major problem now was whether the money would arrive in time. Boogie had to collect it, get on a plane, and arrive at Farmers Market before the four o'clock deadline.

She was only thinking as far as four. After that her mind went blank.

What if Roberto and Brigette were not returned?

What if they were *never* returned?

She shuddered and refused to think the unthinkable.

• • • • •

"Why don't we drive to San Francisco for the weekend?" Gino suggested. "You're supposed to be there anyway, so let's go for it."

"Oh, you drive, too," teased Paige.

"I do things you ain't never even heard of, kiddo."

She smiled. "There's not much *I* haven't heard of."

He was full of enthusiasm. "I kinda fancy a drive. We can take the coast highway—stop off at an inn for the night—hit San Francisco Sunday mornin' an' fly back Monday. What d'you say?"

She sipped her coffee. "You sound like a travel agent."

"C'mon, Paige, take chances."

She laughed. "What the hell do you *think* I'm doing?" She paused for a moment, then gazed at him meaningfully. "I'm a married woman, Gino."

He met her gaze head on. "So what?"

"So I shouldn't even have spent the night, let alone take off for a dirty weekend."

He considered her remark before answering. "So, that's what I am to you, huh? One dirty weekend comin' up."

"Just keep on coming!"

"You got a mouth for a broad."

"And don't you *looove* it!"

"We goin' or what?"

"I think you talked me into it."

．　．　．　．　．

Lucky paced Lennie's study. It was so strange to be in his house, his room, among his things. She picked up a leather-bound script and gazed at it blankly.

She thought of her son. Roberto. He was so strong and full of curiosity and energy. So alive.

If whoever had him so much as *touched* him . . .

She would kill.

She had done it before.

CeeCee timidly entered the room and announced the arrival of the cabdriver Lucky had tracked down with two phone calls.

"Show him in," Lucky said flatly.

A bullnecked man with a dark complexion and a bulbous nose entered the room. He wore ludicrous shorts and a Hawaiian shirt.

Lucky waved a hundred-dollar bill at him. "I want to know everything you can remember about the girl and the little boy you picked up here yesterday afternoon."

The man's eyes stuck to the money like glue. "Picked 'em up at four-thirty," he said, licking fleshy lips. "Took 'em to the corner of Fairfax and Sunset—right outside the Thrifty drugstore. I kinda thought it wasn't exactly the right neighborhood for 'em to be in. Nice-lookin' chick."

"What happened after they got out of your cab?"

"Well she was kinda starin' around as though she was meetin' someone."

"And did anyone approach them?"

"In the T-shirt *she* was wearin', every guy on the street was stoppin'."

"What color was it?"

"Red an' tight, an' she had some kind of writin' on it."

"What did it say?"

He made a face. "I got a memory—not *that* good."

"Was the little boy okay? Or did he seem upset?"

"He was happy. Kept on talkin' about gettin' an ice cream."

"Anything else?"

"I think they went off with some guy, but I'm not sure. The light was green an' I was turnin' the corner."

"What did he look like?"

He shrugged. "I don' know. Young, thin. I only got a glimpse."

She handed him the money.

He stretched it out and held it up to the light.

"It's real," she said.

"I know that. I'm just checkin'. Habit, y'know."

"Would you recognize the man they went off with if you saw him again?"

"Naw."

"Thank you."

"Thank *you*. Easiest money I ever made."

Not much information there. But it showed that wherever they'd gone was of their own free will. Nobody had snatched them off the street.

Lucky thought about Brigette and the cabdriver's telling words. Everyone treated Brigette like a child—including Lucky herself. But she looked like a woman, and a sexy one at that. Maybe some guy had gotten hold of her . . . some guy with big ideas and a dirty mind. . . .

Abruptly Lucky hurried from the study. CeeCee hovered outside. "Where's Brigette's room?"

CeeCee escorted her upstairs, and they entered Brigette's domain. It was a teenage mess.

Lucky stood for a few moments just looking and remembering when she was very young where she used to hide things.

Under the mattress. Nothing. Behind a picture frame. Nothing. Beneath a stack of magazines. Bingo! A small square book with MY DIARY printed on the front.

She opened it, and a scattering of Polaroid pictures fell out. Quickly she scanned them and knew her hunch was right. Some guy had gotten hold of Brigette. And how.

128

The big man swooped down and picked Roberto up before Brigette could do anything. "Mr. Bonnatti wants to see ya," he growled.

Roberto tried vainly to wriggle free. Nobody on Hollywood Boulevard took any notice of the blond teenager and the hulk of a man carrying a small, yelling boy. Brigette figured she could make a run for it—but how could she possibly leave Bobby?

"Who's Mr. Bonnatti?" she asked, trying to sound brave.

"Don't worry about that," said the man. "Just tell the kid to shut up, an' let's go."

Dragging her feet, she followed him back to Tim's apartment.

By the time they got there Tim was sitting on the couch. He looked white, but at least he wasn't lying on the floor with someone's foot at his throat.

"Uh . . . Brigette," he said in a strained voice, indicating Santino. "This man's a friend of mine. We . . . er . . . we were involved in some hassle about money I owed. Everything's okay now."

The hood put Roberto down, and the little boy promptly kicked him on the shin.

Santino beamed. "I'm sorry if we upset ya. Just clearin' up a few matters."

Brigette stared at Tim. Something wasn't right and she knew it. "I want to take Bobby home," she said shakily.

He wouldn't look her in the eye. "You can't," he said. "Not yet. You know we have it all planned."

"I'm gonna be a partner in ya little sting operation," Santino joined in smoothly.

She hated him. He smelled of sickly-sweet after-shave and made her skin crawl.

"I don't think I want to do it anymore," she said uneasily.

Santino leered. "No choice, chicken."

"Wanta go home. Wanta go home," Roberto chanted, jumping up and down.

Santino walked over to Brigette and took her chin in the palm of his hand. "Sweet stuff. Young stuff," he crooned. "How'dja like to make me happy?"

Panic flooded her body. "Don't touch me," she warned, backing away.

"Whatcha gonna do about it?" he asked, and with one fast move he pinned her arms and brought his fleshy lips down on hers, thrusting into her mouth with his thick tongue.

She gagged and began to scream as she struggled free.

Santino whacked her across the side of the face with all his strength. "Just shut up, ya stupid little cunt!" he shouted.

She fell to the floor and started to sob. Roberto ran over and bent to comfort her.

Tim took a deep breath. Life wasn't easy. He didn't want this to happen, but there was nothing *he* could do to stop it.

• • • • •

Zeko was on her case with a vengeance.

"I'm going shopping," Eden announced aloofly.

"Mister Bonnatti said y'ain't t'leave the house."

"Mr. Bonnatti can go fuck himself."

Zeko shrugged. "He gives the orders. I just listens to 'em."

Eden tried another tactic. Maybe she could get the big goon to feel sorry for her. "Look at my face, Zeko," she said mournfully. "I'm all beaten up. I need special creams and lotions to put it right. Please take me out. I won't tell him."

Zeko considered her request and nixed it. He knew better than to cross his boss when it came to a definite order.

"You jerkoff asslicker!" Eden screeched, realizing she was not winning him over. "No wonder you're nothing but a dumb watchdog."

She slammed into her bedroom and tried to think of a way

to escape. Santino had her locked up, a prisoner. Who knew *what* he was planning to do with her next? She had heard stories of mobsters' girlfriends being shipped over the border when they were finished with. Sent away to do time in some foreign brothel. Santino had told her of one girl who ended up hanging herself in a Mexican whorehouse.

She shuddered. The house was rigged with alarms. She couldn't even walk out the front door without bells signaling her departure. And even if she did, Blue Jay Way was high in the Hollywood Hills, and Zeko kept the car keys on a string around his neck.

She picked up a lamp and hurled it across the room, sick with frustration.

Then an idea came to her. A brilliant idea.

There *was* somebody who could save her. One person.

129

Paige Wheeler is in San Francisco. Nobody seems to know where she's staying," said Costa wearily. "I, personally, have checked six of the best hotels. She's not registered. Neither is Gino."

Lucky glanced up. She had just started reading Brigette's diary. "Maybe she never went to San Francisco. Could be she and Gino are shacked up somewhere here. Have Alice and CeeCee start checking. Begin with the Beverly Hills Hotel, and then the Beverly Wilshire."

Costa nodded. "Have you found out anything?"

"I'll let you know."

Brigette's writing was almost illegible and her entries erratic. Lucky started with the most recent. It must have been written on the day before her disappearance.

Dinner with you know who!!! Trader Vic's. Got bombed. Then went back to his place in Hollywood. Did everything!! Everything!!!!! Gave him coke for present. He was pleased. Took nude pictures for fun! Wish I had pix of him. Next time I'll ask him. He's so amazing! I can't believe it! Dread leaving. Stayed all night. Told Alice I was with a girlfriend. She's so easy. I love Tim. I think he loves me!!!!

So, his name was Tim. It was a start. Quickly Lucky flicked back over the pages. It was mostly all the same stuff. *Bored! Boring! Alice is so dumb!* And an occasional *You know who hasn't called yet.*

And then she hit pay dirt. The opening night of the Santangelo.

Fantastic awesome evening!!! Met Tim Wealth! The only Tim Wealth! And he's even better in the flesh, and I mean flesh! Finally did it, with him!!!! Can't believe I did it. But he's so fully cool and brilliant. Totally. I love him of course. Told him I was 18!!!

Lucky dropped the diary and jumped up. Who the hell was Tim Wealth?

She picked up the phone and reached Matt in Atlantic City. "Get hold of the guest list for opening night and tell me who Tim Wealth is."

One thing about Matt—he was completely organized. Within minutes he had the list in front of him. "No Tim Wealth listed."

"Damn! Do you know who he is?"

"No idea. Why? What's up?"

"Nothing I can go into now."

"Maybe Jess knows. Hang on, I'll get her."

Lucky glanced at her watch. It was almost one-thirty. Soon she would have to leave for the airport to meet Boogie and get the money.

Jess came on the line. "Tim Wealth starred in one movie about four years ago. He's a good actor. I don't know why he hasn't done anything since. He just sort of faded into obscurity."

"He was at our opening. Right?"

"I didn't see him."

"Jess—please tell Matt to find out his current address immediately and to call me at once at Lennie's house. It's urgent."

"I don't believe this! I was with Lennie in L.A. last night. He didn't tell me you two were—"

"Is Lennie in L.A.?" Lucky asked, surprised.

"Aren't you with him?"

"No. I'm at his house because—look—I can't go into it now. Where can I reach him?"

Jess was perplexed. She couldn't figure out *what* was going on. "He's staying at his old apartment." She gave Lucky the number.

Costa entered the room. "Gino was registered at the Beverly Wilshire. He checked out an hour ago."

"Shit!" exclaimed Lucky angrily.

"What?" questioned Jess.

"Nothing. Get me that address."

She hung up. Costa looked worn-out. "Why don't you go to the hospital and visit Ria and the baby?" she suggested. "There's nothing else you can do around here."

"I'm coming to the airport with you," he said.

"No, you're not."

"Yes, I am."

"Go visit your baby, Costa. It's just a question of timing now. I think I know who has the kids."

"Calmly you tell me! Who? What?"

"I'll have an address in a minute."

She closed her eyes. Her head was pounding. This was the nightmare of her life. She thought of Lennie and wanted to call him. But what could he do except interfere? She had to do this her way. No outside help. Not even Lennie.

The phone rang. She grabbed it.

"I don't know how I do it, but I always do," Matt said smugly, and he gave her an address for Tim Wealth.

130

A stretch. A yawn Lennie had worked enough for one day. His scribble filled thirty pages. Not bad. He was on a roll, the script was coming nicely.

Maybe he should call Alice—couldn't put off giving her the good news forever. Lazily he reached for the phone, and it rang as his hand hovered over it. It could only be Jess, reporting on her trip. She had taken a ride into New York on a Lear Jet owned by a dissolute record producer who swapped boyfriends the way some people swap Christmas presents.

"Hiya. Good flight? How many attendants did little Mary Sunshine have?" he asked cheerily.

"How'd you know it was me?"

"Because," he explained patiently, "you are the only person who knows where I am."

"Not anymore."

He groaned. "Who have you told?"

There was a smile in her voice. "Lucky."

He tried to sound disinterested. "Oh yeah?"

"I thought you wouldn't mind."

He didn't know whether he minded or not. He wanted to see her—desperately. On the other hand, he wasn't so sure if it was too soon. They both needed time to adjust.

"Why'd you do that?"

"Actually," Jess said, "she's over at your house now."

"Olympia's house," he corrected.

"I don't care who the house belongs to—she's there."

"Doing what?"

"Sounding fraught."

"Can you be more explicit?"

"Call her."

"You're a big help."

"Do it."

"Piss off."

He hung up and made a decision. He wouldn't call, he would go there. He needed to see her more than anything else in the world.

· · · · ·

Brigette knew something was terribly wrong. Roberto and she were caught in an evil trap, and it was all her fault. Fright racked her body as they huddled together in the back of a car with rough thugs on either side. Santino sat in the front, next to a stony-faced driver. He leaned over the seats and chatted pleasantly.

"I got plans for y'two kids," he said. "We're gonna do things together ya thought only the big boys an' girls could do." He leered at Brigette. "Ya think that crap actor was somethin', wait till *we* get it on, chicken."

She shuddered, and held tightly onto Roberto. For the first time in her life she was truly afraid, and not just for herself. For Bobby, who was only a baby. And for Tim. What had they done with him? She'd been hustled from the apartment and made to wait in the car for fifteen minutes. When Santino appeared, Tim was not with him.

"Stop snivelin'," Santino growled at Roberto.

"Where's Tim?" she asked fearfully.

"How was he in the sack?" Santino leered. "Hot stuff, honey? I'll show ya hot stuff. I'll show *both* of ya."

131

There was just time to stop by the address Matt had given her for Tim Wealth before heading full speed to the airport. It turned out to be a house on Laurel Canyon.

The two men "lent" her by Gino's old business associate were low-key and youngish. Both seemed sharp-witted and competent. They called themselves Caveman and The Guardian. A third man drove the car, a 1980 Lincoln with a telephone.

She filled them in on the action, and they nodded as if they had been involved in this sort of scam all their lives.

The house on Laurel Canyon had gates and an electric entry system. The servant who answered was willing to buzz them through after three simple words: "Sparkletts water delivery."

They drove to the back entrance and waited for the door to open. Then Caveman and The Guardian stepped by the startled houseman flashing phony FBI cards and guns.

Lucky followed. She liked their style.

They checked the house quickly and methodically. The ground floor was deserted. Upstairs, the owner of the house sat in the center of a purple circular water bed watching a soap opera and blowing his nose. "God save me!" he twittered, as they invaded his bedroom.

Lucky took command. "Drug squad." She stepped forward. "We have a warrant for Tim Wealth."

The man fluttered well-manicured fingernails. "A scene from one of my own movies! Don't hurt me, I'll do anything you ask."

"Tim Wealth," she said menacingly.

"I haven't seen *him* in weeks. He moved out with two of my favorite Guccis, eight hundred dollars, three cameras, and a clutch of cashmere. Actors! Never again!"

"Do you have an address for him?" she asked authoritatively.

"I don't have one and I don't want one." He fidgeted uncomfortably. "Are you *sure* you're from the drug squad? You look awfully familiar." He squinted. "I think I must see your search-and-entry warrant."

"Look—we have to find him," she said sharply. "And if you don't tell me where we can locate him, then you'll be booked as an accessory. Am I making myself clear?"

"Try his agent, Zack Schaeffer." He peered at her, searching his memory, and then it came to him. "Is this some sort of ridiculous joke?" he asked peevishly. "You're that woman from the Santangelo Hotel in Atlantic City. I was at the opening." He struggled clumsily from the bed, resplendent in purple pajamas. "My God! This is one of those TV shows, isn't it? Where are the cameras? Oh, God! I'll be a laughingstock. I refuse permission, you'll never be able to use it. I'll sue. I'll . . ."

His words floated after them as they hurried from the house.

*   *   *   *   *

On his way to Bel Air, Lennie rehearsed his lines. Nothing intense, yet not too casual. *Hey, I left Olympia.* No. Too impersonal. How about—*Yeah. I finally made the move.* Or even better—*Lucky, what are you doing here? Did you know Olympia and I separated?*

Christ! He felt sixteen. Why couldn't he just tell her his feelings?

He entered the house and sensed something was wrong immediately. Alice lay on a couch in the living room, pale and wan. She clutched a glass of amber liquid, while a middle-aged man of Lilliputian size sat beside her, eyes glued to a flickering television.

"What's going on?" Lennie looked around and didn't like the whole scene. He had clearly told his mother not to bring any of her friends to the house.

"Lennie! My son!" Alice fluttered, sitting up and gesturing dramatically. "They've kidnapped Bobby and Brigette. They've taken the babies."

132

There were three cars parked in the driveway of the Bonnatti residence. Steven pulled up behind a sickly yellow Toyota in the Hertz Ford he had rented at the airport. A call to the hospital in New York on arrival had given him the news that Mary Lou was hanging in there. Carrie had elected to stay with Mary Lou's family at the hospital when he informed her that he had to go immediately to Los Angeles.

"Why?" she had asked, with concern.

"Because sometimes," he had replied calmly, "the law does not cover getting through the day."

"I don't understand. . . ."

It didn't matter whether she understood or not. He knew what he had to do.

He got out of his rented car and rang the doorbell.

Donatella Bonnatti herself answered the door. For years Santino had tried to train her to use servants, but Donatella had no use for people waiting on her. She preferred to be a martyr and do everything herself. "You thinka they clean? No! They cleana like shit!" she would complain hotly. "You thinka they cook? Pasta shit they cook!" So while Santino surrounded himself with bodyguards, Donatella preferred the company of two elderly Italian aunts, who did things the old way and came by the house three times a week.

Today she was on her own. And even though it was Saturday, she had decided to scrub down the vast kitchen floor while Santino and the children were out.

She came to the front door, hair awry, plain features shining with the sweat of hard work, a flowered cotton housedress covering her considerable bulk.

"Whata ya want?" she asked, looking Steven up and down.

Naturally he assumed she was the maid. In one hand she

held an old-fashioned broom which she leaned on as she surveyed him with sharp Sicilian eyes.

He spoke slowly, measuredly. "I need to speak to Santino Bonnatti. It's a matter of urgency."

She sucked on a hard candy. "You gotta the appointment?"

"I flew in from New York. I came straight from the airport. Is Mr. Bonnatti home?"

Donatella was not aware Santino was doing business with Blacks. He told her nothing. She only knew his secretiveness sometimes drove her mad. As her husband, he should share things with her, but he confided nothing.

"Whatsa this about?" she asked.

"Who are you?" Steven replied.

She laughed hoarsely. "You think I'ma the maid, huh? I know, I know." She smoothed down her housedress. "Nobody worka their ass in Beverly Hills. I'ma Mrs. Bonnatti."

. . . . .

Gino and Paige stopped for a leisurely lunch somewhere along the Pacific Coast Highway. They enjoyed fresh lobster and a bottle of wine. They enjoyed each other's company.

In all his years, Gino had never been really involved with a married woman. Oh, sure, he had experienced one-night stands, afternoon matinées and the like. Once, long ago in his youth, he had indulged in a steamy affair with the supersophisticated Clementine Duke, wife of a Senator. But this thing with Paige was different. He was an old man and she allowed him to feel alive. She made him laugh, and he knew he wanted her in his life on a permanent basis.

After lunch he broached the subject casually. "You ever thought about leavin' Ryder?"

They were seated at a table by the window overlooking a magnificent ocean view. She gazed out to sea. "Ryder needs me," she said quietly. "So do my children."

"Bull*shit!*"

"True."

"Your old man wouldn't give a camel's crap if you walked out tomorrow. An' your kids are all grown up."

She looked at him levelly. "Thanks a lot. You certainly know how to make a person feel wanted."

"C'mon, kiddo. *I* want you. That's what I'm sayin'."

"You've got me."

"For a lousy weekend."

"Maybe more might be too much for both of us."

He couldn't figure her out. Why wasn't she jumping? All his life women had jumped.

Maybe that's why he liked her. Paige did what she wanted, *when* she wanted.

"I'd better call the house," he said, getting up from the table. "Otherwise they'll be summonin' the FBI."

She watched him walk from the restaurant. He had style, Gino Santangelo, real style.

Seeing Boogie made Lucky feel safe. He was always at her side in times of trouble, and she knew she could depend on him.

He was his usual understand self in faded army fatigues and scuffed sneakers. Under his arm he carried a leather bag stuffed with the ransom money. His pale-blue eyes darted this way and that as they hurried toward the car.

She told him once again everything she knew. "Do you think we should bring the police in?" she asked anxiously, not quite sure of her own decision.

"No way," he said. "No outside interference."

She was glad he was with her. Since Gino was on the missing list, Boogie was her only security.

"This is what we're going to do," she explained. "We'll make the ransom drop at Farmers Market and hope and pray the children are returned. Caveman will follow the money pick-up—"

"No. I'll do that," Boogie interrupted quickly. "There's nobody better at shadowing than me."

"Good. We'll have a surveillance truck with full telephone contact and radio communication. Everything's being set up." She waved a slip of paper at him. "This is the latest address of the guy I think's involved. Tim Wealth—an out-of-work actor. The Guardian is checking the address now—he'll phone as soon as he comes up with information."

Boogie looked at her penetratingly. "And how are you coping?"

She was silent for a moment. When she finally spoke, her voice was tense, yet laced with steel. "I'll be all right. I just want the children back safely. And when I get them . . ." Her black eyes hardened. ". . . The sonofabitch who took them will wish he never lived."

The Bonnatti living room was immaculate, every piece of furniture polished to a dazzling shine. The damask couch featured plastic coverings on each arm, and there was a black grand piano in one corner with an old lace shawl thrown over it, and lots of fake antique frames filled with family photographs on the top.

Steven didn't care to sit down. He was not there for social niceties. "Mrs. Bonnatti," he said, "your husband is the lowest form of human life." He threw the copy of *Comer* magazine he had brought with him onto a table. "The lady on the front is my fiancée," he said angrily. "Or rather, the face is hers, the body is not."

"Eh! Why you shown me this?" Donatella shrieked. "I no lika these filthy magazines inna my house."

"I'm glad to hear that," Steven said harshly. "But your husband has no such objections. He *publishes* them."

He picked up the magazine and flicked through it until he reached the pictorial spread that purported to be Mary Lou. "Take a look at these pictures, Mrs. Bonnatti." He thrust the magazine toward her. "These are *fake* pictures. You understand me? Fake! Mary Lou Moore's face and somebody else's body."

"I no looka this dirt," Donatella insisted, sorry now she had invited this stranger in. She had hoped to find out something about her husband, but not this sort of something.

"Mary Lou Moore tried to kill herself because of these pictures," he said roughly. "She tried to kill herself because of your *sick, sadistic* husband."

"I don'ta know nothing," Donatella said sulkily.

"No? Well isn't it about time you started finding out? If I were you I—"

The phone rang and he stopped abruptly. Glad of the diversion, Donatella rushed to answer it. If it was Santino she would order him home at once. He would be angry that she had allowed a stranger into the house, especially a *Black* stranger. Santino was always warning her about crime and robberies, and the risk of even stepping out onto the street.

Goddamn Santino. If he was involved with filthy magazines she would never forgive him. He had a publishing company, but they published computer and technical things—Santino had told her so himself.

Ah . . . but could she trust him? He never confided much of anything. She knew he was involved in certain bad things, but over the years she had grown used to his secretive ways concerning business. "Never you bringa anything home," she had once warned him. And he never had.

Now she had pornography in her own house, and the Black man claimed Santino was responsible.

She picked up the phone. "Whosa this?" she shouted.

A husky female voice. "Mrs. Bonnatti? Donatella?"

Impatient. "Yes, yes. Whosa this?"

"There is a house on Blue Jay Way in the Hollywood Hills where your husband keeps his mistress," the voice whispered.

"What? Whata you talking?"

"Mistress. Girlfriend. Sexual playmate." The voice murmured the full address, then added, "Why don't you come over and see for yourself?"

Click.

135

The Irish maid in the New York hotel complained to the night manager when she got off duty at 6:45 P.M. "Darn it, Albert, I can't be gettin' inta room four twenty-five all day."

"Don't worry about it," the long-haired manager replied.

"I ain't *worried*," she replied scornfully. "But I got half me supplies locked up in that big storage cupboard in the bathroom."

"You'll get 'em out tomorrow."

"If he's not lyin' dead in his bed," she sniffed.

"Who?"

"That musician person—Flash."

The night manager twitched his nostrils. He had just returned from vacation and didn't know the legendary Flash was staying with them. "Why do you say a thing like that?" he asked, thinking the woman was a flake but he'd humor her anyway.

"It wouldn't be the first time in this hotel," sniffed the maid. "And that room is too quiet today. He's usually got music playin' and people comin' and goin'."

"Let's go see," suggested the manager, eager to meet the rock star.

The maid laughed derisively. "Look at you! Can't wait to view a body! Shame on you."

"Come on," he encouraged, walking out from behind the desk.

"Go yourself," she said rudely. "I'm off to cook me husband's dinner, and he doesn't take kindly to its bein' late."

She hurried off, and the busy switchboard caught the manager's attention. He fielded a few calls, then decided that maybe he should take the opportunity of meeting the great Flash in person. He removed the passkey from a drawer and left the desk in charge of a stoned porter. Not that he was exactly straight himself. Nothing serious. A couple of Quaaludes just to get him through the night shift. Maybe Flash would have something better to offer him.

Puffed with anticipation, he rang for the rusty elevator.

136

They made it to Farmers Market on Fairfax with twenty minutes to spare. Parked next door in the CBS parking lot was the surveillance van Lucky had requested. Its driver was an ex-detective named Dave.

"Wire both me and Boogie," Lucky instructed. "I'll do the drop and Boogie's going to handle the tail. You'll stick with him and keep in full contact with me."

"No problem," Dave said. He was tall and agile. He would be well compensated for his trouble.

Lucky hoped he was smart. She needed smart more than anything.

• • • • •

Santino had a naturally suspicious nature. And even though the people who worked for him professed to-the-death loyalty, he didn't trust them one inch. Certainly picking up a million bucks cash was too much temptation to put in anyone's path. So he decided to stay along for the ride and see that a couple of hundred thousand didn't vanish along the way. If what Tim Wealth promised was true, the entire operation was a cinch.

Lucky Santangelo must be going through the fucking ceiling, and he was glad. She would go through a whole lot more before she ever saw her kid again—*if* she ever saw her kid again.

Santino smiled to himself. What a day this had turned out to be—there was no revenge sweeter than a revenge long awaited.

• • • • •

Farmers Market was a tourist's paradise, a large complex of open-air souvenir shops, trinket emporiums and a covered food market selling everything from mangos to Italian salami.

Lucky found the B. Dalton bookstore right in the middle.

Slowly she walked toward it, carrying the leather carry-all containing the ransom money. Outwardly she was calm, but a cold anger beat inside her head, and she wanted to scream aloud with fury and frustration.

The bookstore was busy, business was brisk. Eyes watchful, she looked around for the diet book section. A fat woman in white polyester pants perused Jane Fonda's exercise book, but apart from her the area was deserted.

Lucky consulted her watch. Two minutes to four o'clock.

The fat woman put the Fonda book down and ambled off.

Lucky looked at her watch again. One minute to go.

She wondered where Boogie was, but it didn't worry her that she couldn't see him. Boogie could blend into a crowd and vanish.

Four o'clock exactly.

Carefully she placed the leather bag in a corner and left the store by the other entrance. Once outside, her immediate instinct was to go back in and grab the person who made the collection. But she couldn't do that. She had to wait. See if the children were returned. Just wait.

Boogie would take care of that end of it. There was a hidden tracking device in with the money. It wouldn't get far without Boogie.

• • • • •

Santino elected Blackie to make the pickup while he waited in the car with Roberto and Brigette and his other two henchmen. They parked on the street outside K-Mart, a block away. Blackie was large and lantern-jawed, with lank hair and a permanent scowl.

"Don'tcha take long gettin' back here," Santino commanded. He leaned over and patted Brigette on the thigh.

She shrank away from him.

"Teenager an' I can't wait to get it on," Santino leered. "That right, chicken? That right?"

137

Slow down," Paige said. "You're going to kill us. Then you'll be no use to anyone."

"You wanna drive?"

"Frankly, yes."

Gino swerved her Porsche into the side of the road, and they changed places. She buckled her seat belt and instructed him to do the same. He did so reluctantly—taking chances had always been more his style.

Expertly she steered the car back into the flow of traffic on the Pacific Coast Highway. They still had a good two-hour drive to go before hitting L.A.

"I never felt so helpless in my life," Gino groaned. "When I get my hands on the motherfucker who's responsible they'll wish they never lived."

"Don't talk," Paige responded, driving even faster than Gino, but less erratically. "Save your energies. Lucky must be frantic. She'll need you when we get there."

"I should've bin with her," Gino lamented. "Jeez! Who would do a thing like this? Who would *dare?*"

• • • • •

Lennie wanted to call the police.

"You can't do that," Alice said, with a firmness unlike her usual self. "Lucky says everything is under control."

"Under *whose* control?" he shouted angrily. "And why hasn't anyone reached Olympia?"

"We've tried," Alice said, "and she's unreachable."

"Jesus Christ!" he exploded. "Brigette *is* her daughter. She should be here. Or at least know what's going on."

"I keep on trying."

"Where's Lucky now?"

Costa entered the room. "I just heard from her. The money

has been dropped off. Boogie's tailing it. All we can do now is wait and see if the children turn up."

"Well, I can't sit around waiting," Lennie yelled. "Where is she? Give me the phone number of the car."

Reluctantly Costa did so. "She won't like being bothered," he warned. "She wants the line kept clear."

"I don't give a fuck *what* she wants," Lennie shouted. "I'm involved. Too bad if she doesn't like it."

• • • • •

Donatella Bonnatti stared at Steven. "Eh—Mr. Berkeley. You coma see my husband. He no here. So now you go, huh?"

Steven studied her carefully. She was agitated and impatient. Whoever was on the phone had upset her. His hunch told him it wasn't Bonnatti, but it was something to do with Bonnatti.

Donatella stalked to the door. The buttons of her housedress strained, revealing a large bosom and sensible underwear. "You leava now. I have to go out."

Steven nodded. "I'll be back to see Santino."

She was distracted, dying to get rid of him. The pornographic magazine and Santino's involvement didn't seem to matter to her anymore. Something else was on her mind.

"You do whata you wanta do. Okay. Okay."

She hustled him out of the front door and slammed it firmly.

He sat behind the wheel of his rented car, drove down the driveway to the street, parked and waited. Fifteen minutes later the Toyota appeared, Donatella at the wheel.

She set off toward Hollywood.

Steven followed.

138

Eden paced the house restlessly. She attempted to put makeup on her face, but her image was distorted by the marks of Santino's vile fists. Not forever. Thank God. Bruises and black eyes healed. A week, two weeks, and she would be back to normal.

Zeko sat out by the pool facing the house, tossing nuts into his ugly open mouth. He was a cretin. She hated him almost as much as she hated Santino. They were both pigs who thought all women were less than human.

She stared at the kitchen clock. It was past four. Tim was waiting for her, and there was no way she could show up. Screw Bonnatti. She would get away from him eventually— one way or the other.

Outside in the driveway she heard a car pull up. Hopefully she ran to the front window and peered out, only to see Santino emerge. He was accompanied by the two goons he always traveled with, and there was a young teenage blonde and a little boy with them.

Was he bringing his children to see her? She could not believe even Santino would stoop that low.

Quickly she rushed into her bedroom and closed the door. It was cool in there, with just the slight hum of air-conditioning to keep her company.

She heard people enter. There was no way she was coming out to meet them. He couldn't make her. What could he do? Kill her?

• • • • •

"C'mon, chicken," Santino leered, pulling Brigette inside the house.

Her heart was beating so fast she could almost hear it. Alice had told her stories about girls who disappeared from home. "White slavers," Alice had clucked knowingly, "sit next to unsuspecting girls in movie theaters and stick needles in their arms. Then they spirit them away to God knows where."

Brigette had laughed at Alice when she told her lurid tales like that. She had sneered at Lucky when she spoke of possible kidnappers. But now that she realized the seriousness of her situation, she knew how right they both were with their warnings and admonishments.

She wondered what was going on up at the house in Bel Air. Was Lucky there? Olympia? Gino? Lennie? Had they called the police? Were they searching for her and Roberto?

She felt like a little girl again, lost and lonely. And yet she had to be strong for Roberto. He trusted her. He clutched her hand as if his life depended on it. Maybe it did.

She spoke up bravely. "You've got the money," she said, desperately trying to keep the tremor out of her voice. "Now you're supposed to let us go like Tim promised."

Santino cackled. "Tim. Who's Tim?" He threw a glance at one of his hoods. "Any of ya guys know who Tim is?"

"Never heard of him, boss," said Blackie.

"Naw, don' know," agreed the other yes-man.

"C'mon, chicken," Santino urged, pulling Brigette toward the bedroom. "Bring the boy too. He can watch—get an early education." He roared at his own humor. "The three of us gonna make a pretty picture—a pretty picture ta send t'his mommy."

He kicked open the bedroom door.

Eden faced him.

"Out, cunt," he ordered.

"W . . . w . . . what's going on?" she stammered.

"Wait outside an' don't disturb me. Ya unnerstand English?"

Brigette looked at her pleadingly, relieved to see another

female. "This man has kidnapped us," she began to say. "He's—"

The back of his hand caught her across the cheek.

Roberto screamed.

Eden backed from the room as he hit the boy too. She couldn't help them. She couldn't even help herself.

The die was cast. Whatever happened now was out of her hands.

A phone call from The Guardian summoned Lucky to an apartment house off Hollywood Boulevard. Tim Wealth's apartment.

Caveman accompanied her from the car. Contrary to his nickname he wore a sports jacket and neatly pressed pants—he looked like a college graduate, but she knew he carried a solid piece, and hoped he was reliable in times of trouble.

They walked up the outside staircase dodging homecoming students and an irascible old drunk blocking everyone's way.

The Guardian let them in. He had edgy gray eyes that scanned the landscape.

Lucky entered the small apartment and stood stock-still. A body was slumped on the floor. A body which not only had been roughed up but shot in the head.

"Tim Wealth," The Guardian said tersely. "I got here just before he left us."

Lucky held her breath. "And?"

"We got more grief," The Guardian offered grimly. "Have you ever heard of a man named Santino Bonnatti?"

Her heart stopped. "Bonnatti?" she whispered.

The Guardian nodded. "Santino has the children."

Blue Jay Way was a quiet winding street high in the hills above Hollywood. There was not much passing traffic, just the occasional resident running an errand.

Boogie, in the back of the surveillance truck, figured it was the perfect hideaway to keep Roberto and Brigette. He was sure they had hit pay dirt when the Mercedes they were following slowed down. He was more than sure when he observed three men get out of the car, and with them the children. One of the men looked vaguely familiar—but he couldn't put a name to the face.

For a moment he had to decide whether to take them then and there. But the odds were stacked against him. Three guys—probably carrying—and anxious to hang on to a million buckeroos. There would be crossfire. Someone could get hurt, and there was no way he planned to risk endangering Roberto or Brigette. Besides, Lucky would never want them involved in any kind of shoot-out.

He waited until they were all in the house; then he tried to contact Lucky on the car phone. Her driver took the call and told him to wait.

Minutes ticked by slowly. He was patient, thoughtful. The decision was ultimately hers.

When she came on the line he could hear the icy anger in her voice. "Where are you?" she asked urgently.

He gave her the address and the news.

She relayed the information to her driver and told him to get there fast. Then she said as calmly as she could manage, "Was one of the men Santino Bonnatti?"

With dull realization he knew the familiar face was indeed Bonnatti, and the implications became clear.

"How do you want to proceed?" he asked. "Maybe now we should bring the police in."

"It'll take too much time," she replied, mind racing. "Caveman and The Guardian are with me. And you have Dave. We're going to deal with it ourselves—it's the only way."

"I don't know who else is in the house," Boogie said. He had learned a long time ago never to argue with Lucky Santangelo.

"Find out what you can," she replied tensely. "We're on our way."

Boogie left the van and went to the front to alert Dave. "She wants to go with it," he said. "Her kid's in there. Are you with us?"

Dave nodded and patted the concealed .38 he kept strapped to his waist.

"She'll be more than generous," Boogie promised.

"The money doesn't matter," Dave said. "I don't like people who fuck around with children. They need a lesson."

"Amen," said Boogie. "I'm gonna check out the action."

The two years he had spent in the jungles of Vietnam made him light on his feet and able to move stealthily and lightning-fast. He vanished into the deep undergrowth around the side and made his way up a hilly incline of bushes and scrub.

Before long he had a perfect downward view of the house.

* * * * *

Lennie sat in his study and kept on trying the number Costa had given him for the car.

It was continually busy.

He swore to himself and thought of how Lucky must be feeling. She needed him. And if only he could get through to her and find out where she was, he would be there. There was nothing he wouldn't do for her.

Alice came into the room and placed a cup of coffee on the desk. It was the single most thoughtful thing she had ever done for him—but who could sit around drinking coffee at a time like this?

Bingo! Finally he was connecting. The line rang and a man answered.

"Yeah?"

"Put me on to Lucky."

The sound was muffled, then her voice.

"Where are you?" he demanded.

She knew immediately it was he, but this was no time for a reunion.

"I'm taking care of it, Lennie," she said breathlessly.

He exploded with fury. "*You're* taking care of it. What about the police?"

"No police," she said calmly. "Trust me."

"Where are you?" he repeated urgently.

"I can't tell you."

"Like hell you can't!" He had never felt so helpless in his life.

"We're approaching Blue Jay Way," The Guardian said.

"I've got to go," Lucky breathed into the phone. "I'll have the children any minute."

"Where the fuck *are* you?" Lennie screamed.

There was no harm in telling him now. By the time he got there it would be all over.

"No police," she insisted.

"You got it."

Quickly she told him where they were. He threw the phone down and raced from the house.

141

The night manager of the New York hotel stood outside the door of room 425, and knocked several times.

When there was no reply he slipped his passkey in the lock, and entered.

At first he thought they were asleep—the legendary rock star and the fat blonde. They were sprawled grotesquely naked across the bed.

The night manager stood very still and listened for the sound of breathing. He drew closer, observing the signs of an all-night dope party. There were bottles of pills spilled on a bedside table, an empty syringe, a half-filled glassine bag of white powder and other drug paraphernalia.

The night manager sniffed, smelled death and shuddered. It wasn't the first time he had witnessed such a sight, and it probably wouldn't be the last. But he had never seen a famous person dead before.

The room was horribly silent. Only the street sounds outside broke the oppressive hush.

Gingerly he moved even nearer and peered at Flash, who was openmouthed, his rotting teeth on show.

With a stealthy movement he tasted a touch of the white powder lying in the half-empty bag next to the bed.

Cocaine.

He pocketed the bag quickly.

Then he looked at the blonde. She was puffy-faced, her skin a mottled purple. There was something vaguely familiar about her.

Police sirens screamed outside, and he jumped, wondering if they were going to stop. They didn't. They faded into the distance—a regular New York sound.

He supposed he had to do something about this mess.

Jesus. It would be an all-night gig what with the news interest and everything. The press were probably going to go crazy. In fact, the press were going to want to interview him. For sure.

He looked at the unhappy couple one last time and picked up the phone.

• • • • •

The news hit the wire services just in time for the ten o'clock evening news in New York. In Los Angeles it was seven o'clock.

How the media loved a famous death. Even better, a *double* famous death.

And this one had all the ingredients.

Money.

Sex.

Drugs.

And rock 'n' roll.

What more could they ask for?

142

"Take your clothes off, chicken," Santino ordered.

"You'd better leave me alone," Brigette warned, her eyes dilated with fear.

Santino laughed. He had locked the door and pocketed the key. The real world was shut out, and he was alone with this little blond piece of ass whom he couldn't wait to stick it to.

Ah . . . but he was not quite alone. Also in the room was the boy. Lucky Santangelo's son.

If he'd planned it in his most imaginative of dreams, he couldn't have arranged it better.

He took off his jacket and snorted with mirth.

Brigette's eyes were drawn to the snub-nosed revolver he kept in a shoulder holster strapped to his arm. Her skin crawled, and she felt faint as she watched him swagger over to a video camera set on a tripod overlooking the bed and switch it on.

"Okay, quit stallin'. Get your clothes off," he snarled, removing the gun from its holster and pointing it at Roberto, who crouched petrified in a corner. "*Now*, chicken flesh, or the boy's gonna get it."

She was weak with terror. This wasn't happening to her. It was all a horrifying dream.

She began to cry.

"Move your ass in front of the camera," Santino commanded.

Slowly she did as he ordered.

Suddenly Roberto jumped up and ran over to him, pummeling his leg with tiny fists. "Stop it! Stop it! Stop it!" the boy yelled.

Santino shoved the child away with a brutal thrust, sending him skittering across the room.

Brigette's sobs increased, but that didn't bother Santino. He fixed her with a lascivious expression. "Get 'em off, chicken. Now. Or I'll shoot this noisy little fucker right in front of your big blue eyes."

• • • • •

Donatella drove past the house on Blue Jay Way and recognized Santino's car at once. She uttered a long stream of Italian curse words and some English ones as well.

Lying, cheating, whoremongering Casanova *bastardo!*

How dare he. *How dare he!*

Father of her children, faithful husband—or so he had always sworn. She had given him the best years of her life and he was nothing but a rutting gutter dog.

She parked and squeezed her angry bulk from behind the wheel.

• • • • •

As Donatella left her Toyota, the Lincoln pulled up in front of the surveillance truck farther up the hill.

Boogie was there to greet Lucky as she jumped from the car. "Santino's in the house with three other men," he stated quickly. "And there's a woman inside too. This is how I see it: Caveman and The Guardian cause a diversion at the front, while I enter through the back."

"And what will I be doing? Knitting?" she asked acidly.

"You should stay in the car. I'll bring the children safely out. Trust me."

"Your scenario stinks," she said coolly. "I'm coming with you."

"You'll slow me down," he pointed out.

"Bull. I'll follow. If I get left behind, that's my fault."

"It could get dangerous."

She stared at him. "Do you know me, Boogie? Do you know me at all?"

There was no point in continuing the argument. Nobody told Lucky Santangelo what to do.

"I'll brief the guys," he said. "And then we'll move."

· · · · ·

Muttering to herself, Donatella crunched along the short gravel driveway. Before leaving her house she had changed from her housedress into a somber brown suit and sturdy pumps. She had combed her hair and put on scarlet lipstick and blue eye shadow. Donatella had never mastered the art of applying makeup, and she looked a sight.

Still muttering, she rang the doorbell of the house on Blue Jay Way, where she confidently expected to find her husband in the arms of some filthy cheap prostitute.

· · · · ·

"Who's the woman?" Caveman questioned, watching Donatella approach the front door.

"It doesn't matter," Lucky replied. "She'll be helpful as far as a diversion goes. You'll enter behind her—stall a confrontation, think of something to keep a dialogue going at the front—while we hit the back."

"Does the FBI scam work for you?" The Guardian asked, flashing his phony I.D. card.

"Perfect," Lucky said. "Go for it, fellas."

She followed Boogie on his trip into the surrounding underbrush.

· · · · ·

The Hollywood Hills were confusing. So many winding streets, and all with cul-de-sacs and turnings and more winding streets.

Steven had lost Donatella Bonnatti in her yellow Toyota when she turned off Sunset onto Doheny Drive, and now he couldn't find her.

It didn't really matter. He would go back to the Bonnatti residence and wait, for he knew what he was going to do to the scum when they finally came face to face.

· · · · ·

"What the hell is he doing with those kids?" Eden asked Blackie, who was in her kitchen searching for something to stuff in his slobbering mouth.

Blackie made a noncommittal gesture. Today—if only for a few moments—he had possessed a million bucks. What a moment!

He conveniently forgot that today he had also murdered a man. Coldbloodedly and with malice shot him in the head.

"You make me sick," Eden said, her voice full of disgust. "You work for and ass-kiss a man who is lower than dirt." She pushed her face toward him. "Look what he's done to me. What do you think of a man who can do this?"

Blackie threw her a cursory glance. "Who cares?" he said, gnawing on a large piece of cheese.

Eden heard the doorbell ring and held her breath. . . .

• • • • •

"Yeah?" Zeko said suspiciously, opening up a crack.

Donatella gave the front door a hefty kick, hurting her foot in the process. "Whata *you* do here?" she demanded. "Where you putta my husband?"

Zeko's mouth hung slackly open. "Mrs. Bonnatti!" he stuttered.

"Yeah. I'ma Mrs. Bonnatti. So what? So now I coma inside. Outta my way, you biga oaf."

Zeko was stumped. What was the boss going to say about *this?*

He loosened his hold on the door and failed to notice the two men coming up behind her.

"FBI," one of them said, holding up identification. "We're investigating one of your neighbors. We'd like you to answer a few questions."

143

Brigette cowered, naked, in the middle of the big bed. Tears streaked her cheeks. The sick, revolting man had touched her, forced her to pose for the camera. And now he was undressing Bobby and cackling with amusement as the little boy kicked and struggled.

She shuddered at the things he threatened next. He had told her in explicit detail what he was going to do to Bobby, as frenziedly he stripped down to his underwear. He wore boxer shorts with hearts on them, and his erection poked obscenely at the material.

Bobby was screaming, and the very sound of his anguished cries wrenched at her heart. It was her fault Bobby was here. *Her fault.*

Santino's concentration was on the child. He was preparing to commit an act so vile . . . so indecent . . .

* * * * *

Boogie moved swiftly, silently, down through the cactus, weeds and hillside brush.

Lucky managed to stay close behind him, oblivious to the overhanging bushes and branches that scratched and tore at her face and hands.

They were nearing the back of the house. A large swimming pool spread out before them, and around it were glass doors leading into the house.

"We'll bust right through," Boogie muttered, drawing his gun. "You'll have the kids back any minute, I promise you, Lucky, any minute."

* * * * *

"Mrs. Bonnatti?" Eden questioned, shoving past Zeko and confronting the big woman at the front door.

Donatella peered at her. "You gotta my husband here?" she said loudly. "My Santino?"

"Yes. He's here," replied Eden. "But before you see him I think you and I should talk."

"He sleepa with you?" Donatella demanded. "You tell me truth."

The Guardian seized the opportunity to push past Donatella into the house.

"Wait a min—" began a confused Zeko. But Caveman, close behind The Guardian, pulled a gun and said, "Save your words, shithead. Where are the kids?"

"Whosa these people?" shouted Donatella. "Whatsa happening?" -

"Just get against the wall and shut up," Caveman commanded. He gestured to Eden. "You too, sweetheart."

Blackie came lumbering out of the kitchen. Caveman waved him to join the crowd. Blackie tried to duck back, but Caveman said, "One more move and you're dead, fucker." Blackie froze.

An almighty crash came from the back of the house. And then a gunshot.

One.

Two.

Three.

EIGHT
MONTHS
LATER

MAY 1984

144

The air in the courtroom was heavy with silence.

Lucky stared into the distance, her black opal eyes mirroring no emotion, although inside she was churning with unbridled anxiety and tension.

The court clerk began to read the form aloud, his voice a nasal whine.

"On this day of May the fourth, nineteen eighty-four . . . in the State of California. . . ."

Words. So many words. And where were they leading to?

She glanced quickly around the courtroom and fixed on Brigette sitting in the front row. The young teenager was solemn, her pale face expressionless, her blond hair tightly drawn back in a sedate braid.

Lucky was angry that she had been allowed to come. The nightmare was behind Brigette now—there was no reason why she should be reminded.

The court clerk droned on.

Lucky held her breath and hoped . . . prayed . . .

It was a foregone conclusion that she would be found guilty. The newspapers had crucified her long ago. *Lucky Santangelo. The mobster's daughter.* Gino had not been involved in organized crime for over twenty years—and yet the stench remained.

Lucky lifted her chin proudly; she refused to crumble. She was prepared to take whatever they handed out.

"And we, the jury," the clerk continued sonorously, "do find the defendant, Lucky Santangelo," a pause, "guilty of murder in the second degree."

The verdict jolted through her like an electric shock as the courtroom erupted.

Voices.

Noise.

A hundred stampeding feet.

The buzz filled her ears, her eyes, her nose, her throat.

The buzz was suffocating her.

She gazed at the movement in the courtroom, her black eyes glassy. The scurrying figures . . . rats running for . . . God, what *were* they running for?

Telephones. Deadlines. The business of getting the news out first. Supplying the greedy masses with their fix of junk news.

Suddenly a piercing anguished scream shuddered through the courtroom as Brigette leaped to her feet.

"*Nooo!*" the young girl yelled. "*No! No! No! Lucky Santangelo is not guilty. I did it. I shot Santino Bonnatti. I'm the guilty one!*"

EPILOGUE

September the first, 1984, was a beautiful day for a wedding. The sky was blue and cloudless, the sun bright but not unbearably hot. The white house, standing in the middle of lush gardens filled with flowers, seemed peaceful and welcoming.

Roberto, now five and a half, strode around greeting guests in his dark suit. He was a sturdy lad, undeniably good-looking with his long-lashed jet eyes and black curly hair. CeeCee hovered watchfully in the background, ever alert, as were the security guards who ringed the perimeter of the house, and the plainclothes detectives who mingled unobtrusively and checked out the arriving guests.

Costa, Ria, and their baby were among the first to get there. Alice rushed to meet them. She wore ribbons in her dyed red hair, and a bright-green swirling chiffon dress. *People* magazine had just photographed her, and she was dizzy with success. Claudio had been replaced by German Rolf, an aging pop singer with pointed teeth and a tendency to whistle nonstop.

* * * * *

Jess and Matt arrived shortly after. Matt was dressed conservatively in a gray suit, while Jess positively bounced in a polka-dot maternity dress. She was expecting twins any moment, and, as Lennie so rudely joked, she looked like a ripe watermelon just about ready to burst.

* * * * *

Steven Berkeley drove up in a bronze Rolls-Royce, a wedding present from his bride, Mary Lou, who sat beside him. They had done the deed a week after she was released from the hospital.

Carrie accompanied them. She was her usual soignée self. *Women's Wear Daily* had just elected her to their Best Dressed Hall of Fame.

As a wedding present Carrie had handed Steven a copy of

her manuscript. "It's up to you whether I publish or not," she had said. And then she finally revealed who his true father was, because he had every right to know.

Steven had taken Mary Lou to Europe for their honeymoon, and while there he read his mother's story. When they returned, he told Carrie he thought it would be a crime if she *didn't* allow it to be published. Then he took a copy of it, and the relevant documents concerning his parentage, out to California, where he visited Lucky Santangelo in jail.

The newspapers were making Lucky an example. After all, she was a woman who had gotten away with murder once, and they were determined that all the money and influence in the world could not buy her freedom twice. Especially since the man she was accused of shooting was the son of her original victim.

GANGLAND VENDETTA, the headlines had screamed. NO BAIL FOR LUCKY SANTANGELO.

He told her everything. "Our lives seem intertwined in every way," he said before leaving. "I don't know if you ever want to accept it or not, but I'm proud to have you as a sister. And I'll do everything I can to help you."

Not only did Lucky accept him—she convinced Gino he had a son. And although it took him months to believe her story, he finally agreed to meet with Steven and maybe—only maybe—forge some sort of relationship.

* * * * *

Brigette wore a white dress. A virginal dress. A maid-of-honor dress. She looked devastatingly pretty with her pale skin, huge blue eyes and lush body.

Brigette was now one of the richest girls in the world. She had inherited all her mother's fortune, plus she had her own trust funds, which were enormous, and also the allowances from her late grandfather.

Brigette attended a private girls' school in Connecticut and spent the weekends with Lucky—who had willingly taken on the role of legal guardian.

Once a month she had to visit a probation officer—purely a formality to avoid the press screaming she had gotten off scot-free because she was Dimitri Stanislopoulos's granddaughter, had money and powerful contacts in the right places.

Brigette sometimes suffered from nightmares. They were always the same:

Tim Wealth

Smiling

Happy

Saying

"How y' doin', little girl?"

And then she imagined his dead body lying in his apartment, while Santino Bonnatti stripped off her clothes and did his degrading deeds.

She remembered that fateful day in terrifying detail.

The gun.

Santino's gun.

Lying on the table.

Santino. So intent on trying to molest Bobby. His filthy face a smirking mask. She had to stop him. . . .

She crawled, sobbing, across the bed. Reached for the weapon.

Bobby's stubborn baby voice one long scream of terror.

With shaking hands she picked up the gun.

His gun.

Instinctively she pointed and squeezed the trigger.

The explosion threw Santino back, and blood spattered from a gaping hole in his shoulder. He looked at her with surprise and fury spilling from every pore. "Ya little cunt—" he said.

She pulled the trigger again, and a third time.

Thick blood splashed everywhere as he fell to the floor without another word.

And that's what Lucky found when she dashed into the room.

From then on it was all a blur. Lucky prising the gun from her shaking hands, wiping the handle clean, grabbing the tape from the video machine and ordering Boogie to get the children out.

And then a large woman appeared in the doorway and started to scream hysterically and point an accusing finger at Lucky. "You did it!" she wailed. "You whore! You shot a my husband. You killed him. I saw you!"

In the ensuing confusion she and Roberto were hustled away by Boogie, who wrapped them in blankets and spirited them out the back to a waiting car. They were rushed to the house in Bel Air, given sedatives and warned never to mention what had taken place.

The next thing she knew, Lucky was arrested for murder, and Brigette stayed silent, until she could hold her guilty secret no longer. She confessed at the trial. She would have done it before but she was too frightened. After her confession there was complete confusion. Eventually the true facts were revealed, and the incriminating videotape produced. Lucky was released, and Brigette, being a minor, was put on probation for a year only. After all, it was a clear case of self-defense.

She was glad she had confessed. At first Lucky was angry at her, but one day she had taken her by the hand, looked her in the eye and said, "Thank you. What you did took a great deal of courage. And I'm grateful."

Now life was okay. Although it wasn't perfect. She missed her mother. Olympia—she really missed her a lot.

•　•　•　•　•

"Hey," Gino said, "you're lookin' good." He clapped Costa on the shoulder.

"I'm not feeling good," Costa complained mournfully.

"Always bitchin'," Gino laughed. "Always carryin' on."

"My arthritis is bad," Costa groaned. "I've got pains in my shoulder. My—"

"Cut it out!" Gino exclaimed. "Who needs a list of your problems? Think healthy. Stay healthy. It's the only way, pal."

Gino was a wonderful advertisement for his own words. He still looked years younger than his age, although his hair was finally gray, and a slight twinge of bursitis reminded him he was human. But he enjoyed life. He had a beautiful daughter, a grandson to carry on the family tradition, and excellent health. Oh yeh—and he also had a newfound son. Bizarre, but apparently true. Steven was a complex and interesting man; he was just starting to get used to him.

He did not have Paige Wheeler. Of all the women in his life, she was the one he had never been able to possess.

They still saw each other. Afternoons in the Beverly Wilshire, an occasional weekend—but she simply refused to leave Ryder.

Gino kept trying. It gave him a challenge. It kept the juice in his life.

. . . . .

Lennie checked himself out in the mirror. He was nervous as a tiger in the circus. And yet he was also incredibly elated. High. Charged.

For the second time he was taking the step. And this time he was in control of his senses. And this time he knew it was forever.

Lucky Santangelo.

Dangerous.

Stubborn.

Strong.

Crazy.

Sensual.

Everything.

He had thought—once—that Eden was the woman for him. Poor, pathetic Eden, who stood up in court and gave evidence about what had taken place in the bedroom of the house on Blue Jay Way—when she knew nothing. He, of course, had arrived too late. It was all over by the time he got there. Lucky had handled it her way.

Eden and he came face to face one day outside the courtroom. "Lennie." She placed her hand on his arm and stared piercingly into his eyes. "I missed you so much, but Santino kept me a prisoner. Can you understand how difficult it has been for me?"

He felt nothing. It was as if their years together had never been.

"I want to see you, Lennie," she murmured seductively. "I think I could be just about ready to make a commitment."

He tried to let her down gently. But there was no such thing as gently with Eden. "Big star now, huh?" she said venomously. "I knew it would go to your head."

Eden was past history.

He adjusted his tie. Silk tie. White silk shirt. Black Armani suit. And black tennis shoes.

Well—nobody had ever accused him of being conventional.

• • • • •

"Hey—daughter." Gino put his head around the door. "We about ready?"

Lucky turned to look at her father. "You've never called me that before," she said softly.

"Called you what?"

She smiled. "Daughter."

He came into the room. "Y'know somethin'?"

"What?"

"I kinda always forgot t'tell you this—an' I guess it's not important—'cause you know anyway."

"Yes?"

"I love you, kid. I *really* love you. And I'm proud of you. Real proud."

She blinked away tears—because it wouldn't do to cry on her wedding day—and fell into his arms. "I love you too, Daddy."

"Hey—" He gave her a gentle shove. "You're wrinklin' the suit."

Gino. So sartorially splendid. So great-looking. She didn't care about his past—so what that because of him and his public reputation she had been allowed no bail? And seven months spent in jail for a crime she did not commit was tough, but she rode it out—took it like a Santangelo. What she *did* care about was Gino the man. Her father. She loved him, and now she could freely admit it.

"Whyn't we move on out?" Gino suggested. "The guests are ready, an' so is my arm."

He extended it in a courtly fashion, and happily she attached herself.

Lennie was waiting.

· · · · ·

They were married in the garden of the East Hampton house. Lucky Santangelo and Lennie Golden.

Lucky stared at her bridegroom-to-be as she walked toward him. He turned and met her gaze.

Electricity sparked. They were destined to be a lethal combination.

Gino gave his daughter away.

Roberto was a page.

Brigette, the maid of honor.

And Jess, Lennie's best man.

It was a perfect wedding.

Don't miss the iconic "raunchy, brash, and suspenseful" (*The New York Times*) blockbuster novel that started it all

HOLLYWOOD WIVES

40th Anniversary Edition coming soon from Gallery Books!

Keep reading for a sneak peek. . . .

1

Elaine Conti awoke in her luxurious bed in her luxurious Beverly Hills mansion, pressed a button to open the electrically controlled drapes, and was confronted by the sight of a young man clad in a white T-shirt and dirty jeans pissing a perfect arc into her mosaic-tiled swimming pool.

She struggled to sit up, buzzing for Lina, her maid, and at the same time flinging on a marabou-trimmed silk robe and pressing her feet into dusty pink mules.

The young man completed his task, zipped up his jeans, and strolled casually out of view.

"Lina!" Elaine screamed. "Where *are* you?"

The maid appeared, inscrutable, calm, oblivious to her mistress's screams.

"There's an intruder out by the pool," Elaine snapped excitedly. "Get Miguel. Call the police. And make sure all the doors are locked."

Unperturbed, Lina began to collect the debris of clutter from Elaine's bedside table. Dirty Kleenex, a half-finished glass of wine, a rifled box of chocolates.

"Lina!" Elaine yelled.

"No get excited, señora," the maid said stoically. "No intruder. Just boy Miguel sent to do pool. Miguel sick. No come this week."

Elaine flushed angrily. "Why the hell didn't you tell me before?" She flung herself into her bathroom, slamming the door so hard that a framed print sprang off the wall and crashed to the floor, the glass shattering. Stupid maid. Dumb-ass woman. It was impossible to get good help anymore. They came. They went. They did not give a damn if you were raped and ravaged in your own home.

And this *would* have to happen while Ross was away on

location. Miguel would *never* have dared to pretend to be sick if Ross was in town.

Elaine flung off her robe, slipped out of her nightgown, and stepped under the invigorating sharpness of an ice-cold shower. She gritted her teeth. Cold water was best for the skin, tightened everything up. And, God knew, even with the gym and the yoga and the modern-dance class it still all needed tightening.

Not that she was fat. No way. Not a surplus ounce of flesh on her entire body. Pretty good for thirty-nine years of age.

When I was thirteen I was the fattest girl in school. Etta the Elephant they called me. And I deserved the nickname. Only how could a kid of thirteen know about nutrition and diet and exercise and all that stuff? How could a kid of thirteen help it when Grandma Steinberg stuffed her with cakes and latkes, lox and bagels, strudel and chicken dumplings?

Elaine smiled grimly. Etta the Elephant, late of the Bronx, had shown them all. Etta the Elephant, former secretary in New York City, was now slim and svelte. She was called Elaine Conti, and lived in a six-bedroomed, seven-bathroomed, goddam Beverly Hills palace. On the flats, too. Not stuck up in the hills or all the way over in Brentwood. On the flats. Prime real estate.

Etta the Elephant no longer had a sharp nose, mousy hair, gapped teeth, wire-rimmed glasses, and flat tits.

Over the years she had changed. The nose was now retroussé, cute. A perfect Brooke Shields, in fact. The mousy hair was a rich brown, cut short and tipped with golden streaks. Her skin was alabaster white and smooth, thanks to regular facials. Her teeth were capped. White and even. A credit to *Charlie's Angels*. The unbecoming glasses had long been replaced with soft blue contact lenses; without them her eyes were slate-gray and she had to squint to read. Not that she did a lot of reading. Magazines, of course. *Vogue, People, Us*. She skimmed the trades, *Variety* and *The Hollywood Reporter*, concentrating on Army Archerd and Hank Grant. She devoured *Women's Wear Daily* and *Beverly Hills People*, but was not really into what she termed hard news. The day Ronald Reagan was elected President was the only day she gave a passing thought to politics. If Ronald Reagan could do it, how about Ross?

The tits, while nowhere near the Raquel Welch class, were a perfect 36B, thanks to the ministrations of her first husband, Dr. John Saltwood. They stuck defiantly forward; no pull of gravity would ever harm *them*. And if it did, well, back to good old Johnny. She had found him in New York, wasting himself doing plastic surgery for a city hospital. They met at a party and she recognized a plain lonely man not unlike herself. They married a month later, and she had her nose and tits fixed within the year. Then she talked him into going to Beverly Hills and setting up in private practice.

Three years later he was *the* tit man, and she had divorced him and become Mrs. Ross Conti. Funny how things worked out.

Ross Conti. Husband. Movie star. First-class shit.

And she should know. After all, they had been married ten long years and it hadn't all been easy and it wasn't getting any easier and she knew things about Ross Conti that would curl the toes of the little old ladies who still loved him because after all he was hitting fifty and his fans were not exactly teenagers and as each year crept by it was getting more and more difficult and, God knew, financially things were not as good as they had been and each film could be his last and . . .

"Señora." Lina hammered on the bathroom door. "The boy, he go now. He want pay."

Elaine stepped out of the shower. She was outraged. He wanted paying—for what? Pissing in her pool?

She wrapped herself in a fluffy terry-cloth robe and opened the bathroom door. "Tell him," she said grandly, "to piss off."

Lina stared blankly. "Twenny dollar, Meesus Conti. He do it again in three day."

• • • • •

Ross Conti swore silently to himself. Jesus H. Christ. What was happening to him? He couldn't remember his frigging lines. Eight takes and still he was screwing up.

"Just take it easy, Ross," said the director calmly, placing a condescending hand on his shoulder.

Some frigging director. Twenty-three if he's a day. Hair hanging down his back like a witch at Halloween. Levi's so tight the outline of his schlong is like a frigging beacon.

Ross shook the offending hand off. "I'm taking it easy. It's the crowd—they keep distracting me."

"Sure," soothed Chip, signaling to the first assistant. "Calm them down for chrissakes, they're background—not auditioning for Chorus Line."

The first assistant nodded, then made an announcement through his loudspeaker.

"Ready to go again?" asked Chip. Ross nodded. The director turned to a suntanned blonde. "Again, Sharon. Sorry, babe."

Ross burned. *Sorry, babe. What the little prick really means is sorry, babe, but we gotta humor this old fart because he used to be the biggest thing in Hollywood.*

Sharon smiled. "Right on, Chip."

Sure. Right on, Chip. We'll humor the old schmuck. My mother used to love him. She saw all his movies. Creamed her panties every time.

"Makeup," Ross demanded, then added, his voice heavy with sarcasm, "That's if nobody minds."

"Of course not. Anything you want."

Yeah. Anything I want. Because this so-called hotshot needs Ross Conti in his film. Ross Conti means plenty at the box office. Who would line up to see Sharon Richman? Who has even heard of her except a couple million television freaks who tune in to see some schlock program about girl water-ski instructors? Glossy crap. Sharon Richman—a hank of hair and a mouthful of teeth. I wouldn't even screw her if she crawled to my trailer on her hands and knees and begged for it. Well, maybe if she begged.

The makeup girl attended to his needs. Now, *she* was all right. She *knew* who the star was on this picture. Busily she fussed around him, blotting out the shine of sweat around his nose with an outsize powder puff, touching up his eyebrows with a small comb.

He gave her a perfunctory pinch on the ass. She smiled appreciatively. *Come to my trailer later, baby, and I'll show you how to give a star head.*

"Right," said Chip the creep. "Are we ready, Ross?"

We are ready, asshole. He nodded.

"Okay. Let's go, then."

The scene began all right. It was a simple bit of business which involved Ross saying three lines to Sharon's six, then strolling nonchalantly out of shot. The trouble was Sharon. She stared blankly, making him blow his second line every time. *Bitch. She's doing it purposely. Trying to make me look bad.*

"Jesus H. Christ!" Chip finally exploded. "It's not the fucking soliloquy from *Hamlet.*"

Right. That's it. Talking to me like some nothing bit player. Ross turned and stalked from the location without a backward glance.

Chip grimaced at Sharon. "That's what happens when you're dealing with no talent."

"My mommy used to love him," she simpered.

"Then your mommy is an even bigger moron that her daughter."

She giggled. Chip's insults did not bother her. In bed she had him under control, and that was where it *really* mattered.

* * * * *

Elaine Conti drove her pale-blue Mercedes slowly down La Cienega Boulevard. She drove slowly so as not to spoil her nails, which she had just had done at a sensational new nail clinic called the Nail Kiss of Life. Wonderful place, they had wrapped her broken thumbnail so well that even *she* couldn't tell. Elaine loved discovering new places; it gave her a tiny shot of power. She pushed in a Streisand tape and wondered, as she had wondered countless times before, why dear Barbra had never had her nose fixed. In a town so dedicated to the perfect face . . . and God knew she had the money. Still, it certainly had not harmed her career—nor her love life, for that matter.

Elaine frowned and thought about her own love life. Ross

hadn't ventured near her in months. Bastard. Just because *he* didn't feel in the mood.

Elaine had indulged in two affairs during the course of her marriage. Both of them unsatisfactory. She hated affairs, they were so time-consuming. The highs and the lows. The ups and the downs. Was it all worth it? She had decided no, but now she was beginning to wonder.

The last one had taken place over two years ago. She blushed when she thought about it. What absurd risks she had taken. And with a man who could do her absolutely no good at all except fix her teeth, and they were already perfect. Milton Langley, her dentist—and probably everyone else's with money in Beverly Hills. How indiscreet of her to have picked him. But really he had picked her. He had sent his nurse scurrying off on an errand one day, climbed aboard the chair, and made fast and furious love to her. She remembered the day well, because he had climaxed all over her new Sonia Rykiel skirt.

Elaine giggled aloud at the thought, although she hadn't giggled at the time. Milton had poured mouthwash over the damaged garment, and, when his nurse returned, sent her over to Saks to purchase a replacement. After that they had met twice a week in some dreadful motel on Santa Monica for two hot months. One day Elaine had just decided not to go. End of *that* little episode.

The other one wasn't even worth thinking about. An actor on one of Ross's films. She had slept with him twice and regretted both times.

Whenever she mentioned their lack of a sex life to Ross he flew into a rage. "What the frig do you think I am? A machine? I'll get it up when *I* want to—not just because you've read some crap sex magazine that says you should have ten orgasms a day."

Ha! She was lucky if she got ten a year. If it hadn't been for her trusty vibrator she would have been climbing walls.

Maybe his erection would return if the movie he was doing turned out to be a hit.

Yes. That was what Ross needed—a massive shot of success would be good for both of them. There was nothing like success for putting the hard-on back in a man's life.

Carefully she made a left on Melrose. Lunch at Ma Maison was a must on Fridays. Anybody who was anybody and in town invariably showed up. Elaine had a permanent booking.

Patrick Terrail, the owner of Ma Maison, greeted her at the entrance to the small outdoor restaurant. She accepted a kiss on each cheek and followed a waiter to her table, keeping an eagle eye out for anyone she should acknowledge.

Maralee Gray, one of her closest friends, was already waiting. She nursed a spritzer and a sour expression. At thirty-seven Maralee maintained more than a shadow of her past prettiness. In her time she had been voted the most popular girl in high school *and* Miss Hot Rod 1960. That was before she had met, married, and divorced Neil Gray, the film director. Her father, now retired, owned Sanderson Studios. Money had never been Maralee's problem. Only men.

"Darling. I'm not late, am I?" Elaine asked anxiously, brushing cheeks with her friend.

"Not at all. I think I was early." They exchanged you-look-wonderfuls, admired each other's outfit, and cast their eyes around the restaurant.

"And how's Ross making out on location?" Maralee asked, extracting a long black cigarillo from a wafer-thin gold case.

"You know Ross—he makes out wherever he is."

They both laughed. Ross's reputation as a cocksman was an old Hollywood joke.

"Actually he hates everything," she confided. "The script, the director, the crew, the food, the climate—the whole bug-ridden setup, as he so charmingly puts it. But Maralee, believe me"—she leaned confidentially toward her friend—"he's going to be dynamite in this movie. The old Ross Conti—full-force."

"I can believe it," Maralee murmured. "I've never counted him out, you know that."

Elaine nodded. Maralee was a true friend, and there weren't many of them around. In Hollywood you were only as hot as your last hit—and it had been a long time between hits.

"I'm going to have my eyes done," Maralee announced dramatically. "I'm only telling you, and you mustn't mention it to a soul."

"As if I would!" Elaine replied, quite affronted. "Who's doing it?"

"The Palm Springs connection. I'll spend a couple of weeks there—after all, I have the house. Then I'll come back and nobody will know the difference. They'll just think I was vacationing."

"Wonderful idea," Elaine said. Was Maralee stupid or what? Nobody took a vacation in Palm Springs, even if they did have a house there. They either weekended or retired. "When?" she asked, her eyes flicking restlessly round the restaurant.

"As soon as possible. Next week if he can fit me in."

They both stopped talking to observe the entrance of Sylvester Stallone. Elaine threw him a perfunctory wave, but he did not appear to notice her. "Probably needs glasses," she sniffed. "I met him at a party only last week."

Maralee produced a small gold compact and inspected her face. "He won't last," she remarked dismissively, removing a smudge of lipstick from her teeth. "Let's face it, Clark Gable he's not."

• • • • •

"Oh yeah, that's it . . . don't stop . . . don't *ever* stop. Oh yeah, yeah . . . just keep on going, sweetheart, keep right on going."

Ross Conti listened to the words pouring from his mouth and wondered how many times he had uttered them before. Plenty. That was for sure.

On her knees, Stella, the makeup girl, worked diligently on his weak erection. She sucked him as if he were a water pump. Her technique could do with some improvement. But then, in his time, Ross had had some of the best little cocksuckers in the business. Starlets, whose very livelihood depended on doing a good job. Hookers, who specialized. Bored Beverly Hills housewives who had elevated cocksucking to an art.

He felt his erection begin to deflate, and he dug his fingers hard into the girl's scalp. She yelped with pain and stopped what she was doing.

He wasn't sorry. Quick as a flash he tucked himself out of sight and firmly zipped up. "That was great!"

She stared at him in amazement. "But you didn't come."

He could hardly lie. "Sometimes it's better this way," he mumbled mysteriously, reaching for a bottle of tequila on the side table in his hotel room.

"It is?" She continued to stare.

"Sure. Keeps all the juices inside. Keeps me buzzing. That's the way I like it when I'm working." If she believed that she'd believe anything.

"I think I know what you mean," she began enthusiastically. "Sort of like a boxer before a fight—mustn't release that precious energy. You've got to make it work for you."

"Right! You got it!" He smiled, took a slug of tequila from the bottle, and wished she would go.

"Would you like me to . . . do anything?" she asked expectantly, hoping that he would want her to undress and stay.

"There's a million things I'd like you to do," he replied. "But the star has got to get some sleep. You understand, don't you?"

"Of course, Mr. Con—Ross."

He hadn't said she could call him by his first name. Mr. Conti would do nicely. Women. Give them nine inches and they frigging moved in. "Goodnight, Sheila."

"It's Stella."

"Right."

She finally left, and he switched on the television in time for *The Tonight Show*. He knew that he should call Elaine in L.A., but he couldn't be bothered. She would be furious when she heard he had blown his lines and walked off the set. Elaine thought he was on the way out. She was always nagging him about keeping up with what the public wanted. He had done his last movie against her advice, and it bombed at the box office. God, that had pissed him off. A fine love story with a veteran director and a New York stage actress as his leading lady. "Old-fashioned garbage," Elaine had announced baldly. "Sex, violence, and comedy, that's what sells tickets today. And you've got to get in on the act, Ross, before it's too late."

She was right, of course. He did have to get in on the act, because he was no longer Mr. Box Office, not even in the frigging top ten. He was on the slide, and in Hollywood they could smell it.

Johnny Carson was talking to Angie Dickinson. She was flirting, crossing long legs and looking seductive.

Abruptly Ross picked up the phone. "Get me the bell captain," he snapped.

Chip had come groveling to his trailer after his walkout. "Nothing we can't sort out, Ross. If you want to quit today, we can schedule to reshoot the scene first thing in the morning."

He had agreed. At least they knew they were dealing with a star now, and not some nothing has-been.

"Yes, Mr. Conti. This is the bell captain. How may I help you?"

Ross balanced the phone under his chin and reached for the tequila bottle. "Can you be discreet?"

"Of course, sir. It's my job."

"I want a broad."

"Certainly, Mr. Conti. Blonde? Brunette? Redhead?"

"Multicolored for all I care. Just make sure she's got big tits—and I *mean* big ones."

"Yes *sir*!"

"Oh, and you can charge her to my account. Mark it down as room service." Why should *he* pay? Let the film company pick up the tab. He replaced the receiver and walked to the mirror. Fifty. Soon he would be fifty. And it hurt. Badly.

• • • • •

Ross Conti had lived in Hollywood for thirty years. And for twenty-five of those years he had been a star. Arriving in town in 1953, he was soon discovered hauling boxes in a food market on Sunset Boulevard by an aging agent's young wife. She was entranced by his blond good looks, and set about persuading her husband to handle him. In the meantime she was handling him herself—twice a day—and loving every minute.

Her husband discovered their affair on the day Universal decided to sign his young client. In a fit of fury the old agent negotiated the worst deal he possibly could, waited until it was signed, then dropped Ross, and badmouthed him as an untalented stud all over town.

Ross didn't care. He had grown up in the Bronx, spent three years kicking around New York grabbing bit parts here and there, and a Hollywood contract seemed just perfect to him, whatever the terms.

Women adored him. For two years he worked his way through the studio, eventually picking on the pretty mistress of a studio executive, who promptly saw to it that Ross's contract was dropped.

Two years, and all he had done was a few small parts in a series of beachparty movies. Then suddenly—no contract, no prospects, no money.

One day, lounging around Schwab's drugstore on the Strip, he got talking to a girl named Sadie La Salle, a hardworking secretary with the most enormous knockers he had ever seen. She was not a pretty girl. Overweight, suspicions of a mustache, short of leg. But oh those magnificent tits! He surprised himself by asking her for a date. She accepted readily, and they went to the Aware Inn, ate health burgers, and talked about him. He loved every minute of it. How many girls were prepared to discuss him and only him for five solid hours?

Sadie was very smart, a quality Ross had not encountered in a woman before. She refused to go to bed with him on their first date, slapped his hands away when he went after the magic tits, gave him sound advice about his career, and on their second date cooked him the best meal he had ever had.

For six months they had a platonic relationship, seeing each other a couple of times a week, speaking on the phone daily. Ross loved talking to her; she had an answer for every problem. And oh boy, did he ever have problems! He told her about the girls he was screwing, the trouble he was having finding work. Going on interview after interview and getting nowhere was depressing, not to mention terrible for his ego. Sadie was a wonderful listener, plus she cooked him two great meals a week and did his washing.

One night he had a narrow escape while visiting a nubile girlfriend.

Her out-of-town husband returned home sooner than expected, and Ross was forced to drop out her bedroom window desperately clutching his pants. He decided to pay Sadie an unexpected visit and tell her the story, sure she would love it.

When he arrived at her small apartment on Olive Drive he was shocked to discover her entertaining a man, the two of them sitting at her candlelit dining table finishing off a delicious-smelling pot roast. There was wine on the table, and fresh-cut flowers. Sadie was wearing a low-cut dress and seemed flustered to see him.

It had never occurred to him that she had boyfriends, and he was unreasonably pissed off.

"I want you to meet Bernard Leftcovitz," she said primly, eyeing his crumpled clothes and mussed hair with distaste.

He flung himself familiarly into a chair and threw a silent nod in Bernard Leftcovitz's direction. "Get me a drink, hon," he said to Sadie, reaching out to slap her on the ass. "Scotch, plenty of ice."

She glared, but did as he asked. Then he outsat Mr. Leftcovitz, who finally left an hour later.

"Thanks a lot!" she exploded, as soon as the door shut behind him.

Ross grinned. "Wassamatter?"

"You know what's the matter. Walking in here like you own the place, treating me like one of your . . . your . . . goddam women!" She was spluttering with rage. "I hate you. I really hate you! You think you're such a big deal. Well, let me tell you—"

He grabbed her fast. Moved in for the kill—for he knew that's what it would be—a killer scene, all thighs and heat and those amazing mountainous breasts enveloping him.

She pushed him away. "Ross—" she began to object.

He wasn't about to listen to any reasons why they shouldn't. Sadie La Salle was going to be his and screw the Bernard Leftcovitzes of this world.

She was a virgin. Twenty-four years old. A resident of Hollywood and a virgin.

Ross could not believe it. He was delighted. Ten years of making out and she was his first.

The next day he packed up his things and moved in with her. He was two months overdue with his rent anyway, and money was becoming a big problem. Sadie loved having him in her life. She said goodbye to Bernie without a second thought and devoted all her time to Ross. "We have to find you an agent," she fretted, because she knew his failure to land a part in a movie was upsetting him more than he cared to admit. Unfortunately all the agents he visited seemed to have got the message—Ross Conti equaled bad news.

One day she made a major decision. "I'll be your agent," she said quite seriously.

"You'll what?" he roared.

"I'll be your agent. It's a good idea. You'll see."

The next week she gave up her job, withdrew her savings, and soon found a tiny room in a run-down building on Hollywood Boulevard. She stuck a notice on the door—Sadie La Salle, Agent to the Stars. Then she had a phone installed, and was in business.

Ross found the whole thing hysterically funny. What the hell did Sadie know about being an agent?

What she didn't know she soon found out. For six years she had worked as a secretary in a large law firm which specialized in show-business work. She had the legalities down pat, and the rest wasn't difficult. She had a product. Ross Conti. And when the women of America got a good look at him they were going to want to buy.

"I have a great idea," she told him one day, "and I don't want your opinion of it, because it'll work. I know it's going to work."

As it happened he loved her idea, although it was a little crazy, and very expensive. She borrowed the money she needed from her former boss, an uptight jerk named Jeremy Mead who Ross suspected wanted to ball her. Then she had Ross photographed by the Pacific Ocean wearing faded Levi's cutoffs and a smile. And she had the picture blown up and placed on as many billboards as she could afford all across America, with just the words: "WHO IS ROSS CONTI?"

It was magic time. Within weeks everyone was asking, "Who is Ross Conti?" Johnny Carson began making cracks on his show. Letters started to arrive by the sackload, addressed to Ross Conti, Hollywood (Sadie had prudently informed the post office where to forward them). Ross was stopped in the street, mobbed by adoring women, recognized wherever he went. The whole thing took off just as she had predicted it would.

At the peak of it all Sadie flew with her now famous client to New York, where he had been invited to do a guest appearance on The Tonight Show. *They were both ecstatic. New York gave Ross the feel of what it would be like to be a star. Sadie was thrilled that it was she who had done it for him.*

He was marvelous on the show—funny, sexy, and magnetically attractive. By the time they got back to Hollywood the offers were piling up. Sadie sifted through them and finally negotiated an ace three-picture deal for him with Paramount. He never looked back. Success as a movie star was instantaneous.

Six months later he dumped her, signed with a big agency, and married Wendy Warren, a rising young star with an impressive thirty-nine-inch bust. They lived together in much-photographed luxury on top of Mulholland Drive, five minutes from Marlon Brando's retreat. Their marriage lasted only two years and was childless. After that Ross became the Hollywood bachelor. Wild stories, wild pranks, wild parties. Everyone was delighted when in 1964 he married again, this time a Swedish starlet of seventeen with, of course, wonderful breasts. The marriage was stormy and only lasted six months. She divorced him, claiming mental cruelty and half his money. Ross shrugged the whole thing off.

At that time his star was at its peak. Every movie he appeared in was a winner. Until 1969, when he made two disastrous films in a row.

A lot of people were not sorry to observe his fall from superstardom. Sadie La Salle, for one. After his defection from her loving care she had faded from sight for a while, but then she had resurfaced and slowly but surely built herself an empire.

Ross met Elaine when he went for a consultation with her husband. At thirty-nine he thought maybe he needed a little face work. He never got the surgery, but he did get Elaine. She moved in on him without hesitation, and she was exactly what he needed at that time in his life. He found her sympathetic, supportive, and an excellent listener. The tits were nothing to get excited about, but in *bed she was accommodating and warm, and after the aggression of the usual Hollywood starlet he liked that. He decided marriage to Elaine was just what he needed. It did not take a lot of persuasion for her to divorce her husband. They married a week later in Mexico, and his career took a sharp upward swing. It stayed up for five years, then slowly, gradually, it began to slip. And so did their marriage.*

• • • • •

Forty-nine. Heading full-speed toward fifty. And he didn't look a day over forty-two. The blond boyish good looks had aged nicely, although he could do without the graying hair that had to be carefully dyed, and the deep indentations under his piercing blue eyes.

Still, he was in terrific shape. The body was almost as good as new. He stared at his reflection, hardly hearing the discreet knock on the door.

"Yes?" he called out, when the knock was repeated.

"Room service," crooned a feminine voice.

Room service was twenty-two and stacked. Ross made a mental note to tip the bell captain royally.